Claire Lorrimer was born in Sussex and has travelled extensively around the world. She comes from an artistic family, numbering musicians, writers and painters: her mother was the famous romantic novelist Denise Robins. Among her bestselling novels are: *Mavreen, Tamarisk, Chantal, The Wilderling, The Châtelaine, Last Year's Nightingale, Frost in the Sun* and *Ortolans*.

THE SPINNING WHEEL

Claire Lorrimer

CORGI BOOKS

Acknowledgements

I would like to thank Daisy Noakes, Doris Hall, Albert Paul, Marjorie Gardiner, Olive Masterson, Margaret Ward and Bert Healey for their accounts of the hardships overshadowing the lives of the working classes in Sussex in the early years of this century (QueenSpark Books, Brighton). Their ability to find happiness despite the extreme poverty of the times was the initial inspiration for the theme of *The Spinning Wheel*. I would also like to thank, as always, the Edenbridge and East Grinstead libraries for their constant supply of reference books; Peter Willett and Barbara Morris for their assistance with equinal information; Mr W. Woodrow for legal detail; Dr R. Griffiths for First World War medical data; and Mr C. A. Hack for Melton Mowbray background material. Finally, I would like to thank my indispensable editor, Diane Pearson, my invaluable researcher, Penrose Scott, and Joy Tait for her wise counselling. Not least, I must thank my family for their patience and tolerance towards the author.

CL
1991

THE SPINNING
WHEEL

PROLOGUE
January 1903

'How much further do we have to go?'

Cynthia, Lady Merstam, turned to peer anxiously at her sister. How young she looks! she thought, and, with her frown deepening, how pale! 'Only fifteen miles, Dorothy. Are you feeling any better?'

The dark-haired girl seated beside her in the landau shook her head. 'The pain seems to come and go,' she whispered.

So it was not indigestion, the older girl realized with dismay. Her sixteen-year-old sister had first complained of feeling unwell after they had left The Plough Inn, where they had stopped for luncheon. She had supposed that Dorothy, who had had a plentiful helping of jugged hare, followed by apple pie and cream, had over-indulged. Now, as the girl's face screwed up in pain and she clutched at her stomach with a gasp, Cynthia was forced to acknowledge the more likely cause: the jolting of the carriage over the rough roads had brought on premature labour.

Had she made the wrong decision to hire a coach, she wondered? It would have been so much quicker and easier to have caught the train to Brighton. But this would have meant risking someone they knew recognizing them. It would have been too awful if, after all these months of concealing Dorothy's pregnancy from everyone – not least their parents – the truth were now to be discovered. She had planned so carefully, so skilfully, pretending in the early months that her young, unmarried sister was putting on weight as did so many young girls of her age.

When, by the seventh month, concealment was no longer possible, Cynthia had arranged a shipboard cruise in the Mediterranean, knowing that their parents would approve of the suggestion that Dorothy should accompany her married sister in order to broaden her education. Unaware of his young sister-in-law's condition, Cynthia's husband had raised no objection to his wife's choice of companion.

They had returned to England a fortnight before the expected date of birth, at which point Cynthia had written to their parents to say that Dorothy must remain with her for the time being as she had contracted an infectious fever while abroad and was under doctor's orders to remain in bed. She and Dorothy had then departed for Brighton, where Dorothy was to remain in a discreet nursing home until her child was born. The unfortunate baby was then to be taken to an orphanage, its parentage remaining unknown.

This was the only part of Cynthia's plan with which Dorothy had been unhappy to comply. It was her baby, she had protested in floods of tears, albeit a bastard! She knew she could not keep it but she loved the baby's father. However, Gervaise Harvey was still not twenty and his father, the Earl of Kinmuire, would never allow them to marry. The time would come when Gervaise would inherit the title and he was expected to make a suitable match in due course. Dorothy's family held no pretensions to aristocracy. At sixteen, still not 'out', there was no question of Dorothy fending for herself or her child – and she was well aware of it.

Cynthia, ten years older and already married, knew that sentiment must not be allowed to cloud the issue. Not only would Dorothy be a social outcast, but so would their parents. True Victorians, they would have been scandalized had they been aware that their younger daughter had allowed herself to be seduced like some ignorant servant girl. It was more than probable that Papa, a professor, would have turned Dorothy out of the house were he to know the truth. Mama would be held to blame for allowing Dorothy to remain unchaperoned long enough for the two young people to have given way to 'the carnal sin of unmarried passion'. It was by threatening to tell their parents the truth that Cynthia had been able to dissuade her sister from any further talk about keeping in touch with her child.

In many ways, Cynthia thought with a sigh of exasperation, Mama *was* to blame. Dorothy had been a sickly child from birth, as a consequence of which she had been given a great deal of freedom. The governess who had kept such tight control of Dorothy's life had been dismissed when Cynthia had married and their father had tutored Dorothy himself. Unsupervised when she was not ill in bed or doing her lessons, Dorothy had been able to keep assignations with the young titled undergraduate who came to their house in Oxford for his tutorials. The two young people had managed to spend long hours together on the River Cherwell throughout the term, and inevitably were caught up by the heady tide of first love. With the ingenuousness of extreme youth, Gervaise had confessed his love to his father and promptly been packed off to Heidelberg by his intractable parent to complete his education there.

Unaware of what had been happening, Cynthia was appalled when on a summer visit, her little sister had confessed her condition. It had required all Cynthia's practical ingenuity to devise a plan to conceal the truth from her husband and their parents. Until now the plan had worked perfectly and their parents remained unsuspecting. What she had not allowed for, Cynthia told herself bitterly, was that a first baby could be born early. She gave another anxious look at her sister. There should still be two weeks to go, weeks when ostensibly Dorothy was convalescing in their country house near Redhill.

'Could we stop for a minute, Cynthia? I . . . I think I may have had an accident!'

Tears, partly of pain and partly of shame, coursed down Dorothy's cheeks as she stared in dismay at the patches of dampness on her travelling coat spreading slowly on to the seat of the carriage.

'I did not know I was doing it,' she sobbed, but her words were cut short by another stab of pain.

Having given birth herself, Cynthia realized with horror that there was no doubt that Dorothy's waters had broken and that she had gone into labour. With a growing feeling of panic, she stared out of the window. As far as she could ascertain in the grey light of the January afternoon, they were crossing a wide expanse of common land. There was no sign of habitation.

'Where are we now?' she called out to the driver.

'Calking Common, ma'am,' came the reply.

Cynthia frowned. They were not yet over the South Downs, always a slow part of the road to Brighton, with the horses travelling at no more than walking pace.

Dorothy was now slumped sideways, her eyes closed, her hands clenched as she was racked by pains that seemed to be coming with increasing frequency. 'I'm sorry, I'm sorry,' she moaned and then, as she clung to her sister's hand in a desperate plea for reassurance, she whispered: 'Could I have eaten something which has poisoned me? It hurts. Badly. Are we nearly there?'

'Not too far,' Cynthia lied. 'We'll stop at the next village. Perhaps you'll feel better if we have a short rest.'

For a few minutes, Dorothy did not reply. Then she said quietly, 'I think the baby is coming.'

Cynthia bit her lip as she put a comforting arm round her sister's shoulders. The younger girl's pains were rising in crescendo and seemed to be coming at regular intervals. She should not have countenanced a halt for lunch, but then she had not anticipated that one of the horses would cast a shoe and they'd have to find a forge to get it replaced. She glanced out of the window again. They had crossed the common and were driving through a small village. It was growing dark, and now and again Cynthia glimpsed the faint orange glow of a lighted window. Should they stop, she asked herself? They would need medical help, and since Dorothy could not possibly have her baby here in the landau or on the roadside, they would have to seek shelter. Their identities would become

14

known. They *must* try to reach Brighton at all costs.

'The young lady is unwell,' she called out to the coachman. 'Go as fast as you can, please.'

'It's getting dark, ma'am,' the man replied. 'I'd best light the lamps.'

Cynthia fretted while he climbed down and set a match to the two oil lamps on either side of the carriage. She knew it must be done but the extra delay was all but unbearable. Dorothy was moaning now, her cries quite audible to the coachman as he climbed back on to his seat. As they left the village, he urged the horses into a trot. Despite the springs, the carriage jolted over every bump. Two miles beyond the village, Dorothy screamed. She was writhing now and her ungloved hands were digging into Cynthia's arm.

'Stop the coach!' Cynthia ordered. As it drew to a halt and the driver came to the window, she forced herself to keep calm. 'I fear my sister is too ill to go on,' she said. 'You'll have to go back to the village. Find a doctor if you can, but bring help. Do you understand? And please hurry!'

Hearing the cries coming from inside the carriage, the coachman needed no second admonishment to hurry. Nor, indeed, was he as ignorant as his passenger supposed. A married man with six children, he knew a pregnant woman when he saw one and the young lady had been unable to conceal her bulk when he had assisted her into the carriage. Nature being what it was, he reflected as he unhitched one of the carriage horses and rode back towards the village, babies had a way of coming into the world when they thought fit and not always when it was convenient. Nevertheless, a gently reared girl – and this one was barely more than a child – shouldn't have been travelling in her condition.

With a sigh, he looked ahead for the sight of a dwelling where he could enquire of one of the villagers if there was a doctor in the vicinity. He stopped at the first farm cottage he saw. A woman came to the door, holding up an oil lamp to peer at her unexpected visitor.

In answer to the coachman's question, she shook her head. 'Doctor's laid up,' she said flatly. 'Broke his leg last week out hunting. My hubby was one of them as helped carry him back on a gate. If'n you wants doctoring, you'd best ask Nurse Wilks. She be village midwife and next best thing to . . .'

'Where does she live?' the man interrupted, trying to keep his patience. He did not like to leave the ladies on the side of the road unprotected.

'Her lives in number four . . . Beacon Cottages, that is. But like as not you won't find her in. She'll be helping Martha Pritchett with Will's tea most likely, he getting home from work soon after sunset and liking his tea soon as he gets in. Her lives at number three. Beacon Cottages is in Chalk Lane, first on your right 'bout half a mile yonder.'

As the man followed the direction indicated, it started to rain – a cold, steady downpour which decreased visibility. It was some time before he found Beacon Cottages and, as he stood waiting for the door to be opened, the rain dripped down inside the collar of his heavy overcoat. He shivered, thinking anxiously of the problems awaiting if the nurse were unwilling to go with him at this time of the evening and in this dreadful weather.

He need not have concerned himself. The midwife stopped only to go next door to fetch her bag and rain cape. A buxom, smiling Sussex woman, she allowed herself to be lifted astride the steaming back of the carriage horse and clung cheerfully to the driver's waist as she waved goodbye to her neighbour and the two young children who were staring out of the tiny window above.

Two miles away Cynthia glanced repeatedly at the fob watch pinned to the velvet lapel of her travelling costume. She had removed her coat, which she had placed behind Dorothy's head as a makeshift pillow. The coachman had been gone for less than an hour but it seemed an eternity and she was terrified lest the baby should arrive before help came. She had not the faintest idea what she should do, and as Dorothy's moans became anguished screams,

16

she feared her sister was going to die. Frequently Dorothy begged to be allowed to do so, tears of pain and self-pity pouring down her face. She was crouched now on all fours on the narrow floor of the carriage, her hands clawing into the upholstery of the seat and tearing at Cynthia's skirt.

The midwife, when she arrived, paused only to order the coachman to pass her one of the carriage lamps before opening the door and peering inside. She gave a brief 'tut-tut' and, stepping past Cynthia, unceremoniously lifted Dorothy's skirt and petticoat and pulled down her drawers.

'Won't be long now,' she said brightly. Seeing from Cynthia's face that she was not far from hysteria, she added, 'Nothing to worry about as I can see, ma'am. First baby, is it?' She heaved Dorothy on to the seat as if she bore no weight. 'You're doing fine, m'dear, but don't push till I say so. Got here just in time.'

Speechless, Cynthia gazed at the newcomer who seemed as impervious to her own wet apparel as she was to the bizarre scene she was attending. She appeared to be not only immensely capable but also resourceful.

'If you can spare your petticoat, ma'am? We'll need summat to put Baby in.'

'She can't have it here!' Cynthia cried. 'I must get her to Brighton. It's all arranged. Can't you give her something to stop it?'

'Can't stop nature,' Nurse Wilks said cheerfully. As Dorothy's cries quietened momentarily, she added, 'Before its time, is it? Reckon as how the poor young lady never expected to have her first in a carriage! Never you worry, though. I've brought little ones into this world in worse places than this. On your way to Brighton, were you?'

Cynthia nodded. There could be no danger in admitting this much.

'We can't have the young lady being bumped about in a carriage when this is over,' the midwife continued. 'Be at very least a week afore she'll be fit for a journey. Best get a room in Calking, ma'am. The Drover's Arms'll put you up. It's not very grand but clean as a whistle.'

Cynthia had given no thought to 'afterwards'. Now her heart sank. They *must* get to Brighton. The matron of the nursing home had promised to remove the baby after its birth and before Dorothy had had time to become accustomed to it. Now, with the fates so set against their carrying out this plan, would they ever be able to continue their anonymity? It might still be possible. The coachman could take them to the local inn, where she could book a room for herself and Dorothy under assumed names, reward the driver handsomely for his assistance and send him on his way, none the wiser. There was, she decided, no alternative.

Dorothy's child – a boy – was born at eleven o'clock that night after a protracted and difficult birth. Despite the long hours in appallingly cramped, cold conditions, Nurse Wilks had remained infallibly cheerful, encouraging her patient and reassuring Cynthia. She had only once looked concerned, when for a minute or two after its birth the baby gave no sign of life. Hand held to her mouth in a state of shock at all she had been forced to witness, Cynthia had been overcome with a desire for the lifeless infant to remain so. Her own child had been stillborn and if Dorothy's child were likewise so, it would solve so many problems. But the baby had started breathing. After hours of intolerable pain, Dorothy refused even to look at it. The midwife sighed.

'Happens from time to time, ma'am,' she said to Cynthia. 'Give her a day or two and she'll feel different.'

'No!' Cynthia cried involuntarily, adding quickly, 'she's only a child herself and I know she doesn't want to nurse the baby. We'll have to get a bottle for it.'

'Time for that in the morning. Folks round here don't fancy that newfangled way of feeding bairns, so there aren't no bottles in the village shop. Have to go into Burgess Hill if'n that's what you want. First thing is to get it some clothing.' Nurse Wilks smiled cheerfully. 'Happen we could borrow something for the poor little mite from Martha Pritchett.'

She finished her ministrations to Dorothy, who was now

lying exhausted and uncaring in a half-sleep, and turned back to Cynthia. 'Martha Pritchett lives next door to me, ma'am. I delivered her little girl two weeks back and she, being a healthy soul, is not short of milk. Maybe you'd like to have the baby wet-nursed till its mother is feeling better?'

For the first time since the dreadful ordeal had begun, Cynthia began to see a ray of hope. She was exhausted and Dorothy even more so. They could rest at the inn until Dorothy was fit enough to return home to convalesce. The baby could stay with the wet nurse in Calking until she, Cynthia, could make fresh arrangements to leave it at an orphanage. Perhaps, she thought, she could take it into Brighton herself? But she dared not leave Dorothy alone in her weakened state. Who knew what she might blurt out if she left her in the hands of a stranger.

'I would pay this woman well for taking the child!' she said eagerly. 'Do you think she will agree to nurse it?'

Nurse Wilks nodded. 'Her's not the problem. They could do with the money, Will Pritchett being only under-gardener at The Grange. But the cottage is very small and there's two little 'uns as well as new Baby. One up, one down is all the rooms there is. Maybe the young lady wouldn't feel it suitable.'

'No, indeed, my sister would be only too happy to have the baby cared for,' Cynthia broke in. 'We never expected this to happen so soon. We were going to buy a suitable layette in Brighton and engage a nurse for the child there.'

Nurse Wilks nodded, before adding practically, 'Best be on our way, ma'am. It's cold as charity and the sooner the poor young lady's tucked up in a nice warm bed the better. She'll be needing towels and suchlike. I can pick them up at my cottage while you're talking to Martha Pritchett.'

With the horses held to a walking pace lest the jolting cause harm to Dorothy, it was the best part of an hour before the carriage came to a halt outside Beacon Cottages. The rain had stopped and there was no sound other than the faint bleating of sheep on the grassy downland, the dark silhouette of which was just visible beyond the dwellings. One of the horses, long overdue for a feed, neighed suddenly, causing a dog in a distant farmhouse to start barking.

Eight feet above the carriage, behind a tiny casement window of the cottage, four-year-old Alice Pritchett stirred out of her sleep. As the horse neighed a second time, she eased her thin body from beneath the slight weight of her little brother's arm and stared out of the window. Fascinated by the sight beneath her, she rubbed her eyes, wondering if she could be dreaming. A fine carriage with two horses and a coachman outside their cottage! Such a spectacle was rare enough even in the yard of The Drover's Arms.

Pushing her long corn-coloured hair out of her eyes and scratching her head, Alice pressed her nose to the latticed windowpane. It was bitterly cold in the tiny room, which had space for no more than the bed in which she and her brother slept. It was not really a bedroom but part of the upstairs landing which had been curtained off when the arrival of the new baby had necessitated the removal of their bed from their parents' room to make way for the cradle. At the top of the stairs there was now only space enough for a single person to walk sideways into her parents' bedroom.

Alice instantly recognized the first person to leave the carriage as their neighbour, Nurse Wilks. Open-mouthed, she watched as the midwife knocked on the door but, hearing her parents' movements through the thin-walled partition, she scrambled quickly back beneath the quilt. A moment or two later she saw a gleam from their oil lamp through a chink in the curtain and heard her father's voice muttering, 'Whosonever can that be at this hour', as he went downstairs.

Holding her breath, wide awake now as her curiosity mounted, Alice listened to her father's raised voice, then Nurse Wilks's quieter tones. She saw her mother, holding a lighted candle, go downstairs. Alice listened, then knelt once more at the window as the carriage door opened. Her mouth gaped in astonishment as she saw a fine lady climb out of the carriage holding a bundle and, sheltering it beneath her coat, hurry in through their front door.

Now there were more voices, only partly audible to the listening child, followed by the wail of a baby.

'. . . more than enough on your hands with our own little 'un . . .' Alice identified her father's deep tones.

'. . . as easily feed one as two, Will, and we need the money. Please . . .' Those, she knew, were her mother's softer tones, pleading.

'. . . easily die if we can't find . . .' That was Nurse Wilks's voice.

Next came the sound of a voice Alice did not recognize. It was clear, not unlike that of Miss Tester, the school-mistress who sometimes allowed Alice to clean her brass and paid her a halfpenny for the work.

'I do assure you, I will make it well worth your trouble . . .' There was a chink of coins being placed on the scrubbed kitchen table, then her father's voice, mollified, saying, 'T'won't cost nowt to feed the babe till you can make arrangements, ma'am, but it's Mrs Pritchett I'm worried for. T'aint long since she birthed our Jenny and . . .'

'Only for a day or two, Mr Pritchett. I'd be so very grateful.'

'Poor little mite.' That was her mother crooning as she did when she nursed Alice's new baby sister. She was soft-hearted, was her mum, and never spoke sharply to her two-year-old brother, Billy, who'd been born with a foot twisted the wrong way. Sometimes Alice resented the scoldings only she received, often accompanied by a rap on the knuckles, but a glance at Billy's foot – which always made her want to cry – brought understanding. Even now he couldn't walk properly.

Now, more than anything in the world, Alice wished she was brave enough to creep downstairs and see the infant they had been talking about. Was it a little girl, like their baby, Jenny? Or a boy, like Billy? How would her mother manage with two babies? But the steep wooden staircase led directly into the kitchen and she dared not

21

risk being noticed. Reluctantly Alice accepted that she would have to wait until morning to see the new arrival.

Downstairs farewells were being said. Outside, the coachman had turned the horses in the entrance to one of the farm fields. Alice watched as the lady came out of the house and the driver helped her into the carriage. As they drove away, the front door closed and Alice heard her mother say, 'You go on back to bed, Will. You've to be at work in the morning. I'll stay down and see if the poor little mite wants a feed. See that, Will. It's more than two weeks' wages the lady gave us. Now I can buy Alice a winter coat, and those new breeches you're needing. 'Tis like it was God intended, Will.'

'More like an accident, if you ask me, Martha. What's gentry doing driving around the countryside in that condition? It ain't right, no matter Nurse Wilks saying as how the babe was birthed 'afore its time.'

'That's not our business, Will. Best not think on it.'

'Mebbe not, but that there baby is our concern. Get it fed quickly, my girl, if you must, and come back to bed. It's bitter cold here.'

Her father's footsteps went past the curtain. Alice heard the springs of the big brass bedstead groan as he climbed in. She snuggled back beside her brother's warm body, and shivered. It was, she thought, only two weeks past Christmas and, so her Dad had said at teatime, there could soon be snow. She loved Christmas and wished it was not behind them. Most of all, she loved the nativity scene that was always put up in the church – the pretty statue of the Virgin Mary, the animals, the silver paper star and, not least, the cradle with a life-size baby doll in it that was Jesus.

As she cuddled still closer to the warm body of her sleeping brother, Alice considered the story they'd been told in Sunday School about the birth of Jesus. That, too, had happened at Christmas and late at night. The Holy Babe had been unexpected – except by the Wise Men – just like the baby downstairs. If it had had a home to go to and a cradle to lie in, the lady wouldn't have had to bring it here in the middle of the night for her mum to look after.

The following morning Alice, usually reluctant to leave her warm bed, was first to go downstairs. Her mum, already up and dressed, allowed her to pull back the blanket to look at the dark-haired infant, which, she told Alice, was a boy. Her mind still a little confused by thoughts of the infant Jesus, Alice was certain that God had sent this baby on purpose for them to take care of.

'We'll keep him, won't we, Mum?' she said as she gazed down at the child. He was sleeping peacefully in the makeshift cradle her mother had improvised from one of the dresser drawers, their own baby, Jenny, occupying the Pritchett cradle.

'Only for a day or two, Alice,' her mother answered as she riddled the kitchen range and the first glimmer of warmth stole into the room. 'Now lay the table for breakfast while I get Billy dressed, and stop talking. Your dad'll be down shortly.'

Alice's hazel eyes filled with tears of disappointment as she obediently put a loaf of bread on the wooden table, together with a bowl of dripping, and placed a jug of milk on top of the range.

Her father's arrival kept her silent until they had finished their meal and he had departed to work. As soon as the door closed behind him, she tugged at Martha's skirt.

'Please, Mum, can't we keep him? I'll take care of him, honest. He won't be no bother to you.'

'Hush, Alice. You don't understand,' her mother said, not unkindly. 'He don't belong to us. Any road, you got our Jenny to take care of – she's your own sister. This 'un got his own family what'll be wanting him theirselves.'

Martha Pritchett had no way of knowing that, not half a mile away, Cynthia Merstam had different plans for the baby's future. After a sleepless night ministering to Dorothy, she had come to the conclusion that there was nothing to be gained by taking the child to an orphanage when there was a family such as the Pritchetts who might be persuaded to bring him up as their own. For all their

23

obvious poverty, the tiny cottage had been spotlessly clean, and in the circumstances it was ridiculous to be snobbish about an unwanted, illegitimate child. The Pritchetts had no idea who she or Dorothy really were. Like the landlord of The Drover's Arms, they believed her to be a Mrs Robinson and the baby's mother, a Mrs Keynes. If they could be persuaded to keep the infant, it would relieve her of the problem of how to get it to Brighton without leaving Dorothy alone. Although physically her young sister was recovering well from the birth, mentally she was very far from well. When she was not actually sleeping, she was weeping hysterically. Nurse Wilks had said it was not uncommon for a new mother to suffer from depression, especially after Dorothy's ordeal giving birth on the highway and without her husband at hand to comfort and support her. But Cynthia was terrified lest Dorothy might blurt out the truth – that she had no husband and that she was mourning the loss of Gervaise's child.

She called once again to see the Pritchetts at a time when she knew the husband would be home from work. She had already assessed that despite being a man of few words, he was the one who determined how his family's life was conducted. Martha Pritchett, she sensed, was a warm-hearted woman who proudly indicated how – despite the way it had come into the world – the baby was clearly thriving in her care. There was the little girl too, who played into Cynthia's hands, bursting into floods of tears when her father said he would not consider keeping the baby for a whole year.

'Mrs Keynes is very far from well,' Cynthia repeated. 'You must appreciate my problem, Mr Pritchett. The baby was born prematurely and Mrs Keynes had not yet made preparations – no nurse engaged, no nursery. Her husband is abroad and she has no close relative to assist her. Naturally, I would make it worth your while, and I'd pay you now in advance. Surely if your wife has one infant to look after, a second is little extra work? Mrs Pritchett does seem to be managing very well indeed.'

'Tis a fact, Will, what the lady says – I can manage well enough.'

The man's expression remained unchanged, and he ignored the little girl's pleadings as she tugged at the edges of his waistcoat.

'Begging your pardon, ma'am, but it don't seem right somehows. We're poor folk and,' he added with a pertinent wryness, 'we ain't got no nursery either.'

Cynthia permitted herself a gentle smile. 'No, but I can see how beautifully you keep your house and I have every confidence in your wife, Mr Pritchett. It would only be for a year. By then Mrs Keynes will have had time to make proper arrangements.'

'We could do with the money, Will,' Martha said persuasively, and turned to her elder daughter, who had stopped crying and was now promising her father that she would help take care of the baby. 'Hush your mouth, Alice. Tis naught to do with you. Upstairs, now, and see to Billy. I can hear him crying.'

'So do I have your agreement, Mr Pritchett? You'll foster the child for a year?'

When Cynthia left half an hour later, she felt as if a great weight had been lifted off her shoulders. She would leave it to Nurse Wilks to have the baby's birth registered. She dared not undertake the task herself since to give the mother's name as Keynes would be an act of perjury. The place where the father's name should be given would, perforce, have to remain blank, since Nurse Wilks would have no inkling as to who he was. Inevitably, the baby would be presumed to be illegitimate – a factor which might well set the gardener's mind against continuing to harbour the child. On the other hand, he had already accepted a year's advance payment for the baby's keep and by the time he received the certificate, she and Dorothy would be gone and he'd have no way of contacting them. He might, of course, keep the money and despatch the child to the poorhouse or to an orphanage, but somehow she doubted he would stoop to this dishonesty.

Painfully, she accepted the fact that if not being exactly 'dishonest', she was nevertheless guilty of the utmost deception; but in the circumstances, she felt it to be justified. If these simple people could be persuaded to incorporate the child into their own family, Dorothy's infant would undoubtedly fare better than it would in the bleak confines of an orphanage. She must simply hope for the best.

The moment Dorothy was strong enough, she would take her back home to Redhill to complete her convalescence. Meanwhile, Cynthia decided, she would tell Dorothy her child had died. The lie would put paid to her sister's tearful requests to see her baby just once more and her even wilder suggestions that she would keep the child, leave home and somehow find work to support it.

She realized it would be several days before her sister could be moved and during that time she called on the Pritchetts, paid for the baby's board for a year and avoided giving any positive date when they might next expect to see her.

Three days later, having paid Nurse Wilks for her services, Cynthia and her sister departed for Redhill, Cynthia with heartfelt relief that neither she nor Dorothy need ever see the Pritchetts or Calking village again. Dorothy was still very tearful but, with the recuperative powers of youth, was slowly regaining her strength.

In number three Beacon Cottages Will and Martha Pritchett continued the discussion that had occupied their waking hours together ever since they had agreed to Cynthia's plans for the baby.

'More I think on·it, more certain sure I am that that there Mrs Robinson were hiding the truth,' Will said for the umpteenth time. 'All very well her a-tellin' us the little 'un's mother's called Mrs Harriet Keynes, but what about the father? Twice I asked her and there wasn't no ways she was a-going to tell me.'

Martha sighed. In her heart she too suspected something was amiss, but although she had had the child only a few days, she'd nursed him at her breast and he felt as

much her own as Baby Jenny. Then there was Alice –
plumb crazy about the infant!

'The lady said as how she'd write all the details down for
us,' she reminded her scowling husband.

'Yes, she did, surely,' he said sourly, 'and next thing we
hear is she's upped and left The Drover's Arms without so
much as a farewell.'

'Mebbe the mother was took poorly,' Martha suggested.
'T'aint for us to question the lady's reasons, Will. Happen
she'll write soon and then Nurse Wilks can get the baby
registered.'

'Happen she will and happen she won't,' was Will's
brief comment.

When a further week went by and still no letter arrived,
he raised the subject again. 'Reckon as how I was right all
along,' he said. 'That story her fine ladyship tolt us was a
pack of lies. As sure as I'm sitting here, that baby ain't got
no father – some gentleman's bastard, I don't doubt.
Landlord tolt me they didn't leave no address, albeit they
paid their bill right enough. I mean to talk to Vicar about
it cum Sunday.'

Martha shot him an anxious look. 'Why for, Will? We
wus paid to look after the babe and t'aint no business of
ourn if'n he's out of wedlock – 'sides which, we'd look a
right pair of busybodies if'n the lady does write. Happen
she's more important things to see to. Happen she's just
forgot.'

'I'd as soon forget my own name as forget a child left in
strangers' hands,' Will said shortly. 'If'n I'm proved right,
he's off to the poorhouse. I'm not having no illegitimates
under my roof.'

This time, Martha remained silent. One thing she knew
for certain was that her Will was as honest as any man
could be; that they'd been paid to mind the baby for a year
and no matter what the truth of its origins, it would be a
year to the day before Will would consider packing the
poor little thing off to the poorhouse. Meanwhile, Alice,
ever the talkative one of the family, gave them little peace.

'We gotta call him something, Mum. Even the cat's got

a name. Why didn't that lady give him a name? Our Billy's got a name and so's Baby Jenny. I'm going to choose a name. Can I, Dad?'

Will Pritchett shrugged as he rattled the bars of the kitchen range. 'Makes no odds to me,' he said. 'He don't belong to us.'

'He does, he does. He belongs to me!' Alice cried. 'You said his mum's name was Harriet, so I'm going to call him Harry – Harry Pritchett. And he's going to be mine for ever and ever.'

Martha Pritchett sighed. Only she knew how passionate this pretty, fanciful daughter of hers could be. The child was too young to understand the situation. The lady, Mrs Robinson, had said the baby's mother was a Mrs Keynes, so that was the name which would go on his birth certificate when he was registered. If Alice wanted to call him 'Harry' in the meanwhile, there was no harm in it. It was more than likely the infant would be gone in a year's time. Even if Will could be persuaded to let them keep the poor little mite permanently, for all they knew its mother might want it back, or Mrs Robinson might call to collect it.

'Adone-do, Alice,' she said sharply. 'We've a new little'un of our own for you to fuss over. You heard what your dad said. This 'un here don't belong to us. Now be off and wash the dishes.'

For the time being, Alice did as she was told. Her mother's words had not altered her conviction. She knew in her heart that the tiny, dark-haired infant was hers and that he had come to stay.

PART ONE
1915–22

CHAPTER ONE

1915

School was over for the day but for once Harry did not linger in the schoolyard playing tops with the other boys. The urge to hurry home to tell his family his good news superseded the satisfaction of whipping his new peg top with his bootlace and keeping it spinning longer than anyone else's. Socks round his ankles, his left boot unlaced, he ran down the High Street, nearly colliding with the milkman's cart as it emerged from a side street, cans and measuring dips rattling. He grinned mischievously as Sydney Deans let go his pony's reins to raise a fist threateningly in his direction.

'I'll do you, you young varmint!' the milkman yelled after the boy as Harry ran off in the direction of his home as speedily as his hobnailed, steel-capped boots allowed. 'I'll tell your dad, I will!'

Harry slowed his pace, well aware that Mr Deans would do no such thing. There'd been many a Sunday when he'd got up early to help deliver the milk on the morning round, earning himself a threepenny piece and enabling Mr Deans to enjoy a few hours' extra rest. It gave him a special warm feeling of pleasure whenever he could obtain paid work and hand over the small contribution to his mother.

Long before he'd reached his present exalted age of twelve, Harry was aware of the struggle his parents had to make ends meet. With seven children to feed and clothe, and an eighth but newly born, his father's wages as head gardener at The Grange barely met the family's needs. But for the fact that they had no rent to pay now that they were in a tied cottage, there would have been many more occasions when they'd all gone to bed hungry.

A little of Harry's earlier euphoria evaporated as he walked the last mile across Calking Common and the big wrought-iron gates of The Grange came into view. He had been so excited, so proud, when Mr Wilson, the headmaster, had told him he'd won a scholarship to grammar school. When he'd sat the exam last term, he'd given no thought to the family finances. Now, he thought suddenly, if he were to continue with his education, he would not be able to take up the position of stableboy at the big house and, consequently, would not after all be earning the three shillings and sixpence a week which had been promised him. As poor Billy, his crippled elder brother, had died of whooping cough four years ago, he, Harry, would be the first boy in the family to become a wage-earner. He'd been looking forward to this adult status. Moreover, he was well aware how much his family needed the money. Several times of late his dad had handed his wages to Mum with the comment, in that quiet voice of his, 'Not long now 'afore you'll be adding your bit, young Harry.' No, he thought unhappily, he could not see his dad being in the least anxious for him to take up the scholarship.

Would he really mind so much if his father forbade it? he asked himself as he slowed his pace still more. When Mr Debrace, the owner of The Grange, had last Easter offered to give him the job when he left school, he had scarcely been able to believe his good fortune. If he was not at school or doing any odd jobs that were going, he spent as much time as he could at the stables, loving the sight and sounds and smells of the horses, the leathers, the saddle soap – even the smells of metal and boot polish, and of the tobacco smoked by the grooms. Most of all he loved the horses, with whom he had a natural affinity, and it was always a red-letter day when he went riding with the Debrace children.

Harry paused to pick some of the juicy blackberries cascading over the hedgerows, and his thoughts turned to the summer when he and his sister Jenny had met the Debrace children for the first time. Then eight-year-olds, he and Jenny had been sent off for the afternoon to pick a basket of blackberries to take up to the cook at The Grange. It was when they had still been living in the tiny cottage in Chalk Lane, before his father had been offered the head gardener's job at the big house. Disobeying their father's express ruling, the two children had taken a short cut through the shrubbery at the front of the house. They had been spotted by Master Aubrey, the Debraces' son, who was pushing his grandmother's Bath chair across the terrace.

As Harry crammed a fistful of blackberries into his mouth, his dark-brown eyes sparkled with remembered pleasure. Master Aubrey's deaf old grandmother had taken a fancy to him because he, unlike Jenny, had not been afraid to speak into her big brass ear trumpet. The old lady had countermanded the nanny's objections when Master Aubrey had asked if Harry could stay and play French cricket with him. In the meanwhile, Miss Madeleine, who was then only seven, had insisted that Jenny should be allowed to play dolls with her. Even though he and Jenny had been late home for their tea and had earned a thrashing for disobeying their father, this did nothing to lessen Harry's happy remembrance of that day for, despite the fact that he was only the gardener's son and Master Aubrey a young gentleman, they had become friends and remained so ever since.

Aubrey was an asthmatic, as a consequence of which he was physically delicate and behind with his schoolwork. When the sons of the neighbouring gentry, who would normally have been his associates, were sent off to preparatory schools, Aubrey had been kept at home with a daily governess, whom he shared with his young sister. Madeleine, the only daughter, was the second cause of Harry's remembered pleasure at that momentous day of introduction to the Debrace family, for it had marked a turning-point in his life.

As fair as her brother, with soft gold ringlets tied back

33

in blue ribbons to match her organdie dress, little Miss Madeleine was the prettiest child Harry had ever seen. He had fallen instantly in love with her. That he had determined at the age of eight to marry her one day when he was a rich and important man was a closely guarded secret he had shared only with his sister, Alice. Alice, four years older than himself, and a great deal wiser, had tried to caution him that such a dream was doomed to disaster; that no matter how rich Harry might become, he was a working-class boy who would never be acceptable as a husband for a young lady like Miss Madeleine. Remembering that Harry was only a little boy, she consoled herself with the thought that he would soon put aside such childish ideas.

Dismayed by Alice's discouraging reactions to his confession, Harry never spoke of it again. As he grew older, however, he began to appreciate the enormous gulf between himself and the girl he had determined to marry. The differences were endlessly referred to by the Debrace children's nanny – a starched, uniformed, middle-aged woman whose efficiency was matched only by her snobbery. By overt glances or snide remarks, she disparaged Harry's Sussex accent, his manners, his clothes. She had forbidden him to call Aubrey by his Christian name, as Aubrey had suggested, and had been openly disapproving when, in her rather vague way, Mrs Debrace had intervened and permitted what the nanny had called 'undue familiarity' between the two boys. Nor was she mollified when her employer pointed out that the children were all very young and Nanny must not get upset by such trivialities.

Unconsciously, Harry had begun to adopt Aubrey's manner of speech, but he did so only when he was at The Grange. He copied him in many other ways, although Aubrey looked to him as the leader when it came to outdoor pursuits. Invariably Harry was the better at any sporting activity, and it was he who helped Aubrey overcome his innate nervousness – a trait which had been exacerbated since infancy by his over-protective mother.

Always deeply concerned by her son's recurring asthmatic attacks, which, she had once enlightened Harry, could in their severest form prove lethal, Eloise Debrace had cosseted Aubrey to the point of effeminacy. Wishing at least to match – if not to beat – the younger boy, Aubrey had begun to attempt and then to enjoy more masculine pursuits. The two boys went birds'-nesting and fishing and climbed trees that Aubrey would once not have dreamed of ascending. Encouraged by Harry, Aubrey learned to ride on the condition that Harry should accompany him. Before long, they were putting the ponies over small jumps. They shot at rabbits with the twenty-bore gun which Philip Debrace gave his son for his twelfth birthday. A keen shot himself, as well as being an enthusiastic rider to hounds before the war had put paid to hunting, the surgeon had been delighted by his son's development, which generously he attributed to Harry's influence. As a consequence he too encouraged the boys' somewhat unconventional friendship.

'You've been good for my lad,' he'd said last January when Harry, a year younger than Aubrey, had celebrated his twelfth birthday, 'and I want you to know I'm not unaware of it.' He had presented Harry with an air gun, as well as one of his old fishing-rods.

When Harry thought about Mr Debrace's accolade, he couldn't see how he'd earned or why he deserved such a magnificent reward. His parents and Alice frequently pointed out to him that he was greatly privileged to be allowed to go up to the big house to play with the young master, and he knew this to be the case. Occasionally Miss Madeleine would come to watch them playing, even asking to join in their games of croquet or cricket, and once, one unbelievably magical day, Mrs Debrace had included both Harry and Jenny on a day at the seaside in Brighton.

It was a day Harry would never forget. The disapproving nanny had supervised their bathing in the sea, while Mrs Debrace had sat beneath her sunshade, smiling as she watched them. Harry had waded deeper into the sea than the other children despite the rough waves and earned an admiring comment from little Miss Madeleine for his daring. This more than made up for the nanny's muttered reproach about placing himself in danger in order to show off. Miss Madeleine's subsequent references to his bravery on the way home had topped the thrills of riding in the new Daimler motor car; of seeing the ocean and the big promenade, with its open-topped buses driving to and from the West Pier; and of riding on donkeys, for which privilege Mrs Debrace had happily paid. The picnic luncheon, provided by the Debraces' cook, had been a veritable feast for Harry and Jenny, who tasted for the first time sandwiches filled with fresh salmon, coloured jellies, and melon, peaches and grapes from The Grange's hothouses.

As Harry now made his way along the back drive to the gardener's cottage where he lived, he could see no sign of Aubrey or his sister. They were probably enjoying nursery tea, he thought, feeling suddenly hungry. Perhaps, if he were lucky, his mum would give him a piece of bread and dripping to stave off the hunger pangs until his father came in from work. Better still, she might give him a piece of the cut-and-come-again cake she had made last week for the new baby's christening.

Passing the formal gardens surrounding the big grey-stone building that was The Grange, Harry increased his pace. He skirted the wall of the kitchen garden and loped past the potting-sheds before making his way along the footpath to his home. Three up, two down, the cottage was brick-built with a warm, red-tiled roof. Although far too small to accommodate comfortably the ever-increasing Pritchett family, it was nevertheless kept spotless by Martha Pritchett. It lacked luxuries of any kind, but the atmosphere within its walls was one that breathed love and homeliness. Apart from the days when Harry had been thrashed by his father for his misdemeanours, he could not recall any that were unhappy. He loved and respected his parents; adored Alice, who had never disguised the fact that he was her favourite; and got on well with the six other Pritchett children, whom he regarded as his brothers and sisters.

It did not occur to Harry to make comparisons between his home and Aubrey's; to wonder why Aubrey had not only a large bedroom but a bed to himself, while he, Harry, shared his with his two brothers; why the four members of the Debrace family had eight indoor and seven outdoor servants to minister to their needs. It was simply the way things were and would remain unless a man became rich. Money, he realized, was the governing factor. The gentry, like Aubrey's father, inherited money. He, Harry, had no such expectations. However, his hopes of improving his situation had been lifted this afternoon by Mr Wilson, who had been at pains to point out to him that, whereas a stableboy could expect no better than to be promoted to groom, a boy who did well at grammar school could, if he so desired, sit for a scholarship to university.

'Learning, young Harry, is the key to everything worth having in this life,' the headmaster had said, shaking Harry somewhat painfully by one ear lobe as if this would emphasize his point. 'Only a boy as ignorant as you would consider earning three and sixpence a week as the pinnacle of their ambitions. How many books do you think that would buy, eh? And you wishing you had time to read three or four a week! You tell your father you could become a teacher, a clerk, even a doctor like Mr Debrace. That is, *if* you study hard; *if* you mend your speech; *if* you ever learn to wash your hands and brush your hair and not go round looking like a gypsy. And that reminds me, boy. You may be leaving my school this term, but you haven't done so yet. You were sucking one of those filthy gobstoppers in the arithmetic lesson before lunch. Yes or no?'

Harry's affirmative had earned him a stroke with the dreaded cat-o'-four-tails and his bottom still stung. He bore Mr Wilson no grudge, for had he not ended the interview by giving Harry a whole florin as a reward for gaining the scholarship? Grinning happily, Harry kicked open the back door with the toe of his boot.

'Mum,' he shouted through the open door to the scullery, 'Mum, I've got summat to tell you, summat what'll make you think it's Christmas. Here . . .' He put the florin, hot from his sticky, blackberry-stained hand, down on the scrubbed wooden tabletop. 'And that's not all,' he said triumphantly. 'Just listen to this.'

Martha Pritchett pushed a strand of damp hair back from her forehead and tested the heat of the flat iron lying on top of the kitchen range. Replacing it with the cooled iron, she set about once more smoothing the worst of the creases out of a coarse sugar-sacking sheet. Hopefully, she thought, Edna would soon stop wetting the bed. She had enough washing to do of a Monday with the new baby without the daily need to rinse out bedsheets.

Although only in her early forties, Martha looked ten years older. Her thin face was lined and, but for the artificial rosiness of her cheeks caused by the heat of the small scullery, very pale, with dark shadows beneath her eyes. Nurse Wilks had wanted her to buy a bottle of tonic, saying Martha needed the iron to pick up her strength after the birth of this last baby. She and Will had not meant to have any more – but it wasn't easy denying a man his needs and Will had always been healthy and robust. The doctors had advised no more children after she had come so close to death a few years back. Fortunately, the baby seemed none the worse for her poor health and was now crying lustily to be fed. She wondered now how long her milk would last. In some ways it would be less taxing, less tiring, if she put him on a bottle, as Nurse Wilks had suggested, but it would mean getting up in the night and early mornings to heat the milk, not to mention the extra cost of having to buy it.

In a minute she would have to feed the infant, Martha thought, reaching out with one foot to set the cradle rocking. As always when she looked at it, a faint smile of pleasure would steal into her eyes. Will had fashioned it from an old apple crate when Alice, their first baby, was due. She had lined it with a layer of cotton padding and covered the outside with cotton sheeting. Over the top, she had stitched a frilly spotted-muslin cover which she had made from a dress given her by the lady who had employed her before she married Will. Martha had packed it away at the time, knowing she would be unlikely ever to have occasion to wear such a delicate garment but certain that one day it would come in useful. Now the cradle had served eight children, counting this new baby, whom they had christened Sam. The muslin had faded with the years but it still gave her pleasure to look at it.

Glancing at the clock on the mantelshelf – one of the few wedding presents she and Will had not been obliged to sell that year when they'd been unable to meet their bills – she noted that it was almost time for Harry to return from school. Her face softened as she thought of him. Although he was not of her flesh and blood, she loved him as dearly as any of her own. He had a way with him that she found hard to resist. Charm was not a word in her vocabulary, but she came close to it when she once admitted to Alice that Harry could twist her round his little finger without knowing it. He had but to stand before her, his dark hair an unruly mop of black curls, his brown eyes sparkling with mischief, for her to forget what misdeed she'd intended to punish him for.

Alice too had a special love for him. Sometimes Martha felt a little jealous of the relationship between the two children, for it was to Alice Harry always turned when he needed something or was in trouble. Although she realized that with so many little ones demanding her own time and attention, she had little enough to spare for this particular child, Martha was happier now that Alice no longer lived at home and it was to her Harry brought his troubles and his triumphs. On the other hand, she had missed Alice sorely when shortly before her fourteenth birthday, her eldest daughter had gone to work as a maid at Calking Grange. Alice was a good worker and had greatly lightened Martha's load, doing the shopping, putting the clothes through the heavy mangle on washdays, patching, mending, darning. Sometimes she cooked too. Now Jenny, who had taken Alice's place helping Martha in the house, had also left home. When war had broken out, the girl who had had the job of nurserymaid up at the big house had married her soldier sweetheart and Alice had spoken for her sister, explaining to Mrs Debrace that Jenny's youth was more than compensated for by her life-long experience with the little ones. Jenny was given the position.

Soon, Martha thought as she abandoned the ironing and put the baby to her breast, Harry would be off to work for the Debraces, making the fourth member of the family to be employed by them. She herself had benefited from the goodwill of her husband's employer. Mrs Debrace quite often sent down bundles of her children's outgrown clothes -- a blessing Martha was only too happy to accept. Unfortunately, much of this clothing was quite unsuitable for her own children's wear. Her Elsie and Edna could scarcely go to school in Miss Madeleine's black patent-leather pumps, or wear the fine beribboned dresses. The sailor suits were equally unsuitable for Arthur or Ted, and Harry, who was taller and broader than Master Aubrey, could not fit into the coats and breeches the older boy had outgrown. Fortunately, Alice was unusually clever with her needle and, when she had time, remade more practical clothes for the little ones from the expensive materials which she carefully unstitched. Many of the neat patches on Harry's breeches had been cut from a pair of Master Aubrey's trousers!

Harry, Martha thought as she moved the baby to her other breast while listening for the boy's footsteps, was harder on his clothes than any of the other children. Of course, before his death poor Billy had had little occasion to wear out his clothes since he had only been able to hobble from place to place at a snail's pace. It was best not to think of their eldest boy, whose memory still brought tears to Martha's eyes. She turned her thoughts quickly to Arthur and Ted, who were already needing respectable clothes to wear to school. They didn't ruin the toes of their boots by kicking tin cans along the streets the way young Harry did, despite Will's thrashing. Part of Harry's nature

– of which even Will approved – was the way the boy never bore a grudge for the beatings, or tried to lie his way out of trouble, or failed to show affection to everyone in the family. He was popular too with all their neighbours, and the tradesfolk frequently chose him above others to do their odd jobs on a Saturday morning.

'Happy Harry' the neighbours called him, stopping to ruffle the boy's thick, dark curls and often giving him a toffee or an apple for no good reason at all. Those who remembered the circumstances of his birth never held it against him, or if they did so, they kept their feelings to themselves. The women were always anxious to mother the boy, attracted by his bright smile and happy nature. The thought reminded Martha that her Alice had wanted to mother Harry even when she'd been no more than a tiny tot herself.

Martha straightened her aching back and, after changing the baby's wet napkin, she put him back in the cradle. As she reached once more for one of the two flat irons, she heard the door of the cottage burst open and Harry's voice calling to her.

'Mum, Mum!' he was shouting. 'I've got summat to tell you . . .' He sounded excited. She'd let the ironing wait a few minutes longer, Martha thought. It would be nice to sit down for a brief rest, have a cup of tea, and let Harry's happy chatter wash over her, soothe her. She placed the big black kettle on the range and turned to see Harry putting a florin on the table.

'Where'd you find that?' she asked, knowing he could not have earned such a sum even if he'd worked all day. 'Findings isn't keepings, you know, no matter what they say. You'd best hand it in to the constable.'

'Mum, it's mine. I won it. Mr Wilson gave it me for a prize, and it's for you. Is it enough for you to buy a new dress? Or a hat? You said last Sunday yours was getting so old it would fall to bits in church one of these days and put you to shame. *Is* it enough, Mum?'

Martha picked up the coin and held it in her hand admiringly.

'Well, I never did!' she said. 'It's a fine prize, Harry, and seeing as how it's what you want, maybe I will buy a new Sunday hat with it. But you're to keep a sixpence for yourself. Now, what've you won this for, then? Something to do with Christmas?'

Delighted with her obvious surprise and pleasure, and proud of himself for providing it, Harry laughed and sat down at the table opposite her.

'No, Mum, it's for winning the scholarship – to grammar school!' he announced. 'Mr Wilson gave it me. He said I've worked hard for it, though I haven't really – not as hard as Tom nor Bertie. Those exams I did were easy and I finished 'em before the time we was allowed, so I wrote them all out again more neatly so's they'd looked better, and Mr Wilson said that was sensible and maybe why I won it. Mum, what'll I do about the job up at The Grange if Dad lets me go to the grammar? Would I tell Mr Debrace, or would Dad tell him? I'd be half sorry in a way. I've been looking forward to it, being with the horses, but I could still go and work in the holidays, couldn't I? Would Mr Debrace be angry? At me not going, I mean?'

As he paused for breath, Martha said quietly, 'It isn't Mr Debrace as'll be angry, Harry, it's your dad. You know very well he means you to start work now you've finished with school. You know as well as anyone we needs the money.' She gave an anxious sigh. 'Maybe it would be best not to mention this to him – just not tell him about the scholarship. No point upsetting him for no good reason.'

'But Mum . . .' Harry hesitated for a moment and then continued. 'Mum, couldn't you talk Dad round? I mean, if *you* tell him . . . make him see I'd earn much more money if I was educated. Mr Wilson said . . .'

'You've already got as much learning as your dad nor I had – and more'n Alice and Jenny,' Martha broke in. 'The likes of us don't need no more than to read and write and do sums – and you're good at all that.'

Harry remained silent. How could he explain to his mother that there was so much more he wanted to learn – algebra, geometry, Latin, English literature. This past year when Mr Wilson had been able to spare the time, he had kept Harry back after school and started him off on such subjects. Even Aubrey, who was not very bright, had started to learn Latin – a subject insisted upon by his father as a 'key to all languages'.

'You're not good at just arithmetic or composition, Harry, you're a good all-rounder,' Mr Wilson had said when he'd first mooted the idea of Harry sitting for the scholarship. 'If you're prepared to work hard, boy, you'll go far.'

'Mum, you will ask Dad, won't you? Please? I really do want to go to the grammar.'

Aware, though not fully understanding, the degree of Harry's disappointment, Martha as always could not resist his pleas. She nodded, adding in a cautionary tone: 'But I can't see as how your dad'll think different, Harry, so you'd best make up your mind to it.'

The younger children had been put to bed and Harry sent into the front room, which Martha called 'the parlour', when finally she decided the moment was right to discuss Harry's future with Will. He'd finished reading his daily newspaper and was sitting comfortably at the kitchen table, plaiting onions he had grown in their own strip of vegetable garden.

'Done well this year, Mother,' he said with satisfaction. 'This lot should last us a while, eh?'

Martha laid down her knitting needles on her lap, and with instinctive tact, said, 'You done well with all the vegetables this year, Will.' She paused and then added in her quiet voice: 'About Harry . . .'

He glanced sharply at her. 'What about him? Been up to mischief again? I'm telling you, Martha, if . . .'

'No, Will, t'isn't that, surely. It's opposite. He brought home a florin after school today – what he'd won as a prize.'

Will returned to his task. 'Did he, now. Prize for what?'

'Getting himself a scholarship to grammar school.' The words were out and Martha stared anxiously at her husband's face. He was frowning.

'And what good's that going to do?' he said after a moment. 'Waste of time taking the examinations – and I said so at the time, only he seemed to have his heart set on it. You shouldn't have encouraged him, Martha. You and Alice both have put these wild ideas into his head.'

'He wants to go to the grammar, Will.'

Martha's hands were busy once more with her needles.

'Them as wants don't always get!' Will's tone of voice had hardened. 'You ain't forgot what was agreed 'tween us all them years ago, Martha? T'was you as said if'n we took him in, he'd make it up to us soon as he were old enough. Well, he's old enough now, and that's a fact.'

Seeing the distress on his wife's face, Will's voice softened.

'See here, Martha, I don't want to be hard on the lad, but what good's a lot of book learning going to be to him, eh? Sooner or later he's got to buckle down, same as we all had to. I'd a mind to teach him my trade, as well you know, but I let you talk me round, seeing as how he's so good with the horses – and the master said as how when the war was over and the stables was full again, he'd raise our Harry to be groom. The boy's got a certain future, which is more than you can count on in other trades.'

It was seldom her husband spoke at such length, and that he did so now did not escape Martha's attention. She knew he was trying to soften his refusal of her request. It was a long time since those years when they'd been courting – five patient years while they'd saved enough to get married. They'd both been working, Will here in Calking and she in Hove, where she'd been in service. They'd been able to meet only once a month, the bus fare being so costly, but they'd made the most of their few hours together. Will had spoken out about his feelings for her and they had exchanged tokens of their love. Although those times were long past, she never doubted that he did still care very deeply about her. He had nearly fallen ill himself with the worry when she'd had to go into hospital, and there'd been tears in his eyes the day they had brought her home. But since those days, their large family and

44

their work had taken up all their time, leaving none for the romantic moments she had once treasured. Nevertheless, he always did his best to fulfil any of the few requests she made. They seldom disagreed and if there had been any bone of contention between them, she could think of none that wasn't to do with Harry.

Perhaps, she thought now with a flash of wisdom, Will had always been a little jealous of her undisguised love for Harry. Perhaps he resented the fact that already the boy had outstripped him and was so able with any sport or activity he attempted. Perhaps it was no longer enough that he, Will, though unsurpassable where gardens and growing things were concerned, was bested by Harry in book-learning. Perhaps he resented the fact that Harry could ride a horse, was being coached by one of the players for the village cricket team and, not least, had been accepted as a suitable companion for the young master of the house. Perhaps it bothered Will – though it did not disturb her – that Harry was different.

Martha was in no doubt that Harry's difference was a result of the blood that ran in his veins. Though it was more than probable that the circumstances of his birth were shameful, the fact remained that the woman who had brought him to the house had been a lady of quality, and she would not have been so concerned for the baby had it been one of her servants who had birthed him, nor given themselves false names so as not to be traced. From the start Martha had never doubted Harry was a gentleman's by-blow, and as he had grown from infant to child, even his appearance had confirmed this belief. There was a certain delicacy of his bone structure that was different from that of her sons or the other village children.

Part of her could not blame Will for resenting the boy. The yearly payments which had been made for Harry had been more than adequate to pay for his needs while he had been a youngster, but he had grown all too rapidly into a fine, strong lad with a healthy appetite and a never-ending need for longer, larger clothes. A year back, Will would have written to the lady who'd left Harry with them, asking for a bit more money, only he hadn't known where to write. There had never been a letter sent with the postal orders that arrived each January. Although Nurse Wilks, the schoolmaster and the vicar had tried to help trace the two ladies, the vicar, who had been to see the landlord of The Drover's Arms, subsequently told Will he too believed the ladies must have given false names when they'd stayed there. He'd conducted a careful search in the parish records to see if a marriage had been registered in the names of either Keynes or Robinson, had made similar enquiries in Brighton and had finally written to Somerset House, but all to no avail.

Will was bitter about it at the time. 'The ladies must have been rich people,' he'd said, 'as could well afford to pay what was their due to those like us as has to scrape a living, and things'll get even more costly now, what with the war and all.'

He'd been only partly mollified by Martha's reminder that Harry was a fine, healthy lad who would soon be able to earn a good wage and ease Will's burden. Nevertheless, he'd said nothing more about Harry being handed over to the parish.

Staring now at his bowed head, his shoulders already stooped from constant bending over his plants and flowers, Martha felt a wave of love sweep over her in which there was a measure of pity. Will, like herself, was growing old so quickly. His hair was even greyer than her own; his face as lined. He was a good man, a good father, and he had been good to her. Not for him evenings spent down at The Drover's Arms, wasting hard-earned money on beer. More often than not when he finished work up at The Grange, he'd earn a few extra pence mending boots for their neighbours. Now he was teaching young Arthur the craft. Albert, the Debraces' chauffeur until he'd joined the army, had always given Will the old worn-out motor-car tyres from which Will could cut new soles, not charging a penny for them. Will never wasted anything that could be turned to good use, wanting to ease life for her as much as for himself.

Martha reached out a hand and laid it briefly on his shoulder. 'I told Harry you'd like as not want him to work for the Debraces the way you'd arranged it, Will,' she said softly. 'Leave it to me – I'll make him see the sense of it. He's a good boy, and he knows our need.'

Will nodded, aware that Martha herself was disappointed but would now support him as she always had. 'That's it, then,' he said. 'Now how about a cup of tea, Mother?'

Knowing that the discussion about Harry had come to an end, Martha hid her true feelings and went across the room to lift the whistling kettle off the kitchen range.

CHAPTER TWO
1915

'You have done that quite beautifully, my dear.' Eloise Debrace was addressing the sixteen-year-old girl kneeling on the soft Wilton carpet, pins, scissors and reels of cotton spread around her. 'You know, Alice, your stitches are even finer than Françoise's. But then, it was she who told me you were quite talented with your needle.'

Ash-blonde, blue-eyed, the elegant mistress of Calking Grange looked far younger than her middle thirties. There was a dreamy, childlike innocence about her which never failed to arouse the protective instinct in males – be they friend or servant – and which fifteen years ago had enslaved her far older and brilliantly clever husband.

Remembering how all those years ago, when she had first met him, her parents had objected to her marriage to someone in the medical profession, Eloise smiled. Her father had maintained that the social stigma would inevitably bar Philip and the woman he married from the visiting lists of the society into which she, Eloise, had been born. The fact that Philip came from an upper-middle-class family quite as respectable as her own, together with his undoubted brilliance, had eventually overruled their objections. They came to admit that there was something laudable in a young man of Philip's background – he had no need to earn his living – insisting upon putting his life to a worthwhile purpose which would hopefully improve the lives of his fellow men.

It was strange, Eloise thought, how both she and her sister had chosen to marry into 'trade'. Rosamund, some years earlier, had eloped with a young, titled but penniless

Frenchman. The youngest son of a French aristocrat, Félix Verveine was at heart an artist, but instead of applying his talents to painting, he had elected to direct them to the designing of beautiful clothes. His father had disowned him. Félix was managing to support himself in Paris when Rosamund met him. Not long after they were married, first his father and then his elder brother had died. Despite the fact that he had now inherited a title and the family château in Meaux, he was far too deeply involved with his career to abandon it. He declined to use his new title, which he felt was not in keeping with his profession. Many years had since passed and he was now well established, as successful in his chosen world as Philip was proving to be as a surgeon.

Forcing herself to abandon her reverie, Eloise turned her thoughts back to her young maid, bestowing on Alice her vague, sweet smile before making a last inspection of the hem of her new dress. Well satisfied, she walked across her bedroom to stare out of the window. The rain was sleeting down on to the lawns and trees, and the view, which could be so colourful and pleasant in the summer, was now shrouded in a uniform greyness. It was difficult not to be just a little depressed in such weather, she thought. Autumn seemed to have come upon them so suddenly this year and now, without real warning, it was winter. Although usually she did not care to think about such things, the sight of the pools of rain-water lying in the edges of the flowerbeds reminded her of her husband's accounts of the appalling conditions suffered the previous winter by the poor soldiers in the trenches in France.

'If only this horrible war would end,' she said aloud. 'Mr Debrace says there is no chance of it doing so. I suppose, Alice, we should be comforted by the knowledge that your father and my dear husband are too old to be involved in the fighting, your brothers and my son too young.'

Alice stood up, straightening the ankle-length skirt of her grey and white uniform. 'The master is helping our soldiers as best he can, madam,' she said in her quiet voice. 'Mr Standing was telling us at dinnertime that there's no counting the lives the master has saved.'

The older woman turned away from the window and smiled once more at her maid. 'That's quite right, Alice. Mr Debrace was saying only yesterday that he does battle every day in the hospital – not with the enemy but with death. He is a very skilful surgeon. Everyone we know thinks he should be rewarded for his work in the New Year's Honours List. With the long hours he dedicates to the wounded, it would certainly be well deserved.'

Alice, whose own hours were every bit as long as her master's, nevertheless agreed he was overworked. She bent to clear up the sewing materials, and replaced them in their basket. She'd been waiting for over a week to speak to the master about Harry, but Mr Debrace no longer came home at night from Lord Kitchener's hospital in Brighton, as he had used to do before the war. Now he returned only at the weekends, and even then as often as not his Daimler would not come up the drive before nine or ten o'clock on a Saturday night. The mistress, Mrs Debrace, had promised that as soon as she could find a moment when her husband was not too exhausted to be bothered with domestic matters, she would ask him to see Alice so that she could explain her problem.

Alice knew that Harry's future lay in the hands of her employers. No one was held in greater respect by her father than Mr Debrace, and not just on account of his reputation as one of the finest surgeons in the country. 'A good man', 'Fair in all his dealings with his staff', 'Honest' and 'Generous' were the words Alice had heard her father use whenever their employer's name was mentioned. 'He has as much respect for us working men as he does for his own kind,' he'd said to Alice on one occasion. 'He told me once that it's us what's the real backbone of the British Empire. He'd asked me to cut him some bunches of Muscats to take to the hospital and we was standing in the greenhouse when he put his hand on my arm and said: "I'm telling you, Pritchett, it's the courage and fighting spirit of the troops that counts – not the officers who lead them.'''

Nor was her father ignorant of Mr Debrace's kindness to Harry. 'Mark my words, Alice,' he'd said, 'there's not so many of the master's sort as would let his only son make a friend of his gardener's lad.'

When Harry had first told her of their father's refusal to allow him to go to grammar school, Alice had forbidden him to make any mention of his winning the scholarship to young Master Aubrey. If there was speaking to be done on Harry's behalf, she wanted to be the one to do it, not only so that she could impress on the master how important Mr Wilson thought it for Harry's future, but so that she could make Mr Debrace understand why, more than likely, Harry was so especially gifted. Not that Harry considered himself so. He thought his ability to be always top of his class was due to his 'good luck'.

Certainly he had never had to work particularly hard and was as often as not to be found out playing with his schoolfriends in preference to doing his homework. It was simply that he found learning easy to understand, to consign to memory. He was also an avid reader and this, as Mr Wilson so often said to his older pupils, could be an education in itself if they would only read worthwhile classics and not rubbish like *Tiger Tim* and *Rainbow*. They were but two of the much-loved weekly comics that were passed from hand to hand since there were only very few pupils whose parents could afford to buy their children such short-lived luxuries.

Familiar now with all her duties as personal maid to Mrs Debrace, Alice did not have to concentrate her thoughts upon her actions as she prepared her mistress's bath and set about the evening ritual of helping her change for dinner. Her mind remained with Harry, recalling the many small but significant things which had enforced her long-held conviction that his was a special destiny.

On winter evenings, when he could not be out playing hoops or hopscotch or cricket with his friends, Harry would take a candle into the scullery, where it was quiet, and read one of the books Master Aubrey had lent him from his nursery shelves – *Highways of History*, *Our Island Story* or perhaps Harry's favourite, *The Children's Encyclopedia*. Although she was of an age to do so, Edna could still not read, but she loved to sit with Elsie and the younger children listening when Harry could be persuaded to read aloud. How much of it the little girl understood, nobody could be sure. There had been one Christmas when Harry had set himself the task of trying to teach Edna to decipher the simplest words, but she was barely able to memorize the alphabet and he was obliged to abandon the attempt. Jenny, Harry's twin in age, was bright enough but uninterested in school lessons. It was to Alice Harry turned to discuss the books and stories he read, and not wishing to be found ignorant, Alice tried to keep pace with him.

It was not easy. As the most junior of all the housemaids when she had joined the Debrace staff at the age of thirteen, Alice's day had begun at half past five when, with two other maids, she had washed, dressed and gone downstairs to polish the parquet floors in the big reception rooms and sweep and dust the main staircase. Her next task was to carry the two-gallon hot-water cans up to the nurseries and bedrooms. She would accomplish this duty before it was time for breakfast in the servants' hall. Mr Standing, the butler, always sat at the head of the table, with Frederick, the footman, and Françoise, Mrs Debrace's French personal maid, on either side and the rest of the staff in order of their seniority. As Betsy, the tweeny, took her meals with Cook and the kitchen boy in the kitchen, Alice had then been the most junior of the servants and therefore the last to be served.

By eight o'clock she was once more on her feet, helping to make beds, emptying the washbasins, cleaning the washstands, the bathroom and water closet. These tasks done, she had to set about scrubbing the servants' stairway, cleaning their rooms in the attic and Cook's bedroom and sitting-room. There'd barely been time to change into her black afternoon dress, white cap and apron, before she was needed to help Sally, the parlour-maid, serve luncheon. After eating her own midday meal with the other staff, if Mr Standing did not require her for some further task such as cleaning the silver, Alice was given a pile of household mending to do.

It had been her aptitude for this particular job which had come to the notice of Françoise. On hearing that Alice actually enjoyed all forms of sewing, Françoise had spoken to the mistress, suggesting that she train Alice in the duties of ladies' maid. When war broke out, Françoise immediately returned to her own country to be with her family and, young though she was, Alice had been promoted, with a welcome rise in her wages.

She loved her new duties, which were far less onerous and, in caring meticulously for her mistress's many beautiful gowns, gave her some degree of scope for the artistic talents that were only now becoming apparent. Mrs Debrace's brother-in-law was a French couturier of some renown and, as a consequence, Alice's mistress had an extensive wardrobe of very beautiful and fashionable clothes. As vague in this as in all things, Mrs Debrace could never recall which hat, what colour of gloves or fichu draping she should wear with which gown. It was Alice who rearranged the position of the ostrich feather in her hair, who tied the tassel-ended stole most becomingly, to whom her mistress deferred, vowing that Alice had natural good taste.

Her tasks were now a pleasure and Mrs Debrace a considerate and unexacting employer. Although Alice was often told that she need not wait up until her mistress returned from a late dinner party, she always did so, using her time to look through old fashion magazines, such as *La Gazette du Bon Ton*, which Mrs Debrace's sister sent from Paris. When there were no new magazines, she read one of the novels Mrs Debrace herself enjoyed and permitted Alice to borrow.

It was not, however, only her mistress's clothes which Alice admired, but the quiet ordered elegance of Mrs Debrace's large bedroom and her beautiful possessions.

For Alice it was a pleasure to handle the ivory-backed hairbrushes and matching hand mirror, clothes brush and comb which lay on a lace cloth covering the glass-topped, mahogany dressing-table. The initials E. L. D. had been carved into the ivory. They were also inscribed on the little silver-capped glass bottles and jars containing creams, lotions and rosewater which fitted neatly into a heavy, crocodile-leather dressing-case. This case went with Mrs Debrace whenever she travelled, but otherwise stood on a bow-fronted chest of drawers in front of the bay window. In summer it was Alice's task always to keep a vase of fresh flowers on the chest, and in winter, one of her father's carefully forced plants or bowls of hyacinths.

Whenever she turned back the quilted bedcover so prettily patterned with green and pink honeysuckle and roses, Alice dreamed she would one day have a room like this in the house she shared with Harry. She would choose the same colours for the wallpaper, decorate her room with similar pictures of the country-side, and choose the same china ornaments of shepherdesses and their sheep. She would have an adjoining bathroom like her mistress's, with blue-and-white-tiled walls and a bath with gleaming brass taps. Not least, she would keep a big glass jar full of rose-scented bath salts to perfume the water in which she would bathe before donning one of the magnificent Verveine, Poiret or Paquin gowns to wear at dinner.

Alice's dreams were tempered by the more practical side of her nature, and she was well aware that they could never be realized unless Harry were to reach his own goal. He too wanted to be rich one day – not in order to own a beautiful house, but because he passionately wanted a string of horses. Whenever he described his future to her, he envisaged himself as the owner of a fine stallion like the master's, keeping a brood mare and raising bloodstock. To him the stables were far more important than the house in which he would live. 'You can take care of that, Alice,' he would say, laughing, for he was never happier than when they were playing this particular game of make-believe.

Now that Harry had the chance to go to grammar

school, the improbability of their aspirations had given way to a tiny ray of genuine hope. Alice herself was unable to save more than a few pence from her weekly wage of four shillings and sixpence. Two shillings of her earnings went to augment the Pritchett family budget. Since the war, prices had been rising sharply, leaving her with even less to keep herself respectably clothed. Knowing these limitations, she had long ago accepted that it must be Harry who found a way to make them both rich. Harry, like herself, had taken to heart the headmaster's edict that if he worked hard enough, he might even win a scholarship to a university and obtain a degree – others had done it.

As if following Alice's train of thought, Eloise Debrace accepted the big bath towel her maid had been warming by the coal fire and, drying herself, said suddenly, 'I quite forgot to tell you, Alice. Mr Debrace will be home this evening. If he is not too tired, I shall ask if he can see you after dinner.' As Alice's face lit up with a delighted smile, she added: 'Do you know, my dear, you're growing into a very pretty girl! To be honest, when Françoise first drew you to my attention, I thought: "What a plain little thing."' She smiled to soften her words. 'It's quite surprising how often it is the ugly ducklings who grow into the beautiful swans. I quite envy your complexion. You have a good figure too, and with those large hazel eyes, I do not doubt you will soon be attracting a great many admirers.'

Eloise Debrace sat down at her dressing-table, staring short-sightedly at her reflection as Alice lit the tiny brass stove and placed the curling-tongs on top to heat. One of her maid's tasks before dinner was to curl her soft blonde hair, which, unpinned, fell to her waist.

She gave a deep sigh. 'If the casualty lists are anything to go by, Alice, there will be scarcely any young men left for girls of your age to marry. You will all be competing with each other for the few who do return from the war.'

Alice tested the warmth of the curling-tongs and, satisfied, wound a coil of her mistress's hair between the prongs.

'I shall not be competing for a husband, madam,' she said quietly. 'It is not my intention to get married.'

Eloise looked at her in astonishment. 'But Alice, surely that is every girl's aim in life? Don't you want a husband to take care of you? Children?'

'My mum has a husband and eight children, so I know what married life's like and it isn't what I want for myself, madam.'

Eloise was interested. 'But why not, Alice? Your father is a good, kind, hard-working man. I know Mr Debrace thinks very highly of him. As to your brothers and sisters, they are a great credit to your mother's upbringing. Aren't you proud to belong to such a family?'

Alice nodded, but much as she liked her mistress and appreciated the degree of intimacy that had grown up between them, she could not lay herself open to ridicule by voicing her dreams for herself and Harry, dreams she knew full well had but the barest hope of materializing.

'I want to make something of myself, madam,' she said truthfully. 'Things are changing now, aren't they? I mean, there's women doing all kinds of war work in factories and the like . . . jobs what were men's work before there weren't enough men to do them.'

'Jobs *that* were men's work,' Eloise corrected automatically. 'You are right, of course, Alice, though I must confess I'd not thought of it. Tell me, child, if you could be anything in the world you wanted, what would you choose to be?'

Alice smiled. 'I don't know, madam. Be like Monsieur Verveine, I think.'

Eloise was amused. As far as she knew, Alice had seen her brother-in-law only once, when he and her sister, Rosamund, had come to stay for a week before the war. Alice had still been a parlourmaid then. Perhaps the girl had listened to their conversation while she had served the meals. Félix's favourite topic was his couture house in Paris and his plan – now shelved because of the war – to open a London salon. Philip considered Félix to be something of a poseur and thought him pretentious, but then his own interests were centred entirely on his medical work, or horses and hunting. It was a sad day for him when the war had put an end to his favourite sport, and all he could do now – when he had the time, poor man – was to hack round the countryside on his stallion.

Eloise forgot her young maid as her thoughts followed their own train. She was remembering how disappointed Philip had been when, in those early years, his only son had proved to be so delicate and unlikely to reach an age where he, the boy's father, could teach him to ride. It was something of a miracle that Aubrey's dreadful asthmatic attacks had lessened after his seventh birthday. Then, alas, the poor boy had been far too nervous to mount the pony Philip bought him. It was not until the gardener's child, Harry, had appeared on the scene that Aubrey had suddenly felt impelled to show that he was at least the equal of the younger boy. He had begun to take a genuine interest in outdoor activities and, wisely, Philip had allowed the companionship to continue, well aware that Harry's influence on his son was a great deal more effective than his own.

Eloise adored her beautiful fair-haired boy. His nature was similar to her own and although Philip sometimes unkindly referred to him as being a bit of a milksop, she argued that Aubrey was merely an unusually sensitive child. Perhaps it was fortunate that Madeleine was so demanding of her father's time and attention. With her huge, sapphire-blue eyes, heart-shaped face and dainty ways, she could twist her father round her little finger – as indeed she could most people when she chose to do so. Her daughter was a little minx, Eloise thought fondly, and even Nanny spoiled her, enjoying the admiration her young charge received whenever they were in public. When Madeleine stamped her foot and demanded her own way, her red lips curving into a pout, one had the inclination to pick the child up and cajole her into laughing again in preference to scolding her. Only yesterday Eloise had heard her daughter speaking in the most dictatorial way to the nurserymaid, Jenny Pritchett.

It was high time Nanny was replaced by a less indulgent governess, she thought now. Madeleine must learn that it did not do to be rude to one's inferiors, since it was quite unfair to take advantage of those one employed who risked the loss of their job if they answered back. Besides, Jenny was a nice girl, like all the Pritchett children.

Eloise's thoughts returned to Harry Pritchett. She could understand why Alice believed he must go to grammar school for he was an intelligent, well-spoken boy. Aubrey openly admitted that Harry was far cleverer than himself, and on several occasions when she had paid an unexpected visit to the nursery Eloise had come upon Harry assisting her son with his homework.

She really must employ a governess who could teach the children properly, she decided now. Miss Tester, the retired schoolmistress who came daily to give them their lessons, was, according to Philip, quite inadequate. On the other hand, Philip had been talking recently about sending Aubrey to a boarding-school. She herself had opposed the idea, for she knew how spartan the boys' lives could be in such establishments. Philip, however, would not let the matter drop, insisting that Aubrey's health had improved so much he was now quite fit to enjoy a normal education; that he would enjoy, too, the wealth of companionship he lacked at home. Eloise was almost persuaded, knowing that if Harry were indeed to go to grammar school he would have less time to come up to The Grange to keep Aubrey entertained, and her beloved son would greatly miss the company of his only real friend. Perhaps, after all, she should allow Philip to have his way without further protest.

'I think I hear the Daimler,' she said as her ear caught the sound of heavy tyres crunching on the gravel of the drive. She smiled at Alice. 'For once Mr Debrace is early,' she said happily. 'I think that will do for now, Alice. Help me into my dress and I'll go down to welcome him.'

Alice slipped the primrose velvet and ninon gown over her mistress's head and fastened a jet necklace round her throat. Deftly, she fixed a jet and *diamanté* comb into her mistress's softly curled hair and, picking up a chiffon scarf, draped it over Eloise's shoulders.

'Thank you, Alice. I think I look very nice, thanks to your assistance.' As Eloise turned to leave the room, she said over her shoulder: 'And don't worry, my dear, I promise I'll ask my husband to speak to you about Harry.'

Alice felt her heartbeat quicken with nervous excitement as she started to tidy the bedroom. In the next few hours, Harry's whole future might be decided, and it was up to her to speak well enough on his behalf to convince the master that this opportunity must not be missed. If Mr Debrace could be persuaded, then he in turn could convince her father. Somehow she must find the right words, for failure to help Harry was even more unthinkable now than it had ever been.

'Well now, Alice, your mistress said you have something important you wish to tell me about young Harry.'

Philip Debrace curbed the note of irritation that might otherwise have raised his voice. Accustomed as he was to his wife's hopelessly inadequate memory, he could never quite accept her failure to appreciate how exhausting and draining a surgeon's duties were, especially in wartime, when operations were for the most part emergencies and not ones for which he had time to prepare. Only Eloise, he thought, would bother him at this hour with domestic matters involving the household staff. He was, however, completely devoted to his young wife and for that reason never denied a request, however trivial, if it could be fulfilled.

Alice bobbed a curtsey and clasped her hands tightly together in front of her. She was not frightened of this tall, grey-haired man, although he insisted his home was run on much the same disciplined lines as he ran his hospital. All the staff were in agreement that he had never dismissed an employee without good reason, nor denied a genuine excuse for some misdemeanour. He was much respected for the hospital work he did – the more so since he had inherited wealth and could, like any other gentleman, have chosen to lead a life of leisure if he so pleased.

This past year, as a result of the war, he was always pressed for time and could become irritable if some small domestic matter delayed him getting back to his work, but he was normally a man of good temper and, as Mr Standing had pointed out, allowances must be made if he acted out of character. No, Alice thought now, she was not afraid of her employer. Her fear was that he might not consider the future of a mere gardener's boy important enough to warrant the taking of his valuable time.

'Sir, I need your help very badly. Harry has won a scholarship to grammar school and our dad won't let him go. He says he's to start work here in the stables, as was arranged between you and him last Easter, but Mr Wilson – the headmaster, sir – says as how Harry must take this opportunity if he can.'

Philip Debrace looked at the girl's flushed cheeks with a well-concealed sigh of weariness. Why couldn't Eloise deal with such matters without involving him? He was tired – bone-tired after a twelve-hour day operating, and on the drive home he had allowed himself to become thoroughly depressed; angry too at the terrible waste of young lives.

'So what is it you want me to do, Alice?' he asked, forcing himself to give the girl his full attention. She was very young, yet there was an expression of such intensity in her eyes that he caught a little of her urgency.

Before she could reply, there was a knock on the door of his study. He had forgotten that on leaving the dining-room he had instructed the parlourmaid to bring him a cognac.

'Your brandy, sir.' It was, however, a man who had come into the room and was now standing beside Alice, holding a tray with a balloon glass and warmer on it.

'Great Scott, Frederick!' Philip exclaimed at the sight of his former footman. 'What on earth are you doing here?'

It was now over a year since his footman had left to join the Royal Sussex Regiment – a year which had obviously taken its toll. Tall, lanky, his dark hair swept back off his forehead, Frederick looked a changed man, his livery hanging loosely on his thin body.

'I'm on leave, sir,' he said quietly. 'The mistress said I might spend my time here. I hope you don't mind, sir.'

'Good heavens, man, I'm delighted to see you. But what on earth reason have you for spending your precious leave here? You should be making the most of it – having a good time. 'Pon my soul!'

Frederick handed the now warmed glass of brandy to his master.

'I'd most likely have gone home, sir, if I had a home to go to. You may not remember, sir, that I came to you from an orphanage? It was a long time ago – I was bootboy here in those days.'

'Yes, of course. I'd forgotten. Things are pretty rotten out there, aren't they? Don't get leave too often, I'm told. See here, Frederick, you should be enjoying yourself . . .' He broke off to reach in an inner pocket and brought out a Moroccan leather purse. Withdrawing two sovereigns he put them on top of the tray Frederick was still holding. 'There now – get yourself a place to stay in Brighton. Plenty going on there – the Follies on the Palace Pier, music hall at the Hippodrome. Find yourself a pretty girl – there's plenty of them without partners these days – and take her dancing at the Aquarium Hall or the Dome or Sherry's.'

'It's very good of you, sir, but, well . . .' The man's face looked suddenly drawn. 'It's like this, sir. Out there it's noise, mud, rats . . . Mostly, sir, it's the noise of the shells coming over got to me worst. It's nice and quiet and peaceful here, sir, if you don't mind, sir.'

Philip Debrace nodded.

'If it's what you want, Fred, my boy. No need to work, though. Just rest up – go for walks. Take young Alice here into Brighton to the pictures . . . Have a day out. You'd keep him company, wouldn't you, Alice?'

Alice nodded, aware that she was blushing. Fred, however, was looking at her with an eager, expectant gaze.

'If my mum and the mistress give permission, sir.'

'Mrs Debrace will take care of that. Good to see you, anyway, Frederick. And keep this . . .' He returned the coins Frederick had given back to him. 'It's the least those of us who can't be out there to share the horrors can do to make amends. Nasty business, war.'

He repeated the words after Frederick had once again professed his thanks before leaving the room.

'Perhaps if you females ran the world, we wouldn't get into these national confrontations,' he said, as much to himself as Alice. 'If the suffragettes get their way, we'll have women in Parliament yet. Won't get women voting for war. Now then, Alice, you were telling me about your brother. Won a scholarship to grammar school, did he? Good for him. I always said he was a bright lad.'

Alice drew a deep breath.

'Sir, my dad says we need the money Harry'd earn if he comes to work here – and he can't afford for Harry to go to the grammar.'

Philip frowned.

'There are others in the family, aren't there? And you and that younger girl – Jenny, is it? You're both earning.'

'Yes, sir, but there's another baby now.'

'Yes, well, I know things aren't easy what with prices rising all the time. All the same, I should have thought your father would see the long-term advantages of Harry getting a full education. He might make something of himself, that boy, if he's willing to work.'

'Sir, it isn't just that Dad can't see the advantages for Harry. You see, there's more to it. Harry's not his son, not his real son . . .'

Haltingly, she explained the circumstances in which Harry had come to be part of the Pritchett family.

'It isn't that Dad's not fond of him,' she concluded. 'I think he is – in his way. But for some time now the payments haven't been enough to pay for Harry's keep. He even spoke about turning him out. Not that Mum would've let him do that even if he'd really wanted. Anyways, Dad reckoned on Harry paying him back what was owing now he is old enough to be earning. What with our Billy passing on and the others too young still to work, it's sometimes hard to make ends meet. From what Dad said to Mum the other night, he doesn't think it would be fair to sacrifice the needs of the rest of the family just because Harry wanted more learning – leastways, that's the way he put it, sir.'

'I find this very interesting,' Philip said, sipping his brandy thoughtfully. 'Explains quite a lot of things. For one, the boy doesn't look like the rest of you. Mrs Debrace remarked on it once – that Harry was the only one of you who was dark-haired and dark-eyed – but I'd forgotten. Well, well, well.'

'I reckoned as how you wouldn't have known, sir, about Mum and Dad fostering Harry, seeing as how you only came down to live here after Jenny and Harry were born. Mum said it was all over the village at the time, but then it got forgot. People have more to worry about than a bit of gossip about us Pritchetts taking in a child.'

'And there's no inkling as to who his father was?'

'I asked Mum once – that time she thought she wasn't going to live – but she said no, nor ever would we be likely to know. We never talk about it at home, sir – being born out of wedlock not being nice talk anyway – and, of course, Harry doesn't know. I'm the only one as does, sir, and I don't think Mum would ever've talked to me about it but for that time she thought she was going to die. That was the time you took her into your hospital, sir, and paid all the expenses and Dad's mindful of that too, saying as how we're indebted to you, like, and he's not having Harry let you down.'

Philip Debrace put down his brandy glass and eased himself into a more comfortable position in his chair.

'My wife's the one who arranged for your mother to go to hospital – least she could do with the poor woman so incapacitated with her prolapse and so badly in need of attention. Neither Mrs Debrace nor I would want your father feeling indebted, Alice, although, proud man that he is, I suppose it's only natural. Having said that, I'm beginning to see why it would be wrong to deny young

Harry the education he's clearly earned. I've always felt it wrong that children should be penalized for their parents' misdeeds. They've done no harm to anyone.' He shot Alice a piercing glance that was not unkindly. 'So this is why you are speaking up for him? I was wondering why the boy had not come to me himself. It's unlike him to be lacking in courage.'

'I forbade him, sir. I thought you ought to know all the facts and Harry couldn't give them to you, not knowing them himself. Do you think you can talk Dad round, sir? I think it will break Harry's heart if he can't go.'

Mr Debrace smiled.

'We can't have that, can we? I'll tell your father that I'll be responsible for all the lad's expenses, and make up the loss of his wages. Pritchett can be a stubborn man, right enough, but he'll have no point to argue then, will he?'

For a moment, Alice was speechless. When she found her voice, it was to say, 'You'll never regret it, sir, I promise. You'll see. Harry will prove he's worth what you're doing for him. I know he will. I just *know* he will,' she repeated fervently.

Mr Debrace's smile broadened.

'Seems he's got one dedicated advocate in you,' he said. 'I'll say this much, Alice – with you behind him, I don't have any doubt the boy will do well.'

64

CHAPTER THREE

1915

Pamela Kinmuire moved her chair closer to the coal fire
and pulled her warm cashmere stole more tightly around
her shoulders. Despite the fact that the fire had been
recently refuelled by one of the servants, the big room
with its tall ceilings was both draughty and chilly. This
constant cold in the winter months was part of the price
one paid for living in an ancestral home, she thought,
remembering her childhood. Gervaise, her husband, had
bought a house in Eaton Terrace when they were first
married, where modern electricity had been installed and
which she had furnished with every creature comfort. She
would infinitely prefer to be living there.

A thin, angular woman with small, pointed features,
Pamela, Countess of Kinmuire, was striking but not
beautiful to look at. When she chose to be charming, she
could attract the opposite sex, who sensed her innate
weakness of character and her need for a strong man to
dominate and take care of her. Her large, round, blue eyes
were her best feature, although they could as easily fill
with tears of self-pity if she were thwarted, as with smiles
when life ran smoothly.

Life was not running smoothly now, she reflected,
glancing at the sleeping figure of her husband in the big
four-poster bed. Gervaise was dying – and he knew it. It
would not be long before she was bereaved, a widow
obliged to go into mourning, unable to rejoin London
society and enjoy the annual entertainments of the season.
It was so unfair, she thought, as tears filled her eyes.
Gervaise was only thirty-two and it was not even as if he

was one of the war casualties. He had survived the first year of fighting, during which, as an officer in the Leicesters, he had been in some of the worst battles at Neuve Chapelle and Hooge. For his life to end now because of some obscure illness the doctors called Bright's Disease was a cruel twist of fate.

'Don't be such a ninny,' her brother, Cosmo, had replied when she had first written to tell him that Gervaise had not long to live. 'He has no children, so you'll get all his money. You're a nice-looking woman, with a good pedigree. It won't be long before you find yourself another husband.'

Pamela was far from sure she wanted another husband. For one thing, she heartily disliked what she called her marital duties. Fortunately, Gervaise had not demanded them, as, according to her more intimate friends, most husbands did. He was a tolerant man, leaving her for the most part to her own pursuits while involving himself in his preferred sporting activities. The main interest in his life was his horses. The Kinmuire family had owned this big estate on the outskirts of Melton Mowbray for generations, and, being in the heart of hunting country, it was traditional for all the members of the family to live at Maythorpe House from November to April. Even before Gervaise's father, the old earl, had died, Pamela had been obliged to winter here in the Midlands. That she did not nor ever had wished to ride was the one bone of contention between them, for Gervaise did not understand her fear and dislike of horses. The old earl had been more sympathetic.

'The boy seems to forget that the purpose of your marriage is to produce children. Not the best thing for females to go charging round on horseback. Can't hunt when you're *enceinte* anyway!'

There had, of course, been no heir, possibly because after the first year of their marriage she and Gervaise had so seldom shared the marital bed. Pamela was not sorry. She disliked children and she dreaded the pain of childbirth, which her women friends described in awful detail.

Since the onslaught of his disease and the first hint of its possible fatality, Gervaise had started to express his disappointment that they had not had a son. The title would pass to a distant cousin who lived in the States – a man Gervaise had never met and did not communicate with. These past few days, since he had been growing steadily weaker, he had begun to refer to this cousin more frequently and now, as he woke from a light sleep, the matter of the Kinmuire title must have been on his mind, for he said:

'Pamela, I think we should have a talk . . . about your future after I have passed on! Will you pull your chair closer? What I have to say is confidential and I don't want to raise my voice.'

As Pamela approached the bed, she felt a sudden pang of grief, tinged with panic. She did not want Gervaise to die. It was not that she had ever loved him, although he was an extremely good-looking man and considered by all her women friends to be unusually handsome. It was, perhaps, his very sexuality which was least attractive to her. As a very young child in the remote moorlands of Northumberland, she had been the victim of an uncle who, drunk at the time, had still been able to give free rein to his paedophiliac inclinations. Pamela could not recall the occasion in detail, but the memory of her fear and disgust remained, and it disturbed her if a man even held her too close in a dance, kissed her cheek or took possession of her hand.

But for the necessity to do so, Pamela would not have married, despite her father's persuasions. It was her brother, Cosmo, who had talked her into it. She had always hero-worshipped her older brother and was appalled when he confessed to her that he had run up such frighteningly large gambling debts that were it not for the certainty of his eventual inheritance, he would have no hope of repaying them. Their father, the eighteenth Viscount Simcox, was already impoverished due to persistent mismanagement of his estates but was ignorant of his son's profligacy – as indeed was everyone else.

Pamela's marriage into the wealthy Kinmuire family would safeguard her future, Cosmo had pointed out, since their land would have to be sold the moment it became his to dispose of. It was extremely fortunate, he had thought at the time, that his father and Gervaise's were old friends and Pamela was the earl's god-daughter, as a result of which neither Gervaise nor his father had concerned themselves with Cosmo's activities in London.

In her own self-interest, Pamela had agreed to the marriage, and was glad she had done so when, a year later, her father had met an untimely death in a fire caused by an overturned oil lamp in his bedroom. Immediately after the funeral, Cosmo had set about selling everything the family possessed and, with the small sum left over after he had cleared his debts, he had departed to Canada to seek his fortune there.

Somehow Pamela had managed to conceal from Gervaise the true reason for Cosmo's actions and, later, the occasional letters she received from her brother. Despite the fact that Cosmo had promised her he would refrain from indulging his love of gambling ever again, he had been unable to combat the compulsion. Reading between the lines, she soon realized that if he were not betting on horses at race meetings, he was playing for high stakes at cards. Every letter contained a hint that he could do with a loan if she could see her way to help him out of a spot.

Prior to their marriage, Gervaise Harvey had, from time to time, been Pamela's escort at hunt balls or on similar occasions. Pamela was one of the few girls – if not the only one – who had not been obviously vying for his attention, demanding nothing from him but friendship. It was this which had done more to attract Gervaise than any obvious effort on her part to involve him in a romantic association. An only son, he was under pressure from his father to marry so that he might produce an heir. Finally, in 1910, when Gervaise was twenty-seven and Pamela twenty-three, they had been married with great ceremony in St Margaret's, Westminster. The society pages had given prominence to the wedding, which, they intimated, was a great love match.

Despite the fact that neither Pamela nor Gervaise was in the least in love with each other, for the past five years they had been content with the way their marriage had evolved. Gervaise's former bachelor existence had changed only marginally – until the war had broken out – and Pamela's life was much improved – apart from these long winter months in the Midlands. She was free to spend as much money as she pleased: not only could she charge her purchases to Gervaise's accounts but he had also provided her with a generous personal allowance. Unbeknownst to Gervaise, she had from time to time sent money to Cosmo in answer to his pleas for help. Despite his profligate ways, Cosmo was the one man in the world Pamela trusted. From childhood he had protected her, as far as he had been able, and had organized their activities and made life tolerable on the isolated Northumbrian estate.

Looking once more at the recumbent form of her dying husband, Pamela thought with relief that soon Cosmo would be here to help her through the difficult days to come. She had sent him a cable the day the family doctor had informed her she must prepare herself for Gervaise's demise, and sent him the money for his passage home. He was due to arrive at Liverpool within a few days.

Gervaise's dark-brown eyes, looking larger than ever in his drawn face, were now open. He was staring at her so intently, it made her feel uneasy.

'What is it, Gervaise?' she asked. 'Are you in pain?'

Momentarily, his face softened into a smile. 'No, my dear. But my mind is not at ease. Has your brother arrived yet?'

Pamela shook her head. 'He'll be here the day after tomorrow.'

Gervaise was silent for a moment before he said: 'You know I'm dying, Pamela, and there is no point in either of us denying it. This is not the time for pretence, my dear. You are going to need a great deal of courage to face these next months without me, and if only for that reason, I am glad Cosmo will be here to assist you. However, there is another reason, and since time is running out for me, I must now speak honestly to you on a subject I'd hoped we need never discuss. Please bear with me, Pamela, and, if you can, give me your understanding.'

Pamela gave him an uneasy glance. Gervaise's voice was charged with emotion and, instinctively, she was on the defensive.

'If there's anything I can do . . .' she said vaguely.

'This has to do with your future, Pamela. As you know, my title and this house are entailed. I cannot, therefore, leave them to you. However, I have heard this morning from my cousin, Wendell Harvey, who, as you know, I notified of my illness. He has told me that there are no circumstances that would persuade him to live in England. He has a flourishing stud farm in Kentucky, a family and a home there, and does not wish to live the kind of life I live in peacetime in this country. He says that I may do as I please about Maythorpe House. I can, therefore, arrange for you to remain in residence for as long as you wish.'

'Without you, Gervaise, I don't think I would wish to live here,' Pamela said hesitantly. 'As you know, I have always preferred our house in London.'

'I am aware of that, but your brother, Cosmo – he is a hunting man, and I would be prepared, on certain conditions, to arrange with my cousin for Cosmo to take up residence here with all the expenses of upkeep taken care of.'

Pamela's mouth fell open in surprise. As far as she was aware, Gervaise had never liked Cosmo. Now she found it hard to believe that he was contemplating inviting her brother to live in Maythorpe House *with all his expenses paid*.

'I am sure Cosmo would be pleased to agree to any conditions you might name, Gervaise,' she said truthfully. 'He has been unable to put down roots since he sold our family home and went abroad. It would be a great comfort to me to have him close at hand after . . . when you are no longer here.'

'So I had thought,' Gervaise said. 'However, you must first hear what those conditions are, my dear. They involve you also, which is why I'm not waiting for your brother's arrival to explain matters to you. You will have time to consider your part in this before I put the matter to him.'

'I . . . I am to be involved?'

'I have no alternative but to involve you.' Gervaise paused, his eyes closing for a moment before he drew a long breath and continued. 'Many years ago – when I was nineteen, to be precise – I fell in love, very deeply in love, with a young girl. She returned my affection. I wanted to marry her but, of course, my father would not hear of it. He arranged for me to complete my education abroad, effectively preventing me from seeing this girl for several years.'

As he paused to draw breath, Pamela said, frowning, 'Do I need to be told all this, Gervaise? I have no wish to hear . . .'

'But I have to make you understand,' Gervaise broke in. 'The love I shared with this girl – whom I shall call "Mary" for the sake of preserving her anonymity – was not the childish infatuation my father thought it. We were, I suppose, not unlike that ill-fated couple Romeo and Juliet! The thought of never seeing each other again was unbearable. When we met for the last time before I left Oxford, to say goodbye, our feelings were such that we could not contain them.'

His voice took on a note of urgency as, ignoring the look of shock on his wife's face, he declared, 'I know that it was wrong. I should never have allowed myself to . . . I should have realized what the consequences might be. At the time, though, we were determined that no matter how long we must wait, ultimately we would marry. We convinced ourselves that since we were one day to be man and wife, we would be harming no one if we anticipated that day. Do you understand what I am trying to tell you, Pamela?'

Pamela was staring at her husband with disbelief. That

71

Gervaise – the most conventional and honourable of men – had behaved in such a way was all but inconceivable.

'You mean, you *seduced* the girl?'

'I suppose I must accept that accusation. I was the elder . . . the man . . . I should have protected her . . .'

He broke off, looking so distressed that for a moment Pamela forgot her astonishment in genuine concern for him, but before she could ring the hand bell by his bed for his manservant, he eased himself into a sitting position.

'We had both given our word to our parents that we would not write letters to each other, so it was a dreadful shock to me to discover when I returned from abroad, that "Mary" had married someone else; that she had not, after all, loved me enough to wait for me.'

Gervaise paused before adding, 'There is far worse to come. I learned that the girl I loved had had my child – a boy. I went to see the friend who helped "Mary" conceal her condition from everyone. She told me that when the child was born, arrangements had been made for it to be placed anonymously with a foster family. For her peace of mind, "Mary" was told the baby had died.'

Pamela now found herself as much intrigued as shocked by this extraordinary story, which revealed an aspect of her husband's character she had been totally ignorant of.

'Why did the girl not wait for your return?' she asked. 'If, as you implied, she had really fallen so deeply in love with you, surely she could have avoided marriage to someone else?'

'Unfortunately, her parents discovered what had happened – or part of it. "Mary" went into a decline and, under pressure from the family doctor, confessed that she had borne a child. She was still under age and the doctor told her parents. Despite their questioning, she refused to reveal the name of the father or that of the friend who had helped her.'

Gervaise's face had become deathly pale, but he was clearly determined to continue with his story. 'Understandably, "Mary's" parents were horrified and for several months they kept her a virtual prisoner in her room, allowing their friends and neighbours to think she was ill with a suspected appendicitis. This state of affairs could not continue indefinitely, and eventually, under the strictest possible supervision, "Mary" was allowed out. Pressure was put upon her by her parents to marry one of their neighbours – a much older man who had been widowed following the birth of his third child. The man was anxious to find a suitable mother for his young family.'

He drew a long sigh as he added, '"Mary" did not love this man, but she had never ceased to mourn for her lost baby and she was drawn to the widower's children – especially the infant. It was not long before she gave way to the pressure of her parents to see her safely married. You must understand that she was still only eighteen and I only twenty-one, and she knew that even when I returned to England my father would never condone our marriage. She therefore accepted the security of a respectable marriage to the widower.'

His long speech had clearly so exhausted Gervaise that, despite her curiosity, Pamela suggested he might leave the rest of his story until later. He insisted, however, that he must unburden himself, since only by doing so could he explain the necessary conditions he must impose upon Cosmo and herself.

'When eventually I returned to England and discovered "Mary" was married, I resolved to put the past behind me and, as far as I could, forget her,' he said. 'I knew that the day would come when I too must marry in order to continue our family line. My father was both ill and elderly when that day came. It was shortly after I had first met you, my dear. Unlike most young girls, you seemed no more anxious than I for romantic love. Perhaps, I thought, you too had had a disappointment in your first experience of it. Whatever the reason, we seemed well suited, and although I could not offer you the kind of love I have spoken of, I was not proposing marriage empty-handed. I was aware of your father's financial state and at least I could offer you a life free from financial concerns. I think you will agree, the arrangement was fair to us both. As far as I'm aware I have never given you cause for complaint. Nor have I ever reproached you for your failure to provide me with an heir.'

Pamela nodded. Still unable to follow his train of thought, she was instinctively uneasy. 'You have been very patient in that respect. I am not ungrateful,' she said.

Gervaise's expression, unnoticed by her, was ironic. 'It pleases me to hear you say so, my dear. You see, I have now to ask you a great favour not unconnected with this subject. It is not one you may find agreeable but, nevertheless, I must ask it. I want you to find my child, bring him to live here, where, but for the circumstances of his birth, he belongs, and bring him up in a manner befitting my son.'

Pamela's gasp registered the full extent of her shock. 'Bring him here? Your child? Your bastard?' The word was out before she could withhold it. 'I couldn't bring myself to do such a thing, you must know that. What would I tell people? What would they say – think? You cannot ask this of me, Gervaise.'

'I can and do ask it, Pamela. It is not the first time a gentleman has acknowledged his natural offspring. When all is said and done, he *is* a Harvey.'

'Your love child,' Pamela whispered. For the first time, she felt a tinge of jealousy, realizing what that young girl had meant to Gervaise. 'Your son by that girl you loved.'

Gervaise nodded, his face pale but his mouth set in a determined line. 'Yes, the child of our love. I don't mean to hurt you, Pamela, nor even do I expect you to love the boy – merely to bring him up as I would do were my life spared. I had thought of doing so many times, but in the light of the fact that we – you and I – might yet have had children of our own, I put off the decision. Then the war came and . . . well, now I can do what I know in my heart is my duty to my son. Bastard he may be, but through no fault of his. It would be my intention to make you and your brother his legal guardians, if that is possible. The child was left with a working-class family whom I very much doubt would have adopted him. If you and your brother will take on this responsibility for me, I can die in peace.'

Gervaise's voice now held a note of desperation. 'Surely this wouldn't prove too heavy a burden for you, Pamela? The child must be nearing thirteen, by now. You can arrange for him to go to a good boarding-school and you would see him only during his holidays. For the rest of the time, you would be free to do whatever you wished.'

Pamela was silent. Although her first reaction had been one of adamant refusal, Gervaise had indicated that she need really have very little involvement. If she were to agree, the advantages to Cosmo would be numerous. As Gervaise had suggested, she need not spend more than a few months of the year here in the Midlands. They might even leave the boy here during his long summer holidays and she could travel abroad once this tiresome war was over. Cosmo could take over Gervaise's stables and, as a resident of Maythorpe House, he would become an acceptable member of the Cottesmore once hunting started again. Provided he did not resort again to his old gambling habits, his financial status would be assured.

'I must talk it over with Cosmo before I can agree, Gervaise,' she said, prevaricating. 'If I have understood you correctly, he too is to be a guardian to the boy.'

Gervaise nodded. 'While I have been lying here, I have thought a very great deal about involving him as well as you. There are many advantages. Cosmo is a gentleman and in that respect would be a good example for the boy to imitate. He is also an excellent sportsman – and I should like my son to be able to hold his own with a gun, a fishing-rod, on the hunting field. I would like him also to be well mannered and well educated. Cosmo can see to such matters.'

'Yes, of course,' Pamela agreed. 'Nevertheless, Gervaise, the boy is still . . . how would we explain him? What should we call him? You couldn't possibly expect me to acknowledge him as your illegitimate child. That is un-thinkable.'

'I don't expect it. Let him retain the surname he now has. As to who he is – you could say quite simply that he's the son of a distant relative who died recently, leaving him homeless. Such a story wouldn't harm you socially, my dear. You would be seen to be acting most charitably.'

Pamela stood up. 'I see you have considered all this in great depth, Gervaise. Wouldn't it have been fairer to discuss it with me when you first thought up this wild scheme?'

'Perhaps it was cowardly of me not to have done so. On the other hand, it's only since I knew I hadn't long to live that I thought seriously about it. The prospect of death does change one's perspective, you know! Now, it seems that my remaining time on this earth is shorter than I'd hoped, and although I have written twice this past month to "Mary's" friend, I have not had a reply. Either she has not received my letters or, far more likely, she does not wish me to know where the child is.'

Gervaise looked anxiously at his wife. 'Unless I receive a letter from her soon, I'm afraid I'll have to leave it to you and Cosmo to approach her in person. She may well deny that such a child ever existed, or she may tell you, as she told "Mary", that the infant died at birth. One thing is certain, she will reveal nothing that could harm her. I think she regretted that she had told me the truth lest, in a moment of madness, I laid claim to the boy. My father was still alive and would most certainly have guessed whose child it was. For that very reason, she wouldn't tell me where he had been left.'

'If she took such trouble to cover up the facts at the time, what makes you think she will consider them safe with me now?'

Gervaise gave a wry smile. 'As I pointed out in my letters to her, you, my wife, would be the last person who would want the truth known. And I shall not be here to claim the boy as mine. The secret would be in good hands. You would need to reassure her on these points.'

Pamela's face was pale and her eyes avoided his searching gaze. 'You realize you're asking a very great deal of me, Gervaise? Frankly, I'm shocked to learn that you have even considered acknowledging this child. I see no reason why you should after all this time. The boy is illegitimate, so he can't inherit. In any event, the title won't die with you. There is this cousin of yours in America.'

'You may attribute my feelings to guilt, if that explains things. I came close to ruining "Mary's" life. The boy is her child as well as mine and this is the only way I can honour my responsibilities.'

'You say he was left with a working-class family. Does he have their name? Supposing they are not willing to let him go?'

'I'm unaware of his name, but according to my solicitor, unless the foster family adopted him, they do not have any legal standing. Arbuthnot will divulge the name of "Mary's" friend as soon as you and Cosmo agree to become the boy's guardians. I have already explained to her in my letters that I will be leaving no instruction for the boy's name to be changed to Harvey, so your own connection with him, Pamela, and indeed anyone else's, will never be revealed. I can see no valid reason why "Mary's" friend should refuse to give you the information you need. I shall leave a last request to that effect. Of course, the boy must never be told I am his father in case he advertises the fact and jeopardizes your position. I have no more wish for you to become a subject of common gossip than you have, my dear. I understand that not even the fostering family were aware who his mother or her friend really were, so unless you were to tell him, the boy has no way of discovering his true parentage. You can tell him his mother and father are both dead if it suits your purpose, that I am an old friend of his family who, on his deathbed, decided to take a philanthropic interest in their child. It's my hope that with the benefit of the good education I have planned for him, he will be able to rise above the stigma of his illegitimacy. I can do no more for him.'

'It seems to me that you are already seeking to do far too

much!' Pamela said dryly. 'I know that . . . that you haven't long to live, Gervaise, but aren't you letting your conscience bother you unduly? What happened took place a long time ago. It's over and done with. Why raise the issue now?'

Gervaise turned away, his face bitter as he sank back among the pillows. 'Because, as you yourself may discover when death is so near at hand, one is filled with a great need to leave something of oneself behind. I should have done this years ago, when first I learned of the boy's existence. He is my son, Pamela, and in so far as I can redress the wrong I did him and, indeed, his mother, I must make amends.'

'And what of me?' Pamela asked. 'I'm your wife. What right have you to involve me? Don't I come first in your consideration?'

Gervaise turned to face her.

'Your involvement is voluntary, Pamela. You are under no obligation to fulfil these last wishes of mine. I am well aware that I would be placing my burden on your shoulders. Talk it over with your brother. I have no wish to persuade you against your will. It is a request – no more.'

As his wife left the bedroom, Gervaise closed his eyes, aware more than ever before, that the spectre of death was very close. He wished he could see his beloved Dorothy just once more before he died. He wished that he had had just one meeting with his son. Was the boy like him? Like his mother? What kind of childhood was he having? Like so many before him, Gervaise Harvey's regrets as death approached were not for the things he had done with his life, but for the things undone.

Three days later, Harry's father died.

The funeral over, the will read and Gervaise's solicitor and mourners having left the house, Pamela was alone with her brother, Cosmo, the nineteenth Viscount Simcox, in the library of Maythorpe House.

'He's left me nothing, nothing,' Pamela said as she

collapsed into one of the big leather armchairs. Tears, withheld until now, flowed freely from her eyes. She mopped at them feebly with a tiny lace handkerchief while Cosmo poured himself a stiff brandy. He was a thick-set, tall man with a florid complexion and a well-disguised paunch. Although not yet middle-aged, he looked many more than ten years older than his sister. Brown haired, with a military-looking moustache concealing a somewhat weak mouth and chin, he was none the less a strong, reassuring figure who inspired confidence, which was all too often misplaced.

Despite Cosmo's promises to his sister when he had gone to Canada, he had arrived back in England in a far worse financial state than when he left. Not that his appearance gave any outward sign of it. He was wearing conventional funeral garb made originally by his Savile Row tailor, but a little tight now around the girth after four years abroad. He had not yet pawned his gold hunter watch, and an equally expensive cravat pin and cuff links were indications of a man of means. So too were his silver cigarette case and cigar cutter. The years of poverty had taught him that those who looked impoverished were seldom able to get credit; that it was important to imply that one's straits were of a temporary nature, brought about by an unfortunate mishap which could soon be put right.

His sister's letter, he thought as he went to sit down in the chair beside her, could not have come at a more appropriate time. He was being badgered on all sides for repayment of long-overdue debts. His brother-in-law's death was most timely, since he had been able, with confidence, to stave off his Canadian creditors with vague references to a legacy he was returning to England to collect. Now, it seemed, it was not going to prove so easy to get his hands on any of the Harvey money.

'Steady on, old girl,' he said, reaching out to lay a comforting hand on Pamela's shoulder. Black did not become his sister, he thought irrelevantly. She looked pale and peeky. Thank goodness marriage had, so it seemed, not otherwise changed her! There appeared to be no strengthening of her character, no desire to be independent, like some of the Canadian women he had met these past years. In the old days Pamela had looked to him to make all her decisions for her. Now, with Gervaise gone, poor fellow, she was renewing her dependence upon him.

'As I understood the will,' he intoned, 'you're to keep the London house and are getting outright the sum of £5,000, as well as a regular income from the trust fund – a sum I would have thought would keep you quite comfortably in the manner to which you have become accustomed.'

His attempt to jolly his sister into a smile was ineffective. She sniffed into her damp handkerchief.

'But the capital – the bulk of the Harvey fortune – he's left it all in trust for the boy.'

Cosmo cleared his throat. The existence of the child had indeed come as a bit of a bombshell. Who would have imagined that the worthy, high-minded Gervaise, Earl of Kinmuire, had a by-blow tucked away? Still, these things did happen and what was really surprising was that the fellow had admitted his parenthood. Most men would have been only too happy to leave their peccadilloes in obscurity. Most certainly it had come as rather a nasty shock – to put it mildly – when the solicitor had said that the bulk of Gervaise's money was to go to his illegitimate son when he came of age; that only the income from the capital was to go to Pamela.

Neither of them had known she was not to inherit Gervaise's wealth when they'd called to see the solicitor, Arbuthnot, the day after Gervaise's death. They had jointly decided that there was nothing worthwhile to be gained by taking on the guardianship of the old boy's by-blow, and with Gervaise gone, Pamela had lost any inclination she might have had to ease her husband's passing by granting him his dying wish. When she had first relayed Gervaise's wishes to him, Cosmo had been in favour of agreeing to them, tempted as he was by the thought of becoming the life-long tenant of Maythorpe

House and, with his occupation, acquiring Gervaise's magnificent horses. Melton Mowbray was a very acceptable venue – best hunting country in England! But then Pamela had pointed out that with the Harvey capital behind her, they could buy a house wherever Cosmo chose – and all the horses he wanted without taking on the tiresome burden of the child.

With Cosmo's approval, his sister had told the solicitor that for the present anyway she did not feel able to take on this additional responsibility; nor, indeed, did Cosmo, thinking he might well decide to return to Canada. The solicitor had suggested they took some time to think the matter over; that Gervaise's wishes could not be forced upon them and that they might, if they so desired, change their minds at a later stage.

'One thing is clear, I shall certainly not change my mind now,' Pamela was saying, her lips trembling as she regarded her brother's untroubled countenance resentfully. 'Why should I put myself out for Gervaise when he has treated me so disgracefully? I was his wife for five years. How can he put that boy's considerations before mine? You may think me ghoulish, but when I knew Gervaise was dying, I thought about buying a house on the Riviera. I've always wanted to live somewhere warm in the winter. You say I'll have "enough to live on", but that means I shall be very little better off than I was in father's day. I wanted to travel, to go cruising. It's all very well for you, Cosmo, you've travelled all over the world, but I've never had the chance to do so.'

'Bit dangerous with all those German battleships cavorting around the high seas, old thing.'

Pamela had momentarily forgotten the war. Her feelings of outrage, however, quickly resurfaced. 'Why couldn't Gervaise have left the capital to me? He could have left the boy a small legacy if he was so determined. The way it's been tied up, it won't even be mine if anything were to happen to the boy.'

Cosmo stroked his moustache, his eyes thoughtful. 'Yes, pity that . . . Still, nothing we can do about it now.

You've got to remember, Pam, we're a canny lot, us northerners. Like to keep the money in the family. No hope you'll produce an heir now, so in a way, you can understand why the Harvey money's to go to the Yanky earl if the boy doesn't get it.'

'I still don't think it's fair. I'll have barely enough to live on.'

'Come off it, the old boy left you well provided for and things could be a lot worse. I've been thinking, Pam, if we agreed to become the boy's guardians, at least we'd have access to his money. The solicitor said we could "call on such funds as we need". Those were his words. Who's to say what are the *boy's* needs and what are *ours*, eh?'

Pamela's tears ceased flowing as she stared at her brother. 'But Cosmo, you mean you've changed your mind? You think we should agree to undertake this guardianship? Two days ago, you said we needn't do so.'

'Because I couldn't see any real advantage to you,' Cosmo replied truthfully. He refrained from adding that, at the time, he had supposed Pamela would shortly have access to unlimited amounts of money, which, since he would be handling her financial affairs for her, would pay his debts and allow him to set himself up in an agreeable life style. Now that her income was limited, there would be no such possibility.

He drained his brandy glass and refilled it. Returning to his chair, he said, 'Don't you see, old girl, we were assuming Gervaise was leaving you all his worldly goods? As it is, we've now got to make the best of a bad job. We must do as the old boy wanted . . . become the boy's guardians.'

'But I don't want the responsibility, Cosmo. I've never wanted children. I don't even like them. Besides, I don't see how we can spend money which is not ours.'

'Now come off it, old thing. Just think it over like a good girl. I'll be here to share the responsibility with you. We keep on Maythorpe House – for the boy, of course. Therefore, we need to employ servants. So for a start, all the staff wages can be put to the boy's account. Then we'll need food, cars, horses – I can't teach him to ride unless we're both mounted, can I? The expenses we can attribute to his care and education are unlimited.' He gave a quick guffaw. 'Don't you see, old girl? Gervaise has set the accountants an impossible task. Who can prove what we do and do not actually spend on the boy? Just have to be careful not to overdo it, that's all.'

'Yes, I see,' Pamela muttered uneasily. Cosmo sounded very confident and she didn't doubt that he knew what he was talking about. None the less, she didn't want anything to do with the child, let alone the trouble of finding him and explaining him to their friends and neighbours. On the other hand, Cosmo would stay here in England, would be here to support and advise her, to take control of everything. If he really believed this would be financially beneficial to them, she should try to overcome her objections. To do as he suggested would also alleviate some of the bitterness she felt when she had learned the terms of her husband's will. To have left his illegitimate child a few hundred pounds was one thing, but to have left him most of his fortune was beyond forgiveness. Why shouldn't they recoup some of it?

'The sooner we agree to become guardians to the little bastard the better,' Cosmo said cheerfully. 'Don't forget the boy's worth a hell of a lot, and the quicker we have it under our control, the happier I shall be. Now listen to me, old girl, we must go and see Arbuthnot at the earliest opportunity, get the necessary documents signed and find out the name of the woman Gervaise told you would know the boy's whereabouts. We need to handle her very carefully. It mightn't be a bad idea for you to play the part of the grieving widow when we approach her – wanting this last remaining link with your husband, can't have a child of your own, you know the kind of thing. She could withhold the information we need, and if we don't get the boy, the money goes to that American fellow. Think you could do it?'

'I suppose so,' Pamela said doubtfully. 'If you really think it's for the best, Cosmo.'

'No doubt about that,' he said firmly, patting her on the shoulder. 'Just leave everything to me. You do as I say and you've nothing to worry about. You can trust me, old girl.'

The trouble was, thought Pamela as she went upstairs to change, much as she loved her brother and in many respects admired him, she was by no means sure that, where money was concerned, he *was* someone in whom it would be wise to place her trust.

CHAPTER FOUR

1916

Cynthia Merstam paced up and down the morning-room of her large London house as, with a frown of deep concern, she read through the letter she was holding for the second time.

How was it possible, she thought bitterly, that after all these years – thirteen to be precise – she was no longer to be allowed to ignore the past? Except for the once-yearly payment she was obliged to send, anonymously, to the Pritchetts, she had been able to put Dorothy's child out of her mind. When Gervaise had written to her, telling her of the plans he hoped to make for the boy after his death, she had hoped that by omitting to reply the poor man would pass on before he could take the matter any further. She was still finding it difficult to believe – not only that he had asked his wife to make herself responsible for his bastard but that the countess had actually agreed to become a guardian. And what if Dorothy came to hear of it? Her sister was respectably married with three young step-children and had put the past behind her. She never mentioned that poor, unwanted baby she had given birth to in such shocking circumstances.

How fortunate it was that her husband's war work had taken him away yet again, Cynthia reflected now. He always opened the morning post and would have demanded an explanation. Even though the contents of the countess's letter were worded ambiguously, she'd still have been obliged to lie to him as she had lied nearly thirteen years ago to protect Dorothy.

. . . Shortly before his untimely death, my husband requested that I and my brother, the Viscount Simcox, should take on the guardianship of the boy known as Harry Keynes, now aged thirteen years. In order that my husband's last wishes should be granted and that he might die in peace, we have agreed to his request.

My husband told me that you, a former friend of his mother, would be able to assist us in discovering the boy's whereabouts. My brother will be in London on Friday, 1 February, and has asked if you would spare a few moments of your valuable time to discuss the matter. He suggests that you should meet at eleven o'clock at Brown's Hotel, where you can talk undisturbed.

As you will appreciate, dear Lady Merstam, in all our interests we wish this matter to be treated in the strictest confidence. I am sure you will agree that vulgar publicity must be avoided at all costs.

The letter was signed, Pamela, Countess of Kinmuire, and postmarked, Melton Mowbray, Leicestershire.

Cynthia's first instinct was to leave the letter unanswered, as she had Gervaise's, but on second reading she found herself wondering if the last paragraph might possibly contain a veiled threat. If she herself proved unwilling to reveal the Pritchetts' address, there was no other living person who could do so. The countess, were she sufficiently morally motivated, might feel compelled to start making her own investigations – employ a detective, perhaps, who could succeed in unearthing the whole terrible secret. The consequences to poor Dorothy would be beyond reckoning. In all probability her husband would divorce her and . . .

Cynthia stood up, her face pale, her limbs trembling. She must lose no time in replying. As poor Gervaise had said in his letters, there was no necessity for her to reveal Dorothy's name – something she would never do. The countess and her brother sought only the whereabouts of the child. At least the people she was dealing with were respectable and presumably, therefore, trustworthy, she told herself. If she could extract a promise that in exchange for the Pritchetts' name and address, they would guarantee not to enquire further as to the boy's maternal background, she could rely on their word. Dorothy herself need know nothing of this whole unfortunate business. She had doubtless already read the announcement of Gervaise's death in *The Times*. There was therefore no reason why she should take note of the future activities and life style of his widow.

Slowly Cynthia went upstairs to her bedroom and opened her rosewood jewel case. By pressing gently on either rim of the box, a secret drawer was revealed and here she placed the countess's letter. Already reposing there were the two letters she had received from Gervaise, and the one and only account she had from the investigator of the baby's development.

It must now be nine years, she thought, since she had felt impelled to make discreet enquiries about the child who, like it or not, was her nephew. After she had read the report, she'd placed it in the jewel case and never again touched it. Even to see it lying there was to renew those deeply disturbing memories of how she had abandoned Dorothy's baby to such lowly circumstances. The secret of his existence, known only to Gervaise and herself, had always weighed heavily on her conscience. In those early years she had been plagued by recurring nightmares in which she relived those frightening hours in the carriage when she had thought Dorothy might die; the dreadful days and nights which followed. It seemed she would never be allowed to forget the sound of Dorothy's sobs; that over and over again she must endure the discomforts of that primitive roadside inn where, quite alone, she had had to bear the constant fear of discovery. On waking, she was further plagued by memories of the lies she had been obliged to tell; the deception she had practised upon the innocent Pritchetts. Not least, she'd been unable to stop herself wondering what had become of Dorothy's child.

She envied Dorothy, who, though she had mourned the lost baby, was nevertheless reconciled to his death.

It was several years before the nightmares had ceased. After sending the promised yearly payments to the Pritchetts in unidentifiable envelopes, her conscience was partially eased, and subsequently for at least eleven months of the year she could sleep with a quiet mind.

Hurriedly she closed the secret drawer and, locking the jewel case, put the key back in her dressing-table. It occurred to her now that at long last her chance had come to hand over responsibility for Dorothy's child to someone else. Undoubtedly the countess must be a good woman to be so philanthropically intentioned. Albeit belatedly, the boy would have an upbringing more befitting his class. For the second time Cynthia thanked her Maker that her husband was away again. She would write at once and tell Gervaise's widow that she would meet Viscount Simcox in Brown's at the prescribed time.

Two days later Cynthia returned from that meeting aware that a huge burden had been lifted from her shoulders. Lord Simcox had turned out to be a charming man with impeccable manners and an amusing sense of humour. Somehow he'd managed to conduct their discussion as if Dorothy's part in the affair was not only quite unimportant but very understandable. He had appeared totally ignorant of the fact that Dorothy was her sister, thus reassuring Cynthia that Gervaise had kept his word not to reveal their relationship. Moreover, Lord Simcox had reiterated several times that he and the countess had no interest whatever in knowing who the boy's mother was; that they planned to tell him she was dead – which, the viscount had added, for all they knew she was.

When at their parting Cynthia had commented upon his sister's altruism in taking on her late husband's orphaned relative, Lord Simcox had agreed, pointing out that it was quite typical of his sister, who had the most charitable of natures, and in any case had been so devoted to her husband that, whatever the difficulties facing her, she would see them only in the light of fulfilling a dying man's wish.

Enormously reassured by the viscount's attitude, Cynthia returned home convinced, now she had given him the Pritchetts' name and address, that this was the last time she need ever be involved with Dorothy's child.

Cosmo, after a quick lunch at his club, resisted the urge to go on to Crockford's to gamble with the money Pamela had given him to cover his expenses and returned instead to Leicestershire. There he was able, triumphantly, to announce to his sister that he had had Lady Cynthia Merstam eating out of his hand.

'Never doubted our discretion,' he said. 'My word was enough for her. So you see, old girl, you were worrying for nothing.' He took a glass of brandy and sat down in the nearest chair, stretching his legs comfortably in front of him. There was a self-congratulatory smile on his handsome face.

'I'll tell you something else, the silly woman was being very guarded and kept stressing the need for secrecy, so she's not going to let any cats out of the bag.'

He gave a huge yawn. No doubt about it, he told himself, the future looked a great deal rosier than he'd thought it would be when the will was read, and the likelihood of his ever being in dire need again was remote. There had been too many months in Toronto when he'd been stony broke and obliged to resort to borrowing from his Canadian friends. Fortunately, he'd had but to drop his title into the conversation for near strangers to be only too willing to help him out of 'a temporary difficulty' by lending him a few hundred dollars. He had been living on such unrepaid loans at the time Pamela's cable had arrived telling him she needed him back in England.

Cosmo yawned again, his mood one of complete contentment. He had done exactly the right thing in persuading Pamela to accept Gervaise's proposal that they should become the boy's guardians. The gambling instinct, which was so strong in him, had paid off for once. The future held unlimited riches and, meanwhile, he had this big, comfortable seat in Leicestershire to live in, servants to see to his every need and Gervaise's horses in the stables. He could see no reason why he should not buy himself a really fine pair of Purdey's – tailored to fit since Gervaise's were a bit short in the stock for him – and some good Hardy's fishing tackle – all in the boy's name, of course. He might even get rides cut in Filby wood, put a thousand or two young birds in and set himself up with an excellent shoot. No need to involve Pamela, who doubtless would be more than happy to allow him to control the household expenses. Having seen the books, he knew that there was plenty of spare cash to play with.

If at that moment Cosmo had one regret, it was that he had not remained in London to renew his association with the gambling club where he had once spent so much of his time.

'Mum, there's a lady and gen'leman coming down the path.'

Edna's voice, shrill with excitement, gave Martha reason to pause in her work. It was Monday – washday – and she was standing by the stone-built copper in the wash-house outside the back door. Will had lit a good fire beneath it before he'd gone off to work and the water was sending up great clouds of steam. In one hand Martha held a washboard, in the other a pair of corduroy breeches. Lather from the big bar of Sunlight soap had spilled over her reddened hands as she'd rubbed the cloth vigorously over the ridges.

Wearily she straightened her aching back and wiped her hands on her apron. 'S'not the master and mistress, is it?' she asked the child. She could think of no one else who might conceivably be coming to the cottage at this time of the morning.

'No, it ain't,' Edna said emphatically.

As she spoke there was a loud knock on the front door. Hurriedly Martha removed her apron and ran a hand through her hair in an ineffectual attempt to tidy it. On washdays the pins invariably escaped from the bun which held back her long grey-brown hair. Loose strands were now straggling over her forehead and shoulders.

She walked in through the back door and across the kitchen. As she did so there was a second loud rat-tat-tat on the front door. Whoever her visitors were, they sounded as if they were in a hurry! Nervously she pulled the door open.

'Are you Mrs Pritchett, wife of Mr William Pritchett?'

Martha caught her breath as she stared at the speaker. Was this bad news? Could anything have happened to Will? Neither the gentleman who had addressed her nor the lady beside him looked as if they had come from the Red Cross or the Evacuees Agency. The small, dark-haired woman wearing a black velour plush hat with a half veil and a long black fur coat with a deep collar, looked the height of fashion. The man, tall and meticulously attired in a fur-lined overcoat and wearing a black crêpe armband, was carrying a Malacca cane. He was now courteously lifting his black bowler hat to her.

Martha dropped a curtsey. 'Yes, sir, I be Martha Pritchett.'

'Then we have come to the right place,' Pamela said to her brother. 'Perhaps we could come indoors for a minute, Mrs Pritchett? I am the Countess of Kinmuire and this is my brother, Viscount Simcox. We would like to have a word with you and your husband on a matter of some importance.'

Martha took a step backwards and opened the door of the front room. The parlour was always kept immaculately clean and was never used except on special occasions. It was the only room with lino in it. A firescreen stood in front of the empty grate and on the mantelshelf above were Martha's two prized possessions – a Queen Victoria Jubilee commemorative mug and a Crown Derby china vase which she had inherited from her grandmother.

When Will had been promoted to head gardener and they had moved into the cottage, the Debraces had given them an old plum-coloured horsehair sofa and two highbacked, elmwood chairs. Martha now ushered her visitors into the room and bade them be seated. She herself remained standing. Edna, goggle-eyed and runny-nosed, was despatched to the big house to fetch her father.

'Mr Pritchett will be here directly, milady,' Martha said. She was very uneasy, unsure how she should address a countess or a viscount – the first she had ever seen – or, indeed, how she should behave in such exalted company.

'We are in no hurry,' Cosmo said soothingly. He was always at his best with women, whom he could invariably charm into complying with his wishes. One quick glance at Martha and at the poverty of their surroundings convinced him that the matter of Gervaise's child's future was hardly likely to be in dispute.

Pamela, meanwhile, was glancing around her in horror. Was she to take on the care of a child from *this* dreadful background? Was the boy going to turn out to look like that mentally deficient girl who had gawped at them as if they were from another world? All the way down from London in the train she had listened to Cosmo talking cheerfully about their good fortune. He had sounded very convincing but now, face to face with the reality of the situation, her spirits were sinking lower with every moment.

'Would you like me to light the fire, milady?' Martha asked. 'T'wont take but a moment, surely.'

'Please don't trouble,' Cosmo said. 'I take it your husband will not be long?'

'No, sir, indeed he won't. Mr Pritchett works at the big house. You'll have seen The Grange as you passed by on your way here, sir. He's head gardener there.'

'Ah, yes, the Debrace family, is it not? The cab driver who brought us up from the station seemed to know them well.'

'That'll be Alfred Tester,' Martha said. 'He does all the station work.'

'Since he couldn't drive us all the way here, he stopped at the top of the lane and is waiting for us there,' Cosmo said, establishing a relaxed atmosphere in which to conduct the forthcoming discussion. 'How many children do you have, Mrs Pritchett?'

'Eight, sir.'

'Then you must be very hard-working,' Cosmo said genially. 'Times must be quite hard, what with the war and food prices rising so steeply.'

'Yes, sir, that's a fact, surely,' Martha replied. She was still very nervous, but less so now that her visitors appeared to be friendly. She had taken a cautious liking to the handsome gentleman.

'Then we may well have good news for you, Mrs Pritchett,' said Cosmo.

The arrival of Will, cap in hand, with Edna running excitedly in front of him, temporarily halted Cosmo's conversation. As Will came into the room, Cosmo stood up and introduced himself and Pamela.

'I was just telling your wife that we are here to bring you good news,' he said with a friendly smile.

Will glanced quickly at Martha, who came to stand beside him.

'It's about one of your children, Mr Pritchett,' Cosmo said. 'My sister and I are here in the first instance to right a wrong done to you many years ago, aren't we, my dear?'

Well rehearsed by Cosmo on their journey down from London, Pamela now took up her cue. 'You were asked to look after a baby for a year by a stranger who did not give you her real name,' she said, 'and due to circumstances that I need not explain, she never returned to collect the child but abandoned him to your care. Although we know she did continue to send money for his upkeep, she had no right to place this burden on your shoulders. It was a gross injustice which my brother and I now wish to put right.'

Cosmo nodded, and noting the somewhat bitter expression on Will's face, he said quickly, 'I don't doubt there have been times when you've had to put your hand in your pocket for additional expenses, so for a start I wish to reimburse you. I had thought about a hundred pounds? Perhaps if we were to make that guineas, you would feel adequately compensated.'

He busied himself lighting a cigar while he waited for

this statement to sink in. The astonishment on both the Pritchetts' faces was almost comical.

Finally, Will said, 'We've managed all right, but I'll not say we can't do with the money, sir, seeing as Harry ain't really ourn.'

'Quite so,' Cosmo agreed. 'We will discuss in a minute how you would like this sum to be paid to you. I don't suppose you have a bank account? Equally, you would not want to risk keeping such a large amount in the cottage. Perhaps we can arrange a savings account for you at the post office? We'll see. Meanwhile, there are other matters to discuss. The child . . .'

'Harry,' Martha said. 'We call him Harry. He's a good boy, sir. We've treated him like our own.'

'That I don't doubt for one minute,' Cosmo said with easy flattery. 'He is indeed lucky to have such a good home, bearing in mind the circumstances of his birth.'

Martha turned to Edna, who had been standing quietly, staring open-mouthed at the finely dressed lady. 'Outside, Edna,' she said sharply. 'Go and see if Baby Sam is crying. If he is, put the dummy back in his mouth. Be off with you now.'

When, reluctantly, the girl had departed, closing the door behind her, Martha looked uneasily at Will. This was not the same lady who had brought the baby to them that January night. Nor did she think that this was Harry's mother, for she seemed almost uninterested in the conversation. It was the gentleman who was doing all the talking. Who, then, were these people? And what business concerning Harry was it that had brought them here?

'Now about this boy – Harry, you say – I must tell you that he was born out of wedlock to a distant relative of my brother-in-law, the late Earl of Kinmuire. It was a matter of great distress to the earl that he was shortly to depart this world without having accomplished any worthwhile charitable deed. Recalling the child born to his relative – and having no children of his own – he decided to do what he could to assist the unfortunate boy to achieve a life more befitting someone of his parentage. He implored his

94

wife, my sister – who despite her recent bereavement, has travelled here today to see you – to discover the boy's whereabouts and, together with myself, take on his guardianship.'

He must not rush them, Cosmo knew. Country folk were often afraid of the unexpected. He would give them a minute or two to recover from this first shock. He could see that both man and wife were paying him full attention.

'Naturally, you will be wondering at the philanthropy – indeed, the saintliness – that has motivated my sister to take on her husband's self-imposed burden,' he said in conversational tones. 'However, it is not in her nature to refuse the wishes of a dying man, let alone that of her beloved spouse; and nor could I bring myself to allow her to carry this burden alone. We have agreed, therefore, to take the boy under our wing and, as far as is possible, rear him as her husband wished.'

'Take him away?' Martha's protest was out before she had time to think. 'But Harry's our boy, like our own, sir. We – his dad and me, his brothers and sisters – we're his family. We don't worry ourselves none about whether he was born legal or not, we . . .'

'Hush now!' Will intervened sharply. 'As this gentleman said, Mother, the boy isn't rightfully ourn. There's no arguing that.'

Cosmo laid a hand soothingly on Martha's shoulder. She was trembling. 'I do understand how you feel, Mrs Pritchett,' he said. 'You've been his foster mother for so long, it's only natural you don't now want to part with him. However, I am sure you will feel differently when I remind you of the many advantages there will be for the boy. He will be brought up as a gentleman – which, in a manner of speaking, is his birthright – and have proper schooling. It would not be fair for you to hold him back, now would it?'

'Where would you think of taking him?' Will asked thoughtfully. 'Would we see the lad?' Well aware of the distress on his wife's face, he added, 'Mrs Pritchett

95

wouldn't be happy not knowing where he was, not seeing him from time to time.'

Now Pamela intervened. 'Harry would come to my home in Leicestershire,' she said. 'That would be too far for visits to be exchanged. Besides, for him to continue to be part of your family would make the break more difficult for him, don't you agree? A clean break is often the best – and the easiest for a child. He will have to adopt an entirely new way of life and this might be simpler for him if he is not influenced by the old.'

Although Martha could think of little beyond the fact that Harry would be going out of her life, perhaps for ever, Will was trying his best to consider what was best for the boy.

'Harry was to start work weekends and holidays for Mr Debrace – with the horses,' he said. 'It was all agreed.'

'Which is yet another tribute to you,' Cosmo broke in. 'You have arranged the very best you could for him, but his horizons have changed, Pritchett. You must see that. He can now take his rightful place in the world as the son of a gentleman. You would not, I'm sure, wish to impose limitations upon him.'

Will's face took on a stubborn expression. 'T'aint right,' he muttered. 'All these years we've looked after him, spent money on his food, his clothes, and now, when he's old enough to help us, he's to go off and lead a life where he don't have to do no work.'

Cosmo was quick to grasp the implications. 'My dear Pritchett, you must not tar my sister and me with the same brush as those who abandoned him to you. We are honourable people, and I can promise you that any assurances we make will be kept. I do appreciate that our plans to remove the boy will have a detrimental effect upon you and your family. As you so rightly point out, he is old enough now to be contributing towards the family upkeep. However, if you tell me what wages the boy would have received, you have my assurance that we will make this good. And do not thank me, my good man,' he added as Will's attitude began to appear less mulish. 'It's the least we can do for you good people who have cared for the boy for so long. It would be unfair if you were to suffer for no better reason than to satisfy the whim of a dying man.'

Realizing that Cosmo had been carried away by his own rhetoric, Pamela said quickly, 'Not a *whim*, Cosmo dear. It was my poor Gervaise's dying wish.' She pulled a small lace handkerchief from her handbag and dabbed at her eyes.

'But of course, of course,' Cosmo said quickly. 'Now, my dear, I think we should leave Pritchett and his wife to break the news to the boy.' He turned to Martha. 'We shall be going on to Brighton, where we will be spending the night at the Metropole. On our way home tomorrow, we will call again. Perhaps you would be good enough to have the boy here, Mrs Pritchett, so that we may take him home with us? We shall want his birth certificate, of course.'

'T'is locked away, sir. Mrs Pritchett and me thought it best not to leave it lying where the lad could mebbe find it – he having no father, like.'

He noted the look which now passed between Cosmo and Pamela and added, 'Far as we knew, the lady as left him with us didn't have him registered. Leastways, if'n she did, she didn't send us no certificate. We reckoned as how mebbe the lady as borned him didn't have no marriage lines.' He looked down at his boots as he broached the subject that had rankled deep inside him these past twelve years. 'We was told the mother's name was Keynes, Mrs Harriet Keynes, but we didn't have no way to be sure, they disappearing like piskies on a winter's night and not sending us any address nor nothing. Not her nor that Mrs Robinson were to be traced, so's we don't know if'n hers be a real name either. Any road, Vicar said as how the lady hadn't registered him in our parish, like the law says, and he thought we ought to have the baby registered. Vicar said Nurse Wilks, the midwife as brought him into the world, could do it, so she did it one time she was in Lewes, that being the place for our parish, you understand.'

'Very sensible of you,' Cosmo said soothingly. 'You did

the right thing. Have it ready for me tomorrow when I come for the boy, will you?'

Sensing that the moment had come when he could make it clear to the couple that they had no alternative but to let the boy go, Cosmo reached into his coat pocket and withdrew a folded document. He addressed himself to Will. 'For your peace of mind, Pritchett, you should look at these papers. This is the required document establishing my sister and me as the boy's guardians. The legal phraseology is not easy to understand, so there is no need for you to trouble yourself with the details.'

He untied the pink tapes securing the pages and, laying them down on the arm of the settee, he pointed to one of the paragraphs. 'You will see this makes it quite clear: "Pamela, Dowager Countess of Kinmuire, and Viscount Cosmo Simcox of Maythorpe House, Melton Mowbray, Leicestershire, are appointed guardians to the male child, Harry Keynes, minor, born 5 January 1903, in the parish of Calking . . ." And these are our visiting cards to establish our identity.'

Seeing that the man was no more anxious to retain the document than he to leave it, Cosmo retied the tape and replaced it in his coat pocket.

Pamela stood up, her face anxious as she looked up at Cosmo. 'You don't think we should meet the boy first? I mean . . .'

'No, indeed not, my dear,' Cosmo broke in. 'It is for his . . . er, foster parents to explain the position to him in the way they feel is appropriate. Have you told him he is not your own child?'

Martha was weeping and it was Will who said, 'There seemed no point to it, us having long since given up 'specting as how we'd ever hear more from his own folk. He be known hereabouts as Harry Pritchett.'

'Naturally. You are not only a kind man but a thoughtful one, Will Pritchett, and I can see that you understand the advantages to the boy of our proposal. Now come along, my dear, we've already taken too much of these good people's time.'

As they disappeared down the brick path, Martha returned to her kitchen and sank into the nearest chair. She could no longer control her sobs. Will went over to her and with a rare gesture of affection, put his hand on her head and stroked her hair.

'You'll be thinking I'm a hard man,' he said tentatively. 'But we have to do what's best for the boy, Martha. Think on it . . .' he elaborated with a flash of intuition, '. . . t'was you what was so anxious for him to continue his schooling. From what the gen'leman said, he'll have a public school education now and the grammar can't match that, now can it?'

'He'll forget all about us,' Martha wept. 'And what'll Alice say? And the other children? I fed him, raised him alongside our Jenny just as if they was twins. T'aint right, Will, no matter what you say.'

Will sighed. 'There weren't no legal papers signed when we took him on. He ain't ourn, Martha, and those people knows it. I must say, this has been a right turn up for the books. Who'd have thought that after all this time, titled folk would turn up and pay us a hundred guineas for looking after our Harry. You always did reckon on him being sort of "special", and you was right, Martha, I'll say that.'

Aware that his compliment had done little to stem his wife's tears, Will added, 'I mun get back to work. Tell you what, I'll ask Mr Standing if'n Alice can get a bit of time off over dinner – say you've had a bit of bad news. If'n madam can spare her, Alice can nip over for a while. You'll be behind with your work same as me, I don't doubt.'

Alice, he told himself, was a sensible girl with a good head on her shoulders. She'd talk some sense into Martha, for there was no doubting that she'd been even more set on Harry going to the grammar than her mother. She'd even got the master to agree to sponsor the boy, though he, Will, had not yet given his agreement to it. Now, it seemed, that agreement would not be necessary.

Will quickened his pace, anxious now to ensure that his

eldest daughter would be allowed time off to go to her mother. He'd only once before seen his wife give way to tears, when their Billy had died of the whooping cough – and by this he measured the extent of her grief at the forthcoming parting with Harry. Although he had never felt the same degree of love for the boy as had Martha, he was nevertheless fond of him and, secretly, proud of him. Unlike Martha, however, he had never allowed himself to think of the boy as his own flesh and blood.

Told by the butler, Mr Standing, that she might have two hours off to comfort her mother, but unaware of the cause of the distress, Alice ran all the way to the cottage. The pins holding her long thick amber-coloured hair in place fell one by one on the path behind her. When she burst in through the kitchen door, she was surprised to find Martha, tearless now, nursing the baby.

'What's up, Mum?' she asked as she collapsed into one of the kitchen chairs and fought to get her breath back.

Martha looked at her eldest daughter from red-rimmed eyes. It was a moment or two before she could bring herself to recount the momentous events that had taken place an hour previously. 'I know your Dad's right and it's best for Harry he should go,' she ended, near to tears once more. 'But like as not, we'll not see him no more, Alice. It'll be same as if . . . as if he died!'

Alice was shocked into silence. She understood immediately Martha's dilemma, for she too felt similar diverse reactions. This was a heaven-sent opportunity for Harry, but at the same time, she could no more easily bear the thought of the impending parting than her mother.

'Tell me more about the lady, Mum,' she said when she could bring herself to speak. 'She must be a kind person – seeing as how Harry's not her own. There's some as might say working-class children was something to be ashamed of.'

'She seemed nice enough,' Martha admitted. 'Not that it was her as said much. Mostly it was him, what called hisself a viscount, as did the talking. He showed your dad a paper tied up with pink tape. Your dad and me've not ever seen anything like it before. But it were legal like, with lots of red wax seals. They took it away, but they've left cards saying who they was.'

She picked them up off the kitchen table where Will had left them, and handed them to Alice.

'But they were nice people? You liked them, Mum?' Alice persisted.

Martha nodded as she moved the baby to her other breast. Alice stared thoughtfully at the cards. 'I don't see as how we've much choice about it, if'n they're who they say they are,' she said finally. 'I could show these to Mr Debrace. He'd know about such folk, I dare say. We musn't forget those last lot as left Harry with you – them giving false names and all, so's they couldn't be traced.'

Martha looked up anxiously as she patted the baby's back to bring up his wind.

'Your dad and me never thought on that,' she said. 'Yes, Alice, you'd best talk to Mr Debrace soon as ever you can – or Mrs Debrace if'n the master's away at t'hospital. Them folk are coming back tomorrow to – to take Harry away. I'll not let him go lest I know it's to real folk.'

'Mrs Debrace is playing whist this afternoon, so she'll be needing me to help her change into her teagown after luncheon. I'll talk to her then,' Alice said, reassuringly. 'I'd best go back now, Mum, if you're all right, else I'll miss the chance to speak to her.'

Eloise Debrace was looking forward to her afternoon card party. She was therefore in a good mood as Alice divested her of her tailor-made wool dress and helped her into the new champagne silk afternoon gown.

'What an extraordinary story, Alice,' she commented. 'If it's true, then indeed the countess must be a singularly kind woman. I don't think I've ever met her. However, that is neither here nor there. You are quite right, of course. We must assure ourselves that these people are genuine. That, I am pleased to tell you, is easily done. One of my afternoon guests, Lady Peasmarsh, moves very much in court circles. She knows everyone who is anyone. What did you say the countess's name was – Kintyre?'

'No, madam, Kinmuire.'

'Ah, yes! Her husband, the earl, died recently,' Eloise exclaimed. 'Well, that establishes the identity of the countess.'

'Yes, madam. Mum gave me these to show you.'

She handed the two visiting-cards to her mistress.

What a fascinating piece of gossip this would make, Eloise thought, studying the black-rimmed cards as Alice set about repinning her hair. The 'distant relative' of the late Earl of Kinmuire did sound suspicious. Wasn't it far more likely that Harry was the late earl's by-blow? But if so, was it likely his widow, of all people, would succour the boy? Maybe she didn't know the truth. Either way, it would be unkind if she herself were to start such a rumour. It would be all over the place in no time, and although it might do no harm to the countess, who would merely be thought silly if immensely kind, it was hardly fair to Harry. To be branded illegitimate would be to undermine any chance of his integrating into a public school, and bar him from the society of his contemporaries in Leicestershire circles. The unfortunate countess's task was going to be difficult enough, passing a working-class boy off as a distant relative! One had to feel sorry for her – as well as the boy – and she had always had a soft spot for Harry. No, she would not tell Lady Peasmarsh the reason for her enquiries. Let Harry go to his new life with as few extra burdens on his shoulders as possible.

'Leave it to me, Alice. I'll find out what I can. Meanwhile, you may have the day off tomorrow to make your farewells, and to be with your mother, who is understandably distressed. And Alice, when Lord Simcox and his sister call tomorrow to collect Harry, please tell them that I shall be at home and will be very pleased to meet them. It's a pity they didn't make themselves known to me today.'

There was nothing more Alice could do other than to ask Mr Standing if she might have a word with Harry, who was probably helping out in the stables or in the bootroom, perhaps. Someone must tell him what was happening before he went home to face their mum's distress, and prepare him for the fact that his whole world was about to be turned upside down.

Suddenly the impact of her own impending loss struck at Alice's heart. When her mistress departed downstairs, she sat at Eloise's dressing-table and, for once unaware of the beautiful objects adorning it, she rested her head on her hands and wept.

CHAPTER FIVE

1917

Harry sat at the leather-topped desk in the library of Maythorpe House and stared longingly out of the big open windows. His Uncle Cosmo was crossing the beautifully mown lawns in the direction of the stables. Without doubt he would be taking Windsor, or Wellington, the stallion, out for exercise. It was a perfect June day and far in the distance Harry could see the tiny shapes of the haymakers turning the newly cut grass.

Inevitably his thoughts turned to his old home and his depression deepened. What would he not give at this minute, he thought, to be helping in the hayfields round Calking! Even had he been allowed to go riding with Uncle Cosmo – his main pleasure in this new life – he would willingly have exchanged the opportunity for one single day at home.

After eighteen months Harry could still not bring himself to think of this big Leicestershire mansion as home; nor, indeed, of the occupants as relatives. There were days when he was so homesick for his old family, his friends in Calking village, even the Debraces, that it was all he could do not to weep. Tears were unbecoming to a boy of fourteen, unmanly and a sign of effeminacy. This knowledge, and a certain pride in himself, forbade the outward signs of his unhappiness. It must, he knew, be borne in silence.

Perhaps worst of all the reasons for his distress was his unbearable loneliness. Surrounded as he had always been by brothers and sisters, to be quite alone in this huge house, in his big bedroom or, as often as not, in the even larger dining-room was but one of the hateful changes in his new life. There were times when he seriously considered running away, returning to his old home, but he was afraid that doing so might land his family in trouble. According to his guardians, they alone had the authority to arrange his life. That he knew his guardians were no more his blood relatives than the Pritchetts merely added to his confusion.

It was not as if either his so-called Aunt Pamela or Uncle Cosmo were cruel to him, he wrote and told Alice. Uncle Cosmo could even on occasions be quite kind. He had taken Harry fishing for trout in the nearby river and rough shooting in the woods on the estate. He was also teaching him to fence. His Aunt Pamela, as far as Harry could ascertain, taught him nothing beyond what she termed 'the correct behaviour and speech becoming to a gentleman'. Since she never permitted Harry to be present when she had guests and never took him with her when she went calling, there seemed little point in these lessons in decorum. The countess was not, however, someone to be disobeyed. Even the slightest transgression from her long list of dos and don'ts meant instant despatch to his room for the remainder of the day. Provided he obeyed her rules, he was free to roam around the large gardens, to amuse himself as best he could, practising archery or hitting a tennis ball against the kitchen-garden wall; or if the weather was inclement, to help himself to books from the hundreds of volumes in the big library. Most of each day, however, was occupied by lessons which were taught to him by the local vicar, an elderly man who lived alone with his housekeeper in the nearby vicarage.

The Reverend Percy Harrison-Finch was a tall, thin, bespectacled man now approaching his sixtieth year. He was a studious, scholarly cleric who was teaching Harry the classics, mathematics, English and French literature, as well as the French language, to a very high standard. Aunt Pamela had been obliged to engage this tutor, she informed Harry, in preference to sending him to a public school, as had been her original intention, since he would need 'a great deal more than a mere polish before you can hope to be accepted into one of the better schools'. Increasing his general feeling of inferiority in those early weeks following his arrival at his new home, she had added cruelly, 'I cannot endure that dreadful Sussex accent, or your total lack of knowledge of the social mores. I have told you twice already that if there's no servant to draw back a lady's chair, it's for the gentleman present to do so.'

'But it's all so different to home, and there's so much to remember,' Harry had protested in his own defence.

His aunt's voice had been cold as she had reminded him that he should say different '*from*' and not different '*to*'. She seemed to take pleasure in correcting his endless mistakes and he was often reminded of the Debraces' old nanny when she did so. The only sign of affection his aunt ever showed him was when she raised her cheek for his good-night kiss. He sometimes wondered why she did so, and was of the opinion that it must be yet another of her rules of etiquette.

He tried not to think harshly of this woman in whose care he had been placed but who barely concealed her dislike of him. Alice had pointed out before he left home that she must be a generous-hearted lady to have considered taking a strange boy from a working-class home into her family. 'She must have loved her husband very much to be carrying out his wishes,' Alice had said, 'so for that reason alone you can't fail to like her, Harry.'

Harry had tried to do so ever since his arrival in Leicestershire, but so far he had failed. He was pleased whenever she went to London, sometimes for weeks on end, relieving him of the fear that he would run into her in one of the rooms or passages of the big house and be castigated for some further sign of his ignorance. His uncle too was often away, but this he did not welcome, for at such times Aunt Pamela would be even more tight-lipped and critical.

At least Uncle Cosmo's corrections were made in comparative good humour, he thought, as he watched his guardian's tall figure, impressive in riding-breeches and hacking-jacket, turn off the drive and disappear into the stable yard.

'I say, old man, mustn't be too familiar with the stable lads, eh? T'aint done, y'know? Must keep your distance from the servants. Not easy, I know, after the way you've been brought up. Not your fault.'

It seemed to Harry a very far cry from his days in the Debrace household. There Aubrey and he had sat together in the tack room, listening to the men's talk about recent racing events or the triumphs or failures of the village cricket team. Once or twice at a weekend Mr Debrace had made an unexpected appearance, but although the men had all jumped to their feet, he had made them sit down again, handing round his cigarette case before recounting the latest war news. He had always addressed the men by name, asked after their families and sorted out any troubles they might have, whereas Uncle Cosmo called all the staff 'you' – which was perhaps not so surprising since nearly all of them were new and the majority female. Soon after Harry's arrival at Maythorpe House, he had learned that the late earl's family servants – those who had not left to join up – had been dismissed shortly after his death, and that only Mrs Appleby, the old cook, now remained.

Mrs Appleby was Harry's only friend. Whenever he could do so unobserved by his guardians, Harry made his way down the back staircase to the big kitchen and stayed talking to the cook while she raised pastry for one of her special pork pies or stirred some rich sauce or pudding mixture. Although in stature she would have made two of his mother (as he still thought of Martha), Mrs Appleby nevertheless reminded him of her, thus evoking both pain and happiness when he was near her. She alone of all the staff seemed to understand what a huge, cultural hurdle he was having to overcome. It had soon become his habit to take his perplexities to her.

'My aunt keeps telling me I must forget my family – my old family,' he said on one occasion. 'She seems to think I'll settle down better if I do – and I do try, honest I do, Mrs Appleby, but I just can't. Most of all, I miss Alice –

she's my eldest sister. She always sort of looked after me, Mum being so busy with all the little ones, and she promised she'd write regular, but she hasn't.'

Mrs Appleby had grunted, muttering something to herself. 'P'raps her letters have gone astray, m'duck,' she'd said ambiguously. 'I'll have a word with Mr Walker. He's the one as takes in the letters from the postboy.'

'What good will that do?' Harry had enquired innocently. 'I dare say Alice's just forgot me.'

'You're not the sort of lad as gets forgot,' Mrs Appleby had said cheerfully. 'Not with those big brown eyes of yourn – and that smile. Give us one now, m'duck, and I'll give you one of these jam tarts in exchange.'

Odd though it sounded when she called him 'duck', Harry infinitely preferred this Midlands intimacy to his new title of 'Master Harry'. He came close to loving Mrs Appleby, not only for her kindness to him and the fact that she always listened when he wanted to tell her stories about his former life in Calking, but because there was no one else in this gaunt, lonely place to love.

He positively hated his valet, Hicks, an embittered, sour-faced man who had been slightly shell-shocked in France and had been discharged from the army. Formerly a regular soldier employed as a batman, Hicks had had a safe and permanent job which now, through no fault of his own, was denied him. Harry would have felt more sorry for him had he not stated quite openly that he considered it beneath his dignity to 'serve the likes of them as was no better than himself'. He never lost the opportunity of telling Harry that he had always served officers who were gentlemen; that he deeply resented the fact that he, accustomed to better things, should now be responsible for clearing up after Harry and seeing to his clothes. He was even more critical of Harry's mistakes than Aunt Pamela and from the start had resisted Harry's attempts to enlist his friendship. 'Surely you know *that* . . .' he would say scornfully whenever Harry asked haltingly for guidance on some point of etiquette with which he was unfamiliar.

It was Harry's misfortune that Hicks was under orders to accompany him wherever he went, even to the vicarage. Hicks would sit drinking tea and gossiping with the Reverend Harrison-Finch's cook-housekeeper until it was time to conduct Harry home. Once, when Harry had suggested that he was quite capable of walking the mile home without an escort, Hicks had given his smile, which was in part a sneer, saying, 'My orders are to see you don't get talking to the neighbours. Her ladyship don't want the whole village knowing you was raised by a gardener, now do she?'

Hicks made other snide remarks, referring once to the story Harry's Aunt Pamela insisted upon telling everyone who came into contact with him – namely that he was 'a distant relative'.

'Don't seem that *distant* to me!' Hicks had said with emphasis. 'Seems to me you're a mite too like the late earl, judging by that portrait in the dining-room.' And he had muttered something about 'folk as was born the wrong side of the blanket'.

Harry had been barely able to control his hatred of the man. What reason, he wondered, had Hicks to suspect his illegitimacy? At once he recalled how, on a spur-of-the-moment visit to the library, he'd come upon the valet leafing through the papers in one of the drawers of Uncle Cosmo's desk. Perhaps his birth certificate had been in there and Hicks had seen it?

Harry had longed to be able to punch the man in the nose and go on punching him until he retracted the slur, but he was in no position to do so. It might all too easily be the truth. When Alice had broken the news to him that he was to be sent to live with unknown relatives, she had explained the circumstances of his birth; that he was not, as he had always supposed, a Pritchett. The man he had always believed to be his father had gone to the oak chest beneath the dresser where he kept the Bible and produced Harry's birth certificate. Sending everyone but Martha out of the room, Will had explained that he had no father; that his real name was Harry Keynes.

When Harry insisted that it was common knowledge that there had to be two parents to make a child, it was Martha who'd tried to explain to him how Nurse Wilks, not knowing who his father was when she'd registered him, had had to leave the place blank. When he'd told Alice, she had tried to soften the disgrace of his seeming illegitimacy by saying he might well have had a father and maybe his new guardians would know the answer. He had not yet dared to ask Aunt Pamela or Uncle Cosmo about his unknown parents. Mrs Appleby – the only person he had questioned – was regretfully ignorant of his mother's existence, and was curiously reticent whenever he referred to his parentage. It was almost, he thought, as if she didn't want to be questioned about the 'unknown relative' whose child he was supposed to be.

It occurred to him now that having been so long in service to the Kinmuires, Mrs Appleby must know far more about the family history than she had so far revealed. Until now, she had mentioned only the man in America who had inherited the Kinmuire title. Those details she gave him of the late earl's distant cousin were that he was married with a son and daughter who must be about the same age as Harry; and that he bred horses on a ranch in some place called Kentucky; and that she'd heard it said he was a millionaire! The subject invariably diverted Harry from thoughts of his father, for he could think of nothing he would like better than to own a ranch, a stallion, some brood mares, and to raise beautiful blood-stock to replace all those poor horses which were being killed so horribly by the Germans.

It distressed Harry to think of such things, and with a sudden urge for company other than his own, he decided to seek out Mrs Appleby. She never minded if he disturbed her afternoon nap. If he were now to sneak down to the kitchens, with Aunt Pamela visiting friends in Melton Mowbray, Uncle Cosmo out riding and Hicks believing him at work in the library, he was unlikely to be detected.

As he anticipated, he met no one on his way downstairs

but Lil, the tweeny, who always giggled and blushed when he spoke to her. Not long after his arrival at Maythorpe House, he'd come upon the girl carrying two heavy slop pails, her thin, undersized body bent beneath the weight. Without thinking, he had taken one from her and, despite her protests, had carried it as far as the water closet.

'You didn't ought, Master Harry, but thanks ever so,' she had stammered, looking anxiously along the passage as if she had been involved in some dreadful misdeed.

Only then did it occur to Harry that he'd broken yet another of his guardian's edicts – that he was here to be waited on and that the servants were here to wait on him. But he didn't care and knew he would do the same again if circumstances demanded it.

From then on Lil had gazed at him with adoring eyes whenever she espied him. Gradually she had become the go-between, advising Harry when he questioned her whether 'the coast was clear' for him to make his way safely to the forbidden territory of Mrs Appleby's kitchen.

Perhaps, he thought, as he returned Lil's smile and went past her into the kitchen, Mrs Appleby would tell him one of her stories about the late earl. She loved to talk about 'the good old days', as she called them. She had first come to work at Maythorpe House as a girl of eighteen, and could remember way back to the excitement on the day of the late earl's birth. She had been a kitchen maid then and the cook had allowed her to stir the christening cake.

'I'd taken over as cook by the time his lordship was your age, Master Harry,' she had once said to him. 'He was just like you, always sneaking down here for a bite of my ginger parkin or wanting sugar lumps for his pony. Mad about horses he was, same as you, Master Harry. They was good days – and it near broke my heart when he passed on, God rest his soul.'

Harry was surprised now to find Mrs Appleby busy at the kitchen table, packing shortbread into biscuit tins.

'I thought you'd be having your nap,' he said, 'but I was getting awfully bored with my history prep and I hoped I

111

could get you to tell me one of your stories – you know, about what it used to be like here in the good old days.'

'Them days won't never come back, m'duck, make no mistake,' the cook replied. 'As a matter of fact, I've been wanting a chance for a chat. I'll just put these away first.'

As Harry sat down at the table it occurred to him that he'd not had the beaming smile with which she usually welcomed him. It was unlike Mrs Appleby, whose face was the only cheerful, happy one Harry ever saw in his new home, to look so downcast; or, indeed, to speak so mournfully.

As she joined him at the kitchen table, she said, 'Mark my words, Master Harry, his lordship would turn in his grave if he knew how things was since the Good Lord took him. It don't surprise me one little bit, him pacing up and down the gallery the way he does, staring up at them portraits as if he'd lost something.'

'D'you mean you've seen his ghost? That he haunts this house?' Harry asked, intrigued.

'I don't have no doubt about it,' Mrs Appleby said emphatically. 'You've been here over a year now, Master Harry, and my mind's made up. I'm going to tell you what I think, what I thought first day I set eyes on you – but I wasn't sure then. Now I'm certain of it, certain as a body can be . . .'

She raised her heavy frame from the chair and disappeared into her sitting-room. When she returned she was carrying a tattered black cardboard photograph album, which she placed on the table between them. Opening the cover, she revealed four brown sepia snapshots of a boy of about ten years old.

'Look closely now, Master Harry, and tell me what you see.'

Obediently Harry studied the pictures. 'Well, the boy's holding a fishing-rod in this one, and here he's kneeling between two dogs – spaniels, I think. This is the same boy on his pony and that . . . why, it's you, Mrs Appleby.'

Mrs Appleby nodded. 'That's right. Mr Roberts, he was butler in those days, he took that one of his lordship and

112

me together. The young master had been given a box camera for his tenth birthday and he were that proud of it. He was always asking me to take pictures of him, and it were he what gave me this album for a Christmas present.'

She turned the page, this time revealing eight more snapshots.

'But that's me!' Harry exclaimed, then added, frowning, 'But it can't be. He looks just like me, though, doesn't he? 'cepting his clothes are different.'

With a look of satisfaction, Mrs Appleby turned another page. 'See that, Master Harry . . . and that . . . and that! There's every one the spitting image of you. Do you understand what I'm trying to tell you?'

'Not exactly, Mrs Appleby. It is strange though, isn't it? It's like we were twins.'

'No, not twins, Master Harry. It's like you were father and son.'

Harry's mouth fell open as he stared at Mrs Appleby and then back to the pictures. 'But I don't understand. If he was my father, why didn't he look after me? Why didn't he . . .' He broke off as he remembered Alice's story of the lady bringing him to their house when he was newly born and then, for no reason Alice knew, leaving him there. He repeated Alice's story to Mrs Appleby, and then added, 'If *she* didn't want me, why didn't *he* come and get me if he was my father?'

Mrs Appleby patted his hand. 'I reckon we won't never know the answer to that, Master Harry, but it's my guess he like as not didn't know about you until a long time after you was born. You've got to remember, your ma and pa wasn't married, and like it or not, m'duck, your mam would have been disgraced if folk found out she'd had a baby with no marriage lines to make it right.'

'Then he shouldn't have got her in the family way!' Harry burst out.

'It's not for us to judge what makes folk do these things,' Mrs Appleby said. 'I've thought on it more than once, and you being fourteen means you was started when your father was not yet twenty. Who knows but your mam

113

wasn't his first love, but no ways would the old earl have let him get married so young. What I do know was that he was packed off abroad to foreign parts, and we didn't see him for the best part of three years. Some years after that he brought her ladyship back home and their engagement was announced. But I'll tell you something, Master Harry, 'spite of all the celebrations that went on, I never did think his lordship were that anxious to get married. The old earl was getting on a bit, and his lordship told me it was his father as wanted to see him married afore he died. I reckon I know'd him better than anyone, and I'm telling you straight, Master Harry, his heart wasn't in it – and that's a fact.'

Harry very much wanted to believe that this man was his father, a fine upright gentleman respected by everyone, as Mrs Appleby maintained. He'd thought of little else ever since Hicks had first drawn his attention to his likeness to the late earl. Nevertheless, with the single-mindedness of his youth, he could see things only as black or white.

'All the same, Mrs Appleby, it was wrong of him, wasn't it, to do what he did?' Harry insisted.

'That's as maybe, m'duck, but you'll see things different when you're a bit older. You'll find out that there ain't no gentleman as hasn't sown a few wild oats 'afore they was married. Wouldn't be natural if they didn't, and seeing as how you was begot 'afore his Lordship was married, there wasn't no adultery. It's adultery what's one of the ten commandments, Master Harry – the seventh, if my memory serves me right – and your father weren't guilty on that score.'

'We learned the commandments in Sunday school,' Harry told her, 'though no one told us what "adultery" was.'

'Won't do you no good to think about what's past,' Mrs Appleby said evasively, and, in an attempt to cheer him, added, 'Just you think on yourself as being a love child, Master Harry. Your father was a good man and I reckon he wouldn't never have got some poor young lady into trouble if'n he'd not loved her, and that's a fact.'

She closed the album and put it back in her sitting-room. When she returned, it was to say, 'Best not talk about this to anyone, m'duck. Her ladyship wouldn't like it. It'll be our secret. Now here's Lil with the milk churn. When old Ted was up for his tea yesterday, he said as how Buttercup had a fine new calf a week past, so the milk'll be extra creamy, I daresay.'

She handed him a glass of milk and a slice of shortbread. 'Best take them upstairs 'afore that there Hicks comes looking for you. Gets my goat, he do, creeping around like some German spy.'

Harry was in two frames of mind as he returned to the library and seated himself once more at the desk by the window. He no longer doubted he was the illegitimate son of the late Gervaise Harvey. In the long year and a half he had been at Maythorpe House, he had never yet heard a word spoken against the earl, but Harry was not at all sure that he really wanted to be anyone's bastard son. It was all very confusing, and perhaps Mrs Appleby's parting advice to put the subject out of his mind was a sensible one.

He gazed out once more at the sunny garden. Although still early in the season this was proving one of the best summers he could remember, and yet it was the unhappiest. If only Alice would write, then he might better be able to picture what everyone at home was doing. There had not been time to say goodbye to Aubrey, so he'd not had an opportunity to ask him to keep in touch by letter. It was only Aubrey who might have told him how little Miss Madeleine was progressing with her riding. When Harry had left she had been learning to jump. She would be twelve years old still, he reflected, for July was her birthday month.

He wondered now if he could persuade Mrs Appleby to buy a postcard in the village so that he could send Miss Madeleine birthday greetings. He could picture her enjoying a children's party in the big hall with coloured balloons and jellies and perhaps a conjuror to entertain them. She would be wearing one of her pretty dresses with a wide sash around her waist and matching ribbons in her long, fair hair. He himself had grown several inches since he'd come to Maythorpe House and he tried now to imagine how tall Miss Madeleine had grown. Not very much, he supposed. She was so tiny and dainty – like one of the little porcelain dolls she kept in the nursery.

Might Aubrey have missed him, he wondered? Was his asthma better enough for him to go to boarding-school? Alice had said that he, Harry, was to be sent to school by his new guardians and, from the schoolboy annuals Harry had read, he had looked forward to the experience. Now he could see no likelihood of his ever getting there.

The thought of school brought Harry's attention back to the history book lying in front of him. There was a great deal he must commit to memory before his lessons tomorrow with Mr Harrison-Finch. Although his tutor was indulgent in some matters, he expected Harry always to complete the homework he had set him.

'The trouble with you, my boy,' he'd said so many times, 'is that you're lazy – yes, lazy. It's easy for you to learn, so you don't put your whole mind to it. I mean to get you up to a standard that will enable you to get into a decent school, and you've a lot of ground to make up. No fault of yours, of course . . . village school and all that.'

Mr Harrison-Finch was a gentleman – impoverished maybe, but he had been born into an aristocratic family. Despite his calling, he was therefore on friendly terms with many of the well-to-do families in the area surrounding the market town of Melton Mowbray. Sometimes the vicar would break off in the middle of a lesson to regale Harry with stories of the eccentric behaviour of past occupants of the big hunting-lodges. Curiously, he seemed to take great pleasure when Harry laughed at these anecdotes. 'You should smile more often, boy,' he'd say, staring intently into Harry's face as if searching for something there. He would lean forward as he did so, and the strong, overwhelming smell of Eau-de-Cologne would assail Harry's nostrils.

Very occasionally Aunt Pamela would wave one of her

handkerchiefs similarly perfumed and Harry, associating it with his tutor, would shrink away. He vowed that when he was grown up he would never use scent, unless perhaps it was to brush back his hair with bay-rum, as Uncle Cosmo did. He admired his uncle's strong, masculine figure and exceptional good looks, although now, he thought, he was content to resemble the man Mrs Appleby believed to be his father. He must ask Mr Harrison-Finch what he knew about the late earl. The only comment his tutor had so far made about him was that he had not been a church-going man.

Wishing yet again that he were out riding with his uncle, Harry returned to his reading and, as so often happened, was soon absorbed in the contents of his history book. He was thus engaged when Hicks came into the room to tell him that his uncle and aunt had returned and that he was to join her ladyship in the drawing-room for afternoon tea.

'Now see here, old girl, we've got to put a bit of a brake on things,' Cosmo said to his sister. Tea had been cleared away and Harry despatched to his own room to continue his studies. Cosmo had not yet changed from his riding clothes and the room smelled faintly of horses. If Pamela disapproved, she made no mention of it. She was frowning, however, as she regarded him. Aware that her brother had been that morning to see Mr Arbuthnot, she realized instinctively that Cosmo had bad news.

'Explain yourself, Cosmo,' she said briefly.

'Seems we've been overdoing it,' Cosmo said, lighting one of his cigars, despite the fact that there was a perfectly good smoking-room and Pamela did not permit the habit anywhere else but in his bedroom and the billiard room. 'The silly old codger waffled on interminably in that vague way of his, but what it all boiled down to was that he'd had last year's accounts – and he wasn't too happy about them.'

Pamela drew a deep breath. 'Was there anything particular he was querying?' she enquired.

Cosmo grinned. 'Damn near everything,' he replied. 'He droned on about the increase in all the household expenses, the purchase of the Silver Ghost, which he said was an absurd extravagance with the petrol rationing and quite unnecessary seeing that we already have the old Standard and the Morris, reminded me there was a war on and – confound his impertinence! – damn nearly asked me outright why I wasn't fighting for my country.'

'You told him you weren't fit?'

'Naturally, but I don't think the old fool believed me. Asked me how it was my spinal troubles didn't prevent me riding. Seems his clerk had seen me out the other day putting Waterloo over a gate down near Brentingby Bottom. I'll have to think of some other chronic complaint. But that's not what's worrying him, old girl; it's the nine thousand we've managed to chalk up to young Harry's account.'

He allowed the ash on the end of his cigar to drop surreptitiously into the bowl of pot-pourri on the sofa table.

'Seems to me you'd best take the boy with you when you next go to London,' he said thoughtfully. 'We'd be in a bit of a quandary if Arbuthnot happened to meet him and Harry said he'd never been there. That fifty odd guineas we claimed for sightseeing, theatres and suchlike was a bit steep in the first place, as I told you at the time.'

'It's no more unreasonable than your claim for expenses,' Pamela said defensively. 'It's not as if the tailor's bill for Harry could possibly have amounted to the figures you claimed. The boy's clothes didn't total half. The majority were yours, as you very well know.'

'Well, let's not quarrel about it, old thing,' Cosmo said pacifically. 'I'm not denying I did bump it up a bit high. Don't forget, my dear, you do have an income as well as a bit put by, and I do not.'

'Gervaise probably guessed if he left you anything you'd gamble it away,' Pamela said spitefully. But her mood quickly softened. The last person in the world she wished to quarrel with was her brother. 'We'd better both tighten our purse strings,' she said in a more friendly voice. 'But I don't want that boy hanging round Eaton Terrace, Cosmo. You know I don't like children, and besides, he's still so – so uncouth.'

'Oh, I don't know,' Cosmo said reflectively. 'Harry's improved a lot since he's been here. Vowels still a bit suspect, and grammar leaves a lot to be desired, as old Harrison-Finch said in his last report. But on the whole, he's quite presentable. After all, we have explained to everyone that his late mother, a widow, was in poor health and living in very reduced circumstances, so he was looked after by a servant. We agreed this would be the reason we'd give for taking him on, wasn't it, when we discovered he was orphaned?'

'I know all that,' Pamela said testily, 'but I don't want Harry with me in London, Cosmo. It's bad enough having him hanging round here like a lost dog. If you think he should go to London, you take him. You're *in loco parentis* and it's a man's job, not a woman's, to see to that side of his education.'

'Yes, well, we'll see,' said Cosmo, rising to his feet. As he made his way upstairs, shouting to his valet as he went, he reflected that one of these days, he wouldn't mind taking the boy to see a good boxing match; to the gymnasium he'd recently joined; nor, indeed, to his fencing club; and possibly even to a variety theatre. Come to think of it, there was a good show on in London, *The Maid of the Mountains*. Harry might enjoy it.

On the other hand, he decided as his valet came into his bedroom with cans of hot water, he had planned to take Violet Covington. She'd been one of the very minor bit players in *Charley's Aunt* and he'd taken a fancy to her when the show had been on in town. The play was currently on tour but Violet, whose looks were a great deal more notable than her acting ability, had been replaced by some other girl, so that Violet was now 'resting' and available.

No, he decided, no more than his sister did he wish to be encumbered by Harry, especially not when he went racing next week. The boy might tag along and take note of the size of his, Cosmo's, bets! The less Pamela knew of his gambling, the better.

There was no real hurry to take Harry to London, he told himself as his valet laid out fresh clothes for him and went to instruct the maid to bring up more hot water for his bath. The chances of Harry running into Arbuthnot were minimal. The poor old boy was long past the age when he could sit a horse. Nor was that miserable old pansy, Harrison-Finch, likely to spill any beans. Heaven knew Pamela paid him well enough to keep his mouth shut where Harry was concerned. She could be quite crafty when she put her mind to a problem, and so far she'd succeeded in confining the boy's life to the extent that he met and conversed only with Harrison-Finch and Hicks. Fortunately, Harry still remained slightly in awe of his new environment and had made no attempt so far to strike out on his own.

Bathed and dressed in his new maroon velvet smoking-jacket, with its quilted silk collar and cuffs, Cosmo regarded his reflection in the wardrobe mirror with deep satisfaction. At forty he was still a very handsome man and, because of the shortage of men these days, much in demand by various hostesses. Once in a while, he was embarrassed by some silly woman's question as to why he wasn't in uniform. A vague reference to a riding accident and a long-standing injury to his back usually did the trick. Recently, however, he had been sent a white feather by, of course, some person wishing to remain anonymous.

Despite his efforts to forget this direct accusation of cowardice, Cosmo was unable to do so. For one thing, he told himself, it was not true. It took a man of courage to wager fifty guineas on a rank outsider if he didn't have the wherewithal to cover the bet! Nor did he lack for physical courage, although by the sound of it the chaps in France were having a pretty grim time. He might well have applied for a commission and done his stint in the cavalry but for the unfortunate timing of the war.

Gervaise's death and the terms of the poor fellow's will

had afforded him, Cosmo, his chance to get back on his feet. He knew his sister too well to suppose that she could ever carry off this financial coup on her own were he to enlist. Like most women, she was hopelessly ignorant about money. No, Pamela could not manage without him, and yesterday's session with Arbuthnot was a case in point. He'd been able to reassure him to some extent although the old boy had remained uneasy about the large sums attributed to 'incidentals' – effectively the cash Cosmo used at the gambling-tables and racecourses. He'd laughed off the old codger's questions.

'Taxis, tips, treats for the lad,' he'd said vaguely. 'Boys need books, toys, tuck as well as clothes and food. Mustn't deny him just because of the unfortunate circumstances of his birth,' he'd added forcefully. 'One has to take an enlightened attitude these days to illegitimacy. I dare say there'll be plenty more like young Harry by the time this terrible war is over – men on leave, can't really blame them . . .' Thus he had shamed Mr Arbuthnot into silence.

Nor should one blame a chap for making hay while the sun shone, he thought as he went downstairs for his pre-dinner sherry. There'd been some pretty awful disasters for the Allies recently. Now, not half-way through 1917, the Boche submarines were attacking the chaps at sea; the Canadians had had the devil's own job to take Vimy Ridge and no one had managed to stop the bloody Boche using poison gas! According to his *Times* this morning, there was renewed heavy fighting over Messines Ridge. No one was admitting it, of course, but things certainly were not going too well and there was no end to the war in sight.

Sipping his sherry – one of the excellent bottles he'd discovered in Gervaise's cellar – Cosmo picked up *The Times*. It contained a list of the recipients of the King's Birthday Honours. Glancing down to see if anyone he knew had been given a knighthood, his eye caught the name Debrace, Philip James. Certain that he knew the name but unable to place it, he asked Pamela, who had just joined him, if she could do so.

'Really, Cosmo, your memory is like a sieve,' she said,

'except where the names of horses are concerned! That's the man who employed Will Pritchett, the boy's foster father. His wife invited us to call on her the day we fetched Harry but we thought it wiser not to get involved. The man's a surgeon – a brilliant one too, according to a friend of mine who knows him. It's not surprising that he's been knighted. I gather he puts together the pieces sent down on those dreadful hospital trains – or so my friend said. I wasn't particularly interested, but I listened to her because I wanted to make sure we weren't likely to run into the Debraces in London. Seems the husband is far too busy to get involved in the social life, such as it is these days. All the same, Cosmo, it might be a good idea for us to write a letter of congratulations – use it as an excuse to reassure him as to Harry's welfare. Just suppose he were to come up here to see for himself how the boy's faring! From what Harry told me, the man used to take quite an interest in him – was even going to sponsor him to grammar school or some such – and he used to let him play with his own boy. On reflection, I'm surprised he hasn't already written to us asking for news.'

Cosmo nodded. 'If he's really so occupied with his operations, perhaps he's not had time,' he said as he handed Pamela a glass of sherry.

'Mrs Debrace could have written,' Pamela said thoughtfully, 'although, when you think about it, it is unlikely Harry was any concern of hers. I do worry, though, about that girl who keeps writing to him – Alice Pritchett – once a month, on the dot. Of course, I've arranged with Emerson always to give the letters to me, and I burn them at once, but the girl doesn't give up. I expressly forbade Harry to write home, on the grounds that it would be less distressing for his family if he made a clean break, and reminded him of the state his mother was in the day we took him away. You'd have thought the Pritchett girl would have given up by now, wouldn't you, not ever getting a reply to her letters?'

'Perhaps Harry gets Hicks or someone to post letters you don't know about,' Cosmo said.

Pamela laughed. 'You don't know Hicks!' she said. 'He dislikes the boy even more than I do. Hicks is a dreadful snob – thinks he's above being valet to a gardener's illegitimate child.'

'Steady on, old girl,' Cosmo argued. 'In the first place, Hicks doesn't know the boy's illegitimate; and in the second, Harry isn't Pritchett's lad. And I can tell you something else, his mother must have had blue blood in her veins, judging by that Lady Merstam female I met. Think about it, Pam. Would she have gone to all that trouble to conceal the boy's birth if his mother had not been one of our sort? I'll tell you something else, too. The boy's taken to our way of life like a duck to water – sits a horse as if he was born to it – and according to our Rev's reports, he's got a very good brain – "exceptional", the man said. Don't see all that in the lower classes, now, do you?'

Pamela sighed. 'You may be right, but frankly, Cosmo, I prefer not to think about Harry. It is hardly a pleasant subject for me, is it? What wife would enjoy discussing her husband's bastard?'

'Come off it, old girl,' Cosmo said genially. 'It's not as if you were all that smitten by Gervaise. Don't try to tell me you mind that he once lusted after some other female.'

'I'm not saying that,' Pamela replied sharply. 'What I am saying is that I've no wish to be the object of my friends' pity – or, even worse, ridicule. You can get away with that sort of thing if you're royalty – God knows, there are enough Fitz's around! – but not in the society we live in. Yes, some might call me a saint for bringing the boy under my roof, but they'd pity me at the same time for being obliged to do so.'

'I see your point, old girl, but you're letting your imagination run away with you. No one is going to find out the truth. The boy certainly isn't going to spread it around that he's a bastard. And who else knows the truth? Lady Merstam won't talk – that I'm sure of – so stop worrying. I wouldn't have suggested we sign the deed in the first place if I hadn't been certain we'd get our rewards. Just leave everything to me, eh?'

Pamela nodded and, visibly relaxing, sat down on the sofa beside her brother. At least they need not face Harry at dinner, she reflected. It was quite sufficient to have him join them for luncheon. At fourteen, he was still young enough to eat his supper in the nursery wing. If Hicks was in a good mood, he'd probably play cards with him. Hicks, Pamela knew, was partial to a game of two-handed whist. Just so long as she did not have to face those bright, trusting eyes which reminded her so uncomfortably of Gervaise, she did not care what the boy did in the evenings.

Although Pamela was no longer in mourning, she was still uneasily aware of Gervaise's spectre. It was as if his ghost haunted this house, which she was growing daily to dislike more and more. Not that she believed in ghosts, which was perhaps as well, for she couldn't think what Gervaise would do were he by some mysterious fashion to know of hers and Cosmo's plan to appropriate, slowly but surely, his bequest to his son.

Unhappy with this train of thought, Pamela turned her mind to more frivolous matters. When she returned to London next week, she must set about replenishing her wardrobe. Because of the war, fashions seemed to have changed very little this past year, but she was going to need a new coat for the autumn – a Poiret cape, perhaps, with a sable collar, and one of the new turbans for evening wear. In the light of Cosmo's warnings at teatime to curb her expenditure, she would cancel the installation of a new Eagle range for the kitchen and confine herself to the redecorating of her house. She'd been fortunate enough to get hold of a retired painter to do the work. She must also make enquiries about employing a replacement for Emerson, who had tendered his resignation, having decided that, despite his age, he must join the army. Kitchener's poster had taken its toll and two of the outdoor staff also were leaving.

Pamela sighed. Domestic staff, particularly good ones,

were becoming increasingly difficult to find. The women were leaving to go to munitions factories. Even her own friends were doing war work – two had joined the VAD, but she knew she could never stand the sight of wounded or blinded men, still less nurse those who had been gassed and spent their days in the wards coughing themselves into their graves.

No, she thought as Emerson announced that dinner was served, like Cosmo she would let it be known that she was in delicate health. The war would just have to go on without her. She had quite enough to think about with all the worry of the boy upstairs.

CHAPTER SIX

1917

'Do try to keep still, Miss Madeleine,' Alice begged as she put another pin in the shoulder of the dress she was making for the child's thirteenth bithday.

'Sorry,' Madeleine said, offering Alice her very best smile. She had practised it in her mirror many times and had now managed to produce it without screwing up her eyes so tight that they concealed the deep sapphire blue that was so often admired. They were her best feature, although every one of her features was good. She had been at boarding-school only a very short while before she realized that the prettiest girls were always the most popular and that, fortunately, she had been born with this useful advantage. The mistresses never stayed angry with her for long, and the older girls and prefects tended to mother her because she was so small.

Madeleine's best friend, Daphne, was also popular – not because of her looks, for she was singularly plain, but because she was the best lacrosse and netball player in the school. She was intensely patriotic and was always passing on news of the progress of the war, which Madeleine found boring. Not least, Daphne had a crush on her, as a consequence of which she was always willing to help her with her prep and would undertake the tiresome chores when it was Madeleine's turn to refill the ink wells or tidy the classroom.

For the time being it suited Madeleine very well to be at this girls' private boarding-school in Bexhill, where the rules were reasonably lax and the lessons not too onerous. Her only complaint was that she was obliged to wear a gym-slip and other such items of drab school uniform. It added to the pleasures of going home at weekends and during the holidays to know that she could wear all her pretty dresses again.

Mother had allowed her to choose the material in Hanningtons in Brighton for the new dress Alice was making and, judging by her reflection, it was going to be beautiful when it was finished.

'You are clever, Alice,' she said generously. 'I'm hopeless at sewing. We're supposed to be learning to feather stitch at school but I make an awful botch of it. I can't see the point in having sewing classes. When I get married, I'll have someone like you to do the sewing, so what's the point of trying to teach me to do something I hate?'

Alice smiled as she took in a second tuck. 'You never know when it might come in useful, Miss Madeleine.'

But, Alice knew, it was highly unlikely this young girl would ever need to pick up a sewing needle on her own behalf. When Miss Madeleine grew up, she was almost certain to marry a rich young man – in all probability, one of the friends Master Aubrey had made at his public school. Even if there were still a shortage of men after the war, as Lady Debrace had prophesied, Miss Madeleine was so pretty she would have the choice of those who were available.

'I'll have to leave off now, Miss Madeleine,' she said. 'It's time I was helping your mama get dressed. Your father is bringing some American officers back with him for dinner and she's in a right fuss about what they'll like to eat.'

Madeleine laughed as Alice helped her back into her box-pleated linen frock. 'Same as us, I should think,' she said. 'Aubrey says they've an American boy at school and he's not much different except that he wants to play a game called baseball instead of cricket.' She picked up her hairbrush and smoothed the long, fair strands back from her face. 'Thinking about school, Alice, did Harry ever get to his boarding-school?'

Gathering up the folds of Madeleine's half-completed dress, Alice turned away, not wishing the younger girl to see the concern in her eyes. 'No, miss, he didn't,' she said in as level a tone of voice as she could manage. 'His guardians found him a tutor instead.'

Madeleine pouted. 'Harry's an old meany. He never writes to us. You'd think he would at least write to Aubrey, they having been such friends before Harry went away. Mother wouldn't let Aubrey write to him in case it unsettled him. I suppose Harry's having such a good time, he's forgotten all about us.'

'That he hasn't,' Alice said more sharply than she intended. 'He asked me to remember him to all of you, but I only got the letter this morning and you've only just got back from school, Miss Madeleine, so I've not had time to tell you.'

'Oh, do tell now, Alice. What's he doing? Is he riding a lot? What . . .'

'I've just told you, Miss Madeleine, your mama will be waiting for me and I'm late. We'll talk about it some other time.'

Alice hurried out of the room and along the passage in the direction of her mistress's bedroom. Pausing to put the dress she was making on one of the shelves in the sewing-room, she stood for a moment with her back to the door, drawing deep breaths in an effort to calm herself. Tucked inside her apron pocket was Harry's letter, and late though she was, she could not resist the urge to read it yet again, despite the fact that the contents nearly reduced her to tears.

Dear Alice,
I wish you would write to me. I wrote a letter to you but I wasn't allowed to post it. I'm not supposed to post this either but Mrs Appleby – she's the cook here – promised she would, only if you do write back, you mustn't let on you got it else she'll get into trouble.

How is everyone? I hope Mum and Dad and everyone else is well. I expect Sam's getting quite big now. Is Edna all right? I expect Jenny is enjoying her job with the Debraces. How is Elsie? I suppose she'll be leaving school soon. I wish I was there. Please will you give them all my kind regards. I wish you would write but I dare say you are busy. Mrs Appleby says you probably have wrote but your letter's not got to me. She says you'll surely write when you get this letter as she's sure you've not forgot me.

I don't like it here and I miss you all very much. I read in the newspaper about the camps for prisoners of war and this place is a bit like a prison. I don't have any friends and I don't go to school now. I have lessons with a tutor who's called Mr Harrison-Finch. He's the vicar and I don't like him much. He's very clever, so I'm learning quite a lot. My guardian takes me riding when he's here. Mostly both my guardians are in London. I'm not supposed to talk to any of the servants so mostly there's no one to talk to. Hicks, the man who looks after me, plays cards with me sometimes but he doesn't like it when I win. I don't like him very much.

I wish I could see everyone, specially you. I hope you haven't forgot me. I am quite tall now as I've grown a lot.

I've got to finish now as it's Mrs Appleby's afternoon off and she's going to post this in the village, so I'll say goodbye and send love to everyone, as well as Aubrey and Miss Madeleine.

With kind regards, yours truly, Harry.

PS Don't tell anyone else I don't like it here else Mum will worry, I dare say. I've got lots of new clothes which are very posh and a horse of my own and a scout knife. I'm not allowed to join the Boy Scouts.

PPS Mrs Appleby says will you put her name instead of mine on the envelope when you write so as to be sure it gets to me safely.

Alice pushed the letter back into her pocket and, with

tears pricking her eyes, she left the sewing-room and went to join her mistress. Fortunately, Eloise Debrace had her mind on other matters that evening and did not notice Alice's unusual quietness. As soon as she was dressed, she hurried out of her room and went downstairs to make a further inspection of the preparations for her unfamiliar guests.

Alice's thoughts were still preoccupied with Harry's letter as she tidied up the discarded clothes and turned down the bed with automatic care. Try though she might, she simply couldn't understand why her letters to Harry had not reached him. She had written every month since he had left home. Not hearing from him she in turn had begun to suppose that he was so taken with his new life that he had all but forgotten them! Someone, she now suspected – as Mrs Appleby had done – was withholding her letters. She couldn't even be certain that any reply she wrote now to Harry would reach him. She would try, of course, but otherwise there was nothing she could do. It broke her heart to think of him so lonely, so homesick and unhappy.

As she turned out the lights and closed the bedroom door behind her, it occurred to her to wonder if there was any way she could go to see him, since it seemed highly unlikely that he would be allowed to visit his old family. She would have to ask Mr Standing if he knew what the train fare to Leicestershire might cost. In a box in her attic bedroom there were five half-crowns, several sixpences and a threepenny piece – the sum total of her savings. Would that amount to the price of a return ticket, she asked herself? Mr Standing would know.

Eager now to go down to the kitchen, where hopefully she would find the butler, she made her way down the back stairs. As she reached the narrow stone-flagged passage leading to the servants' hall, a man stepped out of the shadows.

'Wait a minute, Alice.'

She recognized Frederick's voice at once and her fear vanished.

130

'Oh, it's you, Fred,' she said. 'Whatever are you doing here? I didn't know you'd got leave again. When did you arrive?'

'A couple of hours ago. I've been waiting to see you, Alice – to talk to you – without all the others around, I mean.'

Alice was grateful for the shadows in the narrow passageway which, she hoped, would hide her blushes. Since that day nearly two years ago when Fred had taken her out for an afternoon in Brighton, he had written with alarming regularity from France. Although he had behaved with the utmost decorum on that outing, treating her as if she had been his young sister, his letters contained a different note and Sally, the parlourmaid to whom Alice had shown one of the letters, said there was little doubt that he was sweet on her.

'He'd know better than to have let on, that day in Brighton, that he was smitten – you being a girl only sixteen,' Sally had said. 'But you're eighteen now, Alice, and I'll say this, you're getting ever so pretty. I don't wonder Fred fancies you!'

'But he's twenty-eight,' Alice had protested. 'Ten years older than me.'

'I don't see the harm in that,' had been Sally's reply. 'He's nice-looking and steady – not like some! And he's got a good job to come back to. Like as not he'll take Mr Standing's place when he retires and you'd be set for life, Alice.'

But Alice knew that the most she had ever felt for Fred was liking and that she would have to love someone very much indeed if she were to be deflected from her dwindling hope that she might one day keep house for Harry.

'You're all right, Fred?' she said now. 'Not wounded nor anything?'

'No, I've been lucky . . . only got my little finger blown off by a bit of shrapnel – and it's worth it to get this extra bit of leave.' He paused, as if uncertain how to continue. 'I wanted to tell you what a lot it means to me getting your letters.'

131

Alice swallowed nervously. 'I'm afraid I didn't write often. There didn't seem much to tell you really.'

It was a weak excuse but Fred let it go.

'You can't know – not being out there – what it means to a bloke to get letters from home, especially if they're from wives and sweethearts. There's times when . . . when it's not too good and you wonder if you'll ever get home again, and if a fellow's just had a letter from Blighty, well, it kind of urges him to pull himself together so's he can get back one day when it's all over.'

Alice had a very good idea of how dreadful the conditions were for the soldiers. One Sunday morning after family prayers, Sir Philip had told all the staff about the men in his hospital and how brave they were, for though they took great pains to hide it, they'd have been lying if they'd said they were not afraid. He'd spoken of the long hours standing in trenches full of mud and water waiting for an attack, or being shelled; of the awful fear of gas; of the cold, the lack of hot food, the rats, the cries of the men who'd been wounded and had to be left in No Man's Land until the shelling was over. Nothing but *nothing*, he had reiterated, was good enough for them.

This was why she had written back to Fred, although she had not really wanted to do so.

'Alice!' Fred reached out and caught her hand in his. She could feel him trembling. 'Alice, I want to ask you . . . I know you're still very young, but . . . I'm not asking for more than an understanding that when – if – I get back, we can start walking out. I'd ask your parents, of course, if they'd have any objections to us . . . well, to us courting.'

Something in the rigidity of Alice's body must have communicated itself to the man, for he lapsed into silence. More than anything in the world at that moment, Alice longed to be able to speak the truth – to tell him that she simply did not harbour the right sort of feelings for him; that she would be raising his hopes unfairly if she indicated that she welcomed his suggestions. At the same time, she knew she could not send him back to the Front

132

believing she did not care whether he lived or died. He had no family and, but for her, there was no one to whom he mattered as an individual.

Gently, she withdrew her hand. 'It wouldn't be right for me to promise anything, Fred,' she said. 'I dare say you'll think I'm silly, but I want to see more of the world before . . . well, before I start going steady. Lady Debrace said as how she'd speak to her sister after the war was over and see if she could get me a job in Monsieur Verveine's *Maison de Couture* in Paris.' Seeing Fred's look of incomprehension, she added quickly, 'It's a sort of fashion house, Fred, where they design and make clothes for important people. Lady Debrace thinks such a lot of my sewing, she says I'm wasting my talents.' Her voice softening once again – for it had risen in her excitement – she added, 'I've never lived anywhere but Calking in all my life, and to go to Paris . . . of course, it might never happen. You have to be very good to get taken on by that sort of place, and Monsieur Verveine might not need any more staff. So you see, Fred, it's best for me not to make any promises, just in case.'

It was a moment or two before Fred spoke. The expression on his face, even in the shadows, revealed his disappointment, but now he said, 'I'd be willing to wait, Alice. And if you did get a job out there, I could always get domestic work somewhere nearby, couldn't I? I've learned a few French words already. Perhaps you're right, anyway, to wait and see what happens. I know it would be wrong to tie you down now when I may not ever get back. Two of our lads got married on their last leave and both of them's dead now and their wives widows afore they hardly knew what married life's like! Meantime, you will come out with me, won't you? I've got five days and if it's still your afternoon off on Wednesday, p'raps we could go into Brighton again. We could go and see Charlie Chaplin – Mr Standing said there's a new film on at the Arcadia. You'd like that, Alice. Remember, last time we didn't have enough time for the cinema?'

'All right, Fred, only we'd go just as . . . as friends, wouldn't we?'

Fred nodded, willing to agree to any terms provided he could be in Alice's company. 'We'll take young Elsie with us, if it'll make you feel happier,' he said generously. ''Tis good to see you, Alice. You're a sight for sore eyes!'

Relaxing now that Fred seemed to have accepted the situation, Alice laughed. 'I should think anything would be a sight for sore eyes after what you've been looking at these past few years,' she said. 'Goodness gracious, just look at the time. I'll just put these in the laundry room and then I've got to get back up to the sewing room. I'm making Miss Madeleine's birthday-party dress and I'll never get it finished this road.'

'Can't you bring it down to the servants' hall?' Fred asked wistfully.

Knowing that she did not want to spend any more time with him than pity dictated, Alice excused herself on the grounds that she needed the dressmaker's dummy and a lot more bits and pieces that Mr Standing would not allow her to bring downstairs.

'I'll see you at supper, then,' Fred said as Alice edged past him and opened the kitchen door. 'It's good to be getting some decent grub again.'

I'll speak to Mum about making him one of her cut-and-come-again cakes to take back off leave with him, Alice thought, knowing that it was not just the least but the most she could do to make up to him for her rejection. Pity, she told herself as she went back upstairs, was no substitute for love – not that she had ever been in love, but Sally was courting and it was clear that her whole world revolved around her boy, who was in the navy. She kept his letters under her pillow, tucked into her chemise, and even when she was at work, she wore the ring he'd given her out of a cracker last Christmas on a ribbon round her neck. When the war was over, he was going to give her a proper engagement ring and they'd get married as quick as ever they could. Sally described their kisses as feeling like she was falling off Beachy Head. The temptation to let him take liberties was almost too strong to resist, she'd said, and she didn't know how she was managing to stay pure.

Alice could not imagine being tempted even to kiss Fred. Betsy, the kitchen maid, thought him the most handsome man she'd ever seen and blushed whenever she saw him. She was knitting him a balaclava, but constantly dropped so many stitches that a year after she'd started it, it was still no more than half done. The rest of the staff teased her, saying the war would be over before ever it was finished and then what use would it be!

Perhaps she should have made something for Fred, Alice thought guiltily; written to him more frequently. It was simply not the same as when she sat down to write to Harry. Doing so made her feel closer to him, and even for a little while as if she was talking to him. Now even more urgently she longed to get out her writing pad and fountain pen and pour out her reassurances that he was very far from forgotten by any of them.

She wondered about his one friend, Mrs Appleby, the cook. At least this meant he was being well fed. Hopefully he was also being well schooled by the tutor, even if he did not like him. What Alice could not understand was why he was kept a prisoner – as he put it; why he was not allowed to make friends with other boys; why his guardians did not take him to London when they went there. Could it be that they were ashamed of him? she asked herself, as she sat down to resume her work on Miss Madeleine's dress.

Her years as Lady Debrace's personal maid had made her realize even more markedly than she had before the many hundreds of differences, some great, some small, between the gentry and the working classes. It was very far from being a gulf created only by accents of speech. She had taken note of her mistress's way of pronouncing words and could, when she chose, speak as if she had had as good an education as Miss Madeleine. No, there were far less obvious pitfalls – so very many things a lady should and should not do. It was easy for someone like Miss Madeleine, who had absorbed them from birth. It was not so easy for someone like herself, who, for the first thirteen years of her life, had spoken and behaved like any other child in the village. She had first to undo the old ways before donning the mantle of the new, and it must be as hard for Harry — harder, probably, because he was compelled to change, whereas she herself could choose how she wished to behave.

When at last the servants' evening meal was over and Alice was free to do as she pleased until her mistress was ready to go to bed, she went at once to her room and, sitting on the iron bedstead, started her letter to Harry. Sally, already in bed, was reading one of the Ruby M. Ayres novels she so enjoyed. She looked at Alice curiously.

'You've not got a secret admirer somewhere you've not told me about, have you?' she asked, only half joking.

'Don't be such a ninny,' Alice answered. 'I'm writing to my brother, Harry.'

'Mr Standing's always talking about him,' Sally said. 'Your Harry'd gone 'afore I started work here. He isn't really your brother, is he? Mr Standing said he went to live with his real family — titled people.'

'I told you, Sally, he's living with guardians. His own parents are dead. But he grew up one of us.'

A deep core of pride had prevented her from allowing Sally to see how deeply hurt she had been when week after week passed without a reply from Harry to her many letters. Even a postcard would have sufficed to let her know that he had not forgotten her, or grown too grand to bother any longer with his old family. Supposing him to be too deeply engrossed in his new life and revelling in all the many advantages that Master Aubrey enjoyed, she had once or twice been tempted to stop writing to him.

Now, his sad little letter safely tucked beneath her pillow, she would wait until Sally was asleep before reading it again, although she knew it would bring tears to her eyes. She felt a great rush of gratitude for whatever instinct had prompted her to keep faith with Harry. She would be able to tell him that although he may never have received her letters, she had not failed to write. It was obvious that, far from forgetting her, he had been forbidden to keep in touch with his old family; that he had been missing her as much as, if not more than, she had missed him. How grateful she was to this Mrs Appleby, who had clearly undertaken the task of acting as a go-between.

It was a very long time since she had felt so filled with joy, Alice thought. There was no longer any need to side-track Sally's questions about Harry and she welcomed the chance to talk about him, albeit with certain reservations.

Sally was leaning on one elbow, her eyes bright with curiosity.

'Harry was your favourite, wasn't he? You don't talk half as much about the other kids in your family. Mr Standing said he was special with the horses,' Sally went on. 'And he said Master Aubrey had him for a friend, but that don't seem right.'

'It wasn't wrong,' Alice said. 'Master Aubrey was delicate when he was little, with his asthma and that, so he didn't have friends of his own kind to play with. Mr Debrace – I mean, Sir Philip – thought our Harry was good for Master Aubrey, and he was too. Harry was clever and he'd have gone to the grammar if his guardians hadn't come to fetch him.'

Sally laughed. 'No doubt about who your favourite is, Alice. One of these days you'll give us all a shock by telling us something bad about Harry. The way you go on, he might be the Prince of Wales.'

'And you're a fine one to talk,' Alice retorted happily. 'The way you go on about your sailor boy, he might be Valentino.'

They both laughed as Sally brought out from beneath her pillow a dog-eared photograph of her cinema screen idol, Valentino, standing outside a tent, dressed as a sheik, with the desert in the background.

'Well, if *he* asked me to marry him, I might have another think about my Herbert,' Sally admitted, for she, like most of the females in the world, came close to swooning at the sight of this silent hero acting out a love scene.

'So now will you read your book or go to sleep,' Alice pleaded. 'Else the mistress will be ringing for me before ever I've started this letter.'

As Sally subsided once more into the pages of her novel, Alice wrote such words of comfort to Harry as she could, followed by:

Mr Standing says I should be able to buy a third-class return ticket for about one pound five shillings and I've half that saved already. As soon as I've enough, I'll come and see you. Please write back and tell me what's the nearest railway station and how I get to Maythorpe House. Shall I ask Mrs Appleby if I can see you when I get there afore I see anyone else? I wouldn't want to come all that way and not see you.

Have you got a photograph you can send me? I might not recognize you if you've grown so much. I'm not changed, although I may get my hair bobbed as lots of girls do these days. Mum's against it and so's Lady Debrace, as she says a woman's hair is her crowning glory, which I think is a quotation.

You mustn't mind not liking your tutor as you didn't like Mr Wilson much when you first started school and it ended up you did like him, so maybe you'll get to like the vicar. I hope you will make some friends soon. Sally, the parlourmaid who came last year, is a good friend to me, and Jenny and me get on better now she's grown up. Now Miss Madeleine is at boarding-school, there's not a lot for Jenny to do except in the holidays, when she's personal maid to her like I am to Lady Debrace. I expect you heard about Mr Debrace being knighted, so he's Sir Philip now, but some of us still forget from time to time and call him Mr Debrace to each other.

Can you find out what's happened to all my letters? I've written so many since you left, I can't count. Now Ted's at school there's only little Sam at home and I think Mum spoils him a bit – sort of makes up for you not being there. Mum's always holding you up as an example to the boys, like how you learned to ride that old bike and rode horses and all that. I think Sam thinks you're a bit like Father Christmas – someone we all talk about but never see!

Dad's put a lot of the flower beds down to vegetables as Sir Philip says we must all do everything possible to help with the war. Fred's home on leave, which they let him have extra because he got a finger shot off. He looks very thin and tired. Although he doesn't say so, I'm sure he's wishing he didn't have to go back out there. I'm very glad you're not old enough. One of the boys in the village who you used to know at school – he was in the seniors when you were starting juniors – he told a lie about his age and got sent to Chichester barracks with a lot of other volunteers although they was all over eighteen. Two months later, his dad found out where he was and went down to the recruiting station and got him sent home. So it didn't do him any good trying to get in before he was old enough.

Sir Philip takes the car to the station and goes into Brighton by train now because of the petrol rationing. Everyone else has gone back to using the carriages and Miss Madeleine is learning to drive the governess cart by herself.

Master Aubrey will be home for his summer holidays soon so I'll tell him your address and if he wants, he can write to you. He quite likes school but can't play games because they bring on attacks when he has to run fast. He's grown a lot too, and is nearly as tall as his father.

I haven't got time for more now, but I'll write again soon as I can. I do hope this gets to you safe this time. Tell Mrs Appleby I'm very grateful she's so kind to you and so would Mum be if she knew. I haven't told her, like you said, because she thinks you are having a nice time where you are. That's why she didn't make any more fuss about you going, though I can't see as how any of us could have stopped it.

Please write again soon as I'll be watching the

postboy every time he rides up to the house.

From your loving

Alice.

Alice's letter, posted by Fred the following morning, reached Maythorpe House the morning after. Unseen by Emerson, it was safely in Mrs Appleby's hands before breakfast.

CHAPTER SEVEN

1917

'We shall combine current affairs with some geography today, dear boy.'

The Reverend Percy Harrison-Finch walked across his study to the chair where Harry was seated and, standing behind it, rested a hand on Harry's shoulder.

'As you know, I had planned to give you some Latin translations today. However, I realize that this exercise does not exactly fill you with enthusiasm . . .' he gave a short laugh, 'so we shall indulge ourselves in something more to your taste, eh?'

Surreptitiously Harry edged sideways in a vain attempt to dislodge his tutor's hand, which, through his shirt, he could feel was hot and sticky. The smell of Eau-de-Cologne was overpowering despite the fact that the big bow windows were opened wide. Outside, the July sun had already raised the temperature into the nineties. While he had enjoyed the heat on the journey here in the dog cart, where their progress had engendered a pleasant cooling breeze, the atmosphere in the vicarage was oppressive.

'I'll get the globe, sir,' he said, welcoming this excuse for widening the space between himself and the vicar. This past year he had become increasingly uneasy in Mr Harrison-Finch's presence. He did not think any longer that he was imagining the man's pale-blue eyes were permanently fastened upon him. Now he was certain of it. It was as if the vicar were unable to cease this persistent staring. Nor was this the only reason for his increasing feeling of discomfort, for he had become aware that his tutor was always finding some reason or other to touch him.

'Use that brain of yours, young man – it's a good one,' he might say but the remark, harmless in itself, meant a warm hand placed on Harry's head, as if to indicate where his brain was lodged. Or, 'There are nine muses, my boy, not ten,' and he would take Harry's hands in his and slowly count them off, finger by finger, 'Caliope, Clio, Euterpe . . .' and so on, retaining Harry's hands until he, Harry, had repeated all the names.

On Harry's birthday at the beginning of the year, he had given him a copy of the poems of Oscar Wilde, on the flyleaf of which he had written: 'For Harry Keynes on his fourteenth birthday – so that he may have a broader vision of our English authors. Yrs affectionately, Percy Harrison-Finch, 5 January 1917.' Following the presentation of this gift, he had given Harry an ambiguous account of Wilde's life, including some even more obscure references to his illicit behaviour, and had read aloud to him 'The Ballad of Reading Gaol'. That Wilde had had a deep and uncontrollable love for a young man by the name of Lord Alfred Douglas was clear enough, but Harry could see no reason why this should result in his being sent to gaol.

The vicar had not enlightened him but promised to do so at some later date. In the meanwhile, he said, Harry must understand that he was entrusting to him a book which, quite possibly, his guardians might feel unsuitable for a boy of his tender years but which he believed Harry was now sufficiently grown up to appreciate. Flattered, Harry had taken the book home in his satchel and omitted to mention it to either his aunt or uncle.

As it happened, he found a great deal of the poetry incomprehensible. Nevertheless, he had also found much of it beautiful and, for some strange reason, the love poems brought memories of little Miss Madeleine into his mind, in particular four verses from 'Roses and Rue'.

Your mouth, it would never smile
For a long, long while,

Then it rippled all over with laughter
Five minutes after.

You were always afraid of a shower,
Just like a flower:
I remember you started and ran
When the rain began.

I remember I never could catch you,
For no one could match you,
You had wonderful, luminous, fleet,
Little wings to your feet.

I remember your hair – did I tie it?
For it always ran riot –
Like a tangled sunbeam of gold:
These things are old.

Of late, he was having strange dreams about Madeleine which seemed to be connected with the poem. He and Aubrey would be deliberately falling off their ponies in an attempt to make her laugh. For a while she would not do so and then, suddenly, she would smile, and Harry would be filled with a wonderful sensation of pleasure. Or he alone would be chasing her through the long, uncut grass of Iron Pit Meadow, allowing her always to remain a little ahead of him, tantalizing himself with the knowledge that he could reach out and touch her if he chose. When finally he did so and they both fell to the ground, yet again he would experience that mysterious, heavenly feeling. In all his dreams, he never failed to see her blue eyes laughing, smiling at him, and the long, ash-blonde, silky strands of her hair.

Mrs Appleby, who was a great believer in analysing dreams – as well as telling futures from tea-leaves – insisted that no one dreamed in colours. Harry knew different.

'Somehow I do not think I have your full attention, dear boy,' Mr Harrison-Finch's voice interrupted Harry's wandering thoughts. 'I trust you are not suffering from a preponderance of sunshine? It can cause headaches, you know, and I noticed that you were not wearing a hat when you came up the drive.'

Harry was unaware that his tutor had been watching for his arrival and now the thought bothered him. 'I am quite well, thank you, sir,' he said.

The vicar nodded. 'In that case, I will continue.' He pointed his paper knife once more to a place on the big globe. 'The United States of America is, as you know, an exceptionally large country with a population very far in excess of our own. We may therefore happily anticipate that we shall no longer suffer a shortage of manpower in our struggle against our enemies. For the last ten days, American troops have been pouring into Europe and, so I understand, they are to be seen quite frequently now in London. It is therefore to be hoped that the war may be brought to a speedier conclusion than we dared to expect. However . . .'

He paused to revolve the globe and pointed now to France. 'You will now indicate to me the positions of Arras, Vimy Ridge and Ypres, all of which battlegrounds being, I hope, familiar to you.'

As Harry took the paper knife from him and did as he was told, Percy Harrison-Finch turned abruptly away. His voice was peculiarly high-pitched as he said, 'Thank God this war will almost certainly be over before you are old enough to be involved, my dear boy. I do not think I could bear . . . that is to say, I would feel . . . it would be a great waste of an excellent brain if you were to meet the fate of so many of our boys out there. The flower of our youth – yes, indeed, the very jewels in our crown! It grieves me beyond belief.'

Not a little embarrassed by this outburst, unrelated, as far as Harry could see, to either current affairs or geography, he remained silent until, suddenly, the man turned and came towards him. His cheeks were flushed, his eyes unnaturally bright as he grasped Harry's hand and held it fiercely between his own.

'You can have no idea what it has meant to me to have you here . . . my pupil, my *raison d'être*. You understand, don't you, my dearest boy, that for someone, someone like myself, one becomes very lonely . . . to have a fresh, untouched mind to mould, to become part of one's life, one's very existence . . . to give meaning to each day . . .'

He broke off and his eyes filled with tears as Harry firmly removed his hand. 'You don't understand what it is I am trying to tell you, do you? Have you no idea, Harry? Has it never occurred to you how . . . how very attached to you I have become? For a year and a half now, you have sat in this room with me and I have tried to teach you everything I know. But there is more . . . much much more than academic knowledge I could impart. You are on the very threshold of manhood and – answer me truthfully – have there not been times when you have longed for something more? The body is as hungry for knowledge as the mind, and you must . . . at your age you must . . . long to have that hunger assuaged. Do you understand me now, dearest boy?'

Harry understood only part of what this distraught man was blurting out in painful gasps. Somehow Mr Harrison-Finch knew of his dreams; knew how, when he woke, the memory of the pleasure was tempered with a sadness born of the fact that he wanted them to be true. He wanted to hold that girl's slim body in his arms; to kiss that small, laughing mouth. He would lie in the darkness thinking about her, remembering lines from the Oscar Wilde poetry book:

> Her little lips, more made to kiss
> Than to cry bitterly for pain,
> Are tremulous as brook-water is,
> Or roses after evening rain.

His tutor could not know of his wild dreams and imaginings, for he did not even know of Miss Madeleine's existence. Harry had told him about Aubrey and how his books and those in the Debrace library had assisted him in his work, but he had never mentioned Aubrey's sister.

To his relief his tutor, as suddenly as he had started this inexplicable diatribe, now seemed to regain normality. He was actually smiling.

'Come now, Harry, I have had the most excellent idea. Really, it is too hot for serious work. We will go down to the Wreake and bathe. You can swim, I take it?'

Harry's face fell. 'No, sir, I've never learned.'

'I'll have to make it my duty for the day to ensure you don't drown, dear boy,' the vicar said with the peculiar little laugh he reserved for the occasions when he thought he had made a joke. 'I will have a word with the cook and she can pack us a picnic luncheon. I don't think we will bother to take that somewhat sour-faced servant of yours with us. We shall walk to the river. I will arrange it. You, meanwhile, can take down Volume A–B of *Chamber's Encyclopedia* from the shelf and look up the entry referring to the Army. There you will find a section on the history of the army of the United States of America. Its development in the last twenty years has been phenomenal.'

There was no such encyclopedia in Maythorpe House, and Harry had long since made up his mind that one of the first things he would do when he was rich enough was buy a set of these volumes, for the facts contained in them fascinated him. He was still reading about the American army when Mr Harrison-Finch came back into the room, carrying two large towels and a picnic hamper. He was beaming.

'All set, dear boy. Let us waste no more of this beautiful day and be on our way.'

Harry was delighted to be out in the open air and more than happy to join in his tutor's discordant rendering of 'Onward Christian Soldiers' as they walked through the meadows in the direction of the river. His companion was perspiring beneath the white panama hat he always wore in summer. He was wearing a white summer jacket over his black trousers. His white dog collar hung loosely round his thin, scraggy neck. Despite his obvious suffering in the heat, he appeared to be in an excellent mood and was playfully knocking the heads off the cow parsley with his walking-stick, pretending to be the famous golfer, Harry Vardon.

'Your namesake, young man,' he said jovially. 'I used to play the game when I was younger. You should get your guardian to teach you.'

Somehow Harry did not think it likely his Uncle Cosmo would do so. There would be other people on a golf course and he was in no doubt now that he was being kept apart from his guardians' friends and neighbours. He was always sent to his own rooms if they had visitors; and if anyone appeared in the distance when he and his uncle were out riding, some excuse would be made to change direction. No one had told Harry the reasons for his being a social outcast, but he assumed it had to do with the fact that he was illegitimate; or else that he had still not entirely lost his Sussex accent and was not fool-proof in matters of etiquette. In this first respect, his speech was almost fault-less, for Mr Harrison-Finch included elocution lessons in Harry's curriculum. Over and over again he would have to repeat such lines as, 'Give me your green glass beads!' and recite passages of Shakespeare, which, his tutor said, would have the added benefit that he could commit them to memory at the same time as learning to articulate correctly.

Strange though the vicar might be at times, he was not really so awful, Harry told himself. He never used the cane and seldom raised his voice. Now, on this perfect summer's day, he was to be allowed to skip lessons and go for a picnic by the river. It seemed a very long while ago since he and Jenny had bathed in the pond on Calking Common – against his father's rules, since they had no bathing-dresses. Aubrey had lent him one of his that special day when Mrs Debrace had taken them to the seaside at Brighton. Today, he supposed, Mr Harrison-Finch would lend him one of his – the vicar was a thin man whose clothing would not be over-large on Harry.

When they reached the riverside, his tutor led the way along the bank until they had left the meadow behind them and reached the outskirts of a wood. The river, dazzling in the sunshine, flowed into the dark-green shadows cast by the overhanging trees.

'It will be cooler here in the shade,' Mr Harrison-Finch announced when they had walked deeper into the wood. 'Moreover,' he added with a chuckle, 'we're not likely to be bothered by Peeping Toms. Wouldn't do to be seen in our nakedness, would it?'

So there were no bathing-dresses wrapped up in the towels, Harry thought with some surprise. He had expected the elderly vicar to be more decorous. His father had never allowed Harry into the scullery when he had taken his bath on a Saturday night. The vicar, however, turned his back as he began to undress. Delighted to rid himself of his own attire, Harry did likewise. As he stripped off the last of his underclothing, he turned to find Mr Harrison-Finch, almost unrecognizable in his nudity, staring at him with such intensity that Harry's face flushed with embarrassment.

'No need to be shy with me, dear boy,' his tutor said in a muffled voice. 'God made us all in his own image, remember.'

There was nothing very godlike about Mr Harrison-Finch's image, Harry thought as he turned his gaze away from the loose-skinned, bony spectacle of his tutor, his body a startling white against the dark background of the trees. Unable to bear the man's scrutiny any longer, he waded into the icy water. Despite the first shock, he was delighted to feel the gentle rush of the river caressing his body. He ducked beneath the water and surfaced, shaking his head. Mr Harrison-Finch was now nearby, swimming a cautious breaststroke.

'Be careful of the can-docks,' he called out. 'Keep your feet well clear if you can. They can drag you under.'

Silly old fool, Harry thought, climbing back on to the bank and jumping in again with childish abandon. The water was beautiful and the river was beautiful and he was happy. He grabbed at a stick drifting past him, threw it into the air and splashed after it. High above his head, he could hear the call of a pair of ringdoves – coo-coo-coo – followed by the sharp squawk of a cock pheasant. Soon the shooting season would be starting and Uncle Cosmo had promised to give him some more practice with his beautiful new Purdey. If only Aubrey could go with them. If only Aubrey and Madeleine and Alice and Jenny could be here now, enjoying this wonderful day and the picnic which was awaiting him. A wave of homesickness engulfed him, replacing his earlier euphoria.

Slowly Harry made his way back upstream towards his tutor, who had already emerged from the water and was drying himself with one of the towels.

'Doesn't do to stay in too long, dear boy,' he called out to Harry. 'You can bathe again after lunch if you want.'

His toes squelching in the mud, Harry scrambled up the bank and took the towel the vicar was holding out to him. As he wrapped it round him, Mr Harrison-Finch leaned over and pulled it away from one shoulder.

'Bit of weed stuck to your back,' he murmured, allowing his hand to run lightly over Harry's skin. 'Goodness me, boy, you are cold. Here, let me give you a good rub down.' He took the ends of the towel from Harry's grasp and, in a voice that might have been used on an infant, intoned: 'Rub-a-dub-dub, three men in a tub! Soon have you dry again. Stand still now, like a good boy. There we go . . .'

Slowly, covered by the folds of the towel, his hands moved downwards from Harry's chest to his stomach. Harry tried to renew his hold on the towel but the man's grasp was surprisingly strong. He was humming now, his eyes averted from Harry's face as he made a feeble pretence of drying Harry's legs before his hands started fumbling at Harry's groin.

'Sir, I can dry myself, please. Please, sir . . .'

'Now, now, Harry. Leave this to me. I want to help you. I can, you know. I will look after you. Don't be afraid. There's no one to see us, I promise you.'

149

Harry had not been so much afraid as embarrassed until the man made reference to the fact that there was nobody about who might be watching them. He knew then that what his tutor was doing to him must be wrong. He could feel his body responding to the rhythmic movements of the man's hands and, horrified, realized that he had no more control now of this part of his anatomy than he had in his dreams – his dreams of Miss Madeleine.

'Don't do that!' he shouted in a horrified voice. 'I don't like it. I don't want you to . . .'

'Please, Harry, please. Don't push me away. Please, don't you understand, I love you. I'll do anything in the world to make you happy. I love you. I know it's wrong but I can't help it. Please, my dearest boy, my darling boy . . .'

Harry wrenched the towel away and, stopping to grab his clothes, he turned and ran as fast as his bare feet allowed, deep into the wood. His horror had turned to disgust, for now he knew what kind of man his tutor was – a man like Oscar Wilde, who had had an unnatural preference for other men. After the vicar had given him the book of poems, he had found a volume in the library called *Famous Trials*, and in it he had read the trial of Oscar Wilde. At the time it had seemed extraordinary but remote, and if he had been moved to any feelings, it had been one of pity for a man who could write so beautifully and yet be so warped. Now, however, he could feel no pity for his tutor – only disgust, and astonishment at his own *naïveté* in not realizing before the true explanation for the vicar's often strange behaviour.

At least the tumult in his loins had subsided, he thought, as he pulled on his clothes, but this did nothing to lessen his revulsion at the thought of having to come face to face with the man. Never again did he wish to hear that voice pleading with him, calling out endearments.

Having ridden all round the vicinity of Maythorpe House, Harry knew exactly where he now was and how he might find his way home through the woods. He would go back and explain to his guardian why he could never have lessons at the vicarage again. Mr Harrison-Finch could make his own explanation to Hicks, who would be waiting to accompany him, Harry, back to the house.

Feeling suddenly far younger than his age, Harry was close to tears as he tied his shoelaces and began the long trek home. If only he were really going home – to Mum and Dad and Alice! Not that he could tell such a story to his parents, but Alice was different. She would understand. She would make him feel better, the way she always did when things went wrong.

Indifferent now to the beauty of this midsummer day, to the squirrels and rabbits and birds he came upon, which normally would have held his interest, Harry scuffled his feet in the leaf mould and slashed viciously at the tree trunks with a hazel switch. He was beginning to wonder if somehow he himself had been to blame for what had happened. He had shown respect towards Mr Harrison-Finch but never affection. It was not even as if he had liked the man. On the other hand, there had been those times when his tutor had ruffled his hair, grasped his shoulder, covered his hand. What he could not understand was how the man had thought that he, Harry, might have been willing to participate in such repulsive conduct. Worst of all was the horrible truth that his body had – albeit momentarily – responded to the man's caresses. Somehow it made him a participant and he hated himself almost as much as he hated Mr Harrison-Finch.

I'll never go back there! I never want to see him again! The words rang in his head so that they became a kind of litany, and they were the first he spoke when, an hour later, he located his uncle in the billiard room.

'Please, sir, I'm never going back. I never want to see him again,' he blurted out as his uncle potted a ball neatly into a middle pocket and turned to look at his ward. The boy was dishevelled, to say the least, and Cosmo had certainly not expected to see him at this hour of the day.

'What's up, old man?' he asked. 'What's this all about?'

151

'Sir, it's him, Mr Harrison-Finch. I'm never going back, not never!' In his distress, Harry had slipped back into his childhood vernacular. 'I hate him. I won't go back.'

'I say, old chap, you are in a miff! Sit down now and let's hear all about it. What's that old Nancy boy been up to?'

Harry was unfamiliar with the term – but in any event, he was not listening. He poured out his story without pausing for breath.

'So you see, sir, I can't go back. I won't.'

He was utterly unprepared for his guardian's reaction. His Uncle Cosmo was actually laughing.

'The devil he did,' he said. 'Who'd have thought the fellow had the guts to try it on. Still, I suppose he thought it worth a try. Must have had a shock when you shot off like that. He'll know you're bound to let the cat out of the bag. The old sinner'll be scared out of his wits now, waiting for the long arm of the law to grab hold of him.'

A little of the horror of the morning left Harry in the face of his uncle's obvious amusement. At the same time, he was still shocked.

'Are you going to tell the constable?' he asked. 'Will they put him in prison?'

Cosmo grimaced. 'Very much doubt if they could. After all, the chap didn't do much, as far as I can gather. A bit of fiddling – that's all.'

'But sir, he . . . he knew it was wrong what he did. He said so. He said he couldn't help it. He said he loved me.'

Even to Harry's own ears, the words sounded ridiculous and he was not surprised this time when Cosmo let out another guffaw.

'Trouble with you, young Harry, is that you've never been to a decent school. If you had, you'd know this sort of thing goes on all the time. Boys with younger boys; masters with older boys. Always happens when there aren't any females around. Doesn't mean much, you know. Never went in for it myself, but plenty did at my school. Goes on in the navy too, when the chaps are at sea for long stretches. Get their relief that way, see?'

'I . . . I hated it!' Harry said violently, but at the same time he did understand what his uncle meant.

Cosmo grinned. 'Yes, well, you made that clear to the old boy, didn't you? He'll know better than to try it on next time.'

'Next time?' Harry asked, aghast.

'Well, I dare say he might try it again. If he does, give him a kick in the privates, what?'

'Yes, but, sir, he's my tutor – at least he was. I don't *have* to go back there, do I?'

Cosmo picked up his cue and deftly potted another ball.

'See no reason why not. Ain't anyone else round here to tutor you. No need to look so horrified, old chap. Tell you what, I'll have a word with him – or Pamela can,' he added, more to himself than to Harry. It wouldn't do to antagonize Harrison-Finch. He knew too much, and the last thing they wanted was all this aired in a police court. There'd be questions asked about the boy for a start. Then there was that troublesome fellow, Arbuthnot, breathing down their necks. They'd got away with murder – well, over a hundred thousand to be precise – and if the solicitor got the idea they weren't taking proper care of the boy, who knew what else he'd look into? No, Pamela could deal with Harrison-Finch. If she was in one of her moods, she could scare the living daylights out of him – threaten him with the loss of his living, or some such.

'Tell you what, old chap. Seeing you've taken the day off anyway, how about a ride this afternoon when it cools down a bit? Wellington could do with a bit of exercise and then, by tomorrow morning, we'll have it all sorted out. That suit you?'

Knowing that the die was already cast and that it didn't really matter whether anything in this new life suited him or not, Harry nodded. It would be nice to go riding. Perhaps he could talk to Uncle Cosmo again about going out on his own when his guardian was away. If he went with one of the grooms and they were told he mustn't be permitted to talk to anyone, maybe his uncle would agree. He might even manage to be happy here at Maythorpe House if he could ride every day. It was what he wanted more than anything else in the world, other than a letter from Alice.

It was two days now since Mrs Appleby had posted his letter. Surely he would get a reply soon. He would go and see Mrs Appleby now – just in case a letter had arrived. If anyone told his Aunt Pamela that he'd been down to the kitchen again, he'd say he couldn't find Hicks and he needed hot water to wash. As he left the billiard room and the grandfather clock in the hall started to chime three o'clock, he realized that he had missed luncheon. Not surprisingly, he was very hungry. Mrs Appleby would probably slip him a slice of jellied pie or cold treacle tart.

Cosmo returned to his game, only half his thoughts still with the boy who had just left the room. No wonder Pamela took such a dislike to the lad, he thought – Harry was the spitting image of his father, a dead giveaway! Just as well she'd taken the portrait down. The older Harry grew, the more like Gervaise he became. Real chip off the old block. Going to be a good-looking chap when he'd completed his growing; girls would be flocking round him. Cosmo had seen the way some of the young maids gazed after him even now. Beryl, the parlourmaid with whom he, Cosmo, often took his pleasure, had even referred to the boy as 'little Master Valentino' and said, moreover, that she'd be happy enough to teach him a few tricks when he was a bit older. It had taken Cosmo some time to persuade her to teach *him* her tricks then and there.

Downstairs in the kitchen, Mrs Appelby was reaching into her apron bib, a broad grin on her face.

'Didn't I tell you, Master Harry? Didn't I say she'd not forgot?'

Aware that Lil was watching them, she passed the letter surreptitiously to him. He did not wait for the food he'd

154

wanted. He gave her a grateful smile and, with Alice's reply to him burning a hole in his pocket, raced upstairs to his room, happier than he had ever felt in the past eighteen months since he had left home.

CHAPTER EIGHT

1918

It was six months before Alice had sufficient money saved
for her fare to Leicestershire. Lady Debrace had, as
always, proved immensely kind when Alice had asked if
she could delay taking the three-day summer holiday that
her mistress generously allowed all her staff. Realizing that
Alice was dreading the thought of having to cross London
from Victoria Station to St Pancras by herself, Lady
Debrace offered to take Alice with her on one of her own
rare visits to the capital to see her mother-in-law, who was
now ensconced in a nursing-home in Harley Street. From
there she paid for a cab to take Alice to St Pancras and
now, at long last, Alice was on her way.

By the time the LMS train, belching steam, drew into
Melton Mowbray station, Alice had made friends with a
kindly, middle-aged woman who was the housekeeper at
Buckminster House. Since this estate adjoined that of the
late Earl of Kinmuire, she was taking the same branch-line
train that would be halting at Saxby, the stop Alice
required.

While they waited to change trains, she told Alice that
both the late Earl of Kinmuire and his wife had been
frequent visitors to Buckminster House and that although
she had seen Viscount Simcox out riding, she had never
encountered Harry. Unaware that Alice was on her way to
see the boy, she had nothing to relate about him other than
that she had heard the countess and her brother were
taking care of an orphan. It seemed that the housekeeper
had heard rumours that Lord Simcox had brought the boy
back with him from Canada, but as she disapproved

strongly of listening to village gossip she knew no more about him.

They parted company when Alice left the train at Saxby and she began the four-mile walk to Maythorpe House. In his last letter Harry had drawn for her a little map, indicating which lanes and footpaths she should take, and another of the house itself by which she could find the servants' entrance and Mrs Appleby. As he had written:

> I wouldn't want her to get her notice on account of helping us see each other, so can you pretend you're visiting her if there's anyone around, which there's almost certain to be. She'll get Lil, the tweeny, to let me know you've arrived and we can hide in the old cricket pavilion and talk as no one ever goes there . . .

Alice was shocked by this need for such deception, but she did not doubt it must be necessary if the countess's cook was involved. Only one thing mattered now and that was to see Harry by whatever means possible.

Mrs Appleby's plan worked without a hitch. Emerson was in the kitchen when Alice arrived.

'You're Mrs Appleby's niece, then. She's expecting you,' he said with a disapproving look at the mud clinging to Alice's boots. 'Walked up from Saxby, have you?'

Before Alice could reply, a fat, motherly looking woman in a clean white apron emerged from what turned out to be her sitting-room. She hurried as fast as her bulk allowed to Alice's side and kissed her.

'Goodness me, Alice. I hardly knew you,' she said with a beaming smile. 'You were only a little bit of a thing when I last saw you. The kettle's on the boil and Lil can make us a cup of tea. I dare say you could do with one after that walk.'

She bustled Alice through the door into her room, where two comfortable basket chairs had been pulled up close to a cheerful coal fire.

'Sit yourself down, Miss Pritchett,' she said in a voice that was several tones quieter. 'I'm that glad you got here safely. Master Harry's been on tenterhooks ever since he got your letter saying you would be coming today. Lil shall go fetch him as soon as she's brought our tea.'

She lowered herself into her chair and waited until Alice had taken off her hat and was seated opposite her before she said, 'I dare say as how you know things aren't right here – not for the boy any road. Us servants aren't supposed to know about it, but as sure as I'm sitting here, the late earl, God rest his soul, is his father. I'll say this much, Miss Pritchett, and I'll stand by it to my dying day, it ain't right the way they've been keeping the boy locked away in this house. Wrong side of the blanket he may have been, and nothing won't alter that, but he's a nice boy, a good boy, and he has a right to a better life than he gets here.'

She paused for breath, during which interval the tweeny brought in a tray of tea and two large slices of cherry cake. Having told the girl that she was to do exactly as she had been instructed earlier, Mrs Appleby poured out the tea and continued to give vent to her feelings.

'I've said time and time again, this house is haunted – has been ever since his lordship died, and it don't surprise me. He'd turn in his grave if he knew what that poor boy suffers. Master Harry's that lonely – and homesick.' She gave Alice a sudden, unexpected smile. 'Talks about you all whenever he can. Reckon I know your family almost as well as you know yourselves, Miss Pritchett. And it's Alice this and Alice that and he goes wild with excitement when your letters come.'

She shook her head, frowning.

'I dare say you realized they was stopping Master Harry getting your letters. T'isn't for the likes of me to interfere with the way they wants to bring the boy up, but one thing I do know – it ain't right to burn letters as come from your own family. His lordship – God rest his soul – was a decent, honourable man, and he wouldn't have done nothing like that. So that's why I decided to do something about it. Right or wrong, I'm not sorry and I'm right glad you're here.'

'I'm very grateful to you, Mrs Appleby,' Alice spoke for the first time. 'You're Harry's only friend and it's been a great comfort to me knowing you've been keeping an eye on him. What I don't understand is why his guardians are behaving in this way. As I understood it at the time, they didn't have to take him away from us. The countess wanted him. Why hasn't she allowed him to come home if she's changed her mind?'

Mrs Appleby snorted. 'Don't make much sense to me neither, 'cepting the money.'

'Money?' Alice echoed. 'What money?'

Mrs Appleby leant forward in her chair and her voice now almost a whisper, she said, 'That Hicks her ladyship employs to look after Master Harry – gaoler more like, if you ask me! – he's a bad lot, I'm telling you. Listens at doors, he does. Hears things not meant for him to hear. Sees things he shouldn't. He's one of the new servants her ladyship got after the late earl died, and she pays all of them over the odds to keep their mouths shut and keep Master Harry out of the way of anyone as comes visiting. But Hicks – he's no more loyal to her ladyship than to anyone else, I imagine – comes down here of an evening and sits gossiping with Mr Emerson and tells him things he's heard upstairs. That's how I know about Master Harry being left a tidy sum of money by his father. She and the viscount have right barneys about the way he's getting through it – her brother, that is. He gambles, you see, and she don't like it. Mind you, he's not such a bad lot – just weak. He's a lot nicer to Master Harry than *she* is.'

Alice was silent as she tried to take in everything Mrs Appleby was telling her. It was as if the woman had bottled up her feelings for so long that, now she had let the cork out, the flow would never stop.

'I'd have given in my notice months ago if it weren't for Master Harry,' she was saying. 'T'isn't like it used to be here in his father's day. But though I've thought about taking another post many a time, I can't bring myself to do it – not while Master Harry needs me. I just hope you'll be able to do something about getting him away from here,

Miss Pritchett. It breaks my heart, thinking of him shut away hours on end in his room with only that Hicks for company, I can tell you.'

She broke off as there was a scuffle at the door and Lil came in.

'Master Harry's gone down to the pavilion and wants you to join him, Miss, and Mr Emerson's in the pantry and I ain't seen Mr Hicks, so you could slip out now if you want, Miss.'

There was a broad grin on the young girl's face and it was clear she was enjoying the conspiracy.

'It'll be perishing cold there, Miss Pritchett,' Mrs Appleby cautioned. 'Best put your hat and coat back on. You'll find your way easy enough. Lil will show you the scullery door and you can nip out there across the lawn and you'll see the pavilion on your right at the far end. Won't be no one looking out of the windows this time of day, and any road, they've gone to London for a week so there's only Emerson and Hicks to worry about. The gardeners won't know who you are and won't ask.'

Alice stood up and held out her hand.

'I can't tell you how grateful I am, Mrs Appleby. I don't suppose I'll see you again as I'll be catching the five o'clock back to London, so I won't have that much time.'

'Don't dilly-dally, then, m'duck,' Mrs Appleby said with a friendly smile. 'Master Harry will tell me all about it, I don't doubt. And you will do what you can to get him home, won't you?'

Although Alice promised faithfully she would find some way to get Harry away from this house, which even Mrs Appleby agreed was like a prison for him, she could not for the moment imagine how this might be done. After she and Harry had hugged and kissed and Alice had had a little cry, she told him that he must not count upon her rescuing him. Sitting beside him on the slatted wooden bench, her arm tucked through his and their hands firmly clasped, she said, 'I don't pretend to know the first thing about the law, Harry, but I do know the countess and her brother was made your legal guardians, because Lady

Debrace was explaining it to Miss Madeleine one time. She said it was the same as if they was your parents, and from then on they would decide what was best for you. I'll speak to Sir Philip, of course, but he's not really anything to do with us, is he, 'cepting Dad and Jenny and me is in his employ.'

Seeing Harry's crestfallen face, she added gently, 'I'm sure he'll do what he can – and now he's a knight, maybe he's got more influence. Oh, Harry, it is so nice to see you. I hardly know you you've grown so much – and you look so grand in those clothes.'

For the first time, Harry smiled.

'Same goes for you, Alice. You've changed a lot. Your eyes have gone all green.'

Alice laughed. 'Silly! They're the same hazel they've always been.'

He grinned. 'Well, you do look different. You're ever so posh.'

Alice laughed again. 'The mistress gave me this suit. I fit her clothes now and she gives me lots of lovely things. Not that I've much chance to wear them, but I wanted you to see me looking nice. You didn't tell me in your letters that your voice had broken!'

Harry grinned as he admitted that there were occasions when it squeaked or croaked, so he had been waiting until it stayed low before he wrote about it.

'You're talking different, too,' Alice said. 'You're like one of them now, Harry – the gentry, I mean. I don't know what Mum and Dad would say.'

For a while they talked about the family, and Harry, wanting every little detail, hung on her words. Then Alice wanted every detail of Harry's life – which he gave her, omitting the unpleasant scene with his tutor the previous summer. Fortunately, Mr Harrison-Finch had never repeated the incident – in fact, he carefully avoided any physical contact with Harry, even so much as the touch of his hand. Only his eyes, following Harry wherever he moved, like a devoted dog pleading for a kind or affectionate word, gave away his inner torment. It was only when Alice looked at her watch and said that she could stay no more than five minutes, that Harry broached the subject to which, above any other, he wanted an answer.

'How's Aubrey, Alice? *And Miss Madeleine?* Do they ever talk about me?'

'Well, Master Aubrey does a lot,' Alice replied, unaware how this reply might be affecting him. 'He always wants to know if I've heard from you. He didn't like school much at first, but he's getting used to it now. He says he'd like it a lot better if you were there.'

'I wish I was,' Harry said. 'And does Miss Madeleine like her school?'

Alice smiled. 'Oh, you know what she's like, Harry – a real butterfly. She'll settle anywhere if the honey's sweet! It doesn't sound like she has to work very hard and she's got loads of friends who, I don't doubt, spoil her. She's so little and pretty – and she knows it! Everyone spoils her – me, too. "Please, Alice, please . . ." she says, and you can't refuse. When Master Aubrey brings one of his friends home, it's quite funny really. They all get tongue-tied and fall over themselves trying to do things for her.'

She shivered, aware suddenly of the cold and the long journey she still had to make to get back to The Grange. She'd be lucky to be back before ten o'clock and, she noticed, it had started to rain.

'I'd best be going,' she said wistfully. Her eyes filled once more with tears as Harry flung his arms round her and hugged her. 'I'll write soon as ever I get back,' she added, hoping to comfort both him and herself. 'Just to let you know I got home safe and sound. And I'll speak to Sir Philip just as soon as I can and let you know what he says.'

As she released herself gently from his grasp, she said anxiously, 'You'd best get back indoors quickly, Harry. Will you get into trouble if that man finds out you aren't in your room?'

Harry shrugged.

'I don't care if I do. I told Hicks I was going to do my maths prep and it would take me ages, so like as not he'll have gone downstairs to talk to Emerson. It's not me but you I'm worried about, Alice. It's got dark and you might get lost.'

'Not me,' Alice said brightly. 'I brought a torch. Sally, the parlourmaid, lent me hers . . .' She broke off to plant one last kiss on Harry's cheek and, before the tears could overwhelm her, she pulled her hat back on her head and half pushed Harry out of the door in front of her.

'Oh, Alice, can't I come with you, at least to the station?'

She pretended not to hear him and, unaware of the wet grass soaking her boots, she hurried off into the darkness. Far away in Eastcaby village, the church clock chimed four o'clock and, hearing it, Alice realized she would have to hurry if she were to reach the station by five. The rain and the darkness would slow her down and she should not have cut it so fine. A few minutes later the ground hardened to gravel as she reached the back drive of Maythorpe House. Harry had told her not to take the short cut across the fields but to keep to the lane leading from the drive directly to Saxby.

If only Harry was with her, she thought as she hurried on through the driving rain, she wouldn't mind the wet, the dark, the need to hasten lest she miss the train. Nothing would matter if they were together. Although the day may have brought pain and anxiety for Harry's future, she would not have forgone those few hours. Their reunion had proved that nothing important had changed in these past two years. He might look different, speak in a different voice and in a different way, but he was still as loving as he had ever been. He still needed her, and her love for him was stronger than ever. She had been right not to give Fred's proposal a second thought, for now more than ever she was determined to spend the rest of her life looking after Harry.

Wild thoughts raced through Alice's head as she ran the last half-mile to Saxby station. If Sir Philip could not or would not set himself against Harry's guardians, perhaps Harry could run away. She would find somewhere for them to go where he would not be found. She could earn money to keep them. It might not be an easy life but they'd manage somehow. There was no hardship she would not endure if it meant lessening his unhappiness, and they could be together.

Back in his room in Maythorpe House, Harry was seated at the window, from which he had drawn back the curtains. He was staring out into the darkness. The rain had stopped and, far away in the distance, he heard the whistle of a train as it steamed into Saxby station. It was too early to be Alice's train. For a moment, he thought only of his concern that she get safely home, then his mind turned to Calking. If only he could be going back there. Lucky Alice, living at The Grange, could see Miss Madeleine whenever she was home from her school. Alice had called her 'pretty', 'little and pretty', but Miss Madeleine had always been so. Now, so it seemed, she was aware of it. Well, why not? If he were there he would spoil her too. He felt fiercely envious of Aubrey's friends who could run errands for her, hear her voice, see the laughter in her eyes. He hoped he would dream about her again tonight. Although he could not dictate his dreams, he was convinced that if he fell asleep thinking of her, she was most likely to feature in them. There were times when he was slightly ashamed when he awoke at the line those dreams had taken. In real life he would not have dared even to hold her hand. As it was, he would dare all manner of intimacies – kiss her, caress her, feel her soft body against his own and the growing tumult inside him.

This was one secret he could not tell Alice for, even if it had not been an improper subject for discussion, he would have been embarrassed to confess that he still nurtured that childish desire to marry Miss Madeleine when he was old enough. Alice had told him all those years ago that such a thing would be impossible. Then he had believed that all he needed was to be rich. It was Alice who had pointed out that he was only a working-class boy and could never marry a girl of Miss Madeleine's background. If this was no longer an insurmountable hurdle because it seemed that both of his real parents had been gentlefolk, there was now an even greater hurdle – his illegitimacy. He had not yet thought of a way to overcome that. He could but hope that he would achieve something of such importance – a deed of great bravery, perhaps, or an outstanding academic honour – that it would encourage Miss Madeleine to overlook the stigma attached to the manner of his birth.

Meanwhile, he consoled himself, he was still only just fifteen, Madeleine not yet fourteen. It would be very many years before either of them was old enough to consider marriage. There was nothing he could do for the time being, although now that Alice had promised to try to get him away from Maythorpe House and his guardians, he could at least hope that he might one day soon find himself back in Calking. He never doubted that Alice would do her utmost to help him. She had never yet failed to do so. He had implicit faith in her and now, although that belief in her persuasiveness was tempered by a more adult understanding of the difficulties involved, it was none the less comforting to know that she intended to help him.

Feeling greatly cheered by such thoughts, Harry drew the curtains, shutting out the damp, dark night, and decided that after all he might as well get down to his maths prep. Much as he disliked Mr Harrison-Finch, he acknowledged his academic abilities. 'Great academic achievement' the man had once said, 'is a key which will open many doors. So work, dear boy, work. You never know when you might need that key.'

Alice's brief references to Miss Madeleine had renewed Harry's determination to be worthy of her one day – whatever the cost.

Sir Philip was frowning as he listened to the neatly uniformed girl standing in front of his desk. His voice held a note of scepticism as he said, 'Really, Alice, your story is unbelievable. Don't misunderstand me,' he added quickly, 'I am not suggesting that you have made this up, but I simply cannot believe there is any truth in what you, yourself, have been told. Perhaps because he is unhappy there, young Harry has . . .'

'Beg pardon for interrupting, sir, but it wasn't Harry who told me. It was the cook, Mrs Appleby,' Alice broke in.

'The cook? Then perhaps she holds some grudge against her employers. I do not wish to sound cynical, Alice, but these things do happen.'

'Sir, I don't think you'd disbelieve Mrs Appleby if you yourself was to speak to her. She was employed by the earl before he died. She was obviously devoted to him and, partly on his account, to Harry.'

Sir Philip sighed. He really did not want to believe what this girl was implying. If it happened to be true, then he was morally bound to look into it, although in point of fact he was not responsible for the boy; for Will, perhaps, and Alice and that other girl, Jenny, who were in his employ, yes; but, much as he had liked young Harry, the boy was no concern of his. On the other hand, he knew his wife was devoted to Alice, thought the world of her, and to tell the truth, he'd noticed her himself this past year – grown very pretty, nice figure, nice eyes, seemed well spoken and intelligent, too. Obviously she believed what she was telling him.

'These are very serious implications, Alice – one might almost say accusations – against highly respectable people. One must be very careful what one says, for, as you may or may not know, there is a law against slander. Now let us reason this out more carefully. You say that the late earl left Harry a lot of money – well, that will be in trust until he is of age, and there have, therefore, to be at least two trustees. The trustees will be accountable. Therefore, I cannot see how – even if such nefarious behaviour as this Mrs Appleby has implied were embarked upon by Harry's guardians – it would not have been noticed by the trustees.'

Or should have been, if they were doing their duty, he thought uneasily. Now that he came to consider the matter, the whole question of Harry's sudden removal to the Midlands had been somewhat strange – hurried, to say the least. He seemed now to recall old Will telling him about some paper or other the countess had shown him, establishing the fact that she and her brother were the boy's legal guardians. But would a simple chap like Pritchett, almost illiterate, have made sense of such a document? And then there was Eloise's belief that Harry was Kinmuire's natural son, a suspicion now endorsed by the family cook. He'd thought it unlikely that a wife could bring herself to 'mother' her husband's bastard. On the other hand, the woman was childless and some females could be excessively maternal, not feeling complete without a child to nurture. He could recall a case where a childless woman had actually stolen an infant and insisted it was her own. However, this theory about the countess's thwarted longing to have a child hardly fitted in with Alice's story that the woman spent as little time as possible in Leicestershire and, when she was there, as little time as possible with the boy.

There could be reasons, he told himself as he dismissed Alice, promising to think the matter over. Lady Kinmuire had been widowed at a relatively young age. Maybe she wished to remarry – or had a lover in London. Maybe she had taken against the boy if, as the cook had informed Alice, he was really so like his father to look at. Women could be funny about such things – neurotic, a lot of them, especially during the menopause. Maybe she had simply not been able, despite all her good intentions, to put up with the boy's accent and habits, although, according to Alice, Harry had grown into 'a proper little gentleman' – whatever that meant.

Dash it all, Sir Philip thought irritably, he was a very busy man – confoundedly busy. Leicestershire was a long way off and he simply could not spare the time to go up there. He was, on the other hand, due to go to a dinner in London next week. If he went earlier than planned, he could make some enquiries about Simcox – fellow must have a club. Alice had spoken about 'gambling too heavily'; chap couldn't do that sort of thing and word not get around. It would probably all turn out to be pie in the sky, but to put Alice's mind at rest, he'd make a few preliminary enquiries.

It was not until much later that night, as he was trying to compose himself for sleep, that Sir Philip Debrace realized it was not just Alice's mind he needed to put at rest but his own as well.

Sir Philip boarded the Brighton Belle and, settling himself comfortably into a first-class compartment, decided after all not to go along to the Pullman carriage and take breakfast. He had too much to think about and it did not concern the success of the speech he had given the previous night on the long-term effects of poison gas on his patients. His thoughts were entirely taken up with the problem of what he must do now to look deeper into the affairs of young Harry Keynes. It seemed as if there was every possibility that at least one of the boy's guardians was turning out to be highly unsuitable for the responsibility he had undertaken. Viscount Simcox was on the verge of being blackballed by his club!

He could not ignore references to overdue payment of bills, Sir Philip thought uneasily, nor unpaid IOUs, nor rumours of a very unpleasant kind about money entrusted to him for a racing bet that had not been honoured when the nag came in. That Simcox had arrived too late to place the bet had been the fellow's excuse, and the creditor concerned could not prove otherwise. Nor, apparently, was this the first time such a thing had happened.

Rumour had it that the viscount had inherited nothing but the family estate from his father and had sold his birthright to pay off his debts. On his return to England when Kinmuire died, it was assumed Simcox had made good in Canada as he was back at the tables. 'However, he must have got through whatever fortune he'd made in Canada since he can't now meet his dues,' Sir Philip's informant had concluded.

Despite these adverse comments, it appeared that Simcox was a likeable enough chap – good on a horse and popular with the ladies. A good shot, too. Fellow's only weakness seemed to be his gambling habits.

Had Simcox been gambling with his own money, Sir Philip asked himself, or his sister's? The earl would certainly have left his wife well provided for. *Or was it Harry's?* Simcox might in all probability have access to it as the boy's guardian. He would have to find out – and the only way to do that was to write to the late earl's solicitor. The man must know who were the trustees, if indeed the lawyer were not one himself.

As soon as he got to the hospital, Sir Philip decided, he'd get his secretary on to the job of finding out who had acted for Lord Kinmuire. Until he found out a bit more, he'd say nothing to Alice. No point in worrying the girl. Funny thing about women – they seemed to have this sixth sense that told them something was wrong even when they hadn't a shred of proof. Eloise had it. Much as he loved his wife, he accepted that she hadn't a brain in her head worth speaking of, and what she did have she often forgot to use. Just occasionally, however, she'd say, 'I really don't like that man you brought home yesterday, Philip,' and sure enough, the fellow would turn out to be a wrong 'un although he, Philip, had not seen it for himself.

Sir Philip's thoughts turned abruptly to his son – the apple of his wife's eye. Eloise had always maintained the boy would turn out well and she'd been right. Aubrey had settled down at his public school – couldn't play games, of course, but was making his mark all the same. His housemaster had said that he was popular both with the boys and the masters, and if he went on the way he was going, he could end up head of house, despite his disability. The boy would be seventeen this summer – almost old enough to be in uniform.

It was a thought which horrified Sir Philip until he reminded himself that Aubrey would never be passed fit, even if the war lasted another year or two. This afternoon he was scheduled to operate on a lad not much older than his son – lost one leg already and today he, Philip, was going to have to amputate the other. What kind of future would there be for the boy? Life was grim enough for the working classes even when they had their youth and strength. His young patient came from a mining family in the north and it was the desperate need for money which had prompted the lad to volunteer. He'd get a pension of sorts, but nothing that would compensate for the loss of both legs.

Sir Philip pulled himself up sharply. It didn't do to get emotionally involved with one's patients, especially not with these relics sent back from France. He must find time to have a word with the almoner about getting all these men up to Roehampton more speedily. Trouble was, they couldn't keep up with the demand for artificial limbs these days. Then there were the plans to be vetted for a convalescent home he was trying to get hold of. No good having a place with endless staircases. They must put in ramps for the chaps on crutches and for the wheelchairs.

Harry and Cosmo Simcox were forgotten as Sir Philip was drawn slowly back into the vortex of what had become for him a normal day.

CHAPTER NINE

1918

It was three months before Sir Philip Debrace was satisfied that he had collected sufficient information to warrant approaching Judge Harmond. Hector Harmond and he had been close friends during their senior years at Eton but then their separate careers after they had left school had limited the opportunities to further their friendship. They had both, however, kept in touch over the intervening years. Sir Philip had no hesitation, therefore, in asking his old friend to lunch at his club with a view to soliciting his advice and, if possible, his assistance.

Now, having exchanged generalities and discussed the progress of the war during an excellent meal, they had adjourned to the morning-room to get down to the purpose of the meeting while enjoying an after-lunch brandy.

Sir Philip waited silently while Hector Harmond cast a practised eye over the various documents the surgeon had produced from his briefcase.

'A pretty kettle of fish, indeed,' the judge exclaimed as he paused to light a cigar. 'That fellow, Simcox, seems to have covered his tracks very skilfully.' He pointed at one of the pieces of paper. 'One imagines he didn't start getting into really deep water until last year. That's when he began reinvesting Kinmuire's capital. That letter to the solicitor chap, Arbuthnot, saying he'd got sound banking experience and knew what he was about, is quite plausible. One wonders whether at that point in time Simcox was genuinely acting for the best or if it was always his intention to sell shares in order to get some ready cash. Criminal offence, whatever his motives. Pretty bad show, especially for a man of his breeding, but there are no limits to the depths to which your inveterate gambler will sink. What exactly are you proposing, Debrace? I haven't quite grasped your involvement in all this.'

'That's exactly my problem,' Sir Philip said. 'I have no legal standing with regard to the boy. However, I feel morally bound to help him if I can.' Very briefly, he explained his connection with the Pritchett family and Harry's unusual relationship with his own son. 'Strange as it must sound to you, Harmond, I feel I owe it in large part to young Harry Keynes that Aubrey can now hold his own with his contemporaries. Be that as it may, both Eloise and I would like to get young Keynes out of this mess if we can.'

The judge nodded, but his expression was doubtful.

'You laymen are all the same – think you can mess around with the law to suit yourselves. Like it or not, these papers here . . .' he shuffled through the papers and produced the document making Lady Pamela and the viscount Harry's guardians, '. . . are perfectly in order.'

Sir Philip leant forward eagerly.

'I assumed as much. However, according to that statement from Arbuthnot, the accounts show that there's damn little left of the money Kinmuire bequeathed the boy. If things go on as they are, there'll be nothing left by the time he's old enough to take charge of it. If that's not criminal, it's certainly irresponsible.'

His friend grinned.

'I don't doubt we've got a case against Simcox which would put him behind bars. What *can* Arbuthnot have been up to? As a trustee, he should have kept a closer eye on the accounts. They were rendered to him yearly, so there's no excuse.'

'Arbuthnot's in his late seventies. Should have retired years ago. Frankly, I felt a bit sorry for him. He had no idea things had gone so wrong until the last lot of accounts came in and then he couldn't pin Simcox down to explain

172

matters. He dillied and dallied, wrote a few letters, and was still dithering when I arrived on the scene and bullied the facts out of him. Unethical, I know, but by then I was already pretty certain that all was not well in the state of Denmark and I was determined to get at the truth. Frankly, I think Arbuthnot was only too relieved to spill the beans. Without doubt, the old boy should have retired years ago – like some of you chaps on the bench, Harmond!'

The judge laughed.

'Just because your lot get too shaky to operate when you're in your last decade, you're jealous of our right to stay in harness.'

Sir Philip responded genially to this friendly jibe.

'The brain can be as vulnerable as the body,' he rejoined. 'Senility can affect a chap in middle age!'

'Have it your own way, Debrace. You always did like arguing. No wonder you were head of the debating society!'

'A long time ago, Harmond. Now, let's get back to the present. It isn't Arbuthnot I'm after. He knows he's slipped up and is prepared to help in any way he can. The point is, what can I do?'

'It looks as if there are good grounds for a case against Simcox and his sister. If it came to court, there's no doubt the press would have a field day with titles involved, not to mention the fact that it looks pretty obvious the boy is Kinmuire's by-blow. If the countess is aware of it, she'd either have to admit it in court or commit perjury.' He took off his steel-rimmed spectacles and regarded Sir Philip thoughtfully. 'I suppose the boy's mother isn't alive?'

'I can't answer that. Anyway, since she or her family went to great lengths to conceal Harry's birth, I doubt she'd be likely to come forward now. As far as I can ascertain, the Pritchetts were given a false name for the mother when the newly born infant was left with them, and the child was registered as Keynes. At the time, various persons in the locality made enquiries, including the vicar, and he's of the opinion no such woman of that name existed. No, Harmond, I'm not concerned with her. My idea is to threaten to discredit Viscount Simcox and the sister – force them to resign their guardianship.'

'Great Scott, man, that sounds like blackmail. Either you do this or else . . . no, no, can't condone that.'

Sir Philip's mouth curved in a half-smile.

'I wasn't intending to involve you, Harmond. I simply want to know how I would stand if Simcox and his sister did resign – if that's the right word – their guardianship. Could an order be made for *me* to act as guardian to the boy? On the grounds that there is no one else to fill the gap?'

'I suppose that might be possible. You're a highly respected man these days. Congratulations on your knighthood, by the way. Saw it in *The Times* and meant to write, but you know how it is?' The judge gave an unexpected chuckle. 'Wonder what the press would have made of it if I'd written and told them you were known at school as Horrible Hackers, the only one of us who actually enjoyed all those grisly dissections of toads and pregnant rats!'

'I suppose you'd have signed yourself "Windbag"?' Sir Philip countered. The smile left his face and he sighed. 'Deuce of a long time ago, eh? Do you realize, Harmond, that those young whippersnappers who used to be our fags may now be called up? Things must be pretty bad now the government has had to put the conscription age up to fifty! Not surprising when you think of those damnable casualty lists.'

Judge Harmond nodded. 'Hardly like to open m'newspaper these days. Did you see they're putting the price of a stamp up by 50 per cent? It's a disgrace – a penny ha'penny indeed! But I suppose the government's got to raise money somehow to pay for this confounded war. Now look here, Hackers, speaking as a friend, I don't think I ought to listen to any more of your plans to sink this Simcox fellow. There's one thing in your favour – he won't want it bandied about that he's an embezzler.

Neither will his sister. My suggestion – off the record, you understand – is that you think up some way to make their voluntary resignation attractive. Persuasion is usually more successful than threats. You'd be surprised how often people are prepared to settle out of court if the offer is attractive enough. Depends how much you're prepared to be out of pocket yourself.'

Sir Philip grinned.

'I'm not exactly penniless, Harmond. I'd be prepared to fork out if it's necessary. According to Arbuthnot, there's enough capital left to send the boy to a good school. He's bright enough and he's a likeable lad – imagine he takes after his father. Arbuthnot admitted the earl had acknowledged the boy as his.'

Harmond stood up.

'I'm in chambers at three, so I'll have to make a move,' he said regretfully. 'Thanks for the lunch, old boy. Next time on me, eh? Meanwhile, let me know how things go. If I can be any help, you've only to get in touch.'

Sir Philip eased himself out of his chair.

'If I'm successful, I might want the name of a good solicitor to draw up new guardianship documents – together with Arbuthnot, of course. Know anyone you can guarantee to keep their mouths shut?'

The judge tut-tutted as he walked with Sir Philip towards the door.

'Can it be you suspect that there are some in our profession who *don't* treat our clients' information as privileged? Come now, Hackers, you medical blokes don't blab out of school, do you?'

Sir Philip laughed.

'Human nature is not infallible, as we both know. If it were, I wouldn't be trying to get young Harry out of the mess he's in, would I? Thanks again, Harmond. I'll fix a meeting with Simcox and tackle him the way you suggest. I was so angry when I found out what he and his sister had been up to I was all for getting them both flung into gaol forthwith! I can see now that yours is by far the better way to achieve my ends. I owe you one, don't I?'

The judge laughed at this allusion to their school days.

'Since you can't do my Latin prep for me, I'll take the favour as squared if you'll stop referring to the plan you have in mind as mine. You're on your own, Hackers. We've not had this conversation. Right?'

They left the club together, parting on terms of excellent understanding. At the corner of Jermyn Street, Sir Philip waved goodbye to his friend and hailed a taxi cab to take him to Curzon Street. He was playing a hunch that he might find the viscount at his own club, or at very least that they would know where to locate the fellow. Now that he knew what he was going to do, he did not intend to waste any more precious time thinking about it.

Pamela was seated at one end of the sofa in the drawing-room of her house in Eaton Terrace. Cosmo was seated at the other end. Sir Philip stood upright with his back to the fireplace, Mr Arbuthnot beside him, looking old and frail, in the large wing chair. Pamela was weeping silently, a small initialled handkerchief held to her eyes.

For once Sir Philip failed to be moved as he usually was by a woman's tears. His expression was implacable as he faced Pamela and her brother with the unpalatable facts of Cosmo's debts.

'Oh, Cosmo, how could you? How could you?' Pamela sobbed. 'You promised . . . you assured me. Oh, how could you?'

Cosmo laid a hand placatingly on her arm.

'I'm dreadfully sorry, old girl. I swear I'd no idea it had got so out of hand. This has all come as much of a shock to me as to you. Fifteen thousand, you say, Sir Philip? I'll pay them off, of course.'

'This is not the time for flights of fancy, sir,' Sir Philip said sternly. 'Unless you have expectations of which I am unaware, you have no hope whatever of paying off those debts. The question now is what is to be done about it. What makes the whole situation a great deal more serious is that the money you used was not yours to gamble with.'

'But Cosmo, why didn't you tell me what you were

doing? Warn me? You told me the interest I was getting on the capital had decreased only because of the war. *You* should have advised me, Mr Arbuthnot,' Pamela said, turning suddenly to the elderly solicitor.

'I made numerous attempts to do so, dear lady,' the old man replied nervously. 'I wrote to you several times and asked you to call and see me.'

Pamela gave her brother a bitter, withering glance. Cosmo had told her not to reply to those letters; said Arbuthnot was fussing about their 'extravagances' and that he'd soon 'sort out the old buffer'.

'There's little point in discussing the past,' Sir Philip intervened. 'It's the future which concerns me. I have a proposition to put to you, Lady Kinmuire, and to you, sir,' he said, nodding towards Cosmo.

Cosmo's face brightened. He had been feeling singularly uneasy ever since he had had Sir Philip's letter demanding – not requesting – that the four of them should have this consultation at Pamela's house. The references to 'discrepancies in the financial affairs of young Keynes' had put the wind up him, to say the least. He'd been clinging to the hope that since, as one of the trustees, he could administer the trust fund as he thought fit, nothing serious could come of any investigation into the boy's finances. Fitness was, after all, a matter of opinion. What he had not taken into account was that this eminent surgeon might take it upon himself to look into his personal affairs and, so it seemed, had discovered most of his debts.

He himself had known about them, of course, but until last year he'd never actually sat down to list them. The total had been so alarming he'd been obliged to find a way to settle at least some of his debts. That was when he'd thought of selling some shares. He kept part of the proceeds in the hope of hitting a lucky streak and being able to replace the money, but he'd been unlucky. A second and third attempt had been equally unsuccessful. Now, when he was on the point of trying his luck once more, Debrace had got wind of his machinations. It had come as an extremely nasty shock.

'What exactly have you in mind, sir?' he prompted Sir Philip uneasily.

'Quite simply, Lord Simcox, that you and your sister should relinquish your guardianship of the boy forthwith. We will not go into the question of whether it was at all wise of the late Lord Kinmuire to have entrusted you with this responsibility in the first place. I don't intend to concern myself with the past. Mr Arbuthnot, together with my solicitor, has prepared a legal document which we have brought with us today and which I trust you and your sister will sign.'

He addressed himself now solely to Cosmo.

'I will summarize it for you. Briefly, you are required to state that as you will be leaving the country, you can no longer meet your obligations to Harry.' He turned to Pamela. 'You, madam, will state that you do not feel you can adequately attend to the upbringing of a boy of fifteen without the support of your brother. You will both state that you feel it is in Harry's best interests that his guardianship should transfer to me.'

Seeing that Cosmo's expression had now become hopeful where before it had been both anxious and guarded, he said quickly, 'In return for your signatures and certain other guarantees, which I will speak of in a minute, I shall make good all your debts, Simcox, and I will give you, madam, an assurance that I shall not call upon you personally to return any of the money that was left by your late husband in trust for the boy. I will not demand that you sell this house to offset your debt to young Keynes, but you will forfeit the interest on what little of the capital remains.'

Tears filled Pamela's eyes. 'But I'll have nothing to live on. Why should I suffer for my brother's misdeeds?'

'Because you knew very well neither you nor he had a right to usurp the boy's money for your use, whatever the purpose,' Sir Philip said sternly.

Cosmo put a hand on his sister's shaking shoulders. 'You've still got that five thousand Gervaise left you, old girl. I didn't touch that. You won't be penniless. The alternative is a court case, and you don't want that, do you?'

Pamela's tears dried, her face was pale as she stared up at her brother. 'It seems as if we have no choice,' she said bitterly. 'We have to agree to Sir Philip's suggestion, don't we, Cosmo? You knew I never wanted to take the boy in the first place and you talked me into it. You'll sign, won't you? I won't go to court.'

'It's only fair to your brother that he first hears all my conditions,' Sir Philip intervened. 'They are namely that you, sir, will leave the country as soon as you are able to obtain a passage abroad. You will also sign the letter I have drafted on your behalf to the present Earl of Kinmuire. It says that, as you will be going to settle in another country, the boy will no longer require the use of Maythorpe House and you are therefore relinquishing the tenancy. I shall write to him requesting that the estate be kept for Harry's use once he comes of age. It is not much of an inheritance for the boy since he now does not have the means to carry the expenses of so large an establishment. However, he may one day do so.'

Pamela's eyes narrowed as she regarded Sir Philip. 'I don't understand why you are doing this. You said that you had never met my late husband, and that the boy is no connection of yours.' Her voice rose hysterically. 'Why is everyone so concerned with this boy? No one considers me. It's not even as if he were Gervaise's son – he's only his bastard.'

'Steady on, old girl,' Cosmo said anxiously, laying a hand on her shoulder. 'Shouldn't have said that. Supposed to be a secret, what? Anyway, there's no denying Harry is Gervaise's flesh and blood, whether you like it or not. Besides, he's a decent enough lad and I've grown quite attached to him. Damn good horseman, I'll say that for him, and you can't say he's been much trouble to us, m'dear.'

Sir Philip's opinion of Cosmo took a slight turn for the better. Simcox sounded perfectly genuine and, moreover, when he himself had talked to Harry the previous day,

179

Harry had professed to like the man. He had made no pretence of liking the countess, whom he considered was the person responsible for keeping him a virtual prisoner these past two and a quarter years.

'It does not say much for your morals, madam, that, feeling as you do about the boy, you nevertheless undertook quite voluntarily to look after him. However, I hope shortly to be relieving you of that duty. As far as you are concerned, I must have your assurances in writing that you will never try to see Harry again; that you, like your brother, will vacate Maythorpe House immediately and will never return there. I should warn you that were such assurances not to be honoured, I would not hesitate to make public your own part in this unsavoury situation, as well as your brother's.'

The quite obvious cough that now emanated from the elderly Arbuthnot reminded Sir Philip that he had determined neither to show his anger and contempt, nor to threaten either the countess or her brother. It was their compliance he needed. In a gentler tone, he said, 'I think that, on reflection, you will consider my suggestions to be extremely generous towards you in the circumstances, and especially to you, Simcox. I am not asking either of you to sign admissions of guilt, although you, sir, have unquestionably been guilty of a very serious crime. You will therefore be able to continue your lives much as they were before you became Harry's guardians. Naturally, you will want to read these affidavits carefully, and I am prepared to give you until tomorrow morning to do so.'

Cosmo was on his feet. His eyes shone, for he was well able to recognize a lucky break when he saw one.

'We shall read them of course, Sir Philip, but I am perfectly willing to take your word as to the contents. I am quite prepared to sign now if you so wish.'

Pamela gave a cry of protest. 'But Cosmo, you will have to leave the country. Where will you go? What will I do without you? You know I cannot cope with builders and tax forms and all those complicated statements from the bank and . . .'

Cosmo turned back to face his sister. 'I should think you'll do a lot better without me, old girl. Let you down, I'm afraid. Probably happen again. I dare say I might go to one of the colonies – Australia, perhaps. Lots of opportunities there. I'd send for you to join me of course, if things went well. Not much alternative anyway, is there, old thing?'

He patted her shoulder but Pamela twisted away from his hand. Tears were falling down her cheeks again and she fumbled to retrieve her handkerchief from the side of the sofa. 'We should never have taken the boy,' she said bitterly. 'We should never have had anything to do with him. Gervaise had no right to ask me. We should have left him in that pigsty, where he belonged.'

Sir Philip stood up, his expression stony. 'Pigsty it may have seemed to your eyes, madam,' he said frostily, 'but I can assure you that the morals of the people living in it are a great deal better than either yours or your brother's. For all your breeding and their lack of it, I would sooner call Martha Pritchett my friend than you, dear lady.'

'You must forgive my sister, sir. She's really not accountable,' Cosmo said quickly. 'Perhaps it would be best if you did return tomorrow. Lady Kinmuire is under a great strain. I do assure you there will be no difficulty. The papers will be signed and sworn.' He glanced at Mr Arbuthnot and hurriedly looked away again as he met the old man's withering glance. There was nothing to be gained, he thought, by asking the fellow what the devil he meant by revealing the family's private affairs to this stranger. Obviously Sir Philip was a man to be reckoned with and it was best not to stir troubled waters.

As he accompanied the two men to the door, he said to Sir Philip, 'About young Harry. Will he be staying at Maythorpe House? I'd quite like the chance to say goodbye to the boy.'

'Harry is already on his way to my house in Sussex,' Sir Philip said in softer tones. 'I will tell him, however, that you wish him well.'

Cosmo nodded.

'Just one more thing, Sir Philip. The horses. Gervaise's stallion, Wellington. Harry'll want to keep him, I dare say, and his own mare, but he needs another year or two before he can handle Wellington. Needs strength, you know, if the old boy's in one of his moods. Wouldn't be safe.'

'Thank you for telling me, Simcox. My head groom will be able to manage him. I had a stallion of my own, but I had to have him put down last year. Broke his fetlock.'

He held out his hand and shook Cosmo's – something he had not expected to do.

'I'll take good care of Wellington – and Harry. I wish you better luck in future, Simcox. Gambling's a mug's game – always has been – and you can consider yourself deuced lucky not to find yourself in gaol. I'll see you tomorrow at my club – Brooks's – with those papers legally signed, I hope, for all our sakes.'

'Count on it, sir,' Cosmo said warmly. 'You can take my word, it's as good as a ten to one on shot!'

With a wry smile, Sir Philip climbed into the waiting taxi cab. He leant out of the window and said, 'Good odds, Simcox, but I'm sure I don't have to tell you, there is no such thing as a racing cert!'

'Oh, Harry, I just can't believe it – you've grown so much. I think you're even taller than Aubrey. Come on, you two, stand back to back so I can measure you.'

Harry blushed as Madeleine caught hold of his arms and manoeuvred him into position. With a book in one hand, she stood on tiptoe and, seemingly unaware of her body balanced against Harry's, laid it across the boys' heads.

'Yes, you are taller,' she said in her high treble. 'Gosh, Harry, it is nice to see you again. Aubrey and I simply couldn't believe it when Daddy told us last night you were coming to live with us. It's absolutely ripping!'

She collapsed laughing into one of the cretonne-covered nursery armchairs and swung her legs over the arm. Her slim ankles and calves covered by black lisle stockings, were fully exposed beneath her short dress. Her large, blue eyes grew suddenly darker.

'I've got to go back to school tomorrow. It's an absolute swizz, just when you've arrived. It's not fair.'

Aubrey picked up a loose cushion from a second chair and aimed it accurately at his sister. 'You've had longer holidays than I have, Pickles, so stop complaining.' He turned to Harry and said, 'Jolly nice seeing you again, Harry. Did the pater tell you he's going to try to get you into my school this coming term? I'm holding thumbs. Sit down, you ass, you look as if you've never seen us before.'

Obediently, Harry sat down in a basket chair opposite Madeleine. 'Sorry if I seem a bit goofy. It's just a bit . . . Seeing you and the nursery – it seems such ages . . .'

'We call it the schoolroom now,' Madeleine told him. 'We have our meals downstairs with Mummy and Daddy so we have only tea up here. That's why we changed things round a bit – to make it our sort of den. We sneak up here whenever there are boring visitors downstairs and pretend we're working.' She stole a sideways glance at Harry. 'You've changed too. You talk differently . . . like us, I mean.'

'Don't be so cheeky,' Aubrey said quickly. 'You know it's rude to make personal remarks.' He grinned at Harry. 'Don't stand any nonsense from her, old chap. She thinks she's the cat's whiskers these days – just because my friends go goggle-eyed when she smiles at them, silly asses!'

'Shut up, you rotter!' Madeleine retorted, aiming the cushion back at her brother's head. 'I suppose you'd rather I was squint-eyed and as fat as Sally, so all your friends could call me Fatso.'

'That's rot – and anyway, Sally's a good sort. She never sneaked to the mater when my fountain pen leaked all over the sheet.'

He turned towards Harry, who was sitting in tongue-tied silence.

'Come on, Harry. We're dying to hear all about it. What was it like in the Midlands? Was it ghastly? The pater said you'd had a pretty rotten time. Did you get caned? I've been caned twice at school, but the second time it brought on one of my attacks. I think Matron must have said something because they haven't done it since. I get extra prep instead.'

Harry listened silently while brother and sister discussed their relative schools. Although their remarks were, in the main, derogatory, it was obvious they both enjoyed boarding-school life. He wondered if it were true that Sir Philip intended sending him to Grafton Abbey with Aubrey. During his brief visit to Maythorpe House, Sir Philip had told Harry only that he was to be his new guardian; that he was to leave Maythorpe House the following day and travel down by train to Calking to live at The Grange.

'I have had a word with your . . . er, foster parents, Harry,' he'd said. 'Much as they would like to have you home, we agreed there really wasn't room for you in their cottage. In all the circumstances I don't feel it would be suitable now that you know you are not . . . er, exactly part of the Pritchett family. There'll be plenty of room for you at The Grange, and the children will be glad to have your company.'

Sir Philip had not enlightened Harry as to the movements of his guardians other than to say that Viscount Simcox would shortly be going abroad. Harry had bade an emotional farewell to Mrs Appleby, who made him promise to write to her and let her know how he was getting on. She would, she said, be giving in her notice and would advise him in due course of her change of address.

'Don't you never forget, Master Harry,' she had impressed on him, 'that you owe this to your Alice. But for her, you might never be leaving this place.'

'I owe it to you too, Mrs Appleby,' Harry had told her. 'It was you who posted my letters and took Alice's in for me.'

He had also felt obliged to call and make his farewells to his tutor. Mr Harrison-Finch had been thunderstruck. He

184

seemed unable to comprehend how this sudden turn in Harry's affairs had come about without his knowledge. There had been a point, highly embarrassing to Harry, when he had thought the man was going to burst into tears. Finally Harry had deposited the pile of books he had borrowed on the vicar's desk, and somehow managed to make his escape.

His tutor was quickly forgotten, however, when, after joining Sir Philip for tea at the hotel in Melton Mowbray where he was staying, his new guardian conducted him to a private corner of the lounge and quietly informed him that he was the late earl's natural son.

Sir Philip had seemed anxious that this news should not come as an unwelcome shock and Harry had been able to reassure him that, after seeing Mrs Appleby's snapshot album, he'd had very few doubts as to his father's identity. He was happy to learn that his father had cared enough about him to provide for his future, and since no one had thought fit to tell him of his father's bequest, it mattered little to him that his former guardians had embezzled most of it. If he felt any distress, he had told Sir Philip, it was that no one – not even Mrs Appleby – could tell him who his mother had been.

Sir Philip had advised him to forget the past and look forward to this new phase of his life; that as Harry Keynes, it was up to him to make his way in the world as best he could and, Sir Philip added kindly, he would always be there to support him.

Later that afternoon a surly Hicks had assisted Harry to pack one of the big leather trunks that had been brought down from the attic. It had G.L.H. embossed on the lid – his father's initials. It was the first thing belonging to his father that he had ever had and Harry was almost as excited to be owning it as he was at the thought of going home.

It was not until he was on the train to London the next morning with Sir Philip that Harry had had time to reflect on the extraordinary speed with which his whole life was changing. He simply could not believe that he would not be living at Maythorpe House any more and that Sir Philip had become his new guardian. He did not doubt that this was all Alice's doing and his feeling of gratitude towards her was no less than his feeling of excitement at the thought that he would be seeing Miss Madeleine again.

Sir Philip was remaining in London and Harry had been put on a train at Victoria Station to undertake his first journey alone to Calking. Long before it steamed out of the platform, the carriage had filled with soldiers going to Brighton on leave and they'd told him fascinating if horrifying tales of their lives in the trenches. His new companions had seen him and his big trunk safely off the train and after a taxi-cab ride to The Grange, he was finally here, in the same room with Aubrey and Miss Madeleine. It was like a dream come true, and he could not believe his good fortune.

'We break up at the end of July,' Madeleine was saying. 'My best friend, Daphne, is coming to spend part of the hols with me, so you'll be able to meet her, Harry. She's a jolly good sport and frightfully good at games, so I'm sure you and Aubrey will like her.'

Harry found his voice. 'If you like her, I'm sure I shall, Miss Madeleine,' he said politely.

Madeleine giggled. 'For heaven's sake, don't keep calling me *Miss* Madeleine. I'm sure Mummy and Daddy wouldn't want you to and I certainly don't.'

'It makes her sound grown up, but she's still just a kid,' Aubrey said in a teasing voice.

Reluctantly, Harry stood up. 'I'm afraid I'll have to go now. I just looked in to say hello before going down to the cottage to see my . . . to see Mum and Dad.'

His hesitation had been momentary but Aubrey understood Harry's dilemma. The poor chap knew that Will and Martha Pritchett were not his real parents and yet it must be very difficult to think otherwise after spending the first twelve years of his life believing they were.

Last night the mater had taken him aside and explained that there would be certain difficulties now that his father had arranged for Harry to come and live with them; that he, Aubrey, must do what he could to ease the situation. Alice was a servant in the house and must therefore take orders from the boy she had always looked on as her brother. It would be best, therefore, if Aubrey could be the one to make Harry's needs known, his mother had pointed out. Jenny had been found another post with a nice family living in Haywards Heath but, despite the difficulties, Alice was to be retained for the time being. Since Alice did not wait at table or clean the bedrooms and, hopefully, was old enough and sensible enough to know her place, the two should not come in contact very often; but it was not going to be easy for Harry, Eloise had maintained, and it was perhaps as well that Harry would be joining him at his boarding-school as soon as it could be arranged.

What his parents did not seem to realize, Aubrey thought now, was that at Harry's age the transition from home tutoring to public school was going to be beastly difficult. It had been difficult enough for him going into a junior house. Because he was now fifteen, Harry would be a senior and totally ignorant of Grafton Abbey mores. The boys would quickly realize how green he was and would try to make his life hell. Fortunately, Harry had grown out as well as up and looked strong enough to box his way out of trouble if any of the prefects tried to bully him. He, Aubrey, must find time to put Harry wise to the dos and don'ts at Grafton Abbey before the poor fellow set foot in the place. One thing Harry could not afford to divulge was that he'd been raised as a gardener's child in the years before anyone had realized he was a distant relative of the late Earl of Kinmuire.

The pater had been unusually reticent when he'd told Aubrey that Harry's guardians had turned out to be rotters and that Harry was coming to live with them, and told him, Aubrey, not to ask a lot of silly questions about matters which were no concern of his when he'd asked why Harry did not have other relatives to look after him. He'd have to find out from Harry – who'd no doubt know – how he'd ever come to be fostered by a family like the

Pritchetts in the first place. This, however, was not the moment and certainly not with Pickles around.

'I'll come downstairs with you,' he said now to Harry. 'Give me a shout if you want any help unpacking your trunk. The mater said you were having the guest room next to mine, so we'll be able to leave the door open at night and jaw if we feel like it.'

'It's not fair,' Madeleine said, jumping to her feet and making a pretence of preventing Harry from leaving the room by tugging on his arm. 'You boys have much more fun than I do. I shall sneak in and have a midnight feast with you both.'

'Don't be so soppy,' Aubrey said scornfully, pushing her none too gently to one side. He gave an exaggerated sigh as he followed Harry downstairs. 'Isn't it the very devil having younger sisters?' he complained. 'There are times Pickles is a real pain in the neck.'

Harry remained in shocked silence. He simply could not believe how Aubrey, who undoubtedly always had been and still was his best friend, could possibly speak so unkindly of Madeleine, still less suggest that she was a nuisance. As far as he was concerned, she was still the sweetest, most beautiful, most attractive girl in the whole world.

CHAPTER TEN

1918

Their arms linked, Harry and Alice made their way along the path to the cottage. Harry had not yet changed from his travelling clothes and, so Alice now told him, he was looking very grown up and elegant.

'The family aren't going to recognize you,' she said. 'Oh, it is good to have you home, Harry. I can't begin to tell you how happy I am to know you've left that horrible place for ever.'

Taller now than Alice, he was obliged to look down when he spoke to her. 'The place wasn't really so horrible,' he said. 'It was the people. I hated them all except Mrs Appleby. She was a real brick! I suppose Uncle Cosmo wasn't really so bad – he and I were quite good friends. He taught me a lot about horses and guns – and fishing.'

Alice looked shocked as she stopped to open the latch of the garden gate. 'How can you say that about him now you know he spent all your money? Sir Philip told me about it when he said you were coming back to live at The Grange.'

'I don't think that all the money's gone,' Harry said thoughtfully. 'Sir Philip said there'd be enough left to pay for me to go to Aubrey's school. I'll just have to find a good job when I finish my education.'

As they walked round to the back door, a small boy of about three came out and, head on one side, stood staring curiously at them.

Alice scooped him up into her arms and said to Harry, 'This is little Sam. He's grown into a big boy now, haven't you, Sam? Last time you saw him, Harry, he was only a baby.'

Harry ruffled the child's hair. 'He looks a bit like Billy. How old are you now, Sam?'

'I's free, sir,' the child answered shyly.

'Great Scott, you mustn't call me sir,' Harry said, laughing. 'I'm not that old.'

Alice put the boy down.

'It isn't because you're old, Harry. It's the way you look in those posh clothes,' she said quietly. 'You don't realize how much you've changed. And I ought to warn you – Mum's been up to all hours cleaning and cooking. She's in a right pucker about you coming to tea.'

Harry had no chance to ask the reason for his mother's anxiety for Alice had already opened the back door and was pushing him ahead of her into the kitchen.

Martha Pritchett had removed her apron and was standing with her back to the kitchen range, a kettle in one hand. She was thinner, greyer than Harry remembered, but otherwise unaltered.

'Hello, Mum,' he said, memories of the past flooding over him as he went to embrace her. She turned quickly away and busied herself putting the kettle on to boil.

'You've grown,' she said as she started to fuss with the crockery laid out on the kitchen table. 'Alice said you had.'

Could it be she was shy of him? Harry wondered. Surely he had not changed as much as all that?

'Sit yourself down,' Martha said. 'Your father and the boys will be home any moment and tea's all ready. Now, go and wash your hands, Sam. You don't half look a fright, and I'd only just got you into clean clothes. Whatever will the visitor think?'

'Mum, I'm not a visitor . . .' Harry started to protest, but broke off as he realized that his mother was wearing her Sunday best clothes and that the best china had been brought out – something which he had never known happen when it was an ordinary family meal.

Sensing a little of Harry's dismay, Alice pushed him into a chair and sat down beside him.

'I expect things have changed a bit since you were last

190

home,' she said, breaking the uncomfortable silence that had fallen. 'Mum and Dad have done quite a bit to make things nicer, haven't you, Mum? We've got a carpet in the parlour and the lino what was in there is in here now. It's easier to clean than the flags – and warmer in the winter.'

'It looks very nice,' Harry said politely, for he had not observed these changes – only the seeming diminution of the size of the room in which he was now sitting. After the huge rooms with their high ceilings at Maythorpe House, the contrast was almost shocking. How did his mother ever manage in such cramped conditions? he asked himself as he thought of Mrs Appleby's vast kitchen, the big servants' hall, the butler's pantry, the big cold scullery.

'Where's Edna, Mum?' Alice asked as once again an awkward silence engulfed them.

'I sent her down to Chalk Lane with Nurse Wilks's shoes what your father mended last night.'

'Doesn't Edna go to school?' Harry asked.

'It was a waste of time,' Alice told him. 'She helps Mum round the house and runs errands. I wrote and told you, didn't I, that Elsie started last term as maid at the convent school for young ladies in Burgess Hill, so you won't see her. That sounds like the boys. Noisy pair of scallywags, aren't they, Mum?'

The back door burst open and Arthur and Ted came in. Twelve and nine years old, they were big boys now and already the room seemed overcrowded. They grinned shyly at Harry.

'Just look at the pair of you!' Martha said sharply before Harry could speak. 'Go upstairs and get out of them dirty clothes this minute – and get yourselves washed up first.'

'Oh, Mum, must we? We was going to play football after tea and . . .'

'I don't mind, if you don't,' Harry said quickly, but Martha, if she heard him, pretended not to do so. As the boys went into the scullery, the back door opened again and Will Pritchett came into the room. He glanced at Harry.

'So you're here,' he said nonchalantly. 'You had a good

day for travelling. Got all my onion sets in this afternoon. Soil's just right.'

Harry, who had stood up to greet his foster father, now sat down again as Will ignored his outstretched hand. He too had aged, Harry thought. He was more stooped than he remembered, his back bent almost to forty-five degrees. He, Harry, had never before realized how back-breaking Will's job must be for all he was so well accustomed to the labour after forty years as a gardener. He felt a sudden pang of pity – and of guilt. If he'd been working alongside the old man, he could have taken on the heavier jobs. He knew from Alice's letters that all the under gardeners had left to join the army and that Will had only a farm girl to help him now. It was the same at Maythorpe House, only Uncle Cosmo had employed girls from the Women's Land Army.

Martha now brewed the tea, and the moment Edna came in she ordered the children to be seated. Throughout the meal she was far sharper about their manners than Harry remembered, insisting that he be served first. Deliberately, he declined to take any of the shop cakes which he could see the younger members of the family eyeing. Accustomed now to eating such treats as part of Mrs Appleby's regular fare, he had not forgotten what it would have meant in the old days to see pink and white coconut pyramids, pin-wheels and one-two-three biscuits on the table. He was conscious, however, of Martha's surreptitious glances.

'You baint eating, Harry,' she said reproachfully. 'I thought as how them pyramids was your fav'rits.'

Harry felt a lump in his throat as he realized that despite the distance she was keeping between them, she still loved him enough to spend her hard-earned money on something she knew he enjoyed. To please her he now helped himself to one of the cakes.

'I was too busy enjoying your damson jam, Mum,' he said. 'Mrs Appleby's isn't half as good as yours.'

'Doant he talk funny!'

Ted's comment struck them all dumb, for Harry's

speech, more even than his clothes, was the cause of the biggest breach between the past and the present.

'You knows my ruling, young Ted,' Will said sharply. 'No talking at mealtimes.' He did not, as Harry half expected, send the boy out of the room.

Edna, who never seemed to understand what was going on, now spoke out. 'Is he really our Harry?' she asked.

'Course I am, Edie,' Harry said quickly. 'You haven't forgotten me, surely? Remember all the stories I used to read to you?'

Edna stuffed another piece of bread and jam into her mouth, her expression blank.

'Her's no better,' Martha said quietly. 'There baint nothing to be done about it, Nurse Wilks said. We just leave her be nowadays.'

Will poured his tea into his saucer, blew on it and returned it to the cup. Having drained it, he said to Harry, 'Does the master know you're here?'

'I suppose so, Dad,' Harry replied. 'It was Lady Debrace who told me you were expecting to see me for tea. Sir Philip is in London. I only arrived back this afternoon.'

'Harry was on a train – two trains,' Alice told the children. 'Same as I went on when I went to visit him in Leicestershire. That's nearly 150 miles from here.'

The children stared at Harry, open-eyed. Realizing their curiosity, he told them every detail he could recall about the journey. Will was not diverted from the point he wished to make.

'The master be your guardian now,' he said. 'You mun do what he tells you. Happen he won't want you traipsing down here too often. Wouldn't be right now you be living in big house.'

So that was how his father wished it to be, Harry thought unhappily. He was only an embarrassment to his former family now. Perhaps he should not have called this man 'Dad' – for both of them knew that Will was not his real father. He wondered what they would say if they knew the late Earl of Kinmuire was his father. Until Sir

Philip had told him the facts, he had still thought of the Pritchetts as his family. He'd been longing to hug his Mum the way he had used to do when he got back from school; to enjoy a rough and tumble with his younger brothers and sisters; to go out in the yard and help his Dad chop firewood or whitewash the privy. Did they still have the old privy out by the wash-house? In the past two years he had become entirely accustomed to having a bath every other night; to using the WC, which never had to be emptied. Given the choice, would he want to give up these things – having his own bedroom, his own bed, the space to read without the little ones rampaging around him?

Perhaps not, he thought unhappily as he watched his father leave the table, shuffle across to his chair by the range, pick up the newspaper and place his spectacles on his nose. They were actions so familiar to him that he found himself waiting for the moment when Will would turn the back page over and fold it so that he could read the sports news. As if on cue, he did so. Now, Harry thought, Mum will ask him if he wants another cup of tea.

''Nother cuppa tea, Will?'

How carefully she always carried the brimming cup from the table and placed it, as she was doing now, on the table by his chair.

He felt a sudden desperate longing for the old days, when his Mum and the girls would clear the table to make room for ludo or shove-halfpenny boards and they'd start playing and begin to get over-excited. His father would put up with it for a while and then bang the arm of the chair with his paper and tell them the next one to raise his voice would get a beating. That was when they'd play 'Silence in the Pig Market, and Let the Old Sow Speak First'. They'd all start giggling and even Mum would smile, though she'd pretend not to. It stood to reason their dad would break the silence threatening them again, and then they'd all shout, 'He's the old sow, he's the old sow!' and Will would pretend they'd gone too far and chase them round the room with his rolled-up paper, and there'd be a fine old rumpus until Mum packed them all off to bed.

Harry rose from the table and went to sit opposite Will in his mother's chair. Beside it was her same old basket full of socks and darning wools. There was a lump in his throat which caused his voice to sound thickened as he said, 'Now I'm home, Dad – up at The Grange, I mean – I'll be able to lend you a hand again in the garden. You still got that big old wheelbarrow?'

Will's face did not emerge above the newspaper. 'Still got 'un,' he said after a pause. 'Not too old to push it myself.'

'I didn't mean that,' Harry said, feeling suddenly close to tears. 'I just meant I'd like to give you a hand – the way I used to. Remember how we . . .'

'Things is diff'rent now,' Will interrupted. 'Wouldn't be fittin'.'

'Why not?' Harry persisted, although he knew the answer.

''Cos it wouldn't,' Will said shortly, returning to his paper.

Instinctively, Harry turned to Martha, who, he noticed, was staring at him with a strange look in her eyes. Was it anxiety? Or pity? Despite being a person of few words, she had always in the past seemed remarkably intuitive where his feelings were concerned. Did she realize how much it was hurting him, somewhere deep down inside, to be made to feel an outsider? He wanted to fling himself into her arms, bury his head in her apron and beg her forgiveness, the way he'd used to do when, as a small boy, he knew he'd behaved badly. But what had he done wrong? He'd not been asked if he wanted to come home when he'd left Maythorpe. He'd not been asked if he'd wanted Sir Philip to become his new guardian. He'd just been told this was the way things were to be. It hadn't once crossed his mind that when he got back to Calking, he wouldn't be renewing his relationship with his foster family, even if he was living at The Grange.

'Lady Debrace said I can come and see you all as often as I want,' he volunteered.

Martha dropped her eyes and started to busy herself clearing away the tea things as she said primly, 'That's very kind of her ladyship, I'm sure.'

So she wasn't going to make him welcome either, Harry thought miserably. There was no 'Come as often as you can.' No, 'That'll be nice.' No, 'We've missed you.'

'Can we play ludo now, Mum?' Little Sam's shrill voice, ignorant of the tension, broke the silence.

'No, you can't. Not when we've got visitors,' Martha said sharply.

It was Alice who came to the rescue. 'Harry's not a visitor, Mum. Anyway, it's time we went, isn't it, Harry? You've all your unpacking to do.'

'Yes, well I dare say,' Martha muttered, folding the tablecloth into a neat square and putting it in the dresser drawer. She looked up as Alice put her arm through Harry's and half pulled him towards the door.

'You can bide a while longer if you want,' she said, not looking at Harry.

'Thanks, Mum, but it really is time we went,' Alice said firmly. 'Bye now, Dad. Don't work too hard.'

'Hard work never did no one no harm,' was Will's laconic response as he nodded his head in Harry's direction.

'It was a lovely tea. Thank you very much,' Harry proffered.

Suddenly Martha spoke. 'Never did say thank you for that nice tea cosy you sent me last Christmas, Harry,' she said. 'It were very nice.'

There was a softness in her tone which did not escape Harry.

'I noticed you weren't using it today,' he said, unable to disguise the reproach.

'Take a cartload of horses to make Mum use that,' Alice said, putting an arm round her mother's shoulders. 'Still got it wrapped in tissue in her souvenir drawer, haven't you, Mum, with all your other precious treasures?'

Martha's cheeks coloured. 'Don't be silly, Alice. I ain't got around to unwrapping it yet, that's all. Now be off, the pair of you, else you'll be late and her ladyship'll be blaming me for it.'

As Harry walked back with Alice towards The Grange, his eyes were thoughtful. 'Has Mum really got that tea cosy put away?' he asked. 'It's not because she didn't like it?'

'Don't you really know, Harry, that Mum loves you? She always has. She's kept everything you've ever given her and no one – not even Dad – is allowed to touch that drawer. Sometimes I think she loves you more'n she loves us lot, her own flesh and blood.'

'It didn't feel like it,' Harry said miserably. 'I felt a stranger, Alice – and that's what Mum and Dad treated me like, and you know it.'

Alice took his hand and squeezed it. 'Can't you understand, Harry? They just can't explain how they feel – not in words, and you know Mum was never one for kissing and hugging and that. It never used to worry you.'

'Well, it does now – it did this afternoon!' Harry said fiercely. 'You just don't know how often I've thought about them, and home, and you, Alice, and I used to think I'd give anything in the world to be back. Then when I do get back – well, it's almost as if they wished I hadn't turned up again, like a bad penny.'

Alice gave a deep sigh. 'The trouble is . . . it's you that's changed, Harry, not them. You mayn't realize it but you just aren't the same boy they used to know. You've grown up, and you look different, and talk different and, well, you just *are* different. You must know it yourself.'

Harry scuffed the toes of his shoes in the gravel. In fact, he was looking very much like the small boy who had left them over two years ago, Alice thought. He was scowling and his voice was astonishingly childish as he blurted out, 'It's not fair! I didn't ask to be different, to be changed! I was perfectly happy the way I used to be. I wish no one had ever found out who I was. I wish . . .'

'No, you don't do no such thing, Harry Keynes,' Alice said, curbing her longing to put her arms round him and

197

comfort him back to smiles. 'You've turned into a very handsome, very nice young gentleman as can hold your own any day with Master Aubrey, and,' she added with a flash of intuition, 'I'll bet Miss Madeleine thinks so too. I saw her tossing those curls about and dancing down them stairs when you came out of the nursery, even if you didn't. Showing off in front of you, she was. I'm real proud of you, Harry, and Mum and Dad are too, and don't you ever start wishing yourself backwards.'

Seeing that Harry was still looking hurt and confused, she tried again. 'You think I don't know how you feel, but I do,' she said. 'In many ways, it's the same for me, though Mum and Dad don't notice it so much, me being in and out every few days. I've learned such a lot from the mistress – about how nice people talk and think and behave. I want to be like her ladyship. I'd like to live the way she does. I shan't always be a lady's maid, you know. Soon as the war's over, her ladyship's going to speak to her sister for me, to see if Monsieur Verveine will give me a job in his couture house. It's something I'd like to do while waiting for you to grow up, Harry.'

'I'm nearly grown up now,' Harry said indignantly. 'I'm fifteen.'

'I know that, silly!' Alice said with a smile. 'But you'll have to be twenty-one before you can choose what you want to do with your life, and I can come and keep house for you.'

It was Harry's turn to smile. 'Remember how we used to plan the way we'd live?' he said.

'I've never forgot it,' Alice answered seriously. 'But it's six years 'afore we can think about doing what we planned, and then we've somehow got to get the money to rent somewhere to live.'

It was the first time Harry had thought with any real regret about the way his former guardians had run through his inheritance. For one thing the sums of money Sir Philip had talked about were outside his comprehension. When Sir Philip had patted him on the back and told him he was taking it all 'like a man', he'd rejected the praise.

'You can't miss losing what you never even knew you had,' he'd said.

Now he could see how useful that money might have proved to be in the future Alice spoke of. Their dreams would have to be shelved until they were rich. So too would that secret dream he still nurtured – that one day he would be important enough to ask Miss Madeleine to marry him.

No, not *Miss* Madeleine. Wonder of wonders, she had asked – no, *told* – him to call her Madeleine. In the brief hour he had spent in her company, their friendship had already changed. She had actually said she regretted that she must go back to school tomorrow just when he'd arrived home.

Quite suddenly he realized he was feeling a great deal happier. As always, Alice was right – he must not 'wish himself backwards'. Perhaps she was right about Mum and Dad, Mum in particular, still loving him but not being able to show it. He wished Martha had made just one gesture, even a small one, like ruffling his hair the way she'd done on the rare occasions in the past when he'd managed to please her. Perhaps she would have shown her feelings if all the other children hadn't been around watching them. As for his dad – well, if he, Harry, saw him working in the garden, he'd go and help whether Will wanted him to or not. Show him he hadn't become too grand to get his hands dirty.

Looking down at his hands, Harry realized with dismay that it was a very, very long while since they had touched the soil; his nails, once grimy and ragged, were now nicely shaped and perfectly clean. Perhaps his father had noticed them and thought he'd grown up a weakling.

He looked up as he and Alice approached the big stone building that from now on was to be his home. How often in the past had he stood in this same spot, looking at this house, hoping for a glimpse of the little golden-haired girl who lived there. How precious those days were when he'd been allowed inside. Now he would be entering those portals not just for an hour or two at Aubrey's invitation, but because he was living there as part of the family. He was to dine that night with Sir Philip and Lady Debrace and both the children. He would be able to see Madeleine, listen to her voice, see her smile.

Suddenly Oscar Wilde's poem, half forgotten, returned to his memory. He recalled the title, 'Roses and Rue', and in particular one short verse:

> And your mouth, it would never smile
> For a long, long while,
> Then it rippled all over with laughter
> Five minutes after.

'Feeling better?' Alice, who had been watching his face, now asked him.

'Yes, lots, thanks, Alice,' he said. 'Maybe things will be better next time I go. I hope so. I do love them, you know – all of them. You, too.'

'I know you do,' Alice said, happy that Harry was feeling easier in his mind. She had felt his hurt as if it had been her own, but now she could feel only joy. No matter what difficulties lay ahead for him, she would help him to overcome them. Nothing mattered measured against the fact that her adored Harry was back with her at last.

There remained but one week before Harry was due to go off to school with Aubrey. Two whole days were fully occupied when Lady Debrace took the boys up to London to buy Harry's uniform. The list seemed amazingly extravagant to him and he hardly dared look at the price labels attached to the sundry articles he appeared to need. Apart from the grey tweed suit and rough coat for everyday wear, there were two pairs of grey flannel trousers, shirts, a school blazer, white flannels and shirts for cricket and tennis, shorts for PT and boxing, games shirts, regulation underwear, Grafton Abbey ties and socks, a school cap, straw boater, raincoat, bathing-dress – the list seemed endless.

When the clothing had been bought and promises

extracted from the Gorringes salesman that all would be despatched by Carter Patterson and delivered to The Grange the following day, there were all the other requisites to be bought – a tuck box, a set of Cash's name tapes which Lady Debrace said cheerfully would have to be sewn on to every item by Alice, a tennis racket, a cricket bat and at least half a dozen different pairs of shoes.

Since there were also items of uniform which Aubrey needed to have replaced, they were unable to accomplish all the shopping in one day, so, much to Harry's delight, they stayed the night at the Savoy Hotel. The following day, with the last of the shopping completed by midday, Eloise hired a taxi cab to drive round London to show Harry the major landmarks. Following lunch at Harrods, the boys were taken to see the musical play, *Chu Chin Chow*.

By the time they returned, exhausted, to The Grange, Harry's uniform had arrived, but it was a further day before the parcel containing the name tapes was delivered. Several times a day, Harry went up to the sewing-room to see how Alice was progressing as, painstakingly, she stitched the tapes on to his clothes and on to the sheets, towels and napkins Lady Debrace had taken from her own linen cupboard for Harry's school use.

Harry's excitement at the thought of going to boarding-school was tempered by Aubrey's insistence that they sit down every evening and go through the list of things Harry should know if he was not to be thought a hopeless ignoramus by the other inmates of Grafton Abbey. He gave Harry a copy of *Stalky and Co.* to read so that he would have some idea of what he might expect at boarding-school.

Aubrey tried to be reassuring. 'At least I'll be around to ask if you get in a mess,' he said. 'By the way, did I tell you my nickname is Whoopers? Because of my cough! I should think they'll call you Swot, or something, because you're so brainy.'

'Who said I was?' Harry asked doubtfully.

'Well, you always used to be,' Aubrey replied, 'and the pater said he'd had a word with your tutor and you were, quote: "above average for your age".' He grinned. 'Best not to let on about that, though. Clever boys aren't frightfully popular. They're looked on as teachers' pets.'

Remembering Mr Harrison-Finch's unhealthy liking for him, Harry shivered.

All too soon, it was the last but one day before he was due to begin this new life at boarding-school, and Harry realized with dismay that he had not repeated that first painful visit to his old home. Somehow there had not seemed to be a 'right' time. He went to see Alice, who was still sewing name tapes into his school clothes. Knowing that it was her half-day, he suggested that he go home with her.

'Why ever not, if that's what you want, Harry?' she said, adding a pair of grey flannels to the neatly folded pile of uniform trousers on the table beside her. As she threaded a needle with a new length of white cotton, she added, 'I'm sure when Dad said you shouldn't lend him a hand in the garden, he didn't mean he didn't want to see you. You know what he's like about "people knowing their place", and, like it or not, Harry, you've moved up in the world now. Dad realizes it even if you don't, but that doesn't mean he and Mum won't be pleased to see you.'

Harry sighed. 'He looked so old, and tired,' he muttered. 'If I'd never had to go away, I'd still be living at home, helping him.'

Alice nodded. 'Then why don't you go home now and dig over Dad's vegetable patch for him? He wasn't able to do it before the frosts because that big old holly tree blew down and Mum wouldn't let him do the sawing because he'd had the influenza. You could cut it up, and Ted and Arthur could help you – they'd enjoy it. Then there's the guttering over the scullery needs replacing. Dad gets dizzy now up the ladder.'

Harry's eyes sparkled with enthusiasm. 'I could make a start while he's at work and then he'd have to let me finish it. I'll go down after lunch and talk to Mum about it. I'll mend the front gate too, Alice. I noticed it was off its hinge.'

He put his arms round her neck and hugged her.

'Get away with you, Harry,' Alice said, the sharpness of her tone mollified by her smile. 'You've gone and unthreaded my needle now, you stupid ninny!'

Martha looked pleased when Harry put the idea to her, although all she said was, 'You mind your Dad's saw. He won't half be angry if'n you mess that up. And mind them good clothes of yourn.'

Harry laughed. 'They're only old ones of Aubrey's. He said it wouldn't matter what I did with them as they're only going to be chucked away when he goes back to school. I want to get as much done as I can before Dad finds out what I'm up to. I reckon with the boys' help, we can get most of the tree cut up before he comes back for his tea. Don't tell him, will you?'

Martha nodded, the hint of a smile curving the corners of her mouth as she said, 'You always was a one as liked surprises, even when you was a little lad. Remember that time you thought of whitewashing the privy to s'prise your Dad and me?'

Feeling happier than he had in years, Harry grinned. 'I'm not likely ever to forget it, Mum, not after the thrashing I got. Whitewash all over my clothes and over your scullery floor and boot marks all the way up the brick path.'

'Reckon as how you'd more in your hair than in privy,' Martha reminisced. 'Took me half an hour getting it out.'

'Yes, but *you* knew I'd only wanted to help,' Harry reminded her. 'You weren't happy when Dad took his belt to me . . . and you gave me a toffee after he'd sent me up to bed.'

Martha's eyes widened in pleasure. 'Now fancy you remembering that after all this time,' she said, and as if embarrassed by the fact that she'd indicated her pleasure, she added in an offhand way, 'Now, I've work to do even if you haven't, and I can't stand here gossiping all day. You'd best be off if'n you don't want a cup of tea.'

'Later, Mum,' Harry said, putting his arms round her unresponsive shoulders. 'I'll be wanting lots of cups of tea by then.'

As he went out to find the saw, he was as filled with contentment as on his previous visit he had been sad. The fact that he and his mum were close again and that it was all due to Alice did not escape his mind. It had never been any different; she always had – and doubtless always would – solve his problems for him.

Harry's first term at Grafton Abbey was unlike anything he had imagined. The physical privations did not trouble him, as Aubrey had warned they might, since for the first twelve years of his life he had known no luxury, had had to share one privy with ten others, had had no hot water to wash in in the mornings. Nor were the masters harsher than Mr Wilson had been, and thanks to his old headmaster, he was used to being beaten! What he had never before experienced was the bullying – the cruel tricks that were played on the weaker boys by the stronger, the ostracizing of those they considered were in any respect different from themselves: a Jewish boy who would never eat bacon or pork, a dark-skinned boy whose home was in India, a boy who wore pebble spectacles, another who had a birthmark on the side of his face. In the village school in Calking such behaviour would have been remarked upon by the teachers and immediately stamped out. At Grafton Abbey the masters seemed to turn a blind eye to such things, leaving it to the prefects to run their own houses.

Harry hated this aspect of boarding-school life, but conversely he loved the good things. Long before the term ended, his ability as a sportsman was noted and he had been chosen to play for the second XI cricket team. He won the house cup for boxing and achieved more points for his house in the end-of-term athletics than any other boy.

Although for the first six weeks of his school career Harry had been excluded from any of the cliques and was dubbed one of the 'outcast oddities' because of his *naïveté* in school affairs, once he had been noticed by the captain of games, the prefects stopped picking on him.

'You've done fearfully well, Keynes,' Aubrey said as they caught the school train up to London. 'You're bound to get a good report after those exam results and old Jenkins is sure to give you a halo – you know what he's like about boys who are good at sports. That's all he cares about. The pater won't half be pleased. I'm not supposed to tell you this but he thought you'd be a bit of a misfit at first.'

'Well, so I was,' Harry said, happy that Aubrey seemed to think well of him. 'You were jolly decent – sticking by me, I mean. I was definitely a Philistine to start with.'

'It'll be heaps better next term,' Aubrey said cheerfully. 'By the way, did I tell you Jenkins says we can share a study? Here – you can have this.' He threw Harry a stick of liquorice. 'Just think, two whole months holiday to do exactly as we please.'

'Do you think Madeleine will meet us at the station?' Harry asked in a voice which he hoped sounded casual.

'Probably. On the other hand, if her best friend's there, they may be doing something girlish and silly together. If it doesn't rain and someone's mowed and marked the lawn, we can have some tennis foursomes. Pickles is hopeless but Daphne's quite good. I'll play with her and you can have Pickles, so it will make us about equal.'

Harry's excitement, which had been building up throughout the term, now increased as Aubrey outlined plans for the summer holidays. Aubrey thought it quite likely that his parents would consider him old enough, now he was sixteen, to take charge if the four of them wanted to go on their own to Brighton to bathe.

'I don't suppose we'll be allowed to go to London because of the confounded Zeppelins,' he said. 'It seems awfully silly seeing the stupid Boche never drop their bombs where they mean to. Our pilots are miles better. Shall you join this new Royal Air Force service if the war lasts long enough, Harry? The pater said I wouldn't pass the medical but I dare say you would with no trouble at all.'

They both laughed and then Aubrey's attention was diverted by the sight of a very pretty VAD who climbed into their carriage at East Croydon. As Aubrey was obviously smitten, Harry tactfully stared out of the window. There was quite a lot of talk about girls among the seniors at school but none of it very romantic. For the most part, they told rude limericks or jokes. There was always a great deal of sniggering when they came to a love scene in a Shakespeare play and, when the lesson was over, they would parody the scene in such a way that everyone would collapse with laughter.

The boy who held the centre of the stage on such occasions was a chap called Burrows, who was reputed to be the only boy in the school who had actually 'done it'. Rumour had it that there was a young woman who owned a tea-shop in Grafton who was willing to go the whole way and that some of the prefects quite often broke bounds to go there. It all depended upon whether she took a fancy to you or not.

Neither Aubrey nor Harry had paid too much attention to the rumours since they were not yet old enough to be prefects and knew that the senior boys would make their lives hellish if they tried to tread on their preserve. Besides, they both agreed, while they would like to know exactly what did happen between men and women, they were far from sure whether or not they would be able to do whatever was required. As far as Aubrey's parents had advised him, this aspect of human nature was not even to be considered until a young man came of age. Five more years – six where Harry was concerned – seemed an unreasonably long time to wait. They had decided, therefore, to put off any serious thoughts about the opposite sex at least until they were prefects.

Madeleine and Daphne were untroubled by such consider-ations. As they swung in the hammock strung between the beech and the maple tree, waiting for the time to pass before they could go in the old Victoria to meet the boys' train, they were concerned mainly with the new fashion adopted by many of the women and girls engaged in war work of cutting their hair short. Daphne thought it would certainly be cooler in hot weather and far less trouble to wash and dry, but Madeleine rather admired her own ash-blonde, silky tresses and happily submitted to the hundred brush-strokes they required every night before she went to bed. Sometimes she would sit in front of her mirror and pile her hair on top of her head to see what she would look like when she was old enough to put it up. She loved it when people told her she was pretty. She adored her doting papa and, although she was too old now to sit on his knee, she would rest in the circle of his arm and listen attentively when he told her that before long she would be breaking all the young men's hearts. It amused her to see the boys Aubrey invited home blushing when she smiled at them, and it was always gratifying when they vied with each other to fetch her sun-hat or a glove, or to retrieve a badly aimed tennis ball.

She was often bored by Daphne's adoration, which had long since ceased to be a novelty, besides which, she needed to practise how she would behave with the young men who at some time in the future would be escorting her to parties and dances. They couldn't *all* get killed, she consoled herself as the casualty lists grew longer and longer. They, the Debraces, had not been unaffected, for one of the gardeners and two of the grooms had been killed in action. Frederick, however, had so far survived. According to Alice, she quite often received letters from him and recently the contents had sounded far more hopeful about the outcome of the war, because of the assistance the Allies were receiving from the Americans. Frederick seemed to think he might be home before Christmas – and, Madeleine reassured herself, if a footman could return safely, so could lots of young officers.

Meanwhile, Aubrey would be home at any moment, bringing Harry with him. Even as small children, Harry had always been far nicer to her than her brother and in that brief time she had seen him before she'd had to go back to school for the summer term, she had observed that, while he had changed to look at, his manner towards her was the same as it had always been.

'You'll like Harry,' she now told her friend. 'He's a bit shy but he'll do anything for you. He once walked all the way down to the village because I said I wanted some hokey-pokey ice, and, guess what, by the time he got back, it had melted.'

The girls were still laughing as Lady Debrace came across the lawn, looking as elegant as always in a creamy-white voile dress and a large-brimmed straw sun-hat.

'If you still mean to meet the boys, you'd better hurry,' she told them. 'The Victoria is waiting at the front door.'

As the two girls tumbled out of the hammock and ran in the direction of the house as fast as their long skirts allowed, Eloise sat down in one of the cane chairs and gave a contented sigh. It was most gratifying, she thought, to be the mother of two such attractive children as Aubrey and Madeleine. Madeleine's friend, jolly as she seemed, looked clumsy and ungainly beside her dainty daughter. As for Aubrey – her beloved son – he was taller than herself now and had grown into a delightfully handsome young man. She must arrange some nice parties for the four young people these holidays. It would be especially good for Harry, who, poor boy, had been shut away for so long in that horrible house in the Midlands without companions of his own age. She must do what she could to make these holidays enjoyable for the boy.

Shocked as Eloise had been by her husband's account of the way Harry's guardians had embezzled his inheritance, she had nevertheless been much impressed by the transformation they had effected in the time he had been with them. When Harry left the Pritchetts, he had been quite unfit for polite society – at best, more intelligent and fractionally more socially adept than the village children. The boy had returned almost unrecognizable. To all intents and purposes, he could now pass as any normal upper-class child but then, Eloise reminded herself, one had to remember his father's background. As Philip had pointed out, breeding was as important in human beings as it was in horses.

According to Alice, the cook at Maythorpe House had maintained that Harry was the spitting image of the late earl. Whether or not this was the case, he was certainly an exceptionally good-looking boy. She had been down to Grafton Abbey with Philip for sports day and felt quite proud to be flanked by two such remarkably handsome youths, one blond, one dark. When Harry had not been competing in an event, the two of them had vied with one another to dance attendance upon her, much to Philip's amusement.

'It doesn't surprise me, my dear. You're one of the prettiest mothers here and that will not go unnoticed by the senior boys. Aubrey and Harry will chalk up quite a lot of credit on your account.'

They and the girls should be back shortly, she thought, as she stood up and walked slowly back to the house. She would instruct Sally to serve tea outside as it was such a beautiful day. They would have it on the terrace. But first the boys would want to get out of their school uniforms. She would allow them to dispense with their blazers as it was so warm. How marvellous it would be if this lovely weather continued for the rest of the holidays.

With a sigh of pleasure, Eloise walked in through the garden door to the cool hallway and rang the bell for the maid.

CHAPTER ELEVEN

1918

This must be the best summer of my whole life, Harry thought as he lay on his back with only a sheet over him, listening to the nightingales singing their hearts out down by Hazel Copse. Yesterday he, Aubrey and Madeleine had been down there to see how the hazelnuts were forming. As children he and the other lads in the village had frequently trespassed on the Debraces' estate to gather the nuts in October, for they were more plentiful in the copse than anywhere else in the neighbourhood. This October he would be back at school, but doubtless Arthur and Ted would be harvesting the nuts when they were ready, especially now that the number of outdoor staff was so reduced and they were even less likely to be detected.

After a sweltering day which had been almost too hot for tennis, darkness had finally fallen and a cool, gentle breeze was blowing apart the bright floral curtains at his open windows. He and Aubrey had been sent to bed at ten o'clock, Madeleine an hour earlier, this being the latest they were ever allowed to stay up other than on party nights, but Harry had found it impossible to sleep. His mind was full of images of Madeleine. This afternoon she had lain against the cushions at the far end of the punt, her fair hair spread around her face. Since the effort of poling was apt to bring on Aubrey's breathing problems, he had been seated opposite her and Harry had been able to watch Madeleine over the top of his friend's head. Despite Lady Debrace's warning to shade themselves from the rays of the August sun, both he and Aubrey had removed their boaters, and Madeleine, her wide-brimmed straw hat.

Madeleine had spent most of the afternoon teasing him, first telling him that he was not poling fast enough and then complaining that he was taking them round in circles. Aubrey's constant brotherly reprimands to his sister to 'shut up, you silly ass!' did nothing to deter Madeleine from her chosen form of amusement. What Aubrey did not realize was that when his gaze was diverted elsewhere, Madeleine would wink mischievously at Harry, as if to imply they were sharing a private joke from which her brother was excluded.

It was really nice having Madeleine to themselves now that her friend had left, he thought, as he tried to find a cool spot on his pillow for his sunburnt cheek. She and Madeleine were far too often sitting whispering to one another, or shut in one or other of their bedrooms trying on clothes or experimenting with new hair styles.

'I can't see why you want them with us,' Aubrey remarked on more than one occasion. 'Girls of that age are nothing but a nuisance, and you shouldn't let Pickles boss you around. She only does it to show off to Daphne. What's more, you encourage her by laughing when she plays the giddy-goat. She and Daphne looked absolute asses doing the bunny-hug.'

'I thought they were quite funny,' Harry had said truthfully. He had also thought Madeleine looked entrancing with her flushed cheeks and fair hair coming loose from her pigtails.

The noise of an owl hooting now coincided with the creak of a door opening.

'That you, Aubrey?' he asked, for sometimes his friend would wander in through the communicating door between their rooms and sit on the end of his bed for a jaw.

There was a soft rustle and then a stifled giggle and Madeleine's voice answered him. 'No, it's me, Maddy. I've just sneaked down to the pantry and got some cakes and stuff. I couldn't sleep so I thought we'd have a midnight feast.'

Harry sat up. He could now just discern Madeleine's small figure standing at the end of his bed.

'I think Aubrey's asleep,' he said. 'I'll go and wake him up.'

'No need to do that, silly,' Madeleine replied. 'The two of us can easily eat what I've got.'

She dumped a bundle somewhere near Harry's feet.

'I put the food in a bath towel, in case anyone saw me,' she said. 'Gosh, it's dark, isn't it? I think I've just stubbed my foot on your shoes.'

She sat down on the side of the bed and bent down to rub her toes.

'Do you think you ought to be here?' Harry asked anxiously. 'I mean, supposing your mother found us? Couldn't we put the food in a drawer or something and eat it tomorrow?'

'Don't be such an idiot,' Madeleine said, sounding cross. 'What's the point of eating in daylight? The whole point about a midnight feast is having it at night. Have you got a torch? My battery's dud so I couldn't bring mine.'

Speechless, Harry opened the drawer of his bedside table and produced his torch. Madeleine took it from him and shone the beam in his face. She giggled. 'You do look funny – all ghost-like. Now look at me.'

She put the torch under her chin and stuck out her tongue. Momentarily, she looked grotesque and Harry had time to find his voice.

'It's awfully late, Madeleine. Don't you think . . .'

He felt her small hand pushing him backwards as she interrupted him, saying, 'Don't be so futile, Harry. We're not committing a crime, for goodness' sake! Of course, if you're in a funk . . .'

It was Harry's turn to interrupt. 'I'm not frightened for me, Madeleine. I'm worried about you.'

'Then stop worrying, and move over. Give me one of your pillows and I'll dish out the food.'

To Harry's dismay, he found himself trembling as she edged up beside him and he could feel the warmth of her body through the thin sheet. She seemed quite impervious to the effect her proximity was having on him – for which he was grateful. He wished very much that Aubrey would wake up and join them. Somehow it would make all the difference. It might even be fun.

Madeleine was unwrapping the bath towel. She pointed the torch at some crumbling jam tarts, two slices of ginger cake and a handful of biscuits.

'Come on, eat up,' she said. 'It's funny how much better food tastes when you know you shouldn't be eating it.'

Appetites were strange things, Harry thought as he bemoaned the sudden loss of his. There was a time in his life when he would have sworn he would never refuse food, let alone delicacies such as jam tarts and cake. It was not so very many years ago that he had gone to bed hungry. Here at The Grange, they ate exceedingly well and were encouraged to do so.

'Eat up, children,' Sir Philip would say. 'There's many a starving Russian who would be pleased to have what you've left on the side of your plate.'

Not only a starving Russian, Harry always thought when his new guardian moralized thus. There were plenty of poor children like the Pritchetts who would be only too happy to consume the Debraces' leftovers.

'Here, have a piece of cake, Harry,' Madeleine urged him as she hunched up her knees. 'We can save the biscuits for another night. I vote we organize a really scrumptious feast on the last day of the hols. Golly, is that someone coming? I'm sure I heard a noise.'

She pulled the sheet over her head and cuddled up to Harry as close as she could get. She's still only a kid, Harry thought, as he tried to edge away from her. Her small, pointed breasts were pressing against his side and he could feel his breath coming in short, uneven gasps. Although none of this was of his doing, he was consumed by guilt, knowing that a boy and a girl should not be in bed together. Even at the Prichetts', Ted, Arthur and Sam slept in a different room from the girls.

His thoughts ceased abruptly as now he too heard the sound of footsteps in the passage. They went past his door and, for a moment, there was silence until the sound of the grandfather clock in the hall struck midnight. He waited, holding his breath. When the last chime died away, he flung back the sheet and climbed out of bed.

'This is a crummy idea, Madeleine,' he said. 'We're lucky no one came in. Go on back to your room, there's a good girl.'

Slowly Madeleine swung her legs over the side of the bed and, pouting, picked up the bath towel and the remains of the 'feast'.

'I never thought you were a funk, Harry Pritchett,' she said scornfully.

'I'm not scared and my name isn't Pritchett – it's Keynes,' Harry was stung to reply. His voice was raised and now, suddenly, the communicating door to Aubrey's room opened and he wandered in, rubbing his eyes.

'What's going on?' he asked. 'For heaven's sake, Pickles, what on earth are *you* doing in here?'

Madeleine tossed her head. 'We were having a midnight feast – and then Harry got the wind up and ruined it. He's nothing but a spoilsport.'

'I don't blame him. If the mater knew you were wandering about at this time of night, she'd have fifty fits. So beat it, Pickles, there's a good girl.'

When his sister had departed, Aubrey turned on the bedside light and stood grinning at Harry, who was now sitting on the edge of his bed.

'I suppose she didn't leave any grub? I say, old chap, are you all right? You're not bothered because Pickles was in a bait, are you? She always sulks when she doesn't get her own way. She'll have forgotten all about it in the morning.'

'I suppose so,' Harry said. 'All the same, she was quite right – I was in a bit of a funk. We thought we heard someone in the passage and I kept wondering what your father would say if he knew Madeleine was in my bed.'

'Yes, well . . . I suppose he wouldn't have been too pleased. It's typical of Pickles – she just does what she feels like and never thinks of the consequences for anyone else. It would have been you who'd have got it in the neck if you'd been caught. I'll give her a good ticking-off in the morning. If she does it again, give me a shout. You're much too soft with her, you silly ass.'

He gave Harry a friendly shove and ambled back to his own room, leaving the door ajar. Within a few minutes, Harry could hear the sound of slight snores and knew that Aubrey was asleep. He, however, had never felt more wide awake. It always made him miserable when he knew he had earned Madeleine's disapproval. If he missed a smash at the tennis net, she would call him 'fathead', or if he dropped something he was carrying for her, he was 'a stupid dolt'. She seemed as unaware how hurtful such remarks were as she was ignorant of the pleasure it gave when she praised him.

Perhaps he *was* a dolt, he thought wryly, to let himself be so affected by a mere schoolgirl. He should try to treat Madeleine as Aubrey did. In some ways he wouldn't be sorry when the holidays were over and he went back to school. At least there were no girls to worry about there. Maybe he'd be picked for the first XV rugger team. Camberwell, the captain, had said he was tall and strong enough now to be considered, although he was a lot younger than the rest of the possible members of the team. He was also to be moved up a year in class because he'd done so well in exams. Jenkins, his housemaster, had said he was wasting his time in the Upper Fifth and, according to his various masters, he should be able to keep up in the Sixth if he put his mind to it. Life would be pretty good, he thought, if only he could forget about Madeleine. However, after tonight's adventure he knew that it was not only love he felt for her. When she had pressed herself against him, he had wanted to put his arms round her, kiss her, touch those small, pointed breasts, explore the mysteries of her female body.

Ashamed of himself yet unable to resist the temptation, Harry gave way to the urge to assuage his frustration, and thus he finally fell asleep.

Eloise was uneasy. Seated in her favourite chair in the shade of the maple tree, she watched the three children as they walked away from her in the direction of the lake. They were going fishing and had taken a picnic lunch so that their day would not be interrupted.

It was as well, she thought, that the holidays were nearly over. In one way they had been as happy as she had planned that day the boys had broken up. Apart from one or two rainy days, the weather could not have been better and the children had been able to spend all their time out in the fresh air. The trouble was, she ought really not still to be calling them children. Aubrey was now as tall as his father and Harry, at six foot, was even taller. They were young men. As for Madeleine, according to Alice, her daughter had started the curse this holidays, which meant that she was now on the threshold of womanhood. There had been other signs, too. Madeleine's behaviour with Harry could only be called provocative. Eloise had not at first noticed it, but one evening, Philip had remarked fondly that their little girl was fast becoming a flirt. He'd seen no harm in it but Eloise, observing the child, realized that her daughter was quite definitely using her feminine charms to beguile Harry – or any other visiting boy – to do as *she* wanted. Invariably, she was successful in getting her own way.

Initially Eloise had found it amusing, for she could see nothing wrong in a woman using her charms to achieve her own ends. But gradually she had begun to notice Harry's reactions and reluctantly she had reached the conclusion that the poor boy was suffering all the pangs of calf love.

Today, as they'd stopped by her chair to say goodbye, Harry in particular had glowed with happiness. He and Aubrey were carrying all the fishing gear and Madeleine, empty-handed, was holding on to Harry's arm in the most possessive manner. She was dancing up and down, laughing at him.

This won't do, Eloise thought. It was something neither she nor Philip had thought of when they had planned for Harry to come and live with them. Like all parents, they had been unaware that their children were about to leave childhood behind them. Innocent they might be – most

216

certainly were – but that very ignorance of how their bodies could betray them, could lead them unknowingly into danger. It would be quite pointless talking to Aubrey, who, in the first place, would probably be shocked if she were to voice her fears, and, in the second, could never see any wrong in Harry, whom he considered his best friend. Nor could she hope for any support from Philip, who could see no wrong in his beloved daughter. To speak to Madeleine might be to put ideas into her head which she was by no means certain were already there. As for Harry – if Philip thought the boy presented any danger to Madeleine, he would send him away at once.

Eloise picked up a glass of home-made blackcurrant cordial and sipped it thoughtfully. Usually when she had a problem, she would take it straight to Philip, or, if it were of a domestic nature, to Cook or Alice. Now she was obliged to concentrate in order to deal with it herself, and her sense of unease increased. In the first place, if Harry were to be sent away, where could he go? Certainly not back to the Pritchetts. Besides, what reason could she give him for his banishment?

Perhaps, she thought, she could arrange for both the boys to be away during part of the Christmas holidays. The following Easter holidays would be no problem, for Philip had this very morning received a letter from Aubrey's godfather asking if the boy was fit enough now to join him on a walking holiday in the Lake District. Aubrey had not been averse to the idea but had asked his father to write back, requesting that Harry be included in the invitation.

Somehow she must think of a way to keep the young people apart over Christmas. Madeleine's friend, Daphne, had written the conventional letter of thanks following her visit to The Grange, and relayed a request from her parents for Madeleine to make a return visit as soon as it could be arranged. If Madeleine were to go to Dorset after the Christmas festivities, the problem would be solved.

In another half-hour, Eloise thought, she must get ready to go down to the Red Cross Hall, where it was her turn to supervise the making of bandages for the Front. She had been doing this for almost four years and had long since lost count of how many thousands of bandages had been sent for use in the field hospitals. Sometimes it seemed impossible that so many were needed, yet all over the country other villages and towns were doing the same.

Sadly, even in Calking nearly half the Red Cross volunteers were in mourning. Among the tradespeople she could think of only two who had not so far received one of those horrible orange telegrams telling them a loved one had been killed or wounded. One of the most difficult tasks Eloise had to undertake was visiting the bereaved. The families seemed honoured by her call but she was unhappily aware of the fact that she had no real comfort to offer them in the face of their losses.

Not a single night went by when she did not include in her prayers her grateful thanks that neither her husband nor her son were of an age to be at risk. Poor Mrs Hobbs, the village baker, had lost both husband and son, and was now struggling to maintain the business with only a boy of fifteen and her young daughter to assist her. She, Eloise, must remember to tell Alice to look out some of her more serviceable clothes to take down to Mrs Hobbs, and perhaps one or two of Madeleine's outgrown frocks for the daughter, although most of those went to Martha Pritchett's girl, Edna.

One of these days, Eloise thought, as she gathered her skirt and walked back towards the house, she must go down and see Martha. It must have been hard for her, losing a child after twelve years of thinking of Harry as hers. Doubtless the woman was pleased to see him again. As for Alice, her happiness was undisguised. If on occasions the girl envied the privileged position Harry now had in the Debrace household, she gave no indication of it and never once, in front of others, did she forget to address him as 'Master Harry'.

Alice came into the room now in answer to Eloise's ring.

'Why don't you come down to the village hall with me, Alice?' Eloise said on an impulse. 'It will do you good to get out in the fresh air on such a lovely day, and we'd certainly welcome another pair of hands.'

'That's very kind of your ladyship,' Alice said, smiling. 'I'd like that very much. Here's your dust coat, Madam, and your gloves. I'll just go and get myself tidy.'

'You never look anything else but tidy,' Eloise said warmly as Alice left the room. Even in her uniform the girl somehow managed to look more elegant than some of Eloise's friends. Alice must be getting on for twenty now, she thought, as she put her straw hat on. Twisting it until the black-velvet bow and red cherries were resting at a becoming angle on one side, she then inserted a pearl hat-pin through the crown and into her coiled hair.

Alice was another girl who had suddenly grown from child to woman, Eloise told herself as she surveyed her reflection. The thought made her feel old, and she gazed anxiously in the mirror to see if her flawless fair complexion had become marred by wrinkles. One's youth was so fleeting, she thought sadly as she closed the bedroom door and made her way downstairs. She must not let her fears for the children ruin these precious years of childhood. Let them all be happy and enjoy themselves while they were still young and full of the energy of youth. In five years' time, her little Madeleine could be a married woman with children of her own.

Disliking the thought, Eloise decided to concentrate instead on her forthcoming visit to the Red Cross meeting. She might have found it less easy to do so had she accompanied her children and Harry to the river. There she would have observed her adolescent daughter jumping up and down on the bank, shouting in her high, treble voice, 'Oh, Harry, you've caught one – a big one! Oh, you clever, clever boy!' and planting a long, voluptuous kiss full on the boy's lips.

CHAPTER TWELVE

1919

'It was very kind of you to send your driver to meet my train, Madam,' Alice said politely as Rosamund Verveine greeted her sister's protégée on her arrival at number two, rue de Sèze. 'I am afraid the porter didn't understand my French very well.'

Rosamund regarded the girl with interest. 'You've grown up since I last saw you, Alice. That must have been the summer before the war broke out.'

'Nearly five years ago, Madame,' Alice replied. 'The mistress asked me to give you her fondest love, and this letter.'

Rosamund took the envelope Alice now extracted from her crocodile-leather handbag, a parting present from the Debrace household. Before opening the letter, Rosamund instructed the waiting chauffeur to take Alice's trunk up to the fourth floor. Then she led the way into an elegant *petit salon*.

'You may sit down, Alice,' she said. 'You must be tired after the journey. I trust you were not seasick?'

'No, Madam, I enjoyed the boat trip very much,' Alice said. While Madame Verveine was reading her sister's letter, she was able to study the wife of her new employer – for it was Monsieur Verveine who had offered her the job of seamstress at his *Maison de Couture*. The elder of the two sisters by ten years, the woman seated opposite her bore little resemblance to Lady Debrace, Alice thought. Her face was lined and she was quite heavily made up. Although the garments she was wearing were in themselves essentially chic, the overall effect was one which

Alice could only describe to herself as 'un-put-together'. Her voice was deep and husky – as if she had just woken from a heavy sleep. The sapphire-blue eyes with which it seemed all the females in the family were blessed were ringed and puffy.

'I see that my sister is already regretting her generosity in arranging for my husband to employ you,' Madame Verveine said. 'Well, we shall have to see if you live up to her recommendation, shall we not? I suppose you might as well come and meet my husband immediately. He is anxious that you should commence work tomorrow as they are very short-handed in the workrooms. There are only ten more weeks to prepare for the show. You may not realize, Alice, that this is the first since before the war, so it is a very important one for my husband. After I have introduced you to Monsieur Verveine, you may go to your room, unpack your things and have an early night. I'll send one of the maids up with a supper tray.'

Without waiting for Alice's comments, she stood up and led the way through the double doors into a smaller room, which she called her husband's *cabinet*. Sitting at a desk covered with large sheets of drawing paper sat the short, elegantly dressed figure of Monsieur Félix Verveine. His black hair, greying slightly at the temples, was sleeked back, his moustache neatly trimmed. On one hand was a ring – a large green onyx, set in gold.

'What is it, *chérie*?' he enquired, peering at his wife over the rim of his gold spectacles. His voice sounded impatient.

'The girl Eloise wrote about so eloquently has arrived,' Rosamund answered. 'I thought you might be interested to meet her.'

With a frown Félix Verveine's glance turned to Alice. His eyes went from the top of her close-fitting velour hat to her buckled court shoes and back again to her face. The frown vanished and his dark thick eyebrows rose as if in surprise.

'Good evening, Mademoiselle . . .'

'Alice Pritchett, Monsieur.'

'Indeed, yes. Take off your coat, Alice.' His voice was peremptory.

Alice did as she was told, feeling slightly unnerved by her new employer's scrutiny. His eyes travelled once more over her body and then he said, 'Did your mistress give you those clothes?'

'Yes, sir. She was very generous about such things. Her clothes are always beautifully cut, but I have had to alter this alpaca skirt to fit me as her ladyship is a little larger than I am.'

Félix Verveine stood up and walked round his desk. He touched the embroidered voile blouse Alice was wearing. 'And this?'

Sensing that the man's voice held a note of criticism, Alice said defensively, 'I'm afraid I did remake it. The large leg-of-mutton sleeves didn't suit me very well and there seemed to be too much material in the style to be . . . well, fashionable. I'd seen a picture in *Vogue* of the new Russian blouse that was to be popular this year and so I modelled a similar design using her ladyship's material.' Her voice trailed into silence.

'And this?' Monsieur Verveine was pointing now to the colourful embroidery with which Alice had decorated the front.

'Perhaps it is a little too . . . too bright . . . ?' she ventured apologetically.

'No, no . . . certainly no! It is exactly as it should be. It is beautifully stitched. I commend you, Mademoiselle.'

He turned to his wife, his face now animated. Having lost its forbidding expression, it was completely transformed, Alice thought with surprise. He had removed his spectacles and she could see his unusually coloured grey eyes dancing with excitement as he pointed to her blouse. An elongated dimple had appeared on the side of his face, making it slightly lopsided yet at the same time lending it a boyish charm. He must once have been an exceedingly handsome young man, she decided and blushed at the unexpected turn her thoughts had taken. What cheek even to be considering the appearance of her middle-aged employer in such terms.

'Look at this, *chérie*!' he continued to his wife. 'See how it hangs quite perfectly from the shoulders. And the collar is charming. I have to say this, the design is an improvement on the one we have been preparing for our exhibition.' He turned back to Alice, waving his arms excitedly. 'You are to bring this to work with you in the morning, Mademoiselle. I wish to show it to Madame Duvalle. She is my *directrice de la maison*.'

He turned once more to his wife. 'It is clear to me that this young lady is more advanced than Eloise led me to suppose. She would be wasted in the sewing-room.' He smiled at Alice. 'We shall discuss this in the morning. You will report to my office at half past eight, Mademoiselle. Is that understood? Now leave me. I have work to do.'

'Yes, sir,' Alice said as Madame Verveine hurried her out of the room. Despite her fatigue and all the emotion of the day, her heart was singing as she was shown by one of the French maids to her room in the attic. Not even Rosamund Verveine's warning that the *directrice*, Madame Duvalle, was a dragon much to be feared could dull her excitement. The coldness of Alice's room beneath the roof, its sparse furnishing, the strange *duvet* on the iron bedstead, went unheeded as she began to unpack her trunk. Tomorrow, she thought, the dream she had nurtured for so long was about to be realized; her career in dressmaking had begun.

The following morning, dressed very simply in a dark navy serge dress, covered by Lady Debrace's discarded double-breasted sac coat, she walked down the rue Cambon on her way to the Maison de Verveine, trying not to let her apprehension of this strange city show.

The February wind bit into her cheeks, burning them to a deep rose colour and stinging her hazel eyes. Occasionally, the smell of roasting coffee beans assailed her nostrils as she passed a café serving *petit déjeuner* to the Parisians, who, like herself, were on their way to work. She had had coffee and croissants in Madame Verveine's kitchen with the staff, who had all giggled and nudged one another as they listened to Alice's halting attempts to speak their language. Her failure to make herself understood had depressed her, for she had persuaded Lady Debrace to pay for a few French lessons with Miss Tester in lieu of a Christmas present and had thought the few phrases she had mastered would be quite intelligible. The spoken word, she now discovered, was far less easy to decipher than the written word and even she could hear that her accent was unmistakably English.

Suddenly her eye caught the black and apricot sign of the Verveine couture house. Her heart beating fiercely with a combination of nervousness and excitement, she pushed open the big glass doors and went inside.

No sooner had she entered the portals than Alice realized that she should have made her way to some back entrance which Madame Verveine had not thought to mention. Her mouth fell open with astonishment as she gazed around her. She had never once imagined that a shop – a dress shop – could look like this. The walls of the vast salon were made of the palest shades of white and brown marble. The floor was covered from wall to wall by a delicate, thick-piled, apricot-coloured carpet. Curtains of a slightly deeper shade hung from the tall windows to the floor, and the same coloured velvet was repeated on the comfortable chairs and sofas, as if for an elegant drawing-room. Above Alice's head hung a number of brilliant crystal chandeliers from which a soft, warm light now filled the room.

While Alice, awestruck, was still staring open-mouthed at her opulent surroundings, a young man in a neat tailcoat and striped trousers approached her. He was shorter than Alice and of a small, delicate build. His eyes – which were not unfriendly – were fringed with exceptionally long, dark lashes and but for his apparel, Alice thought anxiously, she might have mistaken him for a girl. He addressed her in a string of voluble French of which she understood not one word.

'I'm sorry,' she said. 'I am afraid I don't understand. *Je ne comprends pas,'* she essayed in French. 'I'm English. I have come to see Monsieur Verveine.'

The young man's pale face lit up in a charming smile. *'Ah, mais je comprends maintenant,'* he exclaimed. 'I know who it is I now speak to. You must be the English *arpette. Le Maître* has given the instruction that I take you to him.'

The *Maître*, Alice realized, being the 'master', must mean Monsieur Verveine. She nodded, returning the young man's smile.

He held out his hand. 'I present myself, Mademoiselle. I am Jules Bellaire, and as you will soon discover, here I am the factotum. How do you say it in English? I am required to do the tiresome business of others who do not wish to do the less agreeable tasks for themselves.'

Alice laughed. 'I'm Alice Pritchett,' she said. 'I think I should have come to a different entrance.'

Her companion nodded with pretended gravity. 'If Madame Duvalle had seen you, she would have eaten you for her *déjeuner*! Come, Mademoiselle, we will go to *le Maître*.'

As he led the way across the room, a girl in a black satin dress and shoes came in, carrying a huge vase of pale apricot gladioli with fronds of dark-green foliage. She gave a friendly smile as they went past her into a passage.

'That was Amélie,' Jules Bellaire said. 'For her is the task of arranging fresh flowers every morning before the clients arrive.'

The passage was also carpeted, although in a darker, more subdued colour. The walls were a pale duck-egg blue.

'When *le Maître* is working, he does not care for any noise,' Jules explained informatively. He knocked on a door and, without waiting for a reply, opened it and said, 'I have brought Mademoiselle Alice Pritchett to . . .'

'Go away, Jules. Can't you see I'm busy? No, leave the girl here. And don't slam the door.'

Alice could see only the back view of Monsieur Verveine as he stood by the window, his head bent over a bolt of material. He did not sound as if he were in a very good mood and her nervousness returned. As he turned to face her, she could not see his eyes behind his spectacles but she could feel his gaze penetrating her.

'You brought the blouse?'

'Yes, Monsieur.'

'Put it on the table. Madame Duvalle is not here yet, more is the pity. I badly need her advice. However, since *you* are here, let's see what you can make of this.'

He turned and went to the large table, which was covered with sheets of stiff paper, pencils, paints, pastels of different colours. He shuffled among the drawings and pulled one out.

'See this miserable creation? It is no good. It is without inspiration. It is *exécrable*!' Frowning angrily, he tore it in half, threw the pieces on the floor and, sitting down at the table, hit his forehead with the palm of his hand. 'What can one do, I ask you? Imagine you have here in this room a very important client – very important indeed. Imagine that she is demanding a gown which will make her look twenty years younger and twice as feminine. Imagine also that she has figure like this . . .' he outlined a caricature of a female shape on a fresh piece of paper, 'a face like an orange that has wrinkled with age, and a complexion to match. And,' he said in an agonized voice, 'she insists *absolument* on having that fabric.' He stormed back to the window and picked up the bolt of cloth he had been looking at when Alice came in.

Alice could now see the problem with which her employer was faced. The beautiful violet material was patterned with peacock-blue and amber-coloured feathers, intricately interwoven with a trellis design of gold ivy leaves. It could only be very ageing against an orange skin colour.

'Monsieur, perhaps if you were to take this colour . . .' she pointed to one of the feathers in the material, 'and place round the neck here a soft peacock-blue tulle ruffle which tones? You could repeat it on the skirt here, perhaps, and here . . .'

'I cannot see it against your frock. Here, take this.' He

226

pushed the piece of paper on which he had outlined his client's shape, and a box full of coloured pastels towards her. 'Draw what you see in your head.'

'But sir, I cannot draw. I have never learned and I . . .'

'Never mind. It is simply the idea I wish to understand.'

Monsieur Verveine's voice had become high-pitched with impatience. Reluctantly, Alice took up one of the pastels and stared at the sheet of paper, trying to imagine the wrinkled, ageing client. Suddenly the woman's image came into her head and, forgetting where she was and in whose presence, she allowed her hand to move quickly over the page. Before she had completed the picture that was in her mind, Monsieur Verveine pulled it away from her.

'*Exécrable*, but *exécrable*!' he exclaimed. 'Why are you not taught to draw in your English schools? It is the same here in France. However, I shall not complain. You have made me see how it should be done . . . like this . . . and this . . .'

With a few simple strokes, he modified Alice's drawing and the gown came to life beneath his hands. His scowl disappeared and, as the door opened, he beamed at the tall, angular, grey-haired woman who came in.

'Come here, Madame Duvalle, and look at this? It is good, *hein*? You must send Jules immediately to find tulle this colour – six metres, I think. If he cannot match it exactly, then he is to choose a darker, not a paler tone.' He walked over to the window, picked up the bolt of cloth and thrust it into the woman's hands. 'You will give him a sample, of course, and he is to bring the tulle back here immediately. Meanwhile, I shall create. Send Denise to me as soon as I am free. I will use her as *mannequin*. So, Madame Duvalle, at long last, the problem is solved – and largely due to this young woman.'

Madame Duvalle turned and stared at Alice. Her eyes were steely and her expression anything but welcoming. She looked questioningly at her employer.

'I applaud your design, Monsieur, and I am sure *la Duchesse* will approve, but I do not entirely understand . . .'

'But you will, *chère Madame*, you will,' Monsieur

Verveine said, beaming. Waving his hands and gesticulating in a typically French manner, he broke into his own language. Occasionally he pointed to the sketch, then to Alice and then ordered her to give him the blouse which she had brought with her, wrapped carefully in brown paper. Tearing the paper away, he pushed it into the woman's hands, talking as he did so. When finally he fell silent, he looked to his *directrice* as if awaiting her comment.

Alice saw that her thin mouth had tightened, and, limited though her understanding of the language was, she was in no doubt that Madame Duvalle's reply to whatever Monsieur Verveine was proposing was in the negative. His response was to bang the box of pastels down on his desk, his face red with anger. The woman shook her head, her lips now pressed together in a line as stubborn as the stiffness of her body. There was more shouting from Monsieur Verveine and then he suddenly held out both hands in a gesture of resignation. Madame Duvalle's face softened almost to a smile of satisfaction and with several little bows, she said: *'Oui, Monsieur, je comprends. Oui, Monsieur, certainement!'* following which she left the room without a second glance at Alice.

'Nom de Dieu!' Monsieur Verveine expostulated as the door closed behind her. 'Why do I tolerate such a monster?' Noticing Alice, his face broke into an apologetic smile. 'You must not take everything I say seriously, Mademoiselle. Madame is quite expert in all she undertakes. I value her opinion as I do no one else's. It is simply that I become irritated when she points out to me that I am in the wrong.'

His smile widened, the small cleft in his left cheek once more immediately noticeable. 'It is like a battle between us,' he continued. 'She attacks, I defend; she gives a little, I make concessions and the armistice is signed. In this instance, my dear child, the battle was over your future here at the Maison de Verveine. I will tell you presently what we have agreed, but first I wish to ask you some questions. How old are you?'

'Twenty, sir. I shall soon be twenty-one,' Alice said.

'Ah, yes, my wife told me. You are not affianced, Alice? No suitors?'

'I am not engaged to be married. I do . . . I did have a suitor – Sir Philip's footman – but I have made it quite clear to him that I don't wish to be married – to him, or indeed to anyone else.'

Monsieur's bushy eyebrows shot up. 'So, your heart is still your own. But will it remain so?'

'Sir, I have no wish to be a wife or a mother. I wish to be a dressmaker. I expect you will consider me very silly to say this, but I wish one day to be like you. I would like to have my own *maison de couture*.'

Alice had expected laughter, but it was not forth-coming. Monsieur Verveine was leaning back in his chair. He had removed his spectacles and was regarding her thoughtfully.

'If one is to reach for a star, it should be for the brightest star in the sky. Believe me, Mademoiselle, no one achieves success unless they are utterly determined upon it. In this business, you are at no disadvantage being a woman. You are probably aware that there are many successful men – Poiret, Worth, Doucet, Paquin, Molyneaux, Patou. However, there are equally famous women *couturières*, such as Jeanne Lanvin, Madelaine Vionnet, for example, and I have heard there is a certain Gabrielle Chanel who has made quite a name for herself in Deauville – a remarkable lady with some very strange ideas. She has had some success in America and will doubtless do well here in France. We shall see.'

He gave a deep sigh.

'However, we speak of your star, Alice,' he continued, 'which is so far away that for many years to come it can be for you no more than a glimmer in the sky. That is not to say you should lose sight of it. In one respect, you are fortunate. I tell you that it is my opinion – and Madame Duvalle could not deny it – that you have talent. After much fighting, she has agreed finally that you would be wasted as an *arpette* or indeed as one of our embroiderers.

You have the figure and style for a *mannequin* but this, too, would be a waste if my instinct is right. If it is, Mademoiselle Alice Pritchett, and if you are prepared to devote yourself absolutely to learning, it is not beyond the realms of possibility that you might one day become my assistant. However . . .'

Pretending not to hear Alice's gasp of amazement, he leaned back in his chair and, pulling a writing-pad towards him, he began to make notes.

'Number one . . .' he said solemnly, 'you will work in the sewing-room with the *arpettes* for as long as Madame Duvalle thinks appropriate. You will then learn everything that is possible in the cutting-room. You will also go to night classes and learn to draw. I shall pay for your lessons. You will learn from Jules the techniques of matching trimmings to fabrics; you will learn to recognize and understand the qualities of every fabric that exists. You will learn how to be a good *vendeuse*: how you should behave with clients and how to get the best from the members of staff who work with or for you. In short, child, you will do little else for a long time but learn, learn, learn, as once I had to do. Without all this knowledge you will never even touch your star, let alone grasp it. Do you understand what I am saying?'

Speechless, Alice nodded. 'I will do anything at all – everything you tell me,' she whispered.

'Oh, no, *mon enfant*, you will not be taking orders from me. You will have "the dragon" for your teacher – and none better, I promise you. But she will be a hard taskmaster. I do not for one moment doubt that you will often go to your bed in tears. I shall be surprised if you do not many times lose heart. Almost certainly you will be tempted to go back to your own country – to abandon your dreams. It is for you alone to decide what is to be the pinnacle of your achievements. And that brings me to one last point, Mademoiselle. You will try to master the French language.'

He leant forward and gave a sudden unexpected smile. As if they were conspirators, he said, 'I will let you into a secret. Madame Duvalle – a courtesy title since she is unmarried – does in point of fact speak excellent English, but I do not think she will reveal this to you. Until you can comprehend the correct words for the tools of this trade, you will have to make guesses – and that can lead to mistakes, for which she will allow you small mercy. But do not allow her to intimidate you. Now, you may go and report to her. She is expecting you, but first, have I your permission to keep this?'

He held up Alice's Russian blouse.

'I shall copy it for my new collection. You may tell Madame that you have my permission to choose any frock that takes your fancy from those of last year's models still in the stockroom. I think that will be fair compensation, yes?'

Pink-cheeked with pleasure, she backed out of the room. A frock designed and made in the Maison de Verveine would be very much more than adequate compensation, she thought. The trouble was, how did she relay Monsieur Verveine's permission to Madame Duvalle in French when she could barely say more than 'please' and 'thank you'? Monsieur had made it clear that she was to appear ignorant of the fact that his *directrice* spoke English. She would have to ask the nice young man, Jules Bellaire, to translate for her, she thought, grateful that she had at least one friend in this awesomely magnificent establishment where she was now to start work.

By the time her interview with her employer ended, Jules Bellaire had returned with the tulle Monsieur Verveine required, and he was detailed by the unsmiling Madame Duvalle to take Alice on a conducted tour of the premises. Despite the imposing façade of the Maison de Verveine, Alice had no inkling as to the size of the building, which was on four floors. At the back of the establishment in one long room, countless women and girls sat side by side at their sewing-machines. The light seeping through the small windows was poor and the room, bare of carpet, was cold and noisy with the whirring of the machines. No one looked up from their work to glance at the visitors, and at the far end of the room, Alice saw a woman in a dark-coloured dress walking up and down the rows of work tables making sure that the machinists were not pausing to talk or take an unauthorized rest.

She was not greatly cheered by the slight improvement in the atmosphere in the adjoining room, where eight women sat round several large frames sewing tiny jet beads and sequins on to the panels of the skirt of a taffeta ballgown.

Sensing Alice's dismay, Jules shrugged as he led her to the cutting-room, where two men as well as a number of women were cutting into the lengths of beautiful silk, velvet, tweed, satin, taffeta and other costly fabrics, seemingly with as much care as they might have used to cut old newspapers. Jules took her next to the *cabine des mannequins*, where several very beautiful girls were busy making up their faces. The fact that they were in a state of semi-undress did not seem to trouble them as Jules called out a greeting.

One, a tall brunette with huge, dark eyes and a honey-coloured skin, called out to Jules, '*Viens, mon petit! Viens t'assoir!*'

She patted her lap invitingly as if the young man were a child.

'Another time, Simone,' he replied without embarrassment. As they left the room, he said to Alice, 'I will introduce you on another occasion. I think that too many names will be a confusion for you this morning. Here now is the room for retiring for the *vendeuses*.'

Like the workrooms, it had none of the luxury of the rooms Alice had seen downstairs. There, the beautiful colours and furnishings were clearly for the benefit of the clients, who, Jules now informed her, were some of the most prestigious ladies in Paris. Indeed, he said, the ladies came also from all the big cities in Europe to be dressed by Monsieur Verveine.

Desperately Alice tried to memorize the other rooms she was shown – for the telephonists; for the packers, who were surrounded by great piles of new dress-size, cardboard boxes and high stacks of pristine white tissue paper; the fitting-rooms – ten in all; the offices of the business manager, the secretarial staff, the stock-keeper. She lost count of the number of people who in passing Jules identified for her – the receptionist, the canteen manageress and cooks, the cleaning women, a day watchman, the carriage attendant, a delivery man.

'The Maison employs nearly 400 people,' Jules told her as he took her finally to the stockroom. 'This is a big and important establishment, no?'

It was beyond anything she had ever imagined, Alice thought. Lady Debrace had spoken of the beautiful *salon* which she had often visited before the war, but she had not spoken of all that went on behind the scenes. Possibly she had never seen how many people were employed to produce her coats and gowns and suits. All she had told Alice was that there was none superior to her brother-in-law's couture house in Paris.

'For Monsieur Verveine, it has always to be the best,' she had said with a smile. 'It is his nature.'

Although Alice's mind was in a daze, remembering Lady Debrace's words as Jules took her down to the canteen for lunch, some of her earlier euphoria returned. Undoubtedly it was true that her star now seemed a very, very long way away, but *le Maître* himself had said it was within her grasp. If he believed in her, then she had no reason to doubt herself. She had worked all her life and now she would work even harder if, ultimately, it led to her goal.

CHAPTER THIRTEEN

1920

'You really look very pretty when you smile, Alice,' Jules said, as he scooped another mouthful of whipped cream from the top of his tall glass of hot chocolate and put it into his mouth. 'It makes the difference, you understand, between *belle* and *laide*!'

After a year in Paris speaking little else but French, Alice had no difficulty in understanding him. Her smile broadened.

'You would scowl the way I do if you had Madame Duvalle breathing down your neck all day long,' she countered as she sipped her *café au lait*.

Jules stopped a passing waitress and ordered a second *mille feuille*. He had an insatiable appetite for anything sweet and he spent a large proportion of his wages indulging himself. He did not try to persuade Alice to allow him to treat her to similar luxuries, for he knew that she was watching her figure lest she put on too much weight.

He had become her best friend, she thought, as she regarded him across the table. Every other Sunday after attending Mass, he took her to see one of the famous landmarks – Notre-Dame, the palaces of Versailles and Fontainebleau, the house of Victor Hugo, the Louvre and the many museums of modern art. Today he had chosen to take her to the top of the Eiffel Tower so that she could see Paris from almost 1,000 feet up. On every outing, he insisted upon paying her entrance fee, explaining that, unlike herself, he was not dependent solely upon his wages; that he had a rich friend who was very generous towards him.

It was fortunate, Alice reflected, that by the time he first mentioned his rich friend, Madame Verveine had informed her that as a young boy living in the slums of Paris, Jules had been adopted by an actor of some repute, who had taken him under his wing.

'Jules was in many ways fortunate,' she elaborated. 'The actor was a man of good family and he taught Jules to speak well and to behave very differently from the way he had been raised. Jules's real name is Albert Grolle, but not liking the surname, meaning "jackdaw", he invented a new one, and a less ordinary Christian name to go with it. In time he developed a liking for beautiful clothes and applied to my husband for a job as a messenger boy. That was nearly eight years ago. Jules is quite a character and the clients find him amusing.'

It was, Alice realized, the first time she had ever had a man for a friend. She had never been able to talk with such ease or intimacy with poor Frederick! To some degree she had shared her thoughts and feelings with Harry, but because of his youth, she could never bring herself to hurt or worry him and she had kept from him her own personal concerns. The only time she had spoken out was during those last few weeks, when it had become clear to her that he was hopelessly in love with Miss Madeleine. Although he was only fifteen and a half, she realized that his youth did not lessen the intensity of his feelings. As for Miss Madeleine, she appeared to encourage him, perhaps without realizing how provocative she could be.

Alice had waited until he returned to school before writing to warn him that he could only bring unhappiness down upon his head by nurturing such dreams of the Debraces' daughter; that Lady Debrace was concerned, and had determined to try to keep them apart. Harry had not replied to that letter and Alice had no way of knowing whether he had taken her advice. His letters to her, only intermittent now, were full of his new school activities, of the problems and the small triumphs.

Alice never failed to write to him every week, despite the fact that she seemed to be permanently tired. Not only did Madame Duvalle ensure that she worked every bit as hard as the other girls, but she had the language difficulty to contend with, as well as a certain amount of antipathy from her fellow workers. They were conscious of the fact that she was 'different'; that she was to be with them only for a short while before being moved on to another workroom. They considered her *supérieure* because, so Jules explained, she had a ladylike manner and came from a higher class than themselves.

'It simply isn't true,' Alice had told Jules. 'My father is a gardener. It's just that since the age of thirteen, I grew up in the household of the gentry and I suppose it was natural to copy their ways.'

When the long workday ended, Alice had written in one of her letters to Harry, if she was not attending French lessons, then she was going to evening art classes. On Sunday – supposedly a day of rest – she often had homework to do for her teachers.

This Sunday, however, she had completed her French essay by lunchtime and was free to accompany Jules to the Eiffel Tower and afterwards to tea.

'Tell me,' he said now, 'is Madame Verveine quite well? She came to *la Maison* yesterday and I had the impression she was – how shall I put it – not quite herself.'

Alice nodded. It was she who had been instructed yesterday by Madame Duvalle to escort Madame Verveine home in a taxi cab. The unfortunate woman had had so much to drink, she was barely able to stand upright. Alice had called Hortense, her maid, who had put her to bed. It was by no means the first time, but such occasions were never spoken about by the household staff. Although Madame Verveine had treated her with a cool reserve throughout this past year, she had nevertheless been kind enough when the occasion had arisen. Sometimes she would call for Alice to make a small alteration to a dress or stitch a new veil on a hat. Afterwards she would reward Alice with a few francs, insisting that she take this little *pourboire* since she was not her employer. The money Alice thus saved enabled her to buy the French history and art books she wanted. Fortunately, Monsieur Verveine paid for all the drawing materials she needed, as she could not have purchased these from her token wages.

Now she hesitated before replying to Jules's question. She knew that to some extent the Maison Verveine was his life and that he was looked upon by *le Maître* as one whose loyalty to the establishment was absolute; nevertheless, she was unsure whether Jules's discretion could be relied upon outside the premises. On the other hand, she was herself concerned about Madame Verveine. On two occasions when Alice had had to take down a dress from her wardrobe, she had found empty bottles of cognac tucked in the back.

'I think Madame Verveine perhaps drinks a little too much,' she said carefully.

Jules did not look surprised.

'Oh, that is nothing new,' he said. 'Early last year, before you arrived, Alice, she was in a nursing-home for several weeks, and I happen to know that this place is where people who need to be cured of the habit go. I fear Madame must have started drinking again. It is very sad.'

'But why?' Alice asked. 'She has everything – an affectionate husband, two lovely homes, money, beautiful clothes . . .'

Jules shrugged.

'Nevertheless, I have heard it said that she fell in love with an American – a major in the army who came to Paris during the war. Soon after the armistice was signed, he returned to his own country. Perhaps this was why Madame became "ill". *Le Maître* must have known about it – we all did, because at the time she was always buying new clothes in those days and her lover would help her to choose them. For whatever reason, Monsieur pretended ignorance. Maybe this was wise. Who can tell? Madame has no children, so it is possible she is sometimes lonely. As you know, Monsieur is dedicated to *la Maison* and spends much of his time there.'

'I don't see how he could do otherwise,' Alice argued in

her employer's defence. 'There are so many things which only he can do.'

'Madame has no interest in the affairs of *la Maison* – except to buy clothes. It is not surprising to me that she took a lover.'

Alice tried not to feel shocked. This year in Paris had opened her eyes to a world quite different from the one she had known in Calking. In the canteen, when Madame Duvalle and the supervisors were absent, the *mannequins* gossiped. Such and such a lady had been in the salon this morning with her new lover. Monsieur Lachoix had called in to order two more frocks for his mistress. A famous actress, known to have a royal protector, had this morning been fitted for a complete summer wardrobe for a holiday in Biarritz. It was as if either the war had swept away the strict moral conventions of the past, or these hugely rich people ignored them, Alice told herself.

Although in some ways Jules's story of Madame Verveine's American lover was a sad one and Alice pitied the woman, she also felt sorry for her husband. At home, Monsieur was invariably kind and attentive to his wife on the few occasions Alice saw them together. Madame on the other hand, though too well bred to be overtly rude, was often very sharp and critical towards him, or else behaved as if he were not there. On several occasions, Monsieur Verveine had sent Alice out to buy his wife some little surprise – flowers, a box of initialled handkerchiefs, a new English novel, a box of handmade chocolates. Madame received these gifts with a studied indifference which must have caused her husband pain.

'I shall have to go in a minute, Jules,' Alice said. 'Monsieur Verveine has asked me to show him my portfolio at half past five. I am very nervous.'

Jules put an arm affectionately round her shoulders.

'Believe me, Alice, you have no need. I have seen some of your designs, remember? They are exquisite.'

Alice smiled.

'You say that to give me confidence. You are a good friend, Jules, and I love you very much.'

'So we shall be married next spring when the chestnut trees are in bloom, yes?'

It was a standing joke between them, for each knew perfectly well that their relationship was affectionate and no more.

'I will ask Monsieur this evening to design me a wedding dress,' she said, laughing as she stood up. 'Thank you for my tea, Jules. Really, you should not waste your money on me.'

He too stood up, at least a head shorter than herself.

'There is no one else on whom to waste it,' he said simply. 'Besides, Alice, I believe the day will come when you will be a *grande couturière* and I shall remind you of our friendship, so you will feel obliged to give me an excellent position in your magnificent establishment.'

'Who knows but you will have a couture house of your own by then,' Alice rejoined with a smile.

'Ah, but that I would not wish. The work, yes; but the responsibility, no! I shall be your *aide-de-camp*, your Madame Duvalle.'

'Heaven forbid,' Alice laughed. 'I have had quite enough of dragons breathing fire all over me to last a lifetime.'

Half an hour later, with her hair newly tidied and wearing one of her simple afternoon dresses, Alice knocked on the door of Monsieur Verveine's office in the house in the rue de Sèze. He was, as usual, sitting at his desk, but he appeared not to be working.

'Come in, come in,' he said affably. 'You may sit down, Alice. I sent Denise to find you a short while ago, but she said you were out.'

'Yes, Monsieur. I went to the Eiffel Tower with Jules.'

Monsieur Verveine seemed to find this amusing.

'Ah, so that young man has an eye for the future,' he remarked with a smile. 'Perhaps he foresees the day when Madame Duvalle is obliged to retire and you, my dear young lady, take her place? A very shrewd customer is Jules – but that is not a bad thing. He is particularly good with our middle-aged ladies – knows just how to flatter them. They will permit him to be a little outrageous because they know he has *les motifs non sexuels*! You understand me?'

Alice nodded, uncertain how she was expected to reply to such a comment.

'Jules is clever and I like him,' Monsieur Verveine continued. 'He is also very astute with money. I may promote him soon to assist my business manager. However, it is not his future you are here to discuss; it is your own. Pass me your portfolio.'

His face was expressionless as he glanced through the sheets of drawing paper. Very occasionally he made a comment: 'Ah, I see you are at last learning to draw the human figure'; 'Good, your art teacher has been showing you how to exaggerate the length of the neck . . .' He gave a sudden impish smile. 'Of course, none of my clients will ever look quite as beautiful as I make them appear in my drawings, but a long neck, a delicate curve to the shoulder, a graceful posture of the head – all will enhance the initial reaction to a design.'

He came to the end of the sketches and peered closely at Alice.

'No designs, then, of dresses? Suits? Coats? Accessories? You have not lost your interest, I hope?'

'Oh, no, Monsieur – far from it. But Monsieur Grison will not let me paint until my drawing is of a higher standard. He says I must learn to walk before I run.'

'I see! Well, perhaps he is right. Nevertheless, I had hoped . . .'

'Monsieur, my teacher is unaware of it because I was afraid he might be angry, but once or twice in the evenings I have . . . well, I have been tempted to try a few designs . . . Only a few, Monsieur . . .'

Monsieur Verveine did not look angry. On the contrary, he seemed to be amused, and, as always when he smiled, Alice was aware of that special charm which had struck her the day she had first met him.

It was not something she had imagined, she now knew, for half Monsieur's fashionable clients were in love with him. Which was to say, they openly flirted with him in the salon, fluttering their eyelashes and waving their hands in the French fashion as they pretended to dismiss his extravagant flattery. Those who were aware that he had inherited his father's title frequently invited him to their homes and, according to Jules, if they were pretty, as many were, he accepted the invitations. If not, he would excuse himself on the grounds of his wife's ill health.

He was regarding Alice now with a look of amusement in his grey eyes – a look which bordered on the mischievous.

'Very well, you may go and fetch the designs to show me. I promise I will not tell Monsieur Grison about your transgressions.' As Alice hurried, pink-cheeked, out of the room and upstairs to fetch her drawings, Félix Verveine leant back in his chair, his face suddenly thoughtful.

Was he wrong, he asked himself, to be setting such store by this girl? She was very young, very inexperienced in spite of the intensive course of training Madame Duvalle had been giving her. What instinct prompted him to feel that Mademoiselle Alice Pritchett was somehow destined for great things? Was it not, perhaps, a matter of wishful thinking? Would he have been as interested in her that very first day if he had not found her so unusually attractive? He saw many lovely women every day of the week, beautifully groomed, sophisticated, many of them prominent in society. This young English girl could not have been more different, and yet there was something about her which intrigued him – a calm? an inner strength? Certainly, a total innocence – and above all, she had talent.

In the past, he thought as he awaited her return, he had always been attracted by the dark-haired, Latin colouring in a woman. Although he had had many mistresses, Rosamund had been the first blonde he had desired – sufficiently so to want to marry her. He had never doubted on his wedding day that Rosamund and he were perfectly suited. How wrong he had been! She had never responded to his ardent love-making and after only a few years of marriage, he had found himself a new mistress.

In those days he had still hoped that they would have children who might turn their otherwise sterile marriage into a united family. It was certainly not poor Rosamund's fault that she had had a series of miscarriages, followed by the birth of a stillborn child, after which she had refused ever to try again. She had become deeply depressed, and despite the care of the best doctor and specialist who had attended her, she had turned to alcohol to dull her depression. Fortunately, they had eventually been able to overcome the post-natal depression and with it her need for drink.

Their marriage had settled into a new relationship where it was tacitly understood that he no longer expected her to fulfil any of the more intimate wifely duties. They entertained at the Château de St Denis in the town of Meaux, where Rosamund often stayed on after a weekend to enjoy the horse-riding that was her main pleasure. Although the château had remained untouched during the fighting, there had been major battles around the River Marne, on which the town was situated, and the château had been commandeered for Brigade Headquarters. It was now in the process of being restored.

Félix himself had always been and was still totally engrossed with the expansion of his business in Paris, which had risen to become equal to any of the existing world-famous couture houses. He had no regular mistress but very occasionally he would visit Lisette, one of his *mannequins* who was prepared to accommodate him. His heart was not involved, nor even did he find the girl particularly appealing, but she served her purpose and was adequately rewarded. He was forty-one years old and he doubted very much whether any woman would hold him in thrall again.

Then Alice had arrived from England – quaint, shy, nervous. The following morning in his office he had glimpsed the fire behind her quiet subservient manner; become aware of her as a female. It had not been easy to hide his excitement when he had planned her future. He wondered if that astute old woman Madame Duvalle, who knew him better than anyone else in the world, had sensed his underlying reason for wishing to give this untried English girl an opportunity to reach untold heights in the fashion business. Perhaps then, a year ago, he had not known himself why he had been motivated to argue so fiercely with the old dragon on Alice's behalf. Now, twelve months later, he could no longer doubt that his interest in her lay not only in her talent – which continued to show itself – but in the girl herself.

Suddenly apprehensive lest he had been exaggerating her abilities, he hesitated before studying the drawings Alice now gave him. With a sigh of relief, he realized that, far from being a disappointment, they exceeded his hopes. The girl had not only drawn her designs in simple, clear lines but she had named the materials and colours she considered appropriate and had, in addition, made smaller sketches magnifying the design for any embroidery or trimming used in her master drawing. He felt a warm glow of satisfaction, mingled with a certain amount of pride in his own judgement. Nevertheless, he thought, it might be detrimental to Alice's training if he were to praise her too fulsomely.

'These are good – very good,' he said quietly. 'However, there is much room for improvement, as no doubt you are aware. And by the way, you have spelt crêpe de Chine incorrectly. The word has an "e" with a circumflex accent over it, not an "a".'

He wished he had not been quite so disparaging as the colour flooded into Alice's cheeks and her expression changed from excitement to shame.

'Come now, *ma petite*, this is not important,' he said quickly. 'I do not expect you to have perfected your French in one year. Your accent is now excellent and I think I would be correct in saying you understand everything that is said to you without difficulty.'

'Yes, Monsieur,' Alice said. 'I will try to improve my spelling.'

Félix stood up and, walking round his desk, laid his hand on one of her shoulders.

'If it is of encouragement to you, Alice, I will tell you that I see your star shining more brightly than when I last spoke of it. That means it is nearer to your grasp.'

As she turned her head to look up at him, he smiled.

'You are happier now?' he asked softly.

Alice nodded.

'You are very kind, Monsieur,' she said. 'Please don't think that I'm unappreciative of the opportunities you are giving me.'

Reluctantly, Félix removed his hand. He walked across to the window and stood in silence for a moment, his back turned towards her. When he spoke it was to say, 'Living in this house as you do, Alice, it cannot have escaped your notice that Madame Verveine is . . . is from time to time not . . . not very well. I have arranged for her to go into a nursing-home for a few weeks. Afterwards I shall engage a nurse to accompany her to Meaux. My wife will need to convalesce and she is happiest in the country. Fortunately, the restoration of our château is progressing well, so Madame Verveine will be able to stay there in comfort.'

As her employer's statement did not call for a reply, Alice remained silent. He turned now to face her.

'There is something I wish you to do for me,' he said. 'I have arranged a dinner party here at this house next Wednesday. It is for business purposes and I do not wish to cancel it – indeed, I cannot do so, as two of my guests are Americans and have come especially to Paris at my invitation. I could, of course, take them to a restaurant, but I wish the atmosphere to be very informal, and restaurants are not ideal venues for relaxed discussion. As Madame will then be in the nursing-home, I would like you to act as my hostess.'

Alice's eyes widened in disbelief.

'But Monsieur, I wouldn't know what to do . . .'

The seriousness of his expression gave way to a smile and Alice was suddenly conscious of the mesmeric charm her employer could exert by so simple a means. She had seen him smile in similar fashion at an irate client who was complaining that her frock had been made up in the wrong colour; at a *mannequin* whom he had criticized to the point of tears. His smile could reduce the importance, the urgency, the unpleasant aspect of a matter by implication that it was all of no great consequence; that life was too short not to be enjoying it and that all he wanted was for everyone to be as happy, as amused, as himself. Jules had once commented that Monsieur was not unlike the French vaudeville singer, Maurice Chevalier, whom he had seen before the war at the *Folies-Bergère*, although Monsieur was much older of course.

His voice was not unlike the singer's either, Alice thought, especially when he spoke to her in heavily accented English, as he was now doing.

'I would not ask you to do anything of which I did not believe you capable, Alice,' he was saying. 'Two things only are important – that you make my guests feel at ease, and that you speak with enthusiasm for any idea I may be promoting.' His smile broadened. 'Otherwise you need only look charming – and for this purpose, you may ask Madame Duvalle to select a suitable dinner gown from my new collection, together with the appropriate accessories, which you may borrow for the occasion. The servants here are well enough trained. They will ensure the mechanics of the meal will be performed smoothly and I shall arrange the menu. As a young girl, you will not need elaborate jewellery. I shall introduce you as my assistant.'

Alice's every instinct demanded that she protest, but she stayed silent, conscious of the fact that she was deeply indebted to this man for all his many kindnesses to her. To refuse would seem churlish, yet her whole being rebelled against the prospect of having to entertain *le Maître*'s important guests. Surely he could not expect her, plain Alice Pritchett, former lady's maid, to officiate at his dinner table as if she were his social equal? It was, despite her misgivings, immensely flattering to be thought capable.

'I have my reasons for selecting you for this task,' Félix

said gently. 'You have one very important asset – you speak perfect English. It is not often Americans speak French, particularly the women. You will be able to converse with them in their own language while we four men discuss our business after dinner. So it is agreed, yes?'

'I would like to be of assistance, Monsieur, but I don't think I'm qualified . . . that is to say, that I *could* do as you ask,' she murmured.

Ignoring her protest, Félix returned to his desk. His smile had vanished and he replaced his spectacles as he sat down in the big leather chair.

'I am sure you are to be trusted with some very private information,' he said thoughtfully. 'Naturally I do not wish the staff at *la Maison* to know my plans until I am certain they will come to fruition, but you should know that it is my wish to open a *succursale* of Maison Verveine in New York. On Wednesday I hope to reach an understanding with the American gentleman who will be backing this new venture.' His face relaxed suddenly into a smile. 'In truth, I do not think Meester Garfield is much interested in clothes, but his wife is an enthusiastic client of mine. I have been dressing her for the past five years. Her husband is a dollar millionaire and is thus able to indulge his wife's every whim. It is she who is so anxious to have a branch of our couture house on her doorstep.'

'I hope you will be successful in your efforts, Monsieur,' Alice said genuinely. 'I would really like to assist you on Wednesday, but . . .'

'No "buts", my dear child,' Félix broke in. 'I will not permit you to refuse. Believe me, Alice, I know what I am doing and I have every confidence in you.'

If only she had a similar confidence in herself, Alice thought, when finally her employer dismissed her. It was not that she was unaware of how private dinner parties were conducted, for she had more or less grown up in a house where such occasions were too frequent to be notable. She was perfectly well aware how the table would be laid and which cutlery was used for which course, which glass for which wine. It was a question of how she should converse with the guests as if she were one of them. At least, she consoled herself, she would be using her own language. There was, too, the confidence it would give her to be wearing one of Monsieur's incredibly chic dinner gowns, any one of which would have cost a client as much as her father's yearly wage. She had had to spend several weeks with Monsieur's business manager learning, among other things, how expensive the fabrics were which were used to make Monsieur's masterpieces.

To Alice's astonishment, it was 'the dragon' who finally gave her the confidence to play the role Monsieur Verveine had allotted her. Madame Duvalle spent over an hour in the stockroom supervising Alice's dress for the occasion. For once her expression was not forbidding and almost bordered on the maternal as Alice struggled in and out of a variety of dinner gowns and paraded for Madame's inspection. Something seemed to be wrong with each one – it was too old, too fussy, the wrong colour for Alice's pale complexion, too tight across the bosom.

'It is important you should do Monsieur the utmost possible credit,' she said finally before at last approving the gown Alice was wearing. And Madame was right, Alice thought, as she gazed at her reflection in the long mirror. The dress was a deep heather pink georgette over a paler pink silk underslip. It had been beautifully embroidered with silver thread from the boat-shaped neckline down to the lower hip. The long wing panels, hanging from the shoulder to the hemline, were without embroidery but the silver floral design had been repeated on the underslip, where the skirt had been slit from hem to waist at either side.

'It might have been designed especially for you, Alice,' Madame said with a rare warmth in her voice. 'Now we must consider the shoes and then the hair – it is good you have not had yours cut. I think with this gown it should be dressed in soft waves, falling a little over your forehead to the right, and gathered at the back into a chignon. I will ask Amélie to arrange it for you on Wednesday morning – she is clever with the hair. You will look very elegant and I am sure Monsieur will be happy with our choice. This dress is one of his newest designs and he will wish the American ladies to remark upon it. *Alors, mon enfant, bonne chance!*'

Félix was not only pleased but also totally captivated when, on Wednesday evening, Alice descended the front staircase half an hour before the guests were due to arrive.

'You look charming, my dear,' he said, his voice warm with approval. It was quite remarkable, he thought as he took her elbow and led her into the big salon, how often this English girl exceeded his expectations. Looking at the tall, slender figure in a dress which he might indeed have designed especially for her, she was indistinguishable from any other society lady. She was not only beautiful but perfectly poised. But for the slight trembling of her arm beneath his grasp, she gave no sign of nervousness.

'You must trust me, Alice,' he said softly. 'I will never demand that you do something of which you are incapable. I shall feel proud this evening to have such a beautiful and charming hostess.'

'You are very kind, Monsieur Verveine,' Alice said.

'No, no, my dear, tonight when you address me, you must remember to call me Félix. Remember, you are my assistant, my protégée. If the subject arises, you may infer you have connections with the Debrace family. Speak of them as if this were true. Americans are not particularly snobbish but you are a little young to be acting as my hostess, or indeed to be my assistant, so it would be quite understandable if we have family connections. I wish to protect your reputation.'

He rang the bell and one of the footmen came in with three silver cocktail shakers on a tray.

'This is for the benefit of my guests,' Félix said with a smile. 'The shakers contain cocktails called a Martini, a Manhattan and a Bronx. They contain respectively gin with dry vermouth, Bourbon whiskey with sweet vermouth, and gin with vermouth and orange juice. Personally, I abhor all three and shall drink wine as usual. What may I offer you, my dear?'

'I will have a little wine too, if I may,' Alice said quickly, knowing that at least she was familiar with this beverage from her canteen lunches. It seemed that all French people drank wine with their meals as the English drank water, and she had become accustomed to it.

Despite Alice's nervousness, the introductions and the meal passed not only without mishap but almost pleasurably. The two American women, as well as the Parisian wife of Monsieur Verveine's banker, were in rhapsodies over her dress.

'A Verveine, of course,' remarked the wife of the New Yorker Félix was hoping to enlist as his backer. 'Now do you see why I'm so crazy about his dresses, honey?' she enquired of her good-natured husband.

'Does your lovely assistant come with the package?' the American had replied gallantly.

Félix smiled. 'I'm afraid not. I have too great a need of Mademoiselle here in Paris. However, I will happily send some of my best *mannequins* to you for your launch, if such is to come about.'

When the ladies repaired to the *salon* while the men remained with their cigars and cognac to discuss the more serious aspects of their business affairs, Alice found herself plied with questions about England. Following Monsieur Verveine's advice, she related a childhood at The Grange as if she had been born Madeleine Debrace. She had heard so much from Miss Madeleine about her life at school that she was able to speak of her boarding-establishment as if she had actually attended it. She was finally able to speak without pretence when she told them she had a brother, Harry, who was younger than herself and at a public school in Dorset.

Tomorrow, she thought, she would write and tell Harry all about this fairy-tale evening and how successfully she had played her part. If she had any doubts about it, they were dispelled by Félix when the last couple had departed.

'You were *magnifique*!' he told her as he conducted her to the foot of the stairs. 'I am more than grateful to you, Alice, and if you are agreeable, I may ask you to perform these duties again as a personal favour. It was not too disagreeable for you?'

'Oh, no, Monsieur, on the contrary, I really enjoyed myself. I hope the evening was a success for you in your business affairs?'

Félix smiled. 'We are to have a meeting with my *avoué* tomorrow to discuss the legalities. If all goes well, there may be a Maison de Verveine in Fifth Avenue,' he concluded.

'I am very pleased for you,' Alice said sincerely. 'Goodnight, Monsieur. And thank you again for inviting me.'

As he gazed after her, Félix Verveine's heart twisted with longing. More than anything in the world he wished he were following Alice up the staircase to her bedroom. He could not recall a time when he had more urgently desired a woman. Tonight he had not seen Alice as a paid employee but as an equal. It was doubtful a girl such as Alice would consent to become his mistress, he told himself, but the possibility remained, however slight, and he determined to continue with her education the way he had already started.

Upstairs, in her cold attic bedroom, Alice hung the beautiful Verveine gown carefully on a hanger, wondering whether she would ever have the chance to wear such a fairy-tale garment again.

CHAPTER FOURTEEN

1921

Peggy Podmore leant over the back of Harry's chair and ruffled his dark, curly hair, taking care not to disturb the piece of sticking-plaster on his forehead.

'So what has my hero been up to this time? Cricket injury?'

Harry laughed.

'No, silly, it's hockey this term, not cricket. If you want to know, I was in a fight.'

'What, at your age? I thought you considered yourself grown up now.'

Harry stretched out his long legs and grinned.

'So I do, but if you must know, I was saving Sethby Minor – a new boy, to be precise – from one of the school bullies.'

'You were doing *what*?'

Harry paused before replying. He watched the young woman he had just made love to as she crossed the room and picked up a gaudy Chinese silk kimono, with which she covered her naked body. In her mid-thirties, she was well built with an hour-glass figure that might, in later years, run to fat. For the present, she was both voluptuous and sensual. Red-haired, green-eyed, she could have been of Irish extraction but had, in fact, been born in Cornwall. Her voice was pleasantly accented.

At Grafton Abbey Peggy Podmore was known as 'The Grafton Tart', a nickname Harry took care to dispute whenever he heard it. In the first place, she was not a tart, for she never took money from the boys who enjoyed her favours. She accepted presents of chocolates or flowers, but nothing more. Harry had been coming to see her since the end of the summer term and he had grown to like and, quite unexpectedly, to respect her.

'As a matter of fact, one of my fellow prefects, who shall be nameless, was giving Sethby Minor a beating that you could only call sadistic,' he told her. 'Fortunately, I heard the kid yelling his head off as I was on my way past the prefect's study. Naturally, he resented my interference and I was obliged to punch him. He managed to land one here—' Harry touched his forehead, 'before I floored him.'

'What horrible little brutes you schoolboys are,' Peggy said as she came to sit on Harry's knee. 'I suppose I'll have to exempt you. What will happen now? Will the prefect be gated?'

'Of course not. You don't think I'd sneak, do you? Nor will Sethby Minor if he's got any sense. I warned the chap in question not to try it again or I'd give him another punch or two. He knows I've got my boxing colours, so he's not likely to ignore the warning.'

'Good for you, darling,' Peggy said. 'You know, Harry, I'm going to miss you. I hate the thought of you leaving at the end of term. I don't suppose you'll ever come back to Grafton.'

'Yes, I will. There'll be Old Boys' Day for a start, and anyway, you'll have plenty of others to choose from once I've gone.'

'That's not the same,' Peggy said sharply. 'I'm fond of you.'

It was, in fact, an understatement, but she did not intend to enlighten him as to the true extent of her feelings.

'I'm fond of you too,' Harry answered casually. 'I wouldn't be here if I wasn't.'

'That's not true and you know it. You're here for sex, same as all the others.'

Harry looked suddenly thoughtful.

'Perhaps that was true the first time. I was curious – and Aubrey'd told me about you, so naturally I thought it was

252

a good chance to . . . well, to find out what it was all about. To be honest, I hadn't expected to like you, but I did, so that's why I come to see you so often. I couldn't do it if I didn't like you.'

Unexpectedly, Peggy laughed.

'Oh, yes, you could. Lusty young lads of your age can't get enough of it.' Her voice, bordering on the crude, suddenly became wistful. 'I've taught you a few things, haven't I, Harry? One day you'll be grateful – when you get married.'

Harry smiled.

'I'm grateful now, Peg. As to getting married, I'm only eighteen, for goodness' sake! Anyway, I don't see how what *we* do bears any relation to marriage.'

'I don't suppose you do. That's the trouble with your sort – and some of us as well. Naice people' – the mispronunciation was deliberate – 'don't talk about sex, and that's why there are so many married people who wish they weren't. Men just get on top of women and do it – the way you did first time, Harry. They don't know how to give their wives the same pleasure. The wives don't know any better, so it's all one-sided. At least *you'll* know better after all I've taught you.'

Harry stared thoughtfully at Peggy's back as she went to her wardrobe and took a frock off its hanger. He found it disturbing when this young woman spoke so openly about sex and yet, paradoxically, he wanted to see her because she alone could tell him all the things he needed to know. He wished he understood Peggy better. She had never told him why – since it was not for money – she made herself available to the Grafton seniors. On a sudden impulse, he put the question to her.

'Why is it you only have boys here – never men?' he concluded.

Still wearing her kimono, Peggy sat down in the chair opposite him.

'If I tell you why, it's to be our secret, Harry. You understand? I don't have to explain what I do to anyone and I'm only telling you because . . . because I like to

253

think we're sort of friends, which I've certainly not been with any of the others, not even your chum, Debrace.'

'Then I shall consider myself honoured,' Harry said lightly, hoping to ease the tension he could hear in her voice.

'The war's been over so long, it's hard to remember back to the time before it all started,' she said quietly. 'I was in Cornwall then, living with my parents. Mum and Dad ran a bakery and I used to help out in the shop.'

'That explains why you manage The Grafton Tea Shoppe so well,' Harry said. 'You must make quite a good living out of it, Peg.'

'Not so good of late,' Peggy said ruefully. 'There's so many unemployed people now who've not got the money to spend. They say it's over two million out of work.'

'My guardian wrote and told me last week the coal strike's still on and most of the miners are starving. They'll have to go back soon.'

'Reckon they will, poor devils,' Peggy said quietly. 'Anyway, there I was, happy enough living at home and walking out with a boy from the next village. He was apprenticed to a carpenter, so he wasn't earning much and, being quite a bit younger than me, we knew we'd have to wait a few years to get married. We were that in love, it was hard sometimes having to say no to him. He wasn't much older than you but I didn't understand things so well as I did later . . . I didn't realize how hard it must have been for him with me always wanting to kiss and cuddle and all that. Of course, I was a virgin so I'd not had any experience – and nor had he.'

Peggy rose from her chair and walked over to the dressing-table. From the centre drawer, she took out a photograph and handed it to Harry.

'That's him – my John,' she said. 'You can see from that how young he was. Well, that's when war broke out, and he joined up at once. I don't think I've ever felt so bad as I did that day I saw him off at the station. We was both in tears. I was frightened I might never see him again and I think he was scared, too, of what he was going out to. So I made up my mind as I watched his train take him away that on his very first leave we would go the whole hog; that I'd let him do whatever he wanted, and we'd spend every single minute of his leave making love just in case there wasn't a next time.'

Her voice became suddenly bitter.

'He never came back. He was killed in France at Ypres two weeks after he got out there. When I heard, I couldn't think of anything but that he'd died without ever knowing what making love to a woman felt like. I think I went a bit mad and for weeks I wouldn't leave the house. Then suddenly I thought of all the others like him who were going off to war as innocent as he'd been, and I made up my mind I'd do something about it – as a sort of way to make it up to my John. That very day I went up to London and I stood on the platform at Paddington waiting for a troop train to come in. Then I let myself get picked up by the first young soldier who came up to me. He looked young enough not to have had much experience and, when I asked him, he said he'd never had a girl, so I said he could have me if he wanted. I don't even remember what he looked like – only that he was young and that neither of us was too sure how to go about it. It didn't mean much, but sure enough, I felt a whole lot better about John afterwards, so I went on doing it. I took money from the lads in those days – I had to pay the rent of a room and put a bit by in case I ever hit trouble.'

She took the photograph from Harry and replaced it in the drawer. When she came back to him, she looked less distraught.

'I couldn't go home, knowing what Mum and Dad would think about me if they knew. They wouldn't have understood. Anyway, after a year or so, I'd quite a bit of money saved up and by then I was beginning to hate London, and the Zeppelin raids had started and all. I saw this shop advertised, going cheap because of the war, so I came down to Grafton and started serving morning coffee and teas. I wasn't going to go with any more soldiers, but one day one of your boys came in. He looked so like my

John I couldn't take my eyes off him. Then he started flirting with me and, next thing, I told him to come back after I'd shut up the shop – and that's how it's been ever since. He told his friends and I couldn't ever bring myself to say no, seeing as how they were all of an age to leave school and would be going off to the army or navy soon as ever they could.'

'But Peg, the war's over now – it's been over nearly three years.'

'I know. I suppose I do it now for the company. I'll never get married or have kids and there has to be more to life than just serving teas. Does all this change the way you feel about me, Harry?'

'Of course not,' he said, standing up and drawing her into his arms. 'I suppose in a way, I can understand why . . . Well, you don't look like . . . I mean . . .'

'You mean I don't look like your idea of a tart,' Peggy said in her old teasing voice. 'So let that be another lesson to you, young Harry. Things aren't always what they seem, eh? Now it's your turn to tell a few secrets. Why do you always turn red when I ask if you've got a girl who's sweet on you – and don't deny it. Your friend Aubrey, he told me you'd got a crush on his sister.'

Harry grimaced.

'He'd no right to tell tales out of school,' he said. 'Anyway, Madeleine's not "sweet on me", as you put it. She only writes to me once in a blue moon. She's in a Swiss finishing-school, learning French, so I've not seen her for ages. She stays out there every Easter for the skiing.'

'I can tell by your voice she's special,' Peggy said. 'I suppose you'll marry her one of these days when you're a bit older.'

'I doubt it very much. I don't think I really mean much to her. Besides, there are several serious stumbling-blocks.'

'Such as?' Peggy prompted.

'I don't really like talking about it, but . . . Well, you told me about John so I'll tell you my secret . . .' He drew a deep breath and then said flatly, 'I'm illegitimate.'

Peggy shrugged her shoulders.

'You and thousands of others, I imagine, after the war, and I'll bet there's some as won't be branded illegitimate which weren't conceived by their dads. Are you afraid your girl will mind?'

Harry frowned.

'She's led a very sheltered life so I don't suppose she'd even know what the word meant. It's her parents who'd probably object. It's not even as if I've got any money – *any* money, Peg, nor am I ever likely to have enough to keep her in the manner to which she's accustomed. When I was a kid, I didn't think about things like that – I just knew I wanted to marry her. I think I was about eight when I first thought of it. Silly, isn't it?'

'I don't think it's silly,' Peggy said. 'I think it's very romantic, and if she's worth having, Harry, she'll forget about the illegitimacy part of it and wait till you do have enough to get married.'

Harry sighed.

'I can't see that happening somehow. Soon after I leave school at the end of term, my guardian has arranged for me to go out to the States to work on a stud farm belonging to a man who's a kind of relative. He's offered me a job and in lots of ways I'm quite excited about it. There's nothing I'd rather do than work with horses.'

'Nothing?' Peggy asked. 'You're sure about that?'

She pressed her mouth to his and her hand moved down his body, resting momentarily between his legs before moving up again to unbutton his shirt.

Harry's response was immediate, for by now Peggy knew exactly how to arouse him; how to prolong their love-making; how to make each time a new and exciting adventure. He allowed her to undress him and then, when he was naked, she shrugged off her kimono. Her body looked pale in the unlit room, which had grown dark as dusk had fallen. As Harry took her in his arms, it crossed his mind that he was going to miss Peggy terribly when he left Grafton. He'd miss school too, although he knew that in many different ways he had really outgrown it. He was eager to begin a new, adult life. As Peggy drew him down beside her on the unmade bed, he ceased thinking about the future and thought only about the urgency of his need for the unmatchable pleasure of the release this woman afforded him.

Usually when he made love to her, she remained totally silent, only her face and body indicating her response. Now he paused as he bent to kiss her, for he thought he heard her say, 'I love you.'

No, he decided, he must have misheard her. Then, as she moved her head slowly down his body, he was lost once more in the sensations she aroused in him. He had never been quite sure whether her strange methods of making love were generally acceptable or not. She herself had told him once that it was unlikely any 'nice' girl would approve of the way she now used her mouth to excite him – far less be willing to do so! It was something she never did 'with the others' and which, she'd told Harry with a smile, 'would give him something special by which to remember her in the years to come'.

On his way back to school, Harry realized that he was unlikely to see Peggy more than once again. Her eyes had filled with tears when he'd kissed her goodbye, and he had felt the need to comfort her.

'You're my first woman,' he'd said, 'so I can never forget you, can I? Not even if I wanted to – which I don't.'

It was strange, he thought, as he climbed over the school wall and trod the familiar path through the shrubbery and past the gymnasium towards his dormitory – he too felt sad about their impending parting, yet in another way he would be glad to put an end to the relationship. He had told Peggy the truth when he'd said he was fond of her, but of late he had begun to feel that it was Peggy who was doing all the giving, and that he was somehow taking unfair advantage of her. He simply did not have anything to give in return. He did not doubt that as soon as the new term started, one of the other prefects would take his place, just as he had succeeded Aubrey. Whether he liked it or not, Peggy was 'a loose woman' and he knew he should not be using her just to satisfy his body. He could well imagine Alice's face were he ever in a moment of madness to tell her about Peggy. The fact was, he'd be ashamed to do so. Alice would probably berate him for taking advantage of poor Peg's loneliness and for living in a dead soldier's shoes.

As Harry finally made the safety of his dormitory without detection, he forgot Peggy as he considered the likelihood of Alice getting back to England in time to see him before he went off to America. She had written to him a few weeks ago from Paris, telling him that she was doing her utmost to persuade Monsieur Verveine to allow her to take a week's holiday prior to Harry's departure.

It would be hateful if he was unable to see her, Harry thought, as he settled down to sleep. It was over two years since she'd gone to France and in all that time she had been home only once – for a few short days last Christmas. As far as he understood the plans Sir Philip had made for him, he was to go to the Earl of Kinmuire's farm in Kentucky for two years, remaining there until he came of age. After that, Sir Philip had told him, he could make up his own mind about what he wanted to do with his life. If it really was going to be two whole years before he had a chance to see Alice again, she must get back before he left. They would write, of course, the way they always did when they were apart, but there would be no opportunity to enjoy their long talks about life, the past, their plans for the future.

It was not easy to express things in a letter, although he had tried three years ago to explain to Alice how he felt about Madeleine; how he'd realized that summer holiday that he was in love with her and more than ever determined one day to be able to ask her to marry him. It had been several weeks before Alice replied, and when she did, she wrote:

First, you are much too young even to be thinking such nonsense, and second, you'll only make yourself unhappy as I can't see nothing ever coming of it. Miss

Madeleine has grown up used to having everything she wants without thinking of the cost, and isn't the sort to be happy doing without. Besides, her parents will want her to choose someone suitable as can give her the same sort of life and how'd you ever do that?

I'm sorry if I sound like I'm giving you a lecture, but you know me. Someone has to tell you what's right and wrong if you can't see it for yourself . . .

At the time the letter upset Harry far more than he'd been prepared to admit to himself. He was sure that what Alice had really been trying to tell him was that Sir Philip and Lady Debrace would never allow their daughter to marry someone who was illegitimate. It was a stigma which he now realized would go with him through life.

This, more than anything else, convinced him that Alice's advice to try and forget about a future which included Madeleine was the sensible thing to do. It was not so easy to forget her, for she never wrote to Aubrey without including a page or two to him. The writing was childish and ink-blotted, containing nothing but girlish gossip about school and Daphne and various mistresses. Nevertheless, he kept them all, for she wrote as she spoke and each letter made him feel that she was in the same room as him.

Gradually he had been able to keep his emotions under control, and on the few occasions in the holidays when they were both at home together – and these were rare – he was able to treat her more or less as Aubrey did. This last year, since he had been seeing Peggy Podmore, he had thought a great deal less about Madeleine and it was only occasionally, when he glimpsed someone like her in the village or read a piece of poetry which reminded him of her, that he allowed himself to give way to the romantic memories he had pushed to the back of his mind.

Since neither thoughts of Madeleine, Peggy Podmore or Alice brought Harry nearer to sleep, he decided instead to concentrate upon his plans for the Christmas holidays.

Following their now-yearly custom, the Debraces were going out to Switzerland for the skiing and Harry had been invited by his friend Alcott Major to stay with him. As the family lived in London, there would be plenty to do – theatres, museums, art galleries, music-halls. Alcott had access to a nearby squash court and often went riding in Rotten Row.

It seemed that Mrs Alcott, a war widow, permitted her elder son a great deal of freedom and it sounded as if the holiday might be fun. Moreover, Harry thought, as the urge to sleep all but overtook him, he could take the train up to Saxby and visit Mrs Appleby – something he had been promising to do for the past two years, and which he knew would give the old cook, who had retired when the house was shut up, a great deal of pleasure. He might persuade Alcott Major to go with him and, if he was interested, take him to see Maythorpe House, his 'old home'. According to Sir Philip, the house had remained empty all these years, with only a caretaker living in the lodge to ensure that it was kept aired and free of tramps or other undesirables.

Harry did not doubt that the three weeks would pass quickly and pleasantly, and in the New Year the Debraces would be back from Switzerland for the last week of the holiday. Madeleine was finally leaving her Swiss school and was returning home with her parents to prepare for her coming-out next season. Aubrey was going to let him drive his new MG, and had promised to go to London with Harry to choose suitable clothes for him to take to America.

One way and another, Harry decided, he was really looking forward to the Christmas hols.

Surreptitiously, Madeleine stared at Harry across the big drawing-room. Like Aubrey and her father, he was wearing a dinner jacket and he had obviously attempted to smooth back his dark hair – not altogether successfully, for it curled intriguingly over the collar of his snow-white dress shirt. She had quite forgotten, she thought, how exceedingly handsome he was. He was smiling at some quip Aubrey had made and she felt a flutter in the base of her stomach. He really had grown into a very attractive young man. For one thing, he seemed to have lost his shyness and was very self-confident, very grown up. He was talking and laughing without a trace of his old embarrassment. Catching her eye, he came over to greet her and, to her dismay, began teasing her about the loss of her beautiful long hair.

'If I'd been a girl with hair like yours, I would certainly not have given way to fashion,' he'd said with a smile. 'Ah, well, I suppose I'll get used to looking at a boy instead of a girl.'

As she herself half regretted the short cropped 'bob', his remark was all the more annoying. She turned her back on him and did not speak to him again until Sally rang the gong for dinner. As he made no attempt to offer her his arm, she said pointedly, 'Don't they teach you any manners at Grafton?'

Harry neither blushed nor looked put out. 'We don't have girls there, so we get out of practice,' he said easily, adding with mock gallantry, 'Do please allow me to lead you in to dinner, Miss Debrace.'

'It's no good coming the high and mighty with Harry, Pickles,' Aubrey commented as they left the drawing-room. 'You're talking to Grafton's VIP – that means Very Important Person, in case you don't know. Head of house, captain of cricket, got his rugger colours and was boxing champion for the third year running. And that's not all. He could have got a scholarship to Oxford if he'd wanted it. Isn't that right, pater?'

Sir Philip nodded.

'Quite right, old man! However, before we knew he was eligible, Harry had already decided to accept his cousin's invitation to go to Kentucky. Not regretting it, Harry, are you?'

'Most certainly not, sir. I'm looking forward to it.'

So after all she had been wrong in supposing that Harry was her eternal slave, Madeleine told herself. It may have been true three summers ago, but clearly he did not give a fig for her now.

'I suppose now you've left school, you think you're a cut above us poor little schoolgirls,' she said as they seated themselves at the dining-table. 'It may have escaped your memory, Harry Keynes, but I am seventeen and next June I'm being presented. Mother's taking a house in London for the season.'

'I'm sorry I shan't be there to see you in all your glory,' Harry replied. 'I'm sure you will look very beautiful. It's a good thing you'll be decked out in three white feathers. One on its own might be a nasty reminder of the war.'

Aubrey, who had heard this interchange, burst out laughing.

'Fancy you knowing what a deb wears at Buck House on her big day,' he said.

Harry smiled.

'Sally was telling me all about it when she came in to turn down my bed,' he confessed. 'She was so excited you'd have thought it was she, not Madeleine, who was to be presented to the King and Queen.'

For a while, the talk revolved around the Royal Family and especially the handsome Prince of Wales, who had so endeared himself to the working classes. He seemed to have taken to heart their suffering during the post-war depression.

'Mark my words,' Sir Philip said. 'That young man will make a fine king one of these days.'

Aubrey turned to his sister.

'He's only in his mid-twenties, Pickles. Better see if you can catch his attention when you go to court. They say he has an eye for a pretty face. Just think, you might one day be Queen of England.'

'And Empress of India,' Harry added.

Madeleine's mouth pursed in a pout.

'I wish you two would shut up. You're just jealous because I'm going to have such a wonderful time.'

'So is Harry,' Aubrey rejoined. 'I'd give anything to be going to America with him. Tell you what, old chap, if pater will fork out for my passage, I'll come out and visit you.'

'How long will you be away?' Madeleine asked.

'At least two years. Maybe longer.'

'Then we aren't going to see much more of each other, are we?' Madeleine said in a low voice as Frederick cleared away the entrée and brought in the main course.

She sounded so genuinely regretful that Harry was momentarily caught off guard.

'Will you mind?' he asked in a similar undertone.

Madeleine looked at him from beneath her lashes.

'Of course I will. You're . . . well, part of the family now and when I'm away and think about home, you're just part of it.'

'Part of the furniture?' He tried to lighten the exchange.

'Don't be silly, you know what I meant. I . . . we'll miss you.'

Madeleine did not fail to notice the slight flush that now spread across Harry's cheeks. So he isn't entirely unaware of me, she thought. I suppose I'm seeing him differently now I'm grown up. I used to think boys were a nuisance, whereas now, she told herself, I am finding it exciting to be flirting with such a good-looking young man as Harry.

'Remember our midnight feast?' she said softly. 'You were in a blue funk because I got into your bed.'

'Quite right too,' Harry said with difficulty. 'I hope you've learned how to behave properly at your Swiss school.'

'What are you two jawing about?' Aubrey asked from across the table. 'Share the joke.'

'It wasn't a joke. We were talking about my school,' Madeleine said glibly. She turned back to Harry. 'Tell me more about Grafton,' she prompted. 'I suppose there were some girls around on parents' day and things like that. Aubrey says it's like being in a monastery. We didn't meet any boys at my school, except when we went skiing, and then we weren't allowed to talk to them.'

Harry's thoughts turned to Peggy Podmore and, despite the fact that he had long outgrown the habit, he felt himself blushing. The sooner he forgot altogether what had passed between him and Peg the better, he told himself sharply. He ought not even to be thinking of those pleasurable hours he'd spent with her while he was talking to Madeleine.

She was, he decided, even prettier than he remembered – despite the short hair! Her face was thinner and consequently had become more heart-shaped; her eyes seemed an even deeper blue than they had been before. He couldn't be sure, but as dinner progressed he had the impression that she was actually flirting with him. Alice's cautions were forgotten as, the meal finally over, Lady Debrace excused the three 'children' from taking coffee in the drawing-room, and they were able to escape to the old schoolroom.

Madeleine sat down on the horsehair sofa and patted the empty place beside her.

'You give me the fidgets standing there towering over me like a giant,' she said to Harry. 'You're inches taller than Aubrey.'

'Six foot is quite enough for me,' Aubrey rejoined as he bent to light the gas fire. 'Harry's six two, which makes him a frightful nuisance in the cinema for the people in the row behind.'

'Well, I like tall men,' Madeleine said. 'It makes a girl feel little and helpless.'

'You don't need a tall man to do that,' her brother said. 'You always were utterly feeble.'

Madeleine did not react to this jibe but turned to Harry, saying, 'Aren't you going to be chivalrous and defend my honour? Or perhaps *you* think I'm feeble too?'

'No, I don't,' Harry said quickly – too quickly. 'I think you're . . . all right the way you are,' he finished lamely.

'So put that in your pipe and smoke it,' Madeleine addressed her brother. 'Now, why don't you do something useful, like putting on the gramophone. I absolutely adore that American Blues music, don't you, Harry? Aubrey's got some new records.'

As the sound of 'St Louis Blues' filled the room,

Madeleine moved closer to Harry and leaned her body against him. He could not be sure if she did so intentionally or if she were merely using him as a prop. He could smell her newly washed hair, fronds of which were now touching his cheek, and his heart contracted. He knew in that moment that he still loved her – that in all probability he always would. Now, because of Peggy's teachings, he understood exactly what was happening to his body and he realized that he not only loved Madeleine but that he desperately wanted to make love to her.

Aubrey came to join them on the sofa and Madeleine edged even closer to Harry. This contact with him was having a very exciting effect on her, she realized. She wished Aubrey were not in the room and that Harry would kiss her. No boy had yet done so and she wanted to know what it felt like. One of the girls at school had a cousin who had kissed her but she had never been able to describe the sensation adequately. All she had been able to say was that it had been *'formidable'* – a French word which did not have the same meaning in English, for it was used by all of them for anything really wonderful.

'Let's put the light out,' she said boldly. 'There'll be plenty enough to see by with the gas fire.'

As Aubrey walked across to the light switch, Madeleine reached out and touched Harry's hand. She heard the sharp intake of his breath and felt her own heart thundering. To cover her confusion, she gave a quick, nervous laugh and said, 'Remember how we used to put the light out and tell ghost stories? Nanny was always livid when she caught us at it. She said it gave me nightmares afterwards.'

'Well, we're not going to start telling ghost stories now,' Aubrey said yawning. 'At least, I'm not. You two can stay up if you want, but I'm going to bed. I had a rotten night last night. Yesterday afternoon I was helping Albert to fix the exhaust pipe which had come loose on my MG and I must have inhaled some of the fumes when we tested it – gave me one of my attacks.' Yawning again, he bade them both good-night and left the room, closing the door behind him.

'You don't think he left us alone on purpose, do you?' Madeleine whispered.

'No, of course not. Anyway, on purpose for what?' Harry said huskily.

'So we could be alone, silly! Don't you think it's nicer being on our own? I mean, two's company and all that.'

When Harry did not reply, Madeleine twisted herself round to face him. By doing so she blocked the soft glow of firelight, and the space between them was a dark shadow.

'You're awfully quiet,' Madeleine said softly. 'Am I being a bore?'

'Oh, Madeleine, no! You don't understand . . .' He sought desperately for the right words. 'Look, we aren't children any more. We shouldn't . . . I mean, your parents wouldn't like it if . . . Dash it all, Madeleine, you're a very beautiful girl and I – I wouldn't be human if I didn't want . . . to kiss you.'

'Then why don't you?' Madeleine whispered. 'I want you to – honestly, I do. I've been wanting you to ever since you were so horrible to me before dinner. I thought you didn't like me any more. You used to, didn't you?'

'I still do.' Harry breathed the words and then was silent as Madeleine pressed her mouth against his. He crushed her body in his arms and then turned her so that she was lying across his lap, her lips still pressed to his. When she drew back for breath, he said urgently, 'You're so beautiful. I tried to forget you. I wanted to forget you. I love you. I've always loved you. Oh, Madeleine, is it possible you feel anything for me?'

She gave a short, excited laugh.

'Of course, I do. Here, feel my heart. It's racing like mad. Kiss me again, please. Only this time, don't hold me so tight. I thought I was going to suffocate.'

Happier than he had ever been in his life, Harry kissed her a second time, only on this occasion his lips were soft touches on her cheeks, her brow, her neck, before they reached her mouth. She was giving little moans of pleasure and, after a minute or two, she reached for his hand and pressed it against her breast.

With difficulty Harry sought to restrain himself from allowing his hands to roam further over her body, which now felt burning hot to his touch. Madeleine, he reminded himself, was very, very young and completely innocent. She could have no idea how her movements were affecting him; how totally her kisses had aroused him. He knew that if he were to protect her from himself, he must bring these embraces to an end.

Gently he eased himself away from her.

'It's because I love you so much,' he tried to explain. 'What we've been doing – it's for men and women who are married, or at least engaged. It's wrong for us to be kissing and . . . and touching.'

Madeleine was now sitting beside him, her cheeks flushed, her eyes bright.

'Then why don't we get engaged?' she said. 'We don't have to get married. I *want* you to kiss me. I *liked* it.'

'I know – that's natural, but there'll probably be lots of others you want to kiss, and anyway, your parents wouldn't allow us to get engaged. We're both far too young, you especially. Look, Madeleine, I do love you. You mustn't ever forget that, no matter what happens. I'm going away next week and we won't see each other for ages and ages, but I'll come back, I promise. Then, if you still think you'd like to get engaged, it'll be different – we'll be older and you'll have had a chance to meet lots of other young chaps.'

Madeleine's scowl deepened. 'I don't want lots of other young chaps. I want you, Harry. I think I love you. I don't *want* you to go away.'

She flung herself back into his arms, but by now Harry had himself under control. He kissed her gently and then disentangled himself once more from her arms and drew her to her feet.

'We'll have to pretend this hasn't happened,' he said, leading her towards the door. 'I know your parents would be frightfully angry if they knew. But I won't forget,

Madeleine. I'll think of you every moment I'm away. Don't be angry with me. Just trust me to know what's best for you.'

'If you really loved me, you'd do what I want,' Madeleine said childishly. 'Anyway, it's easy to say you won't forget, but I bet you do. I dare say I will too. I dare say by the time you come back to England, I'll be engaged or even married to someone else.'

'Not if you really love me,' Harry said. 'If you do, you'll be like me and wait.'

He kissed her once more, lightly, on top of her head.

'I love you with all my heart,' he said.

Madeleine stared back at him, her eyes stormy.

'I don't believe it,' she said cruelly. 'You're just frightened of my parents. You don't really care what *I* want. If you really loved me, you'd want to go on kissing me. Well, I'm not in the least interested in kissing you any more and I'm certainly not going to promise to wait for you!' With this parting sally, she turned and ran down the passage, opened the door of her bedroom and then slammed it shut.

As unhappy now as a few moments earlier he had been euphoric, Harry walked slowly into his room and lay down on his bed. He could not believe that it was possible so to have mishandled his first – and almost certainly his last – chance of winning Madeleine's love. For a brief moment she had been his – soft, yielding, eager to receive his kisses. Somehow he had failed to make her understand that, far from rejecting her, he had sought only to protect her. Now she no longer believed he loved her, whereas he loved her more than he had ever done before.

You fool! he told himself bitterly. You should have found a better way to explain that it was not from fear of her parents but of yourself that made you stop kissing her. Wanting her as passionately as he had, it would have been all too easy to lose control.

Feeling utterly dejected, Harry reviewed how quickly it had all happened. One minute they had been sparring like brother and sister and then suddenly Madeleine had changed from schoolgirl to woman, catching him unawares. Her voice, her eyes, her words – everything about her had suggested she found him attractive, and it had been Madeleine who had placed herself near him on the sofa, leant against him, touched his hand.

Now she was hurt, angry and was doubtless thinking him a prig, or worse still, uncaring – and he had only his own stupidity to blame!

Totally dispirited, Harry undressed and climbed into bed. He was without hope and knew he must somehow come to terms with the fact that he'd been crazy ever to imagine that he could win Madeleine's love. He must forget her as Alice had once told him to do. Yet he knew it was going to be harder than ever now that he had had a taste of what might have been.

CHAPTER FIFTEEN
1922

Harry looked anxiously down the length of Platform 2 at Victoria Station. The boat train due in from Dover was three minutes late. He didn't mind waiting just so long as Alice was actually on it. Her telegram had said only that she hoped to catch the morning ferry. Later this evening, she would be travelling down to Calking to stay with the Pritchett family, so they wouldn't have long together.

He had already said goodbye to Will, Martha and the children. Realizing that it would be a very long while before he would see them again, it had been a wrench leaving them. It had been a sad moment, also, leaving The Grange. Madeleine, who had maintained a cool distance since their night in the schoolroom, had relented at the last minute and accompanied Aubrey to the station to see him off. Aubrey had done most of the talking but as Harry had stood at the window to wave goodbye, Madeleine had stood on tiptoe when the guard blew his whistle and raised her face for a farewell kiss. Although she had given no other indication of a change of heart and no promise to wait for him, she had whispered, 'I'll never forget you, Harry' – a declaration which had left him even more confused than before.

Now, however, he could not help but feel a growing excitement at the adventure ahead. Aubrey had been filled with envy. Tonight Harry would be staying with his school chum, Alcott Major, and first thing in the morning he would be catching the train to Southampton. Afraid to let his Thomas Cook travel documents out of his sight, he had put them safely in his wallet – a Christmas present from Lady Debrace – and deposited his trunk in the left-luggage office.

There was the sound of a whistle and a train steamed into view, slowing as it pulled alongside the platform. Minutes later doors opened and Harry's view was obscured by the passengers and their porters, who came hurrying towards the barrier where he stood.

Craning his neck, he was able to peer over people's heads in the hope of catching a glimpse of Alice. It was two years since he'd last seen her and he could hardly wait.

'Hello, Harry. It *is* you, isn't it?'

Harry gasped as he stared down at the elegant young woman who had approached him. Dressed in a smart, fur-trimmed tweed coat with cape sleeves and a wide collar tucked under her chin, Alice was all but unrecognizable. On her head was a matching dark green brimless hat sporting a downward-facing feather. Below the hem of her coat, which was a fashionable mid-calf length, he saw light tan-coloured suede boots with a row of tiny black buttons running up from each instep to her ankles. The heels and toe caps were a shiny black patent leather.

'It's me all right,' he said with a grin. 'But I'm still not sure it's you, Alice.'

He bent down and kissed her cheek and then, after another unbelieving stare at her new image, he hugged her.

'Gosh, it's good to see you,' he said. 'Let me take that case. We'll bung it in the left-luggage. I'm taking you out to lunch.'

As Alice followed him across the station concourse, she clung to his arm, unwilling to let go of him even for a minute. He too had changed, she thought. He was taller even than she remembered and he had filled out. He was a young man now. The boy was gone, except that a few dark curls had escaped from beneath his brown felt trilby, and, she noticed, there was a button off his Burberry.

Harry checked in Alice's luggage, gave her the ticket and tucked his arm through hers.

'I was going to take you to a café,' he said, 'but you look so smart, I think I'll take you to the Ritz.'

'A café would do perfectly well, honestly,' Alice protested, but Harry would not hear of it. With perfect aplomb he took her across the station forecourt to the bus stops and found one waiting to go to Piccadilly.

'Let's go on top, shall we?' he suggested. 'It won't be so crowded.'

Was it because Jules was so small that Harry seemed so large? Alice wondered as he eased himself into the seat beside her. His voice too seemed to have deepened.

'I was so afraid you'd miss the ferry,' he said. 'At least now we'll have five or six hours together. I just wish I didn't have to leave tomorrow, but Sir Philip booked my passage on the *Aquitania* ages ago.'

'Let's not think about you leaving when I've only just arrived,' Alice said with an attempt at cheerfulness. 'At least I managed to get my holiday in time. Monsieur Félix only allowed me to come home as a favour. We've been desperately busy over Christmas, and this week there's another rush on for New Year's Eve.'

'He sounds a decent sort of employer to have,' Harry commented. 'I gather from your letters he's been taking a special interest in you. Tell me about this chap, Jules Whatever? You seem to see a lot of him. Is he one of your suitors? I'm sure you must have dozens, the way you look.'

Alice shook her head.

'Didn't I tell you about Jules? He's just a friend, and he's been very good to me.'

'Then I'm sure to like him,' Harry said, smiling. 'Are you trying to tell me you have no admirers, Alice?'

Alice returned his smile.

'I've been far, far too busy to think about such things,' she said.

'I'm glad to hear it,' Harry answered. 'It would be perfectly beastly if you married a Frog and went to live abroad. Besides, I thought you were going to come and keep house for me, or is that all off now you're becoming so grand?'

273

'I'm not grand, as you put it. I'm a very junior assistant to Madame Duvalle, who is herself an assistant to Monsieur Verveine. Perhaps one day . . .' She broke off as she remembered her employer's assurances that one day she might be able to reach out and grasp her star; become a designer. If this dream were to be realized, her earlier idea of keeping house for Harry would not be possible. She would be forced to make an impossible choice, for she wanted both.

'Let's not think about the future now,' she said uneasily. 'You said you were going to America for at least two years – maybe three! I'll probably be bored to tears with my job by then.'

No, she thought, she would not be bored; but she might have failed somewhere along the line to achieve the very high standards she now knew were necessary; or she might lack the talent, the imagination, the inspiration to be able to create new designs year after year.

'We're here, Alice,' Harry said, as he stood up and grasped her hand. He smiled down at her, and for a moment Alice's heart thudded violently and her legs felt too weak to support her.

'Come on, Alice, we're here,' he said again as she paused. She was staring up at him with a look of disbelief.

'What's wrong?' he asked. 'You look terribly pale. You're not feeling ill, are you?'

With difficulty, Alice found her voice. 'Just . . . just a little dizzy,' she said. 'I'm perfectly all right now.'

But she was very far from 'all right', she thought, as she allowed Harry to help her down the steep staircase of the bus and on to the pavement. She was deeply shocked, so much so that she was trembling as Harry shepherded her across the busy street, and her breath was coming in short gasps which she was only just managing to conceal. A moment ago, when Harry had taken her hand in his she had become aware that the love she had always felt for him was very far indeed from being that of a sister for an adored brother. She had had but one thought – one urgent need – that he would take her in his arms and kiss her!

274

She tried to put this ridiculous notion out of her mind. Even though they were not actually related, she and Harry had grown up as brother and sister, she reminded herself. Besides, he was only nineteen years old and she was four years his senior.

Glancing sideways at him, she found herself unable any longer to see him as a child. He was a young man – a devastatingly handsome young man – and her body was responding unerringly to his attraction. The intensity of her feelings frightened her.

'You sure you're all right?' Harry asked again as they reached the hotel. 'You've not said a word for at least ten minutes.'

In a daze Alice followed him into the foyer and allowed him to take her coat and check it into the cloakroom. With an enormous effort of will, she recovered her composure as he led her into the dining-room. He seemed perfectly at ease in these opulent surroundings.

'You've been here before,' she said, managing to smile at him as they were shown to a table by a waiter.

'Once or twice,' Harry admitted, as he studied the wine list the waiter handed to him. 'One of my school chums lives in London – I'm staying with him tonight as a matter of fact – and when I was up here for a spell in the hols, his mother always brought us here to the Ritz. Lady Debrace prefers the Savoy, but this is nearer.'

In a surprisingly masterful way, he suggested dishes from the menu and ordered for both of them. Alice, he was relieved to see, looked quite her old self again. Leaning across the table, he took hold of one of her hands.

'It really is ripping – us being together like this. I've missed you no end,' he said boyishly.

'Have you?' Alice asked. 'Your school life sounded pretty busy, one way and another.'

Harry grinned. 'Well, it was, so don't be angry with me, Alice. I really did write as often as I could.'

No, he thought, that was not quite true. What about all those evenings he had spent with Peggy in her flat over the tea shop? But he couldn't tell Alice about that affair, which he did not regret but of which he sometimes felt ashamed. Looking back, he knew that he would not have given Peg a second glance if she'd not been prepared to let him make love to her. She had taught him to understand his body and he'd done a great deal of growing up that last term. Peg had somehow given him the confidence to behave like a man, although there were some disadvantages in that from time to time – he badly needed to make love to a female, any female!

Seeing Alice's eyes fastened on his face, Harry looked hurriedly away, embarrassed lest she should somehow read his thoughts.

'Tell me about France,' he said quickly. 'Do you like it there – really like it? You said in your letter you could speak the language now without having to translate every word. Gosh, Alice, it's really quite remarkable what's happened to us both. I mean, when you think back to those days when we were both squashed into that tiny back bedroom at Beacon Cottages. We spoke like village kids and behaved like them. Now here you are speaking French as well as proper English – and we're lunching together at the Ritz as if we'd always been accustomed to this way of life.'

Alice didn't reply until the waiter had served their meal and poured the wine Harry had ordered. Then she said, 'Perhaps it isn't so surprising for you, Harry. You were born for it. It's different for me.'

'That's bunkum,' Harry argued hotly. 'I know Sir Philip said the deed left by the Earl of Kinmuire proved I was his son, but no one knows who my mother was. Besides, nothing will ever undo the fact that I'm illegitimate. At least you don't have to carry that stigma throughout your life.'

'You shouldn't worry about that,' Alice said, longing to ease the pain of the disgrace he so clearly felt. 'It's what you are that counts, not what morals your parents had before you were born.'

The tension left Harry's face.

'I know. You've told me that before and, of course,

you're right. I'm going to make good in America, Alice. I'm going to learn everything there is to learn about breeding thoroughbreds and then, when I've saved enough money, I'm going to come back to England and start up my own stables. Sir Philip says I'm to be allowed to live at Maythorpe House if ever I want to. It may take a long time, but I will do it, Alice – and you will be able to come and live there with me.'

Tears sprang to Alice's eyes and she looked quickly down at her plate. The star that was Harry's dream was shining more brightly than her own. Monsieur Félix had said that to reach it she must be single-minded, and she had believed that she was. Now, sitting opposite Harry, from whom she was all too quickly to be parted yet again, she knew that the dictates of her heart came first. If he still wanted her to live with him in some far-off future, she would, without a moment's hesitation, abandon her own star and do so.

In as casual a voice as she could muster, she said lightly, 'Who knows but you'll be married by then and your wife won't want me living in her home.'

Harry scowled, looking suddenly as if he was nine instead of nineteen. 'I shan't ever marry,' he said bitterly. 'If I can't have the girl I want for a wife, then I'll stay single. You were absolutely right, Alice, I was a fool ever to hope Madeleine would feel the same way about me. I made a complete idiot of myself last week. I thought she'd begun to care the way I did and . . . well, I asked her to wait for me – until I got back from America, I mean. She made it perfectly clear that she wasn't going to and . . . well, it's all over, although she did come to the station to say goodbye to me. Perhaps it's just as well I'm going away.'

He had no idea, Alice told herself, how his words hurt her, for they indicated only too obviously that she herself held no special place in his heart; that she was just Alice, his elder 'sister', someone he was fond of and who was part of his childhood. As for Madeleine, it would be wrong to blame her for making Harry so unhappy. She was still very young. This summer during her season, she would meet a vast number of eligible young men and sooner or later she would probably marry one of them. Harry would not even be around to plead his cause.

'I'm sorry,' she said simply. 'It probably is best to try and forget her. She isn't the only girl in the world, you know.'

Harry gave a rueful smile.

'You're quite right, of course. You always are, Alice. I wish you were coming to the States with me. Then you could keep my head pointing in the right direction. Shall I see if there are any jobs going out there that would suit you? I'm sure they must have dressmakers in Kentucky.'

Alice did not attempt to explain to him that she was not a seamstress; that she was training to be a dress designer. Since there was no immediate future that she could see for herself with Harry, she would go back to Paris and pursue her own star. The likelihood of Harry ever wanting to marry her was so improbable that it might as well be forgotten.

What was not forgettable, she thought, as he took her to Victoria Station to catch her train to Calking that evening, was the intensity of her love for him. When he kissed her cheek and hugged her tightly against him before saying goodbye, she realized the folly of trying to deny the reality of her response. Her whole body was trembling with longing as she clung to him, uncontrollable tears coursing down her face.

'Don't cry, Alice. Please don't cry,' he said. 'We'll see each other again soon – and I'll write often, I promise.'

As finally she dragged herself away, her instinct told her that it was a promise he was unlikely to keep.

'Welcome to Blue Ash Farm,' the girl said as Harry's Negro chauffeur opened the door of the Lincoln and went round to the back to unstrap his trunk off the luggage rack. 'Poppa's down at the stables but he'll be back any minute.' She held out her hand and, with a friendly smile, added, 'I'm Cora-Beth, by the way. I guess I'm a kinda cousin of sorts.'

Harry followed her tall figure on to the veranda surrounding the large, rambling white farmhouse. On the train travelling down from New York through Ohio into Kentucky, a loquacious American had informed him that he should not refer to his relative's home as either a 'ranch' or a 'stud'. 'In our part of the world,' he'd said, 'we call 'em farms. Guess it's different where you come from, eh?'

So far, Harry thought, he had found nothing but friendliness from the Americans he'd met during his eight-day journey to his new home. They kept remarking upon his British accent, and those who had visited England during the war were keen anglophiles. This girl – who he recalled was the same age as himself – seemed equally friendly and informal. She was dark-haired and dark-eyed, quite tall for a female, and in her riding-breeches and thick high-necked jersey, looked almost boyish in stature.

'One of the mares has just foaled,' she said, leading the way into a comfortable living room. Indicating a large armchair for Harry's use, she sat down opposite him and stretched out her legs as she explained, 'That's why Poppa's not here to meet you. It's Inveray's first, you see.'

Noticing Harry's puzzled expression, her somewhat large mouth widened into a smile. 'Inveray's one of our mares. Poppa gives all his horses Scottish names – as a kind of compliment to his Scottish forebears. Our stallions get grand names like Grampion and Stornaway. Poppa hasn't called any of them Kinmuire yet. That name's being reserved for the first foal by Man o'War out of one of our mares.'

'I say, that would be something to write home about,' Harry exclaimed for he'd often heard Uncle Cosmo speak of this magnificent American racehorse. 'When's the foal due?'

With a boyish gesture, Cora-Beth slapped the sides of her long legs with her riding crop and let out an unrestrained laugh.

'Never, I should think,' she said. 'For the present, it's no more than a wild idea of Poppa's. Mr Riddle, the old man who owns Man o'War, guards him the way you

English people guard the royal jewels, and he certainly can't be tempted by Poppa's millions. Poppa says everyone has their price, but it doesn't look as if it's anything as simple as money which motivates Mr Samuel Riddle. That horse is his life. Poor Poppa. He's been trying for the past two years to enter a horse to beat him and I think he's realized Man o'War just isn't going to be beaten. Anyway, next best is to get one of our mares covered successfully and then hopefully raise Man o'War's colt or filly to equal his record.'

Harry was surprised to hear a female speak so naturally about horse breeding, but since this young girl did not seem in the least embarrassed by the subject, he assumed this was the way she had been raised. Conversation halted while a black servant came into the room, bearing a large tray of refreshments.

'This is Peter, our butler,' Cora-Beth said. 'I'll introduce you to the rest of the servants later. Don't worry if you can't remember all their names. You'll soon get used to them. Ah, here's Poppa.'

She jumped to her feet and hurried across to greet her father with an affectionate hug.

'Harry's arrived,' she said. 'We've been talking about Man o'War. Is Inveray OK?'

Ignoring her, the man held out his hand to Harry, who had risen to his feet.

'This girl of mine has no manners,' he said without rancour. 'I despair sometimes why I spent all those dollars on having her privately educated. So, you are Harry, Kinmuire's boy. No doubt about that. For a start – you've got the family colouring and the features. Well, welcome to Blue Ash Farm, m'boy. I hope you're going to like it here. We've been looking forward to your arrival, haven't we, Peachcake?'

Cora-Beth hit her father playfully on the arm.

'I wish you'd stop using that silly name, Poppa. I'm nearly nineteen and it's so babyish.'

'Keep your hair on, young lady. I'm getting an old man and I can't help it if from time to time I forget.'

Since this man was to be his new guardian, it was good that even on such a short acquaintance he liked him, Harry decided. Wendell Harvey was almost as tall as himself, thick-set with dark hair slightly peppered with grey and a small military moustache to go with it. His heavily jowled face was creased with laughter lines, and he was beaming as he took out a cigar from a pigskin case and offered one to Harry.

'Just thought you might have started the habit,' he said cheerfully as Harry refused. 'Now, what have you got to say for yourself, eh? Debrace sure did write about you in glowing terms. "Sounds too good to be true," I said to Cora-Beth. "Heaven knows how the poor fellow's going to live up to this reputation – good on horseback; first class tennis player; erudite and clever; highly regarded by his public school." How's your dancing, by the way? Cora-Beth's crazy about it. When she isn't riding, she's playing those confounded jazz records of hers.'

Cora-Beth ruffled her father's hair.

'I'm trying to educate you, Poppa,' she said, grinning at Harry. 'You've got to keep up with the times, you know. You don't want people calling you old-fashioned.'

'I'll tell you this much, Peachcake, I'm old-fashioned enough to demand a little more respect from my daughter. Now go and change out of those clothes. You look like one of the stud hands.'

As Cora-Beth left the room, smiling wickedly at Harry, her father sighed.

'It's entirely my own fault. I spoil the girl,' he said. 'I expect you know her dear mother has passed on, and now that my son, Judd, is at West Point Military Academy, she's all I've got for most of the year. Cora-Beth misses her twin even more than I do. They grew up as close as two peas in a pod, which, I guess, is why Cora-Beth sometimes behaves more like a boy than a girl! It'll be good for her having you around – make up for losing the company of her brother. It's one of the reasons I was so pleased to get your guardian's letter. It came at just the right time. I'd wanted Cora-Beth to stay on at school, go to college, but she wouldn't hear of it. Trouble is, she'd nothing in common with the other girls. Naturally enough being the age they are, most of 'em think of little else but boys and getting themselves prettied up to attract them. My Peachcake should have been a boy like her twin. She's plumb crazy about horses and riding. My fault, I suppose, raising her here on a farm.'

'I think your children have been very lucky to grow up on a ranch – I mean, farm,' Harry said. 'We didn't get any riding at my public school and I missed it terribly. My former guardian, Viscount Simcox, used to take me out quite a bit. We didn't hunt, of course, because of the war.'

'No, well, we can be glad that's all over,' Wendell Harvey said. 'Nearly got dragged into it myself, but I was a bit too old for the game, or so they told me. Judd was hoping it would last long enough for him to put on a uniform, but thank God, it was all finished by then. The boy always wanted to be a soldier – read too many stories about war, I suppose. At least he's realized his ambition to get into West Point. Not many who'd like to make it – only 400 or so from the whole of the country – so I guess I've every right to be proud of him.'

He stood up and looked apologetically at Harry.

'Guess you think we Southerners have no manners,' he said. 'Here I am, going on about Judd when you must be real tired after that journey. I'll ring for Peter. He can show you up to your room. If you feel like it, you can have a bath and bit of a rest before dinner. Eat at eight. Don't change into a DJ the way you do at home – just a decent suit, if you've got one. Only dress up if we've got guests.'

Waving his arm in farewell to Harry, his cigar ash drifted on to the floor rug, where it remained unheeded. His riding-boots, covered in straw, left a similar trail behind him. In the armchair where she had sat, Cora-Beth's riding-crop and gloves lay discarded and forgotten. Remembering the Debraces' meticulous attention to tidiness and cleanliness, Harry was smiling as the white-haired Negro came into the room. He was going to enjoy the friendly informality of Blue Ash Farm. He liked

Wendell Harvey and he thought he was going to like the tomboyish Cora-Beth. However distantly, he was related to these people, and they were already treating him as one of themselves. His first task must be to find out how Wendell Harvey liked to be addressed. As Lord Kinmuire, since he was the Earl? Or didn't Americans bother with titles? Everything was still very new and strange, and he had a lot to learn about this new country and its people.

It was a bit like being in one's first term at school, he thought, as he followed the manservant up a wide staircase and into one of the bedrooms leading off the landing. He felt suddenly tired – and a little homesick. England, Calking, Alice, Aubrey and, of course, Madeleine, seemed very far off. On the globe America had not seemed quite such a long distance away. As soon as he could, he must buy some postcards and send them to Alice, Jenny and to Mrs Appleby, and one each to Elsie, Edna and the boys. He'd given the children a postcard album as a parting present and had promised them faithfully that he would fill it before he came home.

Someone, he noticed, had already unpacked for him. A huge black woman in a colourful pinafore and wearing a bandanna round her head came into the room. Her teeth gleaming white in her smiling face, she informed him that her name was Becky, that she had run his bath and that Mr Harvey's manservant, Jake, was pressing his suit.

'If there's anything else you need, Mr Keynes, you be sure and let Becky know. I's been Mammy to Miss Cora-Beth an' Master Judd since they was born and I sure like lookin' after young folk.'

He could not have had a warmer welcome, Harry thought. Despite her colour, Becky reminded him of Mrs Appleby and, moreover, she had solved the problem for him as to what to call his host. Obviously Mr Harvey had chosen not to use his title.

In spite of the short rest he had been able to take before dinner, it was all he could do to stay awake as the last course of the evening meal was served.

'Bed for you, young fellow,' Mr Harvey said as he observed Harry's attempts to stifle another yawn. As Cora-Beth started to protest, he added, 'Harry's here for the next two years, so you'll have plenty of time to do all the talking you want, Peachcake. See you at breakfast, son, OK?'

He had not realized how tired he was, Harry thought, as he sank gratefully into the comfortable feather bed. Someone had put a stone bottle between the sheets, and, resting his feet on it, within minutes he was asleep.

He awoke next morning with difficulty to hear a loud knocking on his bedroom door. Supposing it might be Becky or Peter, he instructed his caller to come in. The door opened and Cora-Beth stood grinning at him. She was dressed once more in riding-breeches.

'Thought you might like a ride before breakfast,' she said. 'It's cold but the sun's shining.'

Suddenly Harry was wide awake. There was nothing he would enjoy more than a gallop.

'I'll be with you as quickly as I can,' he said, waiting only for her to close the door before jumping out of bed. His riding-clothes were hanging neatly in the wardrobe. Remembering that Cora-Beth had once again chosen to wear a thick jersey in preference to a riding-coat, he found one of his old school sweaters in the chest of drawers and, pulling on his boots, hurried downstairs.

Cora-Beth was waiting for him in the hall. She tucked her arm through his as if they were old friends.

'That outfit sure suits you, Harry,' she said, giving his tall figure an admiring glance as they left the house and walked past the big blue ash tree which, she said, had given the farm its name. 'Usually one of the grooms brings the horses to the house, but I thought you might like to stretch your legs. The stables aren't far away.'

The morning air was crisp and quickly cleared Harry's head.

'How many horses has your father got?' he enquired.

'Around 160, I guess – one more with the new foal. Poppa said last night that you can have the honour of naming her when the time comes. It's a filly, by the way. We've four stallions. The rest are mares.'

'It must be a very large ranch – I mean, farm – to accommodate so many,' Harry said as they turned a corner and the paddocks came into view.

'I think it's about 25,000 acres,' Cora-Beth said vaguely. 'I'm afraid I can't tell you how many men work here. I never thought to count them.'

'I didn't mean to quiz you,' Harry said with an apologetic smile. 'It's just that I promised my friend, Aubrey Debrace, I'd write every detail. He'll get frightfully ratty if I don't.'

Cora-Beth laughed.

'You do sound funny,' she said. 'I suppose we'll get used to your English accent in time. I guess we all sound just as odd to you.'

'A bit,' Harry agreed as they reached the first of a long line of stable blocks, where there was a hive of activity. Men, both white and black, were busily engaged around the horses.

'You'll soon get to know everyone,' Cora-Beth said cheerfully. 'It's all pretty organized. We've a yard foreman for every twenty stalls – each horse has its own, of course. A foreman has several stud hands under him, each of whom is responsible for six, or perhaps seven, mares. Then we employ our number-one stud groom and he has an assistant. The stallions are kept over there . . .' She pointed to a building 100 or so yards away. 'There's a groom for every two horses and the head man, who's been with Poppa since he started up the farm.'

Calling out friendly greetings to each man by name as they passed, Cora-Beth stopped by one of the stud hands and asked him to saddle her own mare, Dalella, and another called Alness for Harry.

'I dare say Poppa will let you exercise Judd's stallion, Roy Bridge, once he knows you're up to it,' she said. She pointed to the great sweep of grassland, where, she told him, the mares were put out in paddocks to graze during the daytime. 'The stallions have high-walled paddocks of their own where they can't get wind of the mares, but I dare say you already know all about breeding blood-stock.'

'No, I don't,' Harry said, 'but I want to learn. One day, if ever I can afford it, I want to have a place like this. I don't suppose I ever will, but I mean to learn how to manage one just in case I do.'

Cora-Beth was smiling.

'Just wait till Poppa hears about that,' she said. 'You'll be his friend for life. The farm is his life . . . more than ever since poor Momma died. And Judd isn't really awfully interested. He's crazy about the army and flying. What he wants to do is to get into the Air Service. I sure do miss him. It's going to be swell having you for company, and more than ever now I know that you're as keen on horses as I am.'

There was certainly no shortage of conversation with this girl, Harry thought as the groom appeared leading two mares, one of whom whinnied as she caught sight of Cora-Beth. He was pleased to see that they had English rather than Western saddles, for he wanted to make a good impression on this first outing and live up to Sir Philip's recommendation.

Cora-Beth led the way on to the dirt track, where, she explained, the initial training of the young horses took place. Harry was soon slightly ahead of her as their canter quickened to a gallop. He slowed down to allow her to catch up with him and they rode neck and neck for the last four furlongs.

'That was just great,' Cora-Beth shouted, her hair blowing across her face, which had been whipped to a deep pink by the wind. 'It's easy to see you're a natural, Harry. You look as if you'd been born on a horse.'

Although pleased by her compliment, Harry remained silent. It would be a long time, if ever, he thought, as they turned their horses' heads back in the direction of the stables, before he confessed to this girl that he had been born to his unknown mother in a carriage somewhere on the road to Brighton! Had Cora-Beth's father told her he was illegitimate, he wondered? Presumably Sir Philip had explained the facts to Mr Harvey.

'Time for breakfast,' Cora-Beth called out in her slow, Southern drawl. 'Gee, I'm hungry, aren't you? Phoebe makes the best waffles you've ever tasted. Just wait till you try them.'

Her friendliness was unforced and genuine, Harry decided. It was not a matter of her father telling her she must 'be nice' to him. As far as he could see, she was the same towards everyone. Maybe she was not the prettiest girl he'd ever met, but she was certainly the easiest to get along with.

Suddenly he felt entirely happy as well as hungry. He no longer doubted that he was going to like it here, and if Cora-Beth had anything to do with it, he would soon start feeling as if Blue Ash Farm was 'home'.

PART TWO

1924—8

CHAPTER SIXTEEN

1924

Wendell Harvey regarded his daughter thoughtfully as she rearranged the big vase of flowers one of the servants had just carried into the room. She was still wearing her riding-clothes and the bright-pink polo-necked jersey matched the colour in her cheeks.

'Harry not back yet?' he asked, as he seated himself by the open fireplace.

Cora-Beth turned and came across the room to plant an affectionate kiss on her father's head.

'He's worried about Gairloch so he's waiting for the vet.'

Wendell nodded.

'Sometimes I think that boy's too conscientious,' he said. 'Dillon doesn't need supervising. After all, I don't pay my head stallion man the kinda wage he gets for being incompetent.'

Cora-Beth sat down in the chair opposite her father and stretched out her long legs to the welcome blaze. On this cold January afternoon, it was already dark outside, and a bitter wind was blowing from the north.

'You know Harry? I think he loves the horses more than anything in the world. Sometimes I wish . . .'

'That he didn't spend quite so much time with them?' her father finished quietly.

'I guess so.' Cora-Beth gave a rueful smile. 'Now tell me I'm jealous, Poppa.'

Wendell's voice was quiet and matter-of-fact as he said, 'I guessed some time ago that you'd fallen for Harry.'

Cora-Beth's head shot up and her expression was full of anxiety.

'Oh, Poppa, does it show? I thought I was managing to hide it.'

'I don't think Harry's aware of it, if that's what's worrying you,' her father said. 'It's only because I know you so well, Peachcake. Used to be a time when Mammy had a job to get you into one of those pretty dresses of yours, remember? All you wanted was to look like your brother.'

'I don't think Harry notices what I look like,' Cora-Beth said with a catch in her voice. 'He treats me like a kid sister. Darn it all, Poppa, I'm only six months younger than he is.'

'I think it's just in Harry's nature to be chivalrous, and friendly,' Wendell said. 'You were the one who set the pattern when he first came to live with us, remember? You made him a replacement for Judd.'

'That's just what he was, at first,' Cora-Beth admitted. 'Then . . . then it happened. We'd been to a party with Nancy and Frank. On the way home, Frank was driving and Harry and I were in the back seat, and Harry put his arm round me. I was half asleep against his shoulder and then . . . suddenly I realized that I wanted him to kiss me. He didn't, of course – at least, only on the cheek, the way he does every night. Poppa, if . . . if he did come to feel the same way about me, would you mind? I mean, you wouldn't disapprove, would you?'

Wendell Harvey drew a deep breath.

'All I want is for you to be happy, Peachcake. Whether or not Harry is the right man for you, it's not for me to say. I like the boy . . . very much indeed. As you know, I don't hold it against him that his father wasn't married to his mother. I explained all that to you and Judd when his guardian wrote and asked me if I'd have him here. We know who his father was, my second cousin, Gervaise Harvey, but no one has ever revealed the name of Harry's mother. She could have been a kitchen maid for all we know and your children . . . Well, they could be throwbacks to either parent.'

He looked enquiringly at his daughter's thoughtful face.

'You understand what I'm saying, don't you, honey? Growing up as you have on a stud farm, you know how important breeding is. Mind you, there's a danger in too much interbreeding and it's no different with human beings. The aristocracy have found that out to their cost and that's why they're often willing to turn a blind eye to the occasional by-blow, provided it's handled discreetly. Nevertheless, Peachcake, if you marry this young man, you're bound to come up against prejudice from time to time. There'll be sections of society who won't accept you, no matter how charming or rich you are. Not that Harry has a penny to his name, but thankfully one thing we're not short of in this family is money, and if that's what is keeping Harry from showing his hand, then you've no worries on that score. What does concern me is that you're both very young. I know Harry is coming of age tomorrow, but you've never had any experience of being in love with anyone else, so one has to ask oneself, how can you be sure this is the real thing?'

'Poppa, I just know it,' Cora-Beth said quietly. 'As for Harry – he has been in love before. To be honest, I'm not sure if "before" is the right word. I think he may *still* be in love with this English girl, Madeleine.'

'You sure about that, honey?'

Cora-Beth shook her head.

'I'm not sure about anything, Poppa. It's just that whenever he gets a letter from her, he won't open it. He takes it away to read in private. If it's from Aubrey Debrace, or that other girl, Alice, he opens it straight away and reads out bits of news to me. He talks quite a lot about the family he grew up with and he's always buying postcards to send them. He tells me endless stories about Alice, and talks about his school quite a bit too. But when he's describing his life at the Debraces', he hardly mentions Madeleine at all. There was just one time when he did. He said that when he was very young, he'd made up his mind to marry her, but that it was a crazy idea and he'd been stupid ever to think of it and Alice had been quite right when she told him so.'

'Sounds like a young boy's adolescent dream to me,' Wendell said as his daughter fell silent. 'At least you have the advantage of being here on the spot to sweet-talk him. Perhaps you should open your heart a little to him, honey, make him aware you've grown into a very pretty young lady.'

Cora-Beth jumped up from her chair and flung herself into her father's arms.

'Have I, Poppa? Really? I know I'm not a wallflower – other boys keep asking me for a date – but Harry just doesn't seem to notice me. When I went to that rodeo with Jerry and I wasn't home until after midnight, Harry didn't even ask me why I was so late – and he knew the time because he'd been down to see if Islay's foal was better. And I only went out with Jerry to make him jealous.'

Wendell put his arm round his daughter and hugged her.

'You go buy yourself a really pretty dress to wear for Harry's coming-of-age party, Peachcake. Cheer yourself up.'

'Poppa, you know I chose something really special the day after we decided on the party,' she reminded him with a smile.

'Then go buy yourself a necklace or something to wear with it,' Wendell replied with his customary generosity. 'Meanwhile, I'll have a word with Harry, let him know I've planned to give him a really dandy pay rise. I'll say this much, the boy's earned it. He's as knowledgeable as any man I've got working for me, and Dillon was saying so only last week. He's a natural, and he studies hard.'

Cora-Beth was smiling now.

'You really like Harry, don't you, Poppa?' she said.

'Sure do. Reckon you two would make a good team – both of you mad about horses! You know, Cora-Beth, with Judd so crazy about aeroplanes and flying, he's never going to want to settle down and run Blue Ash Farm the way I'd hoped. It wouldn't bother your brother one jot if I handed the place over to Harry when I got too old to manage it. The pair of you could live here and look after me in my dotage.'

'Poppa, you're not even within trotting distance of your dotage. Even so, it's a swell idea and I know Harry's crazy about the farm. He's always talking about finding a way to get rich so he can start up a place of his own one day in England.'

'I'll have a word with Judd when he's next on furlough. If he's in favour of the idea, I'll let Harry know what's in my mind. At the same time, Peachcake, if worries about the future are what's been keeping him from showing his feelings for you and he's as much in love with you as you appear to be with him, there's to be no hasty wedding. I'll settle for a good long engagement – to give you both time to be sure.'

'Sure of what?' Harry asked as he came unexpectedly into the room. 'More secrets about my party, Cora-Beth?' He smiled at Wendell. 'I hardly dare go into a room without permission, let alone open a drawer without your daughter throwing a fit and shouting at me, "Don't look – it's a surprise!"'

He ruffled Cora-Beth's hair in an intimate but casual fashion.

'Just wait until *you're* twenty-one in the summer,' he teased her, before turning back to speak to Wendell. 'The colt's doing fine, sir,' he reported. 'Jefferson reckons it was just a touch of colic. I must say there was a moment yesterday when I though we were going to lose him.'

'Never a dull moment, eh?' Wendell commented. He rose to his feet and put an arm affectionately round Harry's shoulders. There was no doubting that this young relative of his made a fine figure of a man, he thought, as he announced that he was going upstairs to change for dinner. He could well understand why his daughter was so smitten with the boy. With his broad shoulders, bright cheerful countenance and easy manner, Harry made an excellent companion and was popular with everyone. The somewhat shy, reserved young man who had arrived from England two years ago had long since disappeared although he had not lost his English accent. He'd gained a great deal of self-confidence.

In some ways, Wendell decided as he went upstairs, he had more in common with Harry than with his own son, Judd. Much as he loved Judd, he was unable to understand the boy's passion for mechanical objects like aeroplanes in preference to living creatures like horses; nor see how Judd could possibly justify equating the two as he did. Not that it would stop him buying his son a small biplane, a Gypsy Moth, for his twenty-first. Judd was doing exceedingly well as an air cadet and he, Wendell, had good cause to be proud of him, but he could see that they were growing apart. It was very different with Cora-Beth. Since she had grown up, they had become the best of buddies. Although he was worried for her, it made him happy to think that she could confide in him her feelings for Harry.

Since money had long since ceased to be a matter of concern to Wendell Harvey, he never stinted on spending it. Generous to a fault, he had booked the ballroom suite at the best hotel in Lexington and a popular jazz band to entertain the several hundred guests whom Cora-Beth had invited for Harry's party. Caterers from Lexington were providing a banquet, and the local bakery had designed a huge oval birthday cake. In the centre in chocolate icing was the shape of a horse about to jump, and twenty-one candles were to form the perimeter fence-posts of the dirt track.

This was but one of Cora-Beth's surprises. Her present to Harry was to be a pair of racing binoculars in a fine leather case with his initials stamped on it; Wendell's, a handsome cheque, since he was aware that Harry had opened an account at the bank and was trying to build up a reserve of cash.

Ignorant of what lay ahead of him, Harry woke on the morning of his birthday with a feeling of pleasurable excitement. Cora-Beth had told him the night before that there were letters and cards awaiting him from England, all of which had 'Not To Be Opened Until 5 Jan.' on the envelopes, so she had extracted a promise from him to leave them on his bedside table until this morning. Now he sat up in bed and looked eagerly at the different handwritings. Leaving until last the one which he knew was from Madeleine, he opened Aubrey's.

Dear Old Thing,

So you've finally made it to manhood! You'll see I've used the term 'old' advisedly. Can't say I feel any different this year from last. I did, however, meet a few rather comely lasses during the Christmas festivities and managed a kiss or two under the mistletoe. Despite this, I am still fancy-free. How about you? I keep expecting to hear you and Cora-Beth are making a go of it? Perhaps you're just playing your cards close to your chest and the first we'll know about it is your engagement.

Somehow I managed to remember that it will shortly be your birthday, so Many Happies, as we used to say at school. I've sent you a perfectly useless present – to wit: a fountain pen – as a small token to mark the Big Day. I dare say you can get far better versions out there!

Life has perked up a bit since The Grange was sold and we moved to Brighton. Pater's as busy as ever, of course, but the mater has kept on the house in London since Madeleine's season, so I spend quite a lot of time in the Great Big City seeing shows, etc. etc. There's a really good train service to Brighton so it's easy to nip between the two.

Pickles is as hopeless as ever! She discards her admirers as often as she discards gloves, and poor Mama spends most of her time comforting the latest reject. I warn them all not to take her seriously, but they all do, poor chaps! The latest is an army officer known to us as Pogo. (Has there been a craze for pogo sticks out there?) Dunbar's a jolly sort of fellow but he's got a bit of a stutter so I don't suppose he'll last long as Pickles makes fun of him!

Thought I might pop down to Grafton again this spring – see if our Peg is still alive and kicking. I think she really took a fancy to you – talked about you all the time when I saw her last summer. I passed on your news.

That's about the limit of my writing endurance time, so you'll have to make do with it! Have a good birthday!

Yours ever, Aubrey P. Debrace.

Smiling, Harry put the letter back in its envelope. It might not have been a very long missive, but it brought Aubrey into the room as if they had not been apart for two whole years.

There was a brightly coloured card from Mrs Appleby, and another from Jenny, signed by all the family. Jenny was helping out in the newsagent-cum-sweet-shop in the village. She and Jack, the boy she had been walking out with, were saving up so that they could buy the shop from old Mr Peabody, who wanted to retire. Poor Elsie had died of the whooping cough just after Harry had gone to America, so now there was only Edna at home in the daytime to help her mother. The boys, of course, were still living at home, Arthur working as a plumber's apprentice and Ted and Sam still at school.

The second letter was from Alice and was, as always, long and full of news. Having expressed her good wishes for his twenty-first birthday, she turned to an account of her own life.

I shan't be coming to New York this spring as I'd hoped because Monsieur Félix has decided to open a branch of the Maison de Verveine in London instead of New York! I'm just so excited, because he says I can be in charge of it. Of course, Madame Duvalle will come over every month to see that I'm doing things the right way and Monsieur Félix intends to spend quite a lot of time in London. He's going to rent an *appartement* (I'm going all French and should have said, a flat!) where I can live and he can stay when he's in England. We'll be going to London for a few days next month to find suitable premises, so I'll be able to go down and see Mum and Dad and the children.

I'm a bit nervous because I'm not sure I'm really ready yet to take on such a big responsibility. Monsieur thinks I am but I know Madame Duvalle doesn't agree. After all, I've only been here five years! It's a great honour and I only hope and pray I won't let Monsieur down. He's had a bad time lately as Madame Verveine has had to go into the nursing-home again. I still do some entertaining for Monsieur Félix when he wants guests at home. It doesn't bother me the way it did the first time. That seems such ages ago, I can barely remember it.

Enough about me – I want to know about you. You said in your last letter that you were just friendly with Cora-Beth but you don't ever write about any other girls, so I do wonder if you aren't more fond of her than you let on. Please tell me the truth. Are you still going to try to get back to England this summer? If you are, and I really do hope so, you must let me know as soon as ever you can so I can get home the same time as you. It would be so wonderful to see you again. I keep the snapshot you sent me by my bed, but although I can see it is you, you look different – so much older. I keep having to tell myself you are grown up now. I really wish I could see you.

From your ever-loving Alice.

Harry felt a glow of pleasure – not least because his darling Alice was making such an obvious success of her career. She deserved no less, for she was the kindest, sweetest, dearest friend he had in the world. He wished very much that she was his real sister. There were times when he felt the need for family ties and the fact was, he had none – unless he could count Wendell Harvey. Not long after his arrival in Kentucky, they'd sat down together one evening with the Harvey family tree and worked out that they were second cousins.

'But for that youthful aberration on your father's part, you and not I would be the Earl of Kinmuire,' Mr Harvey had said.

Slowly, savouring the moment, Harry opened the letter he knew was from Madeleine. He had read her letters to him so many times that he could recognize her large, childish writing at a glance.

Dearest Harry,

This is to wish you many happy returns. I don't have to tell you it was Aubrey who reminded me you'd be twenty-one on the fifth. I hope you have a nice party and lots of fun with that horsy girl you live with. I know you say she's very nice but she can't be all that special or you'd have fallen for her donkeys' years ago. I've fallen in love again – this time it's with a really nice army officer called Pogo. (That's a nickname, by the way. His real name is Lionel Dunbar.) Mummy approves for once. I may decide to marry him. He's mad on polo so he takes me to the Hurlingham Club to watch him play. He's almost as good as you on a horse! Of course, being in the army, he may get posted abroad one of these days and I don't know if I want to leave London – it's such jolly good fun now I'm out.

Aubrey says you might come home for a visit this summer. I do hope you do. We could go to dances and things. He said he forgot to put in his letter that your hero, Steve Donaghue, won the Derby for the third time last year but you probably knew that ages ago. Have you heard the song 'I'm Just Wild About Harry'? I think of you every time I hear it. Pogo gave me a lovely Mah Jong set for Christmas and 'I'm just wild about' the game. Everyone here is. Do you play it in Kentucky?

Just before Christmas, Pogo invited Aubrey and me to go up to Melton Mowbray to hunt. The Prince of Wales was staying in a suite of rooms at Craven Lodge in the middle of the town. Do you know it? Aubrey wanted to drive over to see Maythorpe House but there wasn't time. Your Mr Harvey could easily let it if he wanted as the whole place was full to bursting. Pogo says it always is.

Pogo's family have invited us to go up to Scotland for some salmon fishing in February. Aubrey's keen to go but I'll probably be bored.

I've got to go now as it's time for me to get my new dresses fitted. Do, do, do, do try and come home for the season.

Heaps of love from,
Madeleine.

The ending left Harry's heart soaring, until he recalled the earlier content. This new chap, Dunbar, seemed to have become very much a part of Madeleine's life; Lady Debrace approved of him and obviously Aubrey liked him. Was this going to be the man who won Madeleine's heart? The very thought left him feeling as if there was a great pit where his stomach should be. Part of him accepted that one day she would get married – and not to him. He had nothing to offer her, whereas a fellow like Dunbar obviously had everything. But the other part cried out against the mere idea of her being someone else's wife. No one could possibly love her as much as he did. Did that mean nothing to her? He knew that it did not, and yet she continued writing to him; continued sending her love; continued her demands, repeated in every letter, that he should go back to see her.

He had by now enough saved up to pay his passage and his expenses. He *could* go, but did he really want to? Madeleine was his sole reason for wanting to return to England – although naturally he'd love to see Alice if she happened to be in London. If, however, he were to arrive only to find Madeleine promised to someone else, he would have to suffer again those bitter pangs of regret he'd endured before he came out to Blue Ash Farm. He'd been happy here; he'd settled down and loved the new life he led. He got along splendidly with Wendell Harvey and with Cora-Beth.

Thinking of the girl who would probably be up and dressed and waiting for him to go downstairs, Harry frowned uneasily. He would have to be blind not to have noticed that something in Cora-Beth's manner towards him had changed; that the looks she sometimes gave him were no longer open and friendly but questioning, as if she expected, or was hoping for, something more. She tended to jump like a nervous thoroughbred if he touched her arm or kissed her cheek. She was no longer the easy-going tomboy with whom he had had such a simple and uncomplicated relationship. He'd hoped that it meant no more than that she was growing up and had become aware of herself as a young woman; that as a consequence it was not quite the done thing for her to rush across a room and hug him like a kid sister, or trip him up in the haybarn and fling herself on top of him like a puppy spoiling for a game.

He supposed that he too had changed in his attitude towards her. He'd become more aware of her as an attractive girl with a very feminine figure that the fashionable flat-chested dress styles could not conceal. Now that she was wearing skirts above the knees, as fashion demanded, he'd noticed her long, slender legs and admired her ankles. There had even been times when he'd found himself imagining her with no clothes on at all – the way he had once seen Peggy Podmore – and felt the same keen desire well up in him. He was fast reaching the conclusion that Cora-Beth wanted him to feel more than a friendly affection for her; that perhaps she even wanted him to fall in love with her.

Could he fall in love with anyone else but Madeleine, he asked himself as he got out of bed and started to get dressed? If he kissed Cora-Beth – not on her cheek as was his custom, but on the lips – would he feel that same passionate desire he'd experienced when he'd kissed Madeleine that night in the schoolroom at The Grange?

Nearly all Cora-Beth's friends were what they called

'dating', although many were even younger than she was. He'd seen Nancy and Frank embracing in the back of the car, so closely entwined that it had been impossible to guess what else they were doing. Perhaps he should let Cora-Beth make the running this evening at his party. Perhaps he was being absurdly English to treat girls like Cora-Beth as precious pieces of china not to be touched. He was twenty-one – a man – and it was high time he started living his life to the full. If Madeleine was enjoying herself with her 'Pogo', he could enjoy himself with Cora-Beth, who probably cared about him far more than Madeleine ever had.

By the time Harry went downstairs for breakfast he was in excellent spirits, heightened by an underlying feeling of excitement. This was the day when his adult life was going to begin, he told himself.

Cora-Beth was already at the breakfast table.

'Sorry if I'm late,' Harry said as he sat down. 'I was reading my birthday letters.'

For once Cora-Beth was not in riding-breeches. She wore a linen knee-length frock the colour of sand, and it suited her. She was, Harry thought, really pretty when she chose to be so. As he admired her dress, she smiled.

'All in your honour, Harry. Today's special. Your every wish granted.'

'Then I'll wish for the first and last dance tonight and as many as you can spare in between,' Harry rejoined, and was pleased to see that Cora-Beth was actually blushing.

When he had finished eating, she followed him into the drawing-room and watched him open her present. Harry rested a hand gently on her shoulder.

'It looks as if this is going to be one of the best birthdays I've ever had,' he said. 'I'm awfully pleased with my binoculars – and I'm really looking forward to the party tonight.'

Cora-Beth tilted her head sideways so that for a brief moment her cheek rested against his hand.

'Are you, Harry?' she said softly. 'I am too.'

Wanting this girl to be as happy as he was, Harry put his

hand beneath her chin and raised her face to his. Her lips were parted and he could feel her heartbeat against his chest. She was waiting for him to kiss her, he realized, and it seemed suddenly to be the natural thing to do. He was unprepared for the urgency of her response as his mouth touched hers. Her arms tightened around his neck.

'Oh, Harry, Harry,' she whispered when finally they drew apart. 'I've been waiting and waiting for you to do that. Kiss me again, please.'

With only the briefest moment of hesitation, Harry willingly gave way to the heady temptation of holding this vibrant, passionate young girl in his arms. He too had been waiting, he thought, but he had not realized before that it was for Cora-Beth.

CHAPTER SEVENTEEN
1924

Wendell Harvey drew a sigh of satisfaction as, together with a number of other older parents, he prepared to leave the party. It was after midnight and the youngsters might well continue enjoying themselves into the early hours.

There was no doubt that Harry's twenty-first celebration was proving a phenomenal success. All Lexington society were present and the newspapers had been busy taking photographs and writing up their accounts for the morning editions. When Wendell had been interviewed, he had refused to say how many dollars the shindig was costing him but he admitted it was a lot.

It was worth every cent, he thought, recalling his daughter's happy, excited face and Harry's marked attention to her. Even without his rose-coloured glasses, he realized that dressed in a pretty, long frock with her hair freshly waved, Cora-Beth could hold her own against any other young girl in the room. As his chauffeur drove him back to Blue Ash Farm in the Lincoln, he decided it was love which gave her that special glow, that sparkle, that vivacity which drew the young men round her like flies.

Was it possible, he wondered, that by breakfast time the two youngsters would be reporting to him that they were in love? Despite Harry's obvious attraction for most of the unattached girls in the room, it was in Cora-Beth's company he was most often to be seen. He, himself, would not be sorry. The family connection between Harry and his daughter was sufficiently diffused not to matter and they were very well matched.

Cora-Beth was thinking the same thing as she watched

Harry partner one of her former school friends on the dance floor. If only Harry were to fall in love with her they could have a wonderful life together. Remembering the kiss he had given her after breakfast it seemed as if their relationship might at long last have changed.

She felt her cheeks flush with a mixture of excitement and anxiety. Surely tonight, when they went home, she would discover the truth? She would definitely *not* make the first move. Judd said half the fun of being with girls was when *he* was doing the chasing. She had never expected it would be so hard to pretend lack of interest when her very heart and soul were longing to demonstrate her love.

With an effort she walked across the room to Jerry, who had so often asked her for a date and who, given any encouragement, would have been a frequent visitor to Blue Ash Farm. He beamed with pleasure at her attention and, hoping Harry would notice, Cora-Beth began flirting with him.

Her efforts did not escape Harry's notice and when the dance ended, he excused himself to his partner and went across to her side. Jerry ignored his greeting.

'Jolly good party, don't you think?' Harry said, for he had met Jerry once or twice and rather liked him.

'Oh, *jolly good*! *Absolutely ripping, what?*' Jerry parodied Harry's English voice.

For a moment Harry looked as if he might hit the other boy, but before Cora-Beth could intervene, he relaxed and smiled.

'Sure is *lickin'-spittin' swell!*' he said good-naturedly in a poor imitation of a Southern drawl, whereupon all three burst out laughing.

'You'll never make it as an American, that's for sure,' Cora-Beth said as she tucked her arm through Harry's. 'Let's see if you can waltz better than you can speak our lingo. See you later, Jerry.'

As Harry led her towards the dance floor, she said, 'For one moment I thought you were going to knock poor Jerry sideways.'

Harry smiled down at her.

'What, and ruin this wonderful party you've arranged for me? Actually, I like Jerry. I was just a bit jealous, I suppose. I mean, it's pretty obvious he's crazy about you.'

'Is it?' Cora-Beth asked demurely. 'I don't feel that way about him.'

'I'm glad to hear it,' Harry said truthfully. 'I was looking on you as *my* date tonight.'

The band was playing a new haunting melody, 'What'll I do . . . when you . . . are far . . . away . . .' in a slow waltz rhythm. Cora-Beth melted into the circle of Harry's arms. They were both good dancers and gradually the other couples drifted off the floor and stood in a circle watching them. There was a great round of applause when the dance ended and, flushed with excitement, Cora-Beth responded eagerly to the pressure of Harry's hand as he kept possession of hers.

'I shall always remember this evening, that dance, that song,' she murmured. 'Especially if ever you do go back to England. Do you really think you'll go this summer, Harry?'

He nodded.

'I'd like to go. It's such ages since I saw my foster family and . . . and friends, but I'll be back, Cora-Beth, you can be sure of that. I love it here. I love the countryside, the horses, the farm, the people. Everyone has been so friendly. I don't feel like a stranger any more.'

'You aren't a stranger any more,' Cora-Beth said vehemently. 'Poppa says you're part of our family now. I know your roots are in England, but don't you think you could put down roots here in Kentucky?'

A part of Harry wanted to agree that it was possible, although it would be a very long while yet before he had enough money to buy even a small farm of his own and start up his own line of thorough-breds. Yet despite this being his long-term plan, he still thought of England as 'home', of Alice and the Pritchetts as his 'family', of Aubrey as his best friend. And there was Madeleine . . .

According to Aubrey, Madeleine was still unattached,

even if she did have that army officer dancing attendance on her. Might there be a chance that if he went back to England, he could make her care for him? Even were he able to persuade her to marry him, somehow he could not envisage her being content to live on a ranch among a whole lot of strangers and without the luxuries she took for granted.

Perhaps, after all, he should put Madeleine out of his mind. Even to imagine she could love him was absurd. It would be far more sensible to concentrate his thoughts on the lovely girl at his side. This morning he had felt her attraction and just now, as they danced, he had been convinced it was mutual.

He wished suddenly that he and Cora-Beth could be alone together. He badly wanted to kiss her. Somewhat to his surprise he heard himself telling her so. Cora-Beth's eyes were sparkling, almost luminous, as she squeezed his arm.

'Birthday or no birthday, you'll just have to wait, Harry Keynes,' she said softly, 'and so will I.'

It was a promise of sorts and one Harry found himself constantly remembering as the hours passed. He was surprised by his impatience for the party to end. Finally, the last goodbyes were said and they were free to climb into the family Studebaker and begin the drive back to Blue Ash Farm. Cora-Beth had a warm travelling-rug wrapped round her legs, and they were both muffled in heavy, furlined coats and caps. The night sky, brilliant with stars, was not yet touched by dawn, although a bright half-moon was low in the eastern sky.

A mile or two short of Blue Ash Farm, Harry stopped the car and pulled on the brake. Somewhere in the distance, a dog barked. Simultaneously they turned to face one another and a moment later they were locked in an embrace. Cora-Beth reached up her arms and clung to him as Harry started to kiss her. Soon his lips left her mouth and he covered her eyelids, the tip of her nose, the warm base of her throat with soft, butterfly kisses. She gave little moans of pleasure and Harry felt the quick, fierce response of his body. His senses told him that Cora-Beth was as eager as he for closer intimacies, and she made no attempt to draw back when he unbuttoned her coat and felt for the soft warmth of her breasts. He felt them taughten against his palms and suddenly she slid her body over his right knee so that she was lying against him, between his legs.

The tension inside him was almost beyond bearing. She began to kiss him and, between kisses, she was murmuring endearments. He silenced her with more kisses as he tried to remind himself that this young girl was not only innocent but trusted herself to his care; that her father trusted him, and however uninhibited she might now appear to be, he must not abuse that faith.

'My dearest girl,' he said, his voice husky with longing, 'we've got to stop this. We've just got to.'

Cora-Beth clung to him more tightly.

'I don't want it to stop . . . not now . . . not ever. Oh, Harry, if you knew how I've longed for this,' she said in a breathless little voice. 'There've been so many times when I've lain awake at night longing for you to kiss me, make love to me. I'd almost given up hope that you'd ever see me as a girl . . . a woman. I might just as well have been Judd.'

She gave a short, excited laugh.

'I've been pretty blind, haven't I?' Harry said with a rueful smile. 'The first time I ever saw you, you were in breeches with your hair all over your face and again the next day when you took me out riding. I suppose that set a pattern. It seemed quite enough just to have you as a friend. Besides, I was still feeling a bit cut-up about . . . about the girl I'd left behind in England.'

For a moment, Cora-Beth was quietly thoughtful. Then she said, 'I don't see how she could have turned you down – knowing how you felt about her.'

Harry sighed.

'It wasn't like that. She was still terribly young and anyway, I think I was just a boy to her . . . any boy . . . and she wanted to know what it felt like to be kissed.'

'But you don't love her any more?'

'I don't think so. That's to say, Madeleine is really just a memory now – and not a very happy one. I'm certain she never loved me. According to her brother, she has dozens of admirers. I dare say she'll marry one of them some day soon. At the moment, Aubrey says she's having far too good a time to want to settle down.'

It crossed Cora-Beth's mind that this girl's feelings towards Harry might well change if she were to meet him again after an absence of two years, but she bit back her words, fearing that the suggestion, were she to make it, might put the idea into his head. Let it suffice for the present that he thought he'd been silly to nurture romantic thoughts about his first love.

'Maybe everyone has to suffer the pangs of calf love before they can recognize when it's the real thing,' she said lightly. 'I was head over heels in love with our English teacher when I was about fourteen or fifteen. I guess he never noticed me. I was disgustingly fat and clumsy and exceedingly plain.'

'I don't believe it,' Harry said sincerely. 'If you were, you've certainly made up for it since. I think you're very, very attractive.'

'Do you really, Harry?' Cora-Beth asked breathlessly. 'I want you to feel that way about me. I wish we hadn't got so many clothes on. I wish we could be close – really close. Do you think that's awful?'

'Of course not. It's natural! But it's also dangerous. A chap may think he's in control of himself but if he's really attracted to a girl, it's not so easy to stop at . . . well, just kissing.'

'You mean, you might want to make love to her? Go all the way? Some of the college girls allow petting on a date, but I don't know anyone who's actually done it, other than married people, of course, but they don't tell you about it.'

'Because there's no need for you to know, probably,' Harry said.

'But if you don't know, how can you be sure when

you're really in love and when you just think you are because the person you're with is so attractive?'

'I'm not sure what the answer is to that,' Harry answered truthfully. He was thinking of Peggy Podmore as he added, 'I knew a girl once who I was attracted to – but I didn't love her. I liked her, though.'

Cora-Beth nodded. 'I once asked Judd to explain things to me. All he'd say was that nature meant men and women to be attracted by each other and if they weren't, the species wouldn't reproduce themselves.'

Harry felt a deep rush of tenderness well up inside him. He had not thought it possible that an innocent girl like Cora-Beth could think about such things, let alone voice them.

'It's hard to believe that I could have spent two whole years walking round with blinkers on. Trouble is, I'm not going to be able to see you as a jolly, good-natured tomboy any longer,' he said huskily.

'I'm glad,' Cora-Beth whispered. 'I thought you never would see me as a perfectly ordinary girl. You do care about me a bit, don't you, Harry?'

'A great deal more than "a bit"!' Harry said, smiling. 'And anyway, Miss Harvey, how do you know I'm not falling in love with you?'

Cora-Beth reached out and touched his cheek.

'You mustn't pretend, Harry, not to please me. You can't be in love with two people and I haven't forgotten your English girl, even if you have. She still writes to you, doesn't she?'

This girl's straightforwardness both surprised and unnerved Harry. He knew instinctively that this was no casual conversation and that for Cora-Beth's sake he must be honest. He had always liked her, had grown very fond of her and now he was finding her intensely desirable. But did these feelings constitute love? It had been so different with Madeleine. He had worshipped her, adored her, and even in his dreams, he had desired her.

'Yes, she still writes to me,' Harry answered Cora-Beth's question, 'but the way I feel about you is different

311

and I don't think I can explain. Love's a funny thing, isn't it? I mean, I love Alice – but that's in a different way too. All I am sure of is that right now I don't want to be anywhere else in the world but here, with you.'

With a little cry, Cora-Beth threw herself back into his arms.

'Then let's not think about – worry about – anyone else but us,' she said between kisses. 'Let's just be together as often as we can, *really* get to know each other. Let's pretend we've only just met and this is our first date. Oh, I just can't tell you how happy I am!'

Her mood of euphoria was infectious and for the moment anyway Harry knew that he was every bit as happy about this new relationship as the girl in his arms. He loved kissing her; loved the warmth of her response; loved the feel of her body. Her lack of reserve delighted him and he could not help but be flattered by her attention. When at last they broke apart, he took both her hands in his and kissed each of her palms.

'I don't think either of us will forget tonight,' he said, 'but it will be another day tomorrow and we've got to decide how we're going to behave. If we suddenly start holding hands like this your father is going to wonder what's going on.'

'Oh, Poppa will be pleased,' Cora-Beth said ingenuously. 'He knows how I feel about you, and he's very fond of you.'

'Then he'll surely expect some sort of explanation from me,' Harry said quietly. 'After all, I'm in no position financially to buy a place of my own; even to think about getting married for several years yet. Then there's . . . there's Madeleine. I think I ought to see her again – just once, to reassure myself that all the old feelings really are as dead as I believe. Can you understand this, Cora-Beth?'

There were tears in her eyes as, withdrawing her hands from him, she nodded.

'I asked you to be honest so I've no right to complain because you've spelt it all out. I keep forgetting that . . . that what's been happening tonight is all new to you. It's not to me, Harry. I've known for months that . . . that what I feel for you is special, very special. I'll just have to wait and hope. And if you do find you still love this girl, I'll take it on the chin, as Judd would say. Perhaps we shouldn't say anything to Poppa yet. There's nothing really *to* say, is there?'

'I think there's quite a lot we could say if we wanted to,' Harry replied. 'Your father will probably guess, anyway. I shan't be able to treat you now as if you were my foster sister, Jenny. She was always a tomboy like you, though I dare say she has changed now she's grown up.'

As he drove slowly back towards the farm, Cora-Beth seemed to regain her equilibrium and, taking his cue from her, they talked lightly about Harry's childhood with the Pritchetts. As Blue Ash Farm came into sight, the Pritchetts were forgotten because, to their astonishment, they saw that every window was ablaze with light.

'I can't think what Poppa's doing up at this hour,' Cora-Beth said with a frown as she peered through the windscreen. 'He said he was feeling tired and was going home to bed.'

As they drew to a halt outside the house, old Peter came hurrying out to meet them. Tears were streaming down his black cheeks. All but incoherent in his distress, he said, 'It's Massa Judd, poor Massa Judd! Doctor's with your Pappy now, Miss Cora-Beth, and he's ill with grieving and Jake went off on horseback not half an hour ago to fetch you and Mr Harry back from your party and we's been waitin' and waitin' for you . . .'

Cora-Beth's face was so pale Harry was afraid she was about to faint. She ran indoors, past the old servant, and hurried into the drawing-room. Wendell Harvey was slumped in one of the armchairs and the doctor was standing over him.

'Poppa, what is it? Has Judd had an accident? Is he all right? Are *you* all right? *What's happened, Poppa?*'

Knowing that it could only be bad news, Harry, who had been standing in the doorway, stepped forward and put his arm round Cora-Beth's shoulders. Wendell stared down at the glass of brandy which someone had put into his hands. He seemed unable to speak.

'It couldn't be worse, Cora-Beth,' the doctor said in an undertone. 'I'm afraid Judd has had an accident – in an aeroplane. Your father had a telephone call an hour ago from Judd's commanding officer. We don't know any details yet, but . . . well, I'm afraid you have to know. The aeroplane crashed and your brother was killed instantly. I'm so very, very sorry.'

'Oh, no. Not Judd. Not Judd,' Cora-Beth cried. 'It can't be true. It *isn't* true, is it? Not Judd! Not Judd!'

Helplessly, Harry stood silent as Cora-Beth threw herself into her father's arms.

The doctor came over and drew Harry to one side.

'I'm afraid this has hit Harvey pretty badly. His only son! And Cora-Beth, poor child. Judd was her twin and they were so close as children. I'll give her a sedative before I leave. Meanwhile, there's nothing much either of us can do for them. In cases like this it's sometimes best to leave people alone to grieve.'

As he led Harry out of the room, he patted him on the shoulder.

'Glad you're here, boy. Harvey thinks very highly of you and you'll be a great comfort to him. Terrible way for young Judd to die. It'll help Harvey if he hears his son didn't suffer none. Seems the boy was flying too low, hit one of those darned electricity cables. It was out in the wilds somewhere and it took a while to find him. Dreadful business, dreadful! Harvey was right. He always did say those new-fangled machines were dangerous.'

The doctor stayed for another hour, gave Cora-Beth the promised sedative and a tearful Becky put her to bed. Disregarding the proprieties Harry went in to see her. She was already quite drowsy. Her eyes were red and swollen with crying as she stared at him wretchedly.

'It was such a wonderful evening, Harry. I was so happy . . . so happy . . . and now . . . now this!'

He knelt by the bed and put his arms round her.

'One of the first things I had to learn by heart when I

went to Maythorpe House was a poem by an Englishman, Laurence Binyon. He wrote it for the young men who were dying in the war, but the words may offer a little comfort. I'll quote a few lines, which you could think about when you think of Judd. It goes, "They shall not grow old, as we that are left grow old; Age shall not weary them, nor the years condemn. At the going down of the sun and in the morning We will remember them."'

Tears were streaming down Cora-Beth's face as she clung to Harry's hand. 'But Judd was so young. It's so pointless! I can't believe I'll never see him again . . .'

'Try not to think about that. Remember all the good times you shared.'

'I'll try. I will try,' Cora-Beth whispered, her voice slow and indistinct as the sedative took effect.

Harry stayed with her until her eyes closed and then went to see if there was any way he could offer some comfort to the grief-stricken man downstairs.

He had completely forgotten that this was his twenty-first birthday and that he had finally come of age.

CHAPTER EIGHTEEN
1924

Jules Bellaire sat opposite Alice at a white, wrought-iron table on one of the large terraces outside the Château de St Denis. A sun umbrella sheltered them from the warm May sunshine. On the table lay several large swatches of fabrics which Jules had brought out from Paris for Alice's inspection.

'When will Monsieur Félix be back?' he enquired.

'Not until after lunch,' Alice told him. 'You're to stay until he returns, Jules. He has gone to see Madame Verveine at the nursing-home.'

Jules nodded. He knew *le Maître* went every Tuesday to see his wife, although from all accounts her condition had deteriorated so much she was unable to converse with anyone and, at times, did not even recognize her husband. He visited her none the less, although Jules had no doubt that it was duty rather than love that prompted his assiduous attention.

'Will you be returning to Paris with me, Alice?' he enquired.

She shook her head. 'No, I'll be going tomorrow morning. Monsieur has guests tonight.'

Jules did not look surprised for Alice now frequently stayed at the château. Rumours abounded at the *salon* regarding the relationship between Alice and *le Maître* – all of which he vehemently denied whenever he heard the gossip. The difficulty of convincing the rest of the staff lay in the fact that Alice did not have a particular admirer or male friend, as most of the girls did. Even he had been forced to admit that it was strange for so lovely a young woman to be leading a life devoid of romance.

Moving a pattern of material out of the shaft of sunlight, which might cause it to fade, he said now, 'Are you certain it is wise to be so single-minded about your career, Alice? I speak as your friend. It seems to me that you should leave a little time for romance.'

Alice smiled. 'In the first place, I'm far too busy, and in the second, I've yet to meet anyone I'd want to marry. Anyway, Jules, it would be silly to form attachments here in Paris when I'm going to be living in London.'

Jules smiled. 'Ah, yes! But we have known each other for five years, Alice, and I count myself your friend. Therefore I know that it is not a matter of you using good sense in rejecting advances from young men because you would soon be parted from them. You do not allow such advances in the first instance.'

'I am perfectly happy as I am, Jules, so why should you worry?'

'Because I am devoted to you, as well you know, and I wish to understand you.'

How could she explain her feelings to him, Alice wondered, when even she herself knew that there was not one hope in a million that Harry would ever want to marry her. His letters from Kentucky were painfully clear – he thought he was in love with Wendell Harvey's daughter, Cora-Beth, and Mr Harvey was encouraging the match because he very much wanted Harry to live permanently in America. It was now four months since the twin, Judd, had been killed and, so Harry had explained, Mr Harvey had felt it his duty to find out whether, now his son was dead, the family title would die with him or, as he now seemed to think, it could be passed through the distaff side to his daughter. If this proved to be the case, then by marrying Cora-Beth, Harry would share her right to the Kinmuire estate.

Harry denied in his letters that this fact was influencing him in any way. He was coming home in July, when he would tell her all about his long-term plans to buy his ranch in America. There had been no mention of Alice going out there to keep house for him. Nor would she wish to do so if he were to marry Cora-Beth, no matter how nice the girl was.

It was one thing to accept that she had no future with Harry and quite another to force her heart to give up hope, to stop loving him. It was this she could not begin to try to explain to Jules.

'You'll just have to accept that I am not like other girls,' she said lightly. 'I am not a romantic, my dear Jules.'

'But I think you are. Moreover, it would be a shocking waste if you were not. You've grown into a very beautiful young woman, Alice, and I do not like to see beauty wasted. You would make some man very happy.'

'I shall be perfectly happy living in London with you, Jules,' Alice said. 'You introduced me to Paris and it will be my turn to introduce you to England – not that I know very much about London. We shall have to explore it together.'

'If we have the time,' Jules said with a laugh. 'There will be so much to do in the new *salon*. I am very excited about it.'

'I still can't believe it's really happening,' Alice said. 'I owe so much to Monsieur Félix. But for him, I would never have risen to these heights.'

Jules nodded. 'That is for certain. I think his reasons are two-fold. One, he has from the start recognized your talent; and two, he is in love with you.'

The statement was so matter-of-fact, so unexpected, that Alice gasped. 'You are joking, of course. Monsieur treats me like a daughter.'

Jules fluttered his long, dark lashes. He was grinning impishly. 'That he does not, Alice. When you are in a room with him, his eyes follow you everywhere. He is enchanted by you – and indeed, why not?'

'But I'm just his protégée,' Alice protested. 'I think he's pleased because I've justified his faith in me. I'm not even sure that his main pleasure has not been in proving to Madame Duvalle that he was right about me. It irritates

318

him beyond measure that she is nearly always right about everything.'

Jules laughed, but then added more seriously, 'Nevertheless, you may find yourself in a difficult position before much longer, Alice. It has surprised me that Monsieur has not spoken out before now.'

'Spoken out about what?' Alice asked. 'Even if you were right – an absurd idea – what is there he could do about it? He's a married man, and a Catholic.'

'He could not propose marriage, but he could propose an alternative alliance,' Jules said quickly. 'For very many years he has had mistresses.'

'Really, Jules, you shouldn't be talking like this about Monsieur,' Alice protested. She could not believe he was serious.

'*C'est la vie, n'est-ce-pas?*' Jules continued, shrugging his shoulders. 'Monsieur is a man with normal appetites, after all. You are not only desirable but you have become the inspiration for many of his most successful designs. Like all *artistes*, he is a sensitive man and you never offend his sensibilities. I am not in the least surprised that he has fallen in love with you.'

For a moment Alice was shocked into silence. Then she said, 'Even if you are right, Jules, Monsieur Félix's personal feelings are not my concern. You can't seriously be suggesting that I . . . that I should become his mistress if he were to . . . to want me as such?'

Jules's eyes narrowed thoughtfully. 'Why not? He is kind, he is good, he is very, very rich – and he loves you. In society as it is today, you would be accepted nearly everywhere. Few would snub the acknowledged mistress of Monsieur Verveine. Your future would be entirely secure.'

Alice tried to laugh. 'This is just your usual nonsense, Jules,' she remonstrated. '"Security" may be important to you, but it is not so important to me that I would . . . that I would live with a man who was not my husband. Besides, I would have to love him if . . . if I were to live like that. Anyway, this is quite ridiculous. *Le Maître* always behaves towards me with the utmost propriety, whatever people may be saying to the contrary.'

Jules smiled. 'I do not doubt your word, Alice. But you must not mislead yourself as to his feelings towards you. Do you not agree that he is exceedingly attractive?'

'You really are talking nonsense,' Alice said quickly. But almost immediately followed the thought, was Jules really so far from the mark when he described Monsieur Félix as a very attractive man? She had seen for herself the effect he had on many of his clients; had herself been impressed by his ability to amuse them with his quick wit and entertaining anecdotes. And had she not felt elated when he praised her in that soft, beguiling voice? Flattered when he had looked at her in that particular way which was both critical and yet admiring at the same time?

Nevertheless, Jules could not have been serious in his suggestion that she might for one single instant consider becoming Monsieur's mistress. Her cheeks flamed even at the thought. Not only was her employer old enough to be her father, but he was a married man, and even if he were not, such a relationship would be totally foreign to her upbringing, if not her very nature.

'You really do talk nonsense at times, Jules,' she repeated in a tone which she hoped sounded mockingly reproachful. 'And what is more, we're wasting a lot of valuable time. Monsieur Félix will expect us to have made our choices and we have not even looked at the velvets yet.'

It was past four o'clock before Félix returned from the nursing-home. He looked tired but nevertheless managed a smile as he caught sight of his two employees and walked over to join them.

'What a charming picture you both make,' he said, sinking wearily into the chair Jules had drawn back for him. '"Spring afternoon in *le jardin*". It would make a delightful Renoir.'

'How is Madame Verveine?' Alice asked. 'Did she like the flowers?'

Félix shook his head. 'I'm afraid she was not aware of

them . . . or, indeed, of me. However, I should have expected no more. As you know, the doctors have warned me Madame can only regress. Now, let's see what the pair of you have selected. This one I approve immediately – such a delicate green! It would look well on you, Alice. Do you not agree, Jules?'

A servant arrived with some freshly made *jus de citron* and for the next half-hour the three of them remained with heads bent over the materials which would do so much to enhance Félix's English collection. He was quite determined to open the new *salon* in Albemarle Street with a fashion display that would be the talk of London society.

'The lease for the tenancy of the flat in Charles Street arrived yesterday and I have signed and returned it to the agent,' he told Alice. 'As soon as I can spare you, you are to go over there and make the place habitable. It is quite adequately furnished but I wish it to be in really *bon ton*. Jules, you can accompany Alice and familiarize yourself with London. You must also buy a copy of Debrett and familiarize yourself with the names of those people in society we hope will become our clients. Some, of course, you already know.'

'And the new *salon*, Monsieur?' Jules enquired.

'Work is progressing very well. As you know, I decided to keep the same colour scheme as we have in Paris. I think it will make our international clientele feel at home. I have been assured that the décor will be completed by the end of July, so we shall be able to keep to the schedule we have arranged and open in September. One of your tasks, Alice, will be to engage suitable *mannequins*. You know the kind of girl I like to have. It is not so much the face as the figure and deportment I consider of paramount concern.'

Alice waited until after Jules had departed before raising the subject that was at the forefront of her mind.

'I have been meaning to speak to you about my going to London,' she said. 'I will, of course, be happy to go in a week or two's time, but if it's at all possible, I very much want to be in London in July. You see, Harry is coming over from America for that month and I so want to see him. It's quite likely he will be returning to America to live there permanently, and so it could be my last chance.'

Félix Verveine regarded Alice's flushed cheeks speculatively.

'Ah, yes. Harry! This is the young man who grew up in your family as your brother?'

Alice nodded. 'He and I have always been very close. I really do want to see him.'

Félix drew a deep sigh and leaning back in his chair, raised his dark eyebrows in a wry half-smile.

'You know, Alice, you would not make a very good actress,' he said softly. 'Whenever you speak to me of this Harry of yours, your face and, indeed, your voice reveal that he is of special importance to you. You may tell me that your personal life is not my concern and that it is not for me to comment – and you would be justified – however, I cannot help but make it my concern because I have your future very much at heart. Therefore I now ask you one simple question, do you love this young man?'

If it had been anyone else who had probed into her private feelings, Alice might have been angry, but this man had become a kind of father-figure to her these past years, and despite the motives Jules might attribute to him, she truly believed her employer had her well-being at heart. Besides which, she reminded herself, he had chosen to put her in charge of his new London branch and, naturally, he needed to know if she was single-minded about her future job. Not that he need be worried, she thought with a brief pang of bitterness. Whoever Harry chose to marry now, it would not be her!

Suddenly, she felt the need to confide, to be able to tell some other person that when she was not actually working, her mind and heart were dominated by thoughts of Harry. She did love him, she had always loved him, but now that they were both adults the love she felt for him had taken on a far greater significance. She wanted to mean everything to him – everything a woman could mean to a man. Had he asked her to marry him, she would have

322

sacrificed everything to that end. Would Monsieur Félix –
her friend and mentor – understand how powerful her
feelings were? At least he had a right to know.

Haltingly she attempted to express her emotions and,
not least, the sense of finality and despair she had known
when Harry wrote so affectionately of the American girl,
Cora-Beth.

'The death of her twin brother somehow brought Harry
and her closer together,' she ended her story. 'I think the
only thing now which would prevent his marrying her was
if he discovered he was still in love with your niece.'

Félix nodded. 'That is a possibility! The little minx
seems to have half the young men in London at her feet. I
saw her at Christmas, did I tell you? Such a pretty little
thing – very much the coquette!'

'I would prefer, if he must marry one or the other, that
he chose this Cora-Beth girl,' Alice said softly. 'I think
Madeleine might end up breaking his heart.'

'Then we must hope that your Harry goes back to
America,' Félix said, 'not only for his sake, Alice, but for
mine. I do not want your heart broken, which I fear it
might be if you saw him unhappy.'

'Then you do understand?' Alice said gratefully. 'I
know there's no hope for me, but I shan't be at peace
unless I know he is happy.'

Félix reached across the table top and took Alice's hands
in his. 'Would it surprise you to know that is how I feel
about you?' he asked softly. 'Would it surprise you to
know that in the five years since I first set eyes on you, I
have not looked seriously at another woman? There is not
one night I have not fallen asleep wishing that I were free
to ask you to marry me. No, please do not take your hand
away. You have nothing to fear from me.'

He gave a sudden, unexpected laugh. 'Oh, *ma petite*,
you should see your face! I cannot believe that you were
quite unaware of my growing affection for you. I have
tried to hide it, but I did not imagine I had been entirely
successful.'

No, not entirely, Alice thought, remembering Jules's

reference to the gossip that had circulated among the staff at the *salon*. Nevertheless, until Jules had put the thought into her head, *she* had not once considered the reason for Félix's numerous kindnesses to her. How naïve and stupid she had been! On the other hand, why should a successful man, who could doubtless have any woman he fancied, be interested in her – plain Alice Pritchett from a simple working-class background? He even had a title!

Félix was regarding her with a look of amused tenderness. 'Let me make something quite clear to you, Alice,' he said. 'My personal feelings for you have nothing whatever to do with my admiration for your abilities. Even if I did not like you very much, I should still want you to be manageress of the Maison de Verveine in London. My dear child, what I am now offering you is a future which might not otherwise be available for you to enjoy. In my wife's absence, I would like you to become mistress of the Château de St Denis and to share my Paris house.'

So Jules was right and had once again proved his astuteness, Alice thought. Félix Verveine was suggesting she become his mistress.

'I fear I have shocked you, Alice,' he was saying, albeit with a slight smile lifting the corners of his mouth, 'but as you know, the option of marriage is not open to us. You are, if I am not mistaken, twenty-five years old, which is an age when, I am well aware, you could still meet and fall in love with a far younger man than I. However, from what you have told me, you have already given away your heart and have set aside any thought of another such love. What better arrangement, therefore, than to allow me to take care of you? I am a very wealthy man and I should greatly enjoy providing you with all the beautiful things you should have by right.' His smile deepened as he added, 'I have been told that I am a good lover and I can think of nothing in this world that would give me greater pleasure than to teach you the *plaisirs d'amour*. You would, of course, be free to break off our association at any time you chose. How is it you say in English – no strings attached?'

At last Alice found her voice. 'I couldn't do as you suggest. You know I don't . . . can't . . . I do like you – very, very much. It's just that I wouldn't consider it was right . . . fair . . . feeling as I do about . . . about another man.'

Félix nodded. 'You must not misunderstand me, *ma petite*! I am not suggesting *une affaire du cœur*. I am suggesting an arrangement which I believe might bring both of us a great deal of pleasure. For example, it would make me very happy if I could see you every night across my dinner table; if when I woke in the morning, I would hear you wish me "*Bonjour, chéri!*" in that so charming accent of yours. It would delight me to be able to buy you presents; to take you with me to my friends' houses, to the theatre, to Biarritz, to Cannes – wherever it pleased you to go.'

'Aren't you concerned about the distress such an arrangement would cause Madame Verveine?' Alice questioned uneasily, conscious of the fact that this man belonged to a society whose conventions differed greatly from her own and that by questioning the moral issues, she sounded unworldly, unsophisticated. Without being aware of her movements, she had withdrawn her hands, as if to distance herself from him.

'My wife is unaware of the real world any more. If you think it should be on my conscience that I take advantage of her ignorance, then it is only fair that I should tell you she has, in the past, been unfaithful to me.'

He gave a wry smile. 'Although I pity my wife, I do not feel under any obligation to remain faithful to her. Do you understand my sentiments?'

Alice nodded. 'I suppose so, but I'm not sure if you understand my feelings. You said that you were not expecting "an affair of the heart", but the relationship you suggest . . . I don't know myself if I am capable of it. I know nothing about that kind of thing . . .'

Her cheeks were suffused with colour and Félix's voice was very gentle as he said, 'Surely you must have been lonely at times? Thought how wonderful it would be to have a man's arms around you; someone to hold you, touch you, bring you to life? Have you not read novels, been to the cinema and watched the hero and heroine embracing and realized you have been missing a great deal? I hope to initiate you into this important part of life . . . to teach you about such things.'

For a moment, Alice was silent. Then she said hesitantly, 'Suppose I was unable to respond? I could be a big disappointment to you. Have you thought of that?'

'If I were not able to give you pleasure, *ma petite*, and thus give myself great happiness, then the fault would be mine,' Félix said, smiling once more. 'I have observed you very closely, Alice, and I do not believe you lack a passionate side to your nature for all you choose to appear so cool and so calm. There have been some most tempting glimpses of it when you have become excited about a design or angry with yourself for a failure to meet your own high standards.'

How well this man knew her, Alice thought. She had imagined that she could always at will appear poised and in complete control of her emotions. Nevertheless, she couldn't imagine herself in any form of intimacy with her employer, much as she liked him. Although she did not deny that he was handsome and in many ways attractive, she could not envisage herself in an intimate relationship with him. She had never felt the slightest stirring of her senses when he had embraced her, kissed her in French fashion on both cheeks. She had only ever felt this physical response in Harry's presence. To defy convention, surrender her virginity, to a man she neither loved nor desired must be quite out of the question.

On the other hand, did she wish to end up a spinster – like poor, dried-up Madame Duvalle, whose very *raison d'être* would end when she retired and no longer had her position at the *salon* to sustain her? If she, Alice, could not be married to the man she loved, did it really matter who became her partner?

Félix, who had been watching her face intently, now touched her cheek tenderly with his fingertips. '*Chérie*, this will not do at all,' he said lightly. 'You are looking worried, sad, anxious, confused, whereas my intention is to make you happy, to make us both happy! We could enjoy life, amuse ourselves, together. We could have what you English call "fun" . . . and I do not think there has been a great deal of that commodity in your life so far. Now, if for no other reason than to give me pleasure, will you please smile?'

Despite herself, Alice did so, but her moment of light-heartedness did not last for long.

'Please don't think me ungrateful,' she said tentatively. 'I know you mean well, but, try as I might, I can't think that what you are suggesting would be right – not for either of us. It's not simply a matter of defying conventions although I admit I have been strictly brought up and I think it would break my parents' hearts if ever they came to know I was living with a man who was not my husband. It's that I'm afraid I would disappoint you. I respect you and I am very fond of you and shall always, always be grateful to you; but that isn't enough, is it? You would expect me to respond and I . . . I don't believe I could. I'm very sorry.'

Félix looked unconcerned. It was almost, Alice thought, as if this was the answer he had expected.

'I had made up my mind to put this proposition to you today,' he said, 'but I see now that this was not the right moment to approach you, *ma petite*. Your thoughts, understandably, are with the young man who is shortly returning from America. Naturally you will not want to make any commitment until you are certain that there is no chance he will change his mind and discover that it is after all you he loves. So we shall not speak further of this matter until after you have seen your Harry again. I should have realized the folly of my timing. It is not like me to lack perception and I can only suppose that my enthusiasm overruled my common sense. Let us await the outcome of your reunion with this boy you love.'

This kindly man was certainly not lacking in perception now, Alice thought. Although there was not one single reason why Harry might suddenly see her not as a sister or friend but as a woman he might fall in love with, deep down inside she still hoped that this unlikely miracle could occur.

Suddenly aware that the afternoon sun had cooled, she shivered, an inexplicable feeling of depression engulfing her. She stared at the beautiful garden beyond the terrace, fighting the inclination to weep. She had every justification not to lose hope, she reminded herself. Jules had told her she was attractive, Félix found her so, and she would have had to be blind not to see the admiring glances of strangers when she went to a café or on a promenade with Jules. All Félix's guests who came to dine at the château paid her extravagant compliments. She would be falsely modest not to acknowledge the fact that she had come a very long way since those days when she had been a thin, gawky adolescent. She not only had the figure of a *mannequin* but she had learned from the girls at the *salon* how to walk, how to hold her head up, how to appear perfectly poised. Her dress sense was faultless and Félix had taught her that she could wear eye-catching colours that she wouldn't have thought of choosing for herself. Whatever her beginnings in life, she could now carry herself in the most élite company without the slightest fear of revealing her true origins. If Harry's circumstances had changed so vitally, so too had hers.

With a sense of shock, Alice now realized that the revelation of Félix's feelings for her had, in fact, radically changed her opinion of herself. She was suddenly seeing herself as a desirable young woman – a woman the famous *Maître* of the Maison de Verveine might have wanted to marry had he been free. Since Félix was not going to oppose her wishes to meet Harry in London in July, then there was still a chance – however remote – that she could change Harry's mind about the American girl. As to his feelings for Madeleine, nurtured since he'd been a little boy, even were they to be revived, it seemed unlikely Madeleine would respond to him. She'd been the most sought-after débutante of her year and, according to the occasional letter Alice had had from Lady Debrace, was forever receiving proposals from faithful admirers who danced constant attendance upon her. She very much doubted Madeleine would be prepared to give up the good time she was having to settle down in the country on Harry's salary.

She became suddenly aware again of the man sitting beside her. If he was disappointed by her rejection of his proposal, he was giving no indication of it. She must do what little she could to soften her refusal.

'I will do everything within my power to make the new London *salon* a success,' she said aloud. 'I wouldn't want you to feel that I am any less dedicated than I have ever been.'

Félix acknowledged this somewhat childlike offer of recompense with a genuine smile.

'Ah, but, Alice, suppose this young man were to invite you to return to America with him? What then, *chérie*?'

Yet again, the colour flared into Alice's cheeks.

'I would consider it my duty to remain at the *salon* until you had found a suitable replacement for me,' she said primly.

'I would have expected no less of you, Alice. I was only teasing, for I am well aware you would never let me down,' Félix said with a pretence at seriousness. 'Come now, *chérie*, my guests will be arriving before long and we are not yet changed for dinner. Let us go in, shall we?'

He rose to his feet and offered Alice his arm. His manner seemed to have reverted to normal. It was as if he had never raised the possibility that she might become so much more to him than his personal assistant.

'Tell me about Jules,' he said as they approached the stone steps leading up to the arched doorway into the château. 'He has no qualms about going to live in England?'

Alice shook her head.

'On the contrary, I understand he is greatly looking forward to it.'

'I have it in mind to promote Jules to a more prominent

position in the firm one of these days,' Félix commented. 'In his own way, he is very talented.'

'He has taught me a great deal about the business,' Alice proffered, 'and I know he is totally loyal to the Maison de Verveine. I like him very much.'

'Such types as Jules are invariably *sympathique* to women,' Félix replied. 'I am glad you get along so well with him, Alice. It is important to have good relationships within the business.'

They had by now reached the foot of the staircase.

'*A bientôt!*' he said with a smile. 'I shall see you presently, looking, as always, quite ravishing in one of my creations – the oyster-pink crêpe de Chine with the russet chiffon cape, is it not?'

It did not occur to Alice to question Félix's interest in the dress she was wearing until, her toilet completed, she finally went back downstairs. As she joined him in the *petit salon* he came towards her with a prettily wrapped package in his hands.

'This is a small *cadeau* for you, *ma petite*,' he said. 'I happened to see it on my way back from the nursing-home and I thought it would go particularly well with the dress.'

Alice unwrapped the parcel with a sense of unease. If this was jewellery, she could not possibly accept it, no matter how appropriate it might be for the gown she was wearing. Opening the lid of the box, she gave an involuntary cry of pleasure. Toning exactly with the colour of her crêpe de Chine dress was a long, *pliqué-à-jour* necklace of geometric metal links filled with various shades of pink enamel, interspersed with cornelians.

'It's lovely, Félix, really perfect,' she said. 'But I could not accept . . .'

'Believe me, Alice, it is of very little value,' Félix interrupted her. Deliberately, he refrained from remarking that she had called him by his Christian name for the first time. 'A pretty *bijou*, no more. If it makes you feel any happier, I will tell you that it did not cost me as much as a bouquet of flowers would have done. So put it on, my dear. Allow me to help you.'

Although not entirely convinced that the necklace was without real value, Alice did not protest as Félix fastened it around her neck. Placing a hand on her shoulder, he led her to an ornate, gilded mirror hanging above the carved-stone fireplace.

'There! Was my choice not perfect?' he asked, staring at their reflections with a satisfied smile.

'Thank you,' Alice said, turning to him. 'It was very clever of you to find it. It's really lovely.'

'As, indeed, is the wearer,' Félix replied, taking care not to touch her. 'Whatever pleasure it gives you cannot match the pleasure it gave me to buy this trinket for you.' He gave a wry smile. 'It is not good being a wealthy man and having no one to spend one's money on, you know.'

Suddenly Alice found herself able to laugh.

'Having heard your accountant exclaim at your expenditure on the new London *salon*, I cannot believe you are having difficulty in disposing of your wealth,' she said. 'If the sums he mentioned are to be believed, it puts a most terrible responsibility on my shoulders.'

'One you are quite capable of carrying, Alice,' Félix said, 'and I shall be behind you if you have any problems. I look on this as our joint enterprise.'

Had she not known Félix so well, Alice thought, touching the necklace at her throat, she might now be feeling as if there were some kind of trap closing slowly about her. Fortunately, she told herself, she had no cause to mistrust him. He had never been anything but completely honest with her, as indeed she was with him. As to the necklace, who was to be the judge of its value? In her early childhood, a threepenny piece had seemed like a fortune, whereas Félix Verveine's rich clients thought nothing of paying 3,000 francs to be dressed by him. The value of money was relative and it was becoming an increasingly difficult task for her to reconcile those early years of poverty with her present position. It seemed terribly wrong that her family were still struggling even now to keep their heads above water, that many like them were close to starvation, when the clothes she, Alice, was wearing would have kept them in food for at least half a year.

A long time ago, Alice thought, as she heard the arrival of the first of Félix's dinner guests, she and Harry had longed to be rich in order to buy themselves a house which they could share. Now, she decided, if ever she had that kind of money, she would first ensure that her family would never again, for as long as they lived, be in need.

It was therefore with mixed feelings that Alice managed to give a welcoming smile to the couple who now entered the room and gracefully acknowledged the compliments of the wife of the Belgian ambassador, who was admiring her unique Verveine gown.

CHAPTER NINETEEN

1924

'Oh, Pogo, do let go of my hand. You're all sticky,' Madeleine said as the taxi cab turned into Charlotte Street.

'S-sorry, M-Maddy! Deuced hot. N-not so b-bad for you in that dress.'

'Don't be so ratty, Pickles,' Aubrey said. 'Honestly, Dunbar, I don't see why you put up with her. She does nothing but bait you.'

Captain Lionel Dunbar looked reproachfully at the young man seated opposite him.

'M-Maddy's perfectly j-justified,' he said with his intermittent stutter. 'Should've kept my gloves on, what?'

'I think we've arrived,' the girl sitting next to Aubrey remarked. She looked adoringly at her fair-haired escort. One of this year's débutantes, Primrose was pretty but still far too much of a schoolgirl to interest Aubrey. Madeleine, however, had insisted he bring along a girl to make up a foursome and Primrose was the only girl available at the last minute.

Poor old long-suffering Dunbar, Aubrey thought, as Pogo climbed out on to the pavement and paid the driver. He was Pickles's slave and she treated him like one. It was high time someone took his young sister down a peg. Either that, or she made up her mind to marry the wretched fellow.

They had been to the Maxwells' for drinks and afterwards to see Shaw's *Saint Joan*. His sister had been restless and Dunbar had had to fight queues of people at the bar to buy drinks in the interval. Now, at Madeleine's insistence, they were going to while the night away at the

Cave of Harmony nightclub, where they would all get even hotter dancing the shimmy, the foxtrot or the black bottom. At least the club had a good jazz band, and a first-class cabaret. With a bit of luck, Ernest Milton would be doing his Pirandello 'Man With the Flower on His Lip' act.

Really, he was stupid to have agreed to come here, Aubrey thought as Pogo led the way indoors. The atmosphere was like a Turkish bath and the fumes from people's cigarettes aggravated his asthma. However, once Pickles and Pogo started dancing, they would probably not notice if he slipped quietly away with the goggle-eyed Primrose.

'It's my first time here,' she whispered as they squeezed into a table and a waiter took their orders for drinks. 'I suppose you've been here lots of times, Madeleine?'

'Dozens,' Madeleine said. 'It's our favourite place, isn't it, Pogo?'

'C-certainly is,' he said instantly. Madeleine was still very much an enigma to him. Sometimes she could be quite sharp and critical, and then, when he was about to give up all hope that she would ever accept one of his frequent proposals of marriage, she would suddenly become very affectionate, even allow him to kiss her.

Tonight, he thought, she was looking particularly stunning. The diagonal hem of her pale-blue frock reached nearly up to her knees on one side, and her shoulders were bare, the flimsy bodice held only by narrow sequinned straps no wider than his shoelaces. Her small, rose-bud mouth was a bright cherry red and her huge, sapphire blue eyes were alight with interest.

'Enjoying yourself, M-Maddy?' he asked as Aubrey invited his partner to dance. 'I know you didn't m-much like the p-play. Everyone s-said it was . . . ripping.'

Madeleine appeared not to have heard him.

'Do look, Pogo. Over there by the pillar. I think that's H. G. Wells! One of the reasons I'm mad about this place is because you always see someone really interesting here. Last time we came, we saw Tallulah Bankhead, remember?'

'If you say so, Maddy,' Pogo said. 'I d-don't usually notice other p-people. I'm too busy looking at you.'

Madeleine laughed.

'You know, you really are quite nice sometimes, Pogo,' she said. 'Sorry if I was beastly to you earlier.'

'You c-couldn't be b-beastly if you tried,' Pogo said. He was about to take her hand but, remembering she had found his unpleasantly sticky, he thought better of it. The difficulty was, Maddy made him nervous, and the more anxious he became, the stickier became his palms. 'I know you t-told me not to p-propose again and I p-promised, but I h-had s-some rather b-bad news today. I'm being p-posted, so . . .'

Madeleine now gave him her full attention.

'Oh, do tell, Pogo. Where to? When? I thought you were going to be here in London for ages.'

'S-so did I,' her companion said mournfully. 'But the p-powers that be have decided I'm to go to Jamaica. D-decent p-place, actually. Lots of chaps would like to go in my p-place, but . . . my c-commanding officer says it's not on. D-don't want to leave you, you see.'

'You mean you tried to get out of it? Jamaica? The West Indies?' Madeleine cried. 'But that's a wonderful place to go, Pogo.'

'Yes, I know, g-good place for cricket, sailing, f-fishing and p-polo, but *you* wouldn't be there to watch me p-play. H-have to admit it, old thing, I'm h-head over h-heels in love with you.'

'Oh, Pogo,' Madeleine breathed. 'I do wish you weren't. I mean, I do like you, you know I do. Better than anyone else actually. But I'm not in love with you. At least, I don't think I am.'

Pogo regarded her longingly from beneath sandy-coloured lashes. The summer sun, to which he was so often exposed during his many sporting pursuits, had accentuated his freckles.

'Couldn't you t-try?' he suggested. 'I m-mean, is there honestly no h-hope?'

'Well, I'm not in love with anyone else, if that's

anything to go by,' Madeleine said. 'And I'd miss you a lot if you went away. Are you really going to Jamaica? I mean, it's certain?'

'Absolutely, although I d-don't know when. The CO just said it was advance n-notice.'

The thought of going to live in the West Indies was exciting, Madeleine thought. One of her schoolfriends had married a Bermudan and wrote in the most glowing terms about the life there. It all sounded like one big, never-ending party, and the climate was wonderful all the year round. Pogo's family were very well connected and he had an entrée to every branch of society. He was, moreover, an extremely wealthy young man who thought nothing of taking a string of polo ponies wherever he went. The Dunbar family had houses in London, Scotland, Ireland and a villa in Biarritz, as well as their own yacht. Pogo was even on Christian name terms with some members of the Royal Family.

If she were to marry him as he wanted, and, indeed, as her mother wanted, she would enjoy all these assets. Pogo was six foot two and, although not exactly good-looking, he had a pleasant, friendly face and was a keen athlete. Why, then, was she not in love with him?

As Primrose and her brother rejoined them at the table, Madeleine continued to pursue her own thoughts. She knew it was silly of her and that her mother would be the first to tell her so, but she had never quite forgotten Harry Keynes. There had been something about him which had affected her deep down inside. She had sensed something more than mere adoration in the way he had kissed her and been aware of her body's response. Neither Pogo nor any other of her various escorts had ever aroused that same sensation of longing.

Could that have been love, real love? she asked herself now, as she had many times before. When Harry replied to her letters, her heart never failed to miss a beat as she recognized his handwriting. No one knew of it, but she had a snapshot of him standing beside Aubrey in the garden at The Grange hidden in her handkerchief sachet.

Sometimes, when she had been to a romantic film, or had been kissed good-night by Pogo, she had sat on the edge of her bed, staring at that dark, handsome, boy's face and tried to conjure up the memory of his living presence.

It was a long, long time since he'd gone off to America and now, at last, he was coming back on a month's holiday. In two days' time, she thought, she would actually see him. Would he still be able to arouse in her that same strange feeling that was part sweetness and part pain? He must have grown up now just as she had done. Would they find each other much changed, or would it be like it was when he had come back from school for the holidays?

According to Aubrey, he had a girl in Kentucky he was keen on. Would that have altered the way he'd always felt about *her*? He'd asked her to wait for him, and although she'd been too angry at the time to say that she would, she had nevertheless avoided marriage to anyone else despite the many proposals she'd had. Once she had seen Harry again, she would know if she'd only imagined that special magic between them. Meanwhile, Pogo would just have to wait for an answer.

Despite her parents' invitation to Harry to stay with them in London while he was back in England, he'd written to say that he had already promised to go to Bertie Alcott's home in Cadogan Square. He'd sounded regretful but pointed out that he had committed himself and felt it would be ill-mannered to tell his hostess he had now made other arrangements. He was, however, anxious to see as much of Aubrey and Madeleine as time allowed. His only other commitments were visits to the Pritchetts.

It struck Madeleine that this was surely a waste of time. It was many years since he'd had anything in common with his foster family and she would have expected him to use his sojourn in America as a tactful method of ending the association, of breaking ties that could have no conceivable advantage for him. One was simply not on friendly terms with people like gardeners and their offspring. It was no fault of Harry's that he had been mistakenly put in the care of such people, although there was nothing to be said against the Pritchetts – a decent, hard-working family – other than their class.

According to letters her mother had received from Uncle Félix, Alice Pritchett had done quite amazingly well and was going to be given the new London branch of her uncle's fashion house to manage. She, Madeleine, would have to buy some clothes there once it opened. Everyone seemed to be talking about Verveine creations as being 'the thing'. But Alice was the only one of the Pritchetts who had, from all accounts, risen above her station in life.

As if guessing the trend of his sister's thoughts, Aubrey said suddenly, 'One of my great friends, Harry Keynes, is coming over from the United States next week, Dunbar. I'll introduce you. You two should get along like a house on fire as he's by way of being quite an authority on horses these days. You can show him that string of polo ponies you're so proud of.'

'Splendid! N-nothing I'd l-like more,' Pogo said with his usual enthusiasm. 'Take him down to Hurlingham, eh?'

'Why not?' Aubrey agreed good-naturedly. 'I've booked some centre-court seats for Wimbledon too. He's not a bad tennis player, though cricket's really his game. Thought we might go down to Grafton for the Old Boys' match against the first XI. Too late to get him in the team, though.'

'Keynes, you say?' Pogo asked. 'Can't say I've m-met anyone of that name.'

Madeleine laughed as a feeling of excitement coursed through her.

'He's vaguely connected to the Harveys,' she answered. 'He's been living with the Earl of Kinmuire in Kentucky.'

'Wouldn't surprise me if he marries the old boy's daughter,' Aubrey said. 'We'll know more about that when we see him. Thought I'd go and meet the boat – docks at Southampton. Want to come along, Dunbar?'

'Oh, do let's go, Pogo. I'd love the drive down there. It'ud be fun,' Madeleine said quickly.

'Then we'll g-go in my Bentley,' Pogo suggested. 'Do the old girl good to have a d-decent s-spin.'

'Thought you said the other day you felt sick in a Bentley,' Aubrey said. The look Madeleine gave him would have withered anyone other than her brother. 'Oh, well, please yourself,' he said and, worried lest Primrose should have felt excluded from the conversation, as well as the trip to Southampton, he offered to give her two of his tickets to Wimbledon.

'Oh, I say, Aubrey, that's jolly decent of you,' she said, beaming at him from round, blue eyes. 'Daddy's been trying like mad to get hold of some. He's frightfully keen. Thanks an awful lot!'

Later, when Aubrey had left to take Primrose home, Pogo said, 'She c-couldn't hold a candle to you, Maddy. I n-never know what to say to g-girls like that. Get hopelessly tongue-tied. It's d-different with you – you've always g-got something to t-talk about. W-will you think about it, M-Maddy? Marrying me and coming out to Jamaica, I mean?'

'I don't see how there'd be time,' Madeleine prevaricated. 'You can't get married in five minutes. Weddings take ages to prepare.'

'But we c-could get a special l-licence,' Pogo persisted. 'I d-don't suppose we'll go for at least a m-month. We c-could h-have our honeymoon out there.'

When Madeleine did not reply, he continued eagerly, 'They'd give us m-married quarters, but if you d-didn't like them, we could rent a house – whatever t-took your fancy.'

This suggestion more than any other caught Madeleine's interest. It was all very well living in London, or, when her mother insisted, at the house in Brighton, but they were not *her* houses, and although she was almost twenty she was still very much subject to her parents' control. She could never go anywhere without her mother's permission and prior vetting of her escort. It was only because her mother approved so strongly of Pogo that she was allowed to go out with him to places like this, and then, as often as not, her mother insisted that Aubrey went too. If she married Pogo, she could do exactly as she pleased — and she would be mistress of her own home. Pogo never refused any request she made if it was in his power to satisfy her.

'I'll think about it,' she said. 'But you're not to count on it, Pogo. You do understand that, don't you?'

'Oh, yes, I d-do! Good L-Lord, Maddy, you've no idea how happy you've m-made me. I m-mean, it's absolutely splendid just knowing you'll think about it. S-seriously, I mean.'

'Well, don't go on about it,' Madeleine said irritably. 'It's more than likely I won't want to do it. So you're not to talk about it to anyone. I absolutely forbid it. If you get all serious, I'll begin to wish I hadn't said anything at all.'

Pogo looked suitably crestfallen.

'I really am a s-silly ass s-sometimes, aren't I?' he said apologetically. 'C-can't think why you p-put up with me.'

'Now you're being utterly futile,' Madeleine told him. 'Come on, let's dance. I'm getting bored sitting here.'

Conscious of the fact that his palms were sweating even more markedly than usual, Pogo hurriedly pulled on his white gloves and led his impatient partner on to the floor.

When Harry had kissed Cora-Beth goodbye in Kentucky a week ago, he had been convinced that he loved her. Now, having met Madeleine again, he knew that he loved them both! It had been a wonderful surprise seeing Madeleine with Aubrey and their friend, Lionel Dunbar, on the quayside. She had thrown herself into his arms and hugged him as if she were still a schoolgirl. However, when she disappeared into the powder room at the hotel where they stopped for lunch on the way back to London and Dunbar went off to book a table in the restaurant, he and Aubrey had a moment alone together. Aubrey had laughingly referred to Lionel as Madeleine's 'intended'. They did not appear to be engaged, nor was Madeleine sporting a ring, but Harry had had no opportunity to discover if the army captain was really her fiancé. He was on his way to dine with the Debraces in their London house, where, he assumed, he would discover the facts.

When he reached number six, Cavendish Street, he was shown by a maid into the drawing-room, where Sir Philip and Lady Debrace stood waiting to welcome him.

'Be damned if you haven't grown a few more inches, m'boy,' Sir Philip said, shaking Harry warmly by the hand. 'Filled out too. Hope you haven't acquired one of those Yankee accents in the States?'

Harry laughed as he shook Lady Debrace's outstretched hand.

'No, sir. If anything, I'll have acquired a Southern drawl. Before I forget, Mr Harvey and his daughter have asked me to convey their very kind regards.'

'Deuced bad business, losing his boy like that. Very tragic. People got used to it in the war but now . . . well, time will soften the blow. It usually does.'

'Do sit down, Harry,' Eloise said as she sat on the sofa, patting the cushioned seat beside her. 'Aubrey and Madeleine will be here presently. They are still changing. They went to see that new celluloid "Plastigram" film at the Coliseum and were late back. I haven't seen it yet, but I am told it's quite spectacular. You have to wear these strange spectacles to obtain a kind of three-dimension effect.'

'New-fangled nonsense, if you ask me,' said Sir Philip as he poured Harry a drink. It was the first time Harry had ever seen him do such a thing for himself, but then he had heard that staff were far less easy to come by since the war. Perhaps he no longer had a butler.

'Did the children give you all the news?' Eloise asked. 'I expect you remember Sally, our maid? She married Frederick and they manage our house in Brighton. Poor Frederick, it took him two years to get over Alice's departure to France. You know about her, of course. My brother-in-law is making her manageress of the London salon he's opening in the autumn. Isn't it quite splendid?'

'I'm meeting her tomorrow off the boat train,' Harry replied, 'and we're going down to Calking together. I expect she'll tell me all about the new job then. Despite our interchange of letters, I feel we've rather lost touch over the years, so it'll be wonderful to see her again.'

Before Eloise could comment, Aubrey came into the room.

'Sorry we're late, old boy,' he said. 'Pickles ran into some friends and was trying to make up a party to go dancing tonight. Thank goodness, they couldn't make it. I don't think I could stand another evening just yet at that nightclub she and Dunbar seem so crazy about.'

'You've met Captain Dunbar, haven't you?' Eloise said to Harry. 'Such a very nice young man. Don't tell Madeleine I said so because she'll deny it just to be contrary, but I'm very much hoping the two of them will soon be getting engaged. Captain Dunbar's been around now for over a year and most of Madeleine's suitors last only a few months, so we think it's serious.'

'Oh, the fellow's smitten all right,' Sir Philip said jovially. 'It's that little minx of mine who won't make up her mind to settle down.'

'She's still very young, dear,' Eloise said. 'Give her time.'

'I married you before you were twenty,' Sir Philip said. 'Haven't regretted it, have you, m'dear?'

'No, of course not, my love,' Eloise replied, smiling. 'But things have changed now. Young girls have so much more freedom than we had in my day. Madeleine does more or less whatever she wants.'

'Mummy, that simply isn't true,' Madeleine said as she came hurrying into the drawing-room. 'You and Daddy always want to know where I'm going, what I'm doing, who I'm with. I'm sure American girls don't have all these silly rules, do they, Harry?'

'I can't answer for anyone but Cora-Beth,' Harry said. 'I suppose it's different for her, but she doesn't very often leave Blue Ash Farm and it's way out in the wilds. Mr Harvey does want to know about it if she goes into Lexington – that's our nearest town – but then someone has to drive her there and back, so she's never without an escort. It's different here in London.'

'Very different,' Sir Philip said. 'All you young people think about these days is "having a good time". You'd think there was no tomorrow the way you behave. Aftermath of the war, I suppose.'

'Oh, let's not harp back to the war, Daddy,' Madeleine said as she reached up to plant a kiss on his cheek. 'You haven't told me if you like my new dress?'

They all turned to look at her, but it was Harry's reaction for which Madeleine was watching. Pirouetting in the beaded chiffon dress with its daring low back, she gazed questioningly at him.

'Like it?' she said.

'You shouldn't ask for compliments, Pickles,' Aubrey reproached her. 'I don't think I've ever met anyone more vain than you. Other girls wait to be told they look half-way decent, don't they, Harry?'

Harry laughed.

'I see you two still bicker as much as ever,' he said. 'However, you really do look very nice, Madeleine. It's a lovely dress.'

She did indeed look more stunning than he had ever in his dreams imagined. He could feel his heart thudding furiously and hoped desperately that he'd succeeded in making his voice sound casual.

Madeleine left her father's side and came to tuck her arm through his.

'Don't pay any attention to Aubrey,' she muttered in a voice still audible to her brother. 'He's just jealous because each time the telephone rings it's for me and not for him. And because you're much more handsome than he is.'

'Sucking up now,' Aubrey said, laughing. 'Watch her, Harry! She's an incorrigible flirt. Must have every swain at her feet. I can tell you this much, if I were Lionel Dunbar, I'd have packed her in months ago. Can't imagine why he actually wants to *marry* her.'

'That's quite enough, you two,' Eloise broke in. 'Harry is our guest. He'll think we have no manners at all.'

343

'Oh, Mummy, he's *not* our guest. He's almost one of the family. You seem to have forgotten we were all children together.'

'Then it's high time you stopped behaving like a child, young lady,' her father said. 'Now then, Harry, m'boy – let's hear about this stud farm you're running. Done pretty well for yourself, I gather. You going to marry Harvey's girl? He wrote and told me it was on the cards.'

'I . . . I don't know. I mean, I'm not actually sure,' Harry said, feeling acutely embarrassed. 'I mean, I haven't exactly proposed or anything.'

'So she hasn't turned you down, eh? Well, good luck to you, boy. You're very happy out there, aren't you? Good move sending you off to prove yourself. Pretty sure you would, of course.'

Harry glanced swiftly at Madeleine, but she had turned her back on him so he was unable to see her reactions to her father's comments. Surely she could not be jealous of Cora-Beth, he thought? Aubrey was probably right – she just wanted to be able to number him among her many admirers. By all accounts, she was going to marry Lionel Dunbar.

I'll make her tell me outright, he told himself as the maid rang the gong for dinner. I won't believe it unless she tells me herself. Maybe I'm not too late after all, and there is still a chance.

As he took his hostess's arm and led her into the dining-room, he did not glance again at Madeleine. He dared not do so for he knew one thing for certain – that he had never really fallen out of love with this stunningly beautiful girl.

[...] with the [...]

CHAPTER TWENTY

1924

Alice's heart seemed to be thumping in time with the train wheels as she looked at Harry's glowing face opposite her. His dark eyes were bright with excitement as the train steamed out of Victoria Station on its way to Burgess Hill.

'Do you realize it's two years, six months and six days since I saw you on to a train – possibly this very one – the day before I went to America? It's so wonderful to see you, Alice. You look marvellous. A bit thin, though.'

'I need to be thin, to do justice to Monsieur Félix's clothes,' Alice said, glancing down at her low-waisted frock of indigo-blue jersey. With its large, carved buttons running diagonally from shoulder to hip, it was one of her favourites and so becoming, Félix had told her she might keep it.

'Well, you certainly look very dashing,' Harry said with genuine admiration. 'You know, I wanted to take you to lunch at the Ritz, like we did last time, but it would have made us so late in Calking. Still, there'll be another chance, won't there? You said you'd be in London for several weeks and I'm here for a month.'

'I do have a certain amount of work to do,' Alice said, 'but I can fit in with your plans, Harry. I'm due some holiday time.'

'That's really good news. And talking of news, Alice, you might be interested to hear that Madeleine may be getting engaged to an army officer called Lionel Dunbar. He's really absolutely the right choice for her,' he ended ruefully. 'I mean, he's from the right kind of background and he has more money that he knows what to do with. I can't begin to tell you how beautiful she is these days. She always was pretty, of course, but now . . . Well, she takes one's breath away.'

Alice looked down at her handbag and fiddled meaninglessly with the clasp.

'Are you still in love with her?' she forced herself to ask.

Harry sighed. 'Regrettably, yes! The trouble is, she's got this chap in tow. He's being posted out to the West Indies and he's asked her to marry him and go with him. With my background, I'm not exactly eligible, am I? Not to mention my impecunious state.'

'Is she going?'

'That's just it – she can't make up her mind. Last night, after her parents had gone up to bed, and Aubrey very tactfully made himself scarce, I had a chance to ask her. First she said she was going to marry Dunbar and then . . . Well, she asked me to kiss her, which of course I did, and then she said maybe she wouldn't marry him; that she thought she might be in love with me. Honestly, Alice, I simply don't know what to believe. I told her I still loved her and asked her how she'd feel about going out to Kentucky. She said she wouldn't want to do that – live on a stud farm, miles away from anywhere; that she'd be lonely and miss all her friends.'

'So she doesn't love you enough,' Alice said thoughtfully.

Harry gave her a boyish grin.

'That's what I thought but then, when I kissed her again, she said she did love me; that she was fearfully jealous of Cora-Beth. She hadn't known until Sir Philip mentioned it at dinner last night that I'd been thinking about marrying her. I feel so dreadfully sorry for Cora-Beth, Alice. She's been terribly cut up about her brother. Mr Harvey is devastated too. Thank goodness he has Cora-Beth to comfort him. Do you know, he didn't even care when Mr Riddle agreed to let his stallion, Man o'War, cover one of our mares? That's been one of his life-time

346

ambitions. Man o'War is probably one of the best race horses the world has ever known. Alice, am I boring you with all this?'

Alice smiled.

'No, of course not. I want to know everything about your life out there. You're going back, aren't you?'

Harry nodded.

'For a while anyway. I promised Mr Harvey I would. Of course, he's terribly anxious for me to settle down out there, marry Cora-Beth and become an American citizen, the way his father did years ago. Do you realize that according to some strange Scottish law about dynasties, Cora-Beth is now heir to the title and the Kinmuire estate? Mr Harvey is waiting for confirmation, but it seems pretty certain although it's very unusual. I wonder what my father would have said if he'd known his illegitimate son might yet marry one of the Kinmuires.'

'But you wouldn't marry Cora-Beth for that reason alone, would you?' Alice asked.

'No, certainly not,' Harry said emphatically. 'I'm not interested in titles, and even if I were, it wouldn't be fair to marry Cora-Beth just for that reason. I'd have to be sure I loved her, and I'm not! It was different when I was actually with her – we always get along so well. In a way, it's a bit like being with you, Alice; I can say anything I want to her and she always seems to understand, just like you do. If it wasn't for Madeleine . . .'

'It seems to me as if Madeleine is going to decide matters for you,' Alice said quietly. She was surprised to find how calm and reasonable she sounded, for although she had expected no different, to hear Harry speaking so ardently of his love for another girl felt as if an icy hand were clutching her heart. 'If this army fellow is leaving London, he's sure to want an answer before he goes. If Madeleine does decide to marry him – or get engaged to him – then you'll know where you stand. I suppose not everyone in this life is able to marry the person they love most in the world.'

'Why, Alice,' Harry said, staring at her curiously, 'you

sound as if *you've* fallen in love with someone *you* can't have. Is that true?'

For a moment, Alice toyed with the idea of denying it. Then she said, 'I suppose so. The man I love is in love with someone else. He . . . he only sees me as a . . . a dear friend. I don't think anything will ever change that so it's very stupid of me even to hope . . . to live in the hope that he . . . that it'll ever be different. I dare say in the end I'll settle for second-best.'

'Second-best,' Harry repeated. 'You mean there really is someone special? Why didn't you write and tell me all this, Alice? I tell you all my secrets.'

By now Alice had regained complete control of herself. She forced a laugh.

'Because there's really nothing to tell,' she said. 'I'm much too busy with my career to bother about such things. Are you pleased with me – that I'm to manage the London branch of the Maison de Verveine?'

'Pleased – and tremendously proud,' Harry said fervently. 'In a way, I'm not in the least surprised, but on the other hand, I somehow can't see you as one of these modern, independent career women. I think of the way you used to help Mum when we were kids – how kind and efficient you were even when you were quite small. Somehow I think of you as . . . well, as a mother, I suppose. Now, seeing you sitting there, looking more like a film star than the Alice I used to know, I'm not so sure. Which is the real Alice?'

'This is,' Alice said quickly. 'I don't think I shall ever marry and have children. I love my work. I enjoy what I do. Isn't that enough?'

'Yes, of course,' Harry said, 'but I still think you should have someone to take care of you. You may like what you're doing, but it must be awfully lonely at times.'

'Perhaps! But I have friends – people who do care about me. And there's Jules . . . and Monsieur Félix.'

'That isn't what I meant,' Harry said. 'I meant everyone needs someone to love and to love them.'

'Well, I love you for a start – and there's Mum and Dad

and the kids. I told you Jenny wanted to get married, didn't I?'

It reminded Harry of his plan to give Jenny and her boy some money towards the shop they were saving to buy. Alice thought it a wonderful gesture, and for the remainder of the journey they discussed their joint wish to make Will and Martha Pritchett financially secure for the rest of their lives.

'Although I'm very far from being a rich man as yet,' Harry said with a smile, 'by Mum's and Dad's standards I am. I'm paid an incredibly generous salary and as I have no living expenses, I've been able to save nearly all of it. Then there's the money I've made at the races. Mr Harvey always take us to the Kentucky Derby and we stay in Washington for the Preakness meeting, then go on to some friends of the Harveys in New York. Twice when we were there, I backed the winner of the Belmont Stakes. And, of course, we go to all the Lexington race meetings, being so nearby.'

He grinned as he saw Alice's doubtful expression.

'Don't look so shocked,' he said. 'I haven't become an inveterate gambler like Uncle Cosmo. We only bet when Mr Harvey tells us who to back, and nine times out of ten he's right, so I've nearly doubled my savings. That's how I could afford my passage to England and this holiday. On top of everything, he gave me 500 dollars for my twenty-first birthday and it's this I intend sharing between Jenny and the family.'

'It's a lovely idea, Harry, and very generous of you,' Alice said warmly, 'but you know how proud Dad is. He won't take charity.'

'Then you'll have to make him see sense if I can't, Alice. He'll have to agree for Mum's sake.'

It proved to be the right approach. Martha had been far from well for some time and was in need of another operation. Will, now approaching his seventies, wanted to retire but their savings were insufficient to allow him to do so. Bent almost double, he was still spending forty hours a week gardening for the new owners of The Grange.

It was Martha who finally made the decision to accept Harry's gift. She surprised all of them, not least her husband, when, after listening to Alice's persuasions and Will's stubborn refusal to give way, she said, 'You been master of your house ever since the day I married you, Will Pritchett. I ain't never argued with you but once – and that were when you said it'ud be wrong for us to keep Harry. T'was you, surely, who let me have my way then, so I'm not saying, as I could, that you was wrong and I was right. Seems I was right all the same, and if Harry's got money to spare as he doesn't know what to do with, then it's not for us to deny his right to spend it any whichaway he pleases. I'd be more'n happy to move out of this tied cottage and have the comfort of our own place, and I reckon with what Harry's offered, we'll soon have enough to buy summat small in Calking village, and if'n you doant want to come with me, Will Pritchett, then you can stay on here by yourself. I'll not be wanting to live with a man what's too proud to take a helping hand from someone as was like our own son, and that's a fact.'

Will got up and, as fast as his old body would allow, stormed out into the garden, leaving his children, mouths agape, behind him.

'Oh, Mum, you shouldn't have said them things, surely,' Jenny gasped when she could find her voice. 'Supposing Dad . . . supposing he says he'll stay on here?'

'Wait and see, girl,' Martha said without moving from her chair. 'Just give him a bit of time. Alice, you and Jenny can get the table laid. I've made Harry's favourite coconut cake and there's cold ham and one of your Dad's lettuces all ready. Arthur, go and wash your hands, and you, Ted . . . go upstairs and see what Edna's up to. She can't still be curling her hair. She's been at it all afternoon.'

She turned to look at Harry and suddenly she smiled.

'Wouldn't have known you if'n I passed you in the street,' she said, ''cepting those eyes of yourn. They haven't changed none, nor've you lost them curls. Right handsome little boy you was and now you're a right

350

handsome gentleman.' She looked away, her faded blue eyes resting now on Alice. 'Reckon as how our Alice's another as I can be proud of,' she said. 'Right little tearaway you was, Alice, when you was a little'un, stamping your feet and your eyes blazing if'n you couldn't get your own way. Happen you doant remember back that far, but when I was nursing Harry that first day we had him, you was the one what was going to choose a name for him. You was the one what was going to tek care of him. He were yourn, you kept saying, though he weren't no more yourn than mine.'

'That was a long time ago, Mum,' Alice said quickly. 'A very long time ago. Do you realize I'm twenty-five now, coming on twenty-six?'

'I does know it – and it's high time you was thinking of getting wed, my girl. You get any thinner and there won't be a young man as'll look at you twice. You doant eat enough in those foreign parts, surely. Now here comes your father, so sit yourself down and eat a decent meal for a change.'

As Harry sat down in the chair Martha indicated, he glanced at Will, who, looking rather hot and red-faced, was now taking his place at the head of the table.

''matoes is coming on well,' he said. 'I've brought a few in for tea.'

'That'll be nice,' Martha replied, as if there'd been no earlier ruction. 'Ain't no one as can grow better 'matoes than yourn, Will. Remember her ladyship saying so? Now sit down, Edna, and eat your tea. You remember Harry, doant you?'

'Yes, Mum,' the girl said, smiling at Harry.

Will harrumphed. 'She doant remember nothing,' he said conversationally, 'but she ain't no trouble – does what her mother tells her, no trouble. More'n I can say for you, Harry, when you was a lad.' He gave one of his rare smiles as he looked at his own two sons. 'Wouldn't think it now, would you? A good beating like I gave young Harry now and agin don't do you nothing but good. Remember that when I next take my belt to you.'

So that was the end of the argument, Harry realized. Martha had taken a stand and Will had given way. He felt an enormous sense of gratification mixed with affection for his two foster parents. This visit, he told Alice as the train took them back to London later that evening, had been a very happy one and it was his intention to go down to Calking to see them all again very soon.

'Will I see you tomorrow, Harry?' Alice asked, as the train slowed down on its approach to the station.

'Oh, Alice, I'm afraid not. I promised Madeleine last night I'd go with them to see Dunbar playing polo. In the evening, Aubrey's got tickets for Covent Garden. How about the day after?'

Alice bit back the tears of disappointment that were pricking her eyelids, and parodied a smile.

'Let's see how it goes, shall we?' she said. 'Here's my address. The telephone isn't connected yet but you can drop a note in. If . . . if there's time, I'd like to show you the new *salon* in Albemarle Street.'

'And I'd love to see it,' Harry said. 'I really am sorry about tomorrow, Alice. I'm sure the day after will be fine, but I'll do as you say and leave a note. Maybe one evening we could all go out together – you, Aubrey, Dunbar, Madeleine and me. I could bring along Bertie Alcott too. He's at a loose end and I'd be enormously proud to introduce you. You'd like him.'

'I'm sure I would if he's a friend of yours, Harry, but I think it's not such a good idea for you to include me with Aubrey and Madeleine. It could be awkward for all of us. Have you forgotten that I was once their mother's maid?'

Harry had forgotten. Those days seemed such a very long time ago, and seeing Alice now, so chic, so elegant, it was almost impossible to remember her in her grey-and-white-striped uniform and white cap, calling Madeleine 'Miss' and Aubrey 'Master'! He'd all but forgotten his own early childhood at The Grange, when he had been the gardener's scruffy little lad, graciously permitted by Lady Debrace to play with her son. Would the Debraces have forgotten, he wondered? What would they say if he were to ask Sir Philip if he could marry their daughter? And Madeleine – had she forgotten?

He felt suddenly deeply depressed. It was all very well for him to have told himself that he no longer minded about his illegitimacy. In America, with the Harveys, it somehow had not mattered; nor had they been in the least concerned about how he had been raised, judging him for what he was now. Could the Debraces be as open-minded?

'Alice, they aren't snobs,' he said. 'If they had been, they'd never have allowed me to mix with their children. I honestly don't think they would object to my marrying Madeleine on the grounds of my birth. I know I haven't anything to offer her and that it might be years before I could afford to run a house and give her the kind of life style she's used to, so I wouldn't expect Sir Philip to agree to it for a long while.'

Alice bit her lip.

'It's different for you, Harry. They know your father was of their class. I'm not, nor ever will be. Goodness knows how many years ago, when you first told me you were going to marry Madeleine, I warned you that the gentry don't marry working-class folk. They don't accept them socially either, and, unlike you, I belong to the working classes.'

'It used to be like that, but times have changed,' Harry argued. 'People like Mrs Harry Brown are accepted in society simply because they have enormous sums of money. Aubrey was talking about her only yesterday. She rented the Duchess of Norfolk's mansion in St James's Square and filled it with red and white roses for a party. Everyone was scrabbling to get invited. Dunbar took Madeleine and they had a marvellous time, or so Aubrey said.'

Alice stood up as the train slowed at the platform.

'Maybe I take after my Dad, Harry – too proud to risk a rebuff! And if I don't mind not meeting up with them, why should you?'

Why, indeed, should it bother him so much, Harry thought, as he escorted Alice back to the rented flat in

Charles Street? He found it deeply offensive to think of Alice – his beautiful Alice – being rejected by anyone. Maybe he really would introduce her to Bertie Alcott. Although his friend must be a few years younger than Alice, he was fancy-free, and Alice was so lovely to look at these days, the age difference wouldn't be noticed. Despite everything Alice had said about never marrying or having children, he didn't entirely believe her. She was a sweet, loving person and would make someone a wonderful wife. It wasn't right for her to be spending all her time with this pansy Jules fellow or her elderly patron.

Despite his good intentions, however, all thought of Alice slipped from his mind next day when he accompanied Aubrey and Madeleine to the polo match. Although he was obliged to 'share' Madeleine with Dunbar during lunch and after the game – which he found incredibly exciting – there were long periods during the chukkers when he had her undivided attention. When she thought no one was looking, she reached out and touched his hand and her eyes were soft and inviting. She appeared quite uninterested in Pogo's exploits on the field, even when he scored several goals.

'For goodness' sake, Pickles, stop flirting with Harry,' Aubrey said testily. 'Dunbar's coming over and he'll have fifty fits if he sees you holding Harry's hand. Or are you trying to make the poor fellow jealous?'

'Don't be such a nincompoop,' Madeleine retorted, apparently not in the least disconcerted. 'Harry's an old and dear friend. Why shouldn't I be nice to him? Anyway, if you weren't so futile, you'd know jolly well I've no need to make Pogo jealous.'

Aubrey frowned.

'Oh, we all know he's your adoring slave. But you don't have to be so beastly to him, Pickles. Come on, Harry, let's go to the bar for a drink and leave Pogo the field.'

Ignoring his sister's furious gaze, he dragged Harry away.

'Pickles really is absolutely hopeless,' he said as they walked over to the crowded marquee. 'She simply can't stand the thought of any eligible male not being crazy about her. Ever since the pater told her you might be going to marry Cora-Beth, she's been determined to win you back. You used to be such an ass about her in the old days. Of course, she gets away with it most of the time because she's so pretty.'

'You're making her out to be a bit heartless,' Harry protested awkwardly. 'I'm sure she has no idea how . . . how attractive she is.'

'Well, take it from me, she knows exactly what's she doing. Now then, old chap, let's have some champagne.'

Despite Aubrey's warning, Harry became convinced that Madeleine was not simply flirting with him. During the next fortnight, she divided her attentions equally between him and Dunbar, but, she whispered to Harry one evening in the back of the Bentley, she would much prefer to be with him and she was being nice to Pogo only because she didn't want to hurt his feelings.

'Can't you find an excuse for us to be alone together, Harry?' she asked. 'Then I'd have a chance to explain everything. We never see each other on our own. I'm sure Aubrey tags along on purpose to annoy me.'

'You know that isn't true,' Harry reproached her, although his heart was beating with excitement at the thought that Madeleine was as anxious to be alone with him as he with her. 'It's Aubrey or Dunbar who buy the tickets and arrange things, so naturally they're both around.'

This past fortnight had been crowded with activity. There'd been a whole day's racing at Goodwood, two afternoons at Wimbledon for the semi-finals and finals, the Eton and Harrow cricket match, a day at Henley and invitations to lunch and dinner parties, the theatre, the opera and then on to one of the nightclubs. Harry was able to fit in only two further meetings with Alice – one when she had taken him to see the very impressive new branch of the Maison Verveine, and the other when she had invited him back to the flat to meet Jules. Somewhat surprisingly, Harry thought, he liked Jules. He found the young man witty, intelligent and obviously devoted to Alice.

His holiday in England was flying by, Harry thought on his way back to the Alcotts. Perhaps he should extend it, for he had not yet taken Alice to the promised lunch at the Ritz, or been up to Leicestershire to see Mrs Appleby, or fulfilled his promise to Jenny to go down to Calking to see the shop and meet Jack and his family. He had also promised Mr Harvey that he would go to Maythorpe House and make sure that all was being kept in order there. Somehow all these less exciting duties had had to take second place to the social events Aubrey and Madeleine were constantly arranging for his entertainment.

It was Lionel Dunbar who inadvertently solved two of Harry's problems for him. On hearing that Harry wished to go up to Melton Mowbray for the day, he offered to drive him in the Bentley. He then remembered that he was on duty and said he would be more than willing for Harry to borrow his car.

Madeleine immediately insisted that Harry do so. Aubrey, she said, was committed to a lunch party with Primrose and her parents, but she would love the drive into the country and would happily accompany Harry since she had nothing better to do.

'You really don't mind – lending me the car, I mean?' Harry asked the good-natured army officer. 'I've been driving a great deal in the States but it was either a Packard or a Studebaker.'

'Absolutely n-not, old boy. Shan't need it m'self! Orderly Officer, you s-see! The old girl's insured so you d-don't have to worry if you d-do have a b-bump.'

'You're a darling, Pogo,' Madeleine said, throwing her arms round his neck and kissing his cheek. 'I'll have to ask Mummy, but I'm sure she won't mind. It's such a bore the way she always wants to know where I am and what I'm doing.'

Although Harry's conscience kept him awake that night until the early hours, the temptation of a day alone with Madeleine dulled his feeling of guilt about borrowing

Dunbar's car to further his own pursuit of the girl they both loved. He knew he ought to feel guilty about Cora-Beth, to whom he had not yet written the promised letter, but with a telegram already despatched to Mrs Appleby, advising her of his visit and that he would be bringing a young lady, he told himself that it was too late to change the arrangement.

Lady Debrace seemed more concerned about Harry's ability to drive her daughter safely in so powerful a motor car than about Madeleine's reputation. She was, further-more, suffering a mild migraine and did not feel able to enter into one of the now familiar arguments with her headstrong young daughter about 'conventional behaviour'. Moreover, having read between the lines of Wendell Harvey's letters to her husband, she was certain that Harry and the Harvey girl were going to make a match of it. As for her daughter, Madeleine had shown no signs of dropping Lionel Dunbar, and a quiet word with his mother had confirmed that he had every intention of marrying Madeleine if only she would agree to accept him.

'Enjoy yourselves, my dears,' she said as they prepared to leave. 'And don't be too late back, Maddy. Your father will be home for dinner tonight, and I'm sure he'll expect you to be here.'

As soon as they were out of the traffic and heading northwards up the main A1 trunk road, Madeleine snuggled closer to Harry.

'A whole day to ourselves,' she said, starry-eyed. 'Do you know, I hardly slept last night I was so excited. What are we going to do, Harry? We're not really going to see that old cook, are we?'

Harry eased the big car past a large furniture van and glanced uneasily at the girl beside him. Dressed in a summer frock patterned all over with scarlet poppies, a scarlet silk scarf wound round her head, she looked devastatingly pretty.

'It's a must, I'm afraid, Madeleine. Actually, I'm quite looking forward to it. Mrs Appleby's awfully nice and I think you'll like her.'

His eyes were back on the road and he did not see Madeleine's mouth turn down in a pout.

'But I don't even know her – and anyway, what on earth can you talk about? I mean, you can't socialize with a cook!'

'Madeleine, Mrs Appleby is a person, not just a cook; and in the days when I lived at Maythorpe House, she was enormously kind to me,' Harry said. 'What's more, you probably won't have to do any talking – she'll do it all! There's nothing she likes better than to reminisce about the days when my . . . my father was a boy. She was with the family for years and years. Besides, I've already told her we'd have lunch with her.'

'Lunch,' Madeleine said as if he'd suggested something outrageous. 'Well, I shan't go in with you. I'll wait in the car.'

It was a moment or two before Harry plucked up the courage to say, 'I do hope you won't do that, Madeleine. She'd be terribly hurt. She's sure to have got out the best china and baked a meat pie or something. I'll have to stay at the very least an hour. I can't possibly disappoint her.'

Madeleine was frowning.

'You're as bad as Mummy. She's always on about "doing one's duty to those who have served one well"! Honestly, I don't see why one has to bother. I mean, they get paid for serving you, don't they? Daddy's just as bad – spends half his life visiting patients, most of whom were never able to pay their bills. Oh, well, I suppose if we must . . .'

Madeleine was still very young, Harry told himself as they drove the next ten miles in silence. It was unreasonable of him to expect her to know what it meant to people like Mrs Appleby to receive a visit from an employer. He could remember what a flurry Martha Pritchett used to get into when Lady Debrace stopped in for a cup of tea, and how afterwards she would tell them proudly how her ladyship had sat down and chatted as if she were no grander than Nurse Wilks! It was for just such occasions that Martha kept her best china locked securely in the glass cabinet and saved to get the front room furnished 'fit for visitors'.

Madeleine, however, did not sulk for long. The fact was, she'd been unable to get to sleep the previous night for thinking about Harry. There would surely be lots of occasions during the day when she could get him to kiss her, she told herself. The mere thought brought a tremor to her legs. One of the French girls at her Swiss boarding-school had told her that boys liked a girl to have a '*poitrine*' and they became very excited when they touched a girl's breast; this, she had maintained, explained the fashion for dresses which made a girl look flat-chested – so that as many as possible would not inflame men's passions and would thereby remain virgins.

Deliberately, Madeleine had selected a dress to wear which buttoned down the front to the waist. It should not be too difficult, she thought, to allow one of those buttons to become undone. This, surely, would inflame Harry and make him want to make love to her. Not that she wanted to lose her virginity – nothing as drastic as that! But she wanted to experience again that lovely swooning feeling only he seemed able to invoke.

Harry was not like Pogo, she reflected. For ages now she had been able to make Pogo do whatever she wanted. Although she was reasonably sure that Harry was still in love with her, she was concerned at all the talk there had been about him marrying the American girl. American girls were said to have much more freedom than English ones, and Cora-Beth was older than herself. Was it possible that she had allowed Harry to make love to her? That Harry was now obliged to marry her? He certainly did not seem to be missing her and, unless someone else mentioned her, he never did. Today, somehow, she would find out which of the two of them he really loved.

Not wishing to antagonize Harry, when finally they drew up outside the little cottage in Melton Mowbray to which Mrs Appleby had now retired, Madeleine allowed herself to be persuaded inside. At least the place was clean, she thought, as Mrs Appleby fussed round her and Harry.

'It's that good to see you, Master Harry,' she said when at last they were all seated comfortably round the dining-table. 'And the young lady, of course. Your favourite Melton Mowbray pork pie, Master Harry, and Farmer Bates let me have a nice piece of Stilton special. Now, let me have a good look at you.'

Beaming, she clapped both hands to her cheeks.

'You're more'n ever like your father, may he rest in peace,' she said. She glanced at Madeleine and added falteringly, 'You're not the young lady from America Master Harry wrote about then, Miss Debrace?'

'No, that's Cora-Beth – Miss Harvey,' Harry said quickly. 'Miss Debrace is the daughter of the family I went to live with after I left Maythorpe House.'

Mrs Appleby nodded as she cut into the pork pie.

'I thought as how the name was familiar. It was your father, weren't it, Miss, as sent Master Harry out to America to his relatives?'

'I really don't know much about it,' Madeleine said vaguely. 'I was at school in those days, so things like that weren't discussed in front of me.'

'Likely not,' Mrs Appleby said. 'So you know Master Harry's sister then – Alice Pritchett?'

'Yes, she was my mother's maid,' Madeleine replied. 'And as a matter of fact, she isn't Harry's sister. She runs a fashion house now. I've not seen her for ages.'

'Seems she's done right well for herself,' Mrs Appleby commented. 'Real nice girl, she was. I took a real fancy to her. Remember that day, Master Harry, when she came up to see you and the two of you hid in that there pavilion?'

The reminiscing had begun and, although she paused briefly to hand round the plates and a bowl of crisp salad to go with the pie, there was no way Harry could stop her. He was conscious of the fact that Madeleine was toying with her food and looking increasingly bored. Finally, Mrs Appleby noticed it too.

'Really, I do go on so,' she said apologetically. 'It's just that I don't see that many people these days and when there's company . . . Likely you'll not want to stop for a cup of tea? I dare say you've things to do, and I mustn't keep you.'

Reluctantly, Harry stood up.

'I promised Mr Harvey – he doesn't care to use his title, Mrs Appleby – that I would go and see if all was in order at Maythorpe House. Miss Debrace has never seen the place. It's a long drive back to London, so perhaps we should be on our way.'

Madeleine was already on her feet and was drawing on her gloves.

'Thanks for lunch,' she said. 'I really do think we should go now, Harry. You know Mummy said I mustn't be late back.'

'Yes, of course.' Harry helped the old cook to her feet and put his arms round her. 'You're getting my postcards, aren't you?' he asked as he kissed her on both cheeks. There were tears in her eyes as she gazed up at him.

'I've kept them all, Master Harry – and the snapshots. I put them in the family album your father gave me – you'll remember the one. When the day comes for me to pass on, it'll be yours. I've made sure of that.'

Madeleine was already at the door and, reluctantly, Harry drew himself away.

'It was a lovely meal,' he said as he lifted his hand in farewell, 'and I don't have to tell you – nobody in the world can make a pork pie like yours!'

Had he been on his own, Harry thought as he drove out of Melton Mowbray market town towards Saxby, he would have taken Mrs Appleby with him to Maythorpe House. She would probably have enjoyed the ride in Dunbar's big Bentley. It was such a beautiful day and suddenly he became aware of a surge of relief not to be in London. He was a countryman at heart, and although these past weeks had been tremendous fun, it was lovely to see the grass and trees and a blue sky unclouded by smoke. On an impulse, he removed his cap and threw it on to the back seat.

As he turned into the lane leading to the Maythorpe

estate, he became aware of Madeleine's hand, now ungloved, ruffling the back of his head.

'Your hair's gone all curly, Harry,' she said teasingly. 'It reminds me of when we were little. I used to hate it when Nanny put rags in my hair and, whenever I had a wish, I used to wish that mine was curly like yours.'

'Oh, but you've such beautiful hair, Madeleine,' Harry said. 'I was so sorry when you had it cut. But it still looks lovely.'

He was acutely conscious of the touch of Madeleine's hand, which she seemed disinclined to remove. It rested now on the nape of his neck.

'Look, there's the house,' he said quickly in an attempt to divert his thoughts from the effect she was having on him. 'I did send a telegram to the caretaker to tell him to be here to let me in. The place looks terribly deserted.'

'Good,' said Madeleine quietly as he stopped the car and pulled on the brake. 'Now we really can be alone.'

CHAPTER TWENTY-ONE

1924

Harry switched off the engine and sat staring at the big, grey, stone-built mansion with a sense of shock. When he had first come to Maythorpe House as an ignorant thirteen-year-old who had never before lived in anything grander than a tiny gardener's cottage, he had felt awed and frightened, and unable to grasp that this huge place was now his home. For over two long, deeply unhappy years, it had been a prison. Now, however, almost a decade later, it did not seem nearly so large and he found himself remembering the good things – the warm, cosy atmosphere of Mrs Appleby's kitchen; the wonderful view across the garden and pastures from all the south-facing windows; the pungent smell of the horses, so well loved by Uncle Cosmo, in the well-kept stables; the fascinating portrait of his handsome father in the gallery; the stamp collection and lead soldiers that had once belonged to his father in the shabby old nursery, where he, a homesick boy, had secretly penned so many letters to Alice.

But for his guardians and his lack of friends, he could have been happy here, he thought as he went round the front of the car to open the door for Madeleine. He could be happy here now – if by some miracle Madeleine were to agree to get married and live in this house with him. Even if the miracle happened, would she entertain the idea of living in the Shires? Kentucky had not appealed to her but in Leicestershire she would be in more or less familiar surroundings – and Mr Harvey had said he might live here if he so chose.

He glanced down at the girl beside him.

'What do you think of the place?' he asked anxiously.

Madeleine shrugged.

'It's bigger than I'd imagined – but terribly isolated. Look, there's the caretaker.'

An old man in corduroy breeches and cloth jacket came round the side of the house and touched his cap.

'Mr Keynes, sir? I bin expectin' you. D'you want I should show you round, sir?'

Harry gave him a friendly smile.

'There's no need for you to do that. I'm familiar with the house. We may be here for an hour or two so you can go on home if you wish. I'll drop the key in as I go past the lodge.'

After the caretaker had unlocked the big front door and disappeared down the drive, Harry took Madeleine's arm and led her into the drawing-room. Dustsheets covered all the furniture and were draped over the pictures stacked against the wall. The rugs had been rolled up and smelt strongly of moth balls. Despite the hot sunshine burning through the windows, which Harry now flung open, the room seemed cold and cheerless, and Madeleine shivered.

'I hate empty houses,' she said, clinging to Harry's arm. 'Let's go and look upstairs. I want to see your room . . . the one where they locked you up.'

Harry laughed as he refastened the windows and led Madeleine back into the hall.

'I wasn't locked up. I did have a gaoler, though – a horrible valet called Hicks, whose job it was to make sure I didn't mix with anyone outside the family. I was the black sheep, you see, and Aunt Pamela didn't want the neighbours suspecting I was my father's son.'

'I think your past is terribly romantic,' Madeleine said as they walked slowly up the staircase. 'Aubrey told me all about it when you went off to America. He said your father was the Earl of Kinmuire but he didn't know who your mother was.'

'No more do I,' said Harry, surprised by Madeleine's broad-minded approach to the circumstances of his birth.

'Weren't you a little shocked to hear that I was born out of wedlock.'

'I suppose I was a bit, but as Aubrey said, it was hardly your fault, was it? Anyway, lots of really famous people had illegitimate children. Just look at William IV. He had ten children, the FitzClarences, by Mrs Jordan. So why should you care?'

'I don't any more,' Harry said quietly. 'I would mind though if *you* thought less of me, Madeleine.'

They had reached the door of his room now and, as Harry opened it, Madeleine went past him and sat down on the edge of his old brass bedstead. Her eyes were bright with excitement as she gazed up at him.

'You do love me a little bit, don't you, Harry?' she said. 'I know you try to pretend you don't, but I can tell.'

She held out her hand with deliberate provocation and, drawing him down on the edge of the bed beside her, she gave a little laugh which came from deep in her throat.

'Remember that time I came to your room for a midnight feast and got into your bed? Wouldn't Mummy have been horrified if she'd known?'

'And rightly so,' Harry said huskily. 'I don't think you've any idea just how attractive you are, Madeleine.'

She lay back against the heaped pile of pillows and smiled at him.

'Aren't you going to kiss me, then?' she asked softly.

Harry needed no second invitation. As he gathered her into his arms and pressed his mouth to hers, he had a sudden swift memory of the nights he had lain here in this bed dreaming of her. Now she was no dream, but a warm, trembling reality who seemed as anxious for his embrace as he was to caress her.

'You do love me, don't you?' she whispered. 'You don't have to be shy with me, you know. I've been wanting you to kiss me for absolute ages.' She took one of his hands and drew it towards her breast. 'Does that feel nice?' she asked. 'Say you love me, Harry. Say it.'

'I love you, I love you! I've always loved you – ever since

365

I can remember,' he murmured. 'I've never felt like this about any other girl.'

'Not even the American girl in Kentucky?'

'No, not even her,' Harry admitted. 'It's different – the way I feel about Cora-Beth. She's really nice and we're the best of friends, but . . .'

'But I'm the one you love best,' Madeleine said. 'Oh, Harry, isn't this exciting? I think I'm in love with you. It's never like this with poor old Pogo.'

She reached up and pulled his head down, her lips parted expectantly for a renewal of his kisses. She was aware of Harry's quickened breathing and realized that she had 'inflamed' him, just as the French girl had foretold. She thought that perhaps she had inflamed herself as well, for she was longing to press her body closer to his; to feel his hands on her waist, her legs – even, she thought with a slight shock, beween her legs. The swooning sensation was growing stronger with every moment.

'Please, Harry, please . . .' she murmured, unsure what exactly she was pleading for. 'I do love you . . . I really do!'

With a groan, Harry tightened his arms around her and struggled to keep control of himself as he felt her response. He must take care of her. Madeleine was entirely innocent and had no idea of the strength of his physical need of her. He moved away from her and swung his legs back over the side of the bed.

'My darling girl,' he said, 'much as I hate the idea, we must stop this. Trouble is, I love you far too much. You do understand, don't you?'

'No, I don't,' Madeleine said, frowning. 'Don't you want to go on kissing me?'

'Of course I do – *of course*!' Harry said. 'But kissing is only a step towards making love and I've no right to do that. Only the man you marry has the right to . . . to touch you.' He turned to face her, his dark eyes burning as he stared down at her. 'Will you marry me, Madeleine? Did you mean it when you said just now that you loved me? Do you love me enough to marry me?'

Madeleine sat up, her dreamy, expectant mood shattered by Harry's question. She did love him, there was no doubt about that, but did she want to marry him?

'I don't want to live in America,' she said. 'Not on a ranch.'

Harry caught hold of her hands and held them tightly in his own.

'I know that. We wouldn't have to live there, Madeleine. I could get a job over here in England if that's what you want. I've gained a great deal of experience these past two and a half years and I think I could manage a stud farm quite easily now. In time I hope to have my own stables. We could live here – at Maythorpe House.'

'Here!' Madeleine repeated. 'But it's miles and miles away from London.'

'It's not really so far,' Harry said persuasively. 'And the house is big enough for you to have as many friends as you want to visit you. I know I couldn't begin to give you the kind of life you'd have with Dunbar, but I'd do everything in my power to make you happy.'

'I am happy when I'm with you,' Madeleine said thoughtfully. 'I suppose it could be quite fun – to be married, I mean. Would we be very poor?'

'I'm afraid we would – for a few years anyway,' Harry admitted. 'I've really no right to ask you to marry me. I don't think your mother and father would be at all keen on the idea.'

Madeleine's face took on a new expression. She laughed.

'Oh, I don't pay any attention to what *they* think is best for me. They're so old-fashioned. I'll marry whom I please.'

'My darling Madeleine, you aren't yet twenty, so it'll be a year before you come of age. We couldn't be married without their consent.'

'I don't see why my parents should be against our marriage,' Madeleine said cheerfully as she snuggled against him. 'Daddy's always thought the world of you, and I know Mummy likes you. So does Aubrey.' She gave

367

a sudden giggle. '*He'll* be against it because he won't think I'm nice enough for you. He says I only ever think of myself, but it isn't true. I've thought and thought about us – about us being together like this, and whether you really loved me and how it feels when you kiss me.'

'Oh, darling,' Harry said huskily, 'I've thought about us too. I never dared hope you might love me, so I tried very hard to forget you. I can't believe this is happening, that you aren't going to marry Dunbar. Aubrey seemed to think . . . and I can see that in so many ways it would be a far better match for you. Are you really willing to wait if your parents object?'

'Oh, do stop worrying, Harry,' Madeleine said, ruffling his hair and covering his face with light, teasing kisses. 'I can always talk Daddy round. He's not all that crazy about Pogo anyway – he says he isn't a strong enough character to keep me in order! You're so different from all the other young men I meet. Daddy says it's quite remarkable the way you've always managed to overcome the obstacles in your life. I mean, nobody would ever believe you'd been brought up as a *gardener's* boy! It must give you the pip every time you think about those days.'

'I was very happy with the Pritchetts,' Harry said quietly. 'They were very good to me, especially Alice.'

'Oh, you were her pet. She was always talking about you. Isn't it amazing – her getting on so well with Uncle Félix? Mummy says she's going to run the London *salon*. I shall go and buy some dresses there.'

It crossed Harry's mind that on the kind of salary he received – even if he was lucky enough to be paid as well by an English employer as he was by Wendell Harvey – Madeleine would not be able to afford designer dresses, or any other of those expensive luxuries she took for granted. He felt a sudden deep wave of depression, coupled with uncertainty. Would Madeleine be happy married to him? *Could* she be happy once the novelty of being a married woman wore off? Was he being indescribably presumptuous even to suppose that Sir Philip might consider allowing his only daughter to share her life with a man who could pay for little more than the bare necessities? Moreover, how could he be sure Sir Philip would disregard his illegitimacy, as Madeleine appeared to do? It was one thing for his guardian to tell Harry to forget the circumstances of his birth, but would *he* do so if it meant his beloved daughter had to share that stigma?

He stood up abruptly.

'I'm going to take you home,' he said. 'I must speak to your father. I owe it to him to explain what's happened between us, to get his permission to go on seeing you.'

Madeleine's brows drew together in a scowl.

'You mean we aren't even going to get engaged?' she asked.

Quickly, Harry put his arms round her.

'But of course, if your parents will permit it,' he said. 'I'll talk to your father tonight.'

'I suppose you've got to,' Madeleine said sulkily, but her mood quickly changed. 'All right. But kiss me again before we go, Harry. We mightn't have another chance to be alone like this for ages and ages.'

As Harry's lips met hers, Madeleine gave a long, trembling sigh. She did not want to have to think about problems, whatever they might be. She wanted to stay in Harry's arms and feel the magical thrill his kisses aroused in her. His body was so warm and strong and exciting! She could feel the muscles of his arms jump where her hands were touching him and exulted in the power she seemed to have over him. It was a power he too seemed to possess, she thought, as his kisses became more ardent and her body leapt to life.

'Must we go? Must we?' she whispered. 'Let's stay here all night. Let's sleep together in the same bed, hugging each other like this. Wouldn't it be ripping?'

'I doubt if your parents would think so,' Harry said, forcing himself to draw away from her. 'No more midnight feasts until we're married!' He eased her arms from around his neck and, smiling, planted a quick kiss on the end of her nose. 'There,' he said, 'that will have to last you until we get back to London.'

369

Madeleine had no intention of agreeing to this suggestion and, throughout the long journey back in the car, she remained as close to him as the gear lever allowed, and whenever an opportunity presented itself, leant over and kissed his cheek. Only when Harry warned her that he might collide with a passing vehicle if she continued to do that, did she finally desist.

His mood was both euphoric and anxious as he parked the car outside the Debraces' house. He had no doubt now that Madeleine loved him, but would Sir Philip consider their shared love sufficient grounds for them to marry?

It was Aubrey who brought Harry back to his senses. Seeing the couple's arrival and the manner in which Madeleine was clinging to Harry's arm as they left the car, he persuaded his friend up to his bedroom on the grounds that he must want a wash and brush-up after the long journey. As soon as they were alone, he said awkwardly, 'Look, old chap, you've every right to tell me to mind my own business, but unless I've made two and two equal five, then I think as your friend I ought to speak up. Something's happened between you and Pickles, hasn't it?'

Harry put down the hairbrush with which he had been trying to smooth his unruly curls, and turned to face Madeleine's brother.

'I don't know how you guessed, Aubrey, but you're absolutely right – Madeleine and I love each other. Of course, I've always loved her but I'd no idea she felt the same way about me until she told me this afternoon. I can still hardly believe it. I'm going to tell your father this evening; ask his permission to get engaged. You . . . you don't mind, do you? I mean, you yourself don't have any objections?'

Aubrey remained seated in the armchair by the window, his eyes thoughtful.

'I've absolutely nothing against you personally, old chap,' he said. 'On the contrary, it's because . . . dash it, I'll say it even if it does sound sloppy! It's because I'm so deuced fond of you that I've got to speak out.'

'About what?'

'About Madeleine! Despite the way I sometimes rag her, she is my sister and I do love her, so don't take this as being disloyal. The fact is, Harry, it simply wouldn't work and, if you weren't so blinded by love, you'd see it for yourself. She may *say* she loves you and perhaps she does in her way, but Pickles doesn't think or feel deeply about anything. She never has. All she thinks about is being happy – and that means having the things she thinks will make her happy.'

'And you don't think I can supply them?' Harry asked, unable to hide an edge of bitterness in his voice.

'Look, Harry, it's as simple as this. I don't think you could *afford* to do so. You told me you have to manage on what you earn – dashed bad luck, I know – but for your own sake, you need to face facts. However well they pay chaps like you to look after horses, it can't be all that much! Do you have any idea how extravagant that sister of mine is? The pater gives her fifty pounds a year as a dress allowance and she has nearly always spent it by the end of the first month. From then on, she just buys what she wants and charges it to one or other of the parents' accounts. The pater pays for holidays and he's about to buy her a car, though she can borrow the family car and chauffeur whenever he doesn't want them. Her escorts pay when she goes out to restaurants or parties, so Pickles hasn't the foggiest idea about money. Mother sees to the housekeeping expenses and organizes the servants' wages and so on. Pickles never has to lift a finger. I doubt she has ever in her life packed a suitcase! I don't suppose for one moment she has given a thought to what life might be like if she had to "make do" married to someone who wasn't too well off. Now, having said my bit, I'll shut up. I'm sorry if I've upset you, old thing.'

Harry gave a deep sigh.

'Someone had to knock some sense into me. What you're really saying is that I've no right to ask Madeleine to make sacrifices. I suppose I hadn't let myself think it through – I mean, I was so happy when she said she loved me, I never stopped to think seriously about what I had to offer her. I was more worried . . . well, about the circumstances of my birth.'

Aubrey waved this aside.

'If that were the only stumbling-block, I'd put all my weight behind you if it came to a showdown with the pater. No, Harry, it's your future happiness that bothers me. I know how difficult Pickles can be when she doesn't get her own way. I'd give the two of you a year of happiness at most. I hate talking like this. I know you love her – always have done, haven't you? But you'd be much better off with someone else. When you told me about the American girl, I hoped it meant you'd got over Pickles. She'll probably end up marrying Dunbar. I suppose she simply couldn't resist adding your scalp to her belt.'

Harry flushed.

'It isn't like that. She really does love me,' he said. 'If you'd seen how she was today, you'd know it was true.'

Aubrey stood up and rested a hand on Harry's shoulder.

'Far be it from me to stand in the path of true love,' he said lightly. 'Perhaps I'm quite wrong and Pickles is serious. I just don't want you having to face the pater only to find that she didn't mean half she said. I don't think she has the faintest idea what it would mean to marry a chap without private means, and if she did, I'm afraid she'd change her mind.'

Harry's mouth tightened.

'You have a low opinion of her,' he said. 'I don't. But which of us is right can easily be put to the test. You're her brother, you go and talk to her. Tell her what you've been telling me; explain all the pitfalls. If I'm right about her feelings for me, it will do no harm. If *you* are right . . . Well, better I should face the consequences before there's harm done.'

Aubrey raised his eyebrows, a look of surprise on his face.

'D'you really mean that, old chap? It's not actually any of my business and I'm half regretting I said anything. I'd hate it if Pickles changes her mind and you thought I'd prejudiced her against you.'

'Piffle!' Harry said bluntly. 'We've been close friends for donkey's years and I know you better than to think you'd try to queer my pitch.'

Aubrey grinned.

'Personally, I can't think of anything I'd like more than to have you as a brother-in-law.' His smile faded as he added, 'I just wish I could believe Pickles would make you happy. I'll have a word with her before dinner. You'll stay for a meal, won't you?'

Harry shook his head.

'Your mother isn't expecting me – and anyway, I think it would be best, under the circumstances, if I push off. I'll come round first thing tomorrow morning and we can have another jaw then. If you've changed your mind, I can talk to your father then. What d'you think?'

'I'm not sure what to think,' Aubrey said doubtfully, 'other than that I hope I am wrong. If Pickles really does love you, maybe the pater would give her a decent allowance and you'd manage somehow. At least you've got a house to live in. How did you find Maythorpe, by the way?'

'In pretty good condition, as far as I could see. It was strange going back there after all this time. I hated the place when I lived there and yet today I had the odd sort of feeling that the house was just waiting for me to go and live in it again.'

'Well, it was your family home, wasn't it?' Aubrey said. 'Still is, I suppose. Are you going to say goodbye to Pickles before you go?'

After a moment's pause, Harry answered, 'I don't think so. You can explain to her why I rushed off; that I want to give her time to think things over without me around to distract her. If she's still sure she wants us to get engaged, I'll speak to your father tomorrow.'

He followed Aubrey on to the landing, where, by mutual impulse, they shook hands. Not allowing himself to glance down the passage in the direction of Madeleine's bedroom, Harry descended the big staircase and went out of the house. He would take Dunbar's car back to the barracks and then walk to Cadogan Place, he decided. Aubrey's warnings had unsettled him far more than he had permitted his friend to see. He'd had doubts even before Aubrey had spoken out but, not wishing to acknowledge them, he'd allowed his heart to overrule his head. If only he did not love Madeleine so totally, so hopelessly, he told himself as he drove down Oxford Street towards Marble Arch. He was a poor man, by the Debraces' standards, and he might *never* be able to keep Madeleine in the manner to which she was accustomed, let alone do so in the foreseeable future.

He felt a sudden desperate need to see Alice – to tell her of the momentous happenings of the day and ask her advice. Even if Madeleine were able to convince Aubrey that she loved him and was willing to wait for him, had he the moral right to ask her to do so? Wouldn't she be far better off with Dunbar, who could give her everything she wanted?

But not the depth of love he, Harry, could give her, he told himself, as he turned back towards Charles Street in the hope of finding Alice there. Alice knew about love – she was in love with some fellow who did not return her affection. Poor Alice! It was beginning to seem as if neither of them was ever to achieve their heart's desires, even while making a success of other aspects of their lives. If Alice were not otherwise occupied, he would take her out to dinner somewhere. They had not seen nearly enough of each other during this holiday – and the fault was his. He'd make it up to her this evening, take her somewhere really special.

Unaware of Harry's plans for her, Alice was getting into a taxi with Jules, who, after a long, tiring day getting things straight at the salon, had decided they both deserved a really good meal.

'I could take you to this Hotel Ritz you have spoken of,' he suggested.

Alice's rejection of the idea was instant and Jules did not

question it. Although she had never said so, his instinct had told him immediately he'd seen her with Harry that she was in love with the young man – a devastatingly handsome young man – whose manner towards Alice had been affectionate but certainly not lover-like.

He did not volunteer any further suggestions but took her to one of the few French restaurants he knew in Soho, where hopefully she would not be reminded of the man she loved.

Aubrey, meanwhile, was perched on the edge of his sister's bed while she sat at her dressing-table, twisting her head in front of the triple mirror as she tried to place two matching clips in her hair. Dissatisfied with the effect, she tugged them loose and placed them finally in position on either side of the V-neckline of her dress. Her mouth was set in a stubborn line, and she was scowling.

'I don't see why Harry had to go,' she protested. 'I wanted him to stay. He was going to talk to Daddy – about us.'

Aubrey sighed.

'I'm well aware of that, Pickles. He told me all about it. That's why I want to talk to you. I'm far from sure you know what you're doing. Harry said you'd told him you loved him, but only a fortnight ago you sat here telling me you might well go to Jamaica with Dunbar.'

Madeleine avoided her brother's eyes.

'That's different. I didn't know then that I'd fall in love with Harry.'

'Pickles, this is a serious business. It isn't a matter of choosing between one frock and another. Do you have any idea what you're talking about? Marriage is for life and a wife has got to share her husband's life, for better or for worse.'

'So why shouldn't I be happy married to Harry?' Madeleine's voice took on an accusing note. 'I thought he was your friend – that you liked him?'

'It's because he's my friend that I don't want to see him hurt. Look, Pickles, he hasn't two beans to rub together. Can you honestly see yourself being poor – really poor by

375

our standards? It's different for Harry, he grew up without any money behind him. You've always had everything you ever wanted. You'd certainly not be able to live the way you do now. I very much doubt if you'd be able to afford even half the number of servants we have to run this house. Just look at the state of this room. You take it for granted one of the maids will come in and tidy it for you. Can you honestly see yourself managing without your own maid for a start?'

'Harry said he'd have his own stud farm one of these days – and Mr Harvey owns a stud farm and *he's* a millionaire.'

'For heaven's sake, Pickles! It's because Mr Harvey was already a millionaire that he was able to indulge his fancy to have a stud farm – not the other way round. His family made their money from investment in the railways.'

Madeleine's scowl deepened.

'We only want to get engaged. Anyway, Harry seemed to think we could manage.'

'I dare say he could, with the right wife. But not with you, Pickles. It would be different if you really did love him, but I don't think you do . . . certainly not enough to make the kind of sacrifices that would be necessary if you did marry him.'

'You can't know how I feel,' Madeleine protested. 'Besides, how do you know how much money Harry has?'

'Because he told me. The pater told me his former guardians had frittered away the money his father left him, and Harry told me the amount of the salary Mr Harvey pays him. That's all he has, and it's not all that much more than your dress allowance, Pickles. You might as well face facts.'

For a few moments, Madeleine was silent, then she said truculently, 'Harry should have told me.'

A faint smile crossed Aubrey's face.

'My dear girl, you'd have thought him very ill-bred if he'd talked about money to you, and even if he had, you wouldn't have understood the relevance of what he was saying, any more than he understands how well off we are.

376

I can tell you one thing – the pater won't give you his blessing. When he hears what's in the wind, he'll probably insist Harry goes back to live in America while you both take time to think it over. Is this love you have suddenly discovered going to weather that kind of separation? I very much doubt it.'

'You mean you think Harry will go back and marry that Cora-Beth girl?'

'No, I don't mean that – and you know it! Harry's the faithful type. Dash it all, Madeleine, he's been in love with you since he was a kid. No, it's *your* so-called devotion I'm doubting and, if you're honest, I think you'll agree with me that it wouldn't weather a long separation.'

'I could go back to America with him.'

'No, you couldn't. The pater wouldn't give you the money for your passage and anyway, even if you found the fare, he could force you to come home. You're being utterly childish and well you know it. Besides, you wouldn't want to live in America – you've already said so. Nor would Harry go against Father's dictates. He's very conscious of the fact that he's indebted to him, not just for rescuing him from those awful guardians but for getting him into Grafton Abbey and then arranging for him to work for Mr Harvey. Come on, old girl, be reasonable for once and admit it would be a mistake.'

As Madeleine listened to her brother's quiet, sensible voice, her emotions seesawed from rebellion to anxiety. Part of her refused to accept that, after all, she couldn't have what she wanted. The other part questioned whether in fact she really did want to get engaged to Harry if it meant leading a dreary life waiting for him to make his way in the world. Aubrey's revelations had shocked her, but she did not doubt he knew what he was talking about. Despite his brotherly teasing and criticisms, he was devoted to her and would not be speaking in this fashion unless he felt it was for the best.

Remembering now how she had felt lying on the bed with Harry's arms around her, his mouth against hers, she felt like crying with frustration. She *could* wait for him –

no one could stop her marrying him once she was twenty-one. Yet she knew it was unlikely that Harry's circumstances would have changed to any great degree by then and she certainly had no wish to live in near poverty. Why, oh why, wasn't it Harry who could offer her the life Pogo could give her? It simply wasn't fair!

Tears of self-pity escaped from her eyes and she brushed them away angrily.

'I won't give him up, I won't. I love him,' she protested.

Aubrey rose slowly to his feet. Knowing his sister so well, he was aware that despite her denial, her decision to abandon the idea of marriage to Harry had already been made.

CHAPTER TWENTY-TWO

1924

Cynthia Merstam watched in silence as the nurse arranged the big bunch of gladioli she had brought with her to the nursing-home. The news she had just received from Dorothy's doctor had come as a dreadful shock, and for the moment she could not trust herself to speak.

'They're beautiful, Cynthia,' Dorothy Copley murmured. 'My room is beginning to look like the Chelsea Flower Show. I'm being so spoilt.'

She glanced at Cynthia's face and a look of pity crossed her own. Poor Cynthia, she thought. Doctor Milford must have told her sister the truth and she was taking it very hard. It was strange how other people seemed to mind about her approaching death far more than she did. Her husband, her stepchildren, and now Cynthia.

When the nurse left the room, she held out her hand and touched her sister's cheek.

'Honestly, dearest, I'm not in the least frightened,' she said. 'I don't feel resentful that God has decided to take me before my allotted span. I mind for Norman, of course, and for you and the children, but not for myself.'

Tears rolled down Cynthia's cheeks.

'I don't think I can bear it, Dorothy,' she said in a choked voice. 'I shall miss you so terribly.'

'I know. We've always been so close, haven't we? You've been a wonderful sister to me, dearest. All those years ago, but for you . . .'

'No, don't talk about it,' Cynthia broke in. 'Don't even think about it.'

The dying woman closed her eyes. She was well aware

of her sister's reluctance ever to speak of that fateful year when she had borne Gervaise's child. In a way, it was best forgotten. She had been relatively happy married to Norman and caring for his children. Only occasionally, on the anniversary of her baby's birth, had she allowed herself to think, to regret, to remember. Now, however, she was dying of tuberculosis and, with only a few weeks of life left, the past was very much on her mind.

'So many people have said to me over the years that it is very sad I never bore Norman a child, that I only ever had stepchildren to love. I've wished then that I could say honestly, "But I did have a child of my own, a little boy by the only man I have truly loved." You know, Cynthia, despite all we went through, my only sorrow is that my baby died.'

'But it was for the best that it didn't survive,' Cynthia said quickly. 'You were so anxious to keep it and . . .'

Dorothy shook her head.

'I know, dearest. I would have been disgraced, and you too. But you can't imagine how many times I've thought, "If I'd kept him, he might have lived." I shall die with that feeling of guilt, that it was I who robbed him of life.'

'But that's not true. It was I . . . Dorothy, I'd no idea you felt this way. You must not . . . you cannot re- gret . . .'

Dorothy gave a rueful smile.

'He was Gervaise's baby, Cynthia, and with Gervaise dying, it would have meant part of him lived on. But for this thought, I truly believe I could die in peace.'

Cynthia stood up and walked across to the window, where she stared out across the busy London street. On top of the news she had received, the thought of her beloved sister dying with regrets and a sense of guilt was more than she could bear. How easy it would be to confess that the baby had survived; that he had, according to Sir Philip Debrace, grown into a strong, good-looking boy. Would Dorothy hate her for having deceived her all these years? Would she want to see the boy? He must be a man now, and she, Cynthia, had not the slightest idea where in the world he was. Perhaps Sir Philip knew his where-abouts. But what of Dorothy's reputation, which she herself had guarded so zealously all these years?

As if her thoughts had been transmitted to her sister, Dorothy said, 'I know my son would have grown up to be a fine, good-looking man. How else would he have been with such a father? I wonder sometimes who he would have resembled. Both of us, perhaps. I suppose if he'd been alive, I'd be afraid now to meet him. We'd be like strangers and I couldn't bear that, but at least I could have made some redress.'

Tears filled her eyes as she added, 'My stepchildren are all well placed in life. When Norman dies, they'll be very well off and therefore have no need of my money. Had my son lived, I could have left it to him. I thought of leaving it to you, Cynthia, but you have no need of it. When Father died, he left us both enough to live in comfort for the rest of our lives, regardless of our husbands' support. I've never needed it, and over the years it has accumulated. To whom shall I will it? An orphanage, perhaps, like the one where we were going to leave my new-born baby?'

O God, help me! Cynthia prayed. What should I do? Should I tell her? If I don't tell her now, it will soon be too late and I shall have it for ever on my conscience.

She returned to the bedside and took both Dorothy's thin, blue-veined hands in hers.

'Why have you never spoken of this before?' she asked. 'Why didn't you tell me how you felt?'

Dorothy regarded her with a great love and tenderness.

'Because I didn't want you to share my distress. You've always been such a wonderful sister to me. You risked so much for me. I wanted you to believe that I was as grateful as you that the baby had died and solved the problem for us of concealing the birth. I remember the look of relief on your face when you told me it was all over – that I could return home and forget it ever happened. I suppose to be honest, I too was relieved at the time. But afterwards, especially when I heard Gervaise had died . . .'

Cynthia wiped the tears from her eyes.

'I wish I'd known. Oh, Dorothy, my dearest, how shall I tell you? You shouldn't feel grateful to me. You should hate me. I lied to you. I thought it was for the best. All those years ago, *I lied!* Will you ever forgive me?'

Dorothy's thin, flushed face paled as she regarded her sister's abject figure.

'You say you lied. In what way? What are you trying to tell me, Cynthia? Are you saying that my baby lived?'

Cynthia could not speak for the sobs that now came from her throat. She nodded.

Dorothy let out a deep sigh.

'Perhaps you'll think this one of those strange fancies of a dying person, but somehow I'm not surprised. I think I've always felt deep within me that my child was alive. I used to tell myself that it was because I wanted so much to believe it that I felt that way. Oh, Cynthia, darling, please don't cry. You can have no idea how happy you've made me. As to blaming you, how could I? You have always shown your love for me in the best way you knew how. I can understand why you lied.'

Tears streaking her face, Cynthia looked up.

'You really mean that, Dorothy? Nursing the secret all these years has been very, very hard for me. If I did wrong, then I have suffered for it. Yes, your baby lived. He grew up strong and healthy. Gervaise knew of his existence before he died, and although he wasn't able to acknowledge his son, he left him quite a fortune.'

Urged on by Dorothy, she related the story of Harry's early years with the Pritchetts, the criminal way in which Gervaise's wife and her brother had dissipated the boy's fortune, Sir Philip Debrace's interest in him.

'The last I heard was that he was to be given a good education at the public school which Sir Philip's son was attending. If I were to contact Sir Philip, I might discover more recent news.'

Dorothy lay back against her pillow exhausted. The excitement of Cynthia's revelation had been too much for her and Cynthia now anxiously rang the bell for the nurse. However, before she herself was dismissed so that

Dorothy could rest, her sister extracted a promise from her that she would set about finding out the boy's address and, moreover, that Cynthia would contact her own solicitor and have him draw up a new will making Dorothy's son her sole beneficiary.

'You will have to lie once more, Cynthia – not for either of our sakes but to save my husband the pain of knowing the truth. No one but he, my son, must know I am his mother. You must make him understand the need for secrecy. Perhaps I could tell Norman he was a godson with whom I'd lost touch when his real mother died? You'll think of something. You must make your solicitor realize that I cannot allow Norman to be hurt. He has been such a good, kind husband.'

By the time Cynthia had discovered that Harry Keynes, now twenty-one years old, was living in Kentucky in the United States, Dorothy had but a few days to live. Grasping Dorothy's hand in hers, she said, 'He's employed by Gervaise's relative, the current Earl of Kinmuire, on his stud farm in Kentucky. The earl, so Sir Philip informed me, is greatly attached to your boy. Sir Philip, himself, is likewise full of praise for your son, for whom he has the highest regard. Understandably, he was curious as to the reason for my enquiries, so I told him you were a distant relative, a spinster who had no other relatives and who might wish to get in touch with him. He said his ward was earning his living as an assistant to a stud-farm manager.'

Dorothy gave a weak smile.

'So Gervaise's son takes after him,' she said happily. 'He always had a special affinity with horses.' She gave a small sigh. 'You have made me so happy, dearest. If it is of any consolation to you, I shall die now in peace. Please arrange for the solicitor to come as soon as possible so that I can sign the necessary papers. I wish I'd not had to lie to my poor Norman, but he didn't question my story about a long-lost godchild and assured me he has no need of my money. I shall leave token sums to his dear children.'

The remainder of Cynthia's visit was spent in supporting Dorothy's arm while she wrote a letter that was to be given to the solicitor – a Mr Graham Lytham of Messrs Granby, Hemingford and Bowles – and handed in person to Dorothy's son when he received his gift. Mr Lytham, however, when he called at the nursing-home to obtain Dorothy's signature to her will, was far from happy when his client told him the content of the letter.

'The very last thing I would wish to do in the, er . . . present circumstances,' he said awkwardly, 'is to create any difficulties for you, Mrs Copley. However, your sister, Lady Merstam, is my client and I must point out to you both that, no matter how unlikely you may think it, Mr Keynes could betray your confidence. Lady Merstam has explained to me her lifelong desire to protect your reputation, Mrs Copley, and I fully understand your own wish to protect your husband from information which would, er . . . hurt him. There is also the question of your sister's reputation if her part in this, er . . . concealment were ever to be made public. Neither of you knows personally the young man to whom you intend to entrust your, er . . . secret, and I feel it is my duty to caution you.'

As Cynthia was about to protest, Dorothy held up her hand.

'Mr Lytham is quite right, dearest. We cannot be sure.'

As Cynthia fell silent, the lawyer stole a quick glance at the dying woman and, shocked at the wastage of so young a life, he hastened to lighten Dorothy's obvious distress.

'There is no reason why your, er . . . son should not receive the money you intend to leave him. It could come from "an unknown relative". It is the letter revealing your true relationship to him which poses the possible danger to your family and to Lady Merstam.'

'No, Cynthia, Mr Lytham's advice is sensible,' Dorothy said as Cynthia once again seemed on the point of protest. She gave a wan smile. 'I was being self-indulgent . . . wishing to make a confession and to beg my child's

384

forgiveness for abandoning him. To do so at risk to you or Norman would give me no happiness, dearest. I will leave this letter in your care and you shall decide when and if the moment is right and you feel you can pass it on.' She gave a long, painful sigh. 'You know, Mr Lytham, I am rapidly coming to the conclusion that my bequest might also wait a few more years. My son has only just reached his majority, and I understand he is in no immediate financial need. It might benefit him the more if the money were to be withheld until he is older. My husband has always maintained that it destroys a young man's ambition to succeed in life if he is financially indulged too young. Robert, my stepson, is not to be given his grandfather's inheritance until he is thirty.'

As Mr Lytham nodded his approval, Cynthia looked anxiously at her sister.

'Are you sure about this, Dorothy? It places the responsibility on my shoulders and . . .'

'On whose better?' Dorothy broke in gently. 'There's no one in this world in whom I have greater trust. Come now, Mr Lytham, let me sign these documents while I still have the strength.'

The solicitor gave an embarrassed cough.

'I am afraid they are no longer appropriate, Mrs Copley. That is to say, the wills of individual persons are open to public scrutiny and, in many cases, details are published in the newspapers. Your son – Mr Harry Keynes, is it not? – would therefore know the name of his benefactor. The alternative might be to arrange with your bank manager to transfer these funds into a separate account in your sister's name, er . . . before . . . while you are still, er . . . in a position to do so. Lady Merstam tells me you have your husband's agreement to what was to have been the bequest. I presume he would not therefore question your method for disposing of your money before, er . . . your demise?'

Dorothy smiled.

'Really, Mr Lytham, it's no secret that I am dying, so please don't feel embarrassed to use the word "death". It doesn't frighten me. What does frighten me is that there may not be sufficient time left to me to do as you suggest. Will it take long?'

'A day or two at most, Mrs Copley. Under the circumstances . . .'

'Of course we shall use the utmost expediency,' Cynthia said. 'Mr Lytham will come with me now to your bank, Dorothy, will you not, sir?'

'I'm at your disposal, Lady Mersham,' the lawyer said. 'I need only a letter from you to your bank manager instructing him of your wishes. There will, of course, be papers for you to sign.'

After he had bowed himself out of the room, Cynthia remained behind and, taking pen and paper, took down Dorothy's letter to her dictation.

'You are quite sure about this, Dorothy?' she said as she handed it to her for her signature.

'Absolutely,' Dorothy said. 'This way is best. You have always taken such care of me, dearest. Now I know that when I am gone, you will be watching over my son's welfare.'

There were tears in Cynthia's eyes as she held the thin, wasted body of her adored sister in her arms.

It was the first time in their lives that Dorothy, although younger by ten years, had ever felt the stronger of the two. Wiping away Cynthia's tears, she urged her to be on her way and perform this last task before it was too late.

'I'm dreadfully sorry, Harry, I really am.'

Alice's voice held genuine regret, for although she had never thought Madeleine the right girl for Harry, she would have done anything possible to forward a marriage between them if she truly believed it would make him happy.

'I suppose you aren't particularly surprised,' Harry said as he regarded Alice miserably from the armchair in the living-room of Monsieur Verveine's spacious London flat. Jules had tactfully made himself scarce on the pretext of work to be done at the new *salon* and now, two days after

386

his visit to Maythorpe House, Harry was at last able to unburden himself.

'Aubrey was decent enough to bring Madeleine's letter round by hand,' he continued. 'He realized I'd be knocked out and did his utmost to persuade me it was all for the best.' Biting his lower lip in an effort to control his emotions, he added wretchedly, 'Despite what he says, I know Madeleine does love me. That day we spent together at Maythorpe House – everything was perfect. Of course, I knew it might be ages before we could actually marry, but she said she'd wait. She said she wanted to get engaged, so you see, she can't love Dunbar. Aubrey seemed to think she probably would marry him, but I just don't believe it.'

He looked so dejected, Alice's heart twisted as if the pain were her own.

'Madeleine's still very young – for her age, I mean. Perhaps she doesn't really know what she wants.'

'She wanted me. She wanted me to make love to her. Alice, you can't believe how sweet she is, and how innocent. I love her so much. Life doesn't seem to have much meaning any more.'

Alice crossed the room and rested a hand lightly on Harry's shoulder.

'It'll get better in time,' she said, although even as she spoke, she knew that in her own case it would never get better. In a way she was happy that Harry had chosen to come to her in his distress, yet it highlighted his attitude towards her. She was, as she always had been, a kind of benign, elder sister. He never saw her as other men did – as a woman. Only this afternoon, one of the Maison's new fabric suppliers had asked her out to dinner and made it perfectly plain that he found her attractive. Then there was Félix, who telephoned from Paris every other day because, he said, he missed her so much.

'I suppose you're right,' Harry said gloomily. 'Aubrey said I'd get over it, but I won't, Alice. I dread going back to the States. I know Cora-Beth wants us to get engaged and now Madeleine's turned me down, she'll expect me to propose. But I can't, not feeling the way I do about Madeleine. I'm fond of Cora-Beth, very fond, but it isn't the same as I feel for Madeleine and somehow I'll have to explain that to her. She's been hurt enough with poor old Judd getting killed in that wretched accident.'

'I'm sure she'll understand,' Alice said, willing herself not to touch Harry's dark curls, not to draw his head against her breast for the comfort she so longed to give him. 'You can still be friends – and if that proves too difficult, then you can come home.'

'Home,' Harry repeated in a harsh voice. 'Where is my home, Alice? It used to be with Mum and Dad and you and the kids in Calking. Then it was Maythorpe House, and then The Grange. Finally, it was Blue Ash Farm. I don't really belong anywhere, do I?'

Yes, yes, yes, you belong with me! Alice ached to say. Anywhere I was with you would be home to me. For a moment she hated Madeleine Debrace for making him so unhappy.

'Why?' she asked. '*Why* did Madeleine turn you down?'

Harry drew a deep sigh.

'She said in her letter that she didn't think we could be happy living at Maythorpe House, that she'd be lonely and probably wouldn't make me a very good wife. How can she know that? She said she'd given it a lot of thought and decided she'd just got carried away because it was all such fun. I can't believe that's all our day together meant to her – fun! Aubrey is convinced Madeleine's priorities are "getting her own way" and "having a good time" – and that she wouldn't be able to indulge either if she married someone without considerable private means. That would make her so mercenary, and I don't believe she's like that. Maybe she was just trying to cover up the fact that she minds about my being illegitimate.'

'If that were true, then she couldn't love you very much, Harry,' Alice said quietly. 'If you were happy together, why should she mind about a few snubs from social snobs who barred you from their visiting-lists for such a reason? Such people aren't worth knowing in the first place. Tell me, does Cora-Beth care that your parents weren't married? I take it she knows?'

Harry nodded.

'It's all a bit different in America, Alice,' he said. 'People are less formal, or the people the Harveys know. No one bothers about Mr Harvey's title and nor does he. It's what you make of yourself that matters out there.'

'It's what you are that matters to me,' Alice said impulsively. Afraid lest she had revealed too much, she added quickly, 'Tell me about your visit to Maythorpe House.'

Successfully diverted, Harry said, 'It's a funny thing about that house, Alice. I really hated it when I was there, but this time . . . I sort of felt as if it was where I belonged.'

'Home?' Alice questioned meaningfully.

'I suppose in a way that's what it did feel like. Yet I never knew my father when he lived there – only the stories Mrs Appeby used to tell me about his childhood. Do you know, his lead soldiers are still in the nursery toy cupboard. And his stamp collection.'

'I'd have thought all those things would have been packed away,' Alice said. 'What does Mr Harvey plan to do with the place? It can't stay empty for ever.'

'I don't think he knows, or cares. Whenever I speak of it, he just says it can stay as it is in case I ever want it. I did think that Madeleine and I . . . But I wouldn't want to live there on my own, Alice.'

'I could always come and look after you – keep you company,' Alice said in a casual tone. 'Remember how we used to plan the future, Harry?'

He gave a disparaging smile.

'We were kids, weren't we, and about as unrealistic as only kids can be! But then we couldn't have foreseen your future, or mine. Here you are, about to be launched in your own right as a successful *couturière* and I'm living in a country thousands of miles away, helping to manage a thoroughbred farm.'

Alice drew a deep breath.

389

'We could give up our jobs and start something new at Maythorpe House.'

Harry laughed, not believing Alice might be serious.

'I'd need a great deal more money before I could start up my own stud farm there. And the last thing in the world you'd want would be to give up this opportunity Monsieur Verveine has given you. I'm so proud of you, Alice. I know you must deserve this chance. It's taken five years of your life, but at least you're getting your just rewards now.'

I was silly even to put one toe in the water, Alice told herself angrily. Of course Harry would not want to be burdened with her, even if he could afford to start up his stud at Maythorpe House. Young though he might be, he was going to need a wife, a family, and it was not her, Alice Pritchett, he wanted to marry, not now, not ever!

Somewhat to her surprise, Harry was smiling.

'You know, Alice, when I walked in here I was feeling pretty suicidal. Just talking to you somehow makes me feel better. I'm not quite sure why! I know you never considered Madeleine was the right girl for me and no one in this whole world knows me as well as you do, so I can't ignore your opinion, even though I'd like to. Now that I'm feeling a bit calmer, I can see that it was amazingly presumptuous of me even to imagine that Madeleine might love me enough to sacrifice all the luxuries she's used to, just to be with me! I don't feel poor – not when I remember our childhood! – but of course I am by her standards. I suppose I was conceited enough to imagine that the amount of love I have for her would make up for the deprivations. You'd be quite right to call me an idiotic, romantic fool. It's much to your credit, my darling Alice, that you haven't done so.'

He drew her towards him and planted an affectionate kiss on her forehead.

'Where would I be without you to knock some sense into my thick head?' he said tenderly. He was suddenly aware of her body trembling and, misunderstanding the reason, he added contritely, 'Why, you're cold! It's that flimsy frock you're wearing, and now I come to look at you, Alice, you're much too thin. Come on, let's go out and have a really good meal somewhere. If you like, I could try and get tickets for *The Merry Widow*. It's on at the Lyceum and is supposed to be frightfully good. I think Dunbar has seats for next week and we were all going as a party, but I shan't go with them now. I don't think I could bear to see Madeleine again. It's probably just as well I'm leaving for the States on Saturday week.'

'So soon?' Alice whispered. 'I wish you could stay longer.'

Harry released her and once again his expression was downcast.

'If things had gone differently, I'd thought of extending my holiday, but now there doesn't seem much point. Here in London I'll be bound sooner or later to run into Madeleine. Aubrey says Lady Debrace is taking her down to Brighton for some sea air, but I don't suppose they'll go for long. No, Alice, I'll leave as soon as I can, so let's you and I make the most of today. You're not doing anything?'

Alice shook her head. She had nothing planned, unless it was to go to a cinema show with Jules, and even if she had, there was nothing she would not have cancelled in order to be with Harry. It would, as always when she was with him, be part pain and part pleasure. The effort of concealing her love was almost impossible even though it was imperative. If Harry were ever to know how she felt, he would never again be able to show the same natural affection, albeit of a brotherly nature, which was all she had of his heart. At least now, today, she could ease his suffering, help him forget Madeleine for a little while, make him see that he could still find happiness of a kind without her.

Somehow she managed a smile as she said with deliberate casualness, 'Sounds a wonderful idea, Harry. Give me a moment or two to change my clothes and leave a note for Jules, then we'll go out on the town.'

'We'll think of something to celebrate,' Harry said, returning her smile. 'If it can't be the present, we could celebrate our unknown futures.'

'Why not?' said Alice softly. 'One never knows what the future will bring.'

CHAPTER TWENTY-THREE

1926

It had taken a long while, Harry thought as he glanced fondly at Cora-Beth, before he had got over Madeleine's rejection of him and the shock of her marriage to Dunbar. Aubrey and Cora-Beth had not long returned from a lengthy ride across the lush, undulating pastures and were still wearing jodhpurs and cool, open-necked shirts. Not only had Cora-Beth been incredibly patient and understanding about his reluctance to become engaged these past two years, but during that period of his life she had somehow made it possible for them to renew their old easy friendship. At first he had suggested it might be fairer to everyone if he were to leave Kentucky and find work elsewhere – perhaps even return to England – but Cora-Beth had succeeded in making him see that there was absolutely no need for him to do so.

'You're happy here at Blue Ash Farm, and Poppa would be heartbroken if you left,' she'd said. 'You told me you can't afford to start your own stud yet, and so what would you do if you did go home? We're both still young and there's plenty of time to make up our minds about the future. I'm in no hurry to get married, and anyway, it wouldn't be right while you're still wishing you could be married to someone else. Why don't we go back to the way we used to be? Surely we can be friends, can't we? I'm perfectly willing to try, if you are. Who knows, you may feel different in time.'

Cora-Beth had been quite right. Time had to a very large extent proved the cure he needed. If occasionally he still dreamed of Madeleine, of holding her in his arms, kissing her, he had reconciled himself to the belief that marriage between them could only have ended in disaster. He felt both older and wiser now. Gradually he and Cora-Beth had grown close again until suddenly, at Christmas, he had realized what an indispensable friend and companion she was. There'd been ever more frequent occasions, when he took her to dances and held her in his arms, that he had once more become acutely aware of her in a physical sense. Slowly but inevitably they had drifted back into a loving relationship, culminating three months ago in their engagement.

When Aubrey had accepted one of their many invitations to come on a lengthy visit, it did cross Harry's mind that his resemblance to his sister might bring back painful memories, but although Aubrey had now been here over a week, he, Harry, had felt no desire to wish himself free of his engagement. On the contrary, Aubrey's instant approval of his choice of a wife had added to his own conviction that he had finally made the right decision for his future happiness.

It pleased him too that Cora-Beth seemed to be getting on so well with his best friend. It was probably a very good thing in far more ways than one, Harry reflected, that Aubrey would be living with them here at the farm for several months. It would limit the amount of time he and Cora-Beth could be alone together. The problem was, Cora-Beth could see no reason now that they were engaged why they should not make love.

'We're young and in love and it's natural,' she said in her open, uninhibited way. 'You want to, don't you?'

Of course he did. Sometimes he could not sleep at night for thinking about the one time it had happened. Cora-Beth's ill-disguised eagerness for a repetition of their love-making had become increasingly difficult to resist.

'I suppose you think me shameless for telling you I want you so badly,' she'd told him shyly. 'I know nice girls don't talk about such things.'

It was impossible to be euphemistic about the basic facts of nature when one lived on a stud farm, Harry told himself as he watched Cora-Beth rise from the swing seat where they were sitting and walk across the veranda into the house to fetch a fresh jug of lemonade. It was not unusual for topics such as mating to be discussed at the breakfast table despite Cora-Beth's presence!

A fortnight before Aubrey's arrival, he and Cora-Beth had watched the stallion, Warrior, cover the new roan mare. Sherry, as she was called, had proved as eager for the mating as Warrior and the coupling had been quick and undoubtedly successful. Without being particularly conscious of where they were going, he and Cora-Beth had ended up in the big barn containing bales of straw for the loose boxes. Cora-Beth's foot had slipped between two of the bales and she had tumbled backwards, dragging Harry down on top of her.

Their coupling had been as quick and inevitable as that of the two horses, and although Cora-Beth had cried out once in momentary pain, she had professed herself entirely happy and not in the least guilt-ridden by their union. His own pleasure had been of shorter duration for he was very well aware that he ought somehow to have protected this trusting girl from himself. With a great effort of will, he'd resisted her pleas to go to her bedroom after everyone was asleep. It disturbed him to think of her father perhaps waking to hear him tiptoe down the passage like a shifty thief afraid of discovery. Aubrey's arrival had augmented the difficulty since he had been given the guest room adjoining Harry's.

'Of course I want to meet him,' Cora-Beth had said before Aubrey's arrival. 'I know what a big part he has played in your life and I'm sure I'll like him, but I just wish he wasn't going to stay quite so long. I want to be alone with you, Harry.'

Over the past few days, however, Harry noticed that she seemed reconciled to the fact that they were fast becoming an inseparable threesome. Returning now with the lemonade, she gave Aubrey a quick glance of appraisal.

'You know, you sure are different from the way I'd

imagined you,' she said in her slow drawl as she poured out fresh drinks for them both.

'So what did you imagine?' Aubrey asked with a smile.

'I dunno. I suppose after those stories Harry told us about you being an asthmatic as a child, I'd expected you to be delicate, a thin undersized weakling!'

Aubrey laughed.

'I probably was. Fortunately, I've outgrown those days. I haven't had an attack for years. I get a bit bronchial if I stay in London in the winter. The smoke and fog seem to get on my lungs, but apart from that I'm as fit as Harry now.'

And in a different kind of way, every bit as good-looking, Cora-Beth decided as she bent her head over her glass and sipped the refreshing drink in her hand. The two young men were opposites, Aubrey as fair as Harry was dark. Harry's charm lay in his quick, almost mischievous smile and impulsive eagerness for life; Aubrey was quieter, more placid, with an easy-going, lazy slowness about his movements.

In a funny kind of way, she thought, it was like having Judd back. Aubrey had much the same rather dry sense of humour. Poppa loved having him around and they would both miss him when he went back to England.

'Do you realize, it has taken me two whole years to get you out here?' Harry was saying to his friend. 'Small wonder Cora-Beth was beginning to doubt if you really existed.'

'You know what life's like at home,' Aubrey said. 'One gets caught up in the old social whirl. Anyway, I'm here now and I'll say this much, Harry, old chap, you weren't exaggerating when you said it was beautiful . . . and everything so vast, so spacious.'

'It can also be lonely, living miles from anywhere,' Cora-Beth reminded their guest. 'If it wasn't for Harry . . .' She looked fondly at him and, as he took her hand in his, her cheeks flushed a deeper pink.

'I'd been expecting for ages to hear you two were getting engaged. Can't think what took you so long to get around to it, old chap,' Aubrey said.

Harry gave him a friendly shove on the shoulder.

'It was on the cards for ages, so it was really only a question of making it official,' he explained. 'Now we've got to decide on a wedding date. We'd thought perhaps this time next year.'

So there was no urgency in this love match, Aubrey mused. Was it possible poor old Harry was still carrying a torch for Pickles? It was well over a year since his sister had married Dunbar and gone off to the West Indies, where, according to her spasmodic letters, she was having 'an utterly marvellous' time. He'd relayed the news to Harry, hoping it would put his fickle sister out of his friend's mind once and for all.

Now that he'd met Cora-Beth, he was in no doubt that Harry stood a far greater chance of happiness with her. Although perhaps not in the strictest sense of the word 'beautiful', the American girl had a very pleasing appearance, and despite her height and strong build, an attractive feminine figure. She was good fun to be with and easy to talk to, and in the short time he'd known her she had shown a ready sense of humour.

'We've decided to go on living here at the farm with Poppa,' she was saying. 'There's no point buying another place. Poppa's letting Harry build up his own stud. Did Harry tell you he'd bought a stallion and four mares of his own? Poppa seems to think he bought very well.'

Harry gave a self-deprecating grin.

'I'd never have got such a bargain on my own,' he said. 'Your father was the one who struck the deals; all I did was choose the animals.'

Cora-Beth laughed.

'For all there's no need, Poppa can't resist bargaining,' she said. 'I sometimes wonder what people must think to hear him haggling over a few dollars. Yet there's nobody more generous. He'll give hundreds away at the drop of a hat. He's a guaranteed soft touch for anyone genuinely out of work or in real poverty.'

'My father's much the same,' Aubrey said. 'He was very much against my inclination to break the recent general strike, as most of my friends were doing. He said the miners were being asked to accept wages that were even lower than they'd been before the war and that their working conditions were appalling. My mother helped to run soup kitchens in Brighton for the starving.'

Harry nodded.

'Jenny wrote and told me about it. Fortunately, none of the family was too badly affected. Did you know that poor little Edna died in the influenza epidemic? I was shocked to hear of her death and of so many others all over the country.'

'It affected the rich as well as the poor,' Aubrey said. 'Two of the mater's friends died, but what really devastated her was the death of my Aunt Rosamund. Personally, I think it was a merciful release both for my aunt and for my Uncle Félix, seeing that she had been a helpless invalid for so long. But I suppose the loss of a sister is always sad, whatever the circumstances.'

'You went to Paris for the funeral, didn't you?' Harry said. 'Alice wrote and told me she'd seen you.'

Aubrey's expression changed to one of amusement.

'I must say, Alice really has made something of herself! I simply didn't recognize her at first, and to tell you the truth, I was a bit embarrassed when Uncle Félix came over to talk to me with this perfectly stunning girl on his arm. I just stood there like a goof waiting for him to introduce her. I supposed she was one of his *mannequins*, although her face did look extraordinarily familiar, and then Uncle Félix said, "You know Alice, of course," and the penny dropped.'

Harry laughed.

'I told you Alice had changed two years ago, when I saw her in London,' he said. 'I gather she's making a great success of the English branch of the business.'

Now it was Aubrey's turn to smile.

'There's no doubt about that. Uncle Félix never stopped singing her praises. You know, Harry, I get the impression he takes far more than a professional interest in Alice. There was something about the way he looked at her. That would be a turn up for the books, wouldn't it, if my uncle married your foster sister?'

Harry grimaced.

'You can't be serious, old chap. Your uncle must be years and years older than she is, and anyway, I rather gathered she'd got her sights set on some fellow whose name she wouldn't tell me. You must have been imagining things. Too much champagne, I suspect.'

'Honest to God, Harry, I'm not joking. I know it was a funeral and I'm certainly not suggesting Uncle Félix behaved improperly in any way, but you couldn't help noticing how his eyes kept following her. I'm not surprised. She really did look fearfully glamorous and so . . . well, I suppose the word is sophisticated. As for her French – she's bilingual. I think she'd make my uncle a jolly good wife, and it would be a splendid match for her, wouldn't it? I believe he's awfully well heeled. The pater was saying something to that effect only the other day. There's talk of him opening two new *salons* in New York and Milan. The mater says everyone who's anyone in society wants Verveine clothes these days. They're internationally famous.'

Cora-Beth now joined in the conversation.

'Even I know about them,' she said. 'I've seen them in the fashion magazines and I must say, they sure are special. Poppa says I can go to London or Paris and have them make my trousseau if I want.' She looked at Harry and grinned. 'Not that I think Harry will appreciate how I look. Half the time, you don't notice what I wear, do you, honey?'

'That's not true,' Harry protested, although on reflection he knew that it was. It wasn't so much Cora-Beth's looks which appealed to him as her character.

Cora-Beth's voice gave him no time to consider the matter further.

'Hey, you guys, it's time we went up to change. I forgot to tell you, Poppa's invited the Simkins to dinner.'

'Simkins,' Aubrey repeated. 'Wasn't that the name of your old guardian, Harry?'

Harry laughed.

'No, that was Simcox, numskull! Cosmo Simcox!'

'Does anyone know what happened to him?' Aubrey asked curiously.

'Your father told me he'd gone to Australia and Aunt Pamela had joined him there,' Harry replied. 'I think it's unlikely we'll ever hear from them again. I doubt if anyone could have been much more unhappy than I was living with them at Maythorpe House. But for Alice, I might have remained there indefinitely.'

Realizing that time was passing, the subject was dropped until later that evening when, after the dinner guests had departed, they were enjoying a nightcap with Wendell before going to bed. Alice's name cropped up once more in the conversation.

'I can't wait to meet this Alice you both speak of so often,' Cora-Beth said thoughtfully. 'She sounds a remarkable person.'

Aubrey nodded.

'My mother thought the world of her. It was Mother who arranged for her to go to Paris to train in Uncle Félix's *salon*. I suppose when we were younger, we all rather took Alice for granted, but looking back, one can see what a strong character she had even then. I wonder if Uncle Félix *will* marry her? What do you think, Harry?'

Harry frowned.

'I think you're way off the mark,' he said. 'Monsieur Verveine must be old enough to be her father! Why on earth should she want to tie herself to someone like that?'

'I don't think he's all that old!' Aubrey said laughing. 'I suppose he's in his late forties, early fifties, and Alice is older than you, isn't she?'

'Only by four years,' Harry protested. 'That makes her twenty-seven.'

'The difference in their ages does not seem unduly large to me,' Wendell interposed. 'On the contrary, mature men can make better husbands than younger ones. At least they are established, and they know their own minds.'

'But it's Alice I'm thinking of, sir,' Harry argued. 'It just wouldn't be right.'

'But you can't know that, Harry,' Cora-Beth joined in the debate. 'From what you and Aubrey have told me about Alice's life, she has always had to fend for herself. Perhaps she would welcome security.'

Harry fell silent. Cora-Beth's comment had touched an unexpected core of unease. It hadn't occurred to him that all those years Alice, who had looked after him so persistently and unobtrusively, should have had no one to look after her. At the same time, he wouldn't feel at all happy were she to marry someone she could not possibly love simply to make her life easier, more luxurious. Perhaps if he were to send her money . . . but the thought died almost before it had crossed his mind. He certainly couldn't afford to keep Alice in comfort for the rest of her life. Were it not for the fact that he and Cora-Beth were to continue living here at Blue Ash Farm with her father, he couldn't even have afforded to get married.

'. . . really mustn't look so worried, old chap,' he heard Aubrey saying. 'It's more than likely I just imagined something was going on behind the scenes. Dash it all, we were attending poor Aunt Rosamund's funeral. Even if my aunt had been mentally lost to Uncle Félix years ago, as the mater said, he'd hardly be thinking about marriage to another woman at such a time. It's just that Alice looked so gorgeous, I really wouldn't have blamed him.'

'It sounds very much as if you were the one who was smitten,' Cora-Beth laughed. 'Isn't it time you were thinking of settling down, Aubrey? You're older than Harry, aren't you?'

'Only by a year. But I'm in no hurry to tie the knot. Apart from anything else, I've not met a girl I'd want to spend the rest of my life with – at least, not until I met you, and Harry's pipped me to the post.'

They all laughed, although Aubrey added, 'Honestly, old chap, I'm not joking. I think you're a very lucky fellow – and I just hope you appreciate your good fortune.'

'You bet I do,' Harry said with a warm glance at Cora-

Beth. 'Sometimes I think I was born lucky. Remembering the circumstances of my birth, life could have been very different for me, couldn't it? If the Pritchetts hadn't taken me in, I'd have probably been put in an orphanage and never had the educational advantages or been given the opportunities that have come my way.'

'I've always maintained that most of us get what we deserve in this life,' Wendell said. 'Most of the time, we make our own luck. Speaking of luck, there's a colt I want to buy not far from Lexington – came up for sale just when I was thinking of getting in some new blood. Care to come along, Aubrey? See the town? Have a bit of lunch?'

'That's a first-rate idea,' Harry said, 'because I shall be tied up tomorrow. I promised Dillon I'd be around when the architect brings the plans for the new extension.'

Wendell nodded and turned to his daughter.

'You'll come along, won't you, Peachcake?'

'I don't think I will. I've got things to do, Poppa,' Cora-Beth said vaguely. 'Time we all turned in, don't you think? It's long past midnight.'

Her father's belief that people made their own luck was true, Cora-Beth thought, when by lunchtime the following day Harry had finished his business with the architect and her ruse to have him to herself for a few hours paid off.

'I'll walk back to the stables with you,' she suggested.

Delighted to have her company, Harry linked his arm through hers and they strolled in a leisurely fashion down the shady drive. Suddenly Cora-Beth stopped and put her arms round Harry's neck.

'Do you realize we haven't kissed – not properly – for days and days?' she said. She drew him with her into one of the paddocks bordering the drive. 'I know you find it embarrassing to show your feelings in front of anyone, especially Aubrey,' she said with a mischievous smile, 'but that's just being terribly English. No one will see us here. Anyway, even if Aubrey could see us, I can't believe he'd be shocked. I guess he's wondering why we don't kiss more often.'

Harry smiled as his arms tightened around her.

'Knowing Aubrey, I doubt he's given it a thought,' he said. 'Perhaps you're right about it being "English". At school, it simply wasn't done to show you cared about anything other than cricket. You could get as worked up as you liked about sports.'

'Then imagine I've just scored a century for your side,' Cora-Beth said with a husky little laugh. 'You know, I sometimes wonder whether you do still really and truly love me.'

To prove that his feelings for her had in no way changed, Harry kissed her as she wanted, his tongue probing her mouth, which was raised so invitingly to his. His desire for her was instantaneous and of their own volition his hands began to search and caress her body. Her breasts were taut against his palms and he could feel their rise and fall as her breathing quickened.

When their lips parted, he said, 'Now do you doubt I love you?'

He had expected her denial but she clung to him saying, 'But not enough, Harry. Don't you want me? Don't you know how much I want you? I'm beginning to think you didn't enjoy it that time we did it properly, that you wish you hadn't!'

Tears of mortification were dripping down her cheeks and, horrified, Harry bent to kiss them away.

'That's crazy, Cora-Beth. Of course I want you. It's been torture sometimes being so close to you and unable to touch you, kiss you. I dare say if you could quantify such a thing, my need is far far greater than yours.'

'Then prove it,' Cora-Beth whispered. 'Here, Harry, now! Here, in the long grass. No one will see us. I've always wanted to make love out of doors, in the sunshine. I'm sure nature didn't mean us to have to wait till we get into a bed! And we are engaged. That makes us almost married, doesn't it?'

Harry was touched by her honesty and, as always, aroused by the way she spoke so openly about her physical desires. The fact that he found it less easy to talk about such things to a young girl did not mean he was less

403

impassioned than she was. On the contrary, were she to change her mind now, he would be unbearably disappointed and frustrated. As Cora-Beth had so truly argued, they were engaged and it could not be so wrong to anticipate their actual marriage.

'I do love you, I really do, Cora-Beth,' he said huskily as his arms tightened around her and he kissed her again.

Her tears dried as suddenly as they had appeared. She pulled him down beside her in the long grass, and smiled shyly at him as she undressed.

'You too,' she said. 'Look how tall the grass is. No one will see us.'

Harry's hesitation was short-lived. After all, he told himself, if the worst did happen and she conceived a child, they could advance the wedding. Maybe they should do so in any event. If they were married, they could make love as often as they pleased.

'Let's get married quickly,' he suggested, his arms around her, his lips against her soft cheek. 'What do you think, darling?'

'I don't want to think about anything but this,' Cora-Beth murmured as her hands caressed his shoulders and moved down his body until, with a little gasp, she held him in her cupped hands. Harry could see the sun glistening on the naked patches of her body although she had not yet removed her undergarments.

Thoughts of Wendell Harvey, of possible passers-by, of wedding dates, receded from his mind as his desire for this lovely, passionate girl matched hers for him. The sun was on his back as he swung himself over her and her long legs parted in expectation. Nothing as beautiful as this could be wrong, he told himself. Cora-Beth was right – this was what nature intended and he would prove his love.

When finally they rolled apart and lay, hands entwined, staring up at the cloudless blue sky, Cora-Beth's voice was soft with contentment as she whispered, 'You do love me, I know it now! I was so afraid you'd changed. I thought – it was silly I know, but I thought perhaps seeing Aubrey had reminded you of Madeleine and that it was going to be as awful as it was when you came back from England after that holiday. Harry, I know I've no right to ask, but I want to know – you never did this with *her*, did you?'

Harry shook his head.

'No, I didn't. To be honest, I suppose I did want to, but . . . well, Madeleine was very young and uncertain of herself, her feelings. I wasn't at all sure if she really did love me – and, as you know, it turned out she didn't. But let's not talk about her – not now. She belongs to the past. I don't even think about her any more.'

That was not entirely true, he realized as he and Cora-Beth straightened their clothing and tidied their hair. One evening after dinner Wendell Harvey had demanded that Aubrey tell them about his childhood at The Grange, and how Harry had become involved with the family. Inevitably, Madeleine's name had cropped up and Harry had felt a pang of nostalgia remembering the little girl with her white dresses and long, golden plaits, laughing or stamping her foot if her brother didn't give her her own way. He had a deep yearning for those long-ago summer holiday afternoons spent on the lawns or down by the lake with the two Debrace children.

No, he would not allow sentimental memories of the past to mar his present happiness, Harry determined, as, with his arm around Cora-Beth's shoulders, they resumed their walk. Those early years were best forgotten and he would not allow himself to dwell on them if he could possibly help it.

But the past could raise its head in other ways, he realized, when two days later a letter arrived with a London postmark, bringing him news of the most extraordinary nature. He showed it to Wendell, who was equally mystified. The letter read:

Dear Mr Keynes,

We have to inform you that you are the beneficiary of a large sum of money which our client is holding in trust for you.

There is, however, a crucial condition attaching to

the gift which must be met before the necessary documents can be finalized. We are aware that you are currently residing in the United States and must inform you that it will be necessary for you to come to London and report to our offices with appropriate means of identification. While it might be to your advantage to do so at the earliest opportunity, there is nevertheless no legal urgency for you to make the journey other than at your convenience.

We look forward to hearing from you regarding the above in the near future.

The letter was signed by a Mr Graham Lytham and had been written on notepaper with the heading Granby, Hemingford and Bowles, Solicitors.

'I've never heard of the firm and simply can't imagine what this is all about,' Harry said. 'What's your opinion, sir?'

Wendell smiled.

'For a start, I go right along with the "never look a gift horse in the mouth" proverb,' he said. 'If you're to come into money, then it couldn't be at a more appropriate moment, could it? At the same time, I'm curious as to what this "condition" is. Why, I ask myself, this legal reticence? The solicitor names neither your benefactor nor his client, nor does he explain why you should be the beneficiary. No one from your past comes to mind who might want to do you a good turn?'

Harry shook his head.

'There's no one in my foster family who could afford to give even a few pounds away,' he said, 'and I certainly don't have any rich friends. It's a mystery to me.'

Wendell lit a cigar and puffed on it thoughtfully for a few minutes before saying, 'Those guardians of yours, Harry – the ones who filched your father's legacy from you. Any chance one or other of them has had an attack of conscience and decided to pay it back?'

Harry frowned.

'I suppose Uncle Cosmo could have made good in

Australia. Somehow I can't imagine him ever giving money away – except by mistake on a race course or at the gambling tables! As for Aunt Pamela, she never liked me and in a way I can understand why she resented my existence. I was hardly someone for her to be proud of, was I? I suppose it just could be Uncle Cosmo, although I'd be sad to hear he'd died. He was kind to me in his way.'

'One thing anyway is clear,' Wendell said emphatically, 'you will have to go to England and find out what it's all about. Now, when is it that Aubrey goes home?'

'In six weeks' time. D'you think I should travel with him?'

'I think we should all go,' Wendell replied jovially. 'For one thing, I know Cora-Beth is crazy to buy her trousseau from that fancy *couturier* she's always on about.' He handed back the solicitor's letter. 'For another, if it isn't too far ahead for you to enquire into this, Harry, then I might take up an invitation I've received to attend Newmarket races at the beginning of October. Strathavon covered one of John Bambridge's mares, before your time I think, and he's entering the filly for the Champion Stakes. Bambridge thought I might like to see her run. From what he tells me, she's in with a good chance.'

'Newmarket isn't all that far from Melton Mowbray,' Harry remarked. 'We could go and see Maythorpe House. After all, sir, it is your family seat.'

Wendell grinned.

'Be yours and Cora-Beth's when I turn up my toes,' he said. 'Let's go tell the others what we plan to do. My bet is Peachcake'll be pleased as punch.'

When Cora-Beth heard the news, she threw her arms round her father's neck and hugged him.

'Poppa, it's a splendid idea,' she said. 'Will your Alice be in London, Harry? I've heard so much about her, I'm just longing to meet her. She can help me choose my trousseau, and Harry, I'll want to meet your foster family and the old cook who was so kind to you. Do you think she'll approve of me?'

Harry smiled.

'Mrs Appleby will approve of anyone who has Kinmuire blood in their veins.'

Aubrey, watching the three excitedly making plans, was sensitive enough not to mention the news he had received a few days' earlier from his mother – that Madeleine and Dunbar were coming home with the regiment. They were expected to arrive in London early in December.

No matter how well matched Harry and Cora-Beth appeared to be, Aubrey was rapidly coming to the conclusion that Harry still harboured romantic memories of his sister. If ever her name was mentioned, he quickly changed the conversation with a too obvious show of lack of interest in Pickles's affairs. That she appeared to be having a marvellous time in Jamaica and was being hopelessly indulged by Dunbar had elicited no more than a shrug of Harry's shoulders and a vague comment about his being delighted she was having such a good time.

Perhaps he was just imagining the undercurrent of nostalgia, he told himself as he looked at Cora-Beth's flushed, excited face. She was such a lovely girl and had such a sweet nature that he would be distressed to think Harry might not be able to give her the depths of love she deserved. She had looked unnaturally pensive, uncertain, when he'd spoken of their childhood days at The Grange and Harry's face had lit up with a special glow.

Despite the material and social disadvantages that Harry had suffered as a child, he still seemed to think of those early years as happy ones. Was it because Madeleine had adored him, tagging along behind, begging to be allowed to share their boys' games? She'd thought Harry was wonderful because he was able to mend her bicycle chain; make bows and arrows and catapults; shin up trees to collect birds' eggs for her collection; find dormice nests, badger setts and squirrel dreys. Most of all she had admired him because he was afraid of nothing, and because he invariably treated her like a princess.

Madeleine, Aubrey thought – although he was far too loyal to his sister ever to say so to anyone – was vain, egotistical and spoilt. It was not altogether her fault. Their father had always indulged her every whim, and she was so pretty that all her life she had been admired and given her own way. Harry was far better off with a really nice, loving girl like Cora-Beth. It was a good thing he had finally come to his senses and realized it for himself.

Six weeks later, unaware of what the future held in store for him, Harry boarded the *Berengaria* with Aubrey, Cora-Beth and her father. As he checked into the first-class cabin of the big liner, he had never, he thought, felt happier in his life.

CHAPTER TWENTY-FOUR

1926

'I'm very sorry, Félix, but I cannot accept this.'

Alice handed back the tiny red-leather Cartier box containing a diamond and sapphire engagement ring of great beauty. Her expression was regretful for without doubt it was the loveliest ring she had ever seen. If Félix was disappointed, he gave no sign of it. He was regarding her thoughtfully.

'Is it because it's too soon – after poor Rosamund's death?' he asked. 'If so . . .'

'No, Félix, that's not the reason,' Alice interrupted quickly. 'I'm very, very honoured that you should consider marriage – and I honestly wish things could be different. Truly, I do. I'm grateful to you and I respect you and I am very fond of you, but . . .'

'"But,"' he imitated her voice with a shake of his head. 'Such a little word but so important, yes? What is this "but", *chérie*?'

Seeing the twinkle in Félix's grey eyes, Alice had the impression that he was teasing her. Surely this was an occasion when he should be serious? Two minutes ago when, astonishingly, he had proposed to her, he had looked and sounded serious enough.

'Well?' he prompted. 'What is this great big "but"?'

Alice found her voice.

'For one thing, if I were to accept I would feel obliged to offer something more than . . . than mere affection. I . . . I'm not in love with you, Félix.'

He was seated on the *chaise-longue* where, as a rule, clients reclined while the models displayed a selection of gowns for their approval. The staff of the London *salon* had long since gone home and the place was deserted. Félix put the jewel box back in his pocket and gave an exaggerated sigh.

'You know, Alice, I have reached the conclusion that you are, without intention I admit, the most tantalizing young woman I have ever known. For the first time in my life, I find myself pursuing someone of the opposite sex who does not respond to my advances. It is piquant, to say the least, and I will confess that there have been moments when I asked myself if I was perhaps becoming a little silly in my middle years. Is it not said that "there is no fool like an old fool"? However, I have to confess that although bitterly disappointed when you refused to become my mistress, I consoled myself with the fact that you did so only because such a liaison would be so contrary to your upbringing. I was astonished to discover how disappointed I was . . . in short, *chérie*, how important you had become to me. Now, it seems, I cannot tempt you even with the offer of a respectable marriage. What a blow to my self-esteem, to my masculine ego!'

Despite herself, Alice smiled.

'You know very well my refusal has nothing to do with whether or not I consider you attractive,' she said. 'If it were not for . . . if I didn't . . . if my affections were not already . . .'

'If you were not in love with young Harry Keynes,' Félix interrupted, his face now serious once more. 'You know, my dear, your faithfulness is laudable but not altogether practical. You have told me that the young man is engaged to be married next summer and, so I understand, to a very suitable girl of his own age. Therefore what hope have you of marrying the one man you do love? Is it not youthful romanticism to reject other ways of finding contentment, happiness? You are far too beautiful to remain a spinster, and a young woman like yourself must realize that you are wasting the best years of your life. Would I not be right in thinking that quite soon you will be thirty?'

Her eyes uneasy, Alice now walked across the big empty *salon* and fingered the length of beautifully beaded satin draped over one of the pairs of carved, gilt *torchères*. She was conscious of Félix's eyes following her. He had arrived unexpectedly from Paris half an hour before closing time and was still wearing his camel top coat with its astrakhan collar and a white carnation in the buttonhole. His pigskin gloves and bowler hat were beside him on the sofa, along with his cane and evening paper and a new edition of *Vogue*. As always, he looked immensely distinguished, and, in a mature way, very handsome. There was an authoritative, self-confident manner about the way he held himself that exuded power.

Why, oh why, couldn't she love him? she asked herself. He was, as always, absolutely right in his judgement of her. She was behaving like a silly, romantic girl in believing that Harry was the only person in the world to whom she could give her heart. How many times had her dear friend, Jules, told her that she was wasting her youth? Perhaps, after all, she had been too busy in her pursuit of personal success. Certainly of late nothing had mattered beyond getting the London *salon* established and proving to Félix – as well as to herself – that she was worthy of his trust, his expectations.

The *salon* was now a proven success and Félix's clients no longer asked for him but were happy to rely on her advice. There was even a member of the Royal Family who, having once insisted that it should be *le Maître* and no one else who attended to her needs, now bowed happily to Alice's suggestions. After all these years of immensely hard work and devotion to her self-imposed goal, wasn't it time she allowed herself to enjoy the kind of life Félix was offering her? For whom was she guarding her virginity? How wonderful it must be to sit back and be spoiled, like some of the clients whose husbands clearly adored them and seemed amused and gratified by their wives' desire to look pretty and fashionable.

So why had she returned the ring Félix had presented just now when he had asked her to marry him? It was certainly not because she entertained any hope of a future for herself with Harry. For a while after Harry had returned to Kentucky following his visit to England and his disastrous reunion with Madeleine, she had wondered if he would remain in America, especially when he had written to say that he and Cora-Beth had reverted to their former friendly relationship and had no plans to get engaged. For a few months, she had allowed herself to imagine that Harry would return to Maythorpe Hall and need her, Alice, to look after him. It was a wild, unrealistic dream, quickly dispelled when subsequent letters from him indicated that he and Cora-Beth were growing close again. Now, with their wedding date actually fixed for next summer, she accepted that her future could never be with him.

She turned to look at the man who had done so much to further her career, who had been so unfailingly kind and good to her, who had for seven years been her friend and mentor. For all he was many years older than herself, he was a man very much in his prime, very much involved in new schemes, new ideas. He had a wide circle of friends and acquaintances with whom he was immensely popular – and not just because he was famous. People enjoyed his company, for he was witty, amusing, erudite and generous. That such a man was prepared to marry her – Alice Pritchett, his sister-in-law's former maid – was flattering, to say the very least, and yet . . .

Uneasily, she looked away, turning to stare out at the darkening sky through the uncurtained windows.

Félix rose from his seat and came to stand behind her. She stiffened as, without warning, he put his arms round her waist and drew her against him so that she felt the warmth of his body against her back. His lips were touching her hair as he said softly, 'You are so very beautiful, Alice. It grieves me to see so much beauty wasted.' One of his hands moved up to cup her breast. He had never attempted such intimacy before and now he said:

'If you will not agree to marry me yet, *ma petite*, at least allow me to show you the delights of love while I wait for you to change your mind. Ignorance is not always bliss, you know. It is time you learned more about the forces of passion which motivate men and women – and, indeed, all nature. There is so much more to life than the search for money, power, recognition. We need to be recognized for what we are deep down inside. You must feel that need too.'

Almost with surprise, Alice realized that her body was indeed responding to his embrace. With slow deliberation, he turned her round to face him and, bending his head, he kissed the base of her throat. She felt a quickening of her heartbeat and instinctively her arms reached up and tightened around his neck.

'Alice, Alice,' he was murmuring. *'Comme je t'aime, ma petite. Je t'adore!'*

Then he was kissing her, at first with gentle teasing kisses and then, when she did not draw away, with rising passion. Alice felt as if she was being divided into two people – the one who in her head kept saying, 'No, I don't love him! I don't want him to make love to me!' and the other, quite separate, who was pleading, 'Hold me closer! Don't stop kissing me! I want you to hold me, show me . . .'

For a few moments longer, Félix continued to kiss her and then he drew back. 'Let us combine this pleasure with another,' he said, giving her his charming smile. 'I have booked a table at the Ivy. It has been recommended to me by our client, Lady Diana Cooper. She told me we shall be certain of good food there and, who knows, we may see some famous actors and writers who have begun to patronize the place. We shall celebrate this very important day – the day when Mademoiselle Alice Pritchett finally permitted the man who has adored her for so long to kiss her! I shall not dare to say "make love to her", for that might frighten away the smile on her face. She has no idea how beautiful she is when she smiles. Come, *chérie*, let us go and enjoy ourselves. It is good for the soul to be happy, *non?*'

With Félix in such a jubilant mood, it was impossible not to respond, Alice thought later, as she sat on the *banquette* beside him, eating the delicious quails' eggs in aspic he had ordered for her. She'd had only a sandwich for lunch and the champagne was making her feel light-headed as well as light-hearted. Between courses, Félix held her hand, occasionally lifting it to kiss her fingertips. He had bought a spray of delicately scented violets for her from a flower-girl outside the restaurant, and from time to time he touched them, telling her they reminded him of quiet, leafy lanes in the English countryside and therefore of her. It was impossible to feel other than cherished and Alice ceased worrying about what might happen when the meal was over.

It was only when he was assisting her into her coat, his hand resting momentarily on the nape of her neck, that she became aware of the sudden change in her relationship with Félix. He was behaving as if . . . as if they were already lovers, she told herself. Had she really committed herself? Félix was tucking her black wrap-over coat around her and she was acutely aware of his eyes burning into her; of the touch of his hands as he settled her collar around her neck; of his voice murmuring endearments in his own language.

Surely it was not too late to put right a misunderstanding? she asked herself in sudden panic. She had not meant . . . intended . . . wanted . . . No, that wasn't true! A few hours previously, she *had* wanted him to go on kissing her. Her body had felt incomplete . . . desirous of far more than she had yet experienced.

During the short taxi-cab ride to the flat, Félix held her hand tightly, refusing to allow her to put on her gloves. Once or twice, he pressed a kiss into her palm. He looked happy, youthful, and she sensed his excitement, which stimulated her own even while it frightened her to think that it really was becoming too late to protest. It would be both embarrassing and unfair to rebuff him now when he was so clearly expecting her compliance.

Félix Verveine was far too experienced not to recognize,

when they reached the flat, the conflicting emotions of the young woman beside him. He knew he would gain nothing by trying to rush her, as a younger man might do. He made no move to touch her while they sat drinking the champagne he had brought with him from Paris. Slowly Alice relaxed, and then, as the tenseness left her face and body, he allowed himself to draw close to her until it seemed quite natural that he should be kissing her. Without haste, he led her into the bedroom and while she sat like a small girl waiting to be told what to do, he drew the curtains, allowing only a faint light from the street lamp outside to filter into the room.

'You must not be afraid, my beautiful Alice,' he said as he went to sit beside her and began to unfasten the row of small buttons on her dress. 'I know it is important that the first time should be an occasion you will always remember with pleasure. You must trust me. You do, don't you, *ma petite*?'

Alice closed her eyes as he pushed her gently back against the pillows. She did trust Félix and yet there was a part of her which was crying out, this should be Harry . . . Harry with the dark curly hair and laughing eyes. This is not my dream. Harry . . . Harry . . .

Then Félix's mouth was against her lips, his hands were caressing her body and she was shivering, her nerve ends responding to his touch until she ceased to be aware of any thought beyond her need for this to continue. As her longing rose to a crescendo and her thighs parted shamelessly so that he could do as he pleased with her, she was dimly aware that he had not yet removed his own clothing; that he seemed intent upon satisfying her needs without thought for his own.

When, for the first time in her life, Alice discovered the miraculous sensation of which her body was capable, she was barely conscious of the quick, almost painless way in which Félix broke the barrier of her virginity. Then only did he undress and slip beneath the sheet with which he had covered her throbbing body.

'I had to hurt you, *chérie*, but only a little, I hope. Now it will be better, I promise.' He kissed her tenderly as she lay relaxed in his arms and then he began once again to caress her. She could feel his lips on her breasts, was aware of the power he had to bring them to life, as indeed he could arouse once again the sensation of longing for more. It seemed quite natural when she felt his body harden against her and then begin the slow, thrusting movements within her while he continued to exert his magical touch between her legs. Suddenly she became aware that she was moving with him, that they had become one single person searching for the supreme moment of fulfilment.

That moment of unity was short-lived. Kissing Alice tenderly before he left the bed, Félix disappeared into the bathroom and she was left alone. What had she done? she asked herself as a deep feeling of melancholy swept over her. Somehow, she had betrayed herself and the worst part of it was that, while it had been happening, she had experienced great pleasure. Félix could not have been gentler, more sensitive and appreciative of her needs, and yet now, for some inexplicable reason, she was dangerously close to tears. She wished that he would not in a moment be returning to the room and that she would feel obliged to pretend that she was happy. All she could think of was that she should not have allowed it to happen.

Félix, however, was in the best of spirits and seemed unaware of her dejection. Wrapped in a large white towel, he returned from the bathroom and stood smiling down at her.

'I have run the bath for you, *ma petite*,' he said. 'Then you are to put on one of your prettiest gowns and I shall take you out to a nightclub – a novelty for you, I believe. There I shall hold you in my arms while we dance.'

It was almost as if he sensed her inability to talk, Alice thought, as, covering her naked body with the counterpane, she hurried into the bathroom. Félix did not try to kiss or touch her as she passed by him and for this she was grateful, since she could not explain even to herself the unaccustomed shyness and embarrassment she was experiencing in his presence.

Partly to give herself confidence, but also to please Félix, she chose to wear her most becoming evening-gown, designed by him for the Pavilion d'Élégance at the Paris Exhibition the previous year. The now-famous dress had been created out of cream parchment silk tissue. Flowers and birds in burnt orange and black were embroidered on the bodice and on the loose panels of the overskirt. These were clasped on one hip by the familiar Verveine hallmark – a large, ornate V. When she appeared before him, she was both relieved and amused by the impersonal eye with which he viewed her.

'It's lovely, Alice, but that panel does not hang correctly. It should be more to the left – like this.' He gave it an expert twist and immediately Alice could see the improvement. She smiled.

'I see I still have much to learn from you, Félix,' she said, and then blushed as she realized that he could mis-interpret her meaning. He, however, was at his most buoyant and remained so throughout the night in the festive atmosphere of the Embassy Club. When they were not dancing – and despite his age, Félix appeared in-exhaustible – his topics of conversation revolved around his business and the plans for the new *salon* in Milan.

'I shall have to be in Italy quite a lot in these coming months,' he told her. 'But I shall come to London to see you as often as I can, Alice. I would like nothing better than that you should accompany me, but alas, I cannot spare you here. You know, my dear, I am seriously considering promoting Jules to a more managerial position here in London. What is your opinion? I am aware you think very highly of him and he has always been very popular with our clients. If you were to allow him to take over the reins from time to time, you would not have to work quite so hard, *chérie*.'

Alice endorsed the suggestion wholeheartedly. Her relationship with Jules had settled into a friendly intimacy and she had grown to rely on him more and more as the business expanded. Moreover, in his last letter, Harry had said that Cora-Beth intended to have most of her trousseau made by the Maison de Verveine and something deep within her had rebelled at the thought of supervising the wedding clothes that were to adorn Harry's bride. Now she could delegate the making of the trousseau. Jules would be thrilled to have the responsibility of attending an American millionaire's daughter.

In addition, it answered her need to have more time to visit her mother. Martha Pritchett was dying and although Will was still not aware of it, the doctor had warned Alice that her mother would not last the year. Arrangements would have to be made for her father to be looked after. Jenny and Jack were married now with two small children and the tiny flat over the sweet shop in Calking where they lived was simply not large enough to accommodate another adult. Arthur was in lodgings in Brighton, where he was in full-time employment working as a plumber and Ted had just joined the Merchant Navy.

Since the onset of Martha's illness, Nurse Wilks had taken the eleven-year-old Sam under her wing but somehow lodgings would have to be found for their father. He was crippled with rheumatism and quite unable to fend for himself. The burden of looking after the two old people was falling entirely on poor Jenny's shoulders and although Alice could, and did, contribute financially, she was unable to relieve Jenny for more than half a day on Sunday. She had not as yet written to tell Harry about the seriousness of Martha's illness, for there seemed little point in burdening him with such sad news when there was nothing he could do about it.

It was all of three o'clock in the morning before Félix suggested that they should leave the nightclub.

'With Jules returning tomorrow, we have little time remaining to be alone together,' he said, taking Alice's hand in his and kissing the soft, white skin of her wrist. Unable to ignore the tensing of her body, he added quickly, 'You must never be afraid of me, *ma petite*! I do not take your acquiescence for granted and if you prefer to sleep alone, I shall respect your wishes.'

He had spoken in a low tone that would have seemed casual had it not been for the look in his eyes as they searched her own. He would take a rejection to mean that she had not appreciated him as a lover, she thought. As he moved one finger gently up and down her arm, she was aware of her body responding and memories of the pleasure he had given her returned with frightening intensity. It would not, after all, be so difficult for her to allow him to do as he wished.

Alice's confusion deepened. How was it possible, she wondered yet again, that she could actually want this man to make love to her and yet not love him? Was it enough simply to be fond of someone? Grateful to them? Or was it simply that after all these years her body was starved of love?

The fact that their subsequent intimacy aroused an even greater degree of passion in Alice only added to her confusion, and although Félix expressed his deepest regrets that he must return next day to Paris, Alice was relieved when he left. She wondered if Jules noticed any change in her, but other than to tell her that she was looking tired, he made no comment when she mentioned Félix's unexpected visit. Within minutes, they were engrossed in the suitcase full of fabric samples Jules had brought back with him from Lyons and Félix was forgotten. Her mind was once more on the trousseau they must make for Cora-Beth. Jules immediately appreciated her desire to pass this particular client on to him.

'It is best that I attend to her,' he said. 'It would be too difficult for you to make beautiful the young lady who has won the heart of the man you love. How you must hate her!'

Alice stared at him aghast.

'I have no cause to hate her,' she said quickly. 'She makes Harry happy and that's all I care about. But Jules, how did you know about Harry? I never told you . . .'

Jules patted the back of her hand.

'My dear Alice, one would have had to be blind not to realize how you felt about that young man, seeing you in his presence. I knew almost at once.'

'But you never said anything to me . . .'

'For what purpose? If you had wished to speak of it you would have done so. Before then, I had been puzzled by your behaviour. It was not natural for you to be without friends of the opposite sex, to reject all invitations, even to reject the advances of our dear *Maître*! After I had met your Harry, I understood. For some people, there is one love – and one only. Now he is to be married. In your shoes, I should hate the woman he has chosen to make his wife.'

'Oh, Jules, *you* might do so, but I can't. For Harry's sake, I shall do everything I can to like her.'

'Then you are a saint,' Jules said as Alice laughed.

But she did not feel in the least saintly as she climbed into bed later that night and recalled her all too willing lapse into immorality. How shocked and horrified her poor mother would be if she knew. She would have pressed her daughter into marrying Félix as quickly as it was possible to arrange. Even so, Alice's mind remained unchanged – she couldn't bring herself to marry a man she didn't love.

Yet she could allow him to share her bed, she reproached herself bitterly. She could enjoy all the things he did to her – and doubtless would do so again – knowing she did not love him. What kind of person was she? One thing was for sure – she was no saint!

A day's sailing from New York, Harry was comfortably installed in a deck chair on the First Class deck of the Cunard liner as the big ship ploughed its way smoothly across the relatively calm waters of the Atlantic.

'Alice is an absolute saint,' he was saying to Cora-Beth, who had not long returned from a dip in the indoor swimming-pool, taken during the 'ladies only' session. He and Aubrey had swum earlier with some of the other more energetic male passengers, Wendell declining to do so on the spurious grounds that swimming might make him seasick! 'I know you're going to love her, Cora-Beth. She's a splendid person, isn't she, Aubrey?'

'Absolutely,' Aubrey agreed, with a sideways glance at the girl beside him.

For days on end, they had all been talking excitedly about the forthcoming trip. Wendell had booked state cabins for himself and his daughter and First Class cabins for Aubrey and Harry. As Harry had said, the last time he had crossed the Atlantic, he had travelled steerage! They had all the opulent luxury of the rich and the famous, not to mention the entertainment available both day and night, but now Cora-Beth – usually so effervescent and full of fun and laughter – seemed unnaturally quiet, as if she had something on her mind. They had been discussing the amount of time she would need to spend at the Maison de Verveine organizing her trousseau, when out of the blue she turned to Harry and said, 'Suppose your Alice doesn't like me?'

Not seeming to hear the anxiety in her tone, Harry laughed off the notion.

'Let's go and see if the deck quoits court is free,' Aubrey suggested tactfully, for it was uncharacteristic of this jolly girl to be afraid of anything. 'I know I ate far too much lunch and I need some vigorous exercise.'

He helped Cora-Beth to her feet and said solicitously, 'You're not feeling seasick, are you? You don't have to play if you don't feel up to it.'

'No, I'm fine,' Cora-Beth answered. 'I think it's just the sea air making me sleepy. You coming, Harry?'

'You bet. If we can't find a fourth, I'll take you both on. Ten bob I beat you.'

But the game was not to take place for a while. As they were about to move off, they were approached by two elderly women. The shorter of the two was dressed in a check tweed suit which somewhat unfortunately exaggerated the size of her stocky figure. She was a plain, homely-looking woman. The taller and smarter one wore an expensive three-quarter-length wrap-over coat with a matching scarf collar and skirt.

She inclined her head towards Wendell.

'Please do forgive me for disturbing you, sir. It is Mr Wendell Harvey, isn't it? I'm Lady Merstam and this is my companion, Miss Hanworth.'

Wendell rose politely to his feet and bowed to the two women.

'I think we may have friends in common, Mr Harvey. I noticed on the passenger list that you have a Mr Debrace in your party.' She turned to Aubrey. 'I am acquainted with your parents. You bear a very strong resemblance to your mother, young man.'

Wendell hastily beckoned to a passing deck steward to bring some more chairs. As soon as they were seated, he introduced Cora-Beth and her English fiancé, Harry.

For the first time, Cynthia Merstam's glance rested on the darker of the two young men.

'My congratulations to you both,' she said. 'You are planning to live in England when you're married?'

'Oh, no, in Kentucky, ma'am,' Cora-Beth answered. 'My father has a stud farm there and Harry is going to run it now that Poppa is about to retire.'

'First I heard of my retirement,' Wendell said jovially. 'Tell me, ladies, is this a pleasure cruise?'

Miss Hanworth looked as if she were about to reply but Cynthia said quickly, 'A sea trip for my health. I'd not been too well. Fortunately, I am now quite recovered.'

'Then perhaps you met my father professionally?' Aubrey asked.

'Not as a patient,' Cynthia replied easily, 'but on matters of business. I am better acquainted with your mother.' She turned back to Wendell. 'Do please tell me more about your stud farm, Mr Harvey. Miss Hanworth is a very keen racegoer. Will you be visiting Newmarket?'

Within minutes, Wendell and Miss Hanworth were deep in conversation about horses and their pedigrees, and Cynthia turned once more to Harry.

'Is it your plan to become an American citizen eventually?'

she enquired. 'If your work and your home are to be in the United States, I imagine you have no roots in your native country.'

'In a way, I do have roots in England,' Harry answered politely. 'In Leicestershire, actually. Mr Harvey and my fiancée also have English connections.'

Cynthia nodded.

'I noticed as I approached that you young people were preparing to go somewhere. Please don't curtail your plans on my account. Now that we have met, I'm sure we shall have further occasion to converse. Miss Hanworth and I will remain a little longer and talk to your future father-in-law.'

As they made their way to the deck quoits court, Aubrey turned and grinned at Harry.

'Funny old stick! People like her can be an awful bore. You can't get away from them on board ship,' he commented.

Cora-Beth laughed.

'Poppa wasn't finding the frumpy companion in the least boring,' she said. 'I thought the older one was rather nice, although she did keep staring at you, Harry. Sure you've never met her?'

'Absolutely,' Harry said. 'Come on, the court's free. I'll play with Cora-Beth. Ten bob we win, Aubrey, right?'

When the family were all together once more in the elegant dining-room that evening, Wendell was in excellent good humour.

'Both the ladies play bridge,' he announced, 'and Lady Merstam is getting the purser to fix us up with a fourth. Now I shan't have to spend my evenings watching you three gallivanting round the ballroom. Interesting woman, that Hanworth female. Really knows what she's talking about. She knows our filly but doesn't give her much of a chance in the Champion Stakes. She's backing her for a place, though. Seems Miss Hanworth's father used to own a string of racehorses and she was riding before she could walk.'

He gave a jolly laugh.

'The father was Irish and hopelessly eccentric – couldn't ever bring himself to get rid of non-runners because he was fond of them. Finally, the stables were so full of lame ducks or elderly nags he'd pensioned off, he couldn't afford to buy any fresh blood. I've a mind to ask Miss Hanworth to join our party at Newmarket – she's good company.'

'Why, Poppa, I do believe you're smitten,' Cora-Beth said teasingly. 'What about the other one, Lady Whatnot? She seemed a bit snooty to me. I wonder why she cottoned on to us? As far as I could gather, it didn't sound as if Aubrey's parents were close friends?'

'Lonely, I dare say,' Wendell replied. 'Asked endless questions about Blue Ash Farm and what sort of work Harry did – that kind of thing. As a matter of fact, she seemed more interested in Harry than Aubrey.'

'It's those Valentino good looks of yours – always gets the ladies,' Aubrey joked, earning himself a kick under the table from Harry. 'You'll have to keep an eye on him once you're married,' he added, addressing Cora-Beth.

'Enough of this frivolity,' Wendell said with mock severity. 'The ladies are joining us for coffee in the lounge after dinner and I don't intend to be party to you three exchanging looks and behaving like kids.'

Although Harry was well aware that Aubrey had only been ragging him about Lady Merstam, even he had to admit later that she monopolized him throughout the brief half-hour of their second meeting. Her questions were surprisingly personal. What were his ambitions for the future? Had he always been fond of horses? Had he enjoyed his school life? He had no objections to answering such questions, although he wondered how long it would be before this strange woman began to enquire about his family connections. When asked about his background, it had become his habit simply to say that he'd been orphaned in infancy and brought up by guardians, but Lady Merstam evinced no interest in his childhood or his parents. On reflection, he decided that she was harmless enough and probably lonely, as Mr Harvey had suggested.

For the rest of the voyage when their paths crossed, he maintained a polite friendliness and thought no more about her.

Harry had no way of knowing that, for the past two years, Cynthia had been keeping a close eye on his activities. Through the friendship she had cultivated with Sir Philip's wife, she had been able to make casual enquiries about Sir Philip's ward, Harry Keynes, and had thus learned of Harry's engagement. Since nothing was ever said to the young man's discredit, Cynthia had decided to instruct Mr Lytham to release Dorothy's money to him. No sooner had she done so than she began to have qualms as to whether her decision was justified, bearing in mind that she had still never met Harry. A visit to Mr Lytham had elicited the fact that Harry would be travelling with the Harveys on the *Berengaria* on 14 September. It was then she had made a most untypically impulsive decision to book a return passage on the same liner to enable her to meet her sister's child without his knowledge of her own identity. Now, having achieved her objective, Cynthia was delighted that she had devised this wild scheme, for it had resulted in setting her mind totally at rest. The young man was living up to the reputation the Debraces had given him, and she had every confidence now that there was no likelihood whatever that the boy would dissipate the large sum of money Dorothy had left him.

'A most enjoyable passage,' she said, endorsing Wendell's comment, as the ship docked at Southampton.

Harry was leaning over the rail, his handsome young face bright with excitement as he watched the crowds waiting to welcome their relatives and friends. He turned politely as Cynthia spoke and she held out her gloved hand. With innate good manners, he expressed regret that she would not be accompanying Miss Hanworth to Newmarket and a wish that they might meet again on some other occasion.

'Before long, I hope,' Cynthia murmured as unexpected tears rose to her eyes and she turned hurriedly away.

When next they met – perhaps no longer than in a few days' time – it would not be as strangers. She had made up her mind that when next she saw him, she would, after twenty-three years of regretting his birth, acknowledge him as her nephew with a genuine welcome in her heart.

CHAPTER TWENTY-FIVE

1926

CHAPTER TWENTY-FIVE

1926

Although on their arrival Aubrey returned at once to his parents' London house, Wendell insisted upon taking a suite of rooms for Harry, Cora-Beth and himself at the Savoy. A hotel, he maintained, would enable them to come and go as they pleased without being beholden to a host and hostess, and although the Debraces had been more than hospitable in offering them the comforts of their home, he did not wish to impose on virtual strangers for the month they planned to stay.

Harry was changing into his dinner jacket in preparation for the evening meal when Aubrey suddenly appeared unannounced. His face was white and he slumped into one of the comfortable armchairs with a look of distress.

'Pretty ghastly news, I'm afraid,' he said. 'The pater received a cable from Madeleine at lunchtime. Poor old Dunbar was killed in a riding accident on the polo field yesterday. A broken neck, by the sound of it. Mother cabled back at once to say one or other of us would go out as soon as possible, but we got a second cable from Pickles about an hour ago, saying we'd be too late for the funeral and, in any event, she'd be coming home with the rest of the regiment in eight weeks' time.'

Harry paused in the act of fastening his bow tie and, deeply shocked by Aubrey's announcement, said stupidly, 'But Dunbar was so young. And they'd only been married two years.'

Aubrey nodded.

'It's pretty grim for poor old Pickles, isn't it? Of course, she'll get lots of support from the regiment – I mean, they'll see to the funeral and that sort of thing. All the same, I don't like the thought of her without one of the family there.'

'I really am dreadfully sorry,' Harry said.

Two months, he thought. He would have returned to Kentucky by then. Perhaps in a way, that was just as well. Although it seemed awful to harbour such a thought when the wretched Dunbar was not yet buried, it had nevertheless crossed his mind that Madeleine was now a widow; that given a decent period of time to recover from her grief, she might wish to find another husband.

Hurriedly, almost guiltily, he pushed the thought to the back of his mind. He was in no better position to support Madeleine now than he had been when he had last proposed – unless, of course, he really had come into money. Tomorrow he would be seeing the solicitor and he'd know what the strange letter was all about. But even if he were now to become a comparatively rich man, it could make no difference. He was going to marry Cora-Beth, whom he loved and respected. Their future was planned and Madeleine was not, nor ever could be, part of it.

'The mater was very fond of Dunbar,' Aubrey was saying. 'As a matter of fact, I liked him too, although he wasn't all that bright. Thoroughly decent chap – too nice for Pickles in lots of ways. Still, they seem to have been fairly happy, although I'm not sure Pickles was all that keen on being an army wife. Service life made too many demands on poor old Pogo, I suppose. Still, that's all over now and, as the pater said, she's only just twenty-one. She's bound to marry again.'

Aubrey stood up.

'Will you explain things to Mr Harvey? Why I can't make dinner tonight, I mean. The pater says I'm not to call off any of our other plans – Newmarket, the theatre and so on . . . says there's no need for me to go into mourning and anyway, what could I do if I hang around at home? So I'll be along as planned to take Cora-Beth round the Tower of London while you see your lawyer chap. It's Windsor Castle after lunch, isn't it? Trust the Americans to want to see everything in five minutes.'

He managed a smile as he left the room, but Harry could see that he was more than a little shaken by the news. He wished he need not be the one to put a damper on Cora-Beth's excitement at being in London. The glow left her face when he made his sad announcement while they were having pre-dinner cocktails in the lounge.

'I feel I've no right to be so happy when that poor girl must be heartbroken,' she said. 'Life can be very cruel, can't it?'

For a moment there was silence while the memory of Judd's as well as Pogo's sudden and untimely death clouded all their thoughts. Then Wendell said, 'We must try to look on the bright side. The girl's very young, isn't she? Younger than Aubrey. I dare say she'll find someone else to take care of her. At least there are no young children.'

'Maybe a child would have been a comfort to her at a time like this,' Cora-Beth said. 'I know it would be to me if anything happened to . . . to Harry.'

'I'll have no more of this morbid talk,' Wendell said sharply. 'Now listen here, Harry. I've spoken to Thomas Cook and they're making all the arrangements for us to take in the races at Longchamp and see the Prix de l'Arc de Triomphe. We'll be staying at the George V in Paris and from there we can make the excursions we want to Versailles and Fontainebleau, and there's a stud farm I want to see at Chantilly. That'll interest you, Harry, my boy, as well as the eighteenth-century Condé stables – they accommodate over 200 horses.'

Cora-Beth was smiling again.

'You two and your horses,' she said. 'Sounds like I won't get to see the Gobelin tapestry works or the Sèvres china factory.'

Wendell patted her head.

'You're gonna see just whatever your little heart desires, honey,' he said. 'We'll stay in France as long as it takes.'

'Poppa, there isn't going to be *all* that much time,' Cora-Beth argued with mock reproach. 'Don't forget my main reason for being in Europe is to get my trousseau together. I'll be needing fittings. Did you speak to Alice, Harry?'

Harry nodded.

'I telephoned from my room. She says they are frantically busy but if she can't see you personally, her chief assistant will.'

Because he did not want the atmosphere to become depressed once more, he refrained from passing on Alice's bad news – that Martha Pritchett had a malignant tumour and although neither she nor Will knew it, the doctors had told Alice that she would not recover. Harry had arranged with Alice to go down to Calking the following Sunday to see her.

Alice had sounded distraught, and he could understand why, in the circumstances, she had not shown greater enthusiasm for helping with Cora-Beth's trousseau. Nevertheless, he thought, it would be wonderful to see Alice. It was two long years since he'd last done so and he remembered now that he had not been entirely happy about her. Although she had spoken at length about the new *salon*, she'd evaded any discussion about her personal life.

On Sunday he would find out if there was even a glimmer of truth in Aubrey's suspicions that Félix Verveine was keen on her. He'd not taken Aubrey's remarks seriously, but a hint of unease had remained and even he had been forced to realize that in her letters Alice no longer referred to '*le Maître*' or to 'Monsieur Félix' but used his Christian name. He would, he decided as they left the cocktail lounge and went in to dinner, quickly disabuse her of any idea that she should give her life to an old man with whom she could not possibly be in love. It disturbed him even to think about it. Alice was so beautiful these days that there must be other, younger men, one of whom would be far more suitable as a husband.

Observing Harry's introspection, Cora-Beth could not bring herself to ask the cause of it. Not unnaturally, she assumed that he was thinking about the girl with whom he had once been in love and who was now coming home a young and unattached widow.

'I hope you won't mind my saying that the, er . . . circumstances of your birth and this, er . . . gift are somewhat bizarre, to say the least, Mr Keynes.'

Harry returned the fatherly smile of the solicitor in whose office he was now sitting. Graham Lytham, so he had been told when he had telephoned for an appointment, was the senior partner of the firm.

'Please don't feel any obligation to beat about the bush, sir,' he said quietly. 'I've long since come to terms with my illegitimacy and I'd much prefer that we talk quite freely.'

The older man visibly relaxed.

'That makes everything a lot simpler, Mr Keynes,' he said. 'I thought you might like to know that I am the only member of the firm who has been involved in this matter, and you may be assured that it will continue to be treated with the utmost confidentiality. Now, Mr Keynes, when I wrote to you last August, I advised you that there was a condition attached to this gift. In order to safeguard the good names of your benefactor and my client, the trustee, I have to ask for your assurance that you will never reveal the facts I now intend to make clear to you. Were you to do so, you could do great damage to the reputation of those whose wish it is to benefit you.'

Seeing the look of astonishment on Harry's face, he smiled.

'You will appreciate from what I've been saying that great faith is being put upon your word, but my client has assured me that we may quite safely rely upon it.'

'I'm afraid this is all beyond my comprehension,' Harry said. 'However, I have no wish to harm anyone who wishes me well and if you, sir, will assure me that there are no circumstances which could arise when I might be in

432

duty bound to reveal this information, I will happily give my word.'

'Then may I ask you to sign this declaration of intent?' The solicitor pushed a document across the desk. 'It is an undertaking not to divulge the facts contained in the letter I shall give you.'

Mystified and by now agog with curiosity, Harry read the document. Seeing that it contained no more than a promise of secrecy, he affixed his signature, which Mr Lytham then formally witnessed before crossing the room to a filing cabinet and withdrawing a sealed letter.

'I will leave you alone for a short while, Mr Keynes, so that you may read the contents undisturbed,' he said, handing it to Harry with an encouraging smile.

As the solicitor left the room, closing the door behind him, Harry broke open the seal. The writing was sprawled across the page, the lines sometimes slanting, the pressure of the pen nib often so faint that the letters were barely visible. The writer, he thought, was either very old or very ill. Then the opening words held his gaze: 'My dear son . . .' Harry caught his breath. What secret of his past was now about to be revealed? he wondered, his heart thudding. Barely able to contain his excitement, his eyes scanned the next sentence.

I, your mother, having been given two – at most three – weeks to live, have decided to make a full confession and to beg your forgiveness for any harm I may have done you . . .

There followed an account of the night of Harry's birth and the subsequent falsehoods which had been told to protect the writer from disgrace and possible banishment from her family home.

Thinking it a kindness to me, my sister told me shortly after your birth that you had died. Ignorant, therefore, of your existence, I married two years later but bore no children, although my husband, a widower, had three young children by his first marriage whom I love dearly but who have never occupied your place in my heart.

When I contracted tuberculosis, I confessed to my sister my feelings of guilt that had I kept you and taken care of you, you might yet have lived. She felt obliged to put my mind at rest and told me that you were alive. My joy was and still is unbounded, although I know there is nothing I can do to remedy the stigma of illegitimacy with which I inadvertently branded you. Now that you are a grown man, perhaps you will be less harsh in your judgement of me when I tell you that I loved your father, Gervaise Harvey, with all my heart and would have married him had we been permitted; also that we were both very young – I not yet seventeen and your father only two years older.

By the time you read this, I shall be in another world, but my sister, your aunt, has promised me she will arrange for you to receive the money I wish to leave to you. Neither my husband nor my step-children are in need of it and it is money left to me by my father and which, therefore, I feel free to dispose of as I please.

I know that money can never buy the things in life that really matter. Love, happiness, respect, peace of mind – these are things you must earn for yourself. However, it is my hope that it will ease your path and assist you to achieve your ambitions whatever they may be.

For the first and last time in my life, I sign myself

Your loving mother,
Dorothy Mary Copley

There was a small postscript requesting Harry to forgive his mother's sister, Cynthia, Lady Merstam, into whose hands she was entrusting Harry's legacy.

For a few moments Harry sat immobile as a multitude of thoughts whirled in his head. Now, at last, he knew who his mother had been, knew for certain that Gervaise Harvey was his father, knew how he had come to be placed in the care of the Pritchetts. Now he understood why the woman he had called Aunt Pamela had chosen to become involved, why she had always been unable to hide her dislike of him. Now too he knew that the tall, thin stranger on board ship was his aunt – his only living maternal relation. Not least, he understood the reason for the secrecy Mr Graham Lytham had demanded.

When a few minutes later the solicitor returned, he was carrying a sheaf of papers. He sat down behind his desk and pushed one of them across the table to Harry.

'This is an up-to-date statement of your deposit account at the bank,' he said. 'You will see that you are now quite a wealthy man, Mr Keynes.'

Harry glanced at the figures and gave a barely subdued gasp.

'I'd no idea the sum would be so large.' He paused to smile wryly at Mr Lytham. 'It may surprise you, sir, but at this moment, it's not so much my inherited wealth which gives me so much satisfaction as the fact that I now know who I really am. Although my guardian, Sir Philip Debrace, told me that I was Gervaise Harvey's son, neither he nor anyone else seemed to know who my mother might be. I wish I could have known her.'

The elderly man nodded.

'Lady Merstam anticipated your curiosity and asked me to inform you that she will be happy to receive you at any time convenient to yourself and answer any questions you may have about your mother. However, she was unsure of your sentiments towards her, bearing in mind the blame that must lie at her door for leading your mother to suppose for so many years that you were dead.'

Harry's eyes were thoughtful.

'In some ways it was a very wicked thing to do. On the other hand, my mother makes it quite clear in her letter that Lady Merstam had only her good in mind. At least it is now to Lady Merstam's credit that she has entrusted me with the truth.'

'Her ladyship has asked me to tell you that although she cannot openly acknowledge you as her nephew, it's her hope that you will allow her to do so in private.'

Harry drew a deep breath.

'I can't say I feel any kind of kinship, if that is the word, towards Lady Merstam. I wish her no harm but . . . perhaps I shall feel differently after a second meeting. When she approached our party on board, I thought her manner somewhat diffident and – as the Americans would say – overly curious. I suppose on reflection she was trying to make up her mind whether or not I could be trusted.'

The solicitor cleared his throat. The edge of bitterness in Harry's voice had not escaped him.

'Her ladyship was duty bound to ensure that you were sufficiently mature to manage the inheritance sensibly. Hearing that you had become engaged to be married, Lady Merstam supposed you might now have need of the money which, I am glad to say, has been accumulating while awaiting your collection. If you do not already have an accountant, I wonder if you'd like to make use of your late mother's firm? Their investment manager – a Mr Birch – has had care and control of the money that has been in trust for you.'

Harry smiled. 'I've never had sufficient funds to need professional assistance,' he said, 'so I'd be happy to make use of this gentleman's services.'

'Then I'll arrange a meeting for tomorrow, if that suits you, Mr Keynes,' the solicitor said. 'There'll be more papers for you to sign and a great deal of information Mr Birch will need from you: the name and address of your bank in Kentucky, that kind of thing. He will also want to know how you wish to dispose of your fortune – or, should I say, invest it. If you are not familiar with these matters, I can assure you that his advice will be sound. Unless you have any immediate need for capital, then the interest on so large a sum should be adequate for your current needs.'

Harry nodded.

'Since I'm very gainfully employed managing a stud farm in Kentucky, I'm not in any great need,' he said, 'although I may well equip myself with some new clothes while I'm in London! There is one matter, though, which I would like to mention. Would there be any legal objection to my giving some of this legacy away? I would like to help my foster family, in particular to buy a small property for one of my foster sisters and her husband.'

'My dear Mr Keynes, there are no conditions attaching to this gift other than that of secrecy,' Mr Lytham said gently. 'The money is yours to do with as you wish. You could, if you so chose, gamble the lot away or give it to charity,' he added, smiling at his little joke before saying, 'You have only to tell Mr Birch what you want to do and he will arrange it. I, of course, will be happy to see to any legal points relating to property you may wish to purchase.'

Harry stood up and held out his hand.

'I am most grateful to you, Mr Lytham. May I take it that I am now one of your clients? A highly satisfied one, I might say.'

The solicitor walked round the desk and shook Harry's hand.

'Speaking now not as your legal adviser but as a man almost old enough to be your grandfather, may I make a personal comment? It is simply that in my profession we spend more time than most sorting out difficulties, disagreements, disputes. It is quite rare that I can close a file knowing that all parties are entirely happy with the outcome of a situation. I don't think it would have been in the least unreasonable for you to have reacted to the news you have received with a certain amount of bitterness.' He paused briefly before elaborating. 'There is no doubt about the fact that you are the former Earl of Kinmuire's only son. Had you been born in wedlock you would have inherited the title and the estate, but both have been denied you.'

Harry shrugged his shoulders.

'It really doesn't worry me. I have no aspirations to belong to the nobility. As to the estate, the present earl, Mr Wendell Harvey, has very generously offered me the use of it during my lifetime. All I'm forgoing is a title, and if you had been raised as I was – the "son" of a very indigent gardener – you would consider, as I do, that fate had already bestowed enough benefits on me without adding a title.'

'I'm humbled by your remarks, Mr Keynes,' Mr Lytham said. 'It's a pity the world is not made up of more men of your philosophy. May I ask if it's your intention to remain in this country?'

'I haven't yet made up my mind about the future,' Harry replied. 'I shall be returning to America next month and had planned to stay there indefinitely. I suppose I could now afford to return to England and start up my own stud farm at Maythorpe, but that might not suit my fiancée. My future father-in-law is a widower and, unless he were to come to England with us, I imagine Cora-Beth wouldn't want to leave him.'

'I understand,' Mr Lytham said, shaking Harry's hand once again. 'It's been a great pleasure, Mr Keynes, a genuine one. I look forward to our next meeting. Meanwhile, my very best wishes for your future happiness.'

As Harry walked out into the September sunshine, his first thought was that he must go at once to the Maison de Verveine and tell Alice what had just happened – not, of course, revealing his mother's or Lady Merstam's identities. Alice was desperately worried about Martha, and now he would be able to put her mind at rest. He longed to see the look of relief in her eyes when he told her he had come into a vast sum of money, but realizing that she would almost certainly be very busy with clients, he decided to wait until the evening, when she was nearly always to be found at the flat in Charles Street.

On a sudden impulse, he hailed a passing taxi cab and instructed the driver to take him to the address Mr Lytham had written down for him before he left. He was going to see Lady Merstam.

Harry was shown into the drawing-room by an elderly parlourmaid – a room that reflected the age of its mistress, filled as it was with dark colours, Victorian ornaments, antimacassars, potted plants. Heavy lace curtains had been drawn to protect the furnishings and carpets from fading. His eyes were attracted to a large photograph in a heavily engraved silver frame. It was of a young girl with long, dark hair swept up in a thick cluster of curls above a delicate, heart-shaped face. Her dark eyes were gazing wistfully down at a spray of artificial flowers and a tentative smile lifted the corners of her mouth. Instinctively, Harry knew that this was his mother.

He jumped as the door opened and a voice behind him said, 'Yes, that's my sister, Dorothy. She would have been about the same age then as you are now.'

Harry nodded and sat down in the chair Lady Merstam indicated.

'I hope you will forgive me for calling on you un-announced,' he said. 'I have just been to see Mr Lytham and . . .'

'He telephoned me a short while ago to advise me of your meeting,' Lady Merstam interrupted gently. She leant forward and looked directly into Harry's eyes. 'Now that you know the truth, I hope you will forgive me. I can only say that I loved your mother more than anyone else in the world, that I was determined to protect her even if it meant harming you.'

'I understand your motives, Lady Merstam,' Harry said quietly. 'As it so happens, I came to no harm. You chose a wonderful foster family for me. It was only later, when . . . when Lady Kinmuire took charge of me, that I suffered. Even then, I suppose, I have much for which I should be grateful to her; she educated me, taught me how to behave, how to speak properly. She was very strict, but her methods worked. When Sir Philip sent me to Grafton Abbey, I was able more or less to pass muster.'

Lady Merstam had been listening intently. She sat back now, a look of relief on her face.

'You can't know how many times I reproached myself for allowing that dreadful man, Simcox, to persuade me to reveal your whereabouts. At the time, I had no reason to doubt his integrity and he seemed so charming. When he told me Gervaise wished to benefit you, it eased my conscience to know that some sort of recompense could be made for my denying you access to your own mother. I thought it was safe to entrust Lady Kinmuire and her brother with the secret of your whereabouts since it was not in her interest to reveal you were her husband's child.'

Harry nodded. Somewhat to his surprise, he found himself feeling sorry for this woman, whose distress was evident despite her regal bearing.

'You mustn't reproach yourself,' he said. 'Obviously my father also trusted my former guardians or he wouldn't have suggested they take charge of me. As I drove here, I thought that perhaps we could now put the past behind us. I bear no ill will to anyone, least of all to my poor mother.'

His eyes turned once more to the photograph.

'Please tell me about her,' he said simply. 'I want to know everything. I can only ever know her through you.'

Tears filled Lady Merstam's eyes.

'My dear boy,' she said huskily, 'nothing in this world could give me greater pleasure than to talk about my darling Dorothy. Have you time now at your disposal?'

'All the time in the world,' Harry said, pushing to the back of his mind the fact that he had told Cora-Beth he would certainly be back at the Savoy for lunch. She had both Aubrey and her father to keep her company, he told himself, and if she knew how momentous this day was proving to be for him, she would surely understand.

CHAPTER TWENTY-SIX

1926

Neither Félix nor time had edged Harry from the centre of her heart, Alice thought as she surveyed his glowing face while he regaled her with his astonishing news. They were once more travelling in the familiar train to Burgess Hill, on their way to see Martha, and for a meeting with the owner of the cottage and post office-cum-sweet shop which Harry now hoped to buy.

'It's got a nice little garden at the back where Dad can potter to his heart's content,' she said. 'Mr Peabody's daughter has been running it since he died and Jenny's husband has been managing the post office side of it. The daughter is very anxious to get back to her family in Cornwall and I'm sure she'll be only too pleased to hand over the shop once she knows the money is safe.'

'The solicitor will confirm that,' Harry told her eagerly, 'although he said it could be several weeks before the transfer of deeds can be completed. It's up to Mr Peabody's daughter whether she's prepared to let Jenny and her husband move into the cottage beforehand. The money couldn't have come at a better time, could it, Alice? I'm still finding it hard to believe I'm a rich man.'

'You've not changed your mind about going back to America? I suppose you could now afford to have your stud farm at Maythorpe House if you wanted it.'

Harry shook his head.

'Cora-Beth wouldn't want to leave her father and anyway, I've mixed feelings about Maythorpe. It's strange, really. At times I think I hate the place and at others, I do have a longing to live there. Maybe it's just in my mind that it's my real home, probably because of all those stories Mrs Appleby used to tell me about the days when my father lived there. I was talking last night to Mr Harvey about the place and he agrees it ought not to be left empty. Maybe he'll decide to let it during the hunting season, although he doesn't need the money.'

He leant forward eagerly.

'I can't wait for you to meet Cora-Beth. I know you two will like each other. She's such a splendid girl.'

Alice turned quickly away from that bright, handsome face and stared out of the window. 'Splendid' seemed a strange adjective to use about the girl you were going to marry. Was Harry really in love with her? Or was it a matter of propinquity – as it had been for her when she had drifted into her relationship with Félix?

Somehow it had become an accepted pattern that whenever Félix came to London, Jules would discreetly remove himself to a hotel for the ensuing one or two nights, and Félix would take her out to dinner before returning to the flat to make love to her. Part of her dreaded his arrival, but he was so charming, attentive and affectionate that he always managed to overcome her qualms. It worried her whenever she allowed herself to remember those nights, for despite her conviction that what she allowed to take place was wrong, she nevertheless ended by wanting the pleasure he gave her.

Sitting now so close to Harry that she could have leant over and touched him, she understood why it was wrong. It was never Félix's arms, lips, caresses she wanted – they were no more than a substitute for Harry's. Her mind, heart and body belonged to him and always would. It was so much more difficult to disregard her emotions now that Félix had woken her body to awareness of the physical aspects of her nature. She could no longer look at Harry and see the child he'd once been. A quick glance at his broad, manly shoulders, his long legs, his strong, capable hands, was enough to arouse a trembling, aching need deep down inside her. It was impossible to ignore his sheer masculinity and no amount of will-power was sufficient to quell that instant response over which she had no control. He was her first and last love. And what of Harry's first love – Madeleine Debrace? He'd told her the shocking news about her husband's death and that she would be coming home in a month or two. He had sounded almost relieved that he would be back in Kentucky by then. Was he regretting that he had tied himself to the American girl?

As if in part following Alice's train of thought, Harry said, 'It's proving a godsend having Aubrey around to keep poor Cora-Beth company. I'd no idea how caught up I'd be. He's taking her to the St Leger today at Doncaster. Miss Hanworth – the woman we met on board our ship – is joining them.' He gave a sudden grin which twisted Alice's heart, for it made him look a boy again. 'Cora-Beth says her father hasn't been so taken with a female for almost as long as she can remember. I suppose it's because they have horses in common. She can hardly be called attractive!'

'And the other woman?' Alice questioned. 'The one you said you didn't like so much?'

Harry looked quickly away. He hated having to lie to Alice, of all people in the world, but he had given his word.

'Lady Merstam. She's not so bad when you get to know her. In fact, I had lunch with her a few days ago and she's really quite interesting. Actually, I think she's rather lonely – she has no children and her husband's dead.'

Perhaps fortunately, the subject of Lady Merstam was brought to an abrupt end as the train drew into Burgess Hill station. Within half an hour, Harry was seated at Martha's bedside. Only her eyes were recognizable in the thin, pain-wracked face. Her mind, however, remained as sharp as it had ever been.

'Got a button loose on your sleeve,' she said. 'Get Alice to sew it on for you. Can't have a fine young gentleman like you walking around like you ain't got no one to look after you.'

Somehow, Harry hid his dismay at her appearance and managed a smile. 'I didn't think you'd notice,' he said. 'I should have known better, shouldn't I?'

'Untidiest lad of the lot, you was,' Martha said. 'Wore out your breeches soon as ever Alice'd patched them.' She sighed. 'Goodness knows how we'd have managed in those days without the hand-me-downs from the big house. Couldn't have afforded to keep you all decent, not the rate you was growing.'

'They must have been hard times for you,' Harry said gently. 'As kids, I don't think any of us appreciated how hard you and Dad worked. We had a happy childhood.'

Martha's face softened.

'Funny you should say that. Will and me was asking ourselves only the other day if'n you didn't care to remember those days, being as how you're one of the gentry now.'

'Of course I do. I honestly think they were the happiest days of my life.'

Martha frowned.

'But you're happy now, aren't you? Alice said as how you was going to be married to a real nice American girl. One time Will and me thought as how you might be going to marry Miss Madeleine. Reckon you was sweet on her right enough, even when you was only a little lad.'

'Perhaps. But let's not talk about me. I've something to tell you. It seems I've come into money – a great deal of money. I'm going to be able to buy the shop and the cottage for Jenny.'

The look in Martha's eyes left him in no doubt as to her joy.

'You really mean that, Harry? Now I knows that, I shall die happy. Doctor won't tell me to my face but I've not much longer on this earth.' Her voice took on a note of urgency. 'It's Will I worry about, not Jenny. She's happy enough with her two little 'uns and her Jack, and Sam's happy enough with Nurse Wilks. No, it's Will. I dursn't tell him the truth like I'm telling you. He can't face up to it. If'n Jenny has a bigger place, she can look after him, and the grandchildren will be a comfort to him. He dotes on them. You sure you can afford it, Harry? You getting married and . . .'

'I won't even notice it's gone,' Harry broke in. 'It's money left to me by someone in my real family – and seeing they couldn't look after me when I was born and you and Dad did, it's only right you should have some of it.'

But she wouldn't be here to enjoy it, he said sadly to Alice as they took the train back to London that evening. He had been deeply shocked by the way Will as well as Martha Pritchett had aged. Despite what Martha had said to him about keeping her husband in ignorance of her approaching death, Harry wondered if somehow he knew. There was so little he could do for either of them, except to ensure that the transfer of the sweet-shop to Jenny and her husband took place without delay or mishap.

'You and me and Jenny went to school together,' Mr Peabody's daughter had said to Harry, 'so it's almost in the family like. You can send the money on as soon as you got it and that'll be soon enough for me. Mum and Dad always hoped Jenny and Jack might take over one day, ever since your Jenny used to help Mum out when she had time off. I'll move my things next weekend and Jenny can move in soon as she wants.'

One of Jenny's children was a little girl with long blonde hair and blue eyes, who, wearing a pretty white-frilled party dress in Harry's honour, reminded him painfully of the little Madeleine in those early days at The Grange. Would he ever truly forget her? he asked himself. Could one forget one's first love? It was more than probable she had forgotten *his* existence! As Aubrey had said, it was almost certain that she would marry again when she'd recovered from the shock of Dunbar's death. It was hard to think of her as a grief-stricken widow dressed for once all in black. He presumed she would wear mourning, although she had always hated dark colours.

Alice, on the other hand, was looking especially lovely in a beautifully tailored black coat trimmed with soft grey astrakhan. The fur collar framed her pale face, which for the moment was in profile as she stared out of the window. The sombre colour of her outfit was relieved by a large scarlet and white-spotted ladybird brooch set in gold, which he had barely noticed on the journey down.

'Where did you find that brooch, Alice?' he asked. 'It's most unusual.'

Alice turned to face him, her cheeks now flushed a deep pink.

'Félix – Monsieur Verveine – found it in Milan. He's thinking of including costume jewellery in our *salons*,' she added hurriedly. 'I think it's a splendid idea. Our wealthy clients don't want to be bothered to go rushing round looking for something appropriate. Of course, they have their real jewellery for evenings.'

Obviously Harry had no idea of the worth of the brooch, Alice decided, or else he would have questioned why she had accepted such a gift from Félix. It had been impossible to refuse it, or gifts like it – tokens of his love, he called them – without hurting his feelings.

'I'd like to buy you a piece of real jewellery,' Harry was saying eagerly. 'Pearls, perhaps. What do you think, Alice? Remember that pearl ring I got at the church Christmas party? You said it was your favourite stone. Or did you just say that to please me? I must have been about six years old.'

'I don't remember,' Alice lied quickly. She still had that ring tucked away in her box of mementoes. There were all Harry's letters to her too, from that first, tear-blotched, untidy scrawl from Maythorpe House to the most recent, telling her of his engagement to Cora-Beth. With tears gathering in her eyes, she sought for something to say that might prevent Harry's poignant reminders of the days when he had loved her more than anyone else in the world.

'Félix is incredibly generous to me,' she heard herself saying in a small, brittle voice. 'I have to be careful when I am out with him not to admire something or he'll go straight into the shop and buy it.'

Sensing the change in her, Harry frowned.

'You don't sound awfully happy about having a rich admirer,' he said in what he hoped was a teasing tone of voice. 'I haven't had a chance to tell you yet that Aubrey

446

said he was sure his uncle was going to ask you to marry him. He wasn't joking either, although I told him not to be such a silly ass. As if you'd marry an old man like that.'

'Félix isn't all that much older than I am,' Alice said sharply, but seeing the look on Harry's face, she added, 'although you're quite right. I wouldn't marry him, for the simple reason I don't love him.'

Harry sighed.

'So you're still faithful to that unknown man you once told me about,' he said. 'It's such a waste of you, Alice. You're so beautiful, and nice. You ought to find a really good husband to take care of you.'

'I'm quite capable of taking care of myself, Harry, as you should well know. It's men who need wives to look after them, not women who need husbands, except, of course, to support them financially. I can support myself. You, on the other hand, need a wife to sew on your buttons.'

Harry laughed.

'Trust Mum to notice mine was loose. Alice, you will promise to let me know if . . . when the worst happens. I think she'd want me to be there . . . at the end. Do you think it will be before I go back to America?'

Alice nodded.

'Jenny said the doctor had spoken about it being a matter of weeks. I'll telephone you if I hear anything, but won't you be in France?'

'Only for a week, straight after the Newmarket races, as Mr Harvey wants to take in the big French classic – the Arc de Triomphe – at Longchamp. Then we're sight-seeing. I do wish you could come with us, Alice. Are you sure you're too busy? I know Mr Harvey would be delighted to have you along. He's terribly anxious to meet you and you'd really like him.'

'I couldn't possibly get away,' Alice said quickly. 'We're always up to our eyes in the weeks before Christmas. Anyway, your fiancée is hardly likely to want me tagging along. I'd be a right gooseberry!'

'Cora-Beth wouldn't mind. She isn't like that, Alice,

and she wants to be your friend. I'm beginning to think you're trying to avoid meeting her.'

Although Harry was only in part teasing, Alice realized that he half believed what he was saying. She must be more careful, she thought. Perhaps she should pull herself together and agree to take on the selection of Cora-Beth's trousseau. To hand over the task to Jules could so easily be misconstrued . . . no, not misconstrued, but taken at its face value. The truth was she did not want even to have to meet Harry's future wife, let alone choose the clothes she was going to be wearing to please and attract him.

'You're imagining things, Harry,' she said. 'Miss Harvey has an appointment at the *salon* tomorrow morning, so we'll have every chance to get to know one another.'

Harry smiled.

'I think Cora-Beth is quite nervous about meeting you. I told her you'd kick up an awful fuss if you didn't think she'd make me a good wife.' He laughed at Alice's shocked expression. 'Well, you know you would, Alice. Remember how you tried to put me off Madeleine?'

'That was different,' Alice said quickly. 'Anyway, you know perfectly well it's none of my business whom you choose to marry.' Her voice softened. 'I just want you to be happy, that's all. You've no regrets, have you, Harry? You aren't wishing you hadn't got yourself tied up to Cora-Beth . . . now that Madeleine's free?'

Harry looked quickly away from Alice's searching gaze. She had posed a question he neither wished nor was able to answer. He had pushed the thought to the back of his mind after learning of Dunbar's death, telling himself that it was unseemly to a degree to be thinking of Madeleine in such a way when her husband was barely in his grave. Moreover, it was better not to speculate on an alternative future when he had no option but to honour his betrothal to Cora-Beth.

Aware that Alice was waiting for an answer, he forced himself to smile at her.

'Of course I've no regrets! Just wait till you meet Cora-

Beth, Alice, and you'll understand then why I fell in love with her.'

Realizing that Harry did not intend to discuss Madeleine and that she had no right to probe, Alice allowed the subject to drop.

'If your fiancée is only half as nice a person as you say, Harry, I'm sure I'll like her,' she said.

However, the meeting next day proved to be far more difficult for Alice than she had anticipated. The difficulty lay in the fact that, as Harry had forecast, she could not but like Cora-Beth. Not only was she open and friendly but she had an unexpected, self-effacing charm.

'I'm just not naturally chic,' she said soon after Harry had introduced them and left them together. 'I don't bother much about clothes at home, but I do so want Harry to be proud of me. He's so handsome, he deserves a really elegant wife. Don't you agree?'

'It's just a question of choosing the right clothes for your personality,' Alice said reassuringly. She finished taking Cora-Beth's measurements and led her into her own private office. 'Why don't we look through these fashion drawings?' she suggested. 'You pick out anything you like and I'll tell you if I think it will suit you.'

After perusing them for a few moments, Cora-Beth looked up at Alice with a serious expression in her eyes.

'Alice . . . you don't mind my calling you that, do you?' she said. 'May I ask you something rather personal . . . personal to me, that is?'

As Alice nodded, her face impassive, the younger girl continued, 'You've known Harry all his life and he respects your opinion. Do you think I'll be able to make him happy? Sometimes I wonder . . . I know this must sound silly . . . but I guess I do wonder sometimes if he really loves me.'

Alice was shaken by the remark. After a brief hesitation, she said quietly, 'Harry wouldn't have asked you to marry him if he didn't love you.'

'Yes, but how deeply? You must have known Aubrey's sister; that Harry was crazy about her for years and years.

It could never have occurred to him that she . . . that she might be widowed and . . . well, available again. We're supposed to be getting married next June. Do you think I ought to postpone it?'

Alice frowned.

'How can you know if Madeleine would even consider marrying Harry now that she's free? She turned him down before.'

Cora-Beth nodded.

'Yes, I know. Harry told me, but he really wasn't in a position to support her, was he? Now . . . now that he's come into a lot of money . . .'

For several minutes, Alice didn't speak. Then she said firmly, 'I can only give you my opinion and it isn't even a fair one since I've not seen Madeleine for years, but I used to think she was the most egotistical person I'd ever known. But then, she may well have changed.'

Detecting a dismissive tone to Alice's voice, Cora-Beth said apologetically, 'I suppose I shouldn't be asking for your advice like this, but who else can I confide in? Harry said you've always been like a mother to him and you're the one person in the world whose opinion he trusts.'

Despite her determination not to give any indication of her true feelings, there was a noticeable edge of bitterness in Alice's voice as she said, 'Hardly "a mother" – I'm only four years older than Harry. An elder sister, perhaps!'

Cora-Beth hastened to rectify what she felt had been a tactless remark.

'I hope you didn't think I meant to infer that you looked the part – far from it! It's just that whenever Harry has spoken of you, he gave me quite the wrong impression of a "motherly" kind of person. That's typical of a man, isn't it? They see you in the rôle they want you to occupy.'

Alice gave a wry smile.

'I don't think there'll ever come a time when Harry could see me as other men do. I'll be his devoted "sister" till the day we die.'

This time, there was no mistaking the note of bitterness, and because Cora-Beth herself was in a highly emotional state, she was more sensitive to Alice's feelings than she might otherwise have been. Alice, she thought, with a sudden flash of insight, did not love Harry as a mother or a sister – she loved him as a woman, as she herself loved him!

She was so certain of it that she only just refrained from gasping. If it were true, then Alice must be very unhappy.

Impulsively, she said, 'I so much want us to be friends. We may not see much of each other in the future, me in Kentucky and you over here, but we do have this in common – we both want Harry's happiness. And I want you to know that I'll do anything, everything, in my power to ensure it.'

Unaware that she had betrayed herself, but unwilling to continue the conversation lest she should do so, Alice said in her professional voice, 'Then we must make a start by choosing some really beautiful clothes for your trousseau.' She had no wish to be moved by sympathy or affection for this girl who, despite everything, she found herself liking. Moreover, Cora-Beth was raising questions about Madeleine which Alice herself found deeply disturbing.

On their journeys to and from Calking, Harry had clearly avoided any prolonged discussion about Madeleine's widowhood. It was so unlike him not to tell her his private fears and expectations that it had left her with a nagging sense of unease.

'You *are* going to come to dinner with us soon, aren't you, Alice?' Cora-Beth was saying. 'Harry said he'd passed on Poppa's invitation but that you were too busy at the moment to go out in the evenings.'

'My employer is arriving from Milan tomorrow,' Alice excused herself. 'I always have to catch up on the paperwork before he gets here, but thank you for asking me.' She softened the refusal with a smile, before adding, 'Don't you think we ought to get down to work? We haven't made one decision yet. What about this pyjama suit? Trousers are the new thing for wearing at home in the evening. The spring colours – pinks, greens, yellows – are going to be really fashionable next year. Monsieur Verveine is using them for his summer collection.'

Cora-Beth nodded.

'His clothes sure are stunning, aren't they? Is he nice to work for, Alice? Aubrey said he's typically French but quite amusing.'

'He wouldn't be very amused if he knew I was wasting time gossiping about him with one of our clients,' Alice said, lightening the reproach with a smile. 'Besides, I'm sure you must have other appointments to keep. Harry said you were short of time too.'

'That's true. Poppa wants me to get really well acquainted with your country while we're over here. Harry was going to drive Poppa and me up to Oxford after lunch tomorrow to see the colleges, but he can't come now because he has to see his new accountant, so Aubrey's going to take us. The day after we're going up to Leicestershire to see Poppa's house and then it's New-market. Goodness knows when I'll be able to manage any fittings as we're off to France for a week directly after Newmarket. So which of these shall I choose, Alice? You decide.' Without thinking, she added with a laugh, 'I know, pretend it's *your* trousseau and just make everything up in my size.'

Too late, she saw the colour rise suddenly to Alice's cheeks and realized that her remark had been not only tactless but, if her suspicions were correct, very cruel. She added hastily, 'Anything you like will be fine with me, especially if I end up looking even half as elegant as you do.'

Unnerved by her *faux pas*, Cora-Beth pushed aside the drawings and made her excuses to leave. As soon as she reached the Savoy, she went immediately to join Harry, who was sitting in the foyer reading a newspaper. Finding him alone without the company of her father or Aubrey, she blurted out her gaffe.

Harry stared at her uncomprehendingly.

'I'm sorry, darling, but I simply don't understand what

you're talking about,' he said truthfully. 'What better suggestion than that Alice should put herself in your shoes and make the decisions for you?'

Cora-Beth sighed with exasperation.

'Don't you understand, Harry? That's where Alice would like to be – in my shoes! She's in love with you – I'm absolutely sure of it. That's why it was such a horrible thing to say to her. Really, I feel so rotten about it.'

Harry patted her arm soothingly.

'Come on now, darling, you'd better let me order you a stiff drink so you can down it and come to your senses,' he said fervently. 'I never heard anything so absurd in all my life. Alice is my sister.'

'No, she's not – and you know she's not!' Cora-Beth burst out. 'Don't you see, Harry, it explains everything. Why she hasn't had any other suitors, why she has never married, why she won't tell you the name of the secret lover who doesn't love her. You're the one she loves. I just know it.'

Harry remained calmly unconvinced.

'You really are talking off the top of your head,' he said. 'Of course Alice *loves* me – I love her – but not the way you're implying. There's never been anything like that between us – never! Look, Cora-Beth, it's Alice you're talking about. I've known her all my life and I can assure you, there's nothing romantic about our relationship – nor ever has been.'

He was so adamant that for a moment Cora-Beth began to wonder if indeed she had sensed something that did not exist. Then, remembering the change in the timbre of Alice's voice whenever Harry's name had been mentioned, her flushed cheeks, that note of bitterness, she knew she was right, and she knew too that Harry would not have doubted it if he had seen the look in Alice's eyes when she, Cora-Beth, had suggested she should pretend she was choosing clothes for her own honeymoon with Harry.

By now her first impulsive wish to share this distressing knowledge with Harry was beginning to wane. What purpose was there in drawing his attention to something

Alice herself had clearly tried – and succeeded in – hiding from him all these years?

'Perhaps you're right, honey,' she said. 'Perhaps I've just got love on the brain because I'm in love myself.' She leant forward and rested her hand lightly on his. 'I do wish you could come to Hampton Court with us this afternoon,' she said wistfully. 'Do you *have* to see the lawyer? I know you said it was urgent, but . . .'

'Darling, I did mean it was urgent. Jenny said it could be only a matter of weeks before the end comes for my foster mother. Even if the contracts are drawn up this afternoon, it's still doubtful they can be exchanged before Jenny moves in. She wants to get the place straight before . . . beforehand, so that my foster father won't have to stay on in the cottage on his own. He and Mum have been married nearly thirty years and Alice is afraid he'll go to pieces when the time comes. They're absolutely devoted.'

'I know, I'm sorry,' Cora-Beth said quickly. 'I was being selfish. Anyway, Aubrey says he knows Hampton Court far better than you do,' she added, gently teasing. 'He warned me you'd only get me lost in the maze and that you'd got him lost once when you went there as schoolboys. There he is now, coming through the door.'

Aubrey's fair hair was unmistakable as he removed his trilby and rain-spattered mackintosh and handed them to the cloakroom attendant.

'Hope I'm not late,' he said as he came to join them.

'Right on time, old boy,' Harry said laughing, 'but that doesn't stop you being a rotten sneak. Call yourself my best friend and then tell my best girl I'm an idiot.'

'I don't know what you're talking about, but Cora-Beth would have discovered that soon enough for herself, if she hasn't done so already,' Aubrey countered.

'Now stop it, you two,' Cora-Beth chided them with a laugh. 'I had quite enough of your squabbles in Kentucky. This is my vacation, remember? I intend it to be a happy and *peaceful* one!'

'And so it will be if I have anything to do with it,' Aubrey rejoined, but Harry's attention was elsewhere.

'Look!' he said, nodding towards the hotel entrance. 'There's your father, Cora-Beth, and if I'm not much mistaken, that's Miss Jennifer Hanworth he's got on his arm. I really do believe he's smitten.'

Cora-Beth smiled as she regarded Harry's animated face. She was not the only one, she reflected, who had got love on the brain.

CHAPTER TWENTY-SEVEN

1926

Despite the fact that Maryburgh came only third in the Champion Stakes, Wendell's party of six travelled back to London in the hired Daimler in a festive mood. Jennifer Hanworth had backed it each way and won the princely sum of fifty pounds. She was insisting that she be allowed to buy champagne when they reached the Savoy. Wendell was adamant that she was his guest and that she should spend the money on herself – on a new Verveine dress perhaps!

'That'll put paid to the argument that you can't come to the theatre with me because you've nothing fashionable to wear,' he said jovially.

Cora-Beth winked at Harry and snuggled closer to him, her hand searching for his beneath the fur travelling-rug.

'Love you,' she whispered. 'It's been a perfect few days, hasn't it?'

In one of their brief moments alone during the race meeting, she had told him that she was going to come to his hotel room as soon as they returned to London. It had been weeks, if not months, since he had last made love to her and she simply didn't care if anyone saw her in the passage, she had said persuasively. It was not as if Poppa would notice what they did, she had added. He was much too preoccupied with his new popsie – the redoubtable Miss Hanworth!

The two elderly people really did seem to be getting along remarkably well, Harry reflected. Miss Hanworth was not above telling a few *risqué* stories when she had had a cocktail or two, and they had all been fascinated by the tales of her childhood with her eccentric father in Ireland. Suppose the friendship were to develop, he thought now. Suppose Wendell were to decide that the jolly English lady would make the ideal companion for his old age and ask her to marry him, would Cora-Beth agree to come to England to live? Their afternoon visit to Maythorpe had inspired him with a longing to come home and set up his stud farm there. As Miss Hanworth had eulogized, the stables were magnificent and would be perfect for the enterprise with a few additions and some modernization. As for the house, it was unchanged since the day Harry had taken Madeleine to see it. The memory of that hour spent with such unforgettable passion in his old bedroom had been sufficiently vivid and poignant to force him to leave the room as quickly as he could.

Wendell's interest in the house had been more concerned with its architecture than its family connections.

'Fact of the matter is, I never thought the day would come when I'd inherit the place so I've never felt closely involved. It'll be yours one day, Peachcake, so you and Harry are the ones to decide its future.'

'Well, I think it's a lovely house and I wouldn't mind a bit living here with Harry,' Cora-Beth had said cheerfully. 'I'd want to modernize it, of course, but that would be fun. Maybe we could come over from the States one season. You could come and stay with us, Aubrey.'

'I'd like that very much,' Aubrey had answered, although he doubted if he would. Sitting silently in the car, very much aware of Cora-Beth's proximity to Harry in the back seat, he knew that the time had come for him to ease out of this friendship. The truth was, he was becoming much too fond of Cora-Beth and, as a consequence, painfully jealous of Harry. There were even times when he found himself silently criticizing him for not showing sufficient appreciation of the magnificent girl he'd chosen to marry. He seemed to take her very much for granted, and although he was never anything but kind and thoughtful towards her, his manner lacked the tenderness Aubrey sensed Cora-Beth might have liked.

Perhaps her out-going, cheerful, somewhat boyish manner did not invite tenderness, yet he knew there was a more vulnerable, feminine side to Cora-Beth's nature than Harry was aware of. He, Aubrey, had come to see a different side of her while he had been squiring her round the sights in Harry's absence. She was quieter, more relaxed, when she was alone with him, and he suspected that a great deal of the 'jolly camaraderie' she normally exuded in Harry's presence was assumed in order to amuse and entertain him.

Whether or not he had only imagined this, Aubrey thought, it was just as well that he was not accompanying them to France. He had no wish to play gooseberry, and in any event he had already accepted far too much hospitality from Wendell Harvey. It was time he returned to his own circle of friends and picked up the threads of his social life. If he didn't make the effort soon, he was going to find time hanging very heavily on his hands once Harry and the Harveys returned to Kentucky.

Meanwhile, he had been persuaded by Wendell to join them once more for dinner at the hotel, along with Miss Hanworth.

The anticipated celebration of Maryburgh's near victory and Miss Hanworth's winnings were not, after all, to take place. They were greeted on their arrival by the hall porter with a note sent by hand for Harry. It was from Alice to say that Martha was dying and that she had left for Calking that morning.

'I'll go straight down there,' Harry said at once. 'I just hope I won't be too late.'

Cora-Beth looked at him dejectedly.

'I suppose you really do have to go,' she said. 'Alice will need your support, but Harry, what about tomorrow? We're supposed to be catching the boat train at midday. You . . . you will be back, won't you?'

Harry turned away from her anxious gaze and looked at Wendell.

'I'm dreadfully sorry, sir,' he said. 'I hope you understand. Martha Pritchett was my mother to all intents

458

and purposes for the first thirteen years of my life. Naturally, I'll want to attend her funeral and . . .'

'My dear boy, you've no need to explain matters. Of course, you must be there. Think no more about it. I'll ask Reception to see what can be done about cancelling your reservations – unless, of course, you'd care to come along in Harry's place, Aubrey? What d'you say, young man? Pity to waste the tickets.'

'Could you go, Aubrey?' Harry asked. 'I'd feel a lot easier if I wasn't responsible for messing up the arrangements.'

'I don't see why you all seem to think I need an escort,' Cora-Beth broke in unexpectedly. She was far more disappointed than she intended anyone, least of all Harry, to know. 'I'll be fine with Poppa. It really isn't fair to make poor Aubrey squire me around when he's probably got a hundred and one more interesting things to do.'

'I've absolutely nothing better to do,' Aubrey interposed. 'I've always loved France and, as I can speak a bit of the lingo, maybe I can be of some help.'

'That's settled then,' Wendell said firmly. 'Now off you go, Harry, and give my condolences to your foster family. We'll see you next week when we get back.'

'I'm sorry, darling, I really am,' Harry said as he bent to kiss Cora-Beth goodbye. 'I know you'll have a good time, and Aubrey will take care of you.'

Cora-Beth forced a smile to her lips.

'We'll be fine,' she said lightly. 'Please tell Alice how sad I am for her . . . for all of you.'

It was only when Harry's back was turned as he walked away from her that Aubrey saw the tears glistening on her lashes. She brushed them away quickly and said in a bright, brittle tone, 'Come on, Poppa, where's this champagne you promised us? I'm positively dying of thirst. Aren't you, Aubrey? I forgot to tell you, Miss Hanworth, how pleased I was to hear from Poppa that you're coming out to visit us next May for the Kentucky Derby.'

Only Aubrey realized that she was determined no one

should see how bitterly disappointed she was to be going to France without Harry. Somehow, he told himself, he would have to try to make it up to her. He could take her to one or two places in Montmartre and on the Left Bank that Harry did not know existed. He'd show her a side of Paris the ordinary tourist didn't see and somehow make the week special for her in the only way he could.

Cora-Beth was the last person on Harry's mind as he and Alice tried to help the family bear up to the fact of Martha's death. To his acute distress, Will seemed to be in a state of shock and remained so throughout the funeral two days later, as if his mind was not present. Arthur, Harry and Ted, proudly wearing his Merchant Navy uniform, were three of the pallbearers. Sam, beanpole tall with several inches of wrist showing above the sleeves of his jacket as he struggled determinedly with his share of the weight, was the fourth. Practically the entire population of Calking had turned out to pay their last respects to Martha and, Harry and Alice were touched to see, Sir Philip and Lady Debrace were also present.

'A very sad day, Harry,' Eloise Debrace said as they left the graveyard and walked slowly back to their waiting car. 'Martha Pritchett was a good woman and she'll be greatly missed. Alice tells me the family have made arrangements for Will to go and live with Jenny and her husband.'

'Best thing in the circumstances,' Sir Philip said. 'Sorry we had to meet up on such a sorrowful occasion, my boy. Aubrey tells me you've been tied up this past week with solicitors and the like. Perhaps you can find time to come and lunch with us when things are sorted out down here?'

'I'd like that very much, sir,' Harry replied. 'I've a great deal to tell you. I expect it will be a day or two before I go back to London. If I could come and see you on Thursday or Friday?'

'Thursday would suit us very well, Harry,' Eloise said warmly. She turned to Alice, who had walked over to join them. 'We'd love you to come too, Alice,' she added. 'Would you be able to get away from your work?'

'I'm so sorry, Lady Debrace, but we really are very busy at the *salon*,' Alice said evasively, 'and now, after taking these few days off, I'll have a backlog waiting for me. But thank you for the invitation.'

'My brother-in-law must bring you to dinner one night when the *salon* is closed,' Eloise said unexpectedly. 'Whenever he calls to see us, he does little but talk about the success you've made of the London *salon*. He thinks so highly of you, Alice, and he is no mild taskmaster.'

'Come along, my dear, we mustn't keep Alice from her duties,' Sir Philip broke in. They did not feel their presence at the reception for the mourners was required and were driving back to London. As they left Calking behind them Eloise closed the sliding-window, so that the chauffeur would not overhear their conversation, and said to her husband, 'Did you notice Alice's expression when I suggested Félix bring her to dinner one night? I am more than ever convinced that I'm right and there is something between those two. Félix talks of Alice in such glowing terms, I really think he's in love with her.'

Sir Philip grunted.

'You women are all the same – forever match-making. And talking of matches, I trust you don't imagine Verveine intends to marry the girl. I'm very fond of Alice, as you know, and I think she's to be congratulated for what she has made of herself, but the fact is, she doesn't come from the same background as your brother-in-law.'

Eloise looked at her husband in surprise.

'I have never known you to be snobbish before, Philip,' she said. 'I think it would be a very good match for both of them. They have plenty of interests in common and as for Alice . . . nowadays, if you didn't know her background as we do, you'd never guess that she'd not been born into our class.'

'I grant you that, but can you imagine a wedding with the Pritchett family on Alice's side of the church? Will Pritchett giving her away?'

Eloise laughed.

'Really, Philip, you have no imagination. They could be

married quietly in France. After all, it's only nine months since poor dear Rosamund died, so a big wedding would not be appropriate. Frankly, if Félix did want to marry the girl, I'd be far more concerned about the age difference. Alice should be marrying some nice young man like Harry.'

Sir Philip regarded his wife quizzically.

'Or what about Aubrey? Perhaps your liberal thinking regarding our English class structure would require a little adjustment were your son to bring home a girl of Alice's background.'

Eloise frowned.

'That's not fair, Philip. The Pritchetts were our employees, so of course it would be awkward. Having said that, it would almost be a relief if Aubrey did fall in love. I'm beginning to wonder if he will ever settle down.'

Sir Philip frowned.

'The boy's only twenty-four, for heaven's sake. If he was ten years older, you might have cause to worry, my dear.'

'I know, but he doesn't seem interested in any of the girls in his circle, although their mothers tell me *they* are all in love with *him*! He's invited everywhere . . . which reminds me, Philip, we really must do something about the Harveys. They've given Aubrey so much hospitality, and now this week in France . . .'

'Whatever you say, my dear,' Sir Philip said affably. 'If I were you, I'd stop worrying about your precious son and give some thought to what is to be done about poor little Maddy. I thought of her today at the funeral. I really do think one of us ought to be out there with her.'

Eloise shook her head.

'She made it quite clear that she didn't need us, Philip. I'm sure she has a great many friends who will be supporting her, and I know the colonel and his wife will take care of her on the journey home next month. I thought I might take her down to Brighton for a while and, after Christmas, maybe to Egypt or somewhere like that, to help distract her.'

'I'm afraid I'll be too busy to join you, but you could take Aubrey along to look after you. I'll make some enquiries from Thomas Cook about cruises. It would do you both good.'

Eloise sighed. Although she would not have dreamed of saying so to her husband, who had never in his life been able to see a fault in his only daughter, she herself was not looking forward to these next months. Madeleine could be quite 'difficult' when she was bored, and the restrictions that mourning would put upon her would mean that she couldn't attend the parties and functions she so loved. Her nature was a restless one. Having few resources of her own to fall back on, she demanded entertainment. Madeleine had never been one for reading and she had no hobbies such as painting, studying a musical instrument or even helping on charity committees – all things which occupied Eloise's time.

It was a great pity Madeleine and Pogo had not had a child, she reflected as the car reached the outskirts of London. Her daughter's childlessness was a state of affairs which Eloise suspected was of Madeleine's choice. Even before her marriage, Madeleine had been reading some of Marie Stopes's pamphlets on birth control – Eloise had found them in a drawer when clearing her daughter's bedroom after she had left for the West Indies. On the other hand, Madeleine was still very young and, although Eloise herself had produced her first child in her first year of marriage while still in her teens, she could understand that nowadays young girls preferred to enjoy a little freedom before settling down to a more domestic existence.

Her mind swung back to Alice – and, with more curiosity, to Félix. Her sister's excesses cannot have been easy for him to deal with, especially in the midst of his meteoric climb to prominence in the world of *haute couture*! If he had turned now for comfort to a young, pretty girl like Alice, she for one didn't blame him. Alice was his protégée and it was all too easy to see the analogy between their relationship and that of Bernard Shaw's

Eliza Dolittle and her professor. If Félix were to bring Alice to dinner one night, she, Eloise, would not be in the least embarrassed to have her as a guest, she decided. She'd always liked the girl and admired her artistic sense in those days before the war when Alice had been her maid. How long ago those days now seemed – Maddy only a little girl and now, tragically, she was a widow.

Three days later Eloise sat at the lunch table in her London house with Harry on her right-hand side, and was reminded once again of those early years at Calking Grange.

'I know some people might think I had a deprived childhood,' Harry was saying with his charming smile, 'but I thought I was the luckiest boy in the world being allowed to come and play in your lovely garden with your children. You were very kind to me, Lady Debrace, and I shall never forget those happy days. Looking back, it seems as if it was always summertime.'

Eloise returned his smile.

'One never realizes how fleeting childhood is until it's too late,' she said. 'I think Sir Philip and I always felt that you were a little special, although I must admit we were astonished when Pamela Kinmuire and her brother suddenly arrived and scooped you up like a forgotten parcel. The children missed you terribly.'

'I'm sure Nanny didn't,' Harry said, laughing. 'She never did approve of her charges being allowed to mix with the gardener's child.'

'I'm not at all sure that Martha didn't bring you all up with far better manners than our children had,' Eloise rejoined.

'It was easy enough for her to discipline me,' Harry replied. 'She had only to remind me that if I misbehaved you might not allow me back to play. That was enough to ensure that I was good.'

'You must be delighted with your unexpected windfall,' Sir Philip commented, feeling he had been left out of the conversation too long. 'I always did think it a rum do when that bounder Simcox usurped your inheritance. I take it

Lady Kinmuire is not the "unknown benefactor" you mentioned before lunch?'

'All I can tell you is that it was a late relative who did not wish to be named,' Harry replied evasively.

'Curious, to say the least,' Sir Philip grunted. 'Still, I suppose it makes no odds in the end. The fact is you're now set up for life, and with you about to get married, it couldn't have come at a better time.'

'That's quite right, sir,' Harry agreed. 'I've not really had time for it to sink in yet. It's certainly important to me that I can be independent of my future father-in-law. Mr Harvey is always so generous and, stupid as you may think it, my pride would have suffered if I'd not been able to support my own wife. It's one of the reasons I delayed so long asking Cora-Beth to marry me.'

It was on the tip of Eloise's tongue to ask what other reasons there had been, but the sound of raised voices in the hall arrested her attention. Almost at once the dining-room door was opened and, pushing past an anxious-looking maid, Madeleine burst into the room.

'Surprise!' she said. 'I nearly telephoned you from Liverpool but the London train was just leaving so I didn't have time . . .'

She broke off as she caught sight of Harry.

'I'd no idea *you* were going to be here,' she said, 'although Aubrey did write and say you were travelling back to England together.'

Still wearing her black travelling-coat and hat, she now removed them and handed them to the open-mouthed maid, before going round the table to her mother and kissing her cheek.

'Aren't you pleased to see me, Mummy?' she asked. 'You're looking quite shocked.'

'Oh, my darling, of course I am,' Eloise answered, rising to her feet and hugging the small figure. 'I'm just so astonished . . . you should have let us know. Are you all right? You're looking . . .' Surprisingly well, she thought, but did not say. Her daughter's big blue eyes were bright and clear, unmarked by signs of grief. Although she was wearing a black skirt, she wore with it a black-and-white silk blouse in bold checks, and had a long rainbow-coloured silk scarf knotted round her neck. She looked like any other smartly dressed young woman and not in the least like someone recently widowed.

'I'm absolutely famished,' Madeleine was saying as she went round to her father. 'I haven't had a thing to eat since breakfast on the boat. Hello, Daddy. You're looking as handsome as ever.'

For a moment, Harry could no longer see her as Sir Philip enveloped his daughter in his embrace.

'This is a wonderful surprise,' he was saying. 'Your mother and I have been so worried about you. Sit down, my darling, and Doris shall bring you something to eat.'

Harry, who had risen to his feet, now offered Madeleine his chair.

'Anyway, I really ought to be getting along,' he said. He looked from Sir Philip to his hostess and added, 'This is a family reunion and I'm sure you'd all rather be on your own. Will you excuse me?'

Sir Philip had been on the point of agreeing to this tactful suggestion, but before he could do so Madeleine looked up at Harry, saying, 'But you can't go yet, Harry. We haven't even said hello. There'll be loads of time for me to talk to Mummy and Daddy later. If you don't sit down, I shall feel frightfully guilty for breaking in on your lunch party.'

I should go, this very minute, Harry told himself as he stood hesitantly by Madeleine's chair. Even in this inappropriate setting, his heart was hammering and he could feel his whole body responding to her physical presence. She was looking even more beautiful than when he had last seen her. Her face had fined down and her magnificent eyes looked even larger as they stared into his in appeal.

'I really think I should go . . .' he muttered stupidly, but now Eloise came to his rescue.

'Do stay and have coffee with us while Madeleine has some lunch,' she said. 'We'll have it here at the table,

Doris. Pull up another chair, Harry, and then, Madeleine, you must tell us how you come to be here so unexpectedly.'

'I was just lucky,' Madeleine said airily. 'The major's wife, who had booked an earlier passage, developed appendicitis and couldn't use her ticket, so I took it, and she's travelling back on mine. I simply can't tell you how awful it was out there, Mummy – after poor Pogo's funeral, I mean. Of course, it was horrible and tragic and heartbreaking, but there's a limit to how many commiserations you can bear to listen to, and nobody seemed to understand that the last thing I wanted was to be left alone. I *was* invited to one or two dull little lunches and dinners, but everyone sat around looking as if the end of the world had come. They didn't seem to realize that what I most wanted was to be allowed to forget about it all . . . or anyway, try to. *You* understand, don't you, Daddy?'

Sir Philip looked uneasy.

'Well, I suppose . . . yes, of course, a little distraction. But . . . ah, here's your lunch,' he added with relief. 'Now you must try and eat it all, darling. You need to keep up your strength. You look much too thin to me.'

Madeleine's downcast expression gave way to a smile.

'You're a silly old fusspot, and I love you, but I certainly don't want to be fat. The colonel's wife is absolutely enormous and no matter what she wears, she always looks a dowdy old matron. You'll be pleased to know, Mummy, that she fussed over me like a mother hen. Nearly drove me mad. She was always wanting to put handkerchiefs soaked in lavender water on my forehead, as if I was an invalid. Don't let's talk about it! Thank goodness I'm home now and don't even have to think about it any more. Tell me about you, Harry. Is it true you're engaged? Aubrey said you were but I didn't believe it. Not to the *American* girl?'

'Why ever not?' Eloise broke in sharply. 'Aubrey says Cora-Beth is quite charming and I'm sure if Harry wants to marry her, she's a lovely person.'

Madeleine appeared unconcerned by the gentle reproach.

'I shall have to meet her and judge for myself,' she said, tucking in to the game pie the maid had put in front of her. 'You must bring her round to see me, Harry. After all, I am one of your oldest friends.'

'Cora-Beth and her father are in Paris this week. I'm not sure if there'll be time,' Harry excused himself quickly. 'Aubrey went with them as I had to go to Martha Pritchett's funeral, and I also have some business matters to attend to. We go back to Kentucky the week after they return, so Cora-Beth is going to be pretty busy too. Alice is fitting her out with her trousseau.'

'Is she now? How is Alice?'

'Pretty cut up about her mother,' Harry murmured. 'We all are.'

'So we're all in mourning,' Madeleine said. 'I did wonder about the black armband you're wearing but I thought it might be for Pogo. Of course, you didn't know him very well, did you? Where are you staying, Harry? With the Alcotts?'

'Harry's staying at the Savoy with the Harveys,' Eloise answered. 'Doris, you can bring in the Charlotte Russe now. Miss Madeleine has finished. More coffee, Harry?'

Harry stood up, this time determined that he would remain no longer. Madeleine might be finding conversation easy but he felt tongue-tied.

'I do really think I must go,' he said. 'It was an excellent meal, Lady Debrace, and very nice to see you both again.' He looked down at Madeleine, who had twisted round in her chair and was staring up at him. 'I know you don't like commiserations, but I do want to say how . . . how very sorry I am,' he said awkwardly.

'Oh, I don't mind *you* being sorry for me,' Madeleine said. 'You're sort of part of the family, aren't you?'

Somehow Harry managed to extricate himself from the Debrace household. He declined to take a passing taxi and decided to walk back slowly to the Strand, cutting through the small side streets and avoiding the bustle of Oxford

Street. He was seeking the anonymity of Soho and the theatre world, his feet taking him automatically in the right direction. He wondered stupidly if the shock he had received must be obvious to the passers-by who he occasionally bumped into, or if they supposed he was drunk.

There was only one thought in his head, and that was to put as big a distance between himself and Madeleine as he could. He did not try to talk himself out of the certainty that he still loved her, that the kind of love he felt for Cora-Beth was totally different and of a far lesser calibre than the depth of emotion that even the sight of Madeleine could evoke. Her presence acted as a kind of catalyst. Reason, honour, logic paled into insignificance, leaving only a great void of longing to be able to take her in his arms and hold her.

By the time he reached the hotel, Harry felt exhausted and yet, at the same time, physically restless. His appointment with the accountant was not until four o'clock and he could think of no way to fill the time. He sat down in the foyer of the hotel and ordered himself some black coffee, trying to distract himself with the comings and goings of the hotel guests. It did not help, for every young woman wearing black or of Madeleine's build served only to bring her back to his thoughts.

He toyed with the idea of going round to see Lady Merstam, the woman he could still not think of as his aunt. Perhaps he needed to talk to someone like her – someone who would be quite unbiased and advise him what to do with his life. Had he the right to marry Cora-Beth now that he knew he was still as deeply in love with Madeleine as ever? However awful the circumstances, she was free again, and something in the look in her eyes convinced him that she was not entirely immune to him. He hadn't imagined it. It was a look that somehow lit up her eyes. She had pursed her mouth, as if she was asking to be kissed; tilted her head, as if she were asking him if the spark were still there for him too.

To occupy himself, he walked to the accountant's office

and finally, as it had started to rain, took a taxi back to the hotel. Passing Alice's flat, he decided on the spur of the moment to leave a note asking her to telephone him immediately she returned from work as he wished urgently to speak to her. An hotel, he decided as he made his way up to his bedroom, was no place to be when you were on your own. He wished very much that Cora-Beth and her father were in their suite down the passage-way to distract him, to reassure him with their jolly, friendly company, that he was not making a terrible mistake marrying a girl he did not truly love.

Unwilling to remain alone, he telephoned Bertie Alcott and arranged to meet him for dinner and a revue. Not even the good company of his friend or the proficiency of the artistes in *Blackbirds* could distract him indefinitely.

When he returned once more to the hotel, he put through a telephone call to Cora-Beth. Unfortunately, it was Wendell who answered the phone. Cora-Beth and Aubrey had gone to a nightclub, he told Harry, and they might not be back until late. Had Harry any message?

'Just tell her that . . . that I miss her,' Harry said wretchedly. He felt a traitor for failing to say what he had intended: that he loved her!

The telephone rang almost as soon as he has replaced the receiver. Supposing that Cora-Beth had returned earlier than expected, Harry answered it, determined this time to say what he knew she would want to hear.

It was not Cora-Beth. It was the hall porter to advise him that a young lady was on her way up to see him.

'She wouldn't wait for me to enquire if it was convenient, sir,' the man said apologetically. 'I'm afraid I had already told her that you must be in your room as the key was not here. The young lady said it was a matter of extreme urgency. She gave her name, sir, as Mrs Dunbar.'

'That's all right,' Harry said, replacing the telephone. But it was not. In a few minutes, Madeleine would be knocking on his door and no matter how dishonourable it might be, he knew he would not hesitate to let her in.

CHAPTER TWENTY-EIGHT

1926

For a moment Harry and Madeleine stood staring at each other, then Madeleine pushed the door shut and, turning once more to face him, said, 'I suppose you're going to tell me I shouldn't have come, but I had to see you, Harry. *I just had to!*'

Two large tears welled up in her eyes and rolled down her cheeks.

'Don't be cross with me,' she whispered forlornly.

Gathering his wits, Harry put an arm round her shoulders and led her to the armchair by the curtained window. Helping her out of her coat, he laid it on the bed, together with her hat and gloves, his thoughts in turmoil. Her tears ceasing abruptly, Madeleine curled up in the chair and managed a wistful smile.

'You look quite flabbergasted,' she said. 'I suppose you think I'm awful, coming here alone like this. I'd have come earlier but it was ages and ages before Mummy and Daddy went to bed and I could slip out of the house without anyone seeing me. I'm so glad you're here, Harry. I was afraid you'd be out at a nightclub, or somewhere.'

Harry sat down awkwardly on the edge of the bed.

'Can I order you anything?' he asked. 'Some coffee, or a drink?'

Madeleine shook her head, the waves of her ash-blonde hair shimmering in the light of the overhead chandelier.

'I had a nightcap with Daddy. The poor darling thought I needed it. He and Mummy both think I'm heartbroken about poor Pogo, and of course I am, but I don't have to pretend with you, do I, Harry? The fact is, we weren't *all*

471

that happy together. I mean, we were in a way, we had lots of good times, but I wasn't in love with him. I suppose I shouldn't have married him. It's a sort of relief to be free.'

'You can't . . . You don't mean that,' Harry said, yet something deep inside him, knowing that she did, rejoiced that she'd never loved the man she had married. At the same time, he was shocked. It was only four weeks since the wretched Dunbar had met his untimely death.

'It's such a relief to be able to tell someone,' Madeleine was saying in a breathless voice. 'It's one of the reasons I had to get away from the regiment. Everyone kept saying how sorry they were and how brave I was because I didn't go around weeping all the time, and now Mummy and Daddy are behaving in the same way. Of course, I'm sorry it happened! The funeral was awful and I'm never going to another one as long as I live. But it's all over now and I just want to be allowed to forget about it. Not that I'm going to be allowed to. Mummy says I'll have to go and see Pogo's family tomorrow and, whether I like it or not, I'll have to go into mourning, and I absolutely hate wearing black.'

Her eyes had once more filled with tears. Unable to bear the sight of them, Harry hurried across the room and took both her hands in his. Her skin was warm and soft to his touch and instantly he knew that he shouldn't have allowed himself to go near her. As he tried to draw away, Madeleine clung to him.

'It's such ages and ages since I saw you,' she said in a low, husky voice. 'As soon as I got Aubrey's letter saying you'd be in England, I just had to come back. I've thought of you so often, Harry – lots and lots of times. As soon as I was married to Pogo, I knew I shouldn't have let you go. I thought being married would make everything all right, but it wasn't like that. I never liked it when he made love to me. That's when I knew I should have married you. You're the only one who's ever made me want to do it. Do you remember that afternoon at your old house in Leicestershire?'

'Oh my God,' Harry whispered, unaware that he had spoken aloud. The temptation to pull her to her feet and take her in his arms was overwhelming. At the same time he felt a great unbearable weight of guilt holding him back.

'It's too late for us, Madeleine,' he said. 'I'm engaged to be married.'

Madeleine's eyes narrowed.

'Oh, I knew all about your engagement ages ago, when Aubrey wrote and told me, but you don't love her, do you? Not the way you loved me?'

'No, not the way I loved you,' Harry said, managing at last to release her hands. 'I'll never love anyone in quite that way, Madeleine. I wanted to marry you, but you chose Dunbar.' Despite himself, there was an edge of bitterness in his voice.

Madeleine's reaction was immediate. She jumped to her feet and flung her arms round his neck.

'Only because Aubrey said I wouldn't be able to make you happy. I did love you. *I still do!* That's why I had to come and see you, before it's too late. You don't *have* to marry this American girl. She'd let you go if she knew you still loved me. You do, don't you, Harry? You do still love me?'

With a small cry of defeat, Harry buried his face in her hair.

'Yes, yes, yes,' he murmured. 'I love you. I've always loved you.'

Madeleine leant back in his arms and stared up at him, her eyes shining.

'I just knew it when you looked at me the way you did when I walked into the dining-room at lunchtime. And it's why you left so quickly, wasn't it? In case Mummy and Daddy or I guessed what you were feeling. Oh Harry, if you only knew how happy I am.'

She gave a sudden childish giggle.

'Isn't it lucky everyone's in Paris? I couldn't have come tonight if they'd all been here. Daddy said he thought they'd be back tomorrow but he wasn't sure.'

'Yes, tomorrow evening,' Harry answered with a sinking feeling in the pit of his stomach. 'Look, Madeleine, you must try and understand. I can't hurt Cora-Beth. She waited two and a half years for me to make up my mind. I'm committed now and . . . and more seriously than you realize. We . . . she and I . . . we've been lovers.'

Madeleine's arms tightened around his neck. She gave a short, excited little laugh.

'Why should I care? I'm not a virgin any more, so it means we've both done it with someone else. Anyway, I think men ought to know about things like that. Pogo hadn't ever made love to a girl – not properly, I mean – and it was ages before he found out how to do it properly.'

The mention of Madeleine's husband and her intimate revelations of their married life had a sobering effect upon Harry's emotions. As gently as he could, he drew her arms away and held them at her side.

'You must go home,' he said harshly. 'We aren't being fair to anyone. Perhaps it wouldn't matter if I didn't love you so much. You wouldn't know, but one of the reasons I came back to England was to collect a legacy which I'd been left unexpectedly. It's ironic, isn't it, that now I really am in a position to support a wife, I'm not free to ask you to marry me.'

He let go her arms, his expression deeply unhappy as he added, 'After you married Dunbar and time passed, I thought I was resigned to the fact that I could never have you, or else I would never have proposed to Cora-Beth. It's too late now, Madeleine.'

'It isn't, it isn't!' Madeleine cried. 'Why should we ruin both our lives just because you're afraid to tell her the truth about us? If I were in her shoes, I'd let you go. She can't love you as much as I do.'

She pressed her small body against his while kissing him with a passion which left him weak and helpless to resist her. His arms tightened around her and his lips crushed hers.

'Say it,' she whispered between kisses. 'Say you love me. Say you want me. I want you to make love to me . . .

now. I don't care about tomorrow. Just this once, please Harry. Just this once.'

She half dragged him towards the bed, which had been turned down for the night. Falling backwards on to the pillow, she held out her arms.

'No one will ever know. Just this once, Harry. We may never have another chance.'

It was true that no one need ever know, Harry thought as he hurriedly removed his tail coat and bow tie. No one would be hurt and never in his life had he wanted anything as much as what Madeleine was now offering. If he was to have to go through the rest of his life without her, at least he could take with him the memory of this one time. Cora-Beth would not suffer and Dunbar was beyond suffering. Fate owed them this one brief moment of union, even if it made the subsequent farewells that much harder.

Madeleine was trying ineffectually to unfasten the buttons at the back of her dress.

'Help me,' she commanded. 'I want to take all my clothes off. I want you to take yours off. I want you so much, Harry. You're the only one who can make me feel like this.'

Her cheeks were flushed and to Harry she had never looked more beautiful, more desirable. His hands were trembling as he fumbled with the row of tiny buttons. Impatiently, Madeleine wriggled her shoulders free. Beneath the pale-grey dress, she wore only a thin silk chemise. Through the soft material, her breasts were clearly defined. With a cry, Harry buried his face against them, his hands circling her small waist.

The shrill ringing of the telephone pierced his consciousness and he half raised his head as it rang again, and then again.

'Don't answer it,' Madeleine said urgently. 'Please don't answer it.'

Harry glanced at his wristwatch and saw that it was not far short of midnight. Whoever was ringing him at this time must have something of the utmost urgency to tell him, he thought, yet he made no move to answer it.

As it continued to ring, Madeleine said, 'Leave it. It'll stop in a minute. It can't be important.'

But it might be, Harry thought, as with an effort he detached himself from Madeleine's embrace and stumbled towards the telephone. There could have been an accident – Cora-Beth, Wendell, Aubrey . . .

As if from the adjoining room, he heard Alice's voice. 'Harry, is that you? I hope I didn't wake you. You were ages answering the telephone.'

'No, no, I wasn't asleep,' Harry said weakly as he half fell into the chair. He could think of nothing else to say. Into the silence, Alice's voice came soft and clear.

'Your note implied you wanted to talk to me urgently. I couldn't ring earlier. Félix is in London and we went out to dinner. Is something wrong, Harry? Are you all right?'

From across the room Harry could see Madeleine's blue eyes staring at him, he was not sure if in irritation or in appeal. If anything she looked even more desirable, and yet it was as if the spell he had been under was broken. All his feelings of guilt about deceiving Cora-Beth had returned. The thought crossed his mind how appalled she would be – as, indeed, would Alice, if the telephone allowed her to see as well as to hear him.

'I'm fine, Alice,' he said in what he hoped was a normal tone of voice. 'I was just feeling a bit down this afternoon, that's all. When I left that note, I'd thought we might have dinner somewhere.'

There was a very brief pause before Alice replied, 'With Félix here, I wouldn't have had time. I expect you're missing Cora-Beth, aren't you? Isn't it tomorrow she gets back?'

'That's right. How is Monsieur Verveine?'

'Busy, as always,' Alice said briefly. 'I'll have to go now, Harry. So long as there's nothing wrong . . .'

'No, everything's fine. Thanks again for ringing. Sleep well.'

Alice's soft laugh reached him.

'Pleasant dreams,' she said and then, as she used to say when they were children, 'Good-night, sleep tight, and don't let the bugs bite!'

Madeleine had been watching him through narrowed eyes. When he made no move to rejoin her, she swung her legs over the side of the bed and began to put on her dress.

'I told you not to answer it,' she said in a small, accusing voice as she straightened out her skirt. 'I suppose your wretched Alice has made you feel guilty. It's just like her to be prim and proper. She never did like me very much.'

That was probably true, Harry thought as he fastened the buttons at the back of Madeleine's dress and helped her into her coat. Perhaps in years to come, Madeleine would feel grateful to Alice for her timely intervention. Meanwhile, her proximity was making him regret his change of mind. Her scent filled his nostrils and once more her lips were soft and inviting as she turned and pressed her mouth to his.

'If Cora-Beth broke off the engagement, you'd marry me, wouldn't you?' she said. 'Then we could be together all the time. You do love me, don't you?'

Speechless, Harry nodded.

'Then at least ask her to set you free – while there's still time,' Madeleine said insistently. 'You will ask her, won't you? I love you so much, Harry.'

'I'll . . . think . . . about it,' Harry said hesitantly, but he knew he wouldn't do so. Perhaps if he'd never made love to Cora-Beth, he might have found the courage to ask for his freedom, but it was in anticipation of their marriage that she had maintained her belief there was nothing wrong in such intimacies. Now he had no alternative but to honour her expectations.

It was with a feeling of unbearable loss that he took Madeleine down in the lift and ordered a taxi cab to take her home. Aware that the night porter had seen him throughout these past weeks in the company of Cora-Beth and her father, he ordered the taxi for 'my sister', as much to protect Madeleine's reputation as his own.

After she had left, Harry returned to his room and sat for a long time staring at the crumpled bed. Now he could think of nothing but the happiness he had deliberately forgone, and he knew that if Madeleine were by some miracle to reappear, he wouldn't have the strength to send her away a second time. He tried to feel angry towards Alice for choosing such a moment to telephone him, but he knew that he'd no right to do so. As always Alice had done only what he'd asked. He wondered what would she say if he were to suggest she decide whether or not he had the right to ask Cora-Beth for his freedom.

Without any doubt whatsoever, she would tell him to make up his own mind. How clearly he could remember her saying to him, 'You've got a conscience that'll tell you what's right and wrong, Harry. You dursn't need me to tell you.' That was the little Alice Pritchett of his childhood. How far they'd both come since those days. It was strange to think of how their paths had carried them so far from their humble origins yet almost to the same point in life.

Could Cora-Beth's suspicions that his beloved Alice was secretly in love with him be right? If she could be suspicious of Alice with so little to go on, what would she not suspect if she were to meet Madeleine! He must make sure that they didn't meet. Apart from anything Madeleine might do or say, he knew that if he were in the same room with the girl he loved, he would be unable to control his voice or his expression.

As Madeleine slipped back into her parents' house undetected, she was very far from sharing Harry's depression. Although her little excursion had been frustrating, she did not feel it had been fruitless. Her instincts had been proved right – Harry still loved her. She'd not been entirely truthful in leading him to suppose she'd advanced her return from Jamaica in order to see him while he was in England. She had been unutterably bored with her unexpected widowhood and resentful of the expectations of those around her that she should behave as a grief-stricken wife. Of course she'd been shocked when the accident happened, and in her way she'd been genuinely fond of poor Pogo; but she'd never loved him and he had proved a tongue-tied, inept lover, unable to rouse her to even the smallest degree of passion. There'd been times when she'd thought of Harry and how he alone of all the men she'd met had really attracted her in quite that inexplicable way. Not that she regretted her former decision not to marry him. She would have hated a life of poverty and knew herself quite unfitted for it. It was not until she heard her father speak of Harry's extraordinary, unexpected legacy that it had occurred to her there was now no barrier between them. With his exceptional good looks and charm and her social popularity, his background of illegitimacy would be overlooked. Moreover, a discreet word here and there would ensure that everyone knew the late Earl of Kinmuire had been his father.

As she climbed into bed, Madeleine stretched out sensuously, welcoming the caress of the smooth linen sheets against her body. For a moment she allowed herself to imagine that Harry was there with her, holding her, touching her. Then she forced herself to think on more practical lines. If such dreams were ever to come to reality, she had to think of a way to eliminate the American girl from his life. It was clear that Harry was not prepared to behave 'dishonourably' and break his engagement. It would have to be done by the girl. According to Aubrey, Cora-Beth adored Harry. A way must be found to change her mind – and it was not difficult to think of one.

The plan that now occurred to her had its risks, but they were risks she must take if she were not to lose him. Once Harry was married, there would be no further chance for her.

Madeleine fell asleep while still formulating the finer points of her plan.

'Who is that young woman sitting over there?' Cora-Beth asked Alice. 'Her face seems familiar and yet . . .'

Alice followed Cora-Beth's glance and caught her breath in surprise.

'That's Aubrey's sister, Madeleine Dunbar. I thought she was in the West Indies.'

'So did I,' Cora-Beth admitted, unable to take her eyes away from the girl who had played such a large part in Harry's life. She was like a tiny version of her brother – the same pale-gold head, now bent over a fashion magazine she was showing to one of the *vendeuses*.

Alice's thoughts were in turmoil. Why had Harry not told her when she had telephoned him last night that Madeleine was back in England? Perhaps he didn't know.

'Aubrey said his sister was not due home for another month,' Cora-Beth said. 'She's just been widowed, hasn't she? Such a terrible thing to happen.'

It was terrible, Alice thought, but there was nothing about the animated expression on Madeleine's face which indicated *she* was devastated by the tragedy.

'Will you introduce me, Alice?' Cora-Beth asked. 'I'd like to offer my condolences.'

As if suddenly aware that they were talking about her, Madeleine looked in their direction. With an eager wave of her small, gloved hand, she stood up and came across the *salon*.

'I could see you were busy, Alice, so I didn't interrupt. I've come in for some new clothes. Forgive me, Mrs . . . ? Miss . . . ?'

'This is Miss Harvey,' Alice said quietly. 'Harry's fiancée.'

Madeleine's eyebrows rose above her startling blue eyes. She held out her hand.

'What a pleasant surprise meeting you here,' she said. 'Aubrey has told me so much about you. He promised to invite you home to meet me . . . and my parents, of course. He said you'd all had a marvellous time in Paris.'

'Yes, it was great fun,' Cora-Beth said. 'Your brother is a wonderful person to have around; Poppa thinks the world of him. We got back only yesterday.'

Madeleine gave a small, breathless laugh.

'You should have seen Aubrey's face when he walked

into the house and saw me. Mummy and Daddy had a shock too, but there simply wasn't time to let anyone know I was arriving.' Her voice lowered a tone. 'I expect Aubrey told you about the perfectly terrible thing that happened to . . . to my husband. I simply couldn't bear it out there a moment longer.'

She turned to Alice, who was regarding her thoughtfully.

'I don't think I would have recognized you, Alice, if the salesgirl hadn't told me who you were. Do you realize we haven't met since you packed my school trunk before you went off to Paris? I must say, you look frightfully chic, whereas I look an absolute sight! That's why I'm here – to buy some new clothes. Mummy thinks I should wear black, but nobody wears mourning these days, so I thought I'd choose something not too bright. Aren't the Verveine clothes absolutely divine, Miss Harvey?'

It didn't seem the moment to offer sympathies, so Cora-Beth said, 'Please call me Cora-Beth. Miss Harvey sounds so formal and . . . well, I hope we're going to be friends. Will you be in London for a while? We leave for Kentucky in ten days' time, but although we've got a very busy schedule, I do hope we can meet.'

Madeleine nodded.

'Are you on your way back to your hotel now?' she asked. 'I'm not really in the mood for choosing clothes. Perhaps I can give you a lift? I have my mother's car outside.'

'That's very kind of you, Mrs . . . I mean, Madeleine. Actually I'm going to Harrods. If that's inconvenient . . .'

'Not in the least,' Madeleine said quickly. She nodded in Alice's direction. 'I'll drop in again in a day or two, Alice. I can see you're pretty busy. Oh, look! Isn't that the actress, Gertrude Lawrence, who just came in? I suppose you have quite a number of famous people as clients. Well, if you're finished, Cora-Beth, shall we be on our way? Lovely to see you, Alice, and I must say I think this place is divine. Shall we go?'

There was something about Aubrey's sister, Cora-Beth

thought as she followed her out into the street, which made it impossible for one to criticize her bright, bubbly manner. Her somewhat inconsequential chatter was in some ways childlike, as was the innocent expression of her large eyes. She lacked the quiet reserve so noticeable in Aubrey but the same easy friendliness was there.

'We'll go through Hyde Park, shall we?' Madeleine suggested as she settled herself into the driving seat. 'I do believe the traffic is even worse than it was before I went abroad. Do you drive, Cora-Beth? Aubrey taught me one summer holiday. I was absolutely hopeless at first but I finally managed to master the art.'

She turned into Dover Street and, still chattering, steered the car down Curzon Street and into Park Lane. Seemingly oblivious to the warning blare of horns from other drivers, she crossed the southbound traffic, giving very erratic signals of her intentions, and finally manoeuvred the vehicle into Hyde Park.

'Are you in a frantic hurry?' she asked. 'If not, shall we stop for a moment or two and have a chat? It was such an extraordinary coincidence running into you at Uncle Félix's shop and . . . well, we've lots to talk about, haven't we?'

Not wishing to appear unfriendly and since she really was in no hurry, Cora-Beth raised no objection when Madeleine drew to a halt. It had started to rain and, without the wipers operating, the windscreen was quickly misted, obscuring the view of the dripping plane trees and damp fallen leaves covering the grass.

Madeleine said suddenly, 'I know I should be congratulating you on your engagement to Harry. Now that I've met you, I can see why he wanted to marry you, but I'm worried about you, Cora-Beth. I mean, do you honestly think it'll work out all right – the marriage, I mean?'

Cora-Beth's face mirrored her bewilderment.

'I don't understand. We love each other very much, so I've no reason to doubt that our marriage will be a very happy one.'

'No, of course not – as things *were*,' Madeleine said,

sighing. 'But who could have guessed that poor dear Pogo would fall off his horse? I mean, he often did have falls, but not fatal ones. He was a wonderful rider.'

'Yes, I'm sure . . . and I'm terribly sorry . . . but I don't understand what you're trying to tell me.'

Madeleine's eyes met hers with an unblinking stare.

'Surely Harry must have told you – about us? We were terribly in love. We have been since we were children. We wanted to get married but my parents wouldn't consider it. I'm sure I don't have to tell you about Harry's background and, of course, he was in no position to support a wife. If I'd been older . . . but I was only nineteen, and when Daddy sent Harry off to America to live with you and your father, I was absolutely heartbroken. I married Pogo on the rebound, hoping I'd grow to love him.'

'But you never did?' Cora-Beth looked away from the younger girl's face and stared with unseeing eyes at the gold clasp of her handbag. The implications of Madeleine's revelations were unmistakable: Harry still loved her.

Beside her, Madeleine continued to speak.

'When Harry asked you to marry him, he couldn't have known I'd be released from my marriage. As far as he was concerned, I was for ever beyond his reach. I couldn't have known it either, and although I have to admit it hurt me dreadfully when I heard he'd become engaged to someone else, there was nothing I could do about it. Isn't it strange the way fate sometimes works things out? When I decided to come home from Jamaica, I never expected to see Harry. Knowing he was engaged and far too honourable a person ever to let you down, I'd made up my mind to avoid seeing him . . . but there he was when I walked into the house, lunching with Mummy and Daddy. I simply couldn't believe it.'

Cora-Beth looked up sharply.

'You mean you and Harry have seen each other? He didn't tell me!'

'You mustn't be cross with him, Cora-Beth. The last thing he wants to do is to hurt you, and it's easy to see why he thought it best to say nothing to you. Well, obviously we needed to talk things through, but we couldn't do so in front of Mummy and Daddy, so we met the night before last. We both agreed we'd never let you know we were still as much in love as we'd ever been.'

Cora-Beth's voice was harsh with the pain now stabbing her heart.

'Then why are you telling me? I wish you hadn't.'

Madeleine reached out and laid her hand over one of Cora-Beth's.

'Because I think it's wrong to keep the truth from you. It isn't fair to you. You see, I know what it does to a person when they're married to someone who doesn't return their love – who *can't* return it. Don't you think I tried to love Pogo? I did everything I could to forget Harry, but Pogo guessed the truth. Love isn't something you can pretend, is it? I tried and failed, and all the time I felt horribly guilty because I couldn't give my husband the love he wanted.'

She drew a prolonged sigh.

'I've thought and thought about you and Harry, and I know that if I were in your shoes I'd want to be aware *before* I got married that I was only ever going to have second-best. It seemed so unfair to you to let you go on believing everything was perfect. I thought you had a right to know, and that it was up to me to tell you. Harry never will.'

'How can you know that?' Cora-Beth said fiercely. 'No one is more honest than he is, and if what you say is true, he'll tell me.'

Madeleine drew another long sigh.

'I pleaded with him to do so that night in his room. I told him it was his duty. He kept saying he couldn't hurt you, that we must forget what we felt for each other and that somehow he would find a way to convince you that he really did love you the way you deserved to be loved.'

Cora-Beth's face was very pale.

'What room?' she asked in a small, tight voice.

Madeleine bit her lip.

484

'Did I say that? I didn't mean to tell you. His bedroom was the only place we could think of where we could talk without anyone seeing us. If we'd gone to a restaurant or to one of the public rooms, someone might have recognized us and Harry was afraid you'd hear about it and . . . well, put two and two together.'

Questions burned on Cora-Beth's lips but she didn't ask them. Had they kissed? *Had they made love?* What had happened in that hotel bedroom?

Guessing Cora-Beth's thoughts, Madeleine said, 'Please try not to think badly of us. We both tried very hard not to remember how it had been when we were last together. All the time, we kept going round in circles, wondering how we could work things out so that *you* wouldn't be hurt. But of course, there wasn't any way. I left soon after midnight – Harry got the night porter to get me a taxi home. We pretended I was his sister. I feel so awful about it. I blame myself for rushing off and marrying Pogo the way I did. If I'd waited until I was twenty-one . . . but I didn't, and although Harry says I'm not to blame and it's his worry, not mine, you two might have been perfectly happy married if I hadn't been widowed. Perhaps it's still possible. I don't care about myself. All I want is for Harry to be happy.'

She gave a small, tenuous smile.

'Mummy wants to take me down to Brighton for a sort of convalescent holiday. I don't want to go, but perhaps I should. If I can just stay out of the way until you and Harry have returned to America, perhaps . . .'

'No!' The single word burst from Cora-Beth's lips. 'It wouldn't do any good. I don't think Harry ever did forget you. I've known for years that I was only second-best. Sooner or later he would have met you again and then . . . no, Madeleine, we've got to have this out in the open. I know Harry doesn't want to hurt me, but you're absolutely right when you say I'd be hurt for the rest of my life if he can't love me the . . . the way he loves you. I love him too, you know, and he has only to ask me and I'll give him back his ring if that's what he wants.'

485

For a moment, Madeleine didn't speak. Then, regarding Cora-Beth speculatively, she said, 'He won't do it, Cora-Beth. He said he wouldn't and I know he meant it. He said something about it being his "duty" to marry you, although I'm not quite sure what he meant and he wouldn't explain.'

Cora-Beth's cheeks flushed a deep pink. This girl might not have understood, but she herself knew only too well what Harry had been thinking of. The pain worsened so that it was almost physical as she recalled those few times when he'd made love to her. It had always been at her suggestion, she thought bitterly. If she were to do as this girl was doing and face up to the truth, everything that had happened between her and Harry had been at her instigation. She'd fallen in love with him and gone on and on trying, until finally she'd made him fall in love with her.

'I need to think about all this,' she said weakly. 'I'd like to go back to the hotel now, if you don't mind.'

Madeleine's blue eyes were regarding her in anxious appeal.

'Please try not to hate me,' she said. 'I don't suppose it's possible for you to think now that I'm really your friend. There didn't seem to be anyone else who would tell you the truth, and for your sake as well as Harry's, you had to know. It doesn't matter about me. I forfeited any right to happiness when I married poor Pogo. I don't deserve Harry's love and no one knows that better than I do. Can you forgive me?'

'I don't know,' Cora-Beth said, close to tears. 'I just know I wish you hadn't told me all this. Maybe I ought to know the truth, but I wish I didn't.'

'I'll take you back to the hotel,' Madeleine said gently. She was more than satisfied with what she believed she had achieved. As she drew up outside the Savoy, she felt she could afford to be generous to the distraught girl beside her.

'If it's of any comfort,' she said, 'I promise I won't see or talk to Harry again until or unless you tell me I may do so, and I'll abide by whatever decision you ultimately make.'

That decision, she assured herself as she drove back to her parents' home, was not in any doubt.

CHAPTER TWENTY-NINE

1926

'You look absolutely stunning, Cora-Beth,' Aubrey said as he drew back a chair for her in a quiet corner of the hotel foyer. His voice held genuine warmth and admiration, and Cora-Beth managed a half-hearted smile as she sat down beside him.

'Harry and Poppa won't be down for a little while,' she said. 'When I left them, they were drinking cocktails with Miss Norton so they were late going up to change.'

'Then it sounds as if we have some catching up to do. Shall we go through to the cocktail lounge?' Aubrey said, trying not to let his eyes linger on the girl beside him. She was wearing a simple sleeveless, jade-green dress, a velvet evening cloak over her shoulders. Her only ornament was a diamond and emerald clip which held back her straight, black hair and twinkled in the hotel lights. It seemed to him as if there were something special about her tonight – or perhaps, he told himself wryly, it was just that he had not seen her since their return from Paris and had been looking forward eagerly to this moment.

The smile left Cora-Beth's face as she said, 'Can we stay here, Aubrey? I came down early because I very much want to talk to you – before the others get here.'

They were not due to leave for the theatre for another hour. Wendell had acquired tickets for what was supposed to be the best show in town, *The Constant Nymph*. Although Noël Coward was no longer playing the lead, his young understudy, John Gielgud, was reported to be excellent in the part and a worthy complement for the female star, Edna Best. Despite this, Cora-Beth had toyed with the idea of inventing an excuse not to go. She genuinely had a headache but the real reason was that she was finding it almost impossible to pretend with Harry that she was her usual jolly self. She had lain awake most of the night thinking about Madeleine and all she had told her. The facts were impossible to ignore and yet she could not bring herself to accept that her forthcoming marriage might not take place after all, and that her engagement to Harry must end.

She tried to tell herself that she had heard only Madeleine's side of the story – that it might be no more than a ruse to get her, Cora-Beth, out of the way. The suspicion had not lingered long, for there had been complete conviction in Madeleine's voice and she had made it perfectly easy for Cora-Beth to check the facts. A word to the night porter would confirm whether Madeleine really had been in the hotel the night before last. Assuming that she had, why hadn't Harry told her, Cora-Beth, about it? There would have been nothing to hide if he'd not wanted Madeleine there with him.

'Something's wrong, I can see by your face,' Aubrey prompted gently. 'Out with it, Cora-Beth. You know I'll help if I can.'

Cora-Beth leant forward, biting her lip in her distress.

'I don't think anyone can help me,' she said. 'I'm not even sure if I should ask for your advice, you being Madeleine's brother. On the other hand, you might know the truth . . . at least part of it.'

'My dear girl, try to calm down and start at the beginning. At the moment, it's none of it making much sense.'

Cora-Beth essayed another smile.

'I'm sorry,' she said in a quieter voice. 'It's not very easy to say . . . to talk about. Aubrey, has Madeleine said anything to you . . . about Harry?'

Aubrey frowned. He'd had no heart-to-heart talks with his sister since his return from Paris, but knowing her so well, his suspicions were aroused.

'Only that Harry was having lunch with my parents

when she arrived home, and that he was looking very well but didn't stay long. Does that help?'

Cora-Beth shook her head.

'No, not really. Oh, Aubrey, I guess Madeleine is still in love with Harry. I *know* she is . . . and I think he's still in love with her. I just don't know what to do. Madeleine says he'll never ask me to release him from our engagement and I'm sure she's right.'

Aubrey leant back in his chair, his eyes uneasy and a sinking feeling in the pit of his stomach. Madeleine *had* been behaving strangely. There had been a kind of tense excitement about her that his mother had put down to a latent hysteria brought on by the shock of Dunbar's sudden death. But Pickles had hardly mentioned her late husband and was far more interested in what he, Aubrey, had been doing – how he had enjoyed Paris; what he, Harry and Cora-Beth had done in Kentucky by way of amusement; what Cora-Beth was really like when one got to know her.

Her questioning had been searching and it had taken him all his time to avoid letting his young sister discover how he really felt about Harry's fiancée. Knowing Madeleine, he was only too aware that she'd never been able to keep a confidence and that if she learned he was in love with his best friend's future wife, in no time at all the rest of the family and most of her friends would know about it . . . perhaps even Harry himself.

'I'm sorry,' Cora-Beth said beside him. 'I guess I'm not making myself very clear, am I? I'll tell you the whole story.'

It was a moment or two before she could get up the courage to do so. For one thing, she was terribly afraid she might cry, and that was the last thing she would want to do in a public place. As if aware of her silent struggle, Aubrey took one of her hands in both of his.

'One of our nanny's favourite proverbs was, "A trouble shared is a trouble halved." So out with it, Cora-Beth. I'm your best friend, remember? Or so you said in Paris.'

'We had a wonderful time there, didn't we?' Cora-Beth

said wistfully. 'I was so happy. I wish . . . I wish we'd never come back.'

'You can't wish that more fervently than I do.'

Aubrey had spoken unguardedly, on impulse, and his hands had tightened unconsciously around hers. Cora-Beth, however, was too caught up in her own perplexed emotions to appreciate the meaning of his words.

'Harry and your sister met . . . here . . . at night . . . in this hotel, while we were still in Paris.' The words came out in short, sharp sentences. 'They're still in love. They agreed I mustn't be hurt and that they wouldn't tell me what had happened. Madeleine . . . we ran into each other at the Maison de Verveine and she offered me a lift in her car. Then she told me. She felt I had a right to know . . . because I could be very unhappy married to Harry if he still loved her. Is she still in love with Harry, Aubrey? Do you really think she is? And what's far more important to me, does Harry still love her?'

'My dearest girl,' Aubrey said aghast, 'I'm finding it hard to believe all this. Madeleine's only just lost her husband. It's madness!'

'But she never loved him. She told me so herself. She only married him on the rebound, because she couldn't marry Harry. Now she's free again.'

Aubrey drew a deep breath. More than anything in the world, he wanted to be able to comfort the girl beside him, to make her happy, but she trusted him and he couldn't lie to her.

'I suppose they could still love each other. Frankly, I thought Madeleine had come to her senses when she married Dunbar. Harry couldn't have supported her. It was her choice. But now – well, I suppose now he's come into money of his own . . .'

'But Aubrey, what should I do? He has said nothing to me.'

'Can't you ask him outright? Leave the choice to him?'

'Madeleine said he'd honour his obligations to me, but

I'd hate that. Your sister's quite right. Even if he pretended he still loved me, I'd very soon know once we were married that he didn't. I'm beginning to wonder now if he ever did. I've always come second in his heart to Madeleine, haven't I?'

'Madeleine's my sister and of course I love her, but . . . she's not half the girl you are, Cora-Beth. I don't understand Harry. If I were in his shoes . . .'

He broke off, realizing that once again he had said far more than he'd intended. Cora-Beth was regarding him curiously.

'You're being very kind – trying to make me feel better, aren't you? It was the same when we were in France, you trying all the time to make up for the fact that Harry wasn't there. Oh, I know in the circumstances he couldn't have been, but . . . do you realize how little I've seen of him since we've been in Europe? Far, far less than I've seen of you. I think if it hadn't been for you, I'd have been utterly miserable. You've been a marvellous companion. I shall miss you dreadfully when we go back to the States.'

'Will you?' Aubrey asked in a low, tense voice. 'I doubt it. You and Harry will have a hundred and one things to do, preparing for your wedding and . . .'

'It doesn't look as if there's going to be a wedding, does it?' Cora-Beth interrupted. Tears filled her eyes. 'What am I to do, Aubrey? If I ask him if he's in love with Madeleine and he denies it, I shan't believe him.'

Aubrey's eyes were thoughtful.

'There is another way. Tell him that *you're* having second thoughts about your relationship. Tell him that while we were in Paris, you found yourself beginning to wonder if you really were suited to each other. If you like, you can tell him that I've fallen in love with you and that you've been wondering whether you might not be happier married to me.'

His voice was deliberately devoid of emotion and, not realizing that Aubrey was telling her the truth about himself, she smiled.

'He'd guess that wasn't true. He knows us both too well.'

'Does he? Can anyone know what goes on in another person's heart? Anyway, what is more natural than that I should have fallen in love with you?'

'You're not serious, are you?' Cora-Beth asked. Aubrey did not reply, and with a shock she realized for the first time that he *was*.

'I guess I ought to say I'm dreadfully sorry, but that wouldn't be true. I feel . . . pleased . . . flattered. You won't believe this, Aubrey, but I once told Poppa that if there'd been no Harry, I could easily have fallen in love with you.' Her voice broke. 'If there had been no Harry,' she repeated her own words. 'It rather looks as if that's the way it's going to be, doesn't it?'

'Put him to the test,' Aubrey said urgently. 'If Madeleine's been talking a load of rot, Harry isn't going to let you go just like that. He'll say your change of mind is due to his fault for neglecting you. I would, and then I'd do everything I could to win you back.'

'And if he is in love with Madeleine, he'll agree it's probably right to break off our engagement. Perhaps he'll even tell me about the night he spent with her,' she added bitterly.

'You mustn't jump to conclusions,' Aubrey said loyally. 'I've known Harry nearly all my life and he's straight down the line.'

'You love him too, don't you?' Cora-Beth murmured.

'Unfortunately,' Aubrey said with a sigh. 'If he wasn't my best friend, I'd have put up a fight for you weeks – months ago. You're the only girl I've ever met that I've wanted to marry. Did you mean what you said just now – about if there had been no Harry, I might have had a chance?'

Cora-Beth nodded.

'Perhaps in a way, I did mean it. There's so much about you that's lovable,' she said gently. 'You're the kindest, most thoughtful, considerate person I know. In lots of ways, you're more sensitive than Harry. Half the time I

493

don't think he notices what I'm thinking, feeling, whereas you always do. You know, Aubrey, I think Harry and I got off on the wrong foot. He wasn't really interested in me when we first met and I saw that as a kind of challenge. I found him fascinating and just so attractive. I wanted him to notice me, as a woman, but I was just Poppa's daughter – a good friend. In the end he did notice me, but I doubt if he would have done if I hadn't made the pace.'

'Only because he went out to the States still carrying a torch for Madeleine,' Aubrey said quietly. 'If I were in his shoes . . . well, I can only say I wish to God I were! I suppose I should congratulate myself for hiding my feelings so successfully until now. That night I took you to the Embassy and held you in my arms while we were dancing, I was sure you'd guessed.'

'Oh, Aubrey, I really am sorry. It must have been horrible for you – Poppa and Harry pressing you to escort me all the time. They made you into a sort of proxy fiancé, didn't they?'

Aubrey smiled.

'Believe me, I loved every minute I was with you. The difficult part has been hiding my envy of Harry. There were so many times when it seemed to me as if . . . well, as if he didn't quite appreciate how lucky he was. I was within inches of telling him so.'

Cora-Beth looked at him uneasily.

'Did you mean what you said just now? That you wouldn't mind if I told him how you feel?'

'Why should I be ashamed of the fact that I'm in love with you?' Aubrey said quietly. 'It's the truth – although if you intend to carry out this charade, the bit about you wondering whether you might be growing too fond of me is stretching it, to say the least.'

'I am fond of you – and if I can convince him, it's the only way for me to find out how Harry feels. I've got to know, Aubrey. He and I can't go back home as if nothing had changed. Oh, I wish . . . I *wish* Madeleine hadn't told me.'

'She'd no right to do so,' Aubrey said angrily. 'Pickles never did know when to keep her mouth shut. It was for Harry to speak out – not her.'

'You mustn't be cross with her, Aubrey,' Cora-Beth said reproachfully. 'Don't forget that she only spoke out for *my* sake.'

Aubrey remained silent. Privately, he doubted very much whether his young sister was capable of such altruism. He felt a sudden sweeping pity for Dunbar. He'd been such a jolly, good-natured, likeable fellow. It wasn't much of a memorial to him for his widow to be lining up a replacement husband within weeks of his death!

'When will you talk to Harry?' he asked. 'He'll be down at any minute. Do you want me to make myself scarce?'

'No, don't go. Poppa will be here soon too, so I shan't say anything until after the show. Aubrey . . .' she looked at him in sudden desperate appeal, '. . . if things go the way I think they might, I couldn't bear to go on seeing Harry. I'd want to go straight back home, but I know Poppa would be terribly disappointed. Would it be . . . well, would it be awful of me to ask if you . . . that we could extend the pretence to Poppa? He wouldn't be nearly so upset if he believed *I* was the one who was breaking off the engagement – because of you, I mean.'

Despite Cora-Beth's embarrassment as she made this request – perhaps to relieve it – Aubrey gave his quiet laugh.

'If Harry opts out, you wouldn't be able to keep me away if you tried,' he said. 'I should tell your father outright what my intentions were – strictly honourable, I might say. I shall also curry favour with him in the hope that he'll invite me out to Kentucky again.'

Cora-Beth managed a smile although there were tears in her eyes as she said, 'If Poppa doesn't invite you, I will, Aubrey. You're one of the nicest people I know and I'm just so grateful I know you.'

'Here's Harry and your father now,' Aubrey said. 'And don't worry – you're looking gorgeous and no one will suspect there's anything wrong.'

'Sorry we're late,' Harry said as he approached them and stooped to drop a kiss on top of Cora-Beth's head. 'How's things, Aubrey?'

Somehow, Harry thought, he must not let Cora-Beth see how utterly miserable he felt. He must keep up a semblance of *bonhomie* and force himself to enjoy the evening. If only he could stop thinking about Madeleine . . . but Aubrey was bound to talk about her and it was going to be the most difficult thing in the world to pretend a lack of interest in what he said.

'I think my mother is going to take Madeleine to Brighton next week, sir,' Aubrey was even now replying to Wendell's polite enquiry about his sister. 'Understandably she's a bit depressed, and the mater thinks the sea air will do her good.'

So Madeleine was as unhappy as he was, Harry thought. Now, according to Aubrey, she was leaving London and it was unlikely that he would see her again before he returned to the States. Aware of Cora-Beth's questioning gaze fastened on him, he looked away quickly, hoping against hope that she would not choose this night to come to his room in a quest for love. If she were to do so, he was very far from sure if he could keep up the pretence any longer.

In a desperate attempt to revive some kind of love for her, he reached out and took her hand.

Jules Bellaire regarded Alice thoughtfully. As always, she was looking very beautiful, but tonight there was an air of repressed excitement about her and he was curious to know the reason. She had spent the past twenty-four hours on and off the telephone and had left the *salon* two hours before closing time – unheard of for Alice. When he returned to the flat, she had already concocted a simple supper for them both and, hurrying through it, had said she wished to talk to him.

Now that they were sitting opposite one another, however, a tray of coffee between them, she seemed in no hurry to open the conversation. Did it perhaps concern

Monsieur Félix, he wondered? She had never before discussed her relationship with *le Maître*, although he knew it had long since ceased to be a working partnership only. Alice had never tried to conceal it and must know that he, Jules, was aware of the situation. For one thing, *le Maître* never arrived at the flat without having already advised Jules that he must find other accommodation during his visit.

Once or twice, it had been on the tip of Jules's tongue to ask Alice why she didn't marry the lover who had so much to offer her, but he respected Alice's right to privacy – as indeed, she had always respected his – and the question had never been asked. Now, perhaps, he would have an answer.

'Jules, I have something to tell you that may come as a bit of a shock,' Alice said into the silence. 'I'm leaving.'

'Leaving?' Jules repeated stupidly. 'You mean, to get married?'

For a moment, there was a look of such wistfulness in Alice's eyes that he wished the question unasked.

'No, not that. But I have made up my mind to leave the Maison de Verveine and I'm going to live in Leicestershire.'

'Leicestershire! Where in the name of heaven is that?' Jules asked incredulously. He knew his way around Europe now, but not around the country he lived in.

'It's in the Midlands,' Alice said smiling. 'I shall be living in a big country house miles from anywhere. Actually, that is not quite true. It's near a little market town called Melton Mowbray.'

Jules shrugged his shoulders helplessly.

'I do not understand,' he said simply. 'If you had told me you were leaving to marry Monsieur Félix . . . No, Alice, this sounds *tout à fait fou!*'

'Perhaps it is,' Alice said quietly. 'You know, Jules, many years ago when I first went to work for Monsieur Félix, he said something to me which I've never forgotten. He said that if one is to reach for a star, it should be for the brightest star in the sky. Well, that's what I'm doing,

Jules. I am risking everything that I have for what I truly want.'

Jules leant back in his chair and ran his carefully manicured hands through his dark hair. Realizing at once that he had disarranged it, he smoothed it down again before heaving a deep sigh.

'This "reaching for a star",' he said. 'I am no wiser, *chère* Alice.'

'Harry is my star. You know I've always loved him – always! It's also true to say that he has never loved me. Knowing that, I opted to settle for the second-brightest star – my career. Now I've been given another chance. Harry's fiancée has broken off their engagement and he's not going back to America with her and her father. He's going to settle in England and do what he once dreamed of doing – start up a stud farm at Maythorpe House – the house in Leicestershire I just spoke about. I'm going to put the house in order for him and look after him.'

Jules's face crinkled in a slow smile.

'Ah, so now I begin to make sense of this nonsense. You will marry the man you love and live, as they say in fairy tales, happily ever after.'

There was no answering smile from Alice.

'That's what I would like, Jules, but the chances of such a thing happening are so small that no one but a woman as stupid as I would act on it. Harry is in love with his childhood sweetheart. She married someone else but the poor man was killed recently in a riding accident, so she's available once more. As she was only widowed a few weeks ago, it would not be proper for her and Harry to declare their love openly so soon, and it's to be kept a secret, even from her family, for the next six months. Harry has gone to live in his house in the Midlands and Madeleine is remaining with her parents. It was her family I used to work for as a young girl. In those days, before I went to Paris, I was her mother's personal maid.'

Jules's handsome face was marred by a frown.

'If it is your Harry's intention to marry this girl, what

hope have you that he will change his mind a second time and marry you?'

Alice gave a helpless shrug of her shoulders.

'None that I can justify. I just know I have to go to Maythorpe House and look after him. He needs someone.'

Jules scowled.

'He has no right to use you, Alice. He should employ a housekeeper if he cannot look after himself.'

'That's exactly what he intended to do until I talked him out of it.' Alice smiled. 'It took some doing. He thinks, as you do, that I'm quite mad.'

'It *is* madness, Alice. What about the *salon*? Monsieur will never permit you to take six months' leave and then return, and who will run the *salon* if you go?'

Alice's smile broadened.

'Why, you will, Jules. Monsieur told me not long ago that he was considering putting you in charge. He wanted me to go to Milan to run the new *salon* there, but I refused. You're more than capable of doing my job, as well you know. You managed perfectly well when I was away while my mother was so ill, and that time I was laid up with pleurisy.'

'I am not so sure,' Jules said with a modesty both knew was false. 'And what has Monsieur to say about this – this crazy scheme of yours?'

Alice clasped her hands together and stared at them, frowning.

'That's my biggest concern. I haven't told him. I don't know how I'm going to find the courage to do so. He . . . he's been so good to me. Even after all this time, he still proposes marriage every time he comes to London. I hate the thought that I'll be hurting him.'

Jules's eyes narrowed as he stared thoughtfully at Alice's anxious face. He seemed to be having a battle with himself before finally he spoke.

'I know that many people think men like me gossip as women do. It isn't true – at least not where I am concerned. Now I think the situation demands that I tell you something I have known for some time but have not seen fit to relate to you. Monsieur has been having an affair with one of the Italian *mannequins* in Milan. Oh, I don't doubt that it is you he loves, but it is not in his nature, I think, to be faithful. I hope this does not shock you, Alice.'

Alice's eyes had widened.

'It hurts my pride, perhaps, but not my heart. Are you certain of this, Jules?'

'But *certainement!*' Jules said, breaking into French as he sometimes did when he was excited or wished to be emphatic. 'I was told it by the girl herself when I was in Milan last spring. Her name is Lucia and she is very beautiful – but very stupid. She does not have a fraction of your intelligence, Alice. Monsieur will never marry her.'

'Well, thank you for telling me,' Alice said quietly. 'That will make it easier for me, although I shan't, of course, confess to Monsieur Félix that I know about his mistress. I can't say I blame him. I've never been very . . . how shall I put it? . . . enthusiastic about that side of our relationship. I'm truly fond of him, though, and I owe him so much, I hated the idea of hurting him.'

'So I am glad I told you,' Jules remarked. 'But Alice, are you quite sure this is the right way? That is to say, what will you do if your Harry remains in love with this other woman and marries her? You cannot continue to live in his house with them.'

'No, that I could never do,' Alice admitted. 'I shall come back to London and open a little shop of my own . . . but not for clothes. I don't have the capital to consider a *couture* house, but as you know, I have often told *le Maître* that we should have a place where our clients can buy all their accessories. If Monsieur will allow me, I could open such an establishment not too far from the *salon*. It would complement the Maison and I would not be in competition.'

Jules nodded.

'I see you have thought of everything,' he said. 'That is typical of you, Alice. It is not such a bad idea, although I think this will present certain hardships for you.'

'I know that. For one thing, I couldn't go on living in this expensive flat. It belongs to Monsieur, as you know. I would try to find a small shop with living accommodation above it.'

'From everything you are saying, I suspect you believe this is where your future lies,' Jules said perceptively. 'You don't really believe you can catch and hold your "brightest star".'

'I can hope, can't I?' Alice said fiercely. 'It certainly will not drop down from the sky into my lap. I must fight for what I want – and that's what I'm going to do. If I lose, at least I will have tried!'

Jules stood up and, crossing the room, laid his hand on her shoulder.

'In so far as it is possible for me to love any woman, I love you, Alice. I shall miss you when you go, and I shall try not to wish that you will come back. Although I am a lapsed Catholic, I shall pray for your happiness and I shall go to church and light candles for you.'

There were tears in Alice's eyes as gently he squeezed her shoulder. Covering his hand with her own, she said, 'I hope you find happiness too, Jules. You've been my friend ever since that day I walked into the *salon* in Paris, and I hope you will always be so.'

Jules gave a loud sniff.

'If we remain here talking in this fashion, I shall burst into tears,' he said. 'It's not very late, Alice. Let us go out and find somewhere where we can drink to the future – to yours and mine.'

Why not, Alice thought? Tomorrow, Félix was arriving from Paris and the die would be cast. Hopefully, Félix would not expect her to remain too long at the *salon* after he knew her intentions. Jules needed no instruction to take over. Harry had already departed to Melton Mowbray and was staying at the George Hotel until Maythorpe House could be staffed and made habitable. In the meanwhile, all he wished to concern himself with was preparing the stables for his horses.

As Alice put on her coat and hat and followed Jules out

of the apartment, the look of excited expectancy had returned to her face. At least for the time being there would be no Madeleine to distract Harry. It would all be as, so many years ago, they had planned – the two of them on their own, Harry supporting them and Alice looking after him. She could not wait to begin.

CHAPTER THIRTY

1926-7

Madeleine had never looked lovelier, Harry thought as he regarded her across the table in Fortnum and Mason's restaurant. Her eyes were bright with an excitement only barely contained while they had eaten their lunch. She had come up from Brighton for their first meeting since the Harveys had returned to Kentucky, although she would have come sooner had Harry not vetoed the idea. He had wanted to wait until his engagement to Cora-Beth was formally broken, and this was not done until after she and her father had returned from Ireland, where Miss Hanworth had taken them on a personally conducted tour.

Harry had not gone with them; nor, indeed, had Aubrey. The break would give Cora-Beth time to sort out her feelings, she'd told Harry, and she would make a firm decision one way or another before she came back to London.

'I can't see why she's finding it so difficult to choose between you and Aubrey,' Madeleine had said on the telephone. 'She must know who she's in love with.'

That Cora-Beth finally chose Aubrey came as no surprise to Harry, and he was hard put to conceal his relief. They had parted without acrimony, promising to remain friends and to exchange visits whenever possible, and Wendell had generously offered Harry the continued use of Maythorpe House for as long as he wished. Aubrey's reaction had been somewhat ambiguous.

'Naturally I'm over the moon for myself,' he'd said, 'but I hope you know what you're doing, old boy. Much as I love Pickles, I really can't see her making the perfect little wife, whereas Cora-Beth . . .'

'I've been in love with your sister ever since I can remember,' Harry had interrupted, 'and I can't imagine myself ever falling out of love with her. She's all I want.'

Everything I've ever wanted, he thought now, reaching for her hand surreptitiously beneath the tablecloth.

'I wish we didn't have to wait so long to get married,' Madeleine said in a soft voice. 'I'll never be able to survive without you until next year.'

'Silly girl,' Harry chided her. 'Another few weeks and it will be Christmas, then New Year and we'll be into 1927. Now don't keep me in suspense any longer. What's this splendid news you say you have for me?'

Madeleine squeezed his hand and laughed.

'It's the most amazing piece of luck, Harry darling. Evelyn Pierce telephoned me the day before yesterday – you don't know her, but I've told her all about you! Anyway, she and her husband and half a dozen of their friends are going to Biarritz next week. Evelyn absolutely loathes the winter in England and so they've bought a villa there, and a yacht so they can sail round the Mediterranean, and Harry, *she's invited us to go with them*. I've been dying to tell you but I wanted to see your face when you heard the news. Isn't it just too, too marvellous?'

Seemingly unaware of Harry's expression of dismay, she went on, 'Just think, darling, three whole months without Mummy and Daddy breathing down our necks. Evelyn's terribly modern and she says we can have adjoining rooms and no one will care what we do. Of course, I didn't dare tell Mummy and Daddy you'd be going too, but they won't know so they can't make a fuss. They're so stupidly conventional.'

For the first time, she became aware of Harry's frown.

'What's the matter, darling?' she asked. 'You're not going to be stuffy too, are you?'

Harry was effectively silenced. The last thing he wished to be thought by Madeleine was 'stuffy', yet instinctively he disliked the need for secrecy. As soon as Cora-Beth had

504

freed him from their engagement, he had wanted to go straight to Madeleine's parents and tell them of their plans to marry. Madeleine wouldn't hear of it, declaring they'd have 'fifty fits' if they knew she'd got over Pogo so quickly. Nor would it be unreasonable of them, Harry had decided, since he too felt ill at ease courting Madeleine when poor Dunbar had died only two months ago.

This, however, was not his only reason for declining the invitation, as he tried now to explain. He was in the middle of meetings in Melton Mowbray with an architect and builders who were preparing plans and costings for the modernization and extension of the stables at Maythorpe House. Wendell Harvey was shipping his horses to England in February and the work must be completed by then. Moreover, if he and Madeleine were to be married next summer, work must begin soon on Maythorpe House. While Alice would be there to see to the refurbishing of the place, he must be present to make decisions regarding the modernization of the house itself.

'Don't you see, darling Madeleine, that I can't leave England for three whole months – or even three weeks!'

The excitement had left Madeleine's eyes and now she was scowling, her brows drawn down and her lips pursed.

'No, I don't see why your wretched horses have to come before me,' she declared. 'Anyway, why can't you ask Mr Harvey to keep them a bit longer? And who cares about Maythorpe House? We don't have to live there the moment we get married, do we? We could stay in London. We could rent a house and . . .'

'Madeleine, try to understand. Maythorpe House will be our home. As for the horses, it's going to take time to build up a really good stud and the sooner I can start the better. Besides, I can't impose on Mr Harvey – not now Cora-Beth and I . . . well, I wouldn't feel justified in asking any favours.'

'So you *are* being stuffy,' Madeleine said accusingly. 'Anyway, why can't you get a groom or someone to see to the wretched animals? Ever since Evelyn telephoned me, I've been counting on us being together. It isn't fair! I'm beginning to think you don't really love me at all.'

'Madeleine, please,' Harry said. 'Please try to understand. It isn't that I don't want to be with you – you know I do. If you stop to think about it, we wouldn't really be alone anyway, would we? I mean, I don't know any of your friends and to be perfectly honest, I don't much go for the idea of having to sneak in and out of your room as if we were . . . well, as if we were criminals. I want everything to be perfect for us – a real honeymoon where we're by ourselves and married and . . . please say you understand.'

Madeleine tossed her head.

'Well, if you want me to be honest, I don't. It's a wonderful chance and it'll be enormous fun. Evelyn's parties always are. We can play tennis and bathe and dance, and they'll have charades and fancy dress parties and they've masses of other friends who go out there for the winter. I shan't want to go if you don't come with me.'

Tears had welled up in her eyes and Harry stared at her aghast.

'Please, dearest Madeleine, don't cry. I'd do anything to please you but things are already under way at Maythorpe and I can't cancel everything at this last minute. Perhaps if I'd known about it sooner . . .'

'I don't think it would have made the slightest difference,' Madeleine said accusingly. 'It's the horses, I know it is. Aubrey said you never thought about anything else. Well, perhaps you should have married that stupid American girl after all.'

'You mustn't say that. You know I love you. Anyway, darling, surely you want to see a bit more of your parents? They'll certainly want to see more of you. After all, you've been abroad for the past two years and . . .'

'If you think I'm going to sit at home with Mummy and Daddy and twiddle my thumbs for the next six months, you're very much mistaken. Evelyn said there'll be several other unattached men in the party, and if you won't come as my *vis-à-vis*, then one of them can partner me. I'm not going to be a wallflower if that's what you're hoping.'

506

For a moment, Harry hesitated. Was he being silly? Was he being unfair to Madeleine? One thing he was certain about was that he didn't like the idea of some other unattached man flirting with her. She was so pretty, she would certainly be one of the most popular girls in any party. On the other hand, it would perhaps be easier to face the next few months without her if distance separated them. She was such a darling, impulsive girl, and it was for him to protect her reputation, even if she disregarded it herself. If she were to stay in England, how long would it be before she travelled up to Maythorpe to see him? And then they would of a certainty be unable to behave properly!

To his dismay, Madeleine was now on her feet.

'I think you're perfectly horrible,' she said. 'I'm going straight home and you can go back to that stupid old house of yours. Who wants to live in it anyway, stuck out in the wilds!'

'But Madeleine . . .' Harry protested. 'You promised to come with me to tea with Lady Merstam. She's longing to meet you and . . .'

'And she can go on longing,' Madeleine interrupted. 'I don't want to meet her and I only said I'd go to please you, so why should I, when you don't care in the least about pleasing me?'

Harry paid the bill and they left in silence, sitting side by side in the back of the taxi Madeleine insisted should take her straight to Victoria Station. He was appalled by their quarrel and could think of no way to put things right. It was Madeleine who finally softened. Edging closer to him in the back of the cab, she said, 'I'll be leaving in a fortnight's time. I suppose you'll be far too busy to miss me.'

Immediately, Harry put his arms round her.

'My darling Madeleine, there won't be a single moment when I shall not be missing you. You've simply no idea quite how much I love you. When Cora-Beth told me she'd decided that it was Aubrey she loved more than me, I could have shouted with joy and relief. I'd been so afraid

I was going to lose you for ever. Tell me you do love me, that you will be faithful to me?'

He felt her body soften in his embrace.

'Of course I will, silly,' she said. 'I'm just terribly disappointed, that's all. I kept thinking how marvellous it would be – being together, I mean. I want us to be together all the time.'

'You can't want it as much as I do,' Harry said huskily as she raised her face for his kiss. Neither was aware that the cab had pulled up in the station concourse until the driver, grinning, pointed out the fact. Despite having made up their quarrel, Madeleine would not change her mind about going to tea with Lady Merstam. Relieved to be on good terms with her once more, Harry did not press the point, although he was disappointed, and embarrassed, when later he was obliged to make excuses to his aunt.

Despite his conviction that he had done the right thing in refusing to join Madeleine and her friends in Biarritz, Harry was very lonely in the big, empty house during the remaining weeks before Christmas. As he had anticipated, he was kept busy enough during the day, but in the evenings when he'd not been invited out to dinner by those few of his neighbours he had now met, he wished Alice were there to keep him company. She had tendered her notice to Monsieur Verveine but would not be free to move up to Melton Mowbray until after Christmas.

Alice wanted him to join her in Calking to share Christmas Day with the family, but much as he would have liked to do so, he felt instinctively that he might spoil their fun. The younger members had all but forgotten he used to be part of the family and tended to 'Yes, sir!' and 'No, sir' him, and to behave as if he were the visiting vicar or doctor. Not even Will Pritchett seemed at ease with him, for the old man had become vague and confused since Martha had died and was inclined to stare at him as if he were a stranger.

When Bertie Alcott invited him to spend Christmas in London with his family, Harry readily accepted and wrote at once to ask Lady Merstam if he might take the opportunity to call and see her on Boxing Day. Her reply by return of post made clear to him her pleasure in his proposal.

When the day came, Cynthia Merstam welcomed him with an unaccustomed show of warmth. Looking at the bright, animated face of her nephew, she wished very much that she could share his confidence in the future he was outlining. Although they had met only twice since the fateful day when she had told him about his mother, she had become far fonder of him than she permitted herself to indicate. When he had called to see her earlier in the month, she'd experienced a renewed joy in life which had been sadly absent since poor Dorothy died.

Harry was sitting quietly, leaning towards her, his hands held loosely between his knees. His dark eyes were alight with pleasure as he fingered the monogrammed gold cuff links she had given him as a Christmas present. Realizing how happy he was, Cynthia could not bring herself openly to express her misgivings.

'I'm quite well acquainted with Madeleine's mother,' she said. 'The Debraces struck me as being a very nice family. How fortuitous that your fiancée discovered her feelings for their son, just when you realized you still loved Madeleine.'

Harry gave his quick, boyish smile.

'I know. Wasn't it an amazing coincidence? Of course, Aubrey and Cora-Beth spent a great deal of time alone together after we came to England in September. I now know Aubrey fell in love with her ages ago in Kentucky but, being my friend and the decent sort of chap he is, he kept his feelings to himself. I'm pretty sure they'll end up getting married.'

'So when do you intend to marry Madeleine?'

Harry looked uneasy.

'I don't suppose the wedding can be much before next autumn. It depends on her family. Her parents will expect a decent sort of interval before she marries again. It's difficult for both of us – having to wait, I mean – but in a way, it's probably a good thing. Maythorpe House is badly in need of modernizing and redecoration, and Alice Pritchett – the girl I grew up with who I call my foster-sister – is going to help me to get the house ready. Alice is wonderful at that kind of thing. She was always the capable one of the family. Quite apart from doing up the house, I'll be pretty tied up in the New Year, getting my stud farm going. Your nice friend, Miss Hanworth, has promised to come and give me the benefit of her experience, although I understand Mr Harvey has invited her to Blue Ash Farm for a holiday in the spring.'

He gave a mischievous grin.

'Do you know, Lady Merstam, it wouldn't surprise me one bit to hear Miss Hanworth decides to stay out there? I wouldn't put it past Mr Harvey to marry again. He and Miss Hanworth seem to get on like a house on fire.'

'So I understand,' Cynthia said dryly, having heard from Jennifer Hanworth her side of the story. 'But returning to your affairs, Harry, am I not right in thinking Alice Pritchett is the girl who did so well in the *couture* business? I thought she was running the Maison de Verveine here in London?'

Harry raised his eyebrows in an unconscious gesture of reflection that was a replica of his mother's. It caused Cynthia to let out her breath in a nostalgic sigh.

'Well, she was, but she resigned a few weeks ago. She's going to start up her own business when Madeleine and I are married. Alice and I have always been very close, although we haven't seen a great deal of each other these past few years, with me in America and Alice either in Paris or London.'

'I'd be very interested to meet her,' Cynthia said. 'Perhaps I could invite her to tea while you're still in London, Harry?'

'I'd have enjoyed that, but she went down to Sussex to be with the family over Christmas. She wanted me to go too, but I thought I might spoil their fun. The fact is, I think I embarrass them now, which I find very sad.'

'It's understandable,' Cynthia said, thinking how very

aristocratic Harry looked, despite the rather unkempt appearance of his suit and the pulled thread hanging from one of his waistcoat buttons. His hair too had a somewhat windswept look, the dark curls refusing to lie flat. No one could conceivably have taken this tall, upright young man as a gardener's son. In the past few years his resemblance to Gervaise had become even more marked. How Dorothy would have loved Harry! How tragic it was that her sister had never met him.

'You will bring Madeleine to see me as soon as she returns to England, won't you?' she said. 'I was so sorry not to see her last time you came to tea.'

Harry nodded, the happy expression on his face giving way to a frown.

'I'm afraid it won't be for ages yet,' he said. 'She doesn't think they'll return before March at the earliest.'

Even as he spoke, he half regretted telling his aunt of his plans to marry Madeleine. Only Alice and Aubrey knew of their intentions. Now Lady Merstam knew too, although he believed she would keep his private affairs confidential.

He not only trusted but had grown to like Lady Merstam, who, he sensed, was very lonely. He had suggested he should spend Boxing Day with her from a sense of obligation, but now he was enjoying the company of this quiet, reserved woman, who, he kept having to remind himself, was his aunt. He had not forgotten that it was due to her confidence in him that he was now in a financial position not only to get his own stud started in earnest but to marry Madeleine.

He had succeeded in regaining his sense of proportion regarding Madeleine's holiday in Biarritz and, as he had just told Lady Merstam, it had been more than a little selfish of him to expect the poor girl to remain at home with her parents when such a lovely holiday would help to take her mind off her recent tragedy.

'I had a letter from Madeleine yesterday,' he said now, a smile once more lighting up his face. 'She says they're having a wonderful time. I'm trying not to be jealous, because there are several unattached males in the party so she's never without an escort or a dancing partner. Not that that surprises me. She's such a lovely girl! Quite tiny, but with the most beautiful blue eyes and ash-blonde hair.'

'Then you will make a very handsome couple,' Cynthia said. 'Is Madeleine as interested in horses as you are, Harry?'

He shook his head.

'I can't honestly say she is, although she's a marvellous rider and she has said she will take up hunting again once we're married. Lots of her London friends go to Leicestershire for the hunting season, and so once she's back in the thick of it, there'll be plenty of parties, which she loves. I'm very anxious that she shouldn't feel lonely up there, as I'm counting on her settling down in the country.'

And what if she does not? Cynthia asked herself.

It was a question Alice too asked herself three months later, as she put a big, cut-glass vase of daffodils on the sofa table in the drawing-room of Maythorpe House and stepped back to survey them with a critical eye. Were they too harsh a yellow seen against the pale primrose linen with which she'd had the big sofa recovered? she wondered. Suppose Madeleine were to walk into the room and announce that she heartily disliked yellow and Alice's choice of furniture and, indeed, the transformation of the house itself? Suppose Madeleine were to declare that she had no intention of living here and was returning to London? It would break Harry's heart, for he thought of little else but what would please or displease her. He was determined to ensure that she would be happy here in Leicestershire.

The fact that Alice loved this room best of all was an irrelevance to Harry. His one concern was that Madeleine would approve of it. Surely she couldn't help but do so, Alice thought. The big windows faced south over the garden and allowed the spring sunshine to flood the room with a lovely golden light. When she could find time, she liked nothing better than to fill it with spring flowers – although Harry rarely noticed them. He, as always, was down at the stables. He had made almost as many renovations there as she had in the house.

It was nearly two months now since Mr Harvey had shipped Harry's horses from Kentucky. Since then Harry had bought two English fillies and a second stallion. He now employed two men and six lads, four of whom lived in the rooms over the new stable block. It had been one of Alice's many tasks to furnish them and she had turned out all the unwanted, old-fashioned furniture in Maythorpe and made the stable accommodation comfortable and habitable without dipping too deeply into Harry's budget.

Harry seemed to have no idea how much it was costing to renovate his home, nor, Alice thought smiling, was he particularly interested in how she was accomplishing it.

'You're the one with the artistic eye,' he'd said. 'Madeleine says that whatever you choose will be fine with her. And don't bother about the cost, Alice. I want the house to be a wonderful surprise for her, and I can afford it. She hasn't seen it since I brought her here when I was home on holiday three years ago.'

He wanted Maythorpe to be as perfect as possible. He needed to ensure that once they were married, Madeleine would be less reluctant to leave London to live with him in Leicestershire.

In each of the last two letters he had received from her, she'd talked about buying a house in London and using Maythorpe House only as a country seat. 'We don't want to turn ourselves into dull old country bumpkins, do we, darling? I'm so glad you've found a good head man to manage the horses 'cos I want us to be together *as much as possible!*' He too wanted to spend as much time as he could in her company, but not, if he could avoid it, in London. Once she saw how comfortable and attractive Alice had made the house, she was certain to feel differently, he told himself.

It was perhaps as well that he'd been kept as busily occupied outside as Alice had been inside, he thought now as he walked up from the stables to the house for lunch. There'd been so much to do, he'd scarcely had time to mope. Alice had moved in immediately after Christmas and although Mrs Appleby was too old to be able to work, she was a frequent visitor, assisting Alice in choosing modern equipment for the kitchens and conducting interviews for kitchen staff. She'd proved invaluable since she knew many of the local families in and around Melton Mowbray whose girls were available for domestic duties.

Since Alice had never learned to drive a car, he'd taken time away from his horses to conduct her into Grantham, where she had ordered the materials she wanted. Never one to waste money, Alice had arranged for the old curtains and carpets to be refitted and used in the less important rooms while the main rooms were re-equipped and transformed.

During those long, cold winter evenings, they had made themselves cosy while the work was progressing, Alice curled up, Harry stretched out, in the basket chairs in Mrs Appleby's old sitting-room in front of a blazing fire. Like the two children they'd once been, they'd toasted muffins and played backgammon or cards, drunk steaming mugs of cocoa and filled themselves with Mrs Appleby's homemade fudge. Alice had discarded her smart London clothes and looked half her age in a simple blouse, cardigan and a thick tweed skirt. Her corn-coloured hair was caught back from her temples by a tortoiseshell slide and her face seemed to him to be rounder, fuller, as if country life suited her, and she had put on weight.

As he edged past two workmen who were laying electric cables beneath the hall floor, it occurred to Harry that during the ten weeks Alice had been living at Maythorpe House, he had never once heard her complain, although with the carpet layers, plasterers, decorators, plumbers and electricians hard at work, most of the house was permanently in a state of upheaval. The master bedroom and the drawing-room were completed to Alice's satisfaction and the dining-room almost so.

Quite soon now, Madeleine would be back in England and, according to the last postcard Harry had received from her, was intending to come up to Maythorpe for a weekend. When he'd told Alice this, it was the one time she had looked other than serene, smiling and content.

514

When he'd questioned her, it seemed that she'd not wanted Madeleine to see Maythorpe before it was entirely finished, but he'd laughed at her misgivings, pointing out that those rooms which were completed were quite enough to give Madeleine a clear idea of how lovely, and comfortable, her home was going to be.

Harry had, as always, gone down early to the stables, and it was not, therefore, until lunchtime that Alice handed him a letter brought by the postman during the morning. It was from Wendell Harvey. Harry pushed it across the table for Alice to read. It contained the very welcome news that Cora-Beth was well and enjoying life, that she had joined Aubrey in a skiing party of young people in Switzerland and Aubrey was going out to stay with them in the summer. Wendell hoped that Harry was settling down in his new life and that he was not too broken-hearted about Cora-Beth's change of mind. He wrote:

> Cora-Beth told me you had met up again with your childhood sweetheart and she seems to think the two of you will get married. If that happens my boy, I hope you will continue to live at Maythorpe House. I have always considered it your home rather than mine.
>
> It sure did grieve me when my daughter backed out of your engagement so suddenly, but now it looks as if it will all turn out for the best. I sure hope you'll be very happy.

'He sounds like a very nice man,' Alice commented as she handed back the letter.

Harry nodded.

'One of the best. You never met him, did you? I shall ask both him and Cora-Beth to the wedding, so you'll meet him then. Do you think the house will be finished by September? It's all taking so much longer than I'd expected. I don't want to leave the wedding any later or we shall be into October and I particularly want to sell

Dundee's foal at the yearling bloodstock auctions then. I'm pretty certain Madeleine will want to go abroad for our honeymoon, so I'm hoping I can arrange it for dates that will allow me to get back here by 2 October.'

Looking across the table at Harry's animated face, Alice's first thought was that Madeleine might have other plans and that Harry could be doomed to disappointment. Her heart felt heavy as she reflected how often Madeleine's name sooner or later came into their conversations. She couldn't bear to think how quickly time was speeding by; that all too soon this idyllic interlude would come to an end. Other than that she and Harry were as close now as they'd ever been and were living together in total harmony, she was no closer to his heart.

As always, she remained his companion, his friend, his confidante, and she had failed completely to make him see her as a woman. He talked happily about the future when he and Madeleine were married and she, Alice, was running her own little establishment in London. If occasionally he said, 'Of course, I'll miss you dreadfully,' his tone did not really sound regretful – and why should it, if he had the girl he loved beside him?

Two days later Harry passed another letter to Alice to read.

'It's from Madeleine,' he said, his dark eyes shining. 'She'll be coming home the week after next, and Aubrey is going to bring her here for a weekend party with some of her Biarritz friends. She wants to make it an engagement party – informal, of course, because of Dunbar.'

He paused briefly while Alice read Madeleine's large, untidy scrawl and then said eagerly, 'Will we have any of the guest rooms ready? Will you be able to cope with it all, Alice? I know we're managing with only a skeleton staff but we could get some extra help from the village. There'll be twelve altogether, including Madeleine and ourselves.'

Alice's voice was carefully controlled as she said quietly, 'I don't think you should count me as one of the party. I'm here as your housekeeper. Really, I'd rather not be present.'

Harry gave a loud laugh.

'I never heard anything so silly in my life. You're my sister!' He laughed again. 'And don't pretend you can't be the perfect hostess. I'm not ignorant of the fact that you used to entertain for Monsieur Verveine when he gave private parties for his friends at his château.'

To his consternation, a deep flush spread over Alice's cheeks.

Realizing that he had unintentionally embarrassed her, Harry was now feeling more than a little awkward. The last thing he had meant was to infer that Alice had been Félix Verveine's mistress, yet now he couldn't help but wonder if Aubrey had been right when he'd suspected that this was their relationship. Hoping to rectify his possible gaffe, he said, 'Monsieur Verveine once asked you to marry him, didn't he?'

Alice nodded.

'But you turned him down?'

'For several reasons . . . not least because I don't love him.'

'Then he must have been pretty fed up when you left him to come up here to keep house for me.'

'I don't think he was particularly surprised,' Alice said, in control of her voice once more. 'Anyway, he's interested in someone else now – an Italian girl – so let's forget him, shall we?'

'Willingly,' Harry replied, 'but I'm not going to let you back out of this party, Alice, and that's a fact. If anyone deserves to enjoy themselves, you do. You've worked like a navvy since you've been here, and without a break. Now promise you won't do a disappearing act or I shall write and tell Madeleine the party's not on.'

It was almost with a feeling of relief that Harry returned to his horses. He was not, he decided, very good at analysing female behaviour. He had been astounded when Cora-Beth had announced that she was returning his ring. He'd known that she liked Aubrey immensely and that they'd always got along extremely well, but it hadn't crossed his mind a deeper emotion might have developed.

If Cora-Beth had surprised him, so too had Madeleine, when he'd refused to accompany her to the south of France. He'd expected her to understand that he had far too many genuine commitments even to consider going abroad for three months. Equally confusing had been Alice's announcement that, if he was going up to Leicestershire to open Maythorpe House, she was going with him. Her explanation that she intended leaving the *salon* anyway in order to start up on her own had sounded plausible, yet he'd not forgotten Cora-Beth's suspicions that Alice was in love with him. Not that he had believed it, still less so since Alice had never given him the slightest reason to suppose it could be true. Before he had given his assent to her suggestion – which naturally appealed to him enormously – he'd tried and failed to answer his own doubts, and finally he had simply put them to one side.

Alice's plan had worked smoothly and without a single hitch. These past months had been extremely happy – to all appearances, for Alice as well as for himself. She was enjoying the creativity of the task of renovation, she'd told him, which was proving so much more rewarding than selling designer clothes to wealthy clients. Now, annoyingly, she was spoiling everything by being ridiculously touchy.

'Why don't you admit the truth, Alice, you don't like Madeleine and you don't care if she knows it?' he said bluntly when they resumed the discussion at teatime. 'You never did approve of her, did you? I simply don't understand what you've got against her, and I'm certainly not going to sit back and let you snub her.'

Alice's mouth fell open and then closed again as she realized that Harry had no idea how far he was from the truth in supposing she, Alice Pritchett, intended to snub Madeleine. Her reluctance to be included in the house-party was due entirely to her wish to avoid a snub *from* Madeleine! Harry had clearly forgotten she'd once been Lady Debrace's maid. Dangerously close to tears, she said quietly, 'If you're quite sure you want me around, I'll be there.'

It was on the tip of her tongue to suggest he ask Madeleine first if it was what *she* wanted, but suddenly she was filled with a spirit of defiance. When she'd decided to give up her job and come to Maythorpe with Harry, she'd told Jules it was in the hope, however small, of touching her 'brightest star'. These last three months had brought her no nearer to that goal. The closeness of their day-to-day companionship had not altered to even the smallest degree the direction of Harry's thoughts, or the intensity of his love for Madeleine. Quite simply, he never saw her as other men did. She was his friend, his sister. That was now about to change, she decided as she made her way along the passage to one of the smaller bedrooms she had appropriated for herself. She would *make* Harry see her differently.

Half angrily, half in desperation, Alice opened the doors of her wardrobe and rifled through the dresses hanging there. She had brought with her to Maythorpe only one or two of her Verveine models. Those she had were still fashionable, for Félix's designs were always in advance of the styles of the day. Her eye caught the delicate shades of the oyster-pink crêpe de Chine evening dress with the diaphanous russet-caped bodice. It was the most feminine of all the gowns Félix had designed with her in mind, and the one in which, he maintained, she looked irresistible.

Undressing quickly, Alice slipped the gown over her head and stared at her reflection in the cheval mirror. She would change her hairstyle too, she thought – draw it back behind her ears so that it lay sleek against her head. By doing so, it would enhance her long neck and high cheekbones, and even if it made her look older, the effect would be one of extreme elegance.

Replacing the dress in the cupboard, Alice went to her chest of drawers and withdrew a purple leather jewel case. Félix had refused to allow her to return his gifts when she'd said goodbye to him, and she had agreed to keep them as mementoes of their years together. Taking out the long, *pliqué-à-jour* necklace, she fastened it round her throat, allowing the colourful enamel links to slip between her breasts.

At least, she now thought wryly, her affair with Félix had given her confidence in herself as a woman. He had made her aware of her body and its powers to give and receive love. He had taught her many things about herself, not least that she had no need ever to play the coquette. According to him, her attraction lay in her serenity, her air of mystery, that unconscious habit she had of leaning forward with her head tilted a little to one side while she listened to what was being said to her.

Dear Félix, she thought. They'd had many happy times together and she would always be grateful to him. She was glad that although he had professed his heart was broken when they'd said goodbye, he had already found the Italian girl to comfort him. Not that he had taken his *congé* as final. With that engaging smile of his, he had kissed her, saying, 'One day you will return to me, Alice, and I shall be waiting. One day, you will become my wife.'

'I believe he truly does love you,' Jules had commented as he'd helped her to pack, 'but you will not want to think of this now. *Nom de Dieu*, Alice, this Harry of yours must be a blind man not to realize what he is overlooking.'

Well, she would not allow Harry to 'overlook' her any more, Alice thought as she put the necklace back in its case. He would see a different Alice on the night of Madeleine's arrival with her friends. If for no other reason than that she was utterly different from the Alice he was used to, he would *have* to notice her. She would take her place beside him as his hostess, and if Madeleine was jealous, Harry would have no one but himself to blame.

There was absolutely no doubt in Alice's mind that it had been Madeleine's intention to come between Harry and his fiancée, that it was not by chance she had turned up at the *salon* and asked Alice to introduce her to Cora-Beth. Harry was convinced it was no more than an amazing coincidence when Cora-Beth suddenly switched her allegiance to Aubrey, but the notion had cut no ice with her, Alice. A woman about to marry the man for whom she'd waited so long was unlikely to have such an abrupt change of heart – and one that coincided so aptly with Madeleine's unexpected return to England and her timely widowhood.

There was no proving such suspicions, Alice realized, and even if she had such proof, Harry would be unlikely to condemn Madeleine. He appeared to have forgotten that she'd come close to breaking his heart when she'd turned him down for a richer husband, that she'd only agreed to marry him when she realized he was now a wealthy man. Harry might believe Madeleine 'adored him', as it seemed she was always protesting in her letters, but she hadn't loved him enough to think twice about going abroad for three months without hope of seeing him during that time. Nor had she cared that another woman was choosing how her future home was to be arranged.

'Madeleine has every confidence in you, Alice,' Harry explained. 'After all, you are the artistic one. Madeleine says her mother always maintained you'd been born with natural good taste and a perfect colour sense. It's very sensible of her to hand the décor over to you – and I know you love doing it. I told Madeleine you would.'

Yes, she had loved making a beautiful home for Harry, but this sweet pill had the bitterest of centres. Her creation was for him to share with another woman. Just as all the loveliest gowns she'd designed had always been for other women to wear – women like Madeleine, rich, spoilt, ephemeral. How could Harry, who was so astute in other aspects of his life, be so blind to Madeleine's superficiality?

But not this time, Alice thought. Thanks to Félix's generosity, the Verveine gown was hers and she would wear it in a last ditch attempt to force Harry to acknowledge her not as a valued sister but as a woman he might love.

CHAPTER THIRTY-ONE

1927

'Alice, you look absolutely stunning,' Aubrey said, his voice warm with admiration as he stood up to greet her. The drawing-room was empty. Harry had gone down to the stables for a quick word with his head groom and Madeleine and her friends had not yet appeared.

'It is a lovely dress, isn't it?' Alice said, pleased with the effect of her appearance on Aubrey. It was obvious that for a moment he hadn't recognized her. 'It's a Verveine, needless to say.'

'Let me get you something to drink,' Aubrey offered with his easy good manners. 'Harry said there'll be champagne presently. He's just nipped down to the stables.'

Alice smiled.

'I think if he had his way, he'd move in there,' she said. 'As far as he's concerned, this house is only somewhere to eat and sleep.'

'But it's quite lovely,' Aubrey enthused. 'Pickles described it as "a gloomy old dump", but then you've been busy transforming it, I gather. I've never seen anyone look more surprised than Pickles when she arrived. You're to be congratulated, Alice.'

It was not Madeleine's face but Harry's which Alice had been watching when the first car-load of visitors had arrived at teatime. His gaze had been riveted on Madeleine as she ran across the room and threw herself into his arms. Her face bright with excitement, she had tossed her feather-trimmed, cloche hat on to the sofa and turned to the group of young people she had brought with her.

'Darlings, this is my beloved Harry,' she'd cried, clinging to his arm. Introducing him first to Verity, Helen, Evelyn, Charles and his twin, Christopher, she explained that Charles was Evelyn's husband and it was they who'd been her hosts in Biarritz. As an afterthought, she added, 'Oh, and by the way, everyone, this is Alice Pritchett. She's been doing the interior décor for Harry.'

Only the tall, thin young man called Christopher Pierce had bothered to talk to Alice, and as soon as the maid had brought in tea, she had slipped away to her room, the picture of Harry's adoring face tearing at her heartstrings. The old proverb 'absence makes the heart grow fonder' had been well proven in Harry's case, she told herself as she tried to rekindle her courage. Eventually the sight of the beautiful gown lying ready on the bed had given her the confidence to hold her head high as she went downstairs for the start of the evening's festivities. The fact that dear old Mrs Appleby was in the kitchen supervising the cook and the assortment of maids who had been employed for the weekend gave her further reassurance. Although the old woman was unable to work, she still had her wits about her and had assured Alice that tonight's dinner party would take place without mishap.

'Here's the old boy himself,' Aubrey broke in on her thoughts as the door opened and Harry came in. There were several wisps of hay clinging to his dinner jacket and instinctively Alice went forward to remove them.

For a moment, he stared at her in astonishment, then his eyes crinkled into a smile.

'Great Scott, Alice, I didn't recognize you,' he commented. 'You look . . . I don't know . . . different!'

'I think she looks absolutely stunning,' Aubrey said as Alice stood silent beneath Harry's appraising glance. 'She's going to outshine everyone else.'

'Yes, but where is everyone else?' Harry asked, glancing round the empty room. He was, Alice realized with a sinking heart, looking for Madeleine. The door opened and the tall, thin young man called Christopher Pierce came in. He went straight to Alice's side.

'Any time you want to revamp my house, Miss Pritchett, you have only to lift the telephone. Wherever did you find this beautiful lady, Keynes?' he said effusively.

'Alice is a dress designer, not an interior decorator,' Harry announced laughing. He linked his arm through Alice's. 'We two have known each other all our lives – in fact, we grew up together. Alice is my best friend – well, she and Debrace jointly.'

'Lucky you,' the young man said jocularly but with another admiring glance at Alice. 'By the way, Keynes, I gather congratulations are in order. Maddy let slip you two were engaged.'

'Well, not exactly. That's to say, only informally,' Harry corrected him. A manservant came into the room carrying a magnum of champagne in a silver ice bucket. He was followed by the five house guests, who already appeared to be in high spirits. Madeleine was among them. Dressed in ice-blue silk, she looked more than ever like a Dresden china figurine. Her ash-blonde hair was set in soft waves over her ears. Her small, rosebud mouth had been outlined in bright red. Having carefully guarded herself from the Mediterranean sun, her complexion was camellia white, accentuating the contrasting sapphire blue of her eyes. She broke away from her companions and, grasping Harry's arm, stared up at him questioningly.

'Do you like my dress, darling?' she asked. 'I bought it in Cannes especially to please you.'

'You look beautiful,' Harry said in a husky voice. He wished very much that she had not brought this crowd of friends with her. All he wanted was to be alone with her so that he could kiss her. With so many people around, he could see little hope of finding an opportunity to do so. He could feel her small, warm body pressed against his side and only with an effort did he tear himself away to perform his duties as a host.

Madeleine's attention turned to Christopher, who, being the only presentable bachelor in the holiday party, had acted as her escort. They had enjoyed a casual

524

flirtation and, inevitably because of their constant proximity, it had developed into a discreet affair. Christopher was rich and, being the older twin, heir to a title. For a little while, Madeleine had toyed with the idea of marrying him instead of Harry. Although she was not particularly attracted to him physically, his way of life was very similar to her own – a constant search for entertainment to pass the time. Far from exciting her, Harry's long letters had left her feeling depressed. There was far too much detail about the horses, in which she had little interest, and about the changes Alice was effecting in the house.

The sooner he understood that she, Madeleine, was unwilling to make Maythorpe their main home, the better it would be, although now, she thought as she glanced round the lovely pale-yellow drawing-room, she had to admit that the place made a very agreeable country house. She might buy a London house with some of the money she had inherited from Pogo and they could come up here for the season. Christopher, for one, had been very keen that she should invite him up for the hunting. So too had Charles and Evelyn. It could be fun, and now that she was with Harry once more, she was in no doubt that he was by far the most attractive man she knew. Christopher paled into insignificance and she wondered how she could ever have allowed him to share her bed.

Despite this change of attitude towards her holiday lover, she felt the onset of pique. Instead of fulfilling his promise to be 'sick as a dog with jealousy' seeing her with the man she was going to marry, Chris was hovering over Alice Pritchett in the most lascivious way. There was no denying that Alice had somehow transformed herself this evening. Madeleine was deeply envious of her lovely pink gown, although she knew it would not have suited her. But it was not just the dress – Alice's whole appearance was eye-catching, to say the least. There was almost a film-star quality about her, the effect of extreme elegance. She looked – Madeleine sought for the right word – she looked aristocratic, very much as if she belonged here in this room.

Perhaps Chris would be a little less bowled over if he knew Alice Pritchett's origins, Madeleine thought as, ignoring Charles who was raising his glass of champagne to her, she walked over to the couple.

'Gorgeous frock, Alice,' she said. 'Does Uncle Félix let you borrow his model gowns? Isn't he worried no one will buy them if they've been worn before?'

'Your uncle is a very generous employer,' Alice replied quietly. 'He thought the dress suited me and gave it to me as a present.'

Madeleine nodded.

'That explains it. They're so dreadfully expensive to buy, aren't they?'

The inference that Alice couldn't have afforded to buy her own dress was not lost upon her, nor upon Christopher. Bored now with Madeleine and very much smitten by the beautiful girl beside him, he said spitefully, 'I'd no idea your uncle was in trade, Madeleine.'

For a moment, Madeleine was speechless. Two angry red spots of colour stained her cheeks.

'And I'd no idea you could be so rude, Chris,' she retorted. 'As a matter of fact, my uncle is probably the most famous *couturier* in the world.'

Afraid that he might have created a bad impression on Alice, Christopher said placatingly, 'Come on, old thing, I was only joking. You know me.'

'Yes, and there are times when I wish I didn't,' Madeleine retorted tartly and, turning on her heel, walked away to join Harry, who was talking horses with Charles.

'Sorry about that,' Christopher said to Alice. 'Just thought Maddy was being a bit . . . well, unkind, if you know what I mean.'

Alice gave a wry smile.

'I don't suppose she meant it,' she said lightly. 'Anyway, Madeleine was quite right. I couldn't possibly afford to buy a Verveine dress. Even if I could, I wouldn't. I'm saving up to buy a small shop of my own. In a few months time, I shall be "in trade".'

Christopher looked a bit nonplussed, not quite sure if

this ravishingly beautiful woman was teasing him. He wondered exactly who she was. Obviously she had connections with Keynes, who, according to Madeleine, had family connections with the Earl of Kinmuire. It didn't fit in with the penniless state Alice was claiming for herself. He had no doubt that he wanted to see more of her. It was a long time since he'd felt so attracted by a woman, and she was refreshingly different from the bright young socialites with whom he usually mixed. He sensed there were depths to her which he found intriguing. She made him think of calm, clear water, soothing and, above all, feminine.

The second car-load of visitors, who had arrived late and were therefore late changing for dinner, now followed one another into the room, greeting Madeleine and their friends with much talk and laughter. Although Madeleine introduced them to Harry, to whose arm she was clinging possessively, she did not trouble to introduce Alice. A second young man – almost a prototype of Christopher – came across the room, an eager smile on his round, moon-like face as he said, 'Come on, Pierce, old boy – introduce me. Can't have you hogging the best-looking filly in the room, what?'

He beamed at Alice, aping a courtier-like bow.

'Someone said you were Keynes's sister. Can't say you resemble him, what? Dick Pennystone at your service.'

'Why don't you go away and bore someone else, Stoners,' Christopher said affably. 'And for your information, Miss Pritchett is not Keynes's sister. Now hop it while I try and seduce Miss Pritchett with my scintillating conversation.'

The fact that she now had two men vying for her attention did little to alleviate the pain in Alice's heart as she listened with one ear to Christopher's innocuous flirtation while watching Harry bend his head to catch something Madeleine was whispering in his ear. She saw the familiar bright, eager smile spread across his face and heard his soft laughter as Madeleine stood on tiptoe to straighten his bow tie.

Excusing herself, she slipped out of the room to go down to the kitchen for a quick, reassuring check with Mrs Appleby that the elaborate menu she had ordered had been prepared without mishap. The old cook quickly bustled her out of the big steamy kitchen.

'Lawks-a-mercy, Alice, m'duck,' she said, puffing with her exertions. 'You don't want that pretty dress of yourn all dirtied up. A sight for sore eyes, you are, and that's a fact. Reminds me of that portrait what used to hang in the dining-room – one of the Countesses of Kinmuire it were, name like yourn. Yes, that were Lady Annamarie – a French lady as married the tenth earl.'

Alice laughed.

'Really, Mrs Appleby, you're letting your imagination run away with you. I'm plain Alice Pritchett, the bedraggled little ladies' maid who had to hide in the pavilion with Harry, remember?'

'Them days is long gone,' Mrs Appleby said firmly. ''Tis the future you should be thinking about – yes, and Master Harry too. I'm just hoping that young flibbertigibbet he brought to lunch with me all them years ago has changed as much as you have, Alice. Getting theirselves engaged, Master Harry said, soon as it's decent. From the noise upstairs, it don't sound like there's much mourning being done for that poor husband of hern, God rest his soul.'

'Mrs Dunbar is still very young,' Alice said quickly. 'Now I'd best go back to the guests, Mrs Appleby. I can't tell you how grateful I am. You're a wonder.'

The old woman chuckled.

'Ain't nothing to it, m'duck. Was a time I'd cook for thirty or more – in the old earl's day, that were. Nine courses, counting the savoury.'

Nine courses, Alice repeated to herself as she went back up the servants' stairs to the hall. Even at the Debraces' before the war, they'd seldom entertained for more than twenty at a time and then only six-course meals. How pleased and excited she'd been in those days when Cook had given her some of the uneaten food to take back to the family. Did Harry ever remember those days? He'd been the hungriest of the lot. Most of his conversation then had centred round two subjects – the Debrace children and food. Well, now he'd acquired those two priorities and she must be out of her mind hoping that he might suddenly discover he wanted her too!

Harry had insisted that when they dined, she and not Madeleine should take the senior lady's place at the table, although Alice had argued that Madeleine, as future mistress of Maythorpe, might consider this her right. He, however, was determined that his courtship of Madeleine should be conducted along strictly conventional lines. It was still not yet six months since Dunbar had died, he'd pointed out, and he didn't want Madeleine to be thought uncaring or shallow. It was one thing for her personal friends to know that she was engaged to him, but village people gossiped, and since she was going to be living at Maythorpe, it was up to him to protect her reputation.

It was thus that Alice, seated on Aubrey's left at one end of the long dining-table, could not help but note throughout the meal how attentive Harry was towards Madeleine, who was seated on his right. They were laughing, joking and frequently smiling into one another's eyes. With a concerted effort, Alice tried to eat the various courses the young hired maid was putting in front of her – piping-hot consommé with julienne strips of baby carrots floating on the surface; fillets of sole poached in Chablis; sirloin running with blood-red juices and served with fresh vegetables straight from the kitchen garden. Sipping the wines which Harry had brought up from the late earl's cellar, she forced herself to smile and reply to the flirtatious remarks from her other table companion. At least no one watching her would be aware of the ache in her heart, she told herself as the meat course was cleared away and one of the two maids came in carrying a perfectly risen chocolate soufflé. At the same moment as the girl bent to offer the dish to Madeleine, Madeleine turned to talk to the man on her right. Her left shoulder caught the girl's arm and, as if in slow motion, the soufflé dish slid forwards, the contents splashing on to the edge of the white tablecloth.

Madeleine let out a cry of dismay.

'My dress . . . my new dress,' she wailed. 'There's chocolate all over the skirt!'

In a matter of seconds, Alice's eyes took in the look of horror on the young maid's face, the furious expression on Madeleine's and the distress on Harry's as he leant over to look at the damage. She quickly rose and walked round the table to Madeleine.

'May I see?' she said. 'I don't think it's too serious. If you come upstairs with me, I think I can remove the splashes so there'll be no stain.'

'But it's ruined, utterly ruined,' Madeleine wailed. 'That stupid . . .'

'A regrettable accident,' Alice broke in sharply. She took Madeleine's elbow and propelled her out of her chair. 'Ask Mrs Appleby to give you a clean cloth to put over the mess, Florence,' she instructed the maid. 'I think there's enough soufflé left to go round – the guests can help themselves. Come now, Madeleine, before it begins to dry.'

As they left the room, conversation – which had come to a halt when Madeleine cried out – was quickly resumed. Clearly, the visitors were not intending to let the accident mar their enjoyment of the meal.

'Cold water will do the trick,' Alice said reassuringly as, scarlet in the face, Madeleine followed her upstairs to her room.

'*Then* what am I supposed to do?' Madeleine said furiously. 'Sit around in a soaking-wet dress? That idiot girl!'

'It'll dry in a few minutes if I iron it under a cloth,' Alice answered firmly, curbing her irritation with difficulty. 'There's really nothing to make a fuss about, Madeleine.'

She slipped the dress over Madeleine's head and, leaving her sulking in her satin petticoat, took it to the bathroom, where she quickly sponged away the offending marks. As she had predicted, they soon disappeared and, five minutes later, she returned the dress, freshly ironed, to the waiting Madeleine.

'There, it's as new,' she said, 'so cheer up. If you go

down with a face like that, you'll ruin your dinner party, and it was going so well.'

'*Your* dinner party, you mean,' Madeleine said as she allowed Alice to put the dress over her head. 'I bet my hair's a ghastly mess. Comb it for me, will you?'

It was on the tip of Alice's tongue to tell this spoilt young girl that she was no longer her mother's maid and to comb her own hair, but she could guess Madeleine's reaction. The evening Harry had been hoping would go so well really would end up a disaster if Madeleine threw a tantrum – and Alice knew she was capable of it.

Nevertheless, she was far too angry even to consider obeying Madeleine's orders, spoken in a dictatorial tone she would not herself have used to the servants in Félix's château. Pretending that she had not heard the command, she said, 'I must go and unplug the iron. I won't be a moment.'

The men rose to their feet as Madeleine preceded Alice back into the dining-room. Harry hurried forward to guide Madeleine back to her chair.

'Everything all right?' he enquired anxiously.

'Apparently,' Madeleine said ungraciously. Violet, the second of the two maids, stepped forward and put a plate in front of her.

'Mrs Appleby thought as how you might like a piece of her Bakewell tart, miss,' she said, 'seeing as how the soufflé's gone flat.'

'Gracious me, no,' Madeleine replied. 'I can't stand almonds. I'll have some fruit.'

Conversation was resumed and only Alice was aware that the unfortunate Florence had not reappeared. Violet was managing to serve the savoury and the desert courses without her help. Madeleine seemed to have regained her composure and was talking earnestly to Harry. Suddenly, her voice rose above the general hum of conversation.

'I hope all the staff you've engaged, Alice, aren't as clumsy as that girl. I know this isn't London but surely they've got a decent domestic agency somewhere in the neighbourhood?'

Alice bit her lip, determined not to let her irritation show.

'There wasn't time to engage permanent staff, Madeleine. Harry only told me two weeks ago that you were bringing guests this weekend. These are local girls.'

'Well, at least you could have given them some kind of training,' Madeleine said as the room fell silent. 'After all, Alice, who better than you to pass on your experience? Mother always said you were the best maid we ever had.'

Somehow Alice managed to keep her head high. On most of the faces staring at her, there was only incomprehension, but on Aubrey's there was unmistakable embarrassment. She could not bring herself to look at Harry.

'I say, Harry,' Aubrey broke in hurriedly, 'did the Harveys write and tell you one of the colts they bred has been entered for the Kentucky Derby? Seems it's in with a good chance, too.' He turned to Alice. 'Did you ever meet Miss Hanworth? We're travelling to the States together the week after next – in time for the big race. What do you think, Harry? Shall I bet on it?'

Grateful for Aubrey's tactful intervention, Harry answered, 'I don't see why not. One of my fillies is a half-sister and Burberry – one of the trainers up here – thinks very highly of her prospects.'

Christopher now joined in the conversation, suggesting they might all attend the Leicester race meeting the following day. Alice rose to her feet.

'Why don't we ladies leave the men to their port?' she suggested.

'Yes, let's,' Madeleine said. 'Race talk's a frightful bore if you aren't mad about horses.' She smiled disarmingly at Harry, who was on his feet holding back her chair. 'Don't be *too* long, darling. I thought we'd put the gramophone on and dance later. I've brought some perfectly divine new records.'

As Harry watched her small figure *chassé*-ing from the room, chattering to her female friends, his emotions were in turmoil. He was still finding it hard to believe that she could have been so cruel to Alice, of all people! What could have made her say such a thing? Was it possible Alice had chided her when they were alone upstairs for being ungracious to the unfortunate little serving-girl? The accident had certainly been as much if not more Madeleine's fault than the maid's. Yet he could think of nothing Alice might have said to Madeleine to prompt such a belittling remark. What possible reason could she have had for wanting to 'put Alice in her place' – and come to that, being a maid was no longer Alice's place. Even if he were biased in her favour, it was perfectly obvious from the way Pierce and Pennystone were vying for Alice's attention that they accepted her as their social equal. Not that he had a great opinion of any of the young men Madeleine had chosen to invite here. They seemed a pretty vacuous lot; the women too. There was not one among them who could hold a candle to Alice, either in looks or, he was certain, in character.

The party, which a short while ago had seemed to be going so splendidly, now took on the aura of an ordeal. As host, he knew he must appear to be enjoying himself, yet all he could think of was how upset Alice must be. He was grateful to Aubrey, who seemed to be keeping the conversation going with amusing anecdotes of Blue Ash Farm and the months they had spent together there. From everything Aubrey was saying, it sounded very much as if he and Cora-Beth had been corresponding by return and that the Harveys' invitation to him was on a 'stay as long as you can' basis. Harry was happy for both of them, and more than a little relieved that Cora-Beth was not regretting her decision to break their engagement. He now knew for certain that what he'd felt for her was a close friendship, a deep affection – but never love. That was reserved for Madeleine alone.

It was strange, he thought now, that there could be moments when one came close to disliking one's beloved! He still felt angry and upset by Madeleine's behaviour towards Alice – his Alice, who had worked so hard to have everything perfect for her. He fully intended to demand an explanation. There could not, he realized, be any excuse.

It wasn't going to be easy to forgive Madeleine, although deep down he knew that if she were in his arms now, pleading in that soft, persuasive voice of hers for him to do so, he would be hard put to resist her. He couldn't even be in the same room as her without his whole body being conscious of her presence.

For some inexplicable reason, he found himself thinking of Peggy Podmore when, on one of those post-coital occasions, she had tried to enlighten him as to the power of sexual attraction, particularly of women over men. They had talked of great men in history who had been ruined by a woman – intelligent, intellectual, brilliantly clever men whose reason deserted them when trapped in the snares of obsessive desire. Often men did not distinguish between love and lust, she'd maintained.

Were his feelings for Madeleine born of love – or lust? he asked himself as Pennystone told yet another joke which might well have circulated among the sixth-formers in Grafton Abbey changing-rooms. The decanter circulated a third time and Pennystone, now far from sober, lent sideways and said to Harry, 'Jolly nice port, old boy. Jolly nice party. Should have come with us on holiday – parties every night. Mind you, old boy, Chris went a bit over the top once or twice.' He lent closer. 'Can't keep his hands off the ladies, that's Chris's trouble. One of those chaps who need a lot of it, know what I mean? Can't blame Madeleine, really. All the same, just as well you've got her back in the fold, what?'

Blame Madeleine for what? Harry asked himself with a sinking feeling in the pit of his stomach. Surely this effete, worthless, drunken fellow couldn't have meant to infer that Christopher Pierce and Madeleine . . . Even if it were true, the chap would not have been so indiscreet as to tell him, of all people!

No, he decided, this was ridiculous. Pennystone had been talking gibberish. Madeleine would never in a hundred years have allowed another man to make love to her. She loved him, Harry, and had said so over and over again in her spasmodic letters. Written in her large, childish scrawl with many misspellings, she'd filled the thin airmail pages with her passionate longing to be with him. 'If I close my eyes I can imagine your lips on mine!' 'If only you were here to hold me, touch me. I long to feel your wonderful strong warm hands on my body.' 'I wake up in the night thinking of how it will be when we can make love properly, my dearest, darling boy!' 'I'm wearing my new swimsuit and lying here in the sun thinking of you. Do you realize, I've never seen you undressed? I think about you all the time!'

No, Harry told himself fiercely, he was being utterly reprehensible even to consider taking Pennystone's remark seriously. It was disloyal to a degree to suspect Madeleine might have been unfaithful to him. She'd told him many times that she had only ever been attracted to one man – himself; that she'd hated having to submit to her husband's demands, wanting only him. In her way, he reminded himself, she had remained faithful, even within her marriage. He felt guilty now that he had doubted her even for a moment. How angry she would be if she knew – and rightly so. He would find a way to make it up to her. This evening when they danced, as she'd suggested, he would hold her as close as decency allowed and she would realize, without him saying anything, how deeply he loved and trusted her.

It was not until much later that night – well into the early hours of the morning, when Madeleine crept into his room and into his bed – that he remembered he had intended to ask why she had made that cruel remark to Alice. Then, as he felt her warm, soft body pressing eagerly against his own, all rational thoughts but one ceased – that after all those long, long years of yearning, his dreams of making love to Madeleine were about to come true.

CHAPTER THIRTY-TWO

1927

Alice put the last of her three suitcases on top of the wardrobe. There was no more space beneath the iron bedstead. The floral carpet covering three-quarters of the room was threadbare and the drab brown linoleum surround was cracked and discoloured. Dingy lace curtains masked the small windows looking down into Talbot Street.

Perhaps she should have booked herself into better lodgings, she thought as she sat down wearily on the sagging bed. She had chosen this area between Notting Hill Gate and Bayswater because the rent of a furnished room was low and she had not wanted to eat into her capital. Every penny she had saved would be needed to lease the shop and tiny flat above it, and to purchase her initial stock.

Harry had insisted upon giving her a very generous cheque when she left Maythorpe, turning an obstinately deaf ear when she had declined to take it. 'If anyone has earned it, you have, Alice,' he'd said. 'I just wish you weren't leaving so soon, but I suppose it's selfish of me to expect you to stay on until the autumn, when Madeleine and I are married. You've got your own life to lead. Now promise me you'll let me know if you need anything – anything at all. If you need more capital and the bank won't lend it, put them on to me. I'll be only too willing to act as guarantor. I just wish you'd let me give you more than this.'

She might as well sink her pride and use the money, she thought bitterly. She was going to need it. There was no point in starting up her business in an unfashionable area of London, since she intended to serve the same wealthy clients as shopped at the Maison de Verveine. Rents in the West End were high and she would be hard put to keep solvent in the first year or two until she became known. Jules was going to recommend her, good friend that he was, but things would be tight none the less.

Feeling lower in spirits than she'd ever felt in her life before, Alice turned to the only real friend she had. She went down to the hall, which smelt unpleasantly of boiled cabbage and kippers. Putting some pennies in the telephone meter, she asked the operator for the number of the *salon*. It was several minutes before she was connected and she heard Jules' voice.

'This is the Maison de Verveine. Can I be of assistance?'

'Jules, it's me – Alice,' she said. 'I've just got back to London and I was hoping you might be able to come and have some supper with me. We could go to our trattoria.'

There was a brief pause before Jules burst into a flow of words, partly in English but also in his native language.

'*Ça c'est impossible, Alice!*' He sounded very agitated. 'You have not heard the news? *Mais c'est affreux!* All the dresses are ruined . . . the fire, you see . . . and only three weeks before the Court presentations!'

'Calm yourself, Jules,' Alice broke in. 'As I told you, I've only been back in London a few hours. What fire? What's happened?'

Close to tears, Jules related how a fire had broken out in the attics of the adjoining hotel. It had spread into the attics of the Maison de Verveine and, in their attempts to put out the flames, the firemen had inevitably played their hoses on the upper windows. Water had seeped into the room where all the half-completed garments were hanging. Even worse, it had poured down the chimney and black oily soot had compounded the damage.

'Monsieur Félix is on his way from Milan to Paris, where he will collect two more machinists as well as the two he is conducting from Milan,' Jules concluded. 'Even with their assistance, I do not see it is possible that we have the dresses repaired in time. These new girls do not speak English and somehow I shall have to find time to interpret for them.'

Alice kept her voice quiet as she tried to calm him.

'How many dresses, Jules? You said "repair". Does that mean they are not entirely ruined?'

'Two dozen at least,' Jules wailed. 'Nine Court dresses for the débutantes. The duchess's outfit for her son's wedding. Mrs Stoddart-Jones's costume for her son's wedding. Lady Jane's wedding-gown – and the six bridesmaids' dresses. *Grâce à Dieu*, her mama's dress was untouched. We had most terrible difficulties with her *poitrine*!'

'With four new girls coming to help, surely it can be managed, Jules? Can't some be cleaned? Pullars of Perth can work miracles.'

'But not on that wild silk, Alice. The whole skirt will have to be remade. And the embroidered satin – all the tiny pearls are discoloured! It is a disaster, a catastrophe!'

'You'll manage somehow, Jules,' Alice said, although she was beginning now to understand the magnitude of the problem.

'If you were here, perhaps. It was the first thing *le Maître* said when I telephoned him.' His voice rose once more. 'We have so little time, Alice, and I cannot be everywhere at once. We have the builders and cleaners in and everyone is demanding my attention. It's "Jules this" and "Jules that" and I do not know where to turn.'

'If you think Monsieur Félix would not object, I could come back until you are straight again,' Alice said slowly. Even as she made the suggestion, she half regretted it. Although her parting from Félix had been amicable, she'd felt embarrassed, for there was no doubt that he had never expected her to leave him.

She could hear Jules's voice, gabbling excitedly in French as he enthused about her suggestion. By now she had run out of coins to put in the meter and she cut Jules's short, telling him she would take a taxi straight to the *salon*.

It was with some relief when, quarter of an hour later, she arrived at the Maison de Verveine and saw that the damage was not quite as extensive as Jules had described. It was true that the upper floors of the hotel next door had been gutted, but the roof of the Maison was untouched, although still dripping water. Inside she surveyed the rails of once-beautiful, half-finished gowns with an expert eye. New sleeves for the countess's dress, cleaning and a new skirt only for the Ascot outfit, only five of the six bridesmaids' dresses spoilt, one whole rail of the new season's gowns quite unscathed.

'We'll manage, Jules,' she said. 'When does Monsieur Félix arrive?'

'The day after tomorrow! Tonight I have to arrange to hire extra beds for the flat. The four girls are to sleep in the big bedroom that was yours, Alice. Monsieur Félix is going to a hotel. I shall move elsewhere if you wish to have my small room. It would be best if you are nearby.'

It would be a pleasure to move out of her newly rented room, Alice thought. She had become horribly spoilt over the years, she told herself. There was a time when she would have welcomed any room which held a bed solely for herself and which she need not share with her sisters. Now she had become accustomed to big, airy bedrooms, beautifully appointed and carpeted with luxurious furnishings and bedding.

'I cannot think how you can smile,' Jules was saying as he watched her face. 'All the girls have been in tears and, I confess, I too have come close to weeping.'

'It must have been an awful shock for you,' Alice said, straightening her face. 'But at least the main *salon* is undamaged – and no one was injured.'

'*Grâce à Dieu*! No one injured in the hotel either.' He crossed himself and then pointed to a pile of dresses in a big laundry basket. 'Janet sorted those out today – for the cleaners. They will be collected tomorrow. The charladies have already cleaned the worst of the mess on the floor, but we shall have to have the room and landing redecorated. I would have moved these dresses down to the stockroom but I am afraid to transfer the odour of soot, which, regrettably, still clings to them.'

Alice's professional eye was already assessing the work to be done.

'You have more of this green slipper satin?' she asked. 'We shall need six or seven yards at least. And the pink-and-grey-flecked tweed? Just a new sleeve, I think, and perhaps that lapel. We can give that to Suzanne if Monsieur Félix is bringing her – she's so good with hand-stitching. The blue chiffon will be more difficult – a whole remake would be quickest. The lining and underskirt are unmarked . . .'

Jules's body, which had been tense with incipient hysteria, slowly relaxed as Alice's soft voice continued. When finally she stopped speaking, he was actually smiling.

'All day I have been bemoaning my ill fortune,' he said. 'Now I see that my good fortune has not entirely deserted me. You are back in London, Alice, and, as you say, together we shall manage somehow.'

Alice nodded.

'But only if Monsieur Félix agrees, Jules. We must ask him first.'

'Then I shall put through a telephone call to him this instant,' Jules said, 'unless you wish to speak to him yourself, Alice?'

'No, it could be awkward for him to refuse if I ask,' Alice said as Jules hurried away to make use of the telephone downstairs. He did not question the reason she had given him, but the real reason was that she did not want Félix to imagine that she was using this emergency as a means of becoming re-employed at the Maison. Her long-term plans remained unchanged. It was simply that Jules was her friend and she owed him, as well as Félix, a debt for having helped her in those early years. Now was her opportunity to repay their kindness to her.

During the next week, when Félix tried to express his gratitude for all she was doing, she found she was able to tell him truthfully that it had advantages for her too. There was no time to dwell on those last miserable few days she had spent at Maythorpe. To Félix she said only that it had hurt her to watch Harry and Madeleine so obviously in love. She did not add that Madeleine had found an opportunity to tell her that she and Harry were lovers, that they were perfectly suited and couldn't wait to be married in the autumn.

The very last thing Alice wanted was to be made Madeleine's confidante. She had tried not to think of the two of them together, but she was no longer the innocent virgin she had once been and she was unable to prevent her imagination portraying Madeleine in Harry's arms as once she, herself, had lain in Félix's. It was this more than anything else which had prompted her to tell Harry that she must return to London to start her own business, that she wanted to be fully operational by the following spring, and that if she delayed much longer, this might not be possible.

Kind as always, Harry had not attempted to dissuade her – and even this had hurt. At least now, when she was on her feet fourteen hours a day, answering questions, interpreting for the French and Italian girls, dealing with anxious clients, answering the telephone, chasing up the cleaners, encouraging the overworked, tired cutters, fitters, seamstresses, she had no time to think of Harry and the world up at Maythorpe which would never be hers.

By the end of the second week, it was clear that they would be able to meet their schedules for all their clients. The pressures eased and, at Alice's suggestion, Félix gave all the staff a Monday off and the promise of a generous bonus for each of them on top of their pay for overtime.

'As for you, Alice,' he said when he returned to his office after he had made his announcement, 'you too deserve a break. I have booked a table for us at Boulestin's for tomorrow and bought tickets for *Desert Song*, which is on at Drury Lane theatre.'

As she was about to protest, he put his arm round her shoulder.

'You have worked harder than anyone, *chérie*, and you must allow me to show my appreciation.' He gave his sudden twinkling smile, which always made him look so much younger than his age. 'I speak as your friend, Alice – nothing more. My invitation is not . . . as I think you call it . . . the opening gambit for a renewal of our old relationship.'

Next day, however, during an excellent dinner which he had chosen with great care, he admitted that he had not been entirely truthful.

'There has not been an appropriate moment during this past emergency for me to tell you that I still find you as enchanting as ever, my beautiful Alice. Believe me, I have not found it easy to replace you, and when Jules told me you were in London . . . well, even had there been no fire, I would have come to England as quickly as I could.'

He smiled at her across the table and, with a wicked glint in his eyes, added, 'I will admit that my first glimpse of you after so long a separation did not quite match the image I had kept in my heart. You had sooty black marks on your nose and forehead; your workdress could not have been less elegant and . . . *mon Dieu* . . . your lovely hair looked like the stuffing from an old *chaise-longue*.'

Relaxing, Alice laughed.

'I had more urgent matters to attend to than my appearance, Félix,' she defended herself. 'And you would have been the first to reprimand me if you'd found me sitting idle in the *salon* in a Verveine model doing nothing to help.'

'That is true. But this evening, you are exactly as I had been remembering you, and I have to tell you that I remain totally in love with you and am as determined as ever that you shall become my wife.'

Until now, his tone had been light, but his grey eyes became suddenly serious as he said, 'It's not my intention – nor indeed any of my business – to ask you about the months you spent with your Harry in the country. When Jules told me that you had returned to London, I guessed that there was to be no happy ending to your story, and I am sorry, Alice, truly sorry. I can only say that I think your Harry must be an extraordinarily stupid young man.

542

I myself would never pick the bud if I could have the bloom.'

His compliment gave Alice the opportunity she needed to regain her composure.

'As always, you're very kind, Félix, and yes, naturally, I'm disappointed. But I'm glad for Harry's sake that he has finally got what he always wanted.'

Félix was not to be sidetracked.

'But what of your future, Alice? Do you still wish to deny yourself a husband, children, security? You know that I can offer you these things. I think I might make quite a good family man – anyway, for short periods of time! I would not be unfaithful, Alice – not if we were married.'

'Félix, dear kind Félix, you assured me you wanted no more than friendship when you invited me out,' Alice reminded him with a reproachful smile.

'Ah, yes, *chérie*, but I was not to know you would be wearing my favourite dress. Can I dare hope that it was to please me you chose it?'

Alice laughed.

'I wish I could honestly say "yes" to that, but to tell you the truth, it is the only one I have unpacked. The rest are in my trunk in storage until I find a flat.'

'And I wish you were less truthful, Alice, and at least pretended that you had been attempting to seduce me.'

Somehow, Alice realized, their banter had restored the old, easy relationship between them. They were friends again, good friends, and she could relax and enjoy her evening.

'How are things progressing in Milan?' she asked.

'Well enough! I have found a *directrice* – a woman who was employed by Bertolini – whom I have persuaded to supervise the branch for me. Now I have only to find a good manager for the Paris branch and I can retire.'

Alice looked shocked.

'But you'd never do that, surely? What would you do with your life, Félix?'

'Travel around the world with you, perhaps? There are

many places I would like to see for which there has never been enough time before. And if you will not accompany me, imagine how many beautiful women there must be – Spanish, Mexican, American, Egyptian, Indian – all waiting for me to come and seduce them. Then there is the Château de St Denis. It is greatly in need of attention. I might even re-establish the vineyards, which, as you know, were ruined in the war, and become one of the great French wine producers, like my grandfather. Believe me, Alice, I should not be bored. I should merely be a great deal happier if I could enjoy my pursuits in your company.'

When Alice returned to the flat that night, she found herself thinking of the contrast between the future she had planned for herself and the one Félix had outlined for her. Anyone else, she thought, would consider her out of her mind even to hesitate. Harry was now irrevocably beyond her reach – he had finally achieved his heart's desire. What possible point could there be in clinging to the idea that if she could not be his wife, she did not wish to be anyone else's? Félix was a kind, thoughtful man, a kind, thoughtful lover, and he was offering her everything most girls could possibly desire. With no hope of sharing her life with the man she loved, why was she rejecting second-best with a man she respected and liked, who could make her laugh, and who would without doubt make an excellent husband?

The question still unanswered, Alice finally fell asleep.

'Do you realize I've been sitting here by myself for the past hour without anything to do? You said you'd only be gone for half an hour! It's long past four o'clock, and I'll tell you this much straight from one of your horrible horses' mouths – I'm bored, bored, *bored*!'

Madeleine's mouth was downturned and her darkly pencilled brows were drawn together in an angry frown.

Harry sank wearily into the nearest armchair, making no attempt to cross the room to the sofa where Madeleine lay curled up in front of the fire. He had been up half the night with Sherry, one of his mares which was foaling. She had finally haemorrhaged following a stillbirth and the veterinary surgeon had been unable to save her. Not only had the mare been the start of Harry's breeding-stock but she was the first he had acquired and he'd been greatly attached to her. Clearly, Madeleine did not grasp the significance of what he'd been doing.

'I'm sorry I had to leave you alone for so long,' he said. 'It was unavoidable.'

'I don't understand what you mean by "unavoidable". Surely you're your own boss, aren't you?' Madeleine's voice was accusing. 'It seems to me it always comes down to the same thing, the horses or me, and you choose the horses!'

'Madeleine, that isn't true, and you know it.'

'It's absolutely true. If it wasn't for the wretched horses, you'd agree to come and live in London, but no, you want me to live here once we're married. Well, I'm just not going to. I'm missing all the best parties when I come up at weekends. Anyway, I've bought the house in Pont Street. I signed the papers yesterday.'

Harry's face darkened.

'You promised me you wouldn't buy the house before I'd seen it,' he said, his voice ominously quiet.

'Well, even if I did, it was a stupid promise to make. After all, you're not interested in the house, and anyway, I'm buying it with Pogo's money, not yours.'

She broke off as one of the maids came into the room to draw the curtains, shutting out the darkening September sky. The panes were spattered with rain and the branches of the big elm tree were waving in the rising wind.

'I'm beginning to hate this place,' Madeleine said once the girl had put more coal on the fire and left the room. 'It wasn't so bad in the summer. But now . . . I absolutely dread the winter here.'

Harry remained silent, his heart sinking as he listened to Madeleine's querulous voice. They were not even married yet and she had stayed at Maythorpe only on alternate weekends these past five months, but already she was bored and critical of life in Leicestershire. It was not just resentment at the amount of time he felt it necessary to be down at the stables; it was the absence of entertainment. Madeleine needed people around her all the time – conversation, company, music, dancing, parties. She needed the stimulus of other young people and seemed unable to relax when she was by herself. He'd never yet seen her with a book, gathering flowers for the house, as Alice had once done with such pleasure, or listening to a concert on the wireless. Although he'd made friends with a number of the neighbours and they were invited out to dinner or to the races, her enjoyment was only transitory and ended once they were alone in the house again. Only when he was actually making love to her did she seem to be completely happy in his company, and Madeleine's demands were insatiable. He had begun to feel like one of his own stallions – that he was only needed by Madeleine for the single purpose of satisfying her.

Things would be no better next month, he thought with a deepening anxiety. He would be busy in the early weeks of October at the Newmarket sales, where he was hoping to pick up one or two high-class yearlings. He'd promised Madeleine he would go down to London for Christmas, although even this hadn't really pleased her since they would be spending the time at her parents' home. Sir Philip and Lady Debrace had welcomed Harry as a future son-in-law but had been adamant in their refusal to allow the marriage to take place until the following spring. There must be a minimum of eighteen months between Madeleine's widowhood and remarriage, they insisted.

Madeleine had wanted Harry to ignore their wishes. She was over twenty-one now, she'd protested, and could do as she pleased, but Harry privately agreed with his prospective in-laws that it would not be too hard on them to wait a further six months. It was one of the few times Madeleine had referred to his childhood. 'Just because you had to take orders from my parents in those days, you won't stand up to them now,' she'd said accusingly.

As always when Madeleine was being difficult, Harry sought to excuse her. In the past, her father had openly indulged her and it was not her fault if, as a result, she had been spoilt. Moreover, he told himself, she was still very young. Her marriage to Dunbar had not matured her – if anything, she had continued to be given her own way in everything.

'I'm sorry I had to leave you for so long,' he said now. 'Anyway, darling, at least you will enjoy this evening.'

Harry had been invited out to dinner by the Fitz-Symonds. Nathan FitzSymonds was an extremely wealthy industrialist who had recently bought up one of the big estates near Grantham. His parties were already being noted by the gossip columnists as the most lavish and 'fast' outside London. Harry didn't know their host very well but the man had called to see one of his hunters with a view to buying it for his daughter's twenty-first. It was then he had issued the invitation, which included any friends who might be staying with Harry.

Madeleine's face now brightened.

'I'm going to wear my Jean Patou,' she said. 'It's the very latest fashion and much more daring than Uncle Félix's dresses. It'll be just right.' She stood up and crossing the room went over to kiss Harry. Her lips were warm and inviting, her voice husky as she whispered, 'Shall we make love before we go, or after, or both?' she added with a giggle. She ruffled Harry's dark curls and, as always, he felt his heartbeat quicken. 'Mummy would have fifty million fits if she knew what we did when I come up here for the weekend. She thinks Daphne comes with me, and so long as I have her to chaperon me, nothing will happen. Poor old Daphne – she's never going to find a husband. I think I'd want to die if I was as plain and fat as she is. Thank goodness she lives in Dorset and Mummy never sees her. Daphne's so stupid she'd be bound to let the cat out of the bag.'

She kissed Harry again and announced that she was going upstairs to have a bath, after which she would have a rest in bed before dressing for the party.

'You won't be long, will you, darling?' she whispered, the invitation in her voice unmistakable.

It was Harry's firm intention to follow her upstairs and make love to her, but the fact that he'd had only an hour's sleep last night and a fraught day following gave sheer fatigue the upper hand. He was fast asleep in an armchair when, an hour later, one of the maids woke him to say that Mrs Dunbar had sent a message to warn him he'd be late for the party if he didn't bestir himself.

Throughout the half-hour drive to the FitzSymonds, Madeleine did not speak, making it clear that she intended him to suffer for his neglect. Once at the house, she quickly left his side and disappeared into the mêlée of guests who were already making the most of the big ballroom and were dancing to Jack Hylton's band.

Harry found his way to the improvised bar at the far end of the ballroom, where white-coated waiters were busily serving champagne and spirits for those who preferred them. He was given a large whisky and soda and found himself being addressed by a middle-aged man standing beside him.

'Name's Falmouth, Roland Falmouth. Don't think we've met, what?'

Harry introduced himself.

His companion emptied his glass and took another. By the slight slur in his speech, it was clear that he'd already had several.

'Say this about the FitzSymonds,' the man was saying. 'May not be quite top-drawer and all that, but they put on a damn good show, what? You here for that "do" in August? No? Well, you missed a really good shindig – went on till dawn. Chaps throwing each other into the fishpond – a girl too!' He gave Harry a conspiratorial wink. 'Wearing some sort of flimsy material, clung to all the right parts, know what I mean? The husband was furious and swung a punch at the fellow who'd pulled her in. Don't think they're here tonight.'

He swayed slightly as he peered at a couple on the dance floor. Then he grabbed Harry's arm, spilling some of his whisky as he did so.

'I'll be blowed! See that girl over there, pretty one with that dago-looking chap. Saw her last weekend at that pub in Maidenhead – you know the place, just the ticket for a weekend with a popsie. Well, I was there with a nice little piece, girl in my office as a matter of fact, and blow me, up comes this blonde girl, introduces herself as Adeleine, and then asks me if I'm on my own. I'd noticed her at lunch with that dago chap she's dancing with, but I think she must have had a spat with him or else he wasn't doing his stuff. Anyway, there she was flirting with me. I'll swear to goodness, if I'd played my cards right, I could have had some fun and games with her that night. Makes you think, doesn't it? Small world.'

Harry, bored by the conversation, was only half listening. The noise and the heat were compounding the headache he'd had since he'd been woken by the maid and he was wondering how he was going to survive the next six hours. Madeleine would certainly not want to leave before the end of the party. She was indefatigable – anyway until the following day, when she would stay in bed until late afternoon, catching up on her sleep.

'. . . older than you, old chap, so you wouldn't know how things were before the war. Believe me, it was a different world. Girls who did and nice girls who didn't! Nowadays, as far as I can see, it's a free-for-all. Take that blonde girl – comes from a good family, judging by the way she spoke and dressed. Not that I'm complaining. I say, old chap, I think she's waving to me.'

Harry glanced at the couple his companion indicated and his face whitened with shock. Surely the man could not have been talking about Madeleine? There had to be some mistake.

'Yes, thought it was the same one. Not Adeleine, Madeleine, that was it. Same dago-looking fellow too, I should think. These wogs all look alike, though, don't they? Ah, there's the little woman. Suppose I'll have to go and do my stuff. Take my advice, m'boy, and stay a bachelor. Much more fun these days.'

Harry didn't even notice the man going. Madeleine and

her dance partner had also disappeared. Emptying his whisky glass, he tried to marshal his thoughts. Where had Madeleine been last weekend? Not at Maythorpe, that was certain. Suddenly, he recalled with shocking clarity her explanation of where she was going.

'I've promised to go to Daphne's birthday party. I expect it'll be a fearful bore but I feel I must go, seeing how often she covers for us, darling.'

Daphne, he knew, lived in Dorset, yet his erstwhile companion had seen Madeleine in a hotel in Maidenhead. According to Madeleine, she'd had 'an utterly boring' weekend at Daphne's and the party on the Saturday had been 'a fearful flop'. On Sunday, they'd all been obliged to go to church and after lunch there'd been 'silly, childish card games like racing demon'.

Harry drew a deep breath. This was no more than hearsay and the fellow was certainly half-way to being drunk. He could easily have been mistaken. Yet he had both named and identified Madeleine without any hesitation.

Deep down inside, Harry knew that Madeleine was capable of being unfaithful to him. Making love had become her priority and she'd complained bitterly that his refusal to go down to London on all but the rarest of occasions was leaving her lonely and miserable and horribly frustrated.

At first her eagerness to respond had flattered him and made him feel tremendously happy that she could love him as intensely and passionately as he loved her, but gradually, without quite realizing it, he'd grown to fear that this side of their relationship was the only part which mattered to her.

Hating himself for the compulsion to do so, Harry concealed himself behind one of the marble pillars close to the dance floor and surreptitiously searched for a glimpse of Madeleine's blue dress. The band was playing a tango now and before long she came into view. Her partner's arm was clasped tightly around her waist and, as he watched, she arched her body so that she was leaning backwards on the man's arm, her breasts pointing provocatively towards him. Her lips were parted, her eyes closed, and the sheer sensuousness of her posture was unmistakable. Small wonder that her partner's head was bent over as if he were about to kiss her. Their closeness was such that there might have been no one else in the room. Only two people who were lovers could dance in such a way, he thought as he turned abruptly on his heel and left the room. He was feeling physically sick and he knew he was not yet ready to confront Madeleine. There were several footmen in the big hall and FitzSymonds was talking to one of them.

'Sorry to interrupt, but I've been called away on an emergency,' he said to his host. 'I have to leave at once. I can't locate Mrs Dunbar, the lady who came with me. Could you possibly find her and explain that I have been obliged to go . . . to London, that is, and see that she's taken back to Maythorpe House. I'll get in touch with her as soon as possible.'

As he walked out into the driveway he wondered what had prompted him to say that he was going to London, for he'd had no idea when he'd approached FitzSymonds where he would go. Certainly not back to Maythorpe, where inevitably he would have to face Madeleine. Now, as he climbed into his car and tipped the attendant holding the door for him, he knew that he *would* go to London. He would book in to a hotel and remain there while he decided what to do about the mess he'd made of his life.

Taking the Witham road which led to the Great North Road, he felt a hard lump in his throat and realized that his hands were trembling as they gripped the steering wheel. How was it possible, he asked himself, that you could love someone as overwhelmingly as he had loved Madeleine and then discover that there was no love left? He would never marry her now. Apart from anything else, he would never trust her again. All his plans, all his hopes, all his dreams were in ruins.

For one brief moment, Harry allowed himself to question whether he had perhaps misjudged her; whether his drunken companion had been mistaken; whether Madeleine did, after all, love him as faithfully as he had loved her. But the moment was short-lived. Seeing her now for the first time without the misleading veil of adoration, he realized that she had only ever loved herself. Her happiness had lain in having her whims, her wishes, her pleasures satisfied. She had given nothing but her body – given nothing because there had been nothing else to give.

CHAPTER THIRTY-THREE

1927

A mile beyond Stamford it began to rain and Harry was obliged to slow down as muddy splashes from the wheels of a large van in front obscured his vision. It crossed his mind that he had not checked his petrol gauge and that at this time of night he might well not find a garage open. There was a two-gallon can in the dicky if the worst came to the worst, but with the rain now a hard, steady downpour, he was beginning to regret his impulsive decision to drive to London.

Somewhere at the back of his mind he had thought that he might take refuge with his aunt. Undoubtedly she would be pleased, if surprised, to see him, but now he realized that he couldn't possibly tell the old lady the real reasons why he was breaking off his engagement to Madeleine. It was not simply a matter of his pride, which he needed to preserve; there was the question of Madeleine's reputation, such as it was. Even if he no longer cared about her, Aubrey was her brother and his closest friend. Perhaps, after all, he would book into a hotel.

Tired as he was, it was over an hour before he realized that there was something seriously wrong with the steering of the Bentley. He drew into a lay-by and switched off the engine. Pulling an old hunting mac from the back seat over his head, he opened the door and stepped out on to the rain-soaked road. Within minutes, he established the cause of the car's erratic behaviour. He had a slow puncture and the front, right-hand tyre was now almost completely flat.

At two in the morning, wearing tails and light-soled

patent-leather evening shoes, he was very far from suitably attired for changing the wheel, he thought. On the other hand, he'd passed Baldock several minutes ago, and it would mean a long trek back in the rain, unless he could hitch a lift. He glanced in both directions and realized that the road was almost deserted.

With an effort he pulled himself together. This wasn't the moment to start feeling sorry for himself – and at least he did know how to change a wheel! It was Madeleine's friends, the Pierces and Pennystones of this world, who had never undertaken such menial tasks for themselves, he told himself wryly.

Since there was little point in waiting for the rain to stop, Harry buttoned up his mackintosh and went round to the boot to find the jack. He was still busy jacking up the car when a lorry pulled up behind him. The driver climbed out, grinning. 'Want a hand, guv?' he asked. 'Not your lucky night by the looks of it!'

With the man's help, the spare wheel was soon in place.

'Fancy a cuppa, sir?' he asked. 'There's a transport café open all night a mile or two further on.' Glancing at Harry anxiously, he added, 'Bit scruffy and all, but if you don't mind, guv . . .'

Ten minutes later, in the hot, smoky room, Harry sat tucking into a big plate of eggs and bacon, a steaming hot mug of tea beside him. His companion – on his way to Covent Garden with a load of vegetables – was by now a friend. Curious as to the reason for Harry being on the road dressed as he was at three in the morning, he finally put the question.

Relaxed now, and feeling a good deal better, Harry found himself saying, 'Had a bit of a spat with my girl. Well, a bust-up, I suppose you might say. Should have waited till morning, shouldn't I?'

The lorry driver shook his head.

'Some things is best done quickly, else they doesn't get done at all. Thinking better of it, are you?'

'No!' Harry's voice was sharper than he'd intended.

'No, it's all over, and I dare say it's as well. I've been a bit of an ass one way and another.'

'Good-looking young gent like you won't find no hardship getting yourself another young lady,' the man said encouragingly. 'With all them lads killed in the war, there's plenty of girls as still can't find husbands for all the war was ten years or more ago.'

'I'm not looking for a wife or a girlfriend, old chap,' Harry said. 'I shall remain a bachelor. The more I think about it, the more certain I am that I shan't ever get married now.'

'That's what I said once. Now look at me – married these past fifteen years and eight kids to bring up. I was lucky to get this job when I came out of the army, but like as not I'll get the sack if I don't get a move on.'

Harry took out his wallet and slipped a note across the bare wooden table top. The man went over to the counter, paid for their breakfasts and, returning to the table, handed Harry his change.

'Keep it, my friend,' Harry said, and when the man protested, he added, 'Buy something for those eight kids of yours. I was poor once and I know what a surprise means to a child.'

As he climbed back into his car and resumed his journey, Harry found himself thinking not about Madeleine but about his childhood with the Pritchetts. What he had told his Good Samaritan was true – they had been desperately poor and often hungry, but there had never been a shortage of love. Even if his foster mother had been undemonstrative and more inclined to give slaps than hugs and cuddles, the deep, caring affection had been there underneath. Then there'd been Alice – the skinny little elder sister always there to run to; always quick to put her arms round him and console him; to encourage him; to share his dreams for the future.

One of the first things he would do in London, he told himself as he passed Biggleswade, was go and see Alice. When she learned that he wasn't going to marry Madeleine after all, she would quite possibly offer to leave her job yet again and keep house for him. Not that he would allow her to do so this time. He knew she had returned to the Maison de Verveine and that her plan to open her own premises had been shelved indefinitely. Although she had written at first to say that this was only a temporary measure because of the fire damage, five months had gone by and she'd made no further mention of leaving.

Once or twice, when he'd had time to do so, he had thought about the months she had spent with him restoring Maythorpe. He'd found himself doubting whether she would ever have left the *salon* but for his need of her. It would have been typical of Alice's unselfishness to put her own career second to his needs. He doubted whether she would ever admit it, but at least he could let her know how truly grateful he was, tell her that she was to consider Maythorpe as much her home as his, and that if she chose to come up there for her holidays, they could invite other members of the family to join them. Jack and Jenny had not had a holiday since their honeymoon. Alice would like that.

Harry was obliged to stop yet again to put petrol in his tank from his spare can, but when finally he reached the outskirts of London, the engine sputtered, coughed and finally stopped. Aware suddenly of his fatigue, he realized that it was almost five o'clock. As he sat wondering whether to set off in search of a garage or take a quick nap, a milk lorry turned into the road to make deliveries. The milkman, with a wry glance at Harry's bedraggled appearance, informed him that there was a garage which might be open not quarter of a mile away. There being no sign of a taxi, Harry took the empty can from the back of the car and walked.

By the time he was once more on his way, the city was coming to life. Housewives were opening their front doors to take in the milk. Young boys on bikes were delivering newspapers to the doors of the bigger houses, where skivvies were already whitening the front-door steps. Greengrocers were putting out boxes of vegetables and fruit on stalls in front of their shop windows. It was six o'clock. The rain had stopped and smoke was curling up from the chimneys. There would almost certainly be a fog, he thought, as he took the familiar streets that would lead him to the Alcotts' house in Cadogan Place. Bertie's younger brother – over six foot tall like himself – would lend him some clothes, he thought. Stupidly, he'd not returned to Maythorpe to pack a suitcase before setting off, and he could hardly go and see Lady Merstam, or Alice, in his present attire! His trousers were spattered with mud and his shoes looked as if he'd worn them on a day's hunt.

Neither Bertie nor his brother were at home when Harry arrived. Mrs Alcott, however, was as hospitable as always. When she heard Harry had been driving all night, she insisted upon his going to bed.

'Whatever the emergency which brought you here, you will deal with it better if you've had some sleep,' she said. 'The boys are up in Scotland grouse shooting. Bertie will be sorry to have missed you. You must stay as long as you wish. I'll be glad of your company.'

Despite his state of mind, Harry slept deeply until mid-afternoon. He felt physically much better, but his depression had deepened. Like it or not – and he certainly did not look forward to doing so – he must telephone Madeleine. He had left the message for her, promising to let her know where he was, but he owed it to her to explain his reasons for walking out on her. It had been a cowardly impulse, he told himself. He should have taken her back to Maythorpe and faced her with the facts. The truth was, he could not have borne to hear her trying to deny them, lying to him, perhaps even asking him to forgive her. He was still a little afraid that despite everything, he might succumb to any appeal she chose to make. He'd never yet been able to resist her when, with her arms round his neck, her body pressed against his, she'd pleaded in her soft, childish voice, 'Don't be cross with me, darling. I do love you, I really do.'

Harry finished the late lunch his hostess had insisted upon giving him and, his mouth set in a determined line, went to the telephone in the hallway which, tactfully, Mrs Alcott had said he might use with complete privacy.

Madeleine, the parlourmaid told him, was not yet up although she was awake and had had breakfast and lunch in bed. At Harry's insistence, the girl went upstairs and called Madeleine down to the telephone. Her voice sounded querulous.

'Harry, is that you? Where on earth are you? I've been worried to death. Why didn't you leave me a note or something? I simply didn't know what to say to the FitzSymonds. It really was too bad of you. You've made me very, very angry.'

'If you'll allow me to talk, I'll explain,' Harry said sharply. 'I left for the simple reason that I wanted to avoid seeing you. I needed time to think . . . before I told you that I don't wish to see you again – ever.'

He heard Madeleine's gasp, but before she could speak, he said quickly, 'I was talking to a fellow at the bar while you were dancing. Not knowing you were my fiancée, he told me he'd seen you with your partner last weekend in Maidenhead. In case you have forgotten, Madeleine, you told me you were going to Dorset to spend the weekend with Daphne. Even supposing there'd been a last-minute change in your plans and you were at that hotel quite innocently, you said nothing about it to me when I asked you how you had enjoyed Daphne's birthday party. If you were innocent, Madeleine, that would have been the natural thing to do, wouldn't it?'

She broke in then, protesting that Daphne had been at the hotel with her, that the man she had been seen with was a friend of Daphne's brother and it was purely a coincidence that he'd been invited at the last minute to the FitzSymonds' party, that Daphne would support everything she was telling him if he cared to ask her.

'Just as she has covered for the weekends you have spent at Maythorpe with me,' Harry said bitterly. 'I agreed to the cover-up because I didn't want to upset your parents, and because I wanted us to be together every bit as much as you did. I was worried about your reputation, but seeing that most of the friends you brought with you were behaving in a similar way, I couldn't see how you could be harmed, most especially since we were to be married.'

'Well, if Mummy and Daddy hadn't been so priggish about Pogo, we would have been married ages ago and then I wouldn't have . . . we'd have been together all the time and . . . I wouldn't have been so lonely without you.'

Harry's shoulders sagged wearily as he heard the little-girl note in her voice.

'Would we have been together *all the time*?' He emphasized the words. 'I think not, Madeleine. You didn't want to live *all the time* at Maythorpe and I certainly can't live all the time in London. Sooner or later, we'd have spent time in different houses and you would, as you put it, have been lonely without me. You'd have found someone to replace me, just as you found Christopher Pierce to replace me on your holiday.'

He thought he could hear Madeleine crying, but her words were clear enough as she protested, 'No one could ever replace you . . . You're the only one I've ever really wanted . . . It's just that you were often too tired or busy with those horrible horses and, anyway, I don't see why I have to give up everything I enjoy just because you want to live in the country. As for Chris, nothing would have happened if *you'd* been there, but you wouldn't come with me. Now you're blaming me and it just isn't fair.'

'Perhaps you're right,' Harry said quietly. 'Anyway, you aren't going to have to give up everything you enjoy after all. We aren't suited, Madeleine, and when you've calmed down, you'll realize I'm right.'

'You're just saying that to get your own back because you're cross with me.' Now her voice was petulant as she added, 'I suppose you're wishing you'd married that Cora-Beth girl. Just because she's old-fashioned and stayed faithful all the time . . .'

'She wasn't old-fashioned and, in any case, she has nothing to do with us. Not only do I not wish myself married to her but I'm delighted that she and Aubrey have got together. It wouldn't surprise me in the least, now he's out there, to hear they have got engaged. Be that as it may, I'd like you to leave Maythorpe as soon as possible, Madeleine. Someone will drive you to the station. I shall stay here in London for two days. I think it's best if you and I don't meet for a while. Our engagement was never made formal so we have no need to announce that it's all off. I suggest you tell your parents that you simply don't wish to spend the rest of your life in Leicestershire and the decision was yours.'

There was a long pause before Madeleine spoke again. Then she said anxiously, 'You won't tell Daddy about . . . about Maidenhead, will you? Or Aubrey? They wouldn't understand. Maybe I'll go abroad for a while. Most of my friends are going to Scotland for dull old shooting parties and Alfonso has invited me to travel with him to Cairo. He says I really must see Alexandria and the pyramids and the Sphinx and all that. Then he's offered to take me to visit his family in Seville . . .' She broke off as if realizing that Harry could scarcely be interested in these plans, that merely by mentioning them she'd revealed she'd been considering the possibility.

'Oh, Harry,' she said plaintively. 'I do still love you, really I do. I know you must be very cross with me, but honestly I've only ever done it with someone else once, on my word of honour. I mean, couldn't you possibly overlook it? It's going to be so *difficult* having to explain to everyone. I mean, couldn't we just go on seeing each other and then sort of drift apart? It wouldn't be nearly so embarrassing. Besides, after all the fuss I made about wanting us to get married quickly, Mummy and Daddy would never believe I'd changed my mind so suddenly. Couldn't we pretend we were still engaged – just for a little while?'

The remnants of Harry's anger left him. He felt suddenly years older than this shallow little girl on the other end of the telephone. Who was it who had said, 'There's nothing so dead as a dead love'? It wasn't true – if 'dead' meant 'final', for there was nothing more final than the discovery that you should never have loved at all. As a young boy, he'd put Madeleine on a pedestal, idolized her, projected on to her the character he would have liked her to have. He'd been in love with a dream, not a reality.

'There's been enough pretending already, Madeleine,' he said gently. 'I think you should go to Egypt. I expect you'll have a wonderful time and you'll soon forget about all this. It was partly my fault anyway. I should have known I couldn't make you happy.'

Madeleine's voice brightened.

'Then you do forgive me? Honestly, I didn't mean to hurt you, Harry, truly I didn't. But you're right about us. I suppose we aren't really suited, are we? You loving country life and your horses and things, and me wanting to live in London. But we can still be friends, can't we? We're bound to meet with you and Aubrey being such good chums and us knowing the same people. Mummy and Daddy are sure to invite you to lunch when you're in London. You'll come, won't you?'

Possibly, Harry thought, if for no other reason than that he owed a great deal to the Debraces. He would never be able to forgive Madeleine, as she seemed to expect, but strangely the knowledge that she had indeed been unfaithful no longer had the power to hurt him. It was as if all those years ago she had cast a spell over him and the spell had been lifted. He was free of her – for the first time in seventeen years.

Suitably attired in Alcott Minor's borrowed clothes, Harry went round to visit his aunt. Lady Merstam was delighted to see him. She listened without comment when he informed her that there would now be no wedding next year and that he and Madeleine had decided amicably that they were not suited. Only then did she say, 'I'm glad you've come to your senses before it was too late. I am probably biased, Harry, but frankly, I didn't think the girl was good enough for you. What are your plans now?'

'None, none at all,' Harry said. 'I shall go home and concentrate on my stud. I've tended to neglect it somewhat since Madeleine came back from France.'

'And are the renovations completed?' Cynthia asked.

Harry nodded.

'Thanks to Alice. She was an absolute brick. Did I tell you she'd returned to work at the Maison de Verveine? I'm going round there later to see her. I dare say I'll take her out to dinner and a show. She certainly deserves a treat and I don't think she gets out a lot.'

'No prospective husband, then?' Cynthia enquired. 'Surely if she's as attractive as you have described, she must have admirers.'

'Come to think of it, our Alice has always been a bit of a loner. I suppose she's what you might call a career girl – she loves her work. There was a time when we wondered if she was going to marry *le Maître*, as they call her boss, but he's years older than she is, and anyway, she wasn't in the least in love with him. As a matter of fact, he's Madeleine's uncle by marriage. Years ago, he and his wife – she's now dead – used to stay with the Debraces in Calking. It was Lady Debrace who talked Monsieur Verveine into taking Alice into his *couture* house in the first place.'

'I often think of those years you spent with the Pritchetts,' Cynthia said. 'For a long time, I couldn't do so without a terrible feeling of guilt, but you were happy with them, weren't you, despite the privations?'

Harry smiled.

'Very much so. It taught me one important lesson – that happiness has nothing to do with wealth. I had everything a boy could want when I went to live with Lady Kinmuire and her brother, except the one thing that really mattered – love! I don't think I shall ever forget that day Alice came up to see me and promised that somehow she would get me away from there and take me home. I never doubted she would succeed, and of course, she did.'

He leant back in his chair and stared thoughtfully into the fire.

'I often think about my childhood too,' he said. 'I wonder what my life would have been like if I'd not been illegitimate and had grown up as my father's son at Maythorpe. When I imagine such things, of course my mother would be there too, but try as I do, it's never real and I don't wish it could have happened that way. With Alice to look after me, I didn't really need a mother the way some children do. I loved Alice and trusted her, and because she never failed me, I felt secure. It's all quite different now, of course. We're good friends but obviously I don't depend on her.'

'But you know she'll always be there if you need her,' Cynthia said quietly.

Harry looked surprised.

'I suppose that's true. I've never really thought about it. All I do know is that if ever she needed me, I'd drop everything to help her. But she's tremendously self-sufficient. Alice isn't the sort of person who needs help.'

'Perhaps not,' Cynthia said, 'but we all need love, don't we? And to have someone to give our love to. I loved your mother and, as you know, I tried to protect her, but we don't always go the right away about it, do we? With the benefit of hindsight, I think I should have helped her to elope with Gervaise, even if it had meant poverty and disgrace.'

'You did what you thought best at the time,' Harry said quickly.

'Yes, but sometimes one does not necessarily make the right choice.'

Harry smiled.

'As indeed I have failed to do. First Cora-Beth and now Madeleine. Perhaps I should let you choose the next girl for me.'

Cynthia's somewhat austere expression softened to a half-smile.

'I doubt if that will be necessary, my dear boy. When you meet the right girl, you will realize it for yourself. You'll open your eyes and your heart and you will think, "But of course, this is the one person in the world – the only one – with whom I wish to spend the rest of my life."'

'I hope you're right,' Harry said as he rose to take his leave. 'If it happens, I'll bring her to you for your approval before I ask her to marry me. But as I said earlier, I've no intention of looking for a wife. I've decided to remain a bachelor.'

'We shall see,' Cynthia said as she bent forward stiffly to receive Harry's kiss on her proffered cheek. 'Now off you go and find your Alice. And come and see me again soon.'

With a growing feeling of affection for her, Harry left his aunt's house and took a taxi to the Maison de Verveine. Despite the fact that it was nearly closing time, the *salon* was, as always, busy with clients. At one end of the room a girl was modelling a frock, the client observing it with a critical eye while a *vendeuse* hovered nearby, pointing out the virtues of the dress. Harry caught sight of Jules and hurried over to him.

'Is Alice somewhere around?' he asked. 'She isn't expecting me, but I'd like a quick word with her if that's possible.'

For a moment, Jules did not reply. Then, as if gathering his thoughts together, he said, 'She's upstairs, in the fitting-room, Monsieur Keynes. Do go up if you wish.'

He stood staring up at Harry, a speculative look in his eyes as he watched him take the wide, carpeted stairs two at a time.

A young girl, carrying a bolt of grey-green satin, pointed out the door of the fitting-room. Harry opened it and closed it behind him quietly. Alice was standing by the window, holding what he took to be a bridal veil in her hands. A stout woman was kneeling on the floor, pinning up the hem of the magnificent, creamy-white brocade wedding-dress Alice was modelling. She looked astonishingly beautiful, although as yet he could see only her profile. Then the sewing woman caught sight of him. Alice turned her head and gave an involuntary gasp.

'Harry! What on earth are you doing here?'

'I wanted to see you,' Harry said. 'So I called round on the off-chance.'

'But I didn't know you were in London. I thought . . .'

As she broke off, the fitter rose to her feet.

'Shall I come back and finish this later, Miss Pritchett?'

she said. As Alice nodded, she gathered up her pin-cushions, measuring-tape and scissors, and left them alone.

Harry grinned.

'Stunning dress,' he said. 'Suits you, Alice. Who's the lucky customer? Someone special, I imagine.'

For a moment, Alice did not speak. Then she said quietly, 'It isn't for a customer, Harry. It's for me.'

Harry's mouth dropped open.

'For you?' he repeated stupidly. 'But . . . I don't understand.'

A stiff-backed, velvet-covered *chaise-longue* stood against one wall and Harry sank on to it. Alice moved away from him and stood at the window, her back towards him.

'I'm marrying Félix in two months' time,' she said. 'In Paris, that is. I . . . I thought you knew. Madeleine was in the *salon* a week or two ago and I asked her to tell you. Didn't she do so?'

Harry found his voice.

'No. She must have forgotten.'

'Yes, well, I expect she has a lot on her mind with her own wedding so soon after mine. I did ask her if she would like to be one of my maids of honour, but she declined. I don't think she approved of me marrying her uncle.'

'And for once I agree with her,' Harry said fiercely. 'I simply can't believe what you're telling me. You can't possibly do this, Alice. It's quite ridiculous. It isn't even as if you love the man. Besides, he's years older than you are. You can't possibly marry him,' he repeated.

'The invitations are being printed now,' Alice said stiffly, 'and I *am* going to marry Félix. Maybe I'm not in love with him the way you are with Madeleine, but he's a good man, a kind one, and he loves me. And anyway, he isn't all that old. We plan to have a family as soon as possible. There's room at the château for a whole army of children.'

Harry stood up abruptly and, walking over to Alice, swung her round by the arms so that she was forced to look at him.

'I just don't believe you're going to go through with this. You've let him talk you into it. Anyway, you told me when we were at Maythorpe and he cropped up in our conversation that he was in love with an Italian girl.'

'No, not "in love",' Alice said quietly. 'She was his mistress.'

'And you're prepared to put up with *that*?' Harry asked indignantly.

Alice's eyes narrowed as she said furiously, 'So who are you to moralize, Harry Keynes? Have you led a spotless existence? Has Madeleine? It doesn't seem to have bothered you that she isn't a virgin. It doesn't seem to have bothered either of you that you aren't yet married. So who are you to cast stones at Félix? And anyway, what has my future to do with you?'

'Everything,' Harry said violently. 'You're my sister and of course I care what happens to you. Your future . . .'

He got no further before Alice interrupted him. Her cheeks were bright pink and her eyes blazed as she said, 'I'm not, I'm not! I've never been your sister. Why don't you just go away and let me lead my own life. Go and marry that silly little girl you think you're in love with and let me choose my own husband. I don't care if I never see you again.'

Not knowing whether he was more astonished by her sudden tears or by the outburst preceding them, Harry stood helplessly staring at her. He did the only thing he could think of doing and passed her the handkerchief in his breast pocket. Alice buried her face in it and, still weeping, dropped on to the *chaise-longue*, the beautiful dress lying around her in crumpled folds.

'As a matter of fact, I'm not marrying Madeleine!' he said, as much to give Alice time to recover her composure as to pass on information he felt might interest her. 'We've broken off our engagement. That's what I came to tell you.'

Her face still wet with tears, Alice looked up at him.

'Not marrying Madeleine! But why, what's happened?'

Pleased to see that she was no longer crying – something

he had never yet in his life seen her do before – Harry sat down beside her.

'I found out I didn't love her,' he said. 'It's silly, isn't it? After all these years too! I suppose I'm a fool – anyway, where women are concerned. They teach you practically everything else at school but not how to pick the right girl. I suppose I should have listened to you, Alice. You never did think much of Madeleine, did you?'

Alice did not reply. Her heart was pounding and as Harry took hold of her hand in a perfectly natural grasp, her body began trembling. Aware of it and mistaking its cause, Harry said quickly,

'Please forgive me, Alice. If you really do want to marry Verveine, then I'll try and be pleased for your sake. It's just that it came as such a shock. I suppose if I'm honest, I'd say a very nasty shock. It just hit me suddenly that you weren't going to be Alice – my Alice – any more. That makes me out to be a pretty selfish pig, doesn't it? Do you know, it even crossed my mind in the taxi on the way here that I might be able to persuade you to come back to Maythorpe – to live, I mean. Remember how we planned it as children? Of course, I know it wouldn't be fair. I mean, I realize you must want a husband, children – that kind of thing. Alice, you're not crying again, are you?'

Unable to trust her voice, she shook her head.

'That's all right, then,' Harry said cheerfully. 'Look, Alice, do you have to have this dress fitted now? I mean, could it wait till tomorrow or something? I want to take you out to dinner – and now I suppose we've two things to celebrate, my broken engagement and your forthcoming marriage.' His voice lowered a tone. 'I just wish I could feel more pleased about you. Do you really and truly want to marry him, Alice?'

'Yes – at least, I think I do.'

Harry's face brightened.

'Thinking isn't good enough,' he said. 'Lady Merstam was saying to me only today that when it is the right person, you're absolutely sure about it. No doubts at all.

What about your future home – the château, I mean? Is it really so wonderful?'

'I prefer Maythorpe,' Alice said in a choked voice.

'Do you? Really? In a way, it is your home. You were the one who made it what it is. Oh, Alice, darling Alice, I know I shouldn't ask, but wouldn't you reconsider? Come up and live with me. We get on terribly well and you weren't bored when you were up there alone with me. You weren't, were you?'

'No, I wasn't bored.'

'There you are, then. You could be happy there. I'd be happy if you were there. It isn't as if either of us needs anyone else. When we're together . . .'

He broke off, letting go of Alice's hands as if they were scalding him. His own words, Lady Merstam's words, were rebounding in his head. 'When it's the right girl, you'll just know it in your heart.' The right girl! There had only ever been one -- and he had been too blinded by his love for Madeleine to realize it. Surely not Alice – *his* Alice!

The revelation had come too suddenly for him to trust it. He looked at Alice's damp, tear-streaked face and the straight, unpowdered pink nose and realized that while she might never have looked plainer, she had never looked more lovable. Equally, he had never felt so afraid. Suppose Alice didn't love him? Suppose the idea of marriage to him appalled her? Suppose she wouldn't ditch Félix Verveine after all the time he had waited for her?

'Alice!' Her name escaped his lips. 'Alice, you don't love him, do you? You don't *have* to marry him?'

There was a half-smile now on Alice's face although she would not meet his eyes as she said, 'I never said I did love him, and no, I don't *have* to marry him.' Her voice dropped even lower as she added, 'Although he and I . . . we have been lovers.'

Harry paused only momentarily before he said, 'Just now you told me I was in no position to moralize, and you were right. It's the future that matters, Alice, not the past. I don't care about the past.'

Now Alice was really smiling.

'Remember what we used to say at home? "Don't Care was made to care, Don't Care was hung; Don't Care was put in a pot, and boiled till he was done!"'

Harry pulled her to her feet and, his eyes bright with laughter, he hugged her.

'It was years before I understood what good hanging would do to "Don't Care". Alice, please get out of that dress. Beautiful as it is, I'd far rather see you in your old clothes. Put something on – anything, and let me take you out of this place.'

Half an hour later, with Jules waving them a knowing farewell, Harry and Alice stepped into the street. It was crowded with pedestrians hurrying home to their tea. High above the chimney tops, the sky was black but dotted with a thousand tiny stars. The fog Harry had forecast had never materialized and, judging by the sharp, clear air, there was going to be a frost.

He tucked Alice's ungloved hand into his coat pocket and held it in his own while his eyes searched the traffic for an empty taxi. Alice gave a little cry.

'Look, Harry, up there behind that steeple. Isn't that the evening star?'

Following her pointed finger, Harry nodded.

'That's Venus, I think. Actually it's a planet. I don't think I've ever seen it so bright.'

'Nor I,' whispered Alice.

Whatever its name, it wasn't important, she thought. What mattered was that it hung very low in the sky – so low that she knew she had only to wait just a little longer and she would be able to reach out and touch her brightest star.

1960

'Have you ever seen a ghost, Granny?'

Granny Alice put down the scarf she was knitting for her six-year-old grandson. Still in his riding clothes following a canter round the Maythorpe estate with the groom, Joe Appleby, Gervaise's thick, dark hair was a curly mop, his brown eyes questioning.

'No, darling, I haven't. I think they only exist in story books.'

'Joe says this house used to be haunted. His granny used to see the ghost quite often.'

Alice shook her head.

'That's just village gossip,' she said. 'Joe's granny used to be the cook in the old days when your Grandpa Harry lived here as a little boy. She was the one who started the rumour that your great-grandfather, Gervaise, haunted the gallery.'

'Why?' Gervaise questioned. 'Joe said only unhappy people become ghosts.'

Alice sighed, aware that she would get no peace until her grandson had all the answers he wanted. She went across to the bureau and withdrew a document from one of the drawers.

'This is the Kinmuire family tree,' she said. 'Come and sit on the sofa and I'll explain it to you.'

When the boy was seated beside her, she pointed to a name half-way down the scroll.

'That is your great-grandfather, Gervaise Harvey, the twelfth Earl of Kinmuire, after whom you were named. He married this lady, Pamela, but they had no children of their own, so the title passed to your American great-grandfather, Wendell Harvey. See, he's over here on the right on this branch of the tree. However, Gervaise did have a child – Harry.'

'Grandpa Harry?' the boy questioned.

Alice nodded.

'That's right. Grandpa Harry married me and we had a daughter, Mary, your mother. Meanwhile, your great-grandfather, Wendell, the thirteenth Earl of Kinmuire, had these two children, called Judd and Cora-Beth. Judd died so the title went to Cora-Beth. Titles like the Kinmuires' pass down through a daughter if there are no boys. Granny Cora-Beth married your other grandfather, Aubrey, and they had a child, Judd.'

'He's my daddy,' the boy said, following Alice's pointed finger. 'And when my mummy was 'vacuated to America in the war, she met Daddy and they fell in love and after the war was over, they got married and had me.'

'Indeed they did. And that's why the two branches of the family meet here. One day, you will become the fifteenth Earl of Kinmuire.'

The boy scowled.

'I don't think I want to be a n'earl. I want to be a spaceman. If I was a n'earl, would I be a ghost when I died?'

Alice laughed.

'I don't think so, darling. Happy people don't haunt houses, and I hope you'll always be happy. I think your great-grandfather is happy now. No one has seen his ghost since you were born, and that could be because he has got what he'd always wanted, a direct heir. Grandpa Harry couldn't inherit, but you are Gervaise's great-grandson and so the wheel has come full circle.'

'What wheel?' the child asked.

Alice smiled.

'The spinning wheel,' she murmured with a small sigh of contentment. 'Lunchtime,' she added, knowing that

572

the next question would be, 'What's a spinning wheel?' –
and that this would be a story for another day.

THE END

ORTOLANS
by Claire Lorrimer

ORTOLANS – A magnificent old house, which held a mesmeric grip on those who lived in it, and also hid a secret which the Calverley family were not to discover for four hundred years.

Three fascinating and passionate women were to save, not only themselves, but also the house throughout its violent history.

ELEANOR – Forced into a marriage she did not want, a marriage that left her unfulfilled and prey to a ruthless adventurer who would stop at nothing to claim Ortolans as his own.

SOPHIA – Self-willed and lovely. She was ready to lie, cheat, and risk everything to keep her home.

EMMA – A twentieth-century careerist who was bewitched by Ortolans, but who would not sacrifice her career for either the house or the man she loved.

And when the blackest moment came – when it seemed as though Ortolans was finished – then the house at last gave up its secret.

0 552 13876 2

THE WILDERLING
by Claire Lorrimer

The childhood of Sophia Lucienne Rochford had been a bitter one. Born an aristocrat but raised first as an orphan in a French convent, then as a skivvy in a Paris brothel, she had received little in the way of love or luxury.

When, at sixteen, she found herself restored to her rightful place, as elegant daughter of the Rochford family, she was betrayed yet again, this time by her father.

And so Lucy, with the outward trappings of a society beauty, and the morals of a hard-headed courtesan, decided she would never trust a man again.

0 552 12182 7

LAST YEAR'S NIGHTINGALE
by Claire Lorrimer

Clementine Foster was young, unbelievably innocent, and wildly in love with a man who didn't even know of her existence. When, one golden summer night, she stepped in front of his horse, he took her with all the drunken arrogance of a young aristocrat used to having whatever he wanted. The repercussions of that night were to forge bonds of hate, love, and tragedy in both their lives.

For the child that was born to Clementine ultimately appeared to be the only legitimate heir to the Grayshot inheritance. And, according to the law of the times, she had no right to keep her child if Deveril wanted him.

But Clementine was determined to remove her son, no matter what the cost, no matter what she had to do.

0 552 12565 2

A SELECTED LIST OF FINE NOVELS
AVAILABLE FROM CORGI BOOKS

THE PRICES SHOWN BELOW WERE CORRECT AT THE TIME OF GOING TO PRESS. HOWEVER TRANSWORLD PUBLISHERS RESERVE THE RIGHT TO SHOW NEW RETAIL PRICES ON COVERS WHICH MAY DIFFER FROM THOSE PREVIOUSLY ADVERTISED IN THE TEXT OR ELSEWHERE.

All Corgi/Bantam Books are available at your bookshop or newsagent, or can be ordered from the following address:

Corgi/Bantam Books,
Cash Sales Department,
P.O. Box 11, Falmouth, Cornwall TR10 9EN

UK and B.F.P.O. customers please send a cheque or postal order (no currency) and allow £1.00 for postage and packing for the first book plus 50p for the second book and 30p for each additional book to a maximum charge of £3.00 (7 books plus).

Overseas customers, including Eire, please allow £2.00 for postage and packing for the first book plus £1.00 for the second book and 50p for each subsequent title ordered.

NAME (Block Letters) ....

ADDRESS ....

....